W9-AUJ-991

A TALE OF
LIFE & WAR

CHRISTOPHER
MORIN

A Tale of Life and War

ISBN 13: 978-1-63381-006-8

Designed and produced by
Maine Authors Publishing
558 Main Street, Rockland, Maine 04841
www.maineauthorspublishing.com

Printed in the United States of America

To Grammie, who so patiently read to me as a young child; fueling my imagination and inspiring me in countless ways.

To all the brave men and women, who fought and sacrificed gallantly, to preserve freedom during the most destructive conflict in human history. It is these heroes who deserve our eternal gratitude.

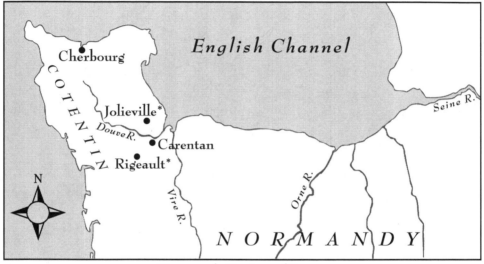

Normandy Region of France

---

*Jolieville and Rigeault are fictional towns

Contents

AUTHOR'S NOTE

In creating this work of fiction, I made every attempt to be as historically accurate as possible. I tried to use as much descriptive detail and period language necessary to give the reader the best understanding of the military situation, the weaponry used, and the overall happenings of the time. Much detail is given to the description of Nazism, the German Wehrmacht, the SS and Gestapo. This is in no way meant to glorify the ideology of fascism, the German armed forces, or the criminal police and paramilitary organizations mentioned above. They do not reflect any political views of the author whatsoever. Some names, locations, battles, and military units mentioned are completely fictional, while others such as the U.S. 9th Air Force, and the U.S. 101st and 82nd Airborne Divisions are real. It was my intention to create an interesting story comprised of many fictitious elements set around actual historical events.

Chapter 1

MORNING

As the sun rose over the slumbering college campus, slivers of light crept through masonry, invading dormitory windows across the sprawling grounds. It was Saturday in central Maine. Winter seemed to have humbly subsided with the deceptively mild mid-April weather, mercifully releasing the state from winter's cold, lingering grasp.

For a few students, the arrival of warmth brought a welcome invitation to arise and embrace everything the new day might offer. For them, jogging shoes were quickly laced, portable CD players strapped on, laundry bags filled, and book bags swung across shoulders. They were the first souls to venture out, piercing the eerie weekend silence that so sharply contrasted with the usually vibrant and bustling campus atmosphere.

Yet the enthusiasm of the few did not spill over into the majority of others. Dozens remained in their beds fast asleep—a result of too much partying and alcohol consumption the night before. Some slept out of sheer laziness, while others enjoyed the small gift of a few extra hours of sleep Saturday morning provided after a week of hard work that preceded the start of final exams. It was morning, and it was springtime at the University of Maine at Orono.

Matthew Switzer lay in his bed entangled in a knot of sheets and blankets that bound his body like a straitjacket—the result of a restless night tossing and turning. The small, dark dorm room was soon illuminated by the onset of morning. A beam of sunshine crept through his curtains and found its target—his face. He let out a small, pitiful groan. His precious slumber had officially terminated, forcing him to rise and face the day. Shaking his throbbing head, hoping to somehow relieve the pain, he glanced at his small electric alarm clock that slowly came into focus. The bright red digits read 7:26. Matthew slowly rose to his feet and stretched his tangled arms, legs, and back long and hard. His body rewarded him with creaks and cracks of loosening pleasure. He looked at the twisted mess of sheets that was his bed and couldn't be enticed to lie back down. He decided it was time to start the day.

"Why didn't I talk to her more? Why couldn't I say the right damn thing? Why did I have to be such a friggin' idiot in front of her? She was so hot. So perfect."

Matthew stood in front of his mirror gathering his soap, shampoo, deodorant, and toothpaste. He berated himself over the previous night's failed attempt at charming the most beautiful woman he had ever laid eyes on. He had gone across campus with his friend Bobby to attend a party the lovely Chi Omega sorority sisters were throwing to celebrate the beginning of the end of the school year. Laden with cases of Natural Light beer, Matt and Bobby easily gained access to the sorority house and spent most of the evening standing around drinking and watching other guys flirt with the girls of their choice.

It was just after one o'clock in the morning when the party started to wind down. Bobby, who was more drunk than Matt, angrily grabbed his friend and charged for the door, realizing he would be sleeping alone again. As they reached the front door, Matthew gazed across the now mostly empty living room, resting his eyes on a girl talking with two of her friends. He was drawn in their direction, abandoning Bobby, who continued to charge out the door and head back toward his dorm.

Walking to within five feet of the three young women, Matt singled out the gorgeous sorority sister who had caught his attention. She was unlike any woman he had ever seen. She was perfect. Her lush, brown, shoulder-length hair was naturally straight and full of volume. Her eyes were big and brown with long, lavish lashes. Her expression was warm and welcoming, with skin so smooth and shiny it appeared flawless. Her smile was natural without hint of sarcasm or dishonesty. Every gleaming ivory tooth hung perfectly inside her mouth. Her lips appeared silky and supple, highlighted by the soft pink lipstick she wore. Her white, V-neck, button-down sweater hugged her upper body and accentuated her every feminine curve. She was well-endowed and it showed. Her jeans fit perfectly and not an ounce of fat was noticeable. To Matthew Switzer, she was perfect.

Noticing she was under close scrutiny by some mystery man, the girl motioned for her friends to casually walk away, which they did, leaving her one on one with Matthew. After eyeing his prize from head to toe, Matt reassured himself of his own physique. He considered himself no slouch and just as good looking as any other college student. He was five foot eleven, with a muscular build and dark blond hair, parted to the right, longer on the top and shaved shorter on the sides. His blue eyes were rich with color that resembled the ocean on a sunny afternoon. His white T-shirt was partially hidden by the untucked, long-sleeved blue denim shirt he wore over it. And his faded black jeans were, in his mind, the perfect match for this evening's ensemble he'd put together in roughly four minutes of dressing. Drunk and full of pulsing testosterone, Matt spoke, blurting out a lame line that he could no longer recall. His pristine goddess reacted as though her ears had been corrupted by his foul language. She abruptly turned her back and walked upstairs to her bedroom, leaving Matt to find his way home alone in a half-drunken stupor. The party was over. Reality came crashing back.

Matt banged his fist hard on the bureau after recalling last night's events.

"What the hell did I say to her?" Matt scolded himself. "Why can't I remember? I wasn't that drunk, was I? She was so hot. I could have salvaged this whole rotten, useless year of school by just having one night with her. Damn it all to hell!"

Matt wrapped a towel around his waist and threw open the door angrily. He walked down the fourth-floor hallway to the men's room, where he hoped a good long shower would help shake the cobwebs from his head and the humiliation from his heart. After cleaning himself up, he dressed hastily and called Bobby. The phone rang four times before the answering machine kicked in. Matt rolled his eyes.

"Hey, shithead, get your ass out of bed and meet me at the commons in ten minutes. I'm hungry," Matt commanded.

He hung up and threw on his tattered white Nikes, still covered in mud from last night's trek home across campus. With student ID and wallet in hand, Matt locked his dorm room door and headed downstairs, crossing the courtyard to the dining commons. Still unable to shake the vision of the beautiful sorority girl, Matt tried to decide what he was going to have for breakfast. He walked briskly under a bright sunlit sky. The entrance to the dining commons was crowded with students waiting for the weekend breakfast to start at nine o'clock. Matt entered the commons and got in line, shaking his head, still asking himself why he had so royally screwed up. Having shaken his hangover, he now felt capable of analyzing last night's social events and perhaps remembering where he had gone wrong.

"Where the hell is Bobby?" Matt muttered as the line began to move. "That idiot is always late for everything. Probably hasn't even gotten dressed yet. I'll bet that numb-nuts crashed in Howie's room last night because he couldn't make it all the way back to *his* room."

He glanced back toward Chamberlain Hall and saw Bobby emerge from the front entrance, looking as though he'd gotten dressed in the dark.

"Yo, Bobby!" shouted Matt from the head of the line. "I'll meet you upstairs. Regular table. Got it?"

Bobby acknowledged the orders with a groggy nod as he rubbed his dirty, tousled black hair with his right hand, trying to tame it.

The line of hungry students buzzing with early-morning conversation moved quickly up the long inclining corridor toward the second-floor cafeteria. Matt slowly worked his tray down the long counter. His mind still preoccupied, he wandered across the cafeteria and sat down at his usual table. Bobby, who had just come through the lunch line, his tray stacked high, joined Matt.

"You know something, man? This place sucks," said Bobby. "I can't ever get those jerks who serve this shit to at least try and cook me what I ask for. I mean, just look at these pancakes; it's like eating rubber!"

"I don't know why you're bitching so much, Bobby. You get the same shit every morning and always complain about the same things. How smart is that?"

"Don't lecture me," replied Bobby, as he stuffed half a pancake into his mouth. "I had a really rough night and I don't need you telling me how I should conduct myself in the cafeteria. Also . . ."

Matt interrupted Bobby before he could spit out his next sentence.

"Don't even go there, man! I know what happened to you last night. You got hammered at the party, struck out with every chick that bothered to look at you, then staggered your sorry ass back to the dorm and passed out. Big fucking deal! At least you didn't make a fool of yourself in front of the most perfect woman God ever created."

Matt suddenly felt embarrassed. He ducked his head and began to shovel scrambled eggs into his mouth, realizing that he probably shouldn't have said what he did. Bobby took a swig of orange juice, belched loudly, and grinned at his friend.

"So, Matty, my boy, tell the old Bobster about your evening after the party's mass exodus." Bobby's previously disgusted tone turned gleefully to prodding sarcasm in the face of his friend's apparent misery.

"Nothin' to tell," snapped Matt.

"Bullshit," said Bobby directly. "Tell me what happened. It's bound to be more interesting than my night."

"I don't know if I want to discuss it," said Matt between bites of bacon. "It's really bothering me to the point of massive distraction. I feel like I've lost the greatest social opportunity of my life. The year is almost over, I'll be graduating in a few weeks, and I think I'll never get another chance like I had last night."

Sensing Matt's despair, Bobby decided to derail the train of teasing, jabbing, and tasteless insults with which he'd planned to mercilessly barrage Matt. He felt genuine sympathy for his friend and realized, noticing Matt's trembling left hand, that now was not the time or place for insensitive jokes. Bobby spoke up.

"Well ... let's talk about it if you want to. If not, I understand."

"Look, Bob, I ... I ... I screwed up royally. I was drunk and not in control of my mouth. After you left I started talking to the most beautiful woman in the whole sorority house. I don't even remember what the hell I said to her. All I know is that I sputtered out some lame lines that caused her to do an about face and leave me hanging. But the part that bugs me the most is that I sensed she was interested in me. I … I don't know, man."

Matt's head dropped to the table. It was apparent to Bobby he didn't want to go on about it any further. "It's okay," Bobby said, at a loss, patting his friend on the shoulder. Matt perked up and looked Bobby square in the eyes.

"It's not okay, Bob," said Matt. "Not only is my social life destroyed forever but my damn academic life might be going down the toilet right behind it!"

"What do you mean, man?" asked Bobby.

"I mean that it took me over three years to declare a History major. I even like history somewhat. I've managed to pass all my classes and get full credit in every required course."

"Yeah, I know," said Bobby. "You done real good. You'll graduate this year, and it only took you the standard four years. Me … I'll be up here forever. You'll have a job somewhere, earning good money while I'm still here failing Chemistry and Biology for the seventh time!"

"You're wrong, Bob. I've passed every class I've taken except one— History 499."

"What's that?"

"It's an upper-level, independent study course on contemporary American history. MacAllister teaches it."

"MacAllister! He's the dean of Liberal Arts and Sciences … and a real ball-buster from what I hear," said Bobby.

"You got that right," replied Matt. "His class is required for a BA in History. Graduate students often take it, too, seeking extra credit toward their master's degree."

"I hear that guy doesn't cut no slack for nobody," said Bobby.

"He uses a cut-and-dried grading system. Either your work passes or fails. There is no 'in between' with that guy," shuddered Matt. "There are only thirteen other students in the class. The first day of the semester, he gave a fifteen-minute lecture on what he considers the importance of contemporary American history. When the time was up, he passed out this friggin' fifty-page booklet that outlines the course objectives and what is required of us to pass the class and graduate."

Matt turned his head to look out the window as if he were afraid to continue the conversation. Gradually he turned his attention back toward his friend, who was now intently listening to every word.

"Go on, man. Tell me more," blurted Bobby as he tried to talk and swallow his bite of blueberry muffin at the same time.

"Well," sighed Matt. "He told us that the booklet should be read that night and all its written requirements and objectives completed in the appropriate time frame in order to pass. He said that the first day of class would be the first and last time everyone would meet together. What he meant was that he wasn't going to lecture or teach us anything. Our responsibility was to read his friggin' glorified syllabus and then act on it accordingly throughout the semester. Dr. MacAllister is one of those 'only the truly gifted shall survive and pass my course while the rest of you go dig ditches until you die' types," said Matt in a sarcastic tone that noticeably lowered the voices of the other students in the cafeteria, who decided to hone in on Matt's conversation.

"So what did the booklet say?" asked Bobby.

"Basically it was a long-winded piece of garbage that gave us our individual assignments ... which we were not allowed to pick for ourselves, I might add. In a nutshell, each student was given a significant event that occurred in the last hundred years and instructed to report on it in any way he or she felt fit. No mention was made of how we were to go about this nightmare of an assignment! After a few days I went to his office for some guidance on the project, and he flatly refused to even discuss it. Then he criticized me for having the audacity to ask for help! In his eyes, that was a sign of failure on my part. He booted me out of his office and told me he expected to see something meaningful and tangible on his desk during finals week if I expected to pass his course."

Bobby sat in amazement at Matt's story, knowing he had taken tough courses at UMO, but had always been given full cooperation from his professors when he needed help on an assignment. Bobby swallowed his last bite of muffin and almost was afraid to ask Matt his next question.

However, curiosity overcame him, and tactfully he asked in a low and concerned voice, "So Matt, what was your assignment?"

Matt sat up a little straighter, then cleared his throat after swallowing a large bite of his scrambled eggs. He shook his head slightly and sighed once again before answering. He knew immediately what he wanted to say, but struggled to get the words out. Matt was in severe denial. He felt if he didn't talk about the assignment, it might quietly fade away without disrupting his march down the graduation aisle. However, Matt was becoming increasingly aware that his unfinished project was lurking on the horizon like an untamed beast, ready to pounce on its unsuspecting prey. He managed to find the words.

"The American GI experience in the European theater during World War II. Can you be any more vague than that? I mean, come on! He expects me to take that immensely broad topic and streamline it into a nice little packaged report to place on his desk come May? I don't know where to even start. It's not like I know anyone who fought in a war over fifty years ago! I don't even have any relatives who served in the military. Neither of my grandfathers were GIs. They were both still in America throughout the war … I think. One worked in a mill or something, and the other … shit … I don't know! My point is that I don't even have anybody I can ask any questions. I don't know anybody who fought in World War II."

Matt shuddered uneasily, as if finally realizing just how bad off he was. He suddenly felt like someone had slapped him in the face with the stiff hand of reality. The denial started to fade. The fault of the matter shifted onto him, rather than the stern MacAllister. The necessity of taking action began to consume him. With one clear thought, Matt's mind started to click. *It's time to do something.*

"So what now?" asked Bobby, stacking up plates and silverware on his empty breakfast tray.

"I guess I'll spend a few all-nighters at the library, researching periodicals and books that hopefully contain some quotes and maybe a few GI stories. Hell, I'll surf the Internet all hours if I have to and download articles, pictures, and shit like that. I'm sure the web has got some veteran sites on it somewhere. I'm sure some old drunken vets at some dingy VFW club have spilled their guts to some historian who wrote the great American novel and plastered it all over the Web. You know something, Bob, I may not be as bad off as I originally thought!"

"Yeah, man, but what about MacAllister's friggin' booklet and its timetables throughout the semester? How did you bullshit your way through that?" asked Bobby.

"All the crap in the booklet was about periodically submitting progress reports and methods of research and proof that we were doing something," said Matt evasively.

"Well ... have you done anything like that?" Bobby prodded sarcastically.

"Hell, yeah," replied Matt in a questionable manner. "I submitted some shit I dug up at the library about GIs in Europe. I even turned in a list of what I thought were good methods of conducting research on the topic. I printed it all up nice and neat and put it in a fancy leather binder. I'm not worried about that shit. I'm confident that if I come up with a really great final report, everything else will come out in the wash in the end. All I want to do is pass. I don't care about enlightening some asshole professor with my newly acquired knowledge on a topic I don't even care about. Know what I mean?"

"I guess so, man," said Bobby. "I hope everything works out for ya, buddy. Keep in mind that you don't have a whole hell of a lot of time on this. I'd really think it was cool if you managed to pull this off, but don't be surprised if your ass is sittin' next to mine up in the bleachers watching the graduates march by during commencement!"

"Don't worry about me," smugly replied Matt. "I may not be UMO's valedictorian, but I can assure you I won't be waving from the crowd next to your dumb ass come mid-May! I'm going to pass that class and shove MacAllister's friggin' course up his ass with my red-hot diploma!"

"I hope you're right, man," said Bobby after wiping his mouth and picking up his tray, signaling his desire to end the conversation. Matt hesitated a second, full of thoughts concerning the final history assignment. For the first time that morning, he was focusing on something other than the beautiful girl who had captivated him the night before.

"C'mon, man," said Bobby impatiently. "I'm done eating and I don't feel like hanging around this lame-ass cafeteria all day!" Bobby carried his tray to the dishwasher and wove his way through the bustling crowd filling the commons. Matt managed one last swig of his orange juice before following his friend to the exit. They headed back to the dormitory.

"Well, I don't know about you, man, but I'm going back to bed to sleep for a few more hours," moaned Bobby, extending his arms high in the air for a good, long stretch.

"Yeah, take that lazy-ass carcass of yours to the shower first. You smell like shit, Bob," replied Matt, shaking his head.

"I love you too, asshole. Good luck on your bullshitting ... er ... I mean history research. Hope MacAllister doesn't come knocking on your door tonight. He's liable to kick your ass before he flunks ya into a good trade school," shouted Bobby as he broke into a trot toward the dorm.

"Whatever you say, Bob," whispered Matt to himself as he watched his friend vanish into Chamberlain Hall. Walking slowly and taking his time, Matt stuffed his hands into his pockets and stared at the ground, his thoughts drowned in deep concentration. His head raced with ideas. He began to see himself in the campus library after hours with piles of books, pictures, and notes scattered around him, signifying all the hard research he would have done. Not to mention the countless hours surfing the Internet and downloading page upon page of golden material that would most assuredly impress the unimpressible MacAllister. Matt's spirits began to rise as he deeply inhaled the fresh morning air one last time before entering the dorm.

He hustled up the stairway to his room on the fourth floor, carefully making sure he didn't step in any dried puddles of beer or vomit graciously left the night before by crazy partygoers. He noticed the halls were still unusually quiet and not many people had discovered it was morning. All the better, as Matt had more thinking to do. With a quick twist of his room key in the lock, Matt was in his quarters. He didn't jump back into bed or immediately turn on his TV as he had done countless times after returning from Saturday breakfast. Instead, he quietly paced back and forth, his hands on top of his head.

"World War II … GIs in Europe … fighting … battles … guns … killing. … What was it like? Where was it done? How was it done? Who were the guys in charge? Where did they go? Who would they have told it to after the war?"

Matt's mind tumbled with questions that seemed to have no immediate answers. The harder he thought, the more his pacing increased and the more frustrated he became. The earlier visions of cramming his mind with research and pulling off the impossible by coming up with a good report faded as the idea of actually having to do something began to rear its ugly head.

"Shit. Where do I begin?"

Matt reluctantly sat down at his desk and pulled out some notes pertaining to what little information he had turned in to MacAllister on his ideas for possible research. The notes made little sense, as they simply were the work of his carelessness, lack of interest, and most pointedly, lack of any basic knowledge on the subject.

"Damn! This is no help," he shouted, flinging his notebook to the floor. The noise startled his neighbor in the next room and he heard an uneasy muffled noise come through the walls. Not being one to want to cause a stir, Matt quietly regained his composure and retrieved the notebook from the already cluttered floor. The harmless red cover emblazoned with the title "HTY 499" was a devilish, taunting reminder of his growing predicament. Placing the notebook back in the desk drawer, he decided to relax for a moment. He sat down on the edge of his bed and folded his arms against his chest. Thoughts of failure entered his mind. The depression he'd felt earlier that morning began to resurface. The previous feelings of possibly completing the assignment and passing the course started to fade and his mind filled with doubt. As he again pondered his predicament, Matt sank back on his bed of tangled sheets. A single recurrent thought, laced with regret, painfully reverberated through his brain.

"Why didn't I talk to her more? Why couldn't I say the right damn thing? Why did I have to be such a friggin' idiot? She was so hot. So perfect. Man, did I really blow my chances with that one! It could've been a really good night for me and an even better morning if only I had been a little more cool and in control! Damn!"

Distraught, he glanced again at the clock. He turned his head away in disgust—it was now 11:14. For Matthew Switzer, morning was officially over.

Chapter 2

THE LIBRARY

The library was a monument to the university. No other building on the UMO campus was bigger or bustled with more activity during the week. Even the Student Union with all its food shops, student supply stores, and relaxing study lounges could not boast a greater daily student attendance than Longfellow Library. It was located directly at the center of the campus.

Students who lived on school grounds found the walk to Longfellow quite pleasant in nice weather. Age-old majestic pines and oak trees that had most likely been just saplings, trembling toward the sunny sky when the school was founded in 1865, surrounded the building. Several old paths scored the earth circling the perimeter. The timeworn dirt routes used by students for decades seemed out of touch with the modern walkways that led to the main entrance.

On the library's quiet and nearly deserted fourth floor, Matt Switzer sat on an old wooden chair at a decrepit desk, ensconced under a set of dim fluorescent lights feebly illuminating a small area. It was now 4:30 on Saturday afternoon. With Bobby out of his hair and his thoughts of the mysteriously striking sorority girl temporarily subdued, Matt found himself haphazardly trying to pursue his history assignment that would make or break his final weeks in college. Scattered on his desk were several worn World War II reference books, encyclopedias, periodicals, and a few current gun magazines containing articles on small arms used in combat during this definitive global conflict.

He sat fidgeting, glancing at the clock on the wall, fooling himself into thinking he was being productive. Maybe if he sat there long enough with many books open and he looked studious, he would miraculously become inspired, and the knowledge the books possessed would seep into his brain via osmosis. His eyes hopelessly scanning chapter titles, occasional pictures, and bold-type captions, Matt became increasingly restless, even panicked. He began sputtering out sentence fragments hoping something would make sense.

"Battle of the Bulge … D-Day invasion … what the frig? … Operation Fortitude objectives … huh? … The Atlantic Wall … Eisenhower's decision to go? What the hell does this all mean?" he whispered pitifully.

A great sinking feeling began to overcome him as he envisioned himself in MacAllister's office at the end of finals week, pleading to be passed and allowed to graduate. He could picture how MacAllister would look, and could hear what he would say. The torturous lecturing on irresponsibility, laziness, disrespectfulness, and lack of effort and enthusiasm would certainly be at the forefront of MacAllister's speech. After speaking his mind, he would then wildly wave in the air whatever Matt had the courage to turn in and, in a highly pretentious tone of voice, yell out what garbage it was before dropping it at Matt's feet, callously branded with a big red F. Matt, having been thoroughly reviled, would then have to salvage what little shred of dignity he had left and exit his teacher's office, wondering how he would explain his failures over the phone to his parents back in South Portland. His parents, completely unaware of the current situation, were fully expecting to see their only son receive his diploma in the next few weeks. The disappointment on their faces and their discontentment with their son would be a scenario Matt couldn't bear to experience.

The lights on the library's top floor suddenly dimmed for a moment before powering back up. Matt looked up at the dangling fluorescent fixtures and decided to take a break. He needed to calm himself. Although he'd occasionally wormed his way out of, or around, past tough assignments, and cleverly slipped by the teacher's best judgments to achieve respectable grades, he was not a cheater and certainly understood the value of hard work and sacrifice. All the same, he didn't always practice what he knew was the right course of action.

One by one the scattered array of books and military references Matt had gathered slammed shut. He stacked them neatly on the desk and stood up slowly to stretch. Glancing left and right, he realized he was alone, with the exception of the sole librarian on duty. As he stood up the librarian looked up from her desk and spoke.

"Can I help you find anything, dear?"

"No thank you, ma'am," replied Matt politely. "I'm just going to take a little stroll and clear my head. I'll be right back. I still have more research to do. Will you be here for a while?"

With a pleasant smile, the aged, graying attendant replied, "Yes, dear, I'll be here until closing time. My shift just started an hour ago. I was hoping you'd stay a while. It often gets lonely up here all by myself."

"I hear that," said Matt. "I'll be right back. I'm gonna leave my books right on the desk. Okay?"

"Yup, that's fine," said the amiable assistant before she resumed her paperwork. Matt jammed his hands into his pockets and walked toward the main stairway. As he did, he spied two iron spiral staircases at the back of the room that could accommodate only one person at a time. They were located on opposite sides of the room and seemed to mysteriously snake downward into a pit of dark nothingness. Curious, Matt approached the one closest to him and peered downward.

"Excuse me?" Matt said to the librarian, who was buried in paperwork, only to pop up abruptly after hearing his voice. "Where do these old iron staircases lead?"

The woman scratched her wrinkled cheek and slowly rose out of her chair. She craned her neck to the left and then to the right, trying to pinpoint Matt's location through the stacks at the other end of the room.

"Where are you, dear? I can't see you," she called out.

"I'm over here, in the back," shouted Matt, waving his right arm in her direction. His signal succeeded, as the librarian started walking his way.

"I'm a trifle deaf in the left ear, dear. Sorry. What was that you said again?" she asked.

"I was just wondering where these old staircases lead," Matt asked, more loudly.

"It's not that bad, dear. You don't have to shout. I'm only a foot away from you," cackled the librarian with a smile. "These are old utility staircases that library staff use primarily for luggin' stuff between floors. They're more convenient than trying to go up and down the main staircases, which usually are busy with students runnin' to and fro. You know what I mean, don't ya, dear?"

Matt nodded his head politely and continued to listen to the librarian, who seemed thrilled she had someone to talk to.

"I never use them myself. My hip, you know, is not as good as it used to be." The librarian turned sideways and pointed to her right hip while wincing a bit to add a little drama to the conversation. "They spiral down to the third floor, then to the second, and eventually to the first," she continued while pointing and twirling her index finger downward to simulate the corkscrew engineering of the staircases. "They really aren't for general use, but we don't pay that much attention to them. If you want to see where they lead, be my guest. I won't snitch on ya, dear." She gave Matt a little pat on the shoulder as she spoke.

"Thanks, ma'am," replied Matt with a polite grin. "I just might do some exploring. Those history books I'm reading are really driving me crazy, and I need a little break."

"Okay. My name is Alice," said the librarian, pointing to a name tag hidden in the folds of her green sweater. "If you need any help finding any type of reference on this floor, just give me a holler, dear." With that, Alice turned around and headed back to her desk.

Matt grabbed the iron handrail and slowly started down the spiral staircase. The lighting was dim, giving the passageway an eerie feel. He could tell the stairs weren't used that often because of the musty smell that dominated the compact airspace. Inhaling deeply, Matt recalled the attic at his grandmother's house. It carried the same stale smell. Twisting and turning with each step, he reached the bottom and emerged into the third floor. Thinking to continue all the way down to the first, he started down again, only to stop curiously. He was on the third floor all right, but he didn't recognize where he was. In the past, he'd spent many hours studying and looking for books here and he thought he knew every square inch of the place. Apparently he was wrong, as he scanned around, but couldn't place where he was. He appeared to be in a small study area, just off the main room. It was drab and contained a few stacks of books and some study tables with lamps. One small, bare window in the corner of the room allowed a beam of sunlight to shine in. The door to the room was closed tightly.

The room appeared to be unoccupied until Matt heard a gentle cough emanate from the corner nearest the window. He glanced around a stack of books to see a young woman sitting by the window, reading a book.

Instantly Matt stepped back and hid himself behind the stacks. His heart pounded wildly and a chill pulsed in the pit of his stomach. His hands trembled as he tried to compose himself. Sitting in the corner was the girl of his dreams—the very one who had haunted him all morning and caused him so much grief. What to do now? That was the question.

Matt wracked his mind, trying to remember every detail about the Chi Omega sorority party. Unfortunately, the amount of beer he'd consumed that evening blocked out just about everything. All he could recall was seeing the girl, approaching her, and her quick departure.

"Damn!" Matt whispered. "What do I do now?" He began to tremble again at the thought of what this beautiful young woman might say if he were to walk up to her and start a conversation. He glanced around the corner of the stack that was shielding him to capture another look at the young beauty. Her brown hair was studiously tied back with small hairpins to prevent its dangling in her face and interfering with her work. She wasn't wearing any makeup, but that failed to detract one bit from her soft, flawless face. Her captivating brown eyes caught the light and seemed to reflect it as pure crystal would. She wore a powder-blue sweater that was V-necked and buttoned, complementing a pair of white jeans and a black belt. White sneakers held laces that matched the color of her sweater. In Matt's eyes she was a pillar of beauty who could do no wrong and could cause him no harm. His courage began to grow.

Matt ran his fingers through his tousled hair. He passed his hand across his face and thanked God he had shaved that morning, then touched the back of his neck to ensure the tag on his T-shirt wasn't sticking up. He made sure both shoelaces on his Nike sneakers were tied and adjusted his belt so he could tuck in his shirt more evenly. With a quick brush of his shirt and pants to remove any dust or lint, Matt felt confident enough that he was physically presentable.

Then came the hard part. A million thoughts suddenly rushed through his mind. He could feel the adrenaline building inside. Without further delay, he stepped out from behind the book stack, in clear view of his heart's desire, just ten feet away. Quietly and without taking his eyes off her, Matt blindly swiped a book from the nearest stack and coolly sauntered up to the table. The girl, apparently well absorbed in her reading, didn't even notice him standing over her.

A few seconds passed, making the situation that much more awkward for the increasingly embarrassed Matt. Nervously, he turned his head from side to side, wondering if anyone was witnessing his social futility. He and the girl were still alone. Feeling the pressure to act build up inside of him, Matt finally spoke.

"Um ... excuse me?"

The girl slowly raised her head and smiled at the stranger hovering above her. She slid her left index finger over the page in her book and rested it halfway down, so as not to lose her place.

"Hi. Can I help you?" she asked in an inquisitive and slightly puzzled manner that one might express when confronted with an apparent total stranger.

"Hi. Ah ... do you remember me?" responded Matt uneasily, his voice cracking like an adolescent's.

"I don't think so. Have we met before?" she replied politely.

"Ah, well ... sort of, I guess," said Matt tensely, clutching the book in his hand and turning his head, afraid to look the woman in the eye for fear of any sign of rejection.

Now very confused and somewhat bothered that her studying was interrupted by a guy who appeared extremely unsettled, the girl closed her hardcover textbook with a thud and waved her hand in the air sarcastically to get Matt's undivided attention.

"Are you okay?" she asked acidly. "Would you mind looking at me instead of the wall? It makes the conversation go a lot easier, and I sense you're feeling a bit uptight about something. Did I do anything wrong?"

Tiny beads of sweat began surfacing on Matt's forehead as he struggled to find words. He looked at the girl and felt his legs start to melt. Sensing her growing impatience at his inability to make sense, Matt finally blurted out some words.

"I'm sorry. I didn't mean to bug ya. I … I see that you're busy studying your … *Elements of Teaching* text," he said, after peering at the cover on the closed book. "My name is Matt Switzer, and we met briefly at the Chi Omega house party last night."

Matt's face cringed and he turned away from the young woman, as if preparing for her to stand up and slap him hard across the cheek. Instead, she curiously stared at Matt's face. A look of disgust slowly emerged on her face as his identity began to register.

"You're that guy that came up to me and my friends at the end of the night! You spouted off all this garbage about … "

Matt abruptly sat down and interrupted her before she could go on. "Wait! Hold it a minute and lemme explain! I was very … "

"Much an asshole!" she said, purposely finishing Matt's sentence. "I don't know who or what you think you are, but after last night I wouldn't even … "

Now it was Matt's turn to interrupt. "Please wait a second and let me explain!"

"No! You're a jerk, and I have better things to do than sit here and listen to your dumb-ass explanation!" She started to gather her things and stood up, intending to leave.

"Please, you gotta believe me. I don't remember what I said. If I offended you in any way, I … I just wanted to apologize and say how sorry I am. I really had a lot to drink last night and … and … and … "

Matt slumped down in his chair unable to go any further. All his problems and fears flashed before him. He pictured the young woman storming away in an angry rage, MacAllister failing him and denying him graduation, the utter disappointment on his parents' faces, and the fear of the unknown that lay in front of him. He started to tremble as a tear gently trickled down his left cheek. All at once he didn't care about his image or who saw his outbreak of emotion. Moreover, he wished the girl who had dominated his thoughts for the past day would simply walk out of his life forever and spare him any further pain or humiliation. Fully expecting to be left alone, Matt was stunned as he felt a gentle hand rest on his right shoulder.

"Hey. Are you all right? Look … I didn't mean to be so nasty … but you really were an obnoxious jerk last night," she scolded.

Matt lifted his head and turned in his chair to face the young lady who now stood beside him with her book pressed against her chest. He briskly wiped away the tear and bit his lower lip, hoping to prevent any further outbursts. He took a deep breath and started again.

"I'm sorry for being such an idiot." Matt managed to cough up a quick little laugh after realizing what a mess he had just created in front of the girl of his dreams. "I feel awful about last night … and I don't even remember what I said." His eyes locked onto her face. She could sense the sincerity in his voice and slowly sat down next to him. He continued.

"Last night I was trying to forget some stupid academic problems I'm facing, and I tried to forget them with about a hundred bottles of Natty Light. When I saw you standing in the corner with your friends, I guess you could say I was filled with 'liquid courage.' I know I started running at the mouth, and I'm deeply sorry if I said anything that upset you. Truly I am sorry. I don't ever drink a lot, I never get drunk, and I'm usually so shy that I can't even approach an attractive person like yourself, let alone talk to one. Please don't hate me. I was a fool last night … a real dumb-ass, like you said before."

Matt's words were sincere and the young woman believed him. She even managed to crack a tiny smile when Matt referred to himself as a "real dumb-ass."

"Look, as I said before, I'm sorry for being so nasty a minute ago. You just really shocked me last night. I thought you might be different than the other guys there. You looked like a nice guy until you came up to me and said what you did."

Matt cringed again at the thought of what may have come out of his mouth.

"I appreciate you taking the time to come up and apologize. I know that wasn't easy to do. A lot of guys would have just forgotten about it and pretended it never happened. Thanks for being sincere and caring."

Matt slowly began to regain his composure and felt better inside after listening to her words. He sat up straight in his chair, itched his nose, and smiled.

"Can we start over?" asked Matt to the girl he dearly hoped would become his new friend. He extended his right hand and politely introduced himself. "Hello, my name is Matthew Switzer. I'm a senior here at UMO and am trying to get my BA in History. When I'm not in class, I specialize in insulting coeds and totally humiliating myself in public places," he added with an easy chuckle.

"Hello, Matt Switzer, my name is Michelle Kessler. I'm also a senior, studying to become an elementary school teacher. My major, as you may have guessed, is Education. I'm a sister at Chi Omega and I love to spend all my free time studying in this library and basically having no life." The two shook hands and smiled at each other.

"Boy, you don't know how much better I feel right now, Michelle. For a while I thought I'd go crazy thinking about what a jerk I must have been to you last night."

"Look, forget it. It's ancient history now as far as I'm concerned. I feel better, too. The important thing is that now we understand each other better," said Michelle.

There was a brief pause in the conversation as both Matt and Michelle looked away from each other, awkwardly trying to figure out what to say next. It was Michelle who finally broke the silence.

"Well … I don't want to keep you from whatever you're doing. I'm just gonna finish this chapter and head back to the Chi Omega house," said Michelle while sitting back down at the table and reopening her textbook.

"That's cool," replied Matt with regained confidence. "I've got some heavy research to continue myself. I'm doing this intense final project for my hardest History class." Matt purposely tried to make his research sound interesting in hopes that he could bait Michelle into asking more about it, thus prolonging the conversation.

"Oh. What are you researching?" she asked softly, without taking her eyes off the page she was reading.

"Ah, you probably wouldn't be interested. It's a pretty lame topic.

Boring as hell and will have absolutely no value to me when I get out into the real world. Know what I mean?"

Michelle looked up from her book and politely cracked a small smile, trying to mask a degree of impatience.

"Well, what's the topic?"

"The American GI experience in the European theater during World War II."

There was a slightly dramatic tone to Matt's voice as he stated the subject of his thesis to Michelle. He wanted the project to sound impressive and extremely important. Something that only certain individuals of his measure could handle and conquer. There was a sense of eagerness and pride in his voice. It was a complete reversal from earlier in the day, when he could barely blurt out the words to Bobby at breakfast without feeling sick and frustrated. "As a matter of fact, I was studying on the fourth floor when I came down here to grab this important history reference book. That's when I saw you sitting here and felt I had to come over and apologize for last night."

Matt gazed at Michelle happily and praised himself for being so clever. He gently patted the book he had swiped off the shelf. It was a real smooth move he'd be sure to remember should he need to pull it from his repertoire again in the future.

Michelle looked down at the book and then up at Matt, who was still foolishly gazing at her. The expression on her face was part confusion and part silly joy. She smiled and shook her head before speaking.

"World War II you said? I don't think you'll find too many soldier stories in that book," remarked Michelle before breaking out into a soft laugh she could no longer cover.

Baffled, Matt frantically looked down and saw the title of the book in his grasp: *The Complete Poems of Emily Dickinson.*

As he read it aloud, Michelle's laughter grew louder. A look of embarrassment showed on Matt's face; although, after a moment of realizing how silly he looked, he started to laugh along with her.

"Well, I guess you're right. I don't think Emily ever shot any Germans," he blurted out between bursts of laughter. "She might have killed them with some badass poetry though!" The two laughed until both were red in the face and out of breath. Michelle was becoming more intrigued with Matt, while Matt was just happy that the girl of his dreams was even talking to him.

"You're a funny guy, Matt Switzer," said Michelle shaking her head. "And it's obvious I won't get through this chapter today." Michelle closed her textbook and leaned back in her chair, gently adjusting her hair away from her face.

"Well, now I'm curious. As a teacher wannabe, I'd like to look at your research and see how far along you've progressed. It'll be good experience for me. Plus, I need a break. Let's go up to the fourth floor and you can tell me all about your assignment. What do you say?"

"Um … sure. You can check out my work … ah … that is … like, if you really want to … I guess. It's pretty heavy stuff, though, I gotta warn ya. Ah … it's not very interesting. Ya know, just a lot of stupid facts and statistics … like, ah, how many people were killed and in what battle … you know … shit like that. Real boring crap," said Matt as he scrambled to keep the conversation going while trying to divert Michelle's attention away from his imaginary research.

"I'm sure there's more to it than that, Matt," said Michelle disbelievingly. "If you have a lot of material down on paper, even if it isn't completely, you know, well organized, I'd like to take a look at it."

Michelle stood up and began thumbing through her *Elements of Teaching* textbook, dexterously licking her fingers before turning each page. Matt leaned over her shoulder.

"Here it is," said Michelle triumphantly. She zig-zagged her finger down it until it rested on a paragraph highlighted in bright yellow.

"I was studying this the other night. Basically it's a teaching theory on how to be objective when reviewing and grading a student's work. It's very interesting. It discusses all kinds of different scenarios a teacher might run into—like if a student was related to the teacher in some way, or if the student was academically or physically challenged, or if they had some distrust or dislike for the teacher."

Matt listened intently and nodded his head agreeably. At this point he wasn't going to dispute anything Michelle asked or wanted from him.

"Okay, if you want to practice on me and my research for a little while … ahh … why not? Grab your stuff and follow me," said Matt with a tad of reluctance lumped in his throat.

Michelle gathered her books and her petite backpack. Matt smiled and grabbed the Emily Dickinson book. Michelle closed her eyes and snickered.

"All right. You got me. I don't need this and I never did. Give me an A for effort though?" asked Matt eagerly.

"Not quite yet. You're cute … but I thought you were cute last night and look where it got me," replied Michelle seriously.

"I'll just leave that one alone," said Matt with a big smile, hoping that would help ease any lingering tension. Matt haphazardly tossed the Dickinson book of poems onto the slick wooden table, where it slid to the far edge and nearly fell off the other side. It had served its purpose and helped break the ice.

"Follow me," said Matt as he walked over to the narrow spiral staircase. Michelle tilted her head and gently tucked a loose strand of her brown hair behind her left ear, being careful not to bump her backpack or hit her head. On the fourth floor, Matt looked around the dimly lit room and saw only Alice, meticulously filling out paperwork at her desk. She lifted her head and lightly waved to acknowledge him and his guest. Matt mimicked the polite gesture in return. Alice dropped her head and continued her work. Matt and Michelle meandered through the tall stacks to his jumbled pile of books and references scattered across the wooden desk where he'd been working.

"Well … um … as you can see, I really was getting into these references big time … and I … kinda lost track of where I, you know, left off," mumbled Matt, while scratching the back of his head and nervously looking around the room.

"Why don't you show me what you've got down on paper so far? We can start there. I'd like to look at your outline so I can get an idea about your thesis statement and main topic of focus and discussion," replied Michelle.

Matt stared at Michelle with the expression of a man who had just seen a ghost and was trying to hide the fact that he had wet his pants. He stumbled to find words that wouldn't make him sound like a complete and utter idiot.

"Ah, Michelle ... I really don't have any of my written material with me right now. All my, you know, statistics and ... data are laid out on an Excel spreadsheet on my hard drive back at the dorm. And ... and ... and my outline and shit ... er ... stuff, I mean, are also on my computer. I got it all on disk and ... well, it's not with me right now. I was just taking some written notes from these references here today," sputtered Matt unconvincingly.

"Okay, let's look at the notes you took. You can tell me about what you were focusing on specifically," replied Michelle.

Matt pulled a chair from under the desk and motioned for Michelle to sit down. He cleared his throat with a loud grumble and began to paw through the scattered mess of references on the desk. After several minutes Matt had done nothing but rearrange the mess and pretend to look through the various books.

"You don't have anything, do you? I can see it in your face," said Michelle with soft sympathy in her voice.

Matt sighed heavily and ran his fingers through his hair while leaning back in his chair. Frustration overtook his spirit. "Well, I got one thing," lamented Matt. "I got one hell of a problem that's just getting worse with each passing minute."

Michelle turned to face Matt. She crossed her legs and folded her hands in her lap as if she were a psychiatrist about to begin a counseling session.

"What's the problem? You're behind on this project and are running out of time? Is that it?"

"Yeah, but ten times worse than that. I haven't done anything at all on it. I basically breezed through all my other courses this semester, on my way to a strong finish. Unfortunately, in order to graduate I have to pass this stupid class. It's an upper level, independent study course on contemporary American history. My professor is some anal jerk named Mac—"

Michelle interrupted Matt before he could spit out the most reviled name in his head.

"MacAllister?" she blurted out. "I know him! I had him for Basic

American History 100 when I was a sophomore! Boy he was a real hard-ass. It was all I could do to get a C in that course!"

"He's one infamous son-of-a-bitch on this campus, that's for sure," scoffed Matt. "But I can't push all the blame onto him. I'm responsible for my own shortcomings on this one. I screwed off and didn't put any effort into this assignment. Now it's going to bite me in the ass and ruin my chances for marching at graduation. I really don't know what to do. I am spinning my wheels, and—oh, Jesus Christ!"

Matt slumped in his chair. He hoped Michelle wouldn't be offended and angry that he had misled her.

"Hey … look, Matt. I know we didn't exactly get off on the right foot, but I feel you're a decent guy. It took courage to apologize earlier, and only someone with decency and feelings would've said the things you said to me. I thank you for helping me realize you're not just another stupid male asshole with no sense of dignity or respect toward women. I think we can help each other out. My classes are pretty well wrapped up until finals begin. Before my exams start, I'd like to get some hands-on teaching practice. All that means is that I can help you organize your work and make observations on how you respond to my teaching advice. I can then whip up a little extra-credit paper that'll look great on my résumé, if my dean likes it."

"Um … that sounds great, Michelle, but how can you help me in such a short space of time? I only got two weeks or so to try to put this thing together. I have no focus and certainly no thesis. I've tried doing research and keep running into dead ends. I … I … I just don't have the willpower or the interest and definitely no time to start something from scratch. I hate war. World War II would've been my absolute last choice—if I had one that is—for a research project. I know very little about it! Please tell me that you're a real history buff and you know all about the American GI experience in the European theater during World War II."

"Sorry, Matt, I hate history. It was my worst subject ever since high school. I really don't know anything about World War II. However, I do know of a source of information that'll solve all your problems and make you the happiest student on campus come graduation day."

"The Internet?" asked Matt somewhat desperately.

"No," replied Michelle. "Not the stupid Internet! Much better than that. My grandfather was a fighter pilot who served in Europe during World War II! He lives down in Bar Harbor! We can visit him. I'm sure he can tell you all kinds of stuff first-hand. That way you won't have to rely on books and periodicals and all this other crap!" Michelle brushed aside the cluttered mess of books on the desk.

"That sounds terrific, Michelle. Wow! You are a real dream come true," said Matt with a renewed sense of hope. "It's a deal!"

Michelle reached into her backpack, pulled out a scrap of paper, and scribbled on it.

"Here's my number. Call me Monday and we'll make arrangements to meet my grandfather at his place. We can talk about what time best fits our schedule after I've talked to him tomorrow, okay?"

"Great. I don't feel so doomed after all!"

Glancing at his watch, Matt noticed that it was now 8:20. The library would be closing soon.

"Jeez, look at the time. Can I walk you out to your car or something?" he asked.

"Sure, I need to get back to the house. Got laundry to do tonight."

The two got up from the desk and headed down the main staircase toward the first-floor lobby. At the main entrance Matt stopped and looked at Michelle as other students began to exit past them.

"Michelle, I don't want to ruin our new friendship or our agreement, but it's killing me. What stupid thing did I say to you last night that made you so angry with me? I honestly don't remember."

Michelle looked Matt square in the eye and smirked. She saw the expectant look in his eyes and relished the moment. With a suspenseful and playful hint of sarcasm, she spoke.

"Well, Mr. Switzer, I can tell you this. I hope your good friend William is as up to the task ahead of you as you need to be."

Michelle pushed the library door open and walked down the stone steps into the night. Confused, Matt followed in step out the door. Michelle purposely did not slow her pace, nor turn around to acknowledge her curious trailer.

Matt raised his voice.

"Uh, Michelle! Who's William?"

Michelle playfully upped her pace to keep Matt from catching her. To compensate, she raised her voice to match his level.

"He's a very close friend of yours! You two do everything together! You tried to introduce me to him last night at the party! You were very eager for us to shake hands!"

Matt stopped in his tracks as Michelle faded into the darkness, with only the dim street lights in the parking lot keeping her from becoming completely invisible. Jamming his hands in his pockets as he habitually did, Matt tilted his head to the left and called out to Michelle again.

"Michelle! I don't know anyone named William! Was he some guy at the party or something?"

"Oh, he was there all right," cracked Michelle facetiously. "I assumed he was very smart because of the way you kept remarking about his enormously large head!"

"What? Michelle? Are you sure that it wasn't you that had too much to drink instead of me? I don't think I've ever known anyone named William!"

"You know him better by his nickname!" hollered Michelle, who was now by her car fumbling through her purse for her keys.

"What nickname?" hollered Matt, still standing stationary on the other side of the parking lot.

"The One-Eyed Sailor!" loudly replied Michelle who had found her keys and slammed the door shut on her white 1997 Ford Escort. As the engine started and the headlights pierced the darkness, Michelle rolled her window down and waved goodbye with a confident, feminine fluttering of her hand and wrist.

"The One-Eyed Sail—?" Matt began, when paralysis gripped his face and destroyed all hint of confusion. He casually looked downward toward his hands jammed firmly into his two front pockets. Then he slowly raised his head.

With a snicker and a slight shake of his head, Matt headed along the path toward Chamberlain Hall.

"Come, William! Let's go home!"

Chapter 3

THE MEETING

On Monday, April 17, Matt peered through the curtains of his dorm room window and quietly observed the streams of frenzied students racing to and from their classes. Commencement exercises were to start Saturday, May 6, with the last final exams ending by 5:00 p.m. Friday.

The weather remained mild with the midday sun shining strongly and unopposed through a cloudless pale blue sky, interrupted only by fluttering birds and the whispered sound of the breeze filtering through the treetops. He glanced at his watch for the umpteenth time, then refocused his stare out the window. It was 1:48.

"Where is she?" muttered Matt to himself with impatience laced in his voice. "Her last class ended a half hour ago. Where could she be? This morning when we talked she told me she'd be here at 1:30. What's taking her so long?"

He heaved a big sigh and abruptly turned away from the window. He plunked himself down on his futon and began idly flipping through pages of a generously illustrated World War II book. He was more concerned with Michelle's whereabouts than the contents of the book. Suddenly Matt's eyes fixated on a grainy picture of two uniformed German soldiers pointing their pistols at the backs of the heads of two men who had been tied up and forced to kneel over a large, open pit. It wasn't the sight of the German executioners that startled Matt the most, but rather the fuzzy contents of the pit, which apparently held several mangled human corpses. After studying the image for several seconds, his eyes wandered down the page to the caption.

"SS executioners pose for the camera at Dachau concentration camp, circa 1942."

With a sudden shiver, he snapped the book shut and stood up.

"Ouch. I'd hate to be those guys. That musta hurt real bad. I bet they had headaches for days! No, wait, they couldn't have. They were dead. Sorry, guys," he said entertainingly to himself without one shred of compassion or remorse. Just then the phone rang.

"Hello?"

"Hi, Matt, it's Michelle." Her soft, feminine voice instantly sent a pleasant shiver through his heart.

"Hey there, Michelle. Where are you? I thought you'd be here by now," questioned Matt.

"I'm sorry. I got hung up when I went home to change my clothes after class. The girls needed some help cleaning up the house before some parents arrived for a visit. I couldn't say no. You know how it is," answered Michelle.

"Yeah, I guess. So, are you on your way now? I've been waiting for you."

"Well, no, not exactly, I'm afraid. I'm still at Chi Omega house and I don't know when I'll be able to leave."

Matt rolled his eyes and switched the phone from his right ear to his left, managing not to entangle himself in the cord. Michelle continued explaining.

"Matt, the good news is I spoke with my grandfather late last night, and he agreed to meet you tomorrow afternoon, if it fits your schedule. I told him you were done with all your other classes and basically had lots of free time to work on this project. So you're in good shape. Hello … hello? Matt, are you still there?"

Matt remained silent for a second before answering.

"Yeah, I'm here. That sounds great, but I get the gut feeling you aren't coming with me. Is that the case? Because if it is, I gotta tell ya that I'd feel pretty uncomfortable traveling to Bar Harbor to visit a man I'd never seen nor talked to, about a subject I really know nothing about. Please tell me you're coming with me."

There was now silence on Michelle's end of the phone that made

Matt feel most uneasy. Abruptly he felt he'd stumbled upon some sort of family problem between Michelle and her grandfather that for whatever reason, caused her not to want to see him. Michelle finally answered.

"Matt, my grandfather has some very old-fashioned values. He won't discuss his war experiences when women are around. He never mentioned to my grandmother or my mother a single combat story or event that occurred while he was fighting in Europe. So it will be useless if I go with you because he won't say a thing about his past as long as I'm there. You do understand, don't you?"

Matt hesitated. "Yeah, I guess so. That doesn't make things any easier, though. I'm pretty shy around strangers."

"It'll be a good test for ya, Matt. It'll show whether you really want to graduate or not. You need to do this, and I know my grandfather can help you. He's the sweetest guy you'll ever meet. I love him to death! Hang on a second and I'll give you the directions to his house in Bar Harbor."

Matt listened as Michelle put down the phone. The voices of chattering women in another room filled the receiver. It was as though he'd been put on hold without any music, just female voices. Michelle returned momentarily and picked up the phone.

"Matt? You still there?"

"Yup. Fire away."

"Okay, here are the directions. Oh, before I forget, my grandfather's name is Henry Mitchell, but he likes to be called Hank."

Michelle dictated the directions, and Matt scratched them down on a piece of paper with a dull pencil. When he was finished he thanked her, said goodbye, and hung up. Disappointed he would have to go alone, he threw up his hands and plopped down on his bed. The bedsprings screeched under the sudden stress. After a few minutes he drifted off to sleep, dreaming about only one thing—Michelle.

The procrastinating slumber didn't last long. As much as he tried to use sleep as a convenient escape from his lingering problems, Matt needed to prepare for his inevitable meeting with Michelle's grandfather. He stood up and began puttering around the room, opening his desk drawers and shuffling the contents aimlessly.

"Well, here's a pad of paper. Might need that for writing some notes," he muttered as he placed the pad on top of his empty L.L. Bean backpack, flung on the floor in the corner of the room. He continued to dig deeper into the desk drawers.

"Hey! Here's a little microcassette tape recorder! This could come in handy."

He opened the recorder and discovered a blank tape already loaded and ready to record. He flipped the device over and snapped open the battery compartment cover where he found two batteries. He smiled happily at the thought of how much effort the tape recorder would save him from during the long-winded and boring conversation he envisioned he'd have to endure.

"Testing, one, two, three," voiced Matt into the mic after simultaneously pushing the "play" and "record" buttons. After watching the tape roll forward for a moment, Matt hit the "rewind" button and listened to the quick little squeal of tape rewinding to the beginning.

"Testing, one, two, three," played back on the tape to Matt's delight.

"This is great. This will really come in handy," he said of his newly discovered toy. The little machine had been a gift from his mother at the start of the school year. She had lovingly bought it for him in hopes that he would use it to record class lectures and aid him with his schoolwork—a very kind and caring gesture. Regrettably, he'd stuffed it in his desk drawer and completely forgotten about it. He hadn't used it once. The thought of his mother's care and willingness to support his academic pursuits caused Matt to feel horrible inside, knowing that he hadn't even had the courtesy to thank his mother for the gift let alone the willingness or responsibility to use it.

Digging even deeper into the desk drawers, Matt unearthed countless items that revealed his laziness and thoughtlessness toward those who had tried to help him through college by providing some little material contribution. Unopened packages of pencils and pens, brand new file folders, pre-stamped envelopes, an unused tape dispenser, a solar-powered calculator, various tiny boxes of thumbtacks, paper clips, and staples were strewn about in one large drawer. Most of it had never been touched at all.

A gnawing sensation developed in the pit of Matt's stomach, accompanied by a shameful feeling of guilt that threatened to consume him. Had he simply wasted his last year of college by doing only enough to get by? Could he have achieved higher grades and more self-respect had he only applied himself a little more? A tear welled up in the corner of his left eye as he stared at the diminutive tape recorder resting in his hand. After a moment's hesitation Matt gathered his reference books and neatly placed them in his backpack, together with a fresh pad of notebook paper, whose first page he titled "Mr. Mitchell's Interview Notes." Matt slid a new pack of pre-sharpened pencils into a side pocket of the backpack together with a few unused pens and 3 x 5 note cards.

"I'm gonna do this and do it right!" he thought firmly while organizing some file folders. Soon the pack was stuffed with every imaginable item he might need for his interview with Henry Mitchell.

The day was slipping by as Matt heard commotion in the hallway outside his door. His neighbors were returning from afternoon classes. It was 4:11 as he sat down at his desk to fire up his computer and begin surfing the Internet for web pages and online articles pertaining to World War II. After doing several searches, Matt hit upon numerous sources of information and began printing out pages of data. The printer hummed and screeched mechanical sounds as each word was electronically transferred from monitor to paper. Matt collected the hefty pile of documents, safely filing them in a folder inside his backpack. The phone rang loudly next to him. His eyes glued on the computer screen, Matt blindly reached for the receiver.

"Hello?"

"Yo, Matt! What's up?"

"Doing some work. Ain't got time to shoot the shit."

It was Bobby. He instantly knew what he wanted. It was getting close to dinnertime and he was ready for supper.

"Okay. You ready, or what?" Bobby inquired.

"Ready for what?" replied Matt, still searching the Internet.

"What the hell do you think, man? Look at the clock. It's almost time for the commons to open, and I'm hungry as hell! You ready to eat, or what?"

Matt rolled his eyes. "Look, I said I have some shit to do. I don't feel like eating right now. Go over without me!" said Matt abruptly.

"Like what? Your classes are over … "

"I'm doing my fucking research project for MacAllister! Remember? I told you all about it the other day? I'm meeting Michelle's grandfather tomorrow afternoon and I have to be ready. I'm working hard right now and I don't want to have my momentum interrupted. Okay, man?"

"Fine! You and your fucking momentum can spend some quality time together tonight without me! I'm going to get something to eat right now, with or without you!" fired back Bobby.

"Have fun, asshole!" replied Matt before hanging up. Turning back to his keyboard he stopped and sighed.

"Shit, I shoulda asked him to come with me tomorrow. Oh, well. Guess I'm flying solo."

It was just after ten o'clock when Matt crawled into bed. He was genuinely tired but felt he had made meaningful progress prior to his meeting with Michelle's grandfather. He clicked off the lamp and quietly fell asleep, oblivious to the endless droning sounds of muffled music, conversation, and the general commotion that never seemed to subside from his neighbors. He had gotten used to them long ago and slept quite easily. His subconscious thoughts and dreams shifted from World War II to Michelle.

Morning came all too soon and Matt fairly leapt out of bed when the alarm sounded. His mind and attitude focused sharply on the task before him. He showered and shaved in less time than it had ever taken him, in all his time at school. Back in his room, he stood in front of his open closet.

"I can't show up there looking like a bum who doesn't care what he throws on in the morning," he pondered. "I have to look somewhat respectable. That'll show ol' grandaddy Mitchell I'm serious about learning."

He reached far back into the closet and pulled out a pair of black dress pants that hadn't been worn once since his mother hung them in there the day he moved in, back in September. Matt took them off the hanger and slowly pulled on the rigid pants that had razor-sharp creases and not a single wrinkle anywhere. Matt then grabbed a white polo shirt and a pair of dark brown dress shoes hidden beneath piles of sneakers and dirty socks. They hadn't been worn since Matt last went to church before the school year started. He combed his hair and studied the directions he had scribbled down when he'd talked with Michelle. Confident he could get to Bar Harbor without getting lost, Matt snatched up his backpack and set out.

Matt hustled down the dorm's back stairway. In the parking lot he hesitated, trying to remember where he had parked. Scanning the lot intently he spotted his trusty vehicle resting dormant in one of the back rows, a dowdy little blue 1984 Volkswagen Rabbit spotted with rust.

Feeling a crisp, penetrating chill in the April air, Matt shivered a bit as he zipped up his lightweight jacket. With one last glance at Michelle's directions, he pulled his sunglasses down over his eyes and puttered out of the parking lot, along the nearest road that led off campus toward Bangor.

The sun shone brightly and soon warmed the car to the extent Matt cracked open the window. Along the roadside, scant patches of snow and ice occasionally showed, hidden under large pines and thick underbrush. What remained of winter would soon be gone.

In Bangor, Matt crossed the Penobscot River and linked up with Route 1A, headed east. After failing to find a song playing on the radio that he liked, Matt snapped it off and sank deeper into his seat. He'd never traveled this route before and it bored him. Being from southern Maine, he was used to more urban landscapes. He loved the hustle and bustle of large cities and wasn't too keen on the slower, more laid-back style of rural downeast Maine. The farther he traveled, the less he saw that impressed him. He couldn't see and appreciate the beauty, the tranquility, and the simplicity of the marvelous landscape unrolling before him.

The surrounding countryside was just waking from its long winter slumber. The trees had shaken off their heavy loads of snow and were stretching toward the heavens, full of life. The numerous lakes and ponds that dotted the area had mostly shed their thick winter coats of ice and revealed the strikingly vibrant blue color of the water they contained. Birds chirped in the trees while deer foraged through the woods without taking notice of the passing traffic. The old car chugged along at a moderate clip, dipping and climbing the long winding hills that formed the outskirts of Ellsworth.

The Rabbit motored down the road, dodging and weaving through the Route 3 traffic heading toward Mount Desert Island. Soon Ellsworth was left far behind. A whole new part of the state of Maine Matt had never seen before unveiled itself. Matt slowed down his car to pay more attention to the majestic coastal scenery that was becoming increasingly evident through his dirty windshield. The clean, brisk, salty smell of the ocean carried heavy on the breeze and curiously tantalized Matt's nostrils. He cracked the window to increase the pleasant aroma. Hailing from the southern Maine city of South Portland, Matt was not unfamiliar with the ocean. He'd spent countless hours at the beach, lying in the sun and frolicking in the surf. Old Orchard Beach was one of his favorite summertime hangouts.

Matt found himself caught up in the ravishing and naturally serene landscape unfolding before him. Waves crashed on rocky shorelines turning the deep blue ocean water into a frothy white spray that was catapulted onto land while majestically sculpted mountains covered with lightly frosted snow-white tree tops rose up toward the sky, dominating the landscape. The sky itself was replete with puffy white cumulus clouds that lazily moved across the sky. The distinct sound of seagulls echoed off in the distance and seemed to sound off in rhythm with the crashing surf. Matt was truly taken in by this unknown land he was treading on for the first time in his life.

Bar Harbor was soon upon the old Rabbit. The world seemed to come to life again as dozens of people and cars appeared from nowhere once Matt entered town. Bar Harbor was truly one of Maine's precious gems, a quaint community nestled in placid paradise along the Maine coast. It was a place where one could easily access both the sea and all it had to offer, as well as the rugged wilderness of nearby Acadia National Park.

With all the natural beauty of the ocean and the landscape, plus the intriguing activity emanating from the various shops, bars, and restaurants that lined the streets of downtown Bar Harbor, Matt was tempted to pull over his car and spend the day perusing the town. He shook off the urge and kept his focus on his goal—meeting with Michelle's grandfather before he failed MacAllister's class. The splendor of Bar Harbor would have to be enjoyed at a later date. If he was lucky, maybe he could come back during the summer and take in the town with Michelle. Maybe.

The busy streets of downtown Bar Harbor faded into the distance behind the billowing exhaust of the Rabbit. Once again nature took over and all things urban simply disappeared. The car slowed as Matt fumbled with Michelle's directions.

"Well, according to this, I should just keep going straight until Eagle Point Road shows up somewhere on the left-hand side. I wish Michelle could've come with me. Woulda made things so much easier."

The road narrowed and began to wind. The trees thickened on both sides, making it harder to see much beyond them. The strong scent of the ocean had weakened but a hint of salt remained in the air. Matt drove on, occasionally passing a small house or cottage sunk deep in the woods. Rounding a small bend in the road, Matt jumped on the brakes. The car screeched and stopped abruptly, triggering Matt's seat belt to hold him securely in place. He backed up a few feet and looked up at a green-and-white street sign partially hidden by overgrown tree branches.

"Eagle Point Road," he read aloud. "This must be the place! Not a minute too soon, either." He turned down the road and slowly proceeded. In the distance, through a clearing in the woods, he could see three houses—two on the right and one on the left. None matched the description Michelle had given him. His eyes scanned the mailboxes at the edge of the road.

"Number six … number eight … number ten. Where the hell is number twelve?" The Rabbit crawled along Eagle Point Road at a snail's pace until he spied a house set back from the road a bit and nestled along the edge of the woods. A carefully constructed stone wall marked the perimeter of the property. A shiny silver mailbox glistened in the sunlight at the end of the paved driveway. Handpainted in cursive blue script, outlined in bright white with an artistic flair, was the word "Mitchell," alongside the number 12.

The Rabbit crept slowly up the driveway and then came to a halt. Matt turned off the engine and gathered up his backpack. Slinging it over his shoulder, he hesitated for a moment and peered around. The house was not exceptionally large or very ornate; however, it had a uniquely warm and rustic charm about it. Though its age was evident, one couldn't help but notice how remarkably well it had been maintained over the years. It wasn't a rich man's mansion or a poor man's shack. It was, in fact, a practical two-story log cabin.

At the top of the stairs leading up to the front door was a porch covered by a shingled roof supported by four beams. A built-in, two-seated swing lazily creaked back and forth when the wind gusted. The porch snaked around the sides of the house to form a larger back porch. A massive stone chimney rose up high against one side of the house discharging small puffs of gray smoke into the air. The smoke blended with the chilly breeze producing an unmistakable wintry aroma that defied the smell of spring.

Windows flanked both sides of the front door. They were also present on the sides of the house and on the second level. Functional wooden shutters adorned each window and were locked in the open position to let the spring sun shine in. Attached to the opposite side of the house from the chimney, a large black steel tank held natural gas, the house's primary source of heating. From all outward appearances, the place looked very hospitable.

With a slam of the car door, Matt wandered up the driveway and onto the front lawn towards the main entrance to the cabin. Before he reached the bottom step his nostrils again caught the salty tang of the ocean. Closing his eyes and listening intently, he could make out the faint sound of waves crashing against a rocky beach in the distance behind the trees that lined the back yard. The ocean must be closer than he'd imagined. As Matt placed one foot on the first step leading to the porch, he instantly recoiled in response to a thunderous sound that sharply cracked through the cool April air.

KA-CHUNK! KA-CHUNK!

Initially taken by surprise, Matt regained his composure as his brain quickly identified the sound. It was one quite familiar in rural areas of the state and one Matt himself was used to hearing. It was the crash of someone splitting wood. Matt turned and walked past the side of the house to the back yard. His shoes gushed in the well-saturated lawn that still held patches of snow. As he rounded the corner Matt saw a gentleman with his back to him wielding a splitting maul. He raised it high above his head and brought it down hard on a block of wood, cleanly splitting it in two.

"Excuse me!" Matt called out. The man turned to face him, resting the maul on his right shoulder. "Good afternoon," said Matt as he slowly walked up to the man. "Are you Mr. Mitchell?" he asked.

"Ayuh. That's me," returned Mitchell warmly. He gingerly shifted the splitting maul from his right shoulder to rest it against a small pile of split wood at his feet. "But please call me Hank. You must be my granddaughter's young friend?" asked Hank as he extended his right hand.

"Yup. You got it. I'm Matt Switzer," Matt replied as he firmly shook hands with Hank. Matt smiled politely and added, "I appreciate your taking the time to see me, sir. I guess Michelle musta told you why I was comin.'"

"Ayuh, I spoke with her on the phone the other day and she mentioned you needed help with some research you're doing for school. That right?" asked Hank as he pulled a white handkerchief from his back pocket and mopped heavy beads of sweat off his brow.

"Yes, sir, um … I understand you did some combat flying during World War II. You were a fighter pilot?" asked Matt sheepishly.

"Yeah. I did some flying during the war. Interested in planes are ya? I could show you some beautifully illustrated books I have on commercial airliners. I even have a book that tells all about the history of the Concorde jet. I'd bet you'd like to take a gander at that!" said Hank enthusiastically.

"Uh, sure. I guess that would be okay?" replied Matt evasively.

"Good enough," answered Hank. "Just follow me into the house and we can sit down and talk more comfortably. Come on up," he added with a wave of his arm, motioning Matt to follow.

Matt stayed a few steps behind to get a better look at Hank. He wore a faded red plaid shirt and rugged tan trousers that were supported with black suspenders. A glasses case bulged in the front pocket of the plaid shirt. Upon his feet were muddied Bean boots. In his back pocket was stuffed a pair of light cotton gardening gloves.

Hank was not a large man, but he wasn't small either. He stood at about five feet, eight inches tall, relatively lean and fit, with only a slight potbelly that didn't quite hang over his black belt. He walked with a trivial slouch and favored his right leg. His face was well weathered and he wore very thick-lensed glasses supported by a weighty nose. His gray hair was cut short, neatly combed, and parted to the right. A receding hairline made his forehead seem larger than it actually was, and Hank made no attempt to conceal it. Hank looked very fit for a man Matt assumed was in his eighties. For a brief second, he could see a glimmer of Michelle in her grandfather, and it made him feel more comfortable.

Hank pulled open the flimsy storm door, then pushed in the heavier wooden front door. Matt followed Hank into the cabin's living room.

"Please excuse me for a moment, Matt. I need to clean up a little before I start to stink and drive you away before we even get a chance to get to know each other. I apologize … I knew you were comin' but that old unsplit log pile just kept callin', and I got so fidgety doin' nothin' that I had to grab my maul and start whackin' at it," said Hank. "I'm just gonna wash up a bit and maybe change my shirt. Go right ahead and check the place out while you wait. Help yourself to a Coke or some iced tea in the fridge. I'll be out in a jiffy." Hank walked down a narrow hallway and into the bathroom, closing the door behind him.

Matt set his backpack on a wooden chair in the corner of the room and started to look around. The muffled sound of running water flowed from behind the bathroom door. The living room revealed some interesting curiosities. A small couch and recliner faced an old television that looked as though it wasn't used much. It was a thirteen-inch Panasonic with no connection to an outside cable, which explained why its built-in antenna was fully extended. Matt couldn't remember the last time he'd seen a television that was operated by a turning dial and not a remote control. A large wooden bookcase built right into the wall housed dozens of old hardcover books. Taking a closer look, Matt found several works on aviation, military and otherwise, which seemed to dominate the case. Also apparent were volumes on American history, European culture, and the Far East. A few classics sprinkled here and there made him cringe back to his high-school English class days. *Treasure Island, Huckleberry Finn, Moby-Dick,* and *A Tale of Two Cities* served as a harsh repellent that made him step back and continue exploring elsewhere.

On the natural, wood-paneled walls hung several paintings of old sailing ships, commercial aircraft, and, most notably, landscapes and ocean scenes. On closer inspection Matt observed the initials "HM" inscribed on the bottom right corner of each one. The walls displaying the paintings matched the polished hardwood floors that appeared to be present in every room of the house. Occasional throw rugs added splashes of color throughout the house.

With the sound of water still running from the bathroom Matt walked into the kitchen immediately adjacent to the living room. It was a little larger than the living room and contained a good-sized refrigerator and dishwasher, both snowy white and quite new. In stark contrast was the cooking stove. It was quite a sight to behold. The black, cast-iron antique was the opulent centerpiece of the room. Its heavy, square body was offset by a lustrous nickel trim that glimmered brightly as the rays of the afternoon sun radiated upon it through the nearby window set above a round wooden table surrounded by three matching chairs.

Supporting the immense weight of the stove were four slender legs shaped like animal paws, which gave the vintage piece an almost lifelike quality. It stood on a red brick hearth that shielded the hardwood floors and the walls from its intense heat. The main oven was concealed by an ornate iron door highlighted with more metallic trim. Built into the door was a round thermometer that measured the interior temperature. Next to the main oven was a smaller door that Matt opened in puzzlement. The little oven section contained wood and wood ash, indicating that the stove was fired by wood and not electricity. Matt was astonished and smiled at its simplicity.

The stovetop had six old burner plates and was perfectly smooth. One plate had a metal lifter that revealed how the plates could be removed without burning the user's hand. Both above and to the sides of the stovetop were metal warming racks that served to keep food hot and added an extra flair to the beauty of the stove. Matt had never seen anything like it.

"That's a real antique beauty, ain't she?"

Matt wheeled around in surprise and saw Hank standing behind him, refreshed and sporting a clean shirt. The fresh scent of Ivory soap caught Matt's nostrils. Hank rubbed the smooth stovetop, eager to show off his prize.

"This belonged to my father," said Hank with a hint of pride. His slightly raspy voice was one Matt identified as belonging to someone who loved to talk endlessly. "He bought it for my mother back in the 1920s as a Christmas present. I think it was the first new appliance they ever owned. My mother managed to hold on to it until she passed away. It stayed in the family all these years and ended up with me. I love her. She was originally designed to operate from wood fire, but I had her converted to gas years ago. Much easier to deal with that way. Less of a hassle for an old fogey like me, ya know!"

"Yeah, it's really neat. I've never seen anything like it before. I bet it cooks up a storm," said Matt with as much of a smile as he could muster. Both men awkwardly fell silent for a moment as each tried to figure out what to say next. Finally, much to Matt's relief, Hank broke the silent stalemate.

"Well, young fella, um … why don't you come with me and I'll show ya some pictures of those planes I mentioned earlier. We can talk for a spell, and you can fill me in on the project you're doing for school. That sound okay?"

"Yeah, that sounds great. Let me go grab my backpack, and I can ask you some preliminary questions I wrote down and show you some of my initial research findings." Matt's voice carried a purposeful tone, as his brain's thesaurus searched for just the right words to flow off his tongue, hoping to impress Hank and prove he was sincere. The old man simply smiled and walked down a narrow hallway toward the study. Matt retrieved his backpack from the chair in the living room and followed Hank into the study.

Hank thumbed through some large picture books lying flat on top of a large, cherrywood rolltop desk in the corner of the room, flanked by two large bookcases. The study seemed to be the largest room on the first floor and possibly the biggest in the house. To Matt it also appeared to be the most interesting.

The centerpiece was another stove. Only this stove was not an antique gem like the one found in the kitchen, but rather a very modern, central-heating wood-burning model. It was a pristine Jøtul stove that rested upon another red brick hearth that mirrored the one in the kitchen. Rather than the traditional iron black, this stove was a rich, dark blue—an elegantly baked-on enamel glaze that gave it a shiny luster. The iron front doors had a Gothic arch design and built-in glass windows that provided a view of the inside. Brass draft-control handles regulated the flow of air.

Directly above the stove was a cherrywood mantel that displayed interesting trinkets. Matt's eye was drawn to a model plane. It was bright silver and easily recognizable as an old warplane.

"Please have a seat and make yourself comfortable," said Hank as he turned away from the books. Matt sat down on a small sofa that faced a large picture window, next to which was a door that led to the back deck. The sun shone through the window onto Matt's face. The natural warmth felt soothing. "Yep, these are good ones. I have a lot of interesting pictures to show you in these books," said Hank enthusiastically, as he pointed his finger to the books he was perusing. "Hey, I'll tell ya what, young fella. Start looking through this one right here, and I'll go get us some drinks." Hank plopped a heavy book in Matt's lap and shuffled down the hall to the kitchen. Matt sighed quietly and turned the pages of a volume that contained nothing but pictures of modern commercial airliners.

"Do you like Coca-Cola?" called Hank loudly from down the hall.

"Yes, Mr. Mitchell. That'll be fine," returned Matt politely. He quickly closed the airliner book and unzipped his backpack. He took out all his notes and research material he had compiled from the Internet the night before and started going over questions he had written down on a notepad.

"Do you take ice with your soda?" hollered Hank.

"Uh, yeah, I like ice with my soda, Mr. Mitchell," Matt replied, masking his mounting impatience.

"Call me Hank, Matt, not Mr. Mitchell," shouted Hank over the sound of ice cubes clinking together in tall glasses and the sizzle of Coke cascading over them.

"Sorry, Mr. Mitch—uh—I mean, Hank," shouted Matt, as he scratched on his pad.

Hank emerged into the study, carefully balancing two tall glasses of icy Coca-Cola on a serving tray. His old hands trembled a bit as he lowered it in front of Matt, who grabbed a glass and took a sip.

"Thank you, Hank," said Matt as he tasted the soda.

"You're welcome, my young friend," returned Hank as he sat down in a brown leather recliner that faced the sofa where Matt was sitting. Hank took a long swallow of Coke and placed his glass on a side table next to his chair.

"This is my favorite room in the house," said Hank proudly. "I do a lot of reading and thinking in here. I'm able to really focus on things. Sometimes when I spend time up at Acadia, I'll come home and reflect on what I've seen. Then have to go paint a picture or write down some thoughts, or simply fall asleep and dream peaceful dreams."

Hank pointed to some of his artwork that lined the walls of the study. Matt recognized the similar themes he'd seen in the living room—rugged wooded landscapes, images of the sea, and vibrant sunsets. Impressive as they were, they failed to stir Matt's interest until his wandering gaze fixed upon the canvas above the stove's mantel. He wondered how he had not noticed the riveting piece of art earlier. He stood up from the sofa to approach the painting, placing his hands on his hips.

"Ayuh. I figured you'd take some interest in that one. Most people who've seen it just can't take their eyes off it. Sometimes I wonder why I painted the damn thing," snarled Hank uncharacteristically.

"It's really cool. It's better than cool … it's awesome!" replied Matt with revitalized enthusiasm. "What are they?"

Hank sighed loudly and slowly pushed himself up from his recliner. "That bright silver plane is an American P-51D Mustang fighter, and the plane chasing it is called a *Focke-Wulf* 190A. That was a German fighter. They're both World War II warplanes," said Hank, as his voice trailed off before another loud sigh.

Matt examined the artwork in detail. The Mustang and the *Focke-Wulf* were engaged in a classic dogfight. In the foreground was the Mustang, its fuselage shot up with bullet holes and its engine lit up by a raging fire that billowed enveloping black smoke. In the background was the *Focke-Wulf*, tearing through clouds, fully intact, with its guns blazing a murderous fire of bullets. The image of the rising sun glowed behind the fighters, as did a detailed green landscape below. The planes themselves were brilliantly detailed.

Matt's eyes focused briefly on the blue-and-white star on the Mustang's tail section and atop the left wing, though he couldn't help being drawn to the large black-and-white swastika on the tail wing of the *Focke-Wulf*. It sent a chill down his spine. Of all the symbols of war he had seen or studied in the past, nothing made him cringe more than the sight of a swastika.

Sensing Matt's fascination with the German fighter, Hank shook his head and sat back down as if he knew what was next.

"Why did you paint the German fighter shooting down the American?" Matt turned and looked at Hank, whose facial expression had turned sour. "I mean, we won the war, right? You were a pilot? You musta shot down hundreds of German planes. So why'd you paint a picture of an American getting shot up and not a German?"

"Son, sit back down," said Hank, folding his arms across his chest and thinking a moment before he spoke. "There are a lot more interesting things I can tell you about than that picture. Why don't you look through this book. I flew many of the aircraft in that book when I was a commercial airline pilot. I can tell you a lot about the origins and history of those planes. Ayuh, they're quite fascinating machines, I can tell ya. Here you go."

Hank plopped the heavy airliner book in Matt's lap. Matt looked again at the Boeing 747 airliner on the cover, frustration welling up inside him. He glanced down at his watch and realized he'd been at Hank's for nearly an hour and accomplished nothing. He decided it was time to stop being polite.

"Hank, I'm not sure what Michelle told you about me and my assignment, but I can't waste time looking at books of commercial jets. I need to find out some information about World War II. And if you were a fighter pilot during the war and killed lots of Germans, great. That would make an awesome report! So please stop showing me these useless books and tell me what it was like to shoot down German planes. I can make it easier for you if you like. Here." Matt handed Hank a list of prepared questions he had written down earlier. "Read these questions I wrote down and I can record your answers with my little tape recorder here." Matt held up his recorder and began cueing up the microcassette inside. "Do we understand each other now? I apologize if I didn't make things more clear earlier. Oh, wait a minute, here's my assignment booklet that kinda explains what I have to do. Take a look at that as well. That may help you organize your thoughts."

Hank sat in silence and glared at his guest before looking at the questions. He finally adjusted his glasses and began reading down the page, his expression growing darker with each sweep of his eyes. Hank removed his glasses and rubbed his eyes as though he were trying to relieve a sudden migraine headache. He then spoke.

"Son, what the hell kinds of questions are these? Do you realize just what in the hell you're asking? Do you have any respect at all for yourself and others? I would be ashamed to ask these types of questions of any veteran!" He then got up out of his chair and began pacing slowly in front of Matt, still grasping the paper in his hand. "How many Germans did I kill? Lord, why is that all they ever what to know? How many planes did I shoot down? How much damage did I inflict on German industry? How many tanks and guns did I blow up? Did I ever kill any civilians on purpose or otherwise? How many of my friends were killed in combat? What was it like to see my friends die? What would possess your young mind to ask questions like these? This isn't research, it's just plain disrespectful, morbid curiosity from a child who has no more concept of that time period than a garden slug!"

Hank dropped the list of questions on the floor and sat back down in the recliner. He picked up the assignment booklet and started to read from it. Matt sat frozen on the sofa, not daring to speak or to move. He figured that any moment he would be asked or forced to leave and then would be faced with losing any chance with Michelle as well as miserably failing MacAllister's course. The depression he'd felt a few days earlier was gradually creeping in again.

"The American GI experience in the European theater during World War II?" said Hank inquisitively. "That's a pretty broad, vague subject, young fella." Matt snapped out of his trance and perked up. He was glad Hank hadn't told him to get out.

"Yes, sir. I know it's very broad. I think my professor made it that way purposely, to see what type of focus we'd concentrate on, or something."

Hank continued to read. "This booklet notes you're supposed to've done research and reported your findings at various times throughout the semester. Have you done this?"

"No, sir," said Matt quietly, hanging his head.

"So am I to understand that you haven't done a damn thing throughout the semester until now? You haven't done any research or chosen a topic to concentrate on? You simply expect me to blurt out some gory war statistics that you'll write down and pass in? Well, my young friend, that ain't gonna cut it." Hank tossed the assignment booklet back to Matt and drank another large swallow from his glass of Coca-Cola.

"I'm sorry, Hank. I messed up. I know that now. I put off and ignored the assignment as long as I could. Now it's too late, and I can't do anything about it. I tried to throw together some facts and figures from crap I downloaded from the Internet and books I got from the library, but that's not gonna work. I thought I could come here and get enough oral history from you to piece something together and pass it in. I guess I was wrong about that, too. I'm sorry I bothered you. I'll go now and leave you alone." Matt began gathering up his things.

"Sit down, boy. I ain't done with you yet," snapped Hank authoritatively. Matt sat back down on the sofa. "I appreciate your honesty, son. Most kids like you would've just told me to go to hell and stormed outta here. That's just the type of lack of respect your generation spreads like wildfire. I'm gonna make a deal with you. If you truly want me to tell you about my war experiences, I will … on the condition you put your best effort into this assignment and do everything in your power to listen and learn what's being taught to you. I ain't got time for bullshit, Matt. Personally, I believe that learning about the progress mankind has made in making life easier and better in the commercial airline industry is of far greater interest than the death and destruction brought about by war; however, I realize your assignment is war-related. I'll help with this, if you really want to be helped."

"Yes, sir! I want your help very much. I promise I'll listen and work hard so I can write a good report. Thank you, Hank. Thank you for understanding my situation," Matt gushed with relief.

"Okay, then. The first thing I want you to do is go home and take this list of questions and burn them. Then I want you to come back here tomorrow afternoon with a clear head and a sharp pencil. Be prepared to listen and learn. I'm gonna take you back to a very difficult time and place for me. Over the next few days I'll tell you a story that will forever change your outlook on life—past and present. Are you prepared for that, son?"

Not knowing quite what to say or how to react, Matt simply nodded as he slung his backpack over his shoulder. Hank put his hand on Matt's shoulder and walked him out the front door.

It was now well into the afternoon and Matt had a long drive back to Orono. The strong smell of the sea carried by the wind flooded Matt's nostrils. As he drove away he could hear *KA-CHUNK, KA-CHUNK!* Hank had returned to his woodpile.

Chapter 4

THE NEXT ENCOUNTER

The next day the Orono campus was covered with an early-morning frost that coated the ground like a fine powdered sugar. The air had a bite to it that drove many ill-prepared students, who had carelessly wandered outside in light clothing, to seek temporary refuge. One such shelter that harbored many cold and weary pupils caught by the unexpected chill between classes was the Bear's Claw, a small restaurant in the Student Union.

At a snugly hidden corner booth sat Matthew Switzer and Michelle Kessler. They had arrived just after the place opened at eight o'clock. Matt sat talking and gesturing while Michelle listened and scribbled notes on a white legal pad. She motioned for him to stop talking by sticking her palm in his face.

"Well, it seems you really didn't accomplish much of anything yesterday. You didn't take any notes or record any conversations or anything! Didn't you tell my grandfather about your assignment? Didn't you ask him any questions or … "

"Look," said Matt calmly. "It's like I was telling you before. We got off on the wrong foot. In the beginning I couldn't get a word in. He just kept shovin' all these airline books and soda at me. Then he made me look at all his artwork and other things around the house. I swear he could've kept me there all day and done nothing but rag on about his antique kitchen stove!"

"Well, why didn't you politely interrupt him and get on with your assignment?" Michelle asked, scribbling on her pad.

"I did," replied Matt unconvincingly. "But … he kinda took things the wrong way and, uh … ” His voice trailed off as his eyes slid down the table, away from Michelle's attentive stare.

“You're not telling me something, Matt. What happened? Did my grandfather lose his temper or something? Did you do something stupid? What? Just tell me. I'm not going to get upset. One part of becoming a good teacher is learning how not to take sides or show favoritism. I'm not gonna go ballistic on you because you might have offended my grandfather. So tell me what happened.”

Matt sat up in the booth and reestablished eye contact with Michelle. He folded his hands together and began to speak with honesty.

“Michelle … it's like this. I got very impatient with Hank. I didn't expect him to act like Martha Stewart and play the part of ‘good host.’ I just wanted him to answer my questions so I could get outta there and write something up. I lost my cool a little bit and he went off on me! I admit I was acting like a bit of an ass, but I was, you know, not accomplishing nothin'. I was mad and he was getting mad with me … and we were … ”

Matt kept groping for the right words but found none. His hands gestured in circles like a pair of spinning car tires mired in mud. Michelle spoke up.

“Jesus, Matt. You really don't have a clue do you? Maybe this whole thing was just a bad idea. I should go now,” she said as she started to pack up her notes.

“No, wait!” Matt blurted out, grabbing for her hand. “I realized that I was wrong with the way I went up there and a lot of the things I said just before I left. I really felt bad and a little embarrassed. Hank told me to come back this afternoon. We're gonna try it again. I think we both know what to expect from each other this time. It'll be better, I know it. I'm sorry if I offended you or Hank. Please just don't go away angry,” pleaded Matt.

With a hint of compassion in her eyes, Michelle sat back down, sipped from her coffee mug, and gave Matt a reassuring look.

“Well, if you're heading back down there this afternoon you'd better get going soon. And if it makes you feel any better, I always hated looking at those stupid old airline books, too!”

They both smiled foolishly. Matt felt a sense of relief and knew today would be more agreeable. Michelle looked at her watch, said goodbye, then rushed off to class. Matt sat in the booth, wondering what his next meeting with Hank would be like. He had no idea what was waiting for him several miles away in Bar Harbor.

The day grew colder and grayer as midday approached. The old blue Rabbit sputtered along the highway headed for Bar Harbor. Despite his heavy winter coat, Matt shivered, cursing the car's heater that chose to work only sporadically and then not at all.

"C'mon, you piece of shit! Pump out some heat!" Matt barked angrily at his mechanically stressed vehicle as he fiddled with the heater controls.

As Matt arrived at 12 Eagle Point Road just before eleven, waves were crashing rhythmically in the distance. He stared up at the cabin. The chimney gently released a small and steady spiral of smoke that danced easily with any hint of wind on this otherwise raw and still forenoon. With shaky confidence, Matt walked up the front steps and gently rapped on the door. There was no answer. He knocked again a little harder and shivered in his shoes until the door finally opened.

"Well, I didn't expect you this early. Figured you'd be along later in the day. No matter. Better this way. We'll cover more ground, which you certainly will need, young fella. Come on in and get warm. Isn't fit for man or beast out there today. Sure glad I got to that old tree yesterday," said Hank as he let Matt in and started down the hallway toward his study.

"Thanks for inviting me back, Hank," said Matt weakly. "I'm sure that we ... "

"Yeah, okay, c'mon in here and sit down," replied Hank curtly without turning to face his young guest. With slight apprehension, Matt reentered the study. He sat down on the sofa in the same spot he had occupied before. Hank was already seated in his chair with his legs crossed and his hands folded. His gaze was fixed on the brilliant glow of the fire in the wood stove. The flames were delightfully soothing as they danced upon the slowly charring wood. The reflection of the firelight mirrored in Hank's glasses as he watched the fiery ballet unfold.

For fear of irritating Hank, Matt quietly unpacked his backpack and made as little sound as possible. He dreaded that shattering the silence would somehow be unwise. As he flipped a few pages on his notepad and cued up his tape recorder, he leaned toward a small table lamp, which provided the only source of light other than the fire. The study held a much darker complexion today, mirroring the gloomy weather outside. Only the light of the flickering fire broke the indomitable tension and gloom that grasped the room and Hank as well.

Several minutes went by and still Hank said nothing, but stared into the fire, a melancholy expression gripping his wrinkled face. Realizing something had to be done to break the icy mood, Matt drew on his courage and spoke up.

"If you like, we can start with some questions ... "

"No. Stop right there," interrupted Hank, as he held up his hand without taking his eyes off the fire. He then slowly stood and focused his eyes on the painting above the mantel that had so attracted Matt's attention the day before. He clasped his hands behind his back and slowly shook his head as his eyes swept over every brushstroke. The image of the burning Mustang fighter being ripped to pieces by the pursuing *Focke-Wulf* captivated Matt's imagination as he wondered about the significance of the painting.

"Goddamn thing!" said Hank abruptly as he quickly turned away and sat back down. His eyes were serious as he focused on Matt. The easygoing charm and polite hospitality he had shown yesterday was gone. He was a different man altogether, and that sent a shiver up Matt's spine. As much as he didn't want to admit it to himself, Matt secretly wished Hank would plop an airline book in his lap and start carrying on as he had done yesterday.

"Son, I hope your attitude has changed since yesterday," Hank said. "All last night I tossed and turned, my head filled with unpleasant things. Things I've learned to suppress over time. Things I don't like to talk about and things that scare the living hell out of me! I understand what your assignment is and I'll do my best to accommodate your research, should you truly be sincere. But like I said before, I ain't got time for bullshit! I talk; you listen, learn, and understand. I haven't talked about the war since I was honorably discharged back in forty-six. Found no reason to. Not to my friends, not to my coworkers, and especially not to my family. I never dreamed a person of your generation would have the slightest bit of interest in what a broken-down old fart like me had to say about something that happened so damn long ago. However, you're here and you really don't have to be, so that tells me something."

Hank drew a long breath and sat up in his chair. He put his hands together as if he were about to pray and spoke again.

"For however long you desire, I promise to tell you about my experiences as an American Air Force combat pilot during my tour of duty in World War II. I'll be as honest and as accurate as I can be. Understand it's been a long time and what I'm going to tell you is something I don't like to talk about. What you take away from this is entirely up to you. Do you understand?" Hank's raspy voice quivered slightly.

"Yes, Hank, I understand," replied Matt softly as he turned on the tape recorder and picked up a pen. His eyes showed an uncertain fear as he looked at Hank leaning toward him.

"Matt, if you're ready for a trip to Hell and back ... I'll take you there. Are you ready?"

"Yes."

The Douglas C-47 Skytrain rumbled through the early-morning sky at an altitude of five thousand feet. Both its Pratt & Whitney radial engines roared loudly as they powered the propellers that sliced through the air with razor-like precision. The olive-green plane and its passengers flew alone without another man-made object in sight. Only the endless expanse of the North Atlantic Ocean was visible. Two hours ago, the C-47 had been safely parked on a narrow runway on a British base located in the Azores, but now it was airborne and isolated over a great ocean.

Twelve American fighter pilots sat silent, peering into the vast nothingness. One pilot was fixated on a copy of the novel *Treasure Island*. Neither the constant drone of the mighty engines nor the occasional jostle of head-on turbulence disrupted his concentration. As were the others, he was young, only twenty-six, and in excellent physical condition. His full, dark brown hair was plastered down by oily hair tonic and covered by an officer's U.S. Army Air Force cap. The eagle on the front of the cap shone brightly, as did the buttons on his dark, olive-drab coat. Both collar lapels displayed brass "U.S." pins, while fighter pilot flight wings adorned the space above his left breast pocket. Lieutenant-rank insignia bars embellished both left and right shoulder loops. His light-colored khaki pants were without wrinkle, while his russet leather shoes completed the impeccable military attire. He remained silent, engrossed in the book. Suddenly, a voice a few seats down broke the silence.

"Hey, Mitchell, whatcha readin'?"

The young pilot lifted his head and locked his dark blue eyes on his fellow airman.

"*Treasure Island*, Righetti," he replied as he scratched an itch on his clean-shaven cheek.

"You thinkin' of joinin' the Navy, Mitchell, or are ya gonna search for buried treasure when we land in England?" cracked Righetti. Some of the other men chuckled.

"It's a classic, Righetti. I'd loan it to you, but it doesn't have any pirate pictures in it. You'd be lost without pictures! Plus all those big English-sounding words would confuse a dumb Brooklyn boy like you," Mitchell replied playfully.

"Hey, don't bash Brooklyn! If it wasn't for dumb Brooklyn guineas like me, them limeys down there in England woulda lost this fight years ago. They'd all be readin' *Mein Kampf* instead of *Treasure Island*. Think about that one, Hank," said Righetti with a confident smile and an extended pointer finger.

"Yeah, you might be right, Sam," replied Hank, making sure to address Righetti by his first name only after he did so first. "Do me a favor and shut up so I can finish this chapter before we land. Can you do that?"

"Whatever you say, Lieutenant," said Sam as he sank back into his seat, still smiling. Hank put his head back down and resumed his reading.

Soon the North Atlantic gave way to the southern English countryside. The C-47 gradually descended over the lush, green landscape toward the makeshift Jefferson Airfield, which was run and controlled by the American 9th Air Force. Jefferson Airfield was not your typical U.K. fighter base. It didn't have the characteristic A-shaped runway layout, nor the various hardstands where numerous fighters were parked inside the perimeter road. The field was much smaller, with fewer accommodations than the prototypical English base. In 1939, it hadn't existed at all. It was hastily constructed and finished in 1940, just before the Battle of Britain commenced. Its location had strategic importance, though it was never given any priority, in terms of fighters or base personnel. Thus it remained largely forgotten, understaffed, and poorly supplied, even as the Americans took it over in late 1943.

The base comprised two large blister hangars, one headquarters building for the commanding officer and his staff, a tower, a mess hall, and several smaller half-pipe-shaped Nissen huts used for barracks and bathroom facilities.

As the C-47 approached the runway, the pilot received landing instructions from the tower. He deployed the landing gear and ordered his copilot to adjust the flaps. He methodically worked the stick and rudder, pulled back the throttle, and taxied the plane to a full stop at the end of the runway. The twirling propellers gradually slowed until they were at complete rest. Looking out the cockpit window, the pilot noticed a vehicle slowly approaching, so he flipped off his headset and climbed back into the cabin.

"Gentlemen, we have arrived," said the pilot to the still-seated group of pilots. The door to the C-47 yawned open, and the men stepped out, saluting the major in the passenger seat of the jeep that rolled out to greet them.

"Captain Al Davenport and Lieutenant Dennis Malloy, sir!" said the pilot, as he and his copilot snapped to attention. The major returned the salute and watched the parade of pilots climb out of the plane.

"At ease, Captain Davenport," ordered the major. "You and your copilot will come with me for a quick debriefing while your plane gets refueled and inspected. We'll get you some food and coffee before we send you on your way. Once we check in with R.A.F. Fighter Command, we'll see if we can get you sufficient fighter cover on your return trip to the Azores. Hop in."

"Yes, sir," responded Al and Dennis in unison as they jumped into the back of the idling jeep behind the grungy mechanic bearing sergeant's stripes sitting at the wheel. The major then turned to the twelve pilots.

"Ten-hut!" shouted the major. The twelve snapped to attention, forming a perfect line parallel with the C-47. "I am Major Jamison. Welcome to Jefferson Airfield. You men will be escorted directly to the barracks where you will stow your gear. You will then be taken to an assembly area where we will begin processing and preparing you for fighter squadron assignment with the 9th Air Force."

As he spoke, several more jeeps rolled up alongside the C-47.

"Gentlemen, before I dismiss you, will Lieutenant Hank Mitchell step forward?" asked Major Jamison.

Hank stepped forward, remaining firm at attention, unaware he was still grasping his copy of *Treasure Island*. Jamison approached him.

"Lieutenant Mitchell, you will immediately report to Colonel Dexter's office in the headquarters building next to the tower," said Jamison as he pointed Hank in right direction.

"Yes, sir," replied Hank, saluting the major with the book still in hand, knocking his own cap off.

"That's a good book, son," said Jamison holding back his disgust. Hank slowly bent down to retrieve his cap while still trying to keep at attention. "But do me a favor and stow it in your duffel bag before you do the same stupid thing in front of the colonel!"

"Yes, sir!" said Hank, recomposing himself.

"Dismissed, Lieutenant!" barked Jamison. Hank picked up his bag and hurried away in the direction of the colonel's office. Behind him he heard Jamison issuing a few more orders before his fellow pilots climbed into the waiting jeeps and sped off toward the barracks. Why had he been singled out? Certainly this must be some disciplinary reprimand. For what, remained a mystery. As Hank passed the guard standing outside the entrance he suddenly wished he were with his fellow pilots, settling into the barracks instead of walking into the building that housed the small base's commanding officer. Upon entering, Hank was greeted by another lieutenant.

"Lieutenant Mitchell?" asked the fellow lieutenant.

"Yes, I'm Mitchell," replied Hank.

"Lieutenant Stevenson. I am one of Colonel Dexter's adjutants. The colonel is detained at the moment, but will see you shortly. Please follow me and I'll escort you to his office where you can wait."

Lieutenant Stevenson led Hank up a narrow flight of stairs. At the top of the steps was a tight and cramped office space where a few officers and general staff sat pecking at typewriters and reviewing military maps of the French coastline. Lieutenant Stevenson bobbed and wove through the maze until he reached a closed door on the far side.

"In here, Lieutenant Mitchell," directed Stevenson.

The door slammed shut behind Hank, catching him off guard and sending a shudder up his spine. What could this business be about? He racked his brain to identify any past wrongdoing that could have landed him in trouble with his new commanding officer. He hesitated as he looked around the small office.

Directly facing him and the door was the colonel's desk, littered with scattered unfinished paperwork. The white walls were bare; several cardboard boxes full of documents, maps, books, and other material were stacked in the corner. Behind the desk was a large picture window that offered a decent view of the airfield. From here Hank could see most of the small base. Looking up, he saw the top of the control tower that was next to the headquarters building. In the distance he could make out perpendicular runways. Nearby were two large, open, steel-blister hangars. One was in clear sight while the view of other was mostly obstructed. Scattered outside the hangars and alongside the runways were three manned anti-aircraft batteries enveloped in brown high-stacked puffy sandbags. Aside from the occasional jeep that sped across the grass field, there was little activity to be seen. The inactivity and the absence of fighter aircraft puzzled Hank. Not one was visible anywhere. Strange for an active U.S. airfield in southern England not to have any fighters in sight. Hank shook his head and walked away from the window. The mounting questions in his mind were giving him a headache. He sat down in a wooden chair opposite the colonel's desk and waited for his arrival. Maybe the colonel would shed some light on the situation.

Several minutes passed as Hank sat patiently. Suddenly, the door swung open and Colonel Dexter barreled inside, rushing around his desk without taking notice of the lingering lieutenant. He sat down and began rifling through papers, not even stopping to acknowledge Hank, who had sprung to his feet and raised his right arm to salute. Hank stood erect and at attention, feeling very awkward that Colonel Dexter was completely ignoring him. He was afraid to speak and decided the best course of action was simply to remain at attention. A small bead of perspiration slowly emerged and began to trickle down his left temple. Finally Dexter broke the silence.

"At ease, Lieutenant," ordered Dexter as he finally found what he was looking for. Hank immediately went from attention to parade rest and breathed an inaudible sigh of relief.

Colonel Dexter still did not make eye contact or formally acknowledge Hank's presence. He began thumbing through the papers in a manila folder and leaned back in his chair as he rapidly processed the contents. Hank studied the colonel and noticed that his uniform was a bit sloppy, even unbuttoned in places. His tie was loose and shirt opened slightly. Even the eagles on his uniform's shoulder loops seemed dingy and unpolished. Very rare for a colonel, and especially a commanding officer, thought Hank. However, he wasn't about to point out any of these flaws, considering he might be in trouble himself. Dexter looked up from his file and glared at Hank.

"Sit, Lieutenant," he ordered.

"Yes, sir."

"Lieutenant Henry Mitchell, formerly of the 232nd Fighter Group, 44th Fighter Squadron of the 9th Air Force operating out of Egypt, North Africa, from February, 1943 to September, 1943." Dexter paused for a moment as his eyes scanned further down Hank's file. "After the collapse and subsequent pullout of the Africa Korps from Tunisia, your squadron was then reassigned to support 15th Army Group during the invasion of Sicily in Operation Husky—more specifically, Patton's 7th Army advance. You've never been shot down yourself and have never lost a wingman to enemy fire. Your flight skills with the Republic P-47 Thunderbolt are listed as 'exceptional' by your former commander, and you have experience with the Curtis P-40 Warhawk and the North American

P-51B Mustang. Your rating by your former commander reflects that you're a noteworthy, textbook combat pilot who was a leader and credit to his squadron. In October of 1943, you were sent back to the States to be treated for an acute case of pneumonia. When you finally recovered after several months, you immediately requested a new tour of duty. One month ago you were flown from New York to the Azores, where you were deposited with the eleven other pilots here today. You trained hard with the Brits stationed there and got into the air every available chance. You twelve pilots formed a pretty tight-knit group and were quoted as saying you'd all like to serve together."

Colonel Dexter closed the file folder and dropped it onto his desk amongst all the other scattered paperwork. He sat up straight in his chair, wrung his hands, and quietly stared at Hank.

"Ahhh, sir, what exactly is … " started Hank in reply before being abruptly cut off by the colonel.

"Seen any air-to-air combat, son?" asked Dexter as he removed his officer's cap from atop his head revealing a mostly bald skull.

"No, sir. I haven't recorded any air-to-air kills," answered Hank.

"I see, Lieutenant," said Dexter as he turned to gaze out the window, fixing his stare on the partially obstructed hangar Hank had glimpsed earlier. "Well, son, I image you're wondering what this is all about, so I'll cut through the bullshit and give it to you straight. You and the eleven other pilots transferred to my command have all elected not to return to the States and to stay in this fight, even though you've flown enough missions to warrant being rotated stateside for pilot instructor duty. I admire men willing to stay in this fight and see it through. That says something about your fortitude and character that I truly admire in a combat pilot. Now, I have reviewed all the files regarding yourself and your comrades. After careful study of yours, I've decided to offer you a mission of the utmost importance, to be carried out before the imminent Allied invasion of Fortress Europe."

Hank sat motionless and tried not to show any emotion that might reveal weakness. He watched the colonel slowly pace back and forth behind his desk, his arms folded tightly against his slipshod uniform. Hank's military stare was cold and hard, and he knew what was coming next. The colonel spoke again.

"Lieutenant, this mission has been classified top secret by my superiors and the top commanders of the U.S. 9th Air Force. At this time I cannot divulge any more information. But before you leave this office, I have to ask you one question. Are you willing to accept a top-secret mission without knowing any of the details beforehand?"

The colonel stood stone-faced and glared directly into the soul of the young combat pilot seated in front of him. Hank's mind raced wildly, as adrenaline coursed through his veins. His heart thumped fiercely as he rose to attention and saluted the colonel.

"Yes, sir!" trumpeted Hank, as his mind became clouded with thoughts of duty, spirit, and great honor. The thought of any danger or risk never entered his head. The dark veil of the unknown never permeated his thoughts. For the moment the adrenaline shielded him.

Colonel Dexter nodded in approval and motioned for Hank to stand at ease. "Very well, son. I was hoping for that answer." Dexter opened the office door and called for Lieutenant Stevenson, who promptly hustled up. "Lieutenant Stevenson, take Lieutenant Mitchell to the barracks and get him settled in. Inform Major Jamison that I would like him to report to my office immediately."

"Yes, sir," said Lieutenant Stevenson, as he saluted. Colonel Dexter then turned to Hank.

"Lieutenant Mitchell, I expect you to get settled in quickly and discuss nothing that has transpired in this office with anyone on this base. You will report to Major Jamison at 1300 hours tomorrow, when you will receive your next set of orders. Stevenson, make sure the lieutenant is taken care of. That will be all, gentlemen." Dexter retreated into his office and closed the door firmly behind him.

The two officers exited the headquarters building, Stevenson in the lead and Mitchell a step behind. They walked across the field towards the barracks. Without breaking stride Stevenson turned his head to Hank and spoke.

"You're from Maine, Lieutenant?"

"Yes, that's correct. Born and raised," answered Hank.

"What town?"

"I grew up in a coastal town named Cape Elizabeth but I was born in the nearby city of Portland, which is the large ... "

"Largest city in the state," interrupted Stevenson. "Yup, I know. I grew up in Portsmouth, New Hampshire. Me and my folks would travel up to Portland all the time. Small world, huh?" he said with a smile.

"Yeah, I guess it is, Lieutenant," replied Hank. "Maybe we'll get a chance to talk about home a little more some time."

"Maybe." Stevenson reached for the door to the barracks and led Hank to the nearest available bunk.

"This one's yours, Lieutenant. Get your stuff stowed away as quickly as possible and get settled. All you boys will be fed a late lunch at 1400 hours. I've got to go find the major right now, so I'll leave you to settle in. Remember the colonel's orders, Lieutenant, and if you need assistance with anything, send a runner to find me."

After Stevenson's departure, Hank found himself surrounded by his fellow flyers. Righetti, whose unmistakable Brooklyn accent drowned out everyone else, cornered him.

"Where'd you go, Hank? Why'd you get special treatment? How come you didn't have to sit through Jamison's half-assed orientation lecture?"

"No particular reason, Sam. The colonel wanted to see me to clear up some misplaced paperwork concerning my file. Nothing more. What about you guys? What's the story so far?" asked Hank, attempting to take the pressure off himself.

"Well, Jamison didn't say much, other than to tell us we'd all be getting assigned to squadrons in the 8th and 9th Air Forces, and that we'd probably be broken up. We ain't even gonna be based here. He said we'd be transported to some base farther north, in preparation for the invasion of Europe. This place is getting stripped down and packed up. I ain't even seen one friggin' fighter here! We don't know how long we're gonna be here or where we're gonna be reassigned, or if we'll even get a chance to log any flight time. Don't make a helluva lot of sense to me," Righetti spouted.

"Where are the other pilots already stationed here?" asked Hank, as he looked around the barracks at the many empty bunks.

"We're it!" shouted Righetti sarcastically as he threw his hands up in the air and turned his head to his ten other pilots. "There ain't any pilots on this base, according to Jamison. Only cooks, mechanics, a couple of MPs and the colonel's staff. I sure hope to hell the Jerries don't find out about this place. One wing of 109s could turn this so-called base into a smoldering pile of shit before we could so much as lob a fucking rock back at 'em! Just don't make any sense at all to me." Righetti backed away and plopped down on his bunk.

"Calm down for a moment and think about it, Sam. If you just think for a second you'll see that the situation makes perfect sense," explained Hank.

"Well, why don't you explain it to all of us, so we'll all feel nice and cozy in our new temporary home," Righetti mocked.

Hank sighed and gently rubbed his forehead to alleviate the growing pain in his skull caused first by the colonel and intensified by Righetti's annoying voice. He gathered his thoughts and spoke to his peers as a teacher would address a classroom of students.

"Obviously, the invasion of Europe is very close. We've known this for a few weeks now. Having just come from the Azores and all requesting to be a part of this theater of operations, it's obvious to me our timing is bad. They know we want to be a part of this upcoming fight, but, unfortunately for us, they don't know what to do with us. This base is obviously in some sort of pre-invasion transition, and we're caught up in it. Simple as that, guys. We'll get our flying orders soon enough and be outta here. Meantime, I say we do our damnedest to fit in and follow orders."

"You might be right there, Mr. Long John Silver, but I think there's more to the story than that," said Righetti. "I think that Colonel Dexter has got something up his sleeve. I'll bet he's got special plans for all us guys."

Hank turned away and lay back on his bunk. The room filled with idle chatter as Hank whispered inaudibly to himself.

"Yeah, Sam, I bet the colonel does have something up his sleeve. I can bet my life on it. I only wish I knew what it was."

The rest of the day passed quickly. Hank and his comrades were fed twice before bedding down for the night. The base remained eerily quiet and vacant. Neither Major Jamison nor Colonel Dexter joined any of the men for either meal. Only a few base mechanics and some personnel from Dexter's staff were present at distant tables in the mess hall when Hank and his men ate. With only the occasional appearance of Lieutenant Stevenson acting as liaison between command and Hank and his fellow officer pilots, all forms of normal military procedure and communication Hank had been accustomed to under previous commands remained shrouded in obscurity.

The darkness of night soon blanketed southern England, entombing the base in uneasy silence and inactivity. Amidst the light snoring of the sleeping occupants within the pilots' barracks, one man remained wide awake. Hank lay motionless on his cot, gazing at the ceiling. No matter how physically or mentally exhausted he felt, he couldn't help but wonder and worry about the top-secret mission he had so fervently, yet perhaps foolishly, volunteered for. Top-secret missions were rarely discussed, even among regular enlisted men with big visions of heroism and even bigger mouths. To most experienced officers, and even the long-time noncoms, top secret meant one thing—death. Hank shuddered at the thought and rolled over on his side.

As he forced himself to close his eyes, they quickly snapped open again. His trained fighter-pilot's ear had picked up the familiar drone of an engine breaking the silence of the cool, dark night. Hank rose off his cot and peered out the barracks' small port of a window. His eyes were fixed on the sky. A gentle breeze blew through the open window, causing Hank's dog tags to clink against each other. He stood there in his white undershirt and boxer shorts and bare feet, as the sound grew louder and louder.

"What is it?"

Hank spun around quickly at the voice behind him. Apparently the sound from outside had caught Righetti's ear, as well.

"I'm not sure. It sounds like a bomber. Definitely four engines," answered Hank quietly.

"You think it's a Jerry?" whispered Righetti nervously.

"I don't know, Sam. But if it was a Jerry, I figure all hell would be breaking loose about now," deduced Hank, continuing to survey the still very quiet airfield.

Without warning the lights along the main runway lit up. In the distance Hank and Sam could see activity in the tower. The sound of approaching aircraft grew louder and louder, awakening several of Hank's comrades and bringing them to the barracks windows. Seconds later a giant, winged shape emerged from the darkness and touched down on the runway. The onlookers identified the unmistakable silhouette of the four-engine bomber.

"Well, I'll be damned. It's a B-24," said Hank as he scratched the top of his head.

"What the fuck is a Liberator doing landing here at this fucked up base in the middle of the night?" asked Righetti irritably.

"Maybe it's damaged and needed to make an emergency landing," replied Hank.

"See any damage?" asked Righetti, as his shorter frame didn't allow him to see past Hank's body and out the small window.

"Nope. No visible damage, anywhere. Wait a minute. That's interesting."

"What?"

"I see 15th Air Force markings on her," exclaimed Hank.

"Move outta the way and lemme see," said Righetti impatiently.

Hank stepped aside, so Sam could look out the window. As he did, the runway lights suddenly cut out, immersing the field in inky darkness.

"Shit, I can't see it now," complained Righetti.

Just then, two jeeps with their headlights carelessly slicing through the darkness drove up to the bomber and greeted the crew. The shadowy figures climbed into the jeeps and sped away toward the main headquarters building.

"Great, more shit that doesn't make sense," moaned Righetti as he lay back down on his cot.

Hank sat on his cot, more confused and worried than ever. Was this bomber landing routine, or something more? Was he reading more into this than he should be? Was the unidentified crew to be involved in the impending top-secret mission, too? More questions than answers clouded his mind to the point he could no longer dwell on them. The answers would come eventually, whether he wanted them to or not. Soon the onslaught of fatigue was too much to overcome, and Hank fell soundly asleep.

The night hours waned into the early hours of morning. A low, dull rumbling in the distance shook the sleep from Hank's now relaxed mind and body. His eyes flickered open. The barracks was still encased in darkness. Again and again he heard the dull, booming sound and rose to look out the window to see if it was raining. To his surprise, the ground and the air were completely dry. Where was the thunder coming from? Surely a storm was brewing and any moment the heavens would open, pouring buckets of rain over southern England, much like it often did over Hank's home in southern Maine. Then reality hit him. He peered in the direction of the English Channel and occupied France.

"Someone's catching hell right now. I just hope it's our guys doing the throwing," mumbled Hank to himself, realizing the thunder he was hearing was most likely the sound of bombs being dropped on German targets along the French coast by way of British Lancaster night bombers. Just then the barracks door swung open and a dark figure approached Hank.

"Lieutenant Mitchell, glad to see you're up. It is now approximately 0500 hours. I will return at 0530 and I expect you dressed and ready to come with me. No questions. Understood?" whispered Lieutenant Stevenson, whose low voice caused a few of the men to stir and roll over in their cots.

"Understood," replied Hank, his heart racing wildly in anticipation. Stevenson did an about-face and quietly walked out of the barracks and disappeared into the darkness and fog. Hank cleaned up and got dressed. It would be light soon.

Stevenson returned at 0530 hours and the two officers walked to the headquarters building before the official reveille sounded. Neither man looked at the other or spoke. Stevenson led and Mitchell simply followed. Stevenson led Hank down an unfamiliar dark, narrow hallway to a heavy door reinforced with solid steel rods. The MP standing guard saluted the two officers and slung his M1 Garand rifle so he could use both arms to unlatch and swing open the heavy door. The lieutenants descended a stairway encompassed by thick concrete walls. The air was heavy and damp. A single, dim light bulb hanging from the ceiling lit the stairway. At the base of the stairs another door blocked their progress. Stevenson turned to Hank and spoke.

"Okay, Lieutenant, this is it." He swung the door open and stepped inside. Hank squinted in the brightly illuminated room, gathered himself, and stood at attention. Stevenson walked to the front of the room and stood next to Major Jamison and Colonel Dexter, who were side by side, staring at Hank. In front of Hank were rows of chairs. Sitting in the first row, with their backs turned to him, were thirteen airmen. Some were officers and some enlisted men. All strangers to Hank.

The room was not small, but somehow seemed cramped. Enlarged maps of France and Germany decorated the walls, stuck with bright red pins indicating major cities, smaller towns, and other unidentifiable places, all representing targets. In the front of the room was a large chalkboard filled with names, timetables, and drawings representing bomber formations. Next to the board was a large screen that faced a movie projector slightly hidden in the back of the room by the door. A sand table displayed a near perfect model of a town. Next to the sand table and between Jamison and Dexter was another table supporting some object with a white tablecloth draped over it, concealing its identity. It was this object that drew Mitchell's attention.

"Take a seat, Lieutenant Mitchell, and we'll get this briefing started," ordered Colonel Dexter. He paced back and forth, his hands clasped behind his back. Hank sat down in the front row, next to another lieutenant who acknowledged his presence with a nod. Dexter pulled a podium from behind the view screen. He spoke.

"Good morning, gentlemen. I am Colonel Daniel Dexter. I am the commanding officer of the now defunct 23rd Fighter Squadron. The 23rd was part of the 96th Fighter Group operating from Jefferson Airfield. For reasons that I cannot divulge at this time, we are in the process of being disbanded and absorbed into various other fighter groups, in preparation for the imminent invasion of Fortress Europe.

"I'm sure you all have many questions pertaining to why you're here and what I have in store for you concerning this special assignment. Rest assured, all your questions will be answered by the time this mission briefing is over.

"Gentlemen, you're here this morning because you have volunteered to participate in a mission vital to the success of the Allied invasion of Europe. Quite simply, your mission is to strike at and eliminate the heart of the Nazi special weapons offensive threat to our invasion forces in occupied France."

All pencils simultaneously stopped and all eyes fixed on the colonel as though he had just ordered every man in the room to be executed immediately.

"That, gentlemen, is the official order from Lieutenant General Lewis H. Brereton, commander of the 9th Air Force. General Spaatz's and General Eisenhower's signatures are also on this top-secret document addressed to me. If I didn't have your attention before, I certainly hope I have it now. Gentlemen, you are going to bomb and destroy a hidden Nazi rocket launch site located on the coast of occupied France. This site poses a serious threat to our invasion forces, as well as a moderate danger to the population, both military and civilian, of southern England. I cannot stress enough the importance of the success of this mission. I expect all of you to perform above and beyond the normal call of duty in preparation and execution of this mission. I am confident that none of you will let me down. With that said, Major Jamison will now brief you on the specifics of this operation. Proceed, Major."

Dexter stepped away from the podium, pulled a white handkerchief from his pocket, and wiped perspiration from his wrinkled brow before stepping to the back of the room as though bearing a tremendous weight on his shoulders. He slumped down in a chair in the back as the confident Jamison gathered his notes and strode up to the podium. The major carried himself in the more soldierly fashion that Hank had come to expect from a U.S. Army Air Force officer, in contrast to the appearance and style of the colonel.

"Gentlemen, I'd like to draw your attention to the sand table next to me," began Jamison. "This model represents the French coastal village of Martinvast on the Cotentin Peninsula. It is located in the Normandy region and has been photographed extensively by U.S. and British aerial reconnaissance planes. As a result, we have an in-depth layout of the village and the surrounding countryside. Now, everybody gather 'round the table."

As the men rose from their seats and huddled around the sand table, Jamison grabbed a wooden pointer and stood at the head of the rectangular table. He took a moment to gather his thoughts and make eye contact with everyone, to ensure he had their full attention.

"I want you all to observe this obscure-looking hill just outside the village."

Jamison lay the tip of the pointer on what appeared to be an ordinary hill away from the small houses, dirt roads, and hedgerows comprising the bulk of Martinvast.

"Look closely now," he emphasized. "Notice that this is not an ordinary hill. G-2 has confirmed this is, indeed, a German bunker containing massive amounts of ordnance, ammunition, food, and possible living space for unknown numbers of German troops comprising a fraction of the *Wehrmacht*'s 7th Army defending the Cotentin peninsula and other regions up the Normandy coast. More importantly, gentlemen, this bunker is believed to house a much more sinister weapon, also in unknown numbers."

Jamison paused to emphasize the importance of the moment. He then moved to the table opposite that supported the concealed object beneath the white tablecloth. Hank and the others eagerly gathered around, anxiously waiting to discover what lay hidden.

"Gentlemen, I want to introduce you to what may be the most destructive weapon to come out of Hitler's Third Reich."

With one gentle tug of the tablecloth, Jamison unveiled the secret as the men squeezed together to gain a closer look at the strange, three-dimensional model that lay before them.

"This is a V-1 rocket, gentlemen," explained Jamison. "The 'V' stands for 'vengeance,' aptly named by Hitler himself. Some of you may have already heard of this weapon, but I assume that the majority of you have not. Very simply, it is a sort of rocket-propelled bomb. Notice the rocket-shaped fuselage. At the tip is the warhead. At the midsection and rear are stabilizing wings, and, most intriguing, is this—the simple gas-and-air-fed jet engine mounted on the back of the rocket. This is the method of propulsion for the weapon. A sophisticated array of internal gyros guides the weapon toward its target. Our G-2 section has informed us this new weapon is being readied for mass deployment against our forces in England as we speak. If the Nazis utilize this weapon to its full potential, it could seriously hamper, if not completely prevent, Allied forces from gaining a foothold in occupied France. It could keep us off the continent, gentlemen, and I, for one, do not want to see that happen."

Jamison stood back to let the gravity of the situation soak in. The rumors and stories of Nazi superweapons had long secretly circulated on the lips of the average American G.I. ever since Hank's deployment to North Africa. To actually see a model of one was a terrifying moment of realization.

"Well, now that I've revealed the target, it's time to reveal how we're going to deal with this particular problem," quipped Jamison. "Gentlemen, please take your seats again.

"We're going to make this short and sweet. This is going to be a simple 'hit and run' operation. One B-24 bomber fully loaded with special bunker-busting five-hundred-pound bombs with forty-five-second, tail-delay fuses supplied by our friends at R.A.F. Bomber Command will drop its ordnance at treetop level and blow the holy Hell out of that Nazi bunker. A direct hit will obliterate the site, destroying any V-1 rockets or other ordnance contained inside. I also want to draw your attention back to the sand table, to these two wooden launch ramps located about one hundred yards south of the bunker."

Jamison wielded his pointer indicating the location of the two V-1 launch ramps.

"These two secondary targets need to be destroyed, as well, and will definitely not survive the ensuing explosion resulting from the destruction of the bunker on the initial strike. The low altitude of the bomb run will help ensure that all ordnance is dropped directly in the pickle barrel."

Jamison reached for a pitcher and poured himself a glass of water, which he drank quickly to ease the strain on his voice caused by his authoritative pitch. After pausing to collect his thoughts, Jamison turned to address an officer who sat comfortably, legs crossed and arms folded. He had an unamiable expression chiseled on his face, one Hank had rarely seen but was keenly aware of. It was the look of a pilot who had extensive combat experience and had become hardened by a long and arduous tour of duty.

"Captain Wheeler, you and your crew will man the B-24 Liberator in this operation. You will also have command of this mission once airborne as strict radio silence will be observed both to and from the target. Radio silence can be broken only on your orders, Captain. Is that point clear?" asked Jamison.

"Clear, sir," muttered Wheeler. "Protection … sir?"

"Yes, I was just getting to that, Captain," replied Jamison. "This is a special operation, gentlemen, requiring nonstandard fighter escort. I am assigning four escort fighters to accompany and protect the bomber to the target and bring her home safely. Ordinarily, we would have at our disposal several squadrons of Republic P-47 Thunderbolts that would be used in an operation like this. However, due to the fact that this fighter group has been disbanded and is in the process of relocating in preparation for the invasion, we have to take what we can get. Yesterday, two North American P-51 Mustangs were delivered straight off the assembly lines back in the States, as well as two used, Lockheed P-38 Lightnings on loan from the Pacific Theater. Unfortunately, they are the only four fighters located on this base. For you superstitious fighter pilots sitting in front of me, I'll have you know that both Lightnings saw combat and have been credited with at least six confirmed, air-to-air kills. All Jap Zeros. Both are well broken in and are serviceable aircraft. As for the Mustangs, they need to be broken in quickly."

Jamison shifted his attention from Captain Wheeler and his bomber crew to Hank and three other officers sitting around him.

"Lieutenant Mitchell, you and 2nd Lieutenant Brady will pilot the Mustangs. Lieutenant Hendricks, you and 2nd Lieutenant Dandridge will pilot the Lightnings. I want the Lightnings to lead the formation and provide low-altitude protection by eliminating any ground fire from either AA or flak batteries that may have been moved up or are camouflaged and not represented on the sand table model. You will also be loaded with reconnaissance cameras to photograph the area before and after the attack. The P-51s will be rolling standard gun cams. I don't anticipate any resistance due to the element of surprise and lack of German 88s in the area. The Krauts are trying not to draw attention to this area of France so they haven't invested much time building up its defenses. G-2 has confirmed this for us.

"Mitchell and Brady, you will be providing high-altitude top cover for the bomber and will bring up the rear of the formation. Your job will be to ax down any enemy fighters that the *Luftwaffe* might have in the area. This will be a non-issue, gentlemen. Due to the excessive bombing the 8th Air Force has employed on Berlin and other targets deep within Germany, the *Luftwaffe* has had to pull back its fighter strength in France to protect the Reich. All in all, boys, the *Luftwaffe* is essentially an empty shell in France. I doubt they can throw up so much as a paper kite at us when we go in. Our intelligence has reported no significant fighter strength anywhere near the target. And if they do manage to get up a fighter or two, it'll most definitely be too far away to pose any sort of threat. We're gonna be in and out of there before they even know what hit them."

Questions began building in Hank's mind as Jamison paused to swallow another glass of water. He had logged only limited flying hours with the P-51 Mustang. Hank's pulse quickened and his throat went dry with an uncertain anxiety detached from the usual mission fears. He began to think that volunteering for this mission had been a bad idea and how much happier he'd be feeling right now if he were back in the barracks with Righetti and the rest of his friends.

"Now for the tough part, gentlemen," Jamison continued. "This will be a daylight mission and will take place in two days—on May 17, at 0600 hours, to be specific. Due to the precision needed for the bombing, daylight is necessary. Plus we need to stay out of the way of the R.A.F. during their night attacks in the area. I advise that every one of you get to know each other as quickly as possible. Officers and enlisted men alike. Study the maps of the area, the sand table, and the model of the V-1. Learn as much as you can, as quickly as you can. Captain

Wheeler will take charge after this briefing and tell you how he wants the operation to be executed. Fighter pilots, our limited ground crew personnel are prepping your planes as we speak. They will be detailed with 96th Fighter Group markings, even though we have been officially disbanded. I suggest you get these planes in the air as soon as possible to become familiar with them before mission time. We will have one more quick briefing the morning of the attack to sew up any loose ends."

Jamison stepped back and stood at parade rest next to Lieutenant Stevenson, who had managed to blend into the background. Colonel Dexter, who had not breathed a word since his initial comments, rose from his chair and walked back to the podium to address the men once more.

"Make no mistake, gentlemen. What we are asking you to accomplish will not be easy, but failure is unacceptable. The lives of many Allied soldiers depend on your success. This mission has been classified top secret. You are not to discuss it with anyone, other than the occupants of this room. This specific mission does not exist, as far as anyone outside this room is concerned. All base personnel, including your crew chiefs, are only aware that one last mission is to occur before we completely shut down base operations and redeploy in preparation for the eventual invasion of Europe. No one knows the target or the specifics of this mission. If any one of you is suspected of leaking information critical to the success of this operation to unauthorized personnel, you will immediately be placed under arrest and subject to court-martial.

"Now, ordinarily you enlisted men present would not be briefed with the officers. However, due to the importance and extremely tight timeframe of this mission, I am allowing it. Gentlemen, it may not look it, but this base is completely secure. No one is allowed in or out. There are no towns nearby, save for Portsmouth, which is strictly off limits. Keep that in mind, gentlemen! This mission has been authorized by the top echelon of the Allied command in the ETO and is in accordance with Operation Fortitude currently being carried out by our forces. The code name for this mission is Operation Vengeance. Now, I know some of you may have questions. We've had to put this together very quickly, and I know all the bases may not have been covered. You all have a tough and long day ahead of you. Lieutenant Stevenson will address any equipment issues you may have and will aid you with preparing your aircraft. Major Jamison is here to answer any questions and will gladly provide any tactical support or leadership you require. Unfortunately I have other duties to perform and orders to carry out and will not be available to you until mission time. If you need to speak with me, go to Major Jamison first. Now, are there any questions I can answer before I end this mission briefing?"

Every man in the room raised his hand.

Chapter 5

SILVER'S SWEETHEART

Hank emerged from the headquarters building and shielded his eyes from the bright afternoon sun. After many hours confined deep in the windowless briefing room, the sun was welcome. The blue sky was clear and peaceful and showed no hint of the fury of 1940 during the Battle of Britain. Hank watched Major Jamison, who was already outside, reach into his pants pocket and pull out a pack of Lucky Strike cigarettes. He snatched up a cigarette and pinched it between his lips. A gentle breeze forced him to cup his hands around the flickering flame of his shiny metallic Zippo lighter. Once the end of the cigarette glowed red, Jamison stuffed his hands in his pockets and walked away without realizing the four fighter pilots were watching him from the doorway.

"I don't know about you guys, but I've got a really bad feeling about that guy and this mission," said Lieutenant Brady gruffly. "What the hell kind of briefing was that? Seven hours of nothing but disorganization, unanswered questions, and bullshit if you ask me. And that Captain Wheeler, what's the story with that guy? Seems to be wrapped a little too tight for my liking."

"I've heard of him," said Lieutenant Hendricks sullenly, while staring at the ground. "Captain Charles Wheeler is his full name. He's primarily been flying Liberators throughout the war, but has been known to take the controls of a B-17 from time to time. In fact, I think he prefers the Flying Fortress to the Liberator. Had quite a few badly shot up, too, but that's neither here nor there. We're all doomed if he's leading this raid."

"What are you driving at, Lieutenant?" asked Hank with concern.

"Chuck Wheeler is a cursed man is what I'm driving at," responded Hendricks. "I never flew with the guy personally, but I knew a lot of pilots who did. Most of them are nothing more than ashes scattered in the wind now. He's been involved with the planning and execution of many disastrous air attacks throughout Italy and North Africa. I can't tell you how many times I've heard he's crashed a bomber on the runway returning from a mission with his entire crew dead and his escort fighters missing."

"That doesn't sound like the man is cursed, Lieutenant, it sounds like he's just had some rotten luck. Fought a good hard war. If you look at it another way, he's lucky. Lucky to still be alive," said Hank.

"That may be, Lieutenant, but I think Captain Wheeler may be 'wrapped too tight' like Brady said. I know he was involved in the attack on the Romanian oil fields at Ploesti and hasn't been quite the same ever since. I'll bet the guy is ready to crack. Probably why he's leading this raid, 'cause he has experience with Liberators on low altitude-bombing attacks like they did at Ploesti—and you all know what happened there. I was told he was completely off his assigned target during the attack, managed to get the majority of his crew killed, and pulled his plane out of danger far sooner than he should have. That doesn't exactly make me want to put my life on the line to protect this man, if you know what I mean," said Hendricks.

"Lieutenant, all these things you've heard about Captain Wheeler are rumors, aren't they?" asked Hank.

"Rumors, stories, truth, lies—call 'em what you want. It's just what I've heard," replied Hendricks.

"Well, whatever the truth is, I think it's best we give Wheeler our full support. We don't have any time to speculate or bitch and complain about what his past record reflects or his present state of mind. Our job is to protect his bomber and its crew. That's what we need to concentrate on, in my opinion. Our lives depend on it."

The young Lieutenant Hendricks reluctantly nodded in agreement and turned away from the group. Lieutenant Brady carefully looked around the grounds to make certain no one else was listening to the conversation before he continued.

"I don't know about the rest of you guys, but I'm more concerned about the lack of information and direction given by Jamison. This morning's briefing was unlike any other I've attended. It seems like this whole mission was an afterthought, slapped together at the last minute. Something ain't right. Both the major and the colonel were too evasive. Notice how neither one could give us a straight answer on just about every question we asked this morning. I have a really uneasy feeling right now. I feel grossly unprepared. And that ain't no way to feel when you're in our line of work."

Tension between the four pilots began to build. Hank's thoughts settled on one predominant, discomforting navigational rumination—the flight path in. His urge to keep silent was only partially outweighed by his sense of duty to his fellow pilots. Hank reluctantly spoke up.

"I tell ya what I feel uneasy about is the route in to the target." The three other men turned their attention to Hank. He took a breath and continued.

"I don't know if you guys noticed, but the flight path Jamison mapped out for us isn't exactly the quickest way in and out of Dodge," noted Hank. "They have us zigzagging back and forth all over the channel before flying a good distance southeast of the Cotentin Peninsula. When we hit coastline, we then have to make a gradual, sweeping turn, flying northwest up along the coast, heading inland, and striking Martinvast from the southeast. Doesn't that seem like an overly complicated navigational route to hit a target essentially due south of our point of origin? I don't know if I can remember all these twists and turns. Too many damn interception points to keep track of."

Hank paused for a moment to let his observation sink in. He expected his fellow pilots to agree with him, whereupon the four would march into Colonel Dexter's office and lodge some form of complaint or concern for the mission's safety. Certainly Hendricks and Dandridge would lead the parade, as they were the chosen pathfinders for the mission, and carried the navigational burden. It was, in fact, Dandridge who spoke up first, but his reply was not what the young Maine pilot expected to hear.

"Mitchell, can't you see that the flight path mapped out for us takes us out of harm's way?" said the cocky Dandridge. "Sure the easiest path in would be to fly straight down the heart of the peninsula and strike from the north, but that takes us directly over Cherbourg and one of the most heavily fortified ports on the French coast. Those Nazi bastards probably have more anti-aircraft batteries ringed around that port city than Berlin itself! I don't know about the rest of you guys, but I'd rather fly a few extra miles out of the way, slip in over the coast where there's minimal fortifications, and hit the target from the side rather than straight on, where every Nazi gun barrel will be pointed right at my nose!"

Dandridge turned away from Hank, who stood silently glaring at the angry pilot. A few seconds passed before Hank looked at both Hendricks and Brady, waiting for their input on the matter. Brady was silent. Hendricks was not.

"A straight path in is not safe, Mitchell," added Hendricks. "By zigzagging, we help avoid detection by enemy ships or fighters. Common sense if you ask me. A formation is harder to target when it's flying an unconventional course. Plus I agree with Dandridge. They want us to avoid Cherbourg—makes sense to me. I'd also tend to believe that a busy port like Cherbourg would have heavier concentrations of surface vessels, U-boats, and fighter aircraft stationed around it, ready to pounce on any Allied threat at a moment's notice."

"Fine, I'll buy that piece about steering clear of Cherbourg, but the rest I can't swallow," Hank fired back. "We're not some convoy on the water, trying to avoid U-boat attacks by zigzagging our course. I just don't see the point of taking a tour of the Northern French coastline that keeps us in the air over enemy-held territory longer than necessary to complete our objective. Plus, the longer we're in the air flying over a lengthier stretch of enemy soil, the more vulnerable we are to attack from ground fire and fighter aircraft. Tell me that makes sense! Doesn't sound like a simple surprise hit-and-run operation to me, gentlemen."

"You believe what you fucking want to believe, Mitchell. I ain't got nothing more to say on the matter," snapped Dandridge. The angry pilot turned his back on his comrades and walked a few steps away from them, slamming his hands into his pockets in search of a cigarette.

The remaining three kept eerily silent, each afraid to speak and reveal any more of their impending mission fears. Just then a jeep rolled up, with Lieutenant Stevenson at the wheel.

"Gentlemen, I'm glad you're all here together. Hop in. I've just been informed your planes are ready. I think it's time we introduce you to your crew chiefs," said Lieutenant Stevenson over the dull roar of the jeep's running engine.

The four pilots climbed in as Stevenson turned sharply and headed toward the mysterious main hangar that had been off limits and out of sight since Hank had arrived on base. The jeep lugged forward under the weight of the added passengers, before coming to an abrupt stop outside the side entrance, since the front way was almost completely obstructed from view by fuel trucks, large crates of equipment, spare parts, and sandbags. A lone MP paced slowly back and forth, guarding the entrance.

The five men scrambled from the jeep and lined up outside a narrow doorway located on the side of the large blister hangar. The sounds of rivet guns, clanking tools, and metal grinding against metal could be heard from within. A second MP patrolled the area surrounding the hangar. He came to attention, with his M1 Garand rifle at his side, on seeing the officers. He saluted Stevenson and allowed him access. Stevenson pulled a key from his pocket, unlocked the door, and led the pilots inside.

Parked within the hangar were the four fighters and the B-24 Liberator. Crawling all over the planes, like ants on an open picnic basket, were several base mechanics covered in grease and whirling wrenches, screwdrivers, and ratchets in the exposed guts of the aircraft engines. The two P-51 Mustangs were lined up side by side, while the two P-38 Lightnings were staggered behind them. In the far back of the hangar was the B-24 Liberator turned sideways to compensate for the tight space. All four engines' cowlings and under-wing fairings had been removed and two mechanics worked feverishly on each engine.

The olive-drab Liberator looked quite different from what Hank had seen landing in the blackness of night. The bomber was a modified B-24G, with a Sperry ball-turret tucked neatly underneath and three heavy .50 caliber machine guns in the nose. Spanning 110 feet, wingtip to wingtip, it measured 67 feet long and weighed in at roughly 56,000 pounds. Maximum speed of the aircraft clocked in at 290 miles per hour, with a cruising speed around 215 miles per hour. Four Pratt & Whitney, R-1830-65, supercharged radial engines each cranked out 1,200 horsepower and provided the raw power needed to safely lift the plane into the air with a full bomb load intended for knocking out targets all across Hitler's Reich. With a range of 2,100 miles fully loaded, the Liberator was more than suited for striking targets deep within Axis territory.

"Mitchell and Brady, you got the Mustangs; Hendricks and Dandridge, go acquaint yourself with those P-38s," commanded Stevenson. Hendricks and Dandridge walked to their waiting fighters and started examining the twin-boomed beauties, famous for terrorizing Axis air forces all over the world. Hank and Lieutenant Brady enthusiastically eyed the striking P-51s.

"I'll take the one on the left," said Brady.

"Guess that leaves me the one on the right," replied Hank with a cheerful smile. Looking at the brand-new warbird excited Hank, as though his parents had just bought him a new car and all he had to do was take the keys and drive to wherever his heart desired.

Hank ran his hand down the side of the Mustang. He could see his reflection in the lustrous aluminum frame that glistened brightly, even in the enclosed hangar. He slowly walked around the fighter, taking in every line, every curve, and every detail down to the smallest rivet. It was truly a marvelous sight to behold, and deep down Hank knew he was fortunate to have the privilege to fly the most potent fighter in the Allied arsenal.

"Finally got her all cleaned up this morning, Lieutenant."

Hank turned to observe a mechanic wearing green HBT coveralls blanketed in dirt and grease standing behind him. The mechanic adjusted the flipped-up brim of his type A-3 cap and spoke again.

"Yup, she was flown over from the States a few days ago. Assembled in Dallas, she's what you'd call brand new, out-of-the-box, Lieutenant. She's a beaut, I must say."

"Yeah, she is—but I wish she had a nice pair of tits to go along with those six machine guns," joked Hank. "Lieutenant Hank Mitchell. This is my crate." The mechanic gave Hank a quick salute before extending his hand to shake.

"Staff Sergeant Frank Russell, sir, but please call me Russ. For the time being, I'm your crew chief," said Frank. "I'm told we're shipping outta here in two days. Do you know where we're gonna be reassigned to, Lieutenant? They haven't told us anything lately."

"I don't know Sergeant. I'm just as much in the dark as you are," said Hank evasively.

"Well, my most recent orders were to get this crate operational and ready for combat. She's ready to go, sir, 'cept she needs to be painted and loaded with ammo. She's fully fueled though," said Russ.

"Painted? I was hoping she'd be left alone. I just love that bare metallic luster," said Hank.

"Well, I agree, sir. To be honest with ya, I wasn't planning on painting the plane. However we were ordered to detail all four fighters with our old fighter-group markings. You can see that the boys are painting 'em up now. The main signature for this group is a black tail and a black spinner. Nose'll stay the same though, sir ... olive drab. She should look pretty sexy after we slap a little makeup on. Agree, sir?"

"Yeah, I can picture it in my mind. That'll give her some flair."

"Well, while we're discussing paint, Lieutenant, I should tell ya that I'm a bit of an artist, too. Painted a few noses in my day. Any thought what you might name her?"

"Gee, I don't know, Russ," replied Hank, taking off his officer's cap to scratch his head. "I don't have a girl back home, so I can't very well ask you to paint the likeness of my sweetheart ... unless Rita Hayworth counts."

Both men chuckled. "Naw, sorry Lieutenant, she's already taken. I've reserved a special spot for her and her only in my imagination. Wouldn't dream of putting her in harm's way either. Can you imagine how awful I'd feel if you brought my plane back with Rita all shot up with Nazi flak? Shit, I can't even think about it, sir!"

"Hey, I got an idea, Russ. You ever read *Treasure Island*?"

"Yup, long time ago, back in school. Pirate book, right?"

"That's right. I'm reading it now, as a matter of fact. What I want you to do is paint a picture of the old Jolly Roger pirate flag on the nose. Then, underneath the flag I want you to write her new name—*Silver's Sweetheart*. I'll bring you my book so you can go by the picture of the pirate flag. How's that sound to you?"

"Sounds just fine, Lieutenant. I'll get to work as soon as I can. Once I get her fully painted, you can take her up for a test flight."

"I'll leave you to it, Russ," said Hank as he turned to focus his attention on the sleek fighter behind it. The P-38J Lightning was truly a marvel to lay eyes upon. The J model was considered one of the best versions to come off the assembly line, and Hank was happy to see two of them sitting in the hangar. The P-38's unconventional design and peculiar appearance caught the eye and imagination of even the most-seasoned pilot. To look at the P-38 made a pilot wonder if it could rocket through the heavens and into the farthest reaches of outer space. The sight of the twin-engine P-38 Lightning tearing through the clouds left its allies in awe and struck terror into the hearts of enemies unfortunate enough to cross its path. Its impressive dual, turbo-charged 1,225-horsepower, 12-cylinder V-1710 Allison engines gave the fighter swiftness and agility that were hard to match. The Germans knew it. The Japanese knew it, too. They had lost scores of fighters at the hands of the P-38 and had finally come to accept the fact that their vaunted Zero fighter was no longer the supreme ruler of the skies in the Pacific Theater. The Germans had had little luck against the Lightning, as well. The ME-109 was becoming obsolete and was outclassed, outrun, and outgunned by the Lightning. The ominous P-38 had wreaked enough havoc on the *Luftwaffe* to have earned the nickname "Fork-Tailed Devil."

Hank gazed up at the front section of the P-38 and stood in awe of the impressive firepower that dauntingly protruded from the nose. The four Browning, .50 caliber machine guns and menacing Hispano, 20mm cannon ensured the destruction of anything that lined up in the pilot's crosshairs. Hank closed his eyes and remembered when he had first flown the P-38 back in training, early in 1942. He remembered struggling with the fighter's awesome power and having a difficult time handling the innovative aircraft. It took many subsequent training flights before he felt comfortable climbing into the cockpit. He wondered what it would be like to fly one in combat. That said, the attraction and newness of the Mustang was far too great to sway him from proposing a swap with Lieutenant Hendricks.

Both Hendricks and Dandridge sat in the cockpits of the Lightnings carefully scrutinizing the instrument panels for any signs of malfunction. Brady had climbed up on the wing of his Mustang and had struck up a conversation with a mechanic who was proudly expressing his admiration for the aircraft. Hank walked around the fighter and approached the B-24 Liberator. Several mechanics were giving it their full attention. Lieutenant Stevenson climbed out of the bomber and began giving instruction to the head mechanic working on the number-four engine. Before Hank could get in on the conversation an unfamiliar voice rumbled from behind him.

"Lieutenant Stevenson, a word please." Hank turned around and saw the stone-faced Captain Wheeler.

"Sir!" said Stevenson to Wheeler, with a quick snap to attention.

"Lieutenant, I need to have my bomber ready and fully loaded by 1700 hours. I want to take her up with my crew for a quick dry run before the actual mission. As a matter of fact, I want the fighters to go up, too. Might as well simulate the real thing as close as possible. Plus it will give us a chance to become more acquainted with each other," commanded Wheeler.

"I'm afraid that's impossible, sir," responded a stunned Stevenson. "The B-24 is not ready yet. She still needs some work."

"What? What the hell are you talking about, Lieutenant? I flew her in here last night and she was running just fine. I want that plane ready to go up by 1700 hours!" yelled Wheeler.

"Sergeant Russell! Come over, please, and explain to the captain what you told me earlier concerning the B-24," ordered Stevenson. Russ turned away from Hank's Mustang and saluted the two officers. Hank pretended to turn his attention away from Stevenson and Wheeler, but continued to eavesdrop on the now heated conversation. Sergeant Russell addressed the captain.

"Captain, with all due respect, sir, my crew discovered several oil leaks coming from all four engines early this morning. We thought we had them all fixed a while ago, but all four are still runnin' way too hot for my likin'. We need to pinpoint all the problems before I can say it's safe to take 'er up. Also, sir, I received orders this morning to modify the supercharged engines to compensate for added weight."

Wheeler's face reddened with anger and he hesitated a moment, choosing his words before unleashing his wrath on Stevenson. "Lieutenant, this is totally unacceptable! Sergeant, I want that plane ready by 1700 hours!" snapped Wheeler, pointing his finger at the bomber.

"Sergeant, you are dismissed," said Stevenson to Russ as he did not want him to hear anything further about the bomber or its purpose. "Captain, with respect, I have orders from the colonel that this bomber is not to leave the hangar until mission time. I assure you that everything will be ready at H-hour on D-Day. Due to the special nature of the upcoming mission, this bomber will not leave this hangar until the specified time. Also, sir, you should know that it is completely against regulations to have live ordnance aboard a bomber during test flights or noncombative maneuvers. The bombs will be loaded the morning of D-Day. If you have a problem with any of this, I suggest you take it up with Major Jamison, but I assure you that he will tell you the same thing, sir."

Wheeler stared hard at Stevenson and crossed his arms defiantly. He then lowered his voice and spoke slowly and directly.

"You mean to stand here and tell me, Lieutenant, that Colonel Dexter intends to endanger this mission and my crew by not allowing us to test fly a modified B-24 Liberator that will be overloaded with high-explosive bombs in territory unfamiliar to us? Not to mention the fact that we're being given almost no prep time and four strangers to protect us. Now just how am I supposed to deal with these ludicrous conditions?"

"Captain, I recommend you deal with the situation as best you can. I have my orders to carry out. I suggest you do the same, sir!" sneered Stevenson as he walked away.

"That's right, Lieutenant! You just keep walking, you little son-of-a-bitch! You're lucky I got more important issues to deal with than stomping your insubordinate ass!" yelled Wheeler, as the noise in the hangar ceased and all eyes and ears tuned on him.

"What the hell are you assholes looking at? Get the fuck back to work, now!" shouted the agitated Wheeler at the gawking maintenance crews. Wheeler turned his attention to Hank, who was still within close earshot.

"You! Mitchell," said Wheeler as he pointed his finger at the lieutenant. "I want you and the other three fighter pilots to report to the briefing room at exactly 1400 hours! Be ready! Tell the others." Wheeler then turned sharply and walked out of the hangar trying to contain his fury. Having overheard the majority of the conversation as well, Hendricks, Brady, and Dandridge climbed off their fighters.

"I told you that guy was coming apart," spoke Hendricks softly. "What are we gonna do now?"

Hank turned to face the three. "We're gonna report to the briefing room at 1400 just like he ordered, Lieutenant," said Hank. "Meantime, I'm going back to my barracks for some rest and quiet. I don't know about you guys, but I want to clear my head a little."

The others agreed some peace and quiet was definitely in order. Hank walked back to his barracks wondering what Righetti and the rest of his old friends were doing. To his shock, he found it completely empty. All the cots were made up and every sign that men had slept there the night before was erased. Puzzled and concerned, Hank looked around for a moment before spying Lieutenant Stevenson walking across the grounds. Hank ran out the door after him.

"Lieutenant Stevenson!" shouted Hank. "What happened to the other pilots that came in with me? It looks like they all packed up and disappeared."

"They flew out this morning during the briefing, Lieutenant Mitchell. A C-47 picked them up and flew 'em out," Stevenson responded.

"Where?"

"I don't know where. Probably some staging area farther north. They'll be reassigned to other units. Units directly involved with preparing for the upcoming invasion would be my guess," said Stevenson. "Now, excuse me, Lieutenant. I have to go see the major."

Stevenson hurried off, leaving a stunned Hank standing alone and motionless. Unable to think, he walked back to the barracks and grabbed his copy of *Treasure Island*. He hustled back to the hangar and gave the book to Russ, who examined the picture of the Jolly Roger in detail. Hank returned to the barracks and climbed onto his cot. Rest was what he needed to clear his throbbing head. Minutes later, Brady, Dandridge, and Hendricks walked into the barracks with all their belongings. Before Hank could open his mouth, Lieutenant Brady spoke.

"Major Jamison ordered us to these barracks. Apparently Captain Wheeler's bomber crew is getting ours."

Hank rested his head back on his pillow as the three other men unpacked gear. Again Hank wondered what he had gotten himself into. More importantly, would he get out of it alive? All questions he couldn't answer.

After Hank had managed a brief nap, Lieutenant Brady awakened him.

"It's briefing time, Lieutenant Mitchell," said Brady, gently shaking Hank awake. The groggy Hank vainly attempted to iron out the wrinkles in his uniform with his hand. Grabbing his cap, he followed the three other officers to the secure briefing room. Captain Wheeler was at the sand table, surrounded by his crew.

"Gentlemen, come in and take a seat," said Wheeler, surrounded by the nine members of his bomber crew, as the four fighter pilots entered the room. "Let's keep things informal, guys. That way we'll be able to go over everything we need to in a shorter amount of time."

"Introductions are the first order of business. For those of you who don't know me, I'm Captain Charles Wheeler, formerly of the 15th Air Force. Before that, I was assigned to the 93rd Bombardment Group of the 8th Air Force. I have flown more than sixteen bombing missions over North Africa, Italy, and Romania, and I have experience flying both B-17 Flying Fortresses and B-24 Liberators. Now, take a minute to introduce yourselves to my bomber crew."

Hank and the three other pilots exchanged introductions with the nine men who comprised Wheeler's crew. Some were friendly, while others seemed distant and uncaring. Hank had experienced being brushed off by fellow airmen before and was used to it. To him, it usually signified an emotionally defensive posture used to prevent becoming too friendly with other airmen who might be killed in combat the very next mission. Everyone took their seats while Captain Wheeler got down to business.

"Gentlemen, I don't want to repeat what Major Jamison covered this morning, so I'll do us all a favor and only discuss what's pertinent to the mission, rather than all the bullshit that isn't." Wheeler's voice oozed sarcasm. The men clapped their hands in approval.

"Directly after takeoff, we'll converge at the rally point and line up in this formation." Wheeler stepped to the blackboard and with white chalk sketched out five aircraft. "The two P-38 Lightnings will take the lead in the formation, side by side, and act as pathfinders. Lieutenants Hendricks and Dandridge will be flying the Lightnings. You will be designated the Blue Element. Hendricks, your call sign will be Blue 1, and, Dandridge, your call sign will be Blue 2. Following the P-38s will be my bomber. The bomber's call sign will be Eagle 1. Watching our tail will be Lieutenant Mitchell and Lieutenant Brady in the P-51s. You guys are the Red Element. Mitchell, you're Red 1, and Brady, you're Red 2. Simple."

Wheeler returned to the podium.

"After we're in the air, we're going to observe strict radio silence. No one is to break that silence unless I give the order. Keep tuned to channel 3. That will be the designated command channel. Unless the situation calls for it, I won't break radio silence until we're lined up and ready to start the bomb run. Once we commence, I want the Lightnings to break formation and gain altitude fast. I'll give the order over the radio. If we're taking flak, then go down to the deck and strafe the hell out of those guns, but keep us in sight. Don't get lost. As for the Mustangs, I also want you guys to gain altitude, but stay in the rear. Keep your eyes on the target and help verify its destruction. Once we've released our payload, we're going to pull up fast and gain as much altitude as we can. Once we've leveled off at five thousand feet, I want everybody to get back in original formation for the flight back to Jefferson Airfield. Questions?"

"Captain, what's our altitude going to be en route to the target?" asked Lieutenant Dandridge.

"We're gonna be on the deck, Lieutenant. I expect to level off at no greater than two hundred feet from the ground all the way to the target," replied Wheeler.

"Isn't that a little low, sir? Two hundred feet doesn't give us much room to safely maneuver, especially if we're in a tight formation and need to pull up suddenly," said Dandridge.

"Gentlemen, this is a low-level, surprise attack. We need to stay on the deck to avoid being detected by enemy radar. It's dangerous, but it's a risk we have to take," said Wheeler.

"What about enemy fighters, sir?" asked Lieutenant Brady. "What happens if the Jerries get planes in the air?"

Wheeler sighed and lowered his head. He took a minute before answering the question. "Major Jamison has done everything in his power to convince me the *Luftwaffe* is not a factor in this mission. He's told me G-2 confirms there are no enemy aircraft based in the immediate area, thus the threat is minimal." Wheeler paused again as he sensed the uneasiness amongst his audience.

"To be perfectly blunt, gentlemen, I think that's a pile of horseshit. Just 'cause intelligence says that there are no airfields close by, doesn't mean those Nazi bastards don't have aircraft stashed in fields under camouflage netting near the target. I fully expect at least one Nazi fighter to greet us before we commence the bomb run," said Wheeler.

"Sir, if we do encounter fighters, how do you want us to handle it? Especially if we're ordered to stay off the radio," asked Lieutenant Hendricks.

"If an enemy fighter is spotted by me or any of my crew, I will break radio silence and give out orders on how to handle it. If any of you fighter pilots see an enemy bandit before me, break radio silence and inform the group. I will then issue orders on how to proceed. Brady, you and Mitchell will be the first option of counterattack if we're jumped. The Mustangs will counter any threat from the air first. I want the Lightnings to stay close, to protect the bomber from threats from the ground and any fighter that might get by the Mustangs."

"Don't worry about that, Cap. No Nazi fighter is gonna get by us," said Brady smugly as he confidently patted Hank's shoulder. The show of fearlessness did not go over well with the two waist gunners from Wheeler's crew. Each rolled his eyes, then shot disturbing glares of disbelief at Brady.

"Good, I hope that's the case. Let's just pray we don't see any fighters at all," said Wheeler. "All right, if there aren't any more questions, I'm done. For the rest of the day, I suggest you all study the sand table and the maps until you know them cold."

The men rose and clustered around the various maps and sand tables, studying every detail. Captain Wheeler pulled his navigator to the side and began talking privately.

"Andy, I want you to come with me and meet with Jamison. I want to make sure you're clear concerning all points of navigation in and around the target. As you know, we're really taking the long way in. It's not a straight shot down and back."

"Yes sir," replied the navigator, as he scribbled some notes on his pad.

Overhearing Wheeler's comments, Hank confronted the captain.

"Captain Wheeler, sir," said Hank. The captain returned Hank's quick salute. "Sir, what are your thoughts about the flight path in to the target?"

"What do you mean, Lieutenant?" asked Wheeler.

"Well, sir, don't you feel this long and complicated route poses a danger to the success of the mission?" Hank pulled Wheeler over to the map hanging on the wall that showed the flight path outlined in bright red ink. "Wouldn't a straight-on approach be less time consuming and hazardous in your opinion, sir?"

"No, Lieutenant," Wheeler answered. "This is the best path in. It's unconventional and would not be expected by the enemy. The route allows us to enter occupied territory over relatively 'soft' ground. It's better to strike the target's soft underbelly rather than hit it straight on. Plus, by making a long, gradual approach from the rear, we don't have to turn directly around to head back home. We just keep flying northwest until we're back over the water. The route bypasses Cherbourg, and that's what we want to do, knowing how heavily fortified its anti-aircraft defenses are. At absolute worst, we'd have to fly over Cherbourg only once, and that would be on the return trip. However, if all goes to plan, we won't fly near it at all, Lieutenant."

Out of the corner of his eye, Hank spied Dandridge smirking and shaking his head. He was silently gloating after Wheeler confirmed what he'd already suspected.

"But sir, don't you feel Major Jamison might have too hastily mapped out this route without considering other options … "

"Major Jamison didn't map out this route, Lieutenant! I did, and he approved it with the colonel. I would appreciate it if you would not question my expertise," interrupted the now agitated Captain. "Clear, Lieutenant?"

"Clear, sir," replied Hank with another brief salute followed by an about-face. Wheeler stepped back toward the podium and raised his voice to address the crowd again.

"Okay, the final mission briefing is on the seventeenth, D-Day, at 0530 hours. We'll be in the air at 0600 hours," said Wheeler. My crew will assist in preparing the bomber for flight. Help out the ground crews in any way possible. You fighter pilots, log as much airtime as possible. Break in your fighters and prepare yourselves as you normally would for any other mission. Come see me if you have any problems or issues before mission time. Don't waste your time going to that son-of-a-bitch Lieutenant Stevenson. Come to me directly. Understood?"

"Yes, sir!" came the resounding reply from all present.

"Good. Dismissed," said Wheeler as he wiped off the chalkboard.

The men lingered in the briefing room after Captain Wheeler's brusque departure. Some stayed and studied the sand table, while others were fascinated by the model of the V-1 rocket. Hank continued to examine the map of the target area and the flight route before deciding it was time to grab some chow from the mess hall.

At sunset the sky became illuminated with fiery colors of red, orange, and yellow, contrasting with the puffy white clouds scattered across the heavens. Hank, Brady, Dandridge, and Hendricks emerged from the mess hall and stopped to marvel at the divine beauty unfolding across the sky.

"Isn't that just glorious," whispered Brady, not wanting to disrupt the blissful serenity surrounding the four officers.

"Yeah, kinda makes you forget there's a war going on," replied Dandridge.

"Someday I'm gonna look at a sky just like this one. Only I won't be here, I'll be back home in Kansas lying in the middle of a wheat field with my arms wrapped around my girl. There won't be any more war, just peace—peace, tranquility, and security in the arms of someone I love. Life will be that simple again," romanticized Brady.

Hendricks shook his head and snickered, before walking back to the barracks. An annoyed Brady followed, with Dandridge right behind. Hank ignored them and continued to gaze up at the brilliant colors stretching far across the horizon into infinity. He dreamed of home and how wonderful it would be watch this same sunset from the rocky shores of Maine, with waves gently breaking across the open ledges and the warm summer breeze sliding over his face. The thought was paradise, if only for an instant.

"Lieutenant Mitchell, sir!"

Hank turned to find Sergeant Russell trotting toward him.

"Sir ... she's ... just about ... " Russ gasped for air as he tried to catch his breath. He bent over and put his hands on his knees hoping to expel the filthy airplane engine exhaust from his lungs. With one big cleansing cough he could again speak clearly.

"Whoa, sorry, sir, I ain't done much runnin' lately. Could you tell?" smiled Russ. "Your crate's all painted and ready to go, sir. You can take her up for a test flight whenever you're ready. First thing tomorrow, if ya want."

Hank looked off in the distance at the large hangar. The trucks and equipment crates obstructing the view inside had been removed and he could see small tractors towing the freshly painted fighters onto the runway. Leading the procession was Hank's new Mustang. The fresh detailing was apparent and Hank's curiosity skyrocketed. He looked at the fighter, then back at the sky.

"Tell ya what, Russ. Why wait? I'm game. Let's take her up right now."

"Now, sir? Are you sure you're comfortable with that? We're losing daylight pretty fast." Russ glanced at his wristwatch.

"Yeah. Why not? I've never flown a Mustang P-51D before and can't wait to see if they're as smooth as I've heard," replied Hank.

"Okay. You're the boss, Lieutenant. Let's go," said Russ.

The two men walked over to the shiny new fighter sitting at the end of the airfield's short runway. The mechanic unhitched the tow rope and drove the tractor back to the hangar. Hank strode around the fighter and marveled at Russ's stylish paint job. Russ climbed up on the wing, leaned over the side of the open cockpit, and began checking the instrument panel.

Hank was drawn to the dark, intimidating feel of the Mustang's jet-black tail. Only the white lettering of the serial number (441973) was visible. On both sides of the fuselage was the United States Army Air Force national emblem or roundel—a brilliant white star encased in a blue, circular disk, flanked by white horizontal bars. The pattern was repeated on the top left and bottom right wings. Flanking the roundel were the squadron's identification code letters, CW, and its aircraft identification letter, M, in bold, black lettering. On the nose was the most impressive and creative work of art Hank had seen on any aircraft he'd had the privilege of piloting. Draped on the side was a fluttering black pirate's flag with a deviously smiling white skull-and-crossbones in the center. Behind the skull's image was a broad pirate's cutlass ominously positioned as if it could leap off the nose and slash down any enemy fighter that dared cross its path. Underneath the pirate's flag was the name *Silver's Sweetheart*, painstakingly painted in flowing, artistic script. It gave the fighter character and a unique identification to which Hank and Russ could personally relate. It was a magnificent rendering showcasing Russ's artistic skills. This Mustang was now ready to soar off into the heavens.

"Whaddaya think, Lieutenant?" asked Russ, as Hank climbed up onto the wing next to him.

"She's gorgeous, Russ." Hank shook his head in astonishment. "She's gonna turn a few heads, for sure."

"She's not only pretty on the outside, sir, but she packs quite a wallop on the inside, too," said Russ as he prepared to show Hank just what this mighty warplane was capable of doing to Hitler's Third Reich. "The standard Allison engine has been replaced by a more powerful, liquid-cooled, Packard/Rolls Royce, Merlin V-1650-7, twelve-cylinder engine. She'll crank out 1,695 horsepower and allow you to fly more smoothly at higher altitudes and pull out of steep dives with less chance of stalling. You can take her as high as 42,000 feet, or ride her at 25,000 at max speed of 437 miles per hour. She's smooth, sir, and I think the second you get this baby into the air you'll notice the difference in handling from any other plane you've flown. Especially at higher altitudes."

Hank listened intently to his crew chief and could feel the enthusiasm and pride in Russ's voice as he continued to describe the features of the P-51 Mustang.

"We've attached two 110-gallon drop tanks to the wings for greater range—about 2,000 miles max. You can ride this baby all the way to Berlin and back, if necessary. In the wings are six Browning .50 caliber machine guns. Three in each wing, packing quite a punch. The drop tanks can also be removed and replaced by ten five-inch rockets or up to 2,000 pounds of bombs."

Hank was impressed.

"Notice the canopy, sir. This is the 'D' model Mustang, also referred to as the P-51D as you said earlier. One of the biggest changes to this fighter is the bubble-top canopy that allows for greater visibility. You can now see more clearly behind you, which is an added bonus for any fighter pilot. And check out this little baby. It's a new, gyroscopic gun sight called the K-14. It's supposed to automatically calculate the range and angle of an enemy target. All ya gotta do is put the pipper on the target and press the trigger. The K-14 will take care of the rest."

Hank listened intently to the advantages of the new gun sight, but immediately disliked its location—much too close to the pilot's head, possibly cutting down forward visibility. Only actual flight time would determine if he was right. He hoped he was wrong. Russ continued his praise of the fighter.

"She cruises at 275 miles per hour and costs about 54,000 dollars. She'll outfly, outgun, and outclass any Nazi piece of shit put up against her, in my opinion, sir. So in short, sir, don't break my aircraft." Russ stepped aside as Hank climbed into the cockpit.

"I don't intend to break *my* bird," Hank firmly replied, as he settled into the pilot's seat. As he sat down he felt something under him. It was a dark, russet-colored, A-2 leather jacket that coincidentally had silver lieutenant's-rank insignia bars on each shoulder loop and a circular, 96th Fighter Group emblem painted onto the left breast. The circular emblem representative of the 96th Fighter Group logo was a ferocious-looking bald eagle in flight, swooping down from the sky with blazing dual machine guns in each talon. The background carried the number "96" in tight red lettering.

"Try that on, Lieutenant. I think it'll fit you okay," said Russ.

Hank slipped on the jacket and zipped it up. It fit snugly and securely. He removed his officer's cap, replacing it with a brown-finished shearling B-6 helmet, goggles, and a radio headset that covered each ear.

"What 'bout a chute, sir? Or a Mae West?" asked Russ.

"No time. I'll risk it. Don't plan on flying over water, anyway," answered Hank, grasping the stick and putting both feet on the rudder pedals.

"You don't even want to put on a flight suit? All right, sir. Fire 'er up!" said Russ excitedly. Hank examined the gauges, switches, and other controls surrounding him. His uncanny instincts with machinery took over. His hands and wits went to work in unison as anything unfamiliar became familiar with the activation of the plane's controls in the correct combination.

"Just like riding a bicycle," Hank thought. "Who needs a manual?"

He went down the pre-flight checklist in his mind, primed the engine, and lifted the guard on the starter switch. With a loud bang the engine fired. The propeller began to turn slowly, gaining momentum until it spun rapidly. Still standing on the wing, Russ leaned toward Hank and shouted over the roar of the Merlin engine.

"Lieutenant, switch over to channel 3 on the radio. I got a Handy-Talkie radio in my jeep and can communicate with you on that channel."

Hank reached down and switched the radio dial to channel 3 and gave Russ the thumbs-up. The engine snarled to 1,300 rpm as Hank monitored the oil pressure gauge for any irregularities. All gauges read normal. Grasping the stick with both hands and depressing the rudder pedals with both feet, he began to get a feel for the plane's maneuvering characteristics. With thumbs extended from his balled-up fists, Hank gestured to Russ to remove the wheel chocks. Russ jumped off the wing and quickly removed the chocks as the prop blast whipped at his coveralls. Russ jogged over to his nearby jeep and grabbed the SCR-536 radio on the passenger seat.

"Lieutenant Mitchell, this is Sergeant Russell. Do you copy? This is a radio check. Charlie, uncle, victor, tango. Over."

Hank secured the fighter's oxygen mask over his face and spoke into the radio transmitter. "I read you loud and clear, Sergeant."

"I've just signaled the tower, sir. You have permission to take off, though they have advised you don't stay up too long, for safety reasons. Over," said Russ.

"Copy that, Sergeant. Will do. Preparing to taxi. Over," said Hank, rolling the bubble canopy shut.

Hank put the Mustang's wing flaps up and released the brakes. The plane rolled forward as Hank steered a serpentine course, making several sharp S-turns to properly line up at the head of the base's shorter runway. Once in position he stared down the open runway. With one final check of the pressure and temperature gauges, he took a deep breath and confidently pushed the throttle forward. The Mustang thrust ahead, gaining speed and momentum. Faster, faster, faster, until reaching the point of no return. As he gently pulled the stick back, the fighter eased off the ground and steadily gained altitude. Looking back through the bubble canopy, Hank watched as Jefferson Airfield became smaller and smaller in the distance.

The fighter leveled off and Hank instantly felt an increase in power and stability unlike any other aircraft he had flown. Cruising through the sky Hank eased the throttle open, gradually gaining speed. Then with youthful exuberance, he opened it full and unleashed the power of the mighty Merlin engine. The P-51 slashed forward with aerodynamic precision and grace. Hank couldn't believe how well it responded to the most sensitive adjustment of the controls. It was almost as if it were flying itself and Hank was nothing more than a comfortable passenger enjoying a ride through the illuminated heavens.

"Damn, she's smooth!" exclaimed Hank as he peeled the oxygen mask off his face, accidentally hitting the K-14 gun sight. He banked hard to the right and headed out toward the coast, ignoring the fact that he wasn't wearing a Mae West life jacket or a parachute. Within minutes the green fields and pastures of the quaint English countryside gave way to the deep blue expanses of the English Channel. Hank cut left and followed the coastline north. As the sun sank toward the horizon, Hank was again drawn to the bright orange, red, and yellow colors that stained the clouds and reflected off the rippling water below. The cockpit lit up with the brilliant colors raining down from the heavens, and Hank became entranced by the peaceful tranquility enveloping him. The splendor of the sun's rays spreading across the sky in a fiery rainbow of colors mesmerized him to the point he no longer heard the roar of the engine or felt the weight of the aircraft hurling him across the sky. The plane seemed to melt away from around him, leaving him as a winged angel soaring through the peaceful unending heavens. No signs of conflict, war, or man's mechanical monsters. Only stillness, harmony, and serenity for as far as Hank's eyes and imagination could take him.

With joyful, adolescent instinct, Hank beamed a wide smile and yanked at the stick, throwing the Mustang into a tight barrel roll—one of Hank's favorite stunt maneuvers. He felt like a child with a new toy. What a magnificent piece of American engineering, complemented perfectly by a British power plant. He began to wonder just how Hitler planned to win this war with such mechanical power and grace opposing him. Not even the looming danger of his secret mission could dampen his spirits.

Slowly the sun dipped below the horizon and the light from the heavens dimmed, turning the sky a dingy gray and blackening the waters. Hank snapped out of his peaceful trance as an angry voice entered his headset over the radio.

"Mustang 9-7-3 this is Gray Goose, come in!" it barked.

Hank hesitated for a moment. *Gray Goose? Who on Earth is Gray Goose?* The message repeated with added intensity.

"Mustang 9-7-3, this is Gray Goose, come in!"

Hank concluded that Gray Goose was the station call sign for Jefferson Airfield and that they must be angry with him for joyriding dangerously over the channel. He pulled his oxygen mask over his face and thumbed the throttle mic.

"Gray Goose, this is Mustang 9-7-3, I read you. Over."

"Lieutenant, you have ventured too far on an unauthorized flight route. You are in serious danger of taking friendly fire from ground AA batteries if you do not return to base immediately! Over!"

Not wanting to irritate the unknown speaker any further, Hank pointed the Mustang back toward Jefferson Airfield.

"Roger, Gray Goose. Returning to base. ETA ten minutes. Mustang 9-7-3 out," said Hank as he signed off, hoping he wasn't in any serious trouble. He glanced back toward the channel and could see bright little flashes of light littering the French coast, followed by faint booms. The reality of war had returned, shattering his brief moment of bliss. He shook his head and clutched the controls, his thumb twitching involuntarily over the trigger-guard on the stick, an all-too-familiar and unpleasant reaction to the sounds of aggression behind him. Soon the tower and two runways of Jefferson Airfield came into view. Hank lined up with the short fighter runway, lowered his landing gear, and glided effortlessly back to Earth. The maiden flight of *Silver's Sweetheart* was a success. As the P-51 came to a full stop, Hank rolled back the canopy and hopped out onto the wing, then the ground. As he unstrapped his leather helmet Sergeant Russell came rushing up.

"Take that damn new K-14 gun sight out and put the old N-3B sight back in, Sergeant," ordered Hank. "Damn thing is right up in my face and cuts my forward visibility in half. I want it out!"

"Aye, aye, sir," replied Russ with a half-hearted salute, as he watched the young pilot walk away into the night.

Chapter 6

THE DAY BEFORE

Matthew Switzer reclined on the couch and stretched his long arms toward the ceiling. The back of his neck creaked as he slowly rubbed the fatigue and stiffness from it. Several hours had passed since Hank had settled into his chair and started his journey into the past. Matt's pocket tape recorder had clicked off hours ago without notice while the pages of his notepad remained largely unfilled. Hank sat in his chair comfortably with his legs crossed and hands folded. His voice had grown hoarse as he told his story in vivid detail. Hank glanced up at the clock hanging on the wall. It read 6:14 p.m. Simultaneously Matt peered down at his wristwatch, confirming the time and wondering when he would be able to head back to Orono. An unpleasant and unexpected chill in the air that defied the normal mid-April weather accompanied the darkness outside Hank's window.

Sensing that Hank had reached a good breaking point in his story, Matt stood up and began organizing his things. Still sitting comfortably, Hank observed Matt's impatient fidgeting and wondered if he had absorbed one word he had said. Nevertheless, it was late and Hank realized it was time for Matt to leave. He stood up as if to give Matt the green light to begin his exit.

"Well I guess I should be heading back now, Mr. Mitchell—I mean Hank," Matt corrected himself. He fumbled with his tape recorder and notes until everything was secure in his backpack. "I sure appreciate all you, uh, shared with me today. It'll be useful in my report … and all … you know," Matt mumbled, trying to be polite. Putting on his coat, he headed for the door.

"Stop right there, boy," ordered Hank.

Matt cringed, as he was in no mood for another lecture. He slowly turned and faced Hank, who stood before him with his arms folded.

"I get the feeling you're unimpressed with the information I've imparted to you today," assumed Hank in a somewhat scholarly tone that irritated Matt as much as did nails across a chalkboard. Matt rolled his eyes and temporarily suppressed the growing frustration boiling inside him.

"Look … it's just that I got this tight deadline, and I got a lot to do, and I need to focus on G.I. combat, not how you felt flying a … uh … Mustang for the first time," clumsily responded Matt. "Look, I'm sure what I got today will help me a little. It was nice meeting you and maybe sometime I'll see you again if I'm down in this area," said Matt as he extended his hand to Hank.

"You aren't very patient, Matt, and you don't listen very well either, I've noticed," Hank retorted. "I really wish I understood your generation, but I must admit I can't, no matter how hard I try. You young fellas assume so much and have so little patience whenever you don't get the answers you want immediately. Life is not that cut-and-dried, son. Sometimes you have to dig a little deeper to find the answers you're looking for. Patience is the key. It certainly is in this situation."

Hank's words were not unfamiliar to Matt. He had heard them before from friends and family. He felt Hank's sincerity, but still struggled with thoughts of failing his class and not graduating.

"We're not done here, mister," added Hank. "I still have a lot more to tell you. Today was just the beginning. I want you to come back here tomorrow at the same time and we'll continue your—lesson, we'll call it."

"I don't know if tomorrow is good for me … I … may have some stuff to … "

"You're the one complaining about time, Matt!" interrupted Hank. "If you're truly serious about this assignment, you better damn well make time!"

Matt paused, unable to respond. The words would not come. He weakly nodded his head and started again for the front door.

"Matt," called out Hank. "I promise to help you in every way I can, as long as you put in the effort to learn. I feel that when I'm done with you you'll have the answers to the questions you're looking for. However, I hope that when we're done you'll take away with you something much greater than the ordinary mundane facts that come from my old, wrinkled head. Hopefully, by then you'll understand what I mean, son."

Matt nodded again, pulled open the front door, and wandered out into the darkness. He drove back to campus in silence, trying to visualize in his mind things working out and everything coming together in the end, but he couldn't. He didn't foresee the current situation with Hank improving for the better, no matter how hard he tried. What would he tell Michelle? What *could* he tell Michelle?

The lights of the busy campus soon showed before him. Chamberlain Hall was a welcome sight to his weary eyes. Stumbling up the stairs to his room, he plopped down on his bed and sighed heavily. Thoughts of calling Michelle crossed his mind, but did not will him to pick up the telephone. He wanted to call her and tell her how crazy he was about her, not how he felt he wasn't getting anywhere with his assignment or with her grandfather. Within minutes the issue was moot; he fell soundly asleep.

The next day Matt left for Bar Harbor earlier than before, ignoring loose-end responsibilities for his other classes. The day was like the one before—unseasonably chilly, with lots of dark clouds and little blue sky. Arriving at Hank's cabin, Matt tried to prepare himself mentally for what was to come. Hank led him into the study, where a warm, inviting fire was burning in the wood stove. It provided warmth, but also a sense of security that eased the tension in the room. Hank went to the kitchen and prepared two glasses of Coke.

"Okay, Mr. Switzer," said Hank optimistically, "are you ready?"

"Yes sir, I believe I am," replied Matt as he put a fresh tape into his recorder.

"Remember: patience, Matt. Patience."

The skies grew dark and overcast over Jefferson Airfield as an unexpected storm system swept down through the English Channel. A sheer curtain of light mist gently moistened the earth, slickening the patches of dirt and oil on the surface of the two runways. The soft and spongy ground slowly became saturated with water and squished loudly under the heels of U.S. army boots. There was no wind, just a steady veil of mist that fell straight down from the sky.

In the early morning hours of May 16, the remaining ground crew personnel lined up the four fighters along the short runway. The two P-38 Lightnings were in front, followed by the two P-51 Mustangs. They awaited the four lieutenant pilots, yet to emerge from the briefing room where Captain Wheeler had them trapped and surrounded by maps, charts, sand tables, and salvos of drilling on correct operational procedures. The morning's briefing had started at 0500 hours and did not cease until 0800. Wheeler finally dismissed his team, which rushed from the building to escape its tomblike conditions.

"Jesus, when did this shit roll in?" asked Lieutenant Dandridge to anyone listening. He zipped up his leather jacket and pulled his officer's peaked cap more securely on his head.

"Well, this'll be a bitch to fly in," flatly replied Lieutenant Hendricks while eyeing the water dripping off the nearby fighters.

"Ain't got much choice. Got to break 'em in today. Only chance to get some practice flight time in before the big show tomorrow," Lieutenant Brady remarked, looking up at the miserably darkened skies.

Hank peered toward the main hangar just as Sergeant Russell emerged from the doorway, shaking his head unappreciatively at the clammy drizzle.

"Damn English weather. Might as well be a goddamned duck," irritably muttered Russ, trotting over to the four pilots.

"Lieutenants Hendricks and Dandridge, you two are cleared for flight in the Lightnings. You're fully fueled and I packed your chutes this morning. They're both on the seats of the fighters. Lieutenants Brady and Mitchell, Lieutenant Stevenson wants you two to come with me."

"What gives, Russ? We need to get into the air, as well," asked Hank, eyeing *Silver's Sweetheart.*

"Tower doesn't want to monitor four fighters in the air at once.

Too much work for a skeleton crew in this ugly weather. They don't want to mistake you for enemy bandits, so they insisted on only two fighters per flight," answered Russ as he wiped a rivulet of water from his grease-smudged face. "For now, Major Jamison wants to get you two outfitted. Once the Lightnings are back on the ground, you and Lieutenant Brady can take the Mustangs up while Lieutenants Hendricks and Dandridge get outfitted. Fair enough, sirs?"

The four pilots nodded. Hendricks and Dandridge headed to the awaiting P-38 Lightnings, while Russ led Hank and Lieutenant Brady back to the main hangar. The roar of both Lightnings' twin engines was soon heard as the fighters sped down the runway and lifted off into the inclement weather. Back in the hangar, Sergeant Russell led Hank and Lieutenant Brady to a doorway at the back end of the building, behind the B-24 Liberator.

"Go right in, sirs. I got to get back to that damn B-24. Gonna be an all-night job before she's ready for any kinda action," sighed Russ, as he saluted the officers and headed over to the unfinished bomber. Hank opened the door and walked into a small room to find Lieutenant Stevenson writing meticulously on a clipboard.

"Come in, gentlemen," said Stevenson without stopping his pencil or looking up. "I'm taking inventory. On the table in the corner you'll find all the available equipment we have for tomorrow's mission. Take only what you feel is essential. I wish we could fully outfit you fighter pilots, but unfortunately we had to give first preference to the bomber crew. It didn't help that 80 percent of our gear and food supplies were packed up and shipped to God-knows-where, as a result of Command shutting us down. Anyway, that's another story. Just take what you can from the table and those lockers next to it," said Stevenson, pointing his pencil in the direction of the equipment before continuing to write.

Hank and Lieutenant Brady looked at each other, then at the table. Hank felt glad that Hendricks and Dandridge were up in the air and that he'd been given first choice of the meager pickings.

As Brady headed for the locker to try on flight jackets, Hank leaned over the wooden table. His eyes locked on a piece of equipment he wanted first and foremost. He reached out and grabbed a Colt .45

caliber pistol, M-1911A1, and russet-leather M3 shoulder holster with the letters "U.S." imprinted on the side. He removed the gun from the holster and released the magazine. It slid out of the stock with ease, revealing the short, stubby bullets staggered atop one another. Satisfied to find a loaded sidearm, He slapped the magazine back into the butt of the gun and reached for two extras that were also fully loaded. He slid them into an Army-green, double-web, M-1923 magazine pocket that he then affixed to his belt. Hank loved the Colt M-1911A1. It was parkerized, with lighter plastic handgrips, and was easy to aim and fire. It was a guaranteed "man-stopper" and a welcome sight to any G.I. fortunate enough to possess one in the heat of battle.

"Pass me one of those, Mitchell, will ya?" said Lieutenant Brady as he pointed to another .45 on the table. Hank grabbed the gun and handed it to Brady, who was fiddling with a life preserver. "This goddamned Mae West! Here, you take it, Hank. It's too small for me," grumbled Brady as he tossed the life vest on the ground at Hank's feet.

Hank grabbed for more gear: a small pocket, prismatic M-1938 compass; M3 trench knife; leather gloves; TL-122B model flashlight; M-1910 canteen; and a first-aid kit containing packets of sulfa powder, small gauze bandages, two red-and-white syrettes of morphine, some iodine swabs, and a tiny pair of scissors. He also spied a Zippo lighter in black, crinkled-paint finish that he snatched up and dropped in his trousers pocket, before stuffing the rest of his findings into a green, Army-canvas satchel that he slung over his shoulder. Lieutenant Brady was far less concerned with his choices that amounted to a jacket, gloves, life preserver, and sidearm.

"Where the hell do think you're gonna stash all that junk? Cockpit is only so big, ya know," said Brady.

"Easy. I just arrange everything neatly in this satchel, hang it on my shoulder, and tuck it under my jacket. I've done it before," answered Hank.

"Mae West don't get in the way?" asked Brady.

"Naw. Sometimes it's a little too snug, but I manage okay. I got pockets, too, you know!" Hank answered sarcastically as if Brady had never thought of actually putting items into his pockets before climbing into the cockpit.

"Gentlemen, before you go, let me write down the description of all you took, so I can properly record our current inventory," ordered Lieutenant Stevenson, his clipboard at the ready. When done, he escorted the two pilots back into the noisy hangar where Russ and two other mechanics were still working feverishly on the B-24's engines.

"Jesus, Mitch, think they'll ever get that bird ready to fly?" asked Brady as both men stared at the bomber's exposed engines.

"They better ... or else tomorrow's mission ain't gonna amount to a whole helluva lot. It'd be pretty interesting flying bomber escort with no bomber, don't ya think?" responded Hank with a chuckle and a smile. "C'mon Brady, let's go see if the P-38s are back. I really wanna log some more flight time. Those P-51s are incredibly agile. Smoothest ride in a fighter I've ever had!"

The two men emerged from the dry hangar and were enveloped once again in the dismal damp English weather. The leaden skies showed no signs of breaking, as the ominous sound of thunder rolled across the heavens. Brady and Mitchell scanned the horizon for any sign of the P-38 Lightnings. Moments later the sound of the twin-boomed monsters roared into earshot.

"There!" cried out Brady, as Lieutenant Hendricks's fighter came into view. Closer and closer, larger and larger, until the plane was practically on top of them. With a nearly picture-perfect approach, Hendricks's Lightning rolled along the water-slicked airstrip, coming to a full stop. Brady and Mitchell watched the Lightning's propellers spin to a safe halt, then walked over to the fighter to greet Hendricks, who had popped open the cockpit and dropped to the ground.

"How'd she feel?" asked Brady.

"Ah, not too bad." Hendricks replaced his leather headgear with his officer's cap. "She's got some kick to her, that's for sure. Not all that much of a different feel from the P-47. State of the art, though."

Sergeant Russell burst from the hangar with his SCR-536 radio.

"Okay, Lieutenant Dandridge, I can see you now! Just keep her level and try to bring her down as gently as possible," shouted Russell into the bulky portable radio. Suddenly all eyes were scanning the sky as Dandridge's Lightning flew into view with one propeller seized up and a black plume of smoke streaming behind the shuddering fighter. "You're doing fine, Lieutenant! Gently ease back on the throttle and line her up with the runway. Don't make any sudden jerks on the stick, or she'll flip over and cartwheel as soon as you hit the ground." Pulling the SCR-536 away from his face, Sergeant Russell barked at the three pilots standing next to him. "Somebody run back to the hangar and get a fire extinguisher!"

"I'll go!" said Brady as he turned and sprinted off.

The Lightning began losing speed and momentum almost to the point of stalling. The smoke thickened as the unbalanced aircraft wobbled left and right while the landing gear was lowered and locked into position.

"That's it, Lieutenant! You got it! Ease her on down," yelled Russell's adrenaline-soaked voice into the radio.

Hank stood with both fists clenched tightly as the fighter descended to within a few feet of the ground. As the wheels screeched against the runway's hard surface, he could see Dandridge struggling frantically in the cockpit and sense his terror. He instinctively started running after the fighter as it rolled along the runway, the smoke from the seized-up engine enveloping him. Russell and Hendricks followed in quick pursuit. The stricken Lightning shuddered to a halt, its right engine spewing streams of yellow and orange flame and billows of black smoke. Lieutenant Dandridge burst open the cockpit and leapt onto the ground, tearing his leather helmet off.

"Stop! Get back now!" he shouted, waving his arms wildly at the three running toward him. "The whole damn cockpit is drenched in oil and she could blow any second!"

Hank, Hendricks, and Russell stopped dead in their tracks and shrank back as Dandridge joined them, his face and clothing covered in foul black oil and smoke. Just then a jeep roared past, with Lieutenant Brady and his fire extinguisher at the ready. Brady jumped out from the vehicle and fearlessly began dousing the engine's blaze, ignoring the warning shouts of Dandridge and the rest. Within minutes the small fire was out.

"You okay, sir?" asked Russell as he handed Dandridge a rag to help clean the oil from his face.

"No, I'm not okay, Sergeant!" wheezed Dandridge as his smoke-congested lungs struggled to filter out the foul air. He dropped to his knees and coughed violently. "What the fuck happened? What kinda death trap did you assholes put me in?" Dandridge continued to choke up smoke from his overwhelmed lungs. "I'm going along nice and easy at an even clip, when all of a sudden the goddamned oil-pressure gauge dropped down to nothing. Before I knew it, a fucking oil line bursts and starts spraying the cockpit—and me! Then the fucking right engine seizes up before I even have a chance to do anything!"

"Don't say any more, Dandridge. We gotta get you inside and checked out by the doc," said Hank as he and Hendricks helped the young pilot back onto his feet.

Another jeep rolled up carrying Lieutenant Stevenson and Major Jamison. The major jumped out and looked over Dandridge.

"Stevenson, get this man over to the infirmary quickly. Have him checked out by Doctor Morgan!" ordered Jamison.

"Yes, sir," replied Stevenson with a quick salute, as he helped Dandridge into the jeep, then peeled out and sped away. Major Jamison turned to the other pilots and Sergeant Russell.

"Did he say anything to you guys? What the hell happened up there? I was in the tower helping monitor the flight when the controllers lost radio contact with him. He even temporarily disappeared from the radar screen. How the hell can that happen? Anybody? Speak freely!"

"Sir, I'll have to take a closer look, but I'm pretty sure the oil pump failed, based on what Lieutenant Dandridge just said and my experience with these P-38s," answered Sergeant Russell.

"Go on," said Jamison, lighting up a cigarette that burned weakly in the damp, cool drizzle.

"Well, sir, for some reason the P-38s don't take to the cold weather very well. We've had a helluva time with some of the few that have flown off this base. The chilly English weather really takes a toll on these fighters. I've seen the damp get into the hydraulics and electrical systems, causing failures of all sorts. We know how to fix them once a problem has occurred, but we have a bitch of a time preventing them. It's more than likely a design problem, sir," explained Russell.

"Who's the crew chief for this aircraft, Sergeant?" asked Jamison.

"That would be Sergeant Burke, sir."

"Get him and his crew out here on the double. I want this fighter brought into the hangar and repaired immediately before mission time tomorrow," said Jamison coldly.

"Begging the major's pardon, sir, but I was ordered by Lieutenant Stevenson to have all available ground crew work on the Liberator until she was ready to go. We still have a lot of armor plat—"

"I understand your predicament, Sergeant, but the situation has changed drastically," interrupted Jamison.

"Permission to speak, sir?" quickly asked Russell.

"What is it, Sergeant?" sighed Jamison.

"Major, we're operatin' with a skeleton maintenance crew as it is. I've already lost my regular assistant crew chief and armorer to reassignment, and even if we work throughout the night without stopping, we may or may not have enough time to finish the remaining work on the bomber or get the remaining aircraft armed and fueled for tomorrow's mission. I can't tell you how much damage that Lightning has sustained because I ain't had a good look at her yet, but I can sure as hell tell ya that it will take at least four men to repair and refit all damage before dawn tomorrow, and that will seriously hamper our efforts on finishing work on the Liberator, sir."

"Noted, Sergeant. Nevertheless, the mission will go on as planned tomorrow and that means that a bomber will go into the air with a four-fighter escort! You find Captain Wheeler and his crew and inform them of the situation. Maybe they can lend a hand arming and fueling the fighters. Hell, get them to help haul the bomb payload, as well. I don't care what you have to do, Sergeant! Get the job done. Colonel Dexter and I expect nothing less! That goes for you three officers, as well!" snapped Jamison before he stormed off out of the drizzle.

"I hope we survive to see the dawn," muttered Russell, as he spat on the ground and climbed into the jeep. "C'mon, guys, we got a shitload of work ahead of us."

"What about our practice flight time?" asked Hank, climbing into the jeep. "We need to get those Mustangs up in the air to make sure they won't fall apart on us, too!"

"Well, according to the major's little speech, I'd say it's been canceled, sir. You better just come with me."

Hank shook his head and cursed under his breath. Russell slammed the jeep into gear and sped away, leaving deep tread marks in the sopping wet grass and bare ground. En route to the hangar, Russ yelled at a few members of his crew who were standing outside watching the black smoke rise from the stricken P-38.

"Get back to work! We ain't got a second to spare! Someone go find Sergeant Burke and tell him he's got to drop what he's doing and get his team wrenching on that smokin' P-38 over there!" Russ slammed on the brakes, causing the three passengers to lurch forward, then back.

"Goddamn brass! Think they can squeeze blood from a stone!" muttered Russ as he entered the hangar. "Burke, where the hell are you?"

"Right where I've been for the past four hours! Patching oil leaks on this damn bomber," replied a voice from under engine number one. Russ turned in the direction of the voice and confronted Sergeant Burke, his hands and face covered in black oil.

"Burke, we got a problem with your bird. She just came down with a seized engine and some fire damage. Damn near killed the pilot."

"What the hell happened?" responded Burke, his arms outstretched and palms pointing upwards. "I had my guys give her a good once-over first thing this morning. She was purring like a kitten. What the hell did they do to my bird?" asked Burke, casting an accusing stare at the three fighter pilots standing behind Russ.

"I don't know what happened, Burke. You know as well as me how the Lightning don't like the cold and damp. My guess is that it's an oil pump problem. Probably had a bad one to begin with," replied Russ.

"Goddamn it!" exclaimed Burke as he peered out the hangar doors at the lightly smoking P-38 Lightning. "What the hell am I supposed to do now, Russ?"

"Jamison wants it towed back inside and to have you and your team fix it immediately."

"Just how the fuck am I supposed to do that, Russ? I got Captain Wheeler up my ass to get this bomber completed and armed by tonight! We're way behind and my guys are exhausted! Even if we finished all the modifications early, it's gonna take us hours to completely fuel and arm it and all the fighters before mission time tomorrow! So explain to me just how the fuck those bastards sitting in HQ doing nothing expect us to pull this off!"

"You're out of line, Sergeant," spoke up Lieutenant Hendricks.

"You can go fuck yourself, sir. I don't care if you got bars on your shoulders or not. You hotshot pilots haven't done a goddamn thing to help us," roared Burke as he pointed a long screwdriver in Hendricks's face. The young lieutenant was so shocked, he was at a loss for any words or disciplinary response. Russ quickly interceded.

"Now just calm down, Burke! I feel exactly the way you do, but that ain't gonna do us one bit of good under the circumstances! We got our orders!"

"You're the head wrench-turner on this base, Russ. What's the plan?" grumbled Burke. Russ thought for a moment.

"Here's what we're gonna do, Burke. Take your two best guys and get that P-38 back in here and in flying shape. I don't care how she looks, just get her flightworthy. I'll take charge of the work on the bomber. I'm gonna whip that bird into shape before dawn if it kills me. Free up one mechanic to assist the pilots here. They're gonna start fueling and arming the fighters right now. Break out the .50 caliber ammo. If it's locked up, bust open the locks, we ain't got a second to spare. I'm gonna round up all of Wheeler's crew and make them assist me with the bomber. They can help with the fueling and arming, and if need be, I'll have 'em do some wrenching. We're gonna make this happen, Burke, I swear it. Move!"

"Yes, sir. That's what I like to hear, Russ," replied Burke with a quick salute before trotting off toward the damaged Lightning. Russ turned back to the three pilots.

"If you guys want to make it through tomorrow alive, you're gonna have to listen to every word I say and do your damnedest to help. We're gonna hafta cut out all military formalities and just get down to work. That means no saluting, no 'sirs,' no nothin' until the work gets done.

Agreed?"

The three pilots nodded their heads in unison.

"Good. Now, let's get to work!" said Russ with renewed enthusiasm, stepping toward the bomber with the trio of pilots in tow. The sounds of grinding metal could be heard all around. Hank knew that the next few hours could very well determine whether he lived or died tomorrow.

Organized chaos ensued in and outside the main hangar as the daylight hours slipped away and yielded to nightfall. Exhausted mechanics scurried around in a sleep-deprived trance, trying desperately to ready the five aircraft for the following day's mission. Slowly but surely, with each turn of the wrench and screwdriver, the aircraft came closer to full fighting readiness. Having changed into greasy coveralls, Hank found himself heavily loaded down with belts of .50 caliber ammunition draped over his shoulders, standing alongside the right wing of his fighter.

"Okay, Lieutenant, just ease up those ammo belts one at a time, and I'll feed 'em in," instructed a young armorer crouched on the open, exposed right wing of Hank's Mustang. Hank slowly lifted the heavy belt of ammunition up to the armorer, who skillfully fed it into the fighter's wing ammo boxes, locking the first round into the ammo feed chute with meticulous care. The armorer realized the importance of carefully arming the guns. Any small mistake could result in a disastrous misfeed or jam that could render them useless in battle and spell certain doom for the pilot. As soon as he passed off the last belt, Hank sprinted back into the hangar, where he hoisted more .50 caliber ammunition from the ammo lockers onto his aching shoulders and hustled back outside. By now the persistent drizzle had finally subsided. The loading process was repeated until the arming mechanic had enough ammo to fully arm both wings.

"Okay, sir, that's enough," said the mechanic. "I need to finish loading in this ammunition. Be easier if I had more light. ... Oh well, I'm okay for now. You can help with the other planes, sir."

Hank nodded and turned to see if help was needed anywhere else. In the corner of the hangar Sergeant Burke was feverishly stripping the blackened and damaged parts from Dandridge's P-38 Lightning. Beneath the nose of the B-24 Liberator, Sergeant Russell was shielding himself from the shower of sparks raining down from the acetylene torch burning hot in his right hand. Additional armor plating was being welded onto the bomber. Members of Captain Wheeler's crew climbed in and out of the aircraft carrying equipment and ammo onboard at an accelerated pace. Just then Lieutenant Hendricks crossed Hank's line of sight carrying boxes of spare parts to Sergeant Burke.

"Just drop 'em over there for now. I'll get to 'em as soon as I can!" said Burke without taking his eyes off his work.

"Mitchell! Give me a hand over here!"

Hank turned his head in the direction of the bellowing voice and saw Brady waving his arms. He hustled over to his wingman and his Mustang, second in line on the runway.

"Help me secure this cowling panel, would ya? Son-of-a-bitch doesn't want to lock into position, and I can't see very well in the dark out here," said Brady in a strained voice. Hank jumped up on the wing alongside Brady and forced the panel back onto the fighter's nose. Both men wiped the dripping sweat from their foreheads as they turned to gaze at the bomber.

"Whaddaya think, Brady?" asked Hank gesturing toward the B-24 in the lit up hangar.

"No way in hell, Mitch. There is no way that bird will be ready to go in a few hours. Not with the modifications they're making. Christ, they've been welding and riveting so much armor plating, I don't see how Wheeler will get that bitch off the ground! Why the hell do they need all that armor?"

"I don't know," replied Hank. "With all that extra plating, plus a full bomb load, he'd be better off strapping wings and an engine onto a battleship and flying that over to France. It might be easier."

"Yeah, you might be right," snickered Brady. "Damn glad I'm not hitching a ride on that bird tomorrow. C'mon … let's concentrate on our own problems and get these fighters ready. Let Wheeler and his crew worry about the bomber."

Hank hurried back to his Mustang, first in line for fueling. A fuel truck pulled up and the driver jumped out and prepared to fuel the Mustang's main tank and both drop tanks under each wing. Hank stepped alongside and helped secure the fuel hose to the aircraft. The sound of fuel gushing through the line filled his eardrums.

"How we lookin' out here?" shouted Russ as he emerged from the hangar. He peeled off his protective gauntlets and goggles, revealing a filthy face washed in oil and soot.

"These three fighters are fully armed, sir. The fuel truck is gonna work its way down the line in the next few minutes once this first Mustang is topped off, sir. Shouldn't be much longer before we can all help out with the bomber and that damaged P-38," answered the mechanic atop Hank's fighter.

"Good!" replied Russ, giving a thumbs-up and turning to Hank. "Sir, I don't think there's much left for you or the other pilots to help out with tonight. Looks like the rest of the burden is in our hands. I appreciate the assistance, though. We wouldn't have gotten this far without you guys pitching in."

"What about the bomb load for the Liberator? Surely we could help load the bombs or stow gear or something?" asked Hank, still willing to aid the exhausted and short-handed ground crews.

"Naw. Not necessary, sir. Captain Wheeler's boys are handling that part. Seems they want to be responsible for their own bird. It's one of those 'You worry 'bout your shit, we'll worry 'bout ours' kinda deals with those guys."

"Just want to be useful, Russ," said Hank.

Just then Hendricks and Brady appeared out of the darkness to join the conversation. Russ continued.

"You pilots should head back to your barracks now and try to get some sleep." Russ squinted at his watch as he tried to make out the time. "If you go now you can still get four or five hours before mission time tomorrow."

"Russ, look at yourself," said Hank. "You're about to fall over. Let us stay and give you a hand."

"You're forgetting that I'm not the one who has to fly this crate tomorrow, Lieutenant. Go. Get some rest. We got everything under control. You'll just be in the way if you stick around. Get lost already!" ordered Russ.

"You're the boss, Sergeant," said Hank with a sarcastic salute. He and the other pilots turned and walked slowly into the darkness toward the barracks. Upon arrival Hank stripped off his filthy coveralls and attempted to clean himself up. Brady and Hendricks followed suit.

"I wonder how Dandridge is doing?" questioned Hendricks aloud. The three men stood silent for a moment.

"Find out tomorrow, I guess," said Brady solemnly.

Half an hour later Hank crawled into his bunk. The sounds of the ground crews frantically finishing their work grew weaker as he drifted into a deep, relaxing sleep. He no longer felt the stress or strain of the upcoming mission. His overtired body, in dire need of rest, would not allow his conscious mind to dwell on the precarious situation any further. Mission time was but a few short hours away.

Chapter 7

OPERATION VENGEANCE

As the night gave way to the predawn hours, the sky over Jefferson Airfield cleared, revealing infinite bright, twinkling stars. The gray overcast skies had finally broken, leaving no doubt the mission would proceed as planned. The fighter pilots slept undisturbed, unknowing what tomorrow would bring. The barracks was peaceful, but would not be for long.

At 0430 hours the door to the sleeping quarters opened and Lieutenant Stevenson entered, shining his flashlight into the faces of the sleeping pilots.

"Let's go, gentlemen!" he ordered. "It is now 0430 hours! You've got one hour to get cleaned up, dressed, and grab some chow. Mission briefing is at 0530 hours, and I suggest you don't be late! Let's go!"

Stevenson turned sharply and moved swiftly out the door with authority. Hank, Brady, and Hendricks each leapt to their feet and made up their bunks in less than a minute. Still in his undershirt and boxer shorts, his dog tags clinking together softly, Hank doused his face and hair with hot water and lathered his cheeks and neck with Burma-Shave applied with a soft-bristled shaving brush. He gently ran his Gillette razor with Pal blades across his face. He grabbed a small package of Milk-i-dent Dental Cream and applied it liberally to his brown Army-issue toothbrush. Finally, he dusted his face with Williams talcum powder and combed his thick brown hair into the accustomed style.

Hustling back to his bunk and duffel bag, Hank began to dress. He first put on his dark olive drab officer's service shirt with silver, lieutenant-rank insignia bar on the right collar and Air Corps service insignia on the left. His flight wings were pinned just above the left breast pocket. He methodically knotted his khaki necktie and pulled on his khaki trousers with officer's belt and brass buckle. He affixed the army-green double-web M-1923 magazine pocket containing the two extra .45 caliber pistol magazines to his belt and tucked his tie into his shirt between the first and second visible buttons. He put on wool socks, laced up his three-quarter-high G.I. boots, and donned his officer's cap. Reaching into his bag again, he pulled out the satchel containing the gear he'd requisitioned the day before. He pulled out the .45 caliber pistol and strapped on the shoulder holster. A quick release of the magazine verified that the gun was loaded, and Hank slid the weapon into the holster securely. The A-2 leather jacket was the final touch. Hank looked in the mirror as he glanced at his watch. The officer he saw staring back at him was confident and ready—the way a fighter pilot should be. It was now 0445 hours.

The three pilots exited the barracks. Looking instinctively in the direction of the main hangar, they saw that it was completely dark and lifeless, as if nothing had happened there the previous night.

"Hey, look over there!" exclaimed Brady, pointing in the direction of the runways.

"Well, I'll be damned," said Hendricks as his eyes locked on the murky outlines of several large, familiar shapes parked in a row along the short strip.

"I never thought they'd pull it off!" said Hank in disbelief. He marveled at the four fighter craft ready for action. The two P-51 Mustangs were parked in front, with Hank's in the lead, while the two larger P-38 Lightnings brought up the rear. Dandridge's bird stood last in line, still showing noticeable signs of scorched metal from yesterday's accident.

"Look over there!" shouted Hendricks as he pointed in the direction of the long runway.

Sitting at the base of the airstrip was the B-24 Liberator. The mighty, mysterious bomber that had drawn so much attention and generated so many unanswered questions was finally revealed in the waning moonlight of the early morning hours. But precious time was slipping away and neither breakfast nor the 0530 briefing would wait.

"Let's go, guys," said Hank, turning toward the dim lights of the mess hall. "We don't have much time."

After breakfast in the mess hall, the three headed to the guarded doorway leading to the briefing room. The MP saluted and opened the door. As they walked down the stairway, Hank could hear voices quietly conversing. It was now 0520 hours. As the three men entered the briefing room it was clear that all personnel were already present. Major Jamison and Lieutenant Stevenson were at the front of the room, whispering to each other, while Captain Wheeler sat to the side, his bomber crew huddled around him. Wheeler was pointing out instructions written on a clipboard in his hand, looking like a basketball coach designing a play during a timeout. In another corner Lieutenant Dandridge sat by himself. He looked tired and still sickly. He was wearing the same clothes he'd had on in yesterday's crash. His hair was a mess and his face was clean, but unshaven. He seemed distracted and didn't notice his fellow pilots. He made no sound other than a subtle coughing spell that repeated every few seconds. Ignoring everything else, Hank and the others went directly to the feeble-looking Lieutenant Dandridge.

"Dandridge? You okay? What happened last night?" blurted Brady, kneeling to the sitting Dandridge's eye level. Dandridge covered his mouth with a balled-up fist and coughed, then looked up at Brady with a stone-faced glare and bloodshot eyes. He spoke softly.

"I spent the night with … with … the Doc. He treated me with … something to ease the pain in my lungs … smoke … oil … my lungs … you know … " answered Dandridge, seeming confused. "I remember coughing and choking … then … sleep. Whatever he gave me … put me to sleep."

"You're not gonna fly today are you? They can't possibly expect you to go up in your condition. Look at yourself! Listen to yourself," pleaded Hendricks.

"I'm all right, Hendricks. Just a little woozy. Need a few minutes to clear my head, that's all. Jamison insisted I not back down for you guys' sake today. I'm flying! That P-38 piece of shit ain't gonna get the best of me!" he declared as he forced himself to sit up in his chair and look straight ahead, the way an officer should before a briefing.

"Let's sit down," said Hank, as he sensed a growing tension in the room. He glanced at the model of the V-1 rocket at the center of the room, then at Captain Wheeler's bomber crew, bundled up in seal-brown shearling. Type A-3 trousers, type B-3 jackets, and type A-6 boots were prevalent throughout the room. Even though it was mid-May, the bomber crew still had to dress warmly in the open-air and unpressurized Liberator.

"Ten-hut!" cried Lieutenant Stevenson, as Major Jamison stepped to the podium. The room snapped to attention and all side conversation ceased.

"Be seated, gentlemen," calmly ordered Jamison. "I'm going to make this briefing as short as possible. I'm sure everyone in this room is ready for some action today, and I want you to get in the air and underway on schedule as orders dictate. First off, the colonel has taken ill this morning and has ordered me to temporarily take charge. The mission will proceed as planned, and you'll all be back here safe and sound before the end of the day. At the conclusion of the mission, I will personally debrief everyone and disclose the details of your next assignment and posting. You, of course, are all aware that this base will no longer play a role in this theater of operations in the coming days—at least not under our control. I will stress again that today's mission is still classified as top secret and you will not discuss it, nor recognize its existence, now or at its conclusion. Anyone who violates this order will be subject to court-martial and will stand a good chance of being lined up in front of a firing squad! With that said, I'll turn things over to Captain Wheeler. Good hunting today, men!"

Jamison stepped down and left the room. Captain Wheeler stood up and took Jamison's place at the podium. He scowled at Lieutenant Stevenson, standing close by at parade rest, and pulled off the white sheet covering the chalkboard behind him.

"Gentlemen, this is it. Here are the target's exact coordinates and here are the rally point's coordinates after takeoff," said Wheeler, indicating the navigation point drawn on the chalkboard. "Once we get in the air we will proceed to the rally point, where we will then get into formation. My bomber will take off before the fighters to get the necessary head start. Once we're together, we'll drop down to the deck at the designated altitude. Then we'll line up in formation and zigzag toward the French coast, following this bearing." Wheeler pointed to the chalkboard. "Blue 1 and 2, the navigational burden is on you as you'll have the lead once we're in formation. You'll act as pathfinders as well as protectors.

"Red 1 and 2, you're the muscle. Keep behind and slightly above the formation, on the lookout for enemy fighters. Remember, the Lightnings will tear up any ground resistance, while the Mustangs cut down anything the Germans are stupid enough to sacrifice in the air. Remember to observe radio silence at all times, unless I give the order to break it. We're not gonna get caught with our pants down! Be prepared to stay close to the deck, gentlemen. We may not get above fifty feet until we're on top of the target."

Wheeler paused a moment to let everything he had said sink in. The room was quiet except for sounds of pencils lightly scratching across small notepads. The tension mounted. Wheeler spoke again.

"I know you're all familiar with your assignments, men. You've studied the target and the mission objectives. I know you all know what to do. Now is the time to shine, gentlemen! Let's make a difference today and give those Nazi sons-a-bitches something to really remember!"

The spirited airmen nodded in unison as they glanced around confidently. The morale in the room heightened rapidly as Wheeler's words sank in. Adrenaline flowed through Hank's veins. He became anxious and antsy in his seat.

"Quickly—any questions?" asked Wheeler.

The room was silent until Hank put up his hand.

"Yes … Lieutenant Mitchell?"

"Sir, will we be issued escape kits?"

"You plan on being shot down, Lieutenant? 'Cause if that's the case, I'm not sure I want you covering my ass today!"

Wheeler's two waist-gunners snickered at their captain's remark. Just then Lieutenant Stevenson stepped forward.

"We've been over this before. Everyone has been outfitted with the gear available to us at this time. Due to the current status of this base, in conjunction with the time-sensitive priority of this mission, we're not able to fully outfit everyone. I suggest you all make do with what you've got!"

Stevenson stepped back while Hank reclined in his chair in silent disgust. Wheeler took control of the floor again and spoke up with authority.

"Let's go to work, gentlemen. It's now 0545. Synchronize all your watches and get to your planes to start preflight!" The men leapt from their chairs and rushed for the exit. Hendricks, Dandridge, Brady, and Hank stood up together and were the last out, save for Lieutenant Stevenson, who stayed behind to secure the room. The four fighter pilots hustled up the stairs into the emerging, early-morning light. As Hank got to his fighter, Sergeant Russell staggered up. Hank looked in horror at his ragged crew chief.

"I threw some equipment into the cockpit that I thought you would need, sir." Hank took a second to examine Russ's appearance before he climbed onto the P-51's wing. His faithful crew chief appeared battered, ready to collapse, having run the gauntlet of extreme physical and emotional pain. His face was bloodied and black with oil and dirt. His coveralls were also filthy, scorched, and torn in several places. The worst sight was his hands, which almost seemed unrecognizable. Covered in black grease, skin cut and cracked, and fingers cramped so badly that Russ could barely extend them, his hands resembled two balled-up monstrosities. Nevertheless, the tough old sergeant didn't try to draw any sympathy to his frightful condition. He simply stared at Hank with bloodshot eyes.

"Sir, I found you some good, angled R.A.F. goggles. They're on the seat."

Hank looked past the rolled-up canopy into the exposed cockpit and saw the goggles on the seat. Beneath them lay a neatly packed parachute. Dangling from the control stick were a white silk scarf and the flying leather helmet Hank had worn on his maiden flight. Last, Russ reached into his pocket and pulled out a dingy old whistle. He handed it to Hank, who clipped it onto his jacket.

"Hang on a second, sir, and I'll climb up and help you get all your gear on," said Russ.

With great effort, the exhausted crew chief climbed up on the wing next to Hank and helped him strap on his life preserver vest and parachute. The remaining contents of Hank's gear were snugly secured in his satchel strapped underneath his leather jacket. Last, Hank pulled on his gloves, wrapped the silk scarf around his neck, and tucked it down into his jacket. The scarf seemed like nothing more than a vain article of clothing flyers used to attract girls, but in fact it was a vital piece of equipment most fighter pilots cherished. It helped cut down on neck chafing and irritation, as the pilot's head was constantly moving, scanning the skies for the unseen enemy waiting to pounce.

Hank climbed into the cockpit and wriggled into the cramped, unforgiving pilot's seat, adjusting it as best he could for greater comfort. He removed his officer's cap and handed it to Russ before pulling on his leather helmet and goggles.

"Do me a favor, Russ … just toss this onto on my bunk after we take off."

Russ nodded.

"Strap yourself in, Lieutenant. You're fully fueled and armed. I gave her a good once-over an hour ago. She's all set to go. You've got one spare drop tank under each wing. Use them first to get to the target. Switch over to the main tank and jettison the spares if you get into any trouble. Crank this baby up and give 'em hell today, sir!"

"I will, Sergeant. Go get cleaned up and get some rest. That's an order!"

"Yes, sir," said Russ, with a smile and a quick salute. "Here, Lieutenant, have a Hershey bar on me," said Russ happily as he handed Hank the coveted brown-wrapped bar of chocolate. Thanking Russ, Hank slid it into his pocket. Russ jumped off the wing and went to check the other fighters and assist the other pilots.

Hank scanned the instrument panel and made sure the ignition switch was off and the parking brake was set. The bomb and gun safety switches were also off. The landing gear control handle was down and set in the correct position. He reached for the control-lock plunger at the base and just forward of the stick. With a firm tug, he released the controls to check for free movement of the stick and rudder pedals. They felt loose and normal. He set the trim tabs and released the hydraulic pressure, with wing flaps and flap handle set in the "up" position. He cranked the canopy shut and pulled his headset on. He secured the A-14 oxygen mask over his face, switched on the radio, and turned the dial to channel 3, per Wheeler's earlier orders. Unlike prior to the maiden flight, Hank meticulously continued the preflight checklist, trying not to overlook even the smallest detail. Finally, he went through the engine startup list.

He primed the engine with three quick shots and instinctively checked to see that the prop was free and clear. With building anticipation and zeal, he lifted the guard on the starter switch. He pressed the switch to "START," and the potent Merlin engine came to life with a throaty bang. Puffs of smoke thundered from the side exhaust stacks just rear of the propeller blades as the engine idled in the cool morning air. The mighty four-blade propeller turned slowly, then rapidly gained momentum until it was a spinning blur. The RPM gauge read 1300 and the oil pressure remained constant and within normal tolerances. Hank moved the stick back and forth until he was satisfied with the feel. The rudder pedals also moved freely, indicating normal function. He then uncaged the gyro instruments and tapped the compass to ensure it wasn't jammed. He rotated the fuel-selector valve to confirm proper fuel flow from the main fuselage tank to both pressed-paper drop tanks beneath the wings. He gripped the stick firmly, extending and retracting his fingers in a rhythmic motion. The adrenaline coursing through his bloodstream heightened his senses. He was ready to go.

One by one the other fighters came to life. Soon all Hank could hear was the sound of turning propellers and roaring engines. He momentarily closed his eyes and listened through his headset, awaiting any last-minute instructions from Wheeler's bomber or the tower. Nothing so far. He looked in the direction of the tower, but saw no activity. He was lead plane and couldn't afford to mess up. For the moment, though, all he could do was wait.

Across the field on the long runway sat the B-24 Liberator. Wheeler's copilot and the rest of his crew were onboard, going through their preflight. From a perch atop the control tower, Lieutenant Stevenson stood with a flare gun, staring at his wristwatch. At precisely 0600, he raised the piece into the air and shot off a large green, glowing flare high into the dawning sky. It descended slowly after giving off a slow, hot-burning green signal.

"Red Element and Blue Element, this is Eagle 1," Wheeler's voice came over the radio. "We are now observing radio silence. Do not break silence unless ordered to do so by me. Out!"

Sitting impatiently in his Mustang, Hank listened to Wheeler's orders and made sure not to respond. He heard nothing from Brady, Hendricks, or Dandridge and assumed they got the message loud and clear. Hank gripped the stick firmly and squirmed in his seat as the rush of the adrenaline coursing through his veins seemed to correspond with the RPMs his propeller was turning under the might of the Mustang's mighty Merlin engine.

Hank watched as the heavily loaded bomber lumbered down the runway, gradually gaining speed. The heavy craft struggled to reach 110 mph; and once it passed the point of no return, Hank could see it shaking violently as it strained to gain altitude. As the bomber slowly vanished from sight, Hank's eyes left the sky and focused on the tower. It was his turn now, and the next green flare sent into the sky would be meant for him. The tension mounted.

The minutes ticked away and still no signal. Hank sat impatiently, double-checking his instruments to verify that everything was functioning properly. He soon found himself simply going through the motions of double-checking.

"Damnit, let's go!" he muttered to himself. He was agitated and couldn't help but wonder if his fellow pilots lined up behind him felt the same aggravation. The idling engine droned on as Hank continued to stare at the tower. Suddenly, a green flare burst into the sky, the bright burning flash rising high into the atmosphere, then gradually disappearing as it fell back to Earth. He felt a wave of relief. It was time to go to work.

Hank looked out the cockpit window. He observed Sergeant Russell race up and quickly remove the wheel chocks. The blast from the propeller blew his cap off, but didn't deter him from saluting Hank as he stepped clear of the plane's path. Hank returned the salute and eased the throttle forward. The stick in his hand was slightly aft of neutral to lock the tail wheel. The P-51 began to roll. Hank executed several broad S-turns with the wing flaps up to line himself up exactly as he wanted. Once in position, he ran up the engine to 2000 RPM, making a final check on the oil pressure, oil temperature, coolant temperature, and fuel pressure gauges. All was normal. He increased power to 2300 RPM and checked the propeller.

With the fighter brought to full power, Hank looked down the runway and into the clear blue skies. He paused to say the simple prayer he had learned as a child from his mother. It gave him comfort before every mission he had flown. He then thrust the throttle forward, and *Silver's Sweetheart* galloped down the strip and raced into the sky, swiftly gaining altitude and leaving Jefferson Airfield and the Earth behind. The English countryside shrank in size beneath him, and soon it was nothing more than a green-and-gold patchwork of rolling meadows and fields stretching eastward toward the turbulent English Channel.

Hank looked left and then right out the canopy, then set course for the rally point. The Mustang sliced through the air with ease, sprinting southeast toward open ocean. Moments later, the two mighty twin-boomed P-38 Lightnings piloted by Hendricks and Dandridge roared violently close overhead and past Hank's fighter. The two pathfinders lined up side by side, with Hendricks taking a slight lead and Dandridge, acting as wingman, staying back a bit to cover him. Hank eased back the throttle to allow the slower Lightnings some room. Just then Lieutenant Brady's Mustang arrived on station. Hank looked behind him and saw his wingman cruising nicely just off his port wing. The four planes maneuvered into the standard "finger four" formation and headed for the rally point and Captain Wheeler's bomber. Lieutenant Hendricks took the lead position, with Dandridge falling in behind as element leader. Hank and Lieutenant Brady maneuvered to the outside and took up wingman positions.

Soon they were over the channel. The sea beneath was rough and choppy, evidenced by the numerous whitecaps dappling the otherwise blue water. Hank scanned the sea looking for signs of enemy naval activity, particularly German E-boats that were a small but constant nuisance to English minesweepers and other Allied shipping operating in the narrow waterway.

"Maybe today I'll really get lucky and get a shot at a surfaced German U-boat," Hank thought. Although the lure of strafing and possibly sinking German naval targets was tempting, he had to stay focused on the mission, and more specifically, on Dandridge's tail, to ensure not getting lost. As he concentrated on staying on course behind Lieutenant Dandridge, he began to carefully examine the scorched metal on the fighter.

"Jesus. It looks worse in the air than on the ground," Hank thought. "She appears to be stable enough, and running smooth, but I'd hate to be flying that crate during a crucial time like this. I hope to hell that he's up to this. That poor son-of-a-bitch!"

Just then, the Mustang shook violently, forcing Hank's attention back to his own fighter. A patch of turbulence rammed the fuselage, causing the Mustang to shudder savagely for a brief moment before settling back down, aided by Hank's capable hand on the stick. He looked to see if any of the other fighters had been affected by the sudden blast, but saw no indication. The formation was intact and maneuvering well.

The four fighters pressed on toward the rally point well over the cold waters of the English Channel. The fighters slowly gained altitude, reaching twenty thousand feet before leveling off. As time passed, the two P-38s decreased their speed. Hank slowed his Mustang to keep pace with the Lightnings and noticed his wingman Brady did the same. The tails of the two leading P-38s began twitching back and forth uneasily, a sure sign that both pathfinder pilots were repeatedly looking to the side and behind them in hopes of spotting the elusive bomber. Hank recognized this and pondered the idea of breaking radio silence and formation to start a more thorough search for Captain Wheeler, but decided to stay in formation and sit tight. The P-38s had a job to do and he wasn't about to get in their way.

Hank watched as the Lightnings reduced power and slowly banked to the left, flying in a large sweeping circle, trying to cover as broad an area of the rally point coordinates as possible. The pursuing Mustangs mimicked the Lightnings' flight path while joining the active search.

Hank scanned the empty skies hoping to find a dot on the horizon.

As time passed Hank began to wonder what to do next. He knew they were in the right place, but couldn't understand why there was no sign of the B-24. What could have happened? The bomber must have had mechanical problems and was forced to abort the mission, he thought. But if that were the case, why didn't they break radio silence and signal the rest of the group? What if they couldn't? What if they had radio trouble? What if they had total engine failure and had to ditch in the channel? What if they crash-landed in the channel? Or worse yet, what if they were jumped by a German fighter patrol and couldn't defend themselves? Maybe they had been shot down and killed instantly.

Suddenly Hank saw Hendricks's P-38 change course. He must have spotted something. The others followed. As their speed increased, Hank noticed a dot on the horizon. The dot grew larger in size as the swift fighters drew nearer until …

"Bingo! There she is," cried Hank.

All the pilots made a straight course to intercept Wheeler's bomber in the distance. Hank was relieved at the sight, though he couldn't help but notice she still appeared to be struggling to stay in the air. It was apparent that all four engines were still straining, even under full power, which undoubtedly contributed to her being slightly off course and out of position.

Hank flew just above and behind the bomber, watching closely as Hendricks and Dandridge flew alongside—Hendricks on the left and Dandridge on the right. Both pilots used hand signals to get Wheeler's attention. Just then the Liberator lurched downward.

Hendricks and Dandridge peeled off out of the bomber's way. Hank was surprised at her rapid descent. Each fighter pilot then nosed downward, pursuing the bomber in a stable, controlled plunge, keeping a safe distance as they went. The Lightnings went first, then Brady's Mustang, with Hank bringing up the rear. The shuddering bomber rocketed downward, passing through ten thousand feet.

"C'mon, guys, get that pregnant cow under control. Straighten her up and fly right," said Hank in pursuit of the bomber. Hank felt the growing G-forces straining his aircraft and body and feared the Liberator would soon be torn apart. His muscles fought against the tremendous weight on the stick, and he knew he had only seconds before he'd have to pull out of the dive or risk blacking out and crashing into the channel.

One by one the fighters in front of him pulled up and leveled off, leaving Hank and the bomber careening downward. They passed through three thousand feet with Hank's Mustang handling more like a runaway freight train then a sleek fighter aircraft. The altimeter spun rapidly like the hands on a clock gone haywire. He was losing control and couldn't stay with the bomber any longer. He had to pull out of the dive now or die. Just as Hank prepared to pull up, he watched and listened as the bomber drastically throttled back with flaps fully extended. The engines started to shake and sputter, but amazingly the Liberator began to level off! Hank followed the bomber's lead. The channel filled the view through the canopy as the Mustang passed through 550 feet. Hank watched as the bomber's flaps retracted and her engines were brought back to full power. With a mighty yank on the stick, Hank leveled off and was shocked to see the bomber now horizontal in front of him. He could only imagine the amount of strength and courage it took for Wheeler and his copilot to pull out of such a death-defying dive. They were flying at two hundred feet.

Wheeler now zigzagged the bomber toward the French coast. Still maintaining radio silence, the two P-38 Lightnings sliced through the air assuming the lead of the formation. The two Mustangs brought up the rear, maintaining a higher, covering altitude. The attacking unit was now in place and the strike plan was still intact and on schedule.

The straight-in distance from the rally point to the French target at Martinvast was roughly ninety-one miles, although the long, sweeping approach would add both distance and time. Even so, Hank knew that the attack force would be on top of the target sooner than anyone truly wished.

The channel below him screamed by with blinding velocity as the powerful Merlin engine propelled *Silver's Sweetheart* ever nearer the French coast. The sea remained rough and the whitecaps visible, but there was still no sign of German naval activity—not one ship or sub visible for miles. The barren seascape was a welcome sight for Hank, who was not looking to lock horns with targets of opportunity until the trip back to England. Yet he remained ever watchful and alert. This was no time to have his force's position revealed to German coastal defenses by some lowly French fisherman sympathetic to the Nazi cause. This was the time to stay sharp and protect the bomber from whatever threat might rear its ugly head.

The small Allied air armada pressed farther and faster into enemy occupied territory. The uneasy waters of the English Channel rapidly gave way to the French Normandy coastline. Hendricks and Dandridge at the lead of the formation were the first to cross into occupied France. After altering courses several times, they made one final broad turn and started the approach to Martinvast from the southeast. As a probing, protective measure, they increased speed, intending to leave the rest of the formation behind. As the Lightnings started to fade from view, Hank became confused.

"Where the hell are they going?" A twinge of fear shot through his stomach as he worried the formation would break down and veer off course should the P-38s maneuver too far ahead and out of sight. Reacting with uncertain instinct, Hank throttled up and flew in formation behind the Lightnings, following them up the coast and inland to the northwest.

Soon Hank could easily make out a small village not heavily fortified with thick German defenses. The propaganda images of Hitler's impenetrable and indestructible Atlantic Wall, ingrained in the minds of most Allied pilots and soldiers, were clearly not evident here. What was evident directly below were small houses and barns, a cathedral with a tall bell tower, winding dirt roads, an occasional milking cow, and even an arbitrarily parked car. However, the most unsettling sight for the pilots, as their fighters pierced the boundaries of occupied France, was one of German soldiers frantically scrambling about from hidden concrete bunkers and strategically placed trenches. The fighters were flying so near the deck that the pilots could just make out the black-and-white eagle swastika decals on the side of the soldiers' steel-green, M1940 helmets. The sight was unnerving to Hank, who solemnly realized the element of surprise was gone.

On the ground, bells started to ring and piercing sirens signaled an alarm. German soldiers poured from buildings, trenches, and bunkers and began pulling camouflage netting from hidden anti-aircraft machine guns and mighty 88mm flak guns. Hank felt his heart sink directly into his stomach as he caught sight of the German weaponry being aimed onto his position. The 88mm guns were especially terrifying as they were known to unleash as many as twenty high-velocity rounds a minute and could easily bring down a bomber with a single direct hit—not to mention the absolutely devastating effects they would have on a fighter at close range.

Before Hank could react, the sky filled with deafening German anti-aircraft fire that violently rocked his fighter and threatened to tear it asunder. Machine gun bullets ripped across the sky and puffs of shrapnel-filled black smoke exploded all around him. German soldiers not manning anti-aircraft batteries drew their personal weapons and fired madly into the sky. MP-40 machine pistol and Kar 98 bolt-action rifle fire mercilessly peppered the heavens as angry German troops behind the triggers hollered inaudible obscenities toward the airborne attackers and orders to each other, in hopes of maintaining some semblance of control on the ground. The flak guns also let loose a horrendous barrage of blue-white muzzle blasts, but could not be aimed accurately or quickly enough to be effective against the low-flying and fast-moving Allied aircraft. Nevertheless, the Germans put as much lead into the air as possible.

Hank looked on as Hendricks tightly maneuvered his fighter, trying to avoid the deadly enemy ground fire. Hendricks let loose a murderous fire of .50 caliber bullets from the nose of his P-38. Pieces of earth carved from the ground kicked up into the air in a perfect linear pattern. German soldiers in the open were instantly cut down by the intense strafing fire blazing from the Lightning's guns.

Gaining some altitude first, Hank observed from above and behind as Lieutenant Dandridge followed Hendricks' example and began a destructive strafing run of his own. His P-38 veered off course and lined up an 88mm gun half hidden in some trees. He swooped down on the target like an eagle going after an unsuspecting lake trout. With the German gun firing frantically and not aimed correctly to be a threat to the marauding fighter, Dandridge unleashed his Hispano 20mm cannon and promptly reduced the German gun emplacement to a smoldering pile of rubble. Nearby troops who hadn't been killed in the blast returned fire with MP-40 machine pistols as Dandridge made his escape hard and fast, his fighter still hounded by bursts of anti-aircraft fire. Hank could see the sparks of pistol fire ricocheting and even punching through the fighter's smooth aluminum twin booms. Undaunted, Dandridge swooped back down to the deck with his guns blazing furiously, kicking up earth and destroying anything crossing his path. German soldiers caught in the track of the hailstorm of fire raining from above were thrown back and cut down by the impact of .50 caliber shells ripping through their bodies. They were immediately silenced and left to drown in thick red pools of their own blood.

Several fires sprang up across the rooftops of the wooden houses and buildings, and the air thickened with the smell of burning oil and cordite. Large explosions ripped through the German bunkers and trenches as the P-38 gunfire touched off small stores of ammunition and fuel. One after another, Hendricks and Dandridge pounced on anything that moved below or seemed like a threat and riddled it with bullets. German troops and anti-aircraft gunnery soon fell silent and were consumed by fire and exploding shells. Black smoke billowed from destroyed gun emplacements, shot-up automobiles, and burning buildings. The organized German resistance to this surprise attack swiftly crumbled into disorganized pockets of nothing more than small-arms fire.

Seeing that the immediate threat on the ground was significantly reduced, the P-38 pilots regrouped and returned to their original flight path. Stunned by the recent battle, Hank snapped out of his trance in time to see Wheeler's bomber and Brady's trailing Mustang fly over the smoldering coastal destruction wreaked by the P-38s. Scattered bursts of anti-aircraft and small arms fire continued to harass the attackers.

No sooner had Hank spotted the Liberator when both waist gunners opened fire on German troops clambering about trying to bring their remaining anti-aircraft defenses to bear on the larger, slower moving bomber. The B-24's tail and ball turret gunners also opened fire, spraying the ground with bullets in an attempt to knock down anything that moved. The tail gunner rattled away at a German 88mm gun emplacement. His .50 caliber slugs sparked off the gun's long barrel until it toppled over and fell silent. The B-24 lumbered on under the strain of its extra heavy load. It adjusted course to match that of the two P-38s on the horizon, making every effort to keep on their tails.

The two P-51 Mustangs formed up and began trailing the Liberator at a higher altitude. Hank tried to concentrate on scanning the skies for enemy fighters, but was constantly drawn to the carnage inflicted below. He activated his reconnaissance camera and signaled Lieutenant Brady to do the same. Hank couldn't help but feel astonished. It had been several months since he had seen any action, and though he hadn't yet fired a shot, the chaos on the ground resulting from the P-38s' initial strike provided a grim reminder that the war was real and he was right back in the middle of it. Just then a blast of 88mm flak rocked his fighter, causing him to struggle to regain control. Fortunately his P-51 wasn't hit directly. The exploding burst was far enough away not to cause any damage.

"Jesus Christ!" he exclaimed, as he fought to steady the fighter. The scarce few remaining anti-aircraft batteries still able to fire had sighted in the higher-flying Mustangs and were trying desperately to knock them out of the sky. Hank looked to his rear and noticed, Lieutenant Brady's fighter wasn't faring any better. The young pilot and wingman struggled to stay on course behind his leader in the midst of the deadly Nazi flak.

At the point of the formation, the two streaking P-38 Lightnings closed up and flew side by side as they left the smoldering coastal village behind and headed inland toward the primary target. The threatening anti-aircraft fire subsided as the fighters roared deeper into the French countryside. In the distance, Hank saw an unsettling sight coming from Dandridge's P-38. He knew instantly he was in trouble.

The rising sun beamed brightly through the patches of broken clouds and cast distinct shadows of the low-flying aircraft on the ground below, Dandridge's port engine trailing black smoke. As the lead P-38s streaked across the French countryside, they encountered only small, annoying and inaccurate bursts of German anti-aircraft fire. Flying into the rising sun, they were soon lost to the view of Captain Wheeler and the pilots in the trailing P-51 Mustangs.

Hank was flying less than half a kilometer above and behind the bomber, with Brady a bit farther back, covering the rear. Attempting to locate the two pathfinders, Hank maneuvered his fighter out of the direct sunlight.

"Where the hell are they? Why do they have to fly so far ahead of the attack group that they're completely out of view?" he thought. "Maybe Wheeler's got a better line of sight on 'em. Maybe Dandridge aborted and Hendricks is escorting him back to base."

Just then Hank glimpsed two objects in the distance, coming directly out of the rising sun ahead of the formation.

"Is that them?" Hank asked. "Did they stray off course and get all turned around or something? Jesus, are we off target?"

Hank continued to watch the approaching planes, fully expecting to see the massive twin-boom signature of the P-38s become visible any second. However, as they came into full view, a frightening rush of adrenaline surged through Hank's system as he witnessed two marauding German ME-109Gs pounce on the B-24 Liberator with unforgiving ferocity. The German fighters hit the bomber head on, strafing it mercilessly with 13mm machine-gun fire ripping from the fighters' upper cowling. The two *Messerschmitts* walked white-hot tracer fire down its fuselage, then roared past before skillfully turning to reengage the target from the rear. This gave Hank a good look at what he was up against.

The two "Gustav" 109s were painted dapple-gray, with toned-down white spotty areas strategically placed along the fuselage, giving them a fearsome resemblance to menacing Pacific Ocean tiger sharks on the hunt. The underside of the aircraft's cowling was painted a bright yellow, as was the rudder that prominently displayed a solid-black swastika, outlined in white. Behind the canopy, along the rear of the fuselage, was a large black German cross, also outlined in white. German crosses also adorned the tops of both wings, assuring that any enemy fighter that crossed their paths knew exactly who they were up against—staunch air warriors of the Reich. The last and most important unit markings Hank desperately strained to identify were typically located under the canopy and on the nose. Ordinarily, it was next to impossible to make them out in the heat of battle, but Hank's keen eyesight was able to zero in on such small details. However, he could spot no *Geschwader* badge under the canopy, nor any unit-marking artistry on the nose. With no exterior insignia to help him, and being relatively unfamiliar with the German fighter units protecting the Atlantic Wall, Hank could not identify the attackers, as the two 109s hit the Liberator once again.

Hank watched as the bomber's right waist gunner took a bead on the German fighter and fired his .50 caliber machine gun in the direction of the attacker without scoring any hits. The 109 peeled off and set himself up for another attack run, while his wingman peppered the bomber from below, shattering the ball turret and killing the gunner before he could get off a shot. The bloodied, lifeless body of the unfortunate victim slipped out of the mangled blood-soaked turret and dropped like a stone to the Earth below.

Ignoring Wheeler's order to maintain radio silence, Hank fired up his transmitter to address his wingman. It was now his turn to join the fight!

"Red 2, this is Red 1, drop your tanks, follow me down, and watch my tail. … I'm going after the lead 109 fighter!" ordered Hank to Lieutenant Brady as he reached down to reset the fuel-selector valve and start drawing fuel from the main fuselage tank. He then jettisoned both his drop tanks.

"Roger, Red 1, I'm right behind you!"

Suddenly Hank's headset filled with static and broken messages from his wingman. He adjusted the radio frequency and began to understand Brady's words.

"Red 1, I've got another bandit on my six … came outta nowhere … can't shake … "

Hank now saw a third ME-109 going after Brady's Mustang, while the first two *Messerschmitts* continued to attack the bomber. The third 109 was directly on Brady's tail, in relentless pursuit. He started to go after the bomber in hopes of disrupting the 109s' attack pattern, but suddenly stopped and did a snap-roll maneuver in Brady's direction. Hank firewalled the throttle and broke hard to get into position behind Brady's attacker. The audacious American pilot figured if he could knock out the third 109 and save Brady, the two of them could go after the 109s attacking the bomber.

Brady's Mustang swept side to side across the sky at full throttle, trying to dodge the heavy enemy cannon fire ripping past the cockpit from the pursuing 109. This 109 had a menacing 30mm *Rheinmetall-Borsig* MK 108 cannon sticking out its nose that was being put to good use by the German pilot behind the trigger. One direct hit from this powerful weapon would destroy Brady's Mustang. Fortunately for Brady, the German pilot hadn't found his mark but certainly had the advantage in this dogfight.

"Red 1, get this guy off me! I can't shake him loose!" cried Brady.

"Red 2, drop the hammer. Gain some altitude and get up in those clouds! You hear me, Brady? Get up in that soup fast! I'm still out of position!" hollered Hank into his mic, trying desperately to aid his wingman.

Hank finally caught up to the 109 and lined up the enemy plane in his crude, N-3B gun sight. Roughly calculating the enemy fighter's range and angle, he then focused on the thin pane of glass behind the quartz, inch-thick windscreen raked back toward him. On it was a small circle of light with a bull's-eye dot in the center, projected there by a thumb-sized bulb. The "pipper," as it was known, was used to line up and destroy enemy targets.

Skillfully leading the target, Hank flipped up the trigger guard, put the pipper directly on the mark, and pressed the trigger button, cutting loose all six of his .50 caliber machine guns. The intense firepower erupting from the Mustang's wings caught the unsuspecting German by surprise, and he immediately broke right to escape the intersecting fire of his attacker. The move was a foolish one; it brought him right into Hank's kill zone. Hank lowered some flaps and pulled hard inside the German's turn.

"I got your ass now, you Nazi son-of-a-bitch!" shouted Hank as he pumped several controlled bursts of machine-gun fire into the fuselage of the 109. As the shells savagely clawed at the 109, pieces of aluminum began to peel off the wings and the engine started to billow smoke. Spent shell casings poured from the Mustang's wings and rained down to Earth below. The Nazi fighter dove to the deck in a desperate attempt to elude its pursuer and escape the deadly firepower bearing down on it. Feeling the strain of heavy G-forces punishing his body, Hank cleverly maneuvered his P-51 and matched his prey's every attempt to escape certain destruction. The fighters twisted and turned in every direction, as machine-gun fire continued to pour from Hank's guns. The French countryside raced by them as both fighters skimmed the treetops and hedgerows with reckless speed, ripping the leaves from their branches as they flew by. Down on the deck, Hank conserved his ammo and concentrated on keeping pace with the fleeing 109.

In a last desperate attempt to escape, the 109 pilot pulled his wounded plane into a steep, high-G climb, apparently hoping Hank would not react in time and fly right past him. Once clear, he would then dive and pounce on the Mustang from above and behind. However, Hank saw the German turn upwards in time and did not overshoot. Instead, he raised his flaps, applied full power, and stayed squarely on the 109s six o'clock, following it vertically upward without blacking out from the high-G maneuver. After a few seconds the 109s smoking Daimler-Benz engine could no longer handle the unbelievable stress being put on it and simply stalled out, as oil and smoke blanketed the cockpit. The ME-109 stopped, suspended in midair for a second or two, before plummeting downward. Hank swooped after the Nazi fighter and pressed home the attack, riddling the German plane with bullets until it exploded before hitting the ground. Hank pulled the P-51 out of the steep dive and started to regain altitude. He had no time to savor his first air-to-air kill, but began to scan the sky for his wingman.

"Red 2, this is Red 1, give me your position. Over." said Hank as he thumbed his throttle mic.

Hank repeated the call, but received nothing but static in return. The Mustang raced up and into the thick clouds above, temporarily impairing his visibility. As the fighter broke out of the clouds, it became apparent that he was both alone and lost. His eyes continued to scan both the sky around him and the Earth below for any signs of his allies. Nothing. With desperation starting to set in, Hank took a reading on his compass and pointed his fighter in the general direction of his last known course heading. He eased back the throttle and cruised at a slower speed and lower altitude as he searched in vain for his wingman or Wheeler's bomber.

"Repeat, this is Red 1 calling Red 2. Give me your position. Over."

Hank paused and listened for a reply, but heard nothing but static. He adjusted the radio frequency and called again.

"Eagle 1 this is Red 1. Do you copy? Over. Blue 1 or Blue 2, this is Red 1. Does anyone read me?"

Suddenly the headset came alive with the garbled, frantic voices of panic-stricken men trying desperately to stay alive. Hank listened intently and tried to tune in the voices crying into his headset.

"Feather prop … !"

"Fire extingu … !"

"Going to lose number … can't hold her!"

"Losing altitu … !"

To his terror, Hank knew exactly what was happening and exactly what he was listening to. The alarmed, fragmented voices calling out in horror, bracketed by static in Hank's headset, were the voices of Captain Wheeler's crew. Hank frantically scanned the sky in a vain attempt to spot the bomber he was ordered to protect and that so desperately needed his help. It was no use. The sky was empty, save for scattered patches of puffy white clouds.

Then, without warning, Hank's headset fell silent. No static, no friendly voices. Only eerie silence that caused Hank's heavy heart to sink deep into his chest. What now? Was he totally alone over enemy territory? Should he press on or abort? These questions swirled in his mind as he reluctantly turned his fighter east toward the coast. As the Mustang slowly banked left, a shiny glint of light caught his eye. He turned to get a better look, and the glint of light became a small speck on the horizon, heading straight for him.

Seconds later Hank made out the unmistakable outline of a P-51 Mustang racing his way. It was Lieutenant Brady! Relief and joy swept over him as he realized his wingman wasn't dead and he wasn't entirely alone over hostile territory.

"Red 2, this is Red 1 … over," called out Hank over the radio.

Realizing that his fighter was heading straight for Brady's head on, Hank banked left and saw his wingman pass him almost wing tip to wing tip. For a brief second, time seemed to stop as he stared at the passing fighter and into what was left of the cockpit. His eyes locked onto Brady's dazed and nearly dead expression. The Mustang's fuselage was badly shot up and smoke billowed from the underbelly. The canopy had been shot out and almost completely torn away, with fragments of shattered Plexiglas skewered into the almost unrecognizable bloody mess that was Lieutenant Brady's face. As the plane swooped by, the tail section of the fighter become enveloped in smoke.

"Jesus Christ!" Hank watched his doomed wingman lose altitude. Just then a gigantic thud rocked Hank's fighter, like a giant wrench being thrown at the side of a metal shed. Without warning another ME-109 appeared on a direct collision course with the P-51, its machine gun muzzles winking mercilessly and scoring random hits on the Mustang's underbelly. With his eyes fixated on the bright yellow nose and prop of the 109 racing at him head on, Hank instinctively cut loose his own guns and returned fire. Before taking evasive action, streams of intersecting machine gun fire ripped across the sky and clawed at the two jousting fighters. Some of his white-hot tracer fire struck the fuselage of the opposing 109, causing it to veer off just seconds before a certain midair collision would have destroyed both fighters. The 109 pulled away to go into a steep, high-G dive and try to escape. He was obviously wounded and wanted nothing more of Hank's P-51. However, the young American pilot would have none of that and again took the fight back down on the deck. The Mustang's Merlin engine sputtered slightly as small wisps of smoke rose from the instrument panel. Hank broke left, firewalled the throttle to the "War Emergency Power" setting, and galloped after the *Luftwaffe* pilot who had most assuredly murdered his wingman.

The smell of burning oil and cordite hung heavy in the cockpit. Hank maneuvered his injured fighter, trying desperately to drop into the 109s six o'clock. The German pilot was not without skill and experience, however. He dashed down to the deck, weaving left and right, not allowing his pursuer to line up a shot. Hank valiantly gave chase, but was unable to harness full power from his fighter. The engine was not firing on all twelve cylinders, allowing the 109 to gradually gain distance and safety. Hank knew if he didn't get lined up for a shot soon, the smaller, more-nimble ME-109 would eventually escape.

The French countryside roared past both fighters still streaking along the deck. This unforgiving arena of combat posed a tremendous hazard. With the vertical element of the fight all but eliminated and the cold, hard ground lurking dangerously close below, there was no room for error. The 109 continued to run with the P-51 in pursuit. Hank kicked the rudder pedals back and forth and fired several small bursts, but none of the shells found its mark. Hank couldn't get the pipper to settle on the target as the 109 was too far ahead and out of range. Hank cursed his luck as his Mustang gradually continued to lose power while his adversary slipped farther and farther away.

Suddenly, German *Flakvierling-38* anti-aircraft fire filled the sky with streams of deadly, high-arching shells. The menacing 20mm four-barreled guns blazed away, sending deadly fire skyward at the dueling fighters above. Hank recoiled in terror, yanking back on the stick to gain altitude. As the Mustang began to climb, Hank noticed the 109 in front of him was also in the line of fire from the batteries below. The pilot who had skillfully eluded Hank was now in danger of being shot down by his own side. Realizing this himself, the German pilot panicked and made a wide, gradual, climbing left turn to escape the ground fire. The unwise move saved him from the friendly fire below but took him directly into the P-51's kill zone. Hank read the turn perfectly, easily closed the distance, and put the 109 in range. He cut loose all six machine guns. The unsuspecting 109 pilot flew directly into the intersecting streams of fire. The shells tore into the side and wing of the 109, igniting its fuel. The burning fighter nose-dived sharply, trailing a stream of black smoke behind it. The German pilot threw open the shattered canopy and leapt from the doomed fighter as flames shot from his ignited clothing. His chute never opened and he hurtled downward before his still-burning body slammed into the ground. Hank's attention was drawn from this gory sight to the fighter as it smashed into a stand of trees, igniting them on impact. He had scored his second air-to-air kill.

Silver's Sweetheart was in rough shape. Numerous hits from both dogfights and small-arms fire from the ground had damaged the engine, punched holes in the fuselage, and were beginning to wreak havoc with the electrical system. Hydraulic and oil pressure was still good, but it would be only a matter of time before it started to fail as well. The P-51 was hurt and there was no guarantee Hank could make it back across the channel to England. In fact, he wasn't at all sure where he was! The air battles had turned him around so much that he couldn't tell just how far inland or in what direction he had traveled. There was no sign of the coastline or the mission's final target. Hank looked at his compass for guidance, only to notice it had been shot out and was now useless. Realizing he was hurt and flying blind over enemy territory, Hank checked the angle of the late morning sun. He couldn't believe how much time had passed since the launch of the mission. There was only one mission now, though—survival!

The Mustang painfully began to climb and turn west as Hank battled with the stick and rudder pedals in a desperate attempt to point the stricken fighter toward friendly territory. The sun beamed into the cockpit, forcing him to shield his eyes. He looked up to offer a short prayer to the Lord, asking for deliverance from harm's way and to get back in one piece. As he did, machine-gun fire peppered the canopy and engine cowling. The canopy cracked and splintered, but did not break away. Smoke poured from the engine as power began to slip from his control.

Startled, he craned his neck in hopes of identifying his attacker, but was blinded by the sun. He had been caught in a trap and he knew it. He had been bounced! His attacker must not have been far off. He'd probably kept above and behind him quietly waiting for his moment to strike, purposely staying hidden in the sun. That was always rule number one in Hank's mind when patrolling for enemy fighters: Always attack with the sun at your back, so your enemy can't see you. Now Hank was about to fall prey to the very strategy he held most sacred.

More machine-gun fire found its mark on Hank's battered fighter. The smoke in the cockpit became thicker as the controls grew less and less responsive. Although he tried to maneuver out of the deadly hailstorm raining down upon him from above and behind, his plane was falling to pieces around him and his efforts were futile. Moreover, he still hadn't visually identified his attacker. Realizing he might be dealt the death blow at any second, Hank decided to try one last-ditch maneuver in a slim but desperate attempt to escape the elusive bogey. He pulled the almost-dead stick over and back as hard as he could and climbed directly into the direction of the sun. Its brilliance poured into the cockpit and blinded him.

He snap-rolled the fighter and dove hard toward the deck. His pursuer was caught off guard, also blinded by the sunlight and forced to look away and miss the escape maneuver Hank had employed. Instead he broke left, out of the sunlight, and leveled off above the Mustang, leaving it safe for the moment.

Surmising his trick had worked, Hank looked up through his damaged canopy and was able to see his adversary for the first time. He used what climbing power was left in his engine to draw nearer to the enemy aircraft. It was a *Focke-Wulf* 190A fighter. Known to the Allies as the "Butcher Bird," it had the familiar dapple-gray paint scheme, yellow on the engine cowling's underside and rudder, yet this fighter looked far more ominous and lethal. Using his keen eyesight, Hank was able to spy an exterior insignia on the FW-190A's upper engine cowling. It was that of a black wolf's head outlined in white. The creature appeared incredibly ferocious, its mouth opened wide and bearing long, hungry, razor-sharp fangs. It made Hank feel like defenseless prey squaring off against a violent, seasoned predator. He struggled to keep his fighting wits about him.

The FW-190A was a fighter-bomber that packed a punch far greater than the aging ME-109. It was stronger, faster, and more agile than the 109. It had a reputation for unforgiving ruthlessness in battle and was not to be underestimated under any circumstance. Its 1,700 horsepower BMW, 801D-2 radial engine gave it the necessary power to keep up with any Allied fighter, while its two 13mm machine guns and four 20mm cannons packed an awe-inspiring offensive punch.

With its big black German crosses painted on the wings and black swastika on the tail, the *Focke-Wulf* 190A looked sinister. It had the guise of a hungry predator on the prowl with its razor-sharp angles and fearsome lines. It was a killing machine, and an invaluable asset to Hitler's war effort. Though the German-occupied skies were often full of *Messerschmitts*, it was the *Focke-Wulf* that commanded the most respect from Allied pilots.

Hank continued to fight his dying aircraft's controls. The stick was loose and the rudder pedals barely responded to even the hardest pressure. Yet, *Silver's Sweetheart* would not surrender. He looked up again at the FW-190A and saw the tail jerk back and forth a bit. It was an indication that the enemy pilot was looking behind him, thinking the Mustang had zeroed in on his six o'clock.

Hank tried desperately to gain altitude and enough speed to get directly behind his adversary and line up a shot, but the P-51 was simply too damaged to maneuver well enough. Smoke poured from the bullet holes in the engine cowling while the smoke in the cockpit nearly overwhelmed Hank. If not for the smoke-venting cracks in the canopy and Hank's protective oxygen mask, he would surely have succumbed by now.

In a last-ditch effort, Hank firewalled the throttle and buried the stick deep in his gut in hopes of getting the fighter's nose up high enough to catch the underbelly of the higher-flying FW-190A with one final burst of gunfire. He would have only one chance at this. He kept his eyes on his gun sight and the target. The nose of the P-51 Mustang rose sluggishly as the flames from the engine cowling grew more intense and hungrily licked back toward Hank in the cockpit. Sweat poured down the young pilot's face as the burning engine bathed him in intense heat. Just when he thought he couldn't hold on anymore, the FW-190 veered into his gun sight. He pressed the trigger with all his fury. The .50 caliber machine guns came to life one final time. The two innermost barrels spit out a small burst of fire that barely grazed the FW-190's underbelly while the four remaining barrels lay dormant. Hank's worst nightmare had just been realized. He was out of ammo! The shots fired from his crippled fighter did not seriously damage the *Focke-Wulf*, but merely alerted its pilot as to the Mustang's whereabouts. The skilled German pilot quickly broke left and dove downward, spotting the Mustang. The P-51's nose was still pitched upward and it continued to gain altitude slowly.

Hank, unsure what to do next, started to panic. He fought with the controls and watched helplessly as his instrument panel sparked wildly, then shorted out completely. Fire now fully enveloped the nose of the plane and was the only thing Hank could see. It was as though he were looking directly into a powerful blast furnace. Without warning, shots from behind ripped into the tail of the aircraft. The prop cranked to a complete stop as the damaged engine died. The nose of the fighter pitched downward as flames spread to the wings. Another blast of machine-gun fire from behind found its mark, and Hank felt the end was near. His mind raced feverishly as burning gruesome death surrounded him. Another blast from behind completely tore away the canopy and the force of the wind and gravity pinned Hank to his seat. He had only seconds to make an attempt to bail out and possibly save his life. He found the strength to unfasten his safety belt, but could not muster enough force from his legs to rise from the seat and climb onto the wing. This was it. He was dead and he knew it. He let out one final scream, closed his eyes, and imagined what it would feel like to slam into the ground and die a fiery, terrible, gruesome death. But just as the encroaching flames started to singe his A-2 jacket, the Mustang, as if acting on its own to save its pilot's life, miraculously flipped over and dropped Hank out.

Caught up in a tremendous blast of wind, Hank cleared the aircraft just seconds before it exploded above him. Fire and debris rained from the sky, threatening to kill him in midair before he could even deploy his chute. He tumbled through the atmosphere not even knowing if he was high enough for his chute to work. He frantically reached for the ripcord and pulled with the meager mental and physical strength he had left. The parachute pack burst open, thrusting a stream of silk into the air. The chute deployed, blossoming into a magnificent half-sphere of white silken thread above his dangling body below. The force of the wind pulled him upward with a quick jerk, before settling and allowing him to float downward with relative ease.

Hank gripped the parachute's lines and stared at the patchwork of green and gold that made up the French countryside below. The cold air blew over his hot, sweaty face. He had bailed out much higher than he'd originally realized. His mind continued to spin as he imagined being back home, riding a roller coaster that he desperately wanted to get off but couldn't. Momentarily, his ears caught the faint sound of an unmistakable rumble, partially drowned out by the wind rushing by. Terrified, he spun around and in the distance saw a horribly frightening sight—the FW-190. It was heading straight for him, like a circling shark zeroing in on a bloody, wounded fish. He looked toward the ground and concluded there was no way he would land before the fighter was upon him. He had heard of disgruntled German pilots who had no compunctions about strafing Allied pilots in midair. This practice was generally frowned upon by both the Allied Air Forces and the *Luftwaffe*, but was never ruled out in the heat of combat.

Hank knew what was coming and realized he was helpless. The FW-190 knifed through the air. Hank swiveled around so he couldn't see the fighter. He closed his eyes and clenched his teeth, waiting for the sensation of machine-gun fire to rip through his defenseless body. The terrifying sound of the *Focke-Wulf*'s engine intensified, and Hank knew it was only a matter of seconds before he would be dead. As the fighter drew within firing range, the wind spun Hank so he was facing his attacker. He instinctively opened his eyes and saw the menacing shape of the German fighter bearing down upon him. He felt a scream escape him as the fighter's machine guns lit up the sky around him. Bullets whizzed by Hank's ears so closely it seemed his eardrums would burst. Several parachute lines were severed and draped over Hank's head, but miraculously no bullet connected with his body.

The FW-190 roared past and made a gradual wide turn to set up another attack run. The parachute was damaged, forcing Hank to fall more rapidly. It proved a fortunate turn of events. Faster and faster the ground grew up toward Hank's dangling legs. He looked up again and saw the FW-190 swoop in for another shot. Just as the machine guns let loose another burst of chattering fire, Hank felt his body crash into a patch of trees. Branch after branch battered his body, as he violently fell downward, his chute ripping apart above him. His leather helmet and goggles were painfully wrenched from his head. Finally the agony of the descent stopped. Hank, only half-conscious and in stabbing pain, found himself dangling from a thick cluster of trees, just a few feet from the ground.

Suddenly there was silence. No sound of rushing wind or roar of an enemy's fighter. For a second, Hank actually believed he was dead. The total silence must be proof of that. As he gradually came to his senses, he felt the tremendous discomfort and fatigue pulsating through his body and sensed the dangerous predicament he was in.

Dangling at least ten feet above the ground, the young pilot put his hands to his chest and managed to release the twisted parachute harness. He dropped to the ground and crumpled on his side. He let out a muffled moan, feeling tremendous pain throb through his right foot and ankle. He lay motionless as his tired mind tried to comprehend all that had just happened. With great difficulty, he managed to sit up, drag himself to a large tree, and rest his back against the trunk.

He went into damage control. He stripped off the Mae West, slowly examined his body, and gently ran his hands down his upper torso and legs, looking for any sign of gross injury. Though he felt no bullet or shrapnel punctures, his entire body was bruised from the tree branches he had slammed into on the way down. Lacerations oozed slivers of blood on his hands and neck where tree branches had penetrated his gloves and scarf. His right foot and ankle were in sheer agony, although he concluded his foot wasn't broken, since he was still able to wiggle his toes inside his boot. Maybe just a bad sprain? Right then it was impossible to tell, and Hank knew it was better to keep the boot on and laced up to avoid excess swelling. Last, he reached up to rub his throbbing left shoulder. Again, nothing felt broken and he was able to move his arm, but not without considerable discomfort and restricted range of motion. He cursed his luck, but deep down he was thankful to be on the ground … and still alive.

Chapter 8

INTO THE LION'S DEN

Matthew Switzer peered at the painting hanging above the mantel that had so captivated him the day before. It now had true meaning and unmistakable realism to it that fueled his imagination. Hank's vividly detailed oral depiction of the savage dogfight over occupied France enabled Matt to visualize the battle in his mind. The painting brought the confrontation to life with each replete brushstroke and made the experience seem tangible to him. For the first time during his visits with the old fighter pilot, Matt was hungry to hear more.

"So it was you who was shot down in this painting," Matt said. "You're flying the Mustang and the plane behind you is that *Focke-Wulf* 190 you described. Right?"

Hank slowly raised his eyes to meet Matt's and responded with a simple nod. The old man seemed worn out and tired. It was also apparent that his memories of the graphic air battle over France fought fifty-six years earlier were still unpleasant and disturbing to him. It was as though all the pain and suffering he had endured had resurfaced in the simple telling of the story. Matt sensed this and remained quiet until Hank decided he was ready to speak.

The fading fire in the wood stove grew dim, and the soft, orange glow of the hot coals was matched only by the sun's rays slowly slipping under the horizon. Hank had been talking for hours, not realizing how quickly the time had passed. He rose from his chair and shuffled over to the small stack of wood piled next to the stove. Reaching for a piece of white birch, he opened the stove's front door, tossed in the wood, and shut it quickly. The birch flared up, reinvigorating the room with inviting warmth and firelight. Hank stopped for a moment and stared quietly at the painting before sitting down again.

"He got the drop on me and blew me out of the sky," admitted the old fighter pilot. Matt could see that it was difficult for Hank to find the words. "So many things went wrong that day over France. Even now I don't know how I was able to get out of that plane. I don't know how I was able to deploy my chute … and I especially don't know how I survived that midair strafing run. That son-of-a-bitch was determined to cut me down, and I can't figure how in the hell he missed me."

Hank lowered his chin and gently rubbed his forehead. He had pondered this question for so many years and was still unable to uncover the answer.

"I guess it was by the good grace of God that I survived," said Hank. "But my problems had only begun once I hit the ground, I assure you of that, my young friend. Ayuh, I almost wished I'd been killed."

Hank looked at his watch and then at Matt. "Getting kinda late, young fella. Almost past supper time. I bet you want to hit the road back to Orono pretty soon. No fun driving in the dark, or the cold, for that matter."

Matt hesitated. He looked at his watch and shuffled some papers in his lap. He felt the need to head back to campus, but he truly didn't want to go. He wanted to hear more of the old man's story and could not bear to leave without more information. He spoke.

"Uh … I think I'd like to give it another hour or two, if you don't mind, Hank. I don't have any other commitments this evening, and I really am not looking forward to the drive back right now. Could you tell me a little more about what happened next … maybe?" Matt sheepishly asked.

Hank observed the young student. It seemed that for the first time since they'd met, Matt was actually showing some true interest in Hank's words. He was starting to write notes on his pad, not relying solely on the tape recorder. He sat more erect on the sofa and didn't yawn as much as he had in the beginning, nor did he continually look at his watch each time he thought Hank wasn't looking. Perhaps he was beginning to take things more seriously. Whatever the case, it was enough to convince the tired old man to keep going a bit longer.

"Okay, my friend. I'm gonna grab us a little snack from the fridge, and then we'll settle back down and you can listen some more. Sound okay?"

"Yes, sir," replied Matt.

Hank returned with a tray of tuna sandwiches and chips. The two sat comfortably by the fire and ate. It grew dark outside and Hank flipped on a dimly powered lamp so Matt could see to write. Hank resumed his story and wondered how long his student's interest would hold out. He knew Matt was getting into the story, but he just hoped it was for all the right reasons and not for the ones he feared.

The injured pilot rested a minute and took long, cleansing breaths to help ease his pain and settle his nerves. He slowly unwrapped the bloodied silk scarf from around his neck and pulled off his bloodstained gloves. Unzipping his leather jacket, he reached for the army satchel tucked underneath. It was still there, thank God. He'd feared it might've been wrenched away and lost during the parachute drop. He ripped into a packet of sulfa powder and rubbed it onto his cut hands and neck, wincing at the sting of the harsh astringent. He spit on his hands to ease the sting, but it didn't help much. His mouth and throat intensely dry, Hank reached for his canteen. He unscrewed the cap and raised it to his chapped lips. The cold water went down smoothly, refreshing him and quenching his burning thirst.

Hank was exhausted and longed to lie under the tree and sleep for as long as it took to recharge his drained, battered body. However, he knew that was a bad idea. It was certain the FW-190 pilot had radioed his position to the local German command and that search parties would soon be combing the area looking for wreckage and survivors. No sooner had this thought crossed his mind than he heard the low drone of aircraft engines. Foolishly, he got up and hobbled out into the open to scan the skies. He couldn't see a thing until, without warning, a German Fiesler Storche buzzed overhead, skimming the treetops. Off in the distance another Storche appeared, flying in long, gradual circles, looking for movement on the ground. The flimsy-looking Fiesler Storche was hardly an intimidating sight. In contrast to the deadly *Focke-Wulf* 190, it was small, thin, lightly armed, and looked as if it were constructed from insubstantial paper and string. However, the plane possessed one horrifying quality. It had the ability to fly low and slow, allowing the pilot to swiftly and easily spot downed Allied airmen. Terrified, Hank limped back to the sparse cover of the trees. He was now a hunted man and on the run!

It was still daylight and Hank feared exposing himself while the sun was still up. However, he knew it was just a matter of time before a hostile search plane would spot his parachute caught in the tree branches high above him and report his position. Before he knew it, German soldiers would be crawling all over the area and he would become a prisoner of war. This was not an option. He had to get away and find friendly help. A sympathetic French civilian or an organized group like the French Resistance was his only chance of getting back to Allied territory and into the cockpit of a new P-51.

Reaching into his satchel again, Hank pulled out his compass and laid it in the palm of his left hand. The needle slowly wavered left, then right, until it eventually pointed north. He marked the reading and looked due east. He didn't know where he was or what direction was the safest to travel. He only knew that, based on his last directional reading in the air and the location of his target on the Cotentin Peninsula, east brought him closer to the English Channel and any chance for escape. East was the answer. He would travel east.

Hank stuffed his scarf and gloves into the satchel with the rest of his supplies. He looked up and spied his tattered parachute, leather helmet, and goggles dangling from several bent tree limbs. Nothing could be done about that. He had to leave them for the German foot patrols to find. He secured the satchel under his zipped-up leather jacket and waited for the German patrols overhead to move on before he left the scant protection of the trees. The planes eventually gave up the search, moving on to a new area. Hank hobbled out into an open field traveling east.

Hank was in French *Bocage* country. The surrounding terrain was a mixture of woodlands and pastures often separated by thick, tall hedgerows—dense, old-growth plantings, used by many local farmers and landowners as natural property boundaries. They were an impressive sight and also an intimidating one, as they could easily hide many unseen dangers. Hank kept a close eye out for any signs of movement. As he made his way along as slowly and silently as possible, several questions raced through his mind. He looked at the silver insignia bars on the shoulders of his jacket and felt the small metallic dog tags dangling from his neck under his shirt. Should he toss his gun and supplies away, remove all U.S. Army Air Force rank insignia and his dog tags, and try to look like a native civilian? Or should he stay looking the way he was?

"No goddamned escape kit," he grumbled. "What the hell were those bastards in charge at Jefferson thinking?" Hank fumbled along, entering a sparsely forested area that helped shield him from air reconnaissance. He pulled his .45 pistol from his shoulder holster and checked it over as he walked along.

"This thing is either going to help save my life or get me killed outright," he sighed. "How long can I last in a firefight with just this? Against one or two soldiers I may stand a chance, but against a platoon or even a squad—hell, I'm dead!" Thoughts of close-quarter combat ran through Hank's mind. He wondered just how good a shot he was and what it would feel like to shoot an enemy face to face. Killing a man with a handgun at close range would certainly feel much different than shooting down an enemy plane. Maybe much worse than seeing Lieutenant Brady's dead body hurtling through the sky or the burning German pilot plummeting to the ground. Hank put the .45 back in the holster and limped on through the woods. The pain in his ankle and shoulder had become almost unbearable. Sweat glistened on his forehead and streamed down his back. He loosened his tie and unbuttoned his collar as he trudged on.

The woods were alive with the sounds of chirping birds and scampering animals. He thought about home and the time he had spent in the thick Maine woods with his father. The experiences were always relaxing and pleasant. He wished the present circumstances were the same. The wind blew through the treetops, causing them to sway with a peacefulness that almost made Hank forget about his predicament. The throbbing pain in his foot and shoulder stretched all the way to his stomach, which grumbled uncontrollably and threatened to give away his position. Remembering the small gift bestowed upon him by his crew chief before takeoff, Hank reached into his jacket pocket and pulled out the Hershey bar. Peeling off the wrapper with anticipation, Hank devoured the Pennsylvania chocolate in two quick bites. The sweet morsel slipped down his throat and tamed his angry stomach. He stuffed the wrapper in his pocket and continued eastward, stumbling over uneven ground.

All thoughts of stripping off his gear and rank insignia disappeared as the sun started to go down and the air became cooler. It was May, but the deep shade and steady breeze made it feel more like late October. Hank's perspiration felt like an icy stream each time the chilly air swept across his face. Ignoring the pain and fearing the possibility of developing a fever, he zipped up his jacket and stuffed his hands into his pockets, pulling them out only to balance and steady himself on the broken ground.

"If I'm captured, then my dog tags and officer's rank insignia will save me," he thought. "Especially if I'm found by troops from the *Luftwaffe*. They'll see that I'm a flyer, too, and they'll treat me with more decency than the average *Wehrmacht* soldier."

Hank stopped dead in his tracks and wiped the last thought from his brain.

"I am *not* going to be a POW! I will not be captured! I am going to find help and get out of this situation. I will not become a prisoner of the German Army!" He pulled out his compass and took another reading. He was still heading east, hopefully toward safety.

Hank emerged from the protective cover of trees and pushed on through wide-open meadows partially walled off by a line of tall hedgerows. Uneasy about being out in the open, he found a path that led into another, larger patch of woods and to the base of a small hill. He struggled on his injured foot to reach the crest. The hill was not particularly high and the slope not steep, but he felt as if he had just scaled Mount Everest. Surveying the countryside below, he spied a narrow dirt road that cut through the forested area that lay ahead. It ranged east to west and would provide easier going for the injured flyer.

He started down toward the road, but hesitated. Using it would make the journey quicker and easier, but it he was certain to run into someone along the way and that someone would not necessarily be friendly.

"Damn! That road could be swarming with German patrols at any time. I could turn a corner and walk into a whole damn German company marching along in formation," Hank realized. "Maybe they'd think I was Dorothy skipping down the yellow brick road. Hell, maybe they'd even help me find the Wizard of Oz!" The young pilot's attempt to find humor in his situation did nothing to stem the fear of capture as he contemplated the dirt road below him. "I've got to risk it! I can't get out of here without help from someone. If I don't make contact with a local Frenchman sympathetic to the Allied cause, I'll be captured and maybe even killed by the Germans. Shit! I have to try."

Having convinced himself of what he must do, the downed airman eased his way to the bottom of the hill and onto the road. He drew his pistol and crept along silently like a hunter stalking undiscovered prey. His injured foot throbbed with every step and his shoulder ached each time he tried to move it. Unable to fully straighten up, he lurked along the roadway like a hunchbacked monster.

An hour or two passed and the sun dipped toward the horizon. The course took him across swampy, flooded fields and in and out of the cover of trees. Hank looked at the shattered face of his wristwatch and wondered what time it was. He stopped and knelt to rest his weary body. The water in his canteen was almost gone and the pain ripping through his injured foot had become more than he could tolerate. He had made very little progress. As he rested he felt his heart pound deep within his chest as sweat poured down his face. He pulled out his scarf and mopped the cool perspiration from his brow before stuffing it back in his satchel. He then holstered his sidearm and took deep breaths.

Hank closed his eyes and wondered, *How far have I gone? How many miles have I walked? How much farther … ?* The questions flowed through his mind like water in a lively stream. He struggled to his feet and limped along, drawing on every ounce of reserve energy.

Hank concentrated on the sound of his heavy boots crunching into the soft dirt and brush. He paused a moment to rest his foot and startled at the continued sound of boots impacting the road. Terrified, he staggered off the road, ducked behind a large tree, and scanned the small bend in the road ahead of him. The sound of footsteps grew louder as the young pilot's heart raced. Momentarily, a man rounded the curve walking in Hank's direction. He was an older man with white hair on the sides of his head and a bushy white mustache hiding his upper lip. He wore tan trousers and a white, long-sleeved shirt. A pair of black suspenders held his pants up, while a tattered brown hat perched atop his head. Strapped on his back was a large handmade basket filled with small pieces of kindling and firewood. Sensing he was a local, Hank decided to make his move.

As the man drew closer, Hank leaped out onto the road, waving his cocked .45 in the man's face. The terrified Frenchman froze in his tracks, trembling with fright at the sight of the armed airman and his weapon.

Not knowing what to say or do, Hank gestured and blurted out, "Me American! Need help! Me hurt! American … you understand … American?" Hank repeated the word "American" several times while pointing to his chest with his free hand. He kept his pistol trained on the old man, whose eyes were fixed on the gun's barrel.

"Understand me? Understand English? American. Need help!" Hank babbled like a caveman. He saw that the stranger was unarmed, terrified, and on the verge of collapsing from fright and lowered his pistol, thinking this might help calm the situation. The old man, still trembling with fear, looked up at Hank and managed to utter a few words.

"*Américain? Oui … américain. Je comprends … américain,*" the panicked old man said hesitantly.

Hank didn't understand the fragmented French, but continued to try to communicate with more halted English and hand gestures.

Hank pointed to his chest and said, "Me pilot. Me shot down by Nazi." As he spoke, he gestured with his left hand to simulate a plane crashing to the ground. The old man cringed at hearing the word "Nazi." He obviously understood the word and it bothered him. In an attempt to further diffuse the situation, Hank thought a personal introduction was in order.

"Ah, my name is Henry Mitchell," said Hank, remembering that his mother always insisted he introduce himself properly as Henry, and not Hank. "I'm a lieutenant in the United States Army Air Force." He pointed to his rank insignia bars, in the hope the old man would recognize the military symbols. The man slowly lowered his hands and pointed to his own chest.

"*Henri? Je comprends. Je m'appelle Maurice Tessier. Bonjour, mon ami américain. Venez avec moi maintenant.*" The old man turned and motioned for Hank to follow. Hank did not know whether to trust the old fellow or not, but he was exhausted and badly hurt. His choices were limited and he had to risk it. He tucked his pistol into its holster and hobbled toward the old man, who stopped him from going any further, bent over, and reached for Hank's injured foot. He grabbed at Hank's ankle and squeezed hard, causing Hank to wince in pain.

"*Le pied?*" inquired the old man, pointing to Hank's foot.

"Yeah, my foot's hurt bad. It hurts to walk on," Hank replied.

"*Je comprends. Ici.*" The old man extended his arm to the wounded pilot. Hank put his arm around the man's shoulders and used him as a walking crutch. He shifted the weight of his injured foot and felt great relief as the two men slowly walked along the dirt road. They said nothing to each other. Hank tried his best to accommodate the burdened Frenchman who was now supporting the weight of a full-grown man as well as his bundle of firewood. In the growing darkness Hank noticed a sudden, yet subtle urgency in the Frenchman's steps.

"*Vite, vite, mon ami!*" whispered Maurice. Hank did his best to hasten his steps, but his strength was gone and he felt he might collapse at any moment. Only the fear of running into a hidden German patrol kept him moving.

The two men struggled down the road until they reached a small path that led to a large arching stone bridge spanning a slow-running stream. As the two crossed the bridge Hank saw in the distance a small, dark, wooden cottage with a dilapidated barn adjacent to it. Thin wisps of smoke rose from the cottage's chimney. Now, all that lay in front of the two weary travelers was an open meadow where a few cows leisurely grazed.

"*Ma maison,*" said Maurice, pointing to the cottage. The two made their way across the meadow. Hank gazed up at the twinkling bright stars littered across the heavens. At the cottage door Maurice groaned with fatigue as he let go of Hank and undid the straps holding the basket of firewood to his back. As the basket hit the ground Maurice massaged his aching neck and shoulders. As his rescuer found relief, Hank selfishly wished his human crutch would return. Maurice picked up the basket of wood and slowly pushed open the wooden door.

The two men entered the dark house. Hank, still not satisfied that he was safe, slowly reached for his gun. Sensing a trap, he readied himself as he imagined the dreaded German Gestapo leaping out of every dark corner and taking him captive. Maurice made no sudden moves, but carried the basket of wood to the fireplace in the corner. He laid two small logs on the bed of glowing embers and blew on them until they became engulfed with bright, flickering flames.

Maurice lit a candle on the kitchen table and motioned for Hank to sit, which he was more than happy to do. Just then a noise came from another room. Hank instinctively reached for his pistol and raised it as an old woman entered the room. At the sight of the stranger sitting at the table with his weapon drawn, she let out a scream and dropped the bowl of potatoes she was carrying. Hank flinched and almost squeezed the trigger as Maurice immediately leapt between the two, his arms flapping up and down. He grabbed the old woman and covered her mouth so she could not scream again. He then calmly motioned for Hank to put down his gun.

"Lily! Lily!" repeated Maurice. "*Il est américain. Il est bien! Il est bien!*" Tears ran down Lily's cheeks as she embraced Maurice and stared at the young American pilot. Maurice gently pulled the old woman toward the fire and whispered what Hank could only assume were reassuring and comforting words in her ear. The old woman dropped her head and watched her teardrops as they hit the hard wooden floor. She shook her head and remained silent as Maurice continued to whisper. Finally she picked her head up and bit down on her wrinkled lower lip to help stop the tears. Maurice turned and pointed at Hank.

"*Lily*," he said. "*C'est Henri. Il est un pilote américain. Il est gravement blessé.*"

The old woman let out a long, tired sigh and wiped the tears from her face. She looked at Maurice, nodded her head, then timidly approached the injured pilot and sat down next to him. She wore a long, faded blue dress covered by a dirty white apron. A white bonnet atop her head covered most of her long white hair done up in a bun and secured with small hairpins. She pointed at Hank's gun. Hank sensed her discomfort and didn't hesitate to strap it back into his shoulder holster. That wasn't enough, though. The woman pointed at it again and gestured at Hank to remove it completely. Hank hesitated a second, but understood. With great pain he unstrapped the shoulder holster with the secured .45 and laid it on the table out of reach, together with his satchel of meager supplies. The old woman gave Hank a feeble smile, then reached over to help him get up out of the chair.

Maurice quickly stepped over and stopped Lily. *"Il est gravement blessé, Lily! Ne le déplacez pas lui!"* exclaimed Maurice.

Lily replied, *"Allez-vous en, Maurice! Depechez-vous!"* With that Maurice sighed, turned away angrily and threw more logs on the fire.

Lily helped Hank into the bedroom adjacent to the kitchen. She took off his jacket, helped him remove his tie, and pointed to the bed. She lit a candle on the night table next to the bed and one on the bedroom dresser, promptly closing all the curtains.

"Allongez-vous, s'il vous plaît," she said.

Hank did not understand her and stood next to the bed. Lily repeated herself and indicated she wanted him to lie down. Hank eased down onto the bed, and as his head hit the soft pillows it seemed for a moment nothing in the world could feel so comfortable. Lily rolled up her long sleeves and looked down at the young pilot. She spoke softly.

"Je ne parle pas anglais, Henri. Où avez-vous mal?" Hank said nothing. His puzzled expression prompted another question.

"Est-ce que ça vous fait mal ici?" she asked, touching Hank's wounded ankle.

Hank winced as a sharp pain ripped through his ankle and foot. He realized that Lily was asking him where it hurt, and nodded his head. Lily replied with a nod of her own and proceeded to unlace Hank's boot. At first he protested but soon gave in, realizing that Lily was simply trying to help him. The old woman loosened the laces and parted them as much as she could before attempting to pull off the three-quarter-high boot. Knowing what was going to happen next, Hank closed his eyes, gritted his teeth, and turned his weary head away. He could not stomach the thought of seeing his boot come off and watching a bloody, and shattered toe drop out onto the floor in some French farmer's cottage.

Lily pulled the boot off slowly with some difficulty. Hank let out a muffled cry of pain as his foot and ankle throbbed unbearably. Lily tenderly pulled off his wool sock and examined the injured foot. Hank was relieved to see that all five pudgy toes were still there. But the foot was now swelling rapidly and bulging out on the side, colored a discomfiting black and purple. Lily ran her wrinkled fingers along the side of the foot and the ankle, feeling for any breaks. She found none. She pointed to Hank's toes and made a wiggling motion with her fingers. Hank understood and with great pain was able to slightly wiggle them. The old woman nodded with approval and interlaced her fingers with the injured pilot's toes. At first Hank winced with pain; however, as Lily squeezed, massaged, and manipulated, the sensation turned from pain to relief. Hank felt his toes creak and crack while the throbbing temporarily subsided. The old woman's touch felt soothing.

"C'est foulé," were the only words Lily muttered as she tended to the injured foot. Turning her head, Lily projected her voice back to the kitchen. "Maurice! L'eau maintenant, s'il vous plait." Hank could hear Maurice stir in the kitchen before the front door creaked open, then shut.

Lily turned her attention to Hank's painful left shoulder. She motioned for him to sit up in the bed. Hank obliged, showcasing the pain in his upper back as well as his shoulder. Lily took notice and knew her work was far from over. She felt and massaged all around Hank's joint, then said, "C'est disloqué un peu." Again, Hank didn't understand. She took his numb left arm and extended it fully to the side so the arm was aligned with the shoulder, parallel to the ground. She then placed his hand on her shoulder. With both her hands on his shoulder, one on top and one beneath, she squeezed them together and jerked upward, causing a pronounced crunching sound. Hank let out a quick yelp at the unexpected pain, but was amazed at how quickly it subsided and how much better his shoulder felt. He realized he must have dislocated it when he crashed through the trees after bailing out.

"*C'est bien?*" asked Lily, nodding her head affirmatively.

"Yeah, it feels much better," replied Hank, as wonderful tingling sensations danced up and down his arm, giving him back the full range of motion he had desired hours earlier.

With that, Hank wanted to lie back and drop off into a deep sleep, but Lily would have none of that. She gestured for him to stand, which he did with great difficulty. Lily started to undo the buttons of Hank's shirt. Hank got the message and finished the job himself, removing both his olive-drab officer's shirt and white cotton undershirt. Lily twirled her index finger, and Hank turned his bare back toward her. Starting at the base of his back, Lily vigorously kneaded Hank's muscles and spine with a deep-penetrating, massaging motion. It felt heavenly. As she worked her way to Hank's hunched-over upper back, the young pilot winced again in pain. Lily had zeroed in on what she was looking for. Her skillful hands went to work again, this time working on a slipped disk. She rubbed and pressed deep and hard into Hank's back, and he could feel his upper vertebrae aligning into proper position. The cartilaginous disk slipped back into place, and Hank instantly felt his upper torso straighten.

Lily then turned her back to Hank and reached her arms behind her. She grabbed the unsuspecting pilot under the arms and lifted him backwards, right off the floor. Hank's back arched across the back of the much smaller woman's and cracked loudly. After hearing that, Lily abruptly released the young pilot and let him slide back to the bed.

Hank lay face up and drifted toward sleep. He could fight it no more. His body wanted to cry out and thank the old woman for the relief she had provided it, but total exhaustion prevented any semblance of thanks. Moments later the front door gently creaked open again. Lily turned toward the kitchen.

"*Maurice?*" she quietly called out.

"*Oui, c'est moi,*" answered Maurice, entering the bedroom with a wooden bucket of water. "*Votre l'eau, ma femme.*"

"*Merci, Maurice,*" said Lily. The old man silently turned around and exited the bedroom. Lily pulled the bucket close to the bed and

Hank heard her whisper, "*Henri? Henri?*" He moaned, barely conscious. She sighed and gently pulled Hank's swollen foot over the side of the bed, into the bucket of chilly liquid. Hank twitched as his foot became immersed in the water. Lily got up and went back into the kitchen. She found the red-and-white syrettes of morphine hidden in Hank's satchel. With one in hand she went back to Hank's bedside, lifted his injured foot from the bucket, and injected the painkiller directly into it. Hank didn't even twitch. Placing the foot back in the bucket, Lily rose up, pulled the ragged quilt over Hank's body, and adjusted the pillow under his head. She blew out both candles and stood in the dimly lit doorway as he sank gratefully into sleep at last.

The darkness of night slowly gave way to the dim light of early morning. As the sun brightened the early hours of the day, Hank awoke from his deep sleep to find his injured foot immersed in the bucket of now lukewarm water. As he attempted to sit up he accidentally knocked over the bucket and watched as the water spilled across the bedroom floor. Lily, who was in the kitchen, heard the commotion and came to investigate. Eyeing the puddle on the floor, she waved her bony finger at Hank in a scolding manner. She muttered a few words in French as she mopped up the spill with a large dishrag.

Hank tried to apologize, but Lily quickly silenced him. She greatly feared the danger and horror she and Maurice would face should some Nazi soldier or sympathizer pass by undetected and hear English coming from the small Tessier cottage. She motioned for Hank to lie back down so his profile would not be visible in the bedroom window—even with the tattered drapes drawn.

"*Henri … ici,*" said Lily. She handed Hank the now empty wooden bucket and pointed downward. The puzzled pilot failed to understand what the old woman was trying to communicate. Lily repeated herself and pointed directly at Hank's crotch. Hank looked at her with a puzzled glance, then down toward where she was pointing.

Hank finally grasped what the old woman wanted him to do. He nodded and sat up on the bed. Realizing that her patient understood, Lily turned around and went back into the kitchen. Hank relieved himself and set the half-filled bucket on the floor. He zipped up and reached for his shirt, minus his tie, which he rolled up and stuck in his pants pocket. Lily came back into the room and snatched up the bucket, scurried outside, and emptied it onto the grass far from the cottage and the grazing cows. At the farm's fresh-water stone well, she rinsed the pail and scooped up another bucket of cool, clean water. When she returned, Hank was fully dressed except for his injured foot. Lily placed the fresh water bucket on the floor and motioned for Hank to soak the foot again. Hank lifted his foot into the bucket and felt the cold penetrate his swollen foot. The throbbing sensation had diminished drastically and the discoloration wasn't as apparent as the day before. He sat quietly and let the foot go numb in the chilly water.

Lily sat down on the bed and gently rubbed and prodded Hank's shoulder and upper back, feeling for tender spots and any further signs of slipped or damaged disks. She had trained hands that could almost effortlessly rub away the pain. His shoulder and back were already much improved as a result of the therapeutic treatment the old woman had administered. He felt his strength gradually returning throughout his body. As Lily massaged, the pilot turned and posed a question.

"Are you a doctor?" Hank asked without remembering that she didn't speak English. Somehow, though, she understood what he was asking. She walked over to a small closet in the corner of the room masked by a flower-print curtain. Pulling back the curtain, she reached for an old white hat and handed it to her patient. Hank recognized it as a World War I nurse's cap. The front had a large red cross emblazoned on it. As Hank touched the cross he noticed that the emblem wasn't the only red on the hat. Specks of dried blood were splattered all over it. Hank respectfully handed it back to Lily.

"So, you were a nurse during the Great War?" Hank said.

Again Lily did not comprehend the words, but knew what Hank was saying. She replied with a meek "*Oui.*"

Just then Maurice burst through the front door and slammed it shut behind him. Startled, Lily dashed into the kitchen to see what was the matter. Sensing danger, Hank got up and followed her.

With a terrified look carved deep into his weathered face, Maurice cried, "*Les soldats allemands croisent la passerelle!*"

"*Mon Dieu,*" exclaimed Lily as she hurried to the small window adjacent to the front door to see what was happening outside. Hank could see her face fill with terror as they watched three German infantry soldiers led by an officer stride over the stone bridge, making their way across the meadow toward the cottage. Two fanned out to search in and around the barn while the others continued toward the cottage. The sight of the Germans brandishing unslung Kar 98 rifles almost made Lily crumple to the floor. Maurice pulled her away from the window and thrust her into the bedroom. Instinctively the old woman knew what to do.

"*Henri! Vite, vite, maintenant!*" shrieked Lily as she frantically motioned for Hank to hide in the closet. Hank hobbled into the recess behind the curtain. As Lily thrust his leather jacket, socks, and boots at him, Hank stopped her and said, "My gun! Where's my gun?" making his right hand and fingers look like a pointing pistol. Lily hurried into the kitchen, grabbed the loaded weapon and the airman's satchel of supplies, and rushed back into the bedroom. Hank stuffed all his belongings behind him in the cramped closet and yanked the curtain shut with a swish. Lily dropped to her knees and used her dress to wipe up the water Hank had spilled on the bedroom floor. She then rushed into the kitchen with the bucket, quickly rolled up her sleeves, poured the remaining water into her tiny sink, and began to act like she was washing dirty dishes.

In the closet, Hank raised his .45 close to his face. The barrel of the gun rested against his right cheek. He cocked the hammer and waited for what was to come next. He could hear Lily and Maurice stir in the kitchen but did not know what was happening. Regardless of who entered the bedroom, whether it be friend or foe, Hank was ready to shoot and kill if necessary to keep from being captured.

Maurice sat down calmly at the kitchen table. He knew it was now his turn to get into character. He reached for a coffee cup on a nearby shelf. Without hesitation, Lily whirled around and filled the mug with fresh milk—the only beverage handy at the moment. Maurice lifted the mug to his lips and peered out the window.

Hank Mitchell stood buried as far back as possible in the bedroom closet, with only a ragged curtain shielding him from certain capture and possibly instant death, as he heard a loud pounding on the door. He remained motionless with his cocked sidearm at the ready. He listened intently to the sounds of two pairs of boots impacting the wooden kitchen floor and unfamiliar voices speaking German.

"*Sprechen Sie Deutsch?*" was the first clear question Hank heard from who he guessed was the officer in charge addressing Lily. It was followed by a quick, "*Verstehen Sie?*" There was no response from either Lily or Maurice. The next sound Hank heard was the sharp snap of fingers followed by boot heels clicking.

"*Maurice et Lily Tessier? Parlez-vous allemand?*" asked the other German in the room.

"*Oui … mais je ne parle pas allemand,*" Hank heard Lily answer while Maurice remained silent. Then the same German-sounding voice assailed Lily with a stream of questions in heavily accented French, which she answered tersely. Upon hearing the old woman's replies the soldier translated the conversation into German for his commander.

Hank's finger twitched over the trigger of his Colt .45 as he listened to the inharmonious exchange of French and German discourse. He did not altogether understand what was being discussed, but certainly recognized the harsh tones and knew full well that the Germans badly wanted something. Hank heard the officer ask a question containing a word he understood perfectly—*Amerikaner!* He gripped his handgun and readied himself to burst out of hiding and do whatever needed to be done. Lily repeated the French word "*Américain*" several times, saying "no" immediately after. She was protecting him.

Hank listened intently as the voices ceased and the sound of jackboots began to echo through the house. Without warning, the German officer walked into the bedroom and examined the bed. Hank could clearly hear and feel the impact of the German's boots as they clomped across the hard, wooden bedroom floor. Hank held his breath and slowly trained the barrel of his gun chest-high on the curtain in front of him as the boots approached the closet and stopped. Hank glanced down and saw the tips of the black leather boots. Suddenly he heard the sound of the front door bursting open. The booted feet whirled around and walked from the bedroom as the sounds of German conversation ensued.

"*Sind Sie schon fertig?*" asked the officer.

An unfamiliar voice replied, "*Jawohl, mein Herr. Es gibt nichts hier.*" He then added, "*Niemand ist hier.*"

The German officer stated in a very sarcastic tone, "*Das ist gut. Gehen Sie!*"

"*Sehr gut, mein Herr,*" responded the new soldier.

The officer said in a heavily German-accented tone, "*Au revoir, Monsieur et Madame Tessier.*" With that he left, slamming the door behind him. Lily dropped to the floor and started to weep. She covered her face with her hands and tried in vain to hold back her anguish. Maurice knelt beside her and held her hands tightly as he whispered comforting words, to no avail. The couple started conversing in hushed French.

The exchange grew more intense as Hank slowly peeled back the curtain and limped out of the closet, his gun still in hand. Entering the kitchen he could only imagine what his caregivers were discussing. At the sight of the injured airman, both stopped arguing and rose from the floor. Lily gestured for Hank to sit and take pressure from his injured foot. The three sat at the table, where Hank listened as Lily and Maurice resumed their debate. Although he could not understand what was being said, Hank instinctively knew that the old couple were trying to determine whether to continue to harbor the downed Allied airman or demand that he leave. Hank could not read the intentions of either as both seemed unable to agree.

Finally Hank stood up. Lily and Maurice stopped talking and looked at the pilot. Hank pointed to the door and then himself, indicating that he should leave. Injured or not injured, he did not want to endanger the old couple any longer.

Hank blurted out, "I have to go. I can't stay here and risk your lives. You've been very kind and I appreciate your help and care. I'll keep moving east and hopefully link up with the French Resistance ... "

Just then Maurice cut him off and said, "*Non! Non Resistance ici! Nazis, oui! Resistance, non!*"

Hank understood. The old man was telling him that the area was crawling with Germans, but no members of the French Resistance, a very unsettling fact.

"Just the same," said Hank, "I think it's best I clear out of here." He limped back into the bedroom and opened the closet to gather his gear. Lily and Maurice looked at each other and without saying a word came to a hard decision. The young airman reentered the kitchen, whereupon Lily and Maurice pounced on him. The old woman snatched away his satchel and jacket and threw them on the living room floor. Maurice put his hands on Hank's shoulders, forcing the airman back down onto the kitchen chair.

"What are you two doing?"

"*Vous ne laissez pas, Henri,*" replied Maurice. "*Vous resterez avec nous pour maintenant,*" added the old man slowly and emphatically.

Although Hank didn't understand the words, he got the idea. Maurice and Lily wanted him to stay. Although he feared endangering their lives he realized his only chance was to follow their direction and ultimately find a way back across the channel to England. He would not last a single day or night out on his own. He would inevitably be found and captured by the Germans.

"Okay," said Hank reluctantly. "How do you propose we handle this situation, my friends?" That was indeed the question. Hopefully, the old French couple had the right answer—for his sake and theirs.

.

Chapter 9

THE SHADOW IN THE BARN

M aurice and Lily worked feverishly throughout the remainder of the day, acting as if nothing had happened earlier. Maurice tended his cows grazing in the meadow and made frequent trips to the barn, carrying something with him each time. Lily kept quite busy inside the cottage, providing care and assistance to her young American patient who had been banished to the closed and closely guarded bedroom. Hank lay in the bed, with his injured foot again immersed in a bucket of chilly water. He remained dressed in his uniform, even under the covers, to be ready for anything. His satchel and shoulder holster were under the bed, tucked behind heavy winter blankets and clothing. Although there was no door separating the bedroom from the kitchen, Lily hung a bed sheet in the doorframe for added privacy and secrecy. The tiny bedroom window had been shuttered from the outside and covered with tattered drapes on the inside.

In the kitchen, Lily prepared dinner from what meager foodstuffs she had. While meticulous in her preparation, she somehow managed to keep one eye on her patient and one on the kitchen window to watch for uninvited guests. Fortunately all she observed was the slowly setting sun and her husband moving back and forth with his milking cows and small flock of chickens. A large black pot hung over the burning fire in the fireplace. In it simmered a watered-down soup broth filled with garden vegetables, the majority of which were potatoes. Hank could smell the weak aroma wafting from the kitchen and felt his mouth water. His stomach felt like an empty cavern echoing with cries of hunger.

The front door opened slowly and Maurice crept inside. He took off his hat and peered through the window in the direction of the stone bridge. All seemed peaceful and quiet.

"*Est-il prêt encore, Maurice?*" asked Lily as she began to set the table in preparation for dinner.

Maurice answered his wife with a weary, "*Oui.*"

The old woman smiled slightly and said a simple word of praise, "*Bien.*"

Restless and hungry, Hank sat up in bed and pulled his much healed foot from the bucket of water. He dried it with a bedside towel and slipped on his G.I. sock. Hearing movement in the next room, Lily pulled back the curtain and gestured for Hank to join them at the table. Still walking with a slight limp, Hank came and sat down. Lily ladled some soup into bowls and placed them in front of the American and her weary husband. Next she brought a plate with a small wheel of cheese and some thick slices of sausage. Last, she reached into a cabinet and pulled out a nearly empty bottle of red wine and rationed out three small servings. The meal didn't look like much, but to everyone seated at the table it was a feast fit for royalty. Lily encouraged the two men to start eating, after which she sat down and took a small portion for herself. Hank purposely ate slowly, making sure he did not devour his meal too quickly. Maurice simply sat with his head lowered and spooned his soup down his throat in a rhythmic pattern.

The three ate and sipped their wine in silence. Maurice and Lily did not speak to Hank nor each other, and the young pilot knew it was better for everyone if he kept his American mouth shut and did not sputter out any words in a land where English was foreign and could be deadly if heard by unforgiving ears. When everyone was finished Lily rose and cleared away the dishes. She peeked out the window again, as did her husband. As the sun vanished under the horizon, the unpleasant yet familiar thud of heavy artillery and anti-aircraft fire filled the air. Hank closed his eyes and listened to the deadly symphony playing outside, and tried to gauge how far away it was with each boom he heard. As darkness began to envelop the continent, the sounds of war intensified. Hank could hear the German 88mm anti-aircraft batteries firing in the distance, as well as the sounds of British Lancaster bombers flying overhead. He wondered just how far from the coast he was. His dogfights with the *Luftwaffe* fighters had turned him every which way and it was impossible to tell how far off course and inland he had traveled. He really didn't know where he was. He needed to find out.

Hank looked out the kitchen window at the distant flashes of light. The sky was lit with tracer fire that burned white-hot from the guns on the ground below. Giant searchlights aimed toward the heavens projected great beams of light that the Germans hoped would illuminate and reveal the formations of British bombers penetrating their airspace. Carried by the wind, the faint voices of German troops touched Hank's ears and made his stomach churn. They were close ... much too close for comfort. Lily glanced at Maurice, then at Hank. Maurice nodded his head, wiped his mouth with a white cloth, then stood up from the table.

The young pilot looked up at Maurice, then at Lily. Maurice peered out the front window, then slowly and cautiously opened the door. He waved for Hank to follow him. Puzzled, Hank looked at Lily as if to ask her what was going on. The old woman said nothing and went into the bedroom to retrieve Hank's belongings. Hank reluctantly followed Maurice outside, carrying all his gear. For a brief moment the American pilot wondered if he'd been betrayed and was being led into a trap. Thoughts of multiple German soldiers emerging from the darkness with weapons at the ready raced through his mind.

Maurice led Hank toward the barn. At the front doors Hank stopped, sensing something was terribly wrong. He dropped his gear and drew his pistol as the sounds of intermittent anti-aircraft fire echoed in the distance.

"*Henri ... c'est bien,*" said Maurice reassuringly. He moved his hands up and down, motioning for his young friend to lower his gun. Not convinced, Hank stood firm. Shrugging, Maurice unlatched the twin front doors, revealing the vast darkness of the barn's interior. Maurice stepped inside and reached for a small, rusty kerosene lantern that he lit and kept very dim. He held up the light and swung it around to prove to Hank the barn was empty. All of the Tessiers' cows and chickens, what scarce few they had left, were outside, asleep in the meadow or roosting in the bushes. Hank cautiously picked up his belongings and crept inside with wide eyes and one finger still on the trigger.

Maurice closed the doors behind them. The lantern he was holding grew brighter with a twist of the knob. Hank took a moment to don his leather jacket as his eyes scanned his new surroundings. Satisfied there was no danger, he holstered his pistol. Maurice stood back and said nothing, like a landlord letting a prospective tenant make up his mind about whether or not he liked an apartment.

The barn was much bigger than the cottage. Hank estimated it was about fifty feet long and twenty feet wide. Large individual stalls for housing and milking cows flanked the sides. From the walls hung various farming tools: a pitchfork, a scythe, an ax, and a large sledgehammer. There were no windows. A smaller pen lined with a trough for feeding hogs or chickens spanned the back. Large sacks of feed lay on the dirt and straw floor next to the trough. Two wooden steps descended into this area of the barn that was walled off by adjacent livestock stalls on either side.

Directly above the hog pen was a hayloft, half full of baled hay, accessed by a ladder that ran upward from the base of the pen through a square hole in its floor. It immediately caught Hank's attention as a comfortable yet shielded hiding spot. It was starting to make sense now. The old French couple was willing to hide Hank in their barn and Maurice had spent the day preparing it.

Hank looked at the old man and nodded his head to show he now understood. Maurice pointed out the loft to Hank and gestured that this was where he should hide and sleep. He then pointed to the pen and gestured that it was where he should relieve himself rather than using the outhouse. Again Hank understood. He gathered his gear and climbed the ladder to the loft. Maurice followed him up a few rungs to hand him the rusty lantern. Hank grabbed it and gave Maurice a quick salute of thanks. Maurice returned the gesture and said, "*Bonsoir, mon ami. Je vais au lit maintenant. J'ai travaillé beaucoup aujourd'hui.*" With that the old man walked from the barn and latched the doors behind him. Hank stashed his gear, removed his boot, and lay back in a soft mound of loose hay. With his gun close at his side, he blew out the lantern and settled down for a long night's rest.

Daylight revealed overcast skies and an early-morning fog that shrouded the Tessier farm. The dreary weather kept the Allied air forces temporarily grounded and put an acting halt to the intense coastal bombing. Hank awoke to the feeling of someone gently nudging his shoulder. He stirred slightly, then opened his eyes upon the smiling face of Lily standing over him. Without a word she reached into her dress pockets and pulled out some scraps of bread and cheese. As the young pilot ate, she massaged his injured foot and examined his shoulder and back. To her satisfaction, Hank's physical condition was markedly improved. The old woman finished her brief therapy session and started back down the ladder.

"Wait!" called out Hank rather loudly. "Can you tell me where I am exactly?"

The old Frenchwoman waved one hand wildly back and forth while holding the ladder with the other, trying to silence the pilot before he blurted out more words in English. Seeing Lily's agitated state, Hank quickly fell silent. Lily climbed back up the ladder and confronted her patient. She scolded Hank vigorously in incomprehensible French. He stared blankly, not understanding. She pointed to her mouth as she closed it tightly. She then walked around the loft, swishing the scattered hay under her feet to purposely make unnecessary noise. She stopped abruptly and shook her head to indicate this was not acceptable. Hank started to get the picture.

Without another word, he reached for his satchel and pulled out his compass, laying it flat on the palm of his hand and showing it to the old woman. She watched the compass needle float back and forth until it rested on north. As the needle stopped, Lily looked up at Hank who shrugged his shoulders and looked all around in puzzlement, as though he were lost. The old woman nodded and motioned for Hank to put away his compass. She pointed at the bucket of water sitting nearby, which she had brought up while he was asleep, and started down the ladder again.

Feeling he was being blatantly ignored, Hank defiantly opened his mouth to speak out. Just then Lily glared at him and uttered a single word.

"*Jolieville.*"

She pointed at the bucket again, climbed down the ladder, and walked out of the barn.

Hank scratched his head and tried desperately to recall whether he had seen a town or village named Jolieville on any map or the sand table he had so thoroughly studied back in the briefing room at Jefferson Airfield. He racked his brain but could not remember the name Jolieville. Despondent, he knelt down by the bucket of lukewarm water and splashed some on his face and neck. Using the silk scarf in his satchel, he wiped away the sweat and dirt from his face, neck, and hands, then wrung out the dirty scarf in the corner of the loft.

Not knowing what was going to happen next or how long he would be confined to the Tessiers' barn, Hank settled down and rested, using his mind and imagination to entertain him. He lay on his back with his hands folded on his chest, peering around the barn and listening attentively to every sound from outside. The barn had no windows and was relatively dark, with the exception of several cracks and small holes in the aging wooden walls and ceiling that allowed small beams of sunlight to penetrate. One such gap was located in the loft's wall directly behind his head. On discovering this, the young pilot crawled to it and peered outside. From the hole, he could see part of the yard and the front of the cottage—perfect for monitoring the comings and goings of both Lily and Maurice. He reached into his satchel and pulled out his M3 trench knife, poking and scraping at the hole to carve out a bigger aperture.

He caught glimpses of Lily carrying laundry from a nearby clothesline and Maurice passing by once or twice with buckets of fresh milk collected from his cows. He noticed how each casually ignored the barn and did nothing to draw any attention to it. The Tessiers had earned Hank's trust, and the young pilot rolled over, feeling confident he was safe.

Hours passed and the young American eventually grew restless and bored. He wanted to leave the loft and explore his surroundings, but knew that was impossible and possibly suicidal. As the sun set, the sound of German artillery fire became louder and more frequent. Hank concentrated on the bombardment and tried to guess how far away it was. Suddenly his concentration was interrupted as the barn doors slowly began to open. Startled, he reached for his pistol and peered downward at the doors while keeping himself hidden. To his relief, it was only Maurice leading his three milking cows into their stalls for the night. Hank would have roommates this evening. Maurice secured the cows in their stalls and tended to them briefly, never acknowledging his guest in the loft above. Hank realized that this odd theatrical performance would have to be played out continuously in order to maintain secrecy and his overall safety. Hank would try to be invisible. He would speak only when spoken to and do everything he was told. He would become a shadow.

Darkness once again fell upon the French countryside. Hank lay stretched out in the loft and rubbed his swollen foot. It felt much better. He looked out his peephole and saw that the cottage was completely dark with the windows covered by makeshift curtains. The familiar booming sounds of intense artillery and ground anti-aircraft fire filled the night air. As he lay in the darkness, he began to drift off to sleep.

Suddenly, beams of bright white light shot through the cracks and holes in the barn. Hank sat up, frightened, as the eerily illuminated wooden structure slowly went dark again.

"What the hell was that?" he whispered.

The droning sound of four-engined bombers could be heard off in the distance, but drawing closer. As the planes neared, ground artillery fire erupted. Again the barn lit up as beams of bright white light shot through every crack and crevice. Stark shadows danced wickedly across the walls of the barn only to fade and disappear as the light diminished. Hank's curiosity overpowered his better judgment and willed him to climb down from the loft, open the barn doors, and gaze upward at the show of war unfolding around him. Once more the sky lit up with bright white light, followed by intense ground fire. Hank watched in awe as dozens of large, low-flying British bombers roared overhead and disappeared into the darkness. Several swarming squadrons of escorting British Mosquito night fighters followed.

"That's it," said Hank to himself. "The Krauts are shooting off incendiary flares to help locate the approaching bombers."

Hank looked off into the distance as white-hot high-arching *Flakvierling-38* anti-aircraft fire pierced the night sky alongside huge narrow illuminating beams from nearby German searchlights. Sirens wailed, while flames touched off by burning wreckage from a downed British bomber scorched the countryside. He stood motionless and in awe amidst the horrific noise and destruction around him.

As Hank stared skyward, he was caught off guard as someone grabbed him from behind and thrust him back into the barn. With a thud he hit the floor face down. Instinctively, he reached for his .45, only to discover that neither it nor the holster was there. He had stupidly left them both in the hayloft! He whirled around and scrambled to his feet to face his attacker. The shadowy figure closed and latched the barn door, then quickly struck a match to light a candle.

"*Henri, vous êtes un imbécile stupide!*" cried out a voice in an agitated whisper. "*Les soldats allemands sont partout!*"

Much to his relief, Hank could make out the wrinkled face of Maurice illuminated by the soft glow of the candlelight. Maurice grabbed a milking bucket and turned it upside down in one of the stalls. He sat down on it and placed the dimly lit taper on a little shelf beside him. He gestured for Hank to sit as well. The young pilot found another bucket and joined his French friend. The two men hunkered down close to one another under the pitiful light of the flickering candle flame. Not saying a word, Hank stared at Maurice as he listened to the faint artillery booms off in the distance.

The old Frenchman pulled a folded scrap of paper from his coat pocket. Hank watched intently as Maurice slowly and carefully unfolded it. Hank's eyes lit up after the last fold was removed. It was a map! It was a regional map that was old, stained, written in French, and had sections that were almost illegible, but it was a map, nonetheless.

"*Nord et sud. Est et ouest,*" Maurice whispered. "*L'Ocean Atlantique.*"

Hank nodded his head, indicating he understood that Maurice was pointing out compass directions and the whereabouts of the Atlantic Ocean.

"*Normandie.*" Maurice made a broad, sweeping movement across the land area shown on the map. Hank easily recognized Normandy and had seen it on the maps and sand tables back at Jefferson Airfield.

Maurice moved his finger across the paper until it rested on a marked town. "*Ste. Mère Eglise*," he said, pausing. Maurice then pulled his finger down the map to another town, when he spoke again. "*Ste. Marie du Mont.*" Last, the old Frenchman shifted his finger to an unmarked point roughly between and to the northeast of Ste. Mère Eglise and Ste. Marie du Mont. He tapped twice and looked at Hank.

"*Jolieville est ici, mon ami*," he said, abruptly ending the geography lesson. Maurice folded the map, stood up, and handed it to Hank. "*Pour vous*," he said, blowing out the candle and quietly slipping out the barn door.

Hank climbed back into the loft with the map still in hand. Though it was late and he was tired, he couldn't help but unfold it and examine every mark, line, and geographical symbol on it. The fact that it was written in French and depicted measures of distance in meters and kilometers rather than feet and miles was of no consequence. Hank was spellbound by the old piece of paper now in his possession. Ignoring the danger of exposure, he pulled out his G.I. flashlight and shined it on the map while he reexamined it.

Hank's eyes darted feverishly, looking for any familiar town, city, or landmark that he would have seen back at Jefferson Airfield. He could not find Martinvast or even Cherbourg, although this was not surprising, since he realized the area depicted was very local, and he could well be farther from the target than he originally thought. He ran his fingers up and down the small stretch of coastline and tried to formulate some answers to the questions buzzing around in his head.

"Jesus, I'm a lot closer to the coast than I thought. I musta got turned around and driven back toward the water during those dogfights. If this is the eastern base of the Cotentin Peninsula, then Martinvast is several miles inland up to the northwest."

It began to dawn on Hank just how far away the target was. He and Brady had been bounced before they even had a chance to get near it. The likelihood that Captain Wheeler and his bomber had been able to fend off their attackers, fly on to the strike zone, successfully release and hit the target, and then make the journey back to base in England was remote, even if Hendricks and Dandridge had been able to regroup and provide cover.

"Maybe Wheeler did hit the target," he wondered. "Maybe the two P-38s found him and took down the attacking *Focke-Wulf* 190 that nailed me and any other lingering *Messerschmitts*. Maybe they're all back at Jefferson being debriefed by Dexter and Jamison about the success of the mission, minus the loss of the two Mustangs."

The fact that he was so near the coast and not buried inland was encouraging. If he could make his way to the coast undetected, maybe he could smuggle his way aboard a French fishing vessel or some kind of merchant or supply ship that could transport him back to friendly waters. Visions of being lowered into the English Channel on a raft awaiting a passing British warship became more and more appealing. Hank eventually switched off the flashlight, tucked the folded map in the front pocket of his shirt, and drifted off to sleep to the sound of dying artillery fire. Visions of sweet and stealthy escape back to England filled his dreams.

Lily returned to the barn early the next morning. The sun had barely begun to rise and it was still quite dark outside. A predawn mist hung heavy in the air and the ground glistened with dew. The old woman crept into the barn and up the ladder with another bucket of hot water. She gently awoke the sleeping American. Hank slowly opened his eyes and sat up as the old woman reached into her pockets and produced more scraps of bread and a little sausage with cheese. He graciously accepted the offering and devoured it as Lily checked over his injuries. She poked and prodded at Hank's back, probing for tender spots. Whenever Hank grimaced, the old World War I nurse rubbed and massaged away his discomfort. Moving from the back to the foot, Lily repeated the massage therapy, leaving Hank comfortable and relaxed. Hank beamed a great smile in recognition of the old woman's kindness. Her treatment didn't stop there, though. She reached for the bucket of warm water, then pulled out a cloth, small bar of soap, and a straight-edged razor from her pocket. She scrubbed away dirt and grime from Hank's face with the soapy cloth and warm water, then skillfully and carefully scraped away several days of beard growth with the razor. When finished, Lily stood up, descended the ladder, and stopped to clean the corner of the pen below the loft where Hank had relieved himself during the night. He watched in silence as she exited the barn and thanked God such benevolent and humane people had saved him. Hank's only other visitor that morning was Maurice, who led his three cows out to pasture.

Hank's plans of escaping undetected back to England swirled in his head. How would he communicate his intentions to Lily and Maurice? How could they disguise and deliver him to the French Resistance? Where would they go and how long would it take? Frustration and impatience set in as the difficult questions mounted. Hank strapped on his shoulder holster and .45 pistol while gathering his meager belongings in his satchel, keeping it close at all times. He affixed his extra magazines to his belt and kept his socks and boots on and laced up tight. The sense of readiness helped ease his mounting impatience and inactivity. The time to leave had to come soon.

As the day wore on, the young pilot became increasingly restless and impatient. Instead of quietly sitting up in the loft, he foolishly paced up and down the barn's hard wooden floorboards. The sound of his G.I. boots impacting the wooden floor echoed throughout the barn, but he was oblivious to the noise.

Time was beginning to wear down the American, who felt as much a captive to it as he did the barn. He looked down at his wristwatch that had been shattered during his bailout. He angrily tore it off and threw it to the ground. It bounced into one of the cow stalls. Hank continued to pace and again pulled out his map, studying it intently until he had become familiar with its every foreign word, distance marking, and geographic expression. It only fueled his desire to get moving again and find a way back to friendly territory.

Frustrated, Hank climbed back up into the loft and lay down. He pulled out his Zippo lighter and lit it. He watched the flame flicker for a moment before flipping the cover shut with a click, repeating the action several times before tiring of it. As sheer boredom gave way to simple laziness, he closed his eyes and drifted off to sleep.

The sounds of strange French voices snapped him to attention. He sat up abruptly and wiggled over to his peephole. The voices grew louder and more distinguishable. The door to the Tessier cottage opened and Lily appeared. Two strangers stepped into Hank's view—a young, well-dressed, slender-looking woman and an equally well-dressed, but chubby young boy holding her hand. The woman wore a blue-and-white floral-print dress with a matching styled hat and bright white gloves. Walking in nylons and high-heeled dress shoes failed to hinder her fast-paced step. A black leather purse hung from her shoulder. She wore shoulder-length black hair and makeup. As Hank scrutinized her appearance, he was reminded of how his mother used to look getting ready for church when he was a little boy. Lily, in contrast, looked haggard and withdrawn, with her hair hanging in a tangled mess and her clothing dirty and tattered.

The two women conversed loudly, with the younger woman doing the majority of the talking. Lily stood motionless and shook her head once or twice as the younger woman gestured about things Hank couldn't begin to understand. Clinging to the young woman's hand was a chubby little boy dressed in a white shirt and bow tie beneath a gray suit jacket and matching short pants, black suspenders, white knee-high socks, and black-and-white leather shoes. A beret covered most of his blond hair. Hank deduced the boy was maybe seven or eight years old and the woman was most likely his mother.

As the two women spoke, the boy pulled away from his mother's grasp and ran off across the meadow. She ignored the boy's youthful exuberance and all but forced her way into the cottage, with Lily behind her. The door slammed shut, although Hank could still hear the woman's voice carrying on endlessly, with barely a word in reply from Lily. From the meadow Hank could hear faint scolding cries as Maurice shouted at the youngster, who was apparently running, laughing, and getting in the old man's way.

Hank could hear the Frenchwoman speaking inside the cottage with confidence and authority, as if she were the host and Lily the guest, although he couldn't understand what was being said. After several long minutes, she opened the front door and walked out, again with Lily in tow. Hank watched from his peephole as the pair stood by the front door. He noticed the poorly concealed, grim look on Lily's face. The young woman took a step forward and looked around for the boy, who was nowhere to be found.

"*Pierre! Où êtes-vous!*" called out the young woman.

"*Ici!*" shouted the little boy.

Hank froze instinctively as every fiber in his being was struck with surprise at the sound of the boy's voice coming from inside the barn! He slowly turned his head away from the peephole and stealthily crawled to the edge of the loft, peeking downward. The boy popped up from behind one of the cow stalls and ran to the front doors, which he threw open with all his might before running outside.

Jesus Christ! How the hell did he get in here? wildly thought Hank. *He couldn't have come in the front doors. ... I would've heard him plain as day! How did he do it?*

Hank crawled back to the peephole in time to see the boy playfully run up to his mother. He reached into his pocket and pulled out a half-wrapped bar of chocolate that he hastily began to devour before the two made their departure across the meadow and over the stone bridge, back to the road. As soon as they were gone both Maurice and Lily rushed into the barn and latched the doors behind them.

Hank climbed down from the loft and confronted his two friends who were trying to contain their horror. Lily grasped Hank's hand and spoke to him in nonsensical French. Maurice spoke up, too, and soon the old couple were questioning Hank together and getting absolutely nowhere. Hank gestured at both of them to stop so he could speak. Ignoring the danger of blurting out sentences in English, Hank asserted, "He didn't see me! I swear to both of you—he didn't see me! It's okay!"

Maurice and Lily didn't understand the English, but his tone and expressions gradually made them comprehend.

"I don't know how the hell he got in here, but I know he didn't see me! We're okay!"

Maurice and Lily fell silent and motioned for Hank to return to the loft. The couple sadly turned away and cautiously exited the barn, latching the doors behind them. Hank felt awful and wondered if this unfortunate episode would adversely affect the positive manner with which they had treated him so far. Not wanting to dwell on it, and still selfishly obsessed with plans of leaving, Hank climbed back into the loft and pulled out his map once again.

Night fell. The stars were hidden behind cloudy skies; however, the never-ending symphony of war played on. As on previous nights, hurtling German anti-aircraft fire lit up the heavens in response to the droning sounds of approaching British bombers. The Tessier cottage was dark with the old couple hunkered down inside.

Inside the barn Hank watched the bright light from the slow-burning German tracer fire slide through the cracks in the walls and ceiling. Once again the eerie light show produced ghostly shadows that seemed to dance across the walls and floorboards. It was as if the dead slain earlier in the war were rising up to face combat and redeem their loved ones. Hank remained restless and singleminded. Escape became his obsession. Escape from the barn and escape from enemy territory altogether. His mind raced and he couldn't sleep. He tossed and turned until he could no longer stand it. He got up and climbed down the ladder as the ghostly shadows danced across the walls, in rhythm with the sounds of war outside. Unimpressed, he turned back around, unzipped his pants, and let loose a hard golden stream of urine into the corner pen.

As he zipped up, Hank was startled by a thunderous boom. The barn rattled violently, loosening a board at the base of the back wall.

"Damn, that was close," he whispered. He envisioned a stray German artillery shell or maybe even a bomb had landed in the woods somewhere near the Tessier land. As he reached to pick up the fallen board, he noticed two others were loose as well. In fact, they were not even nailed in at all! Hank pulled out all three to reveal a nice and neat opening a man might possibly squeeze through, perfectly sized for a child.

"So that's how that little bastard got in here," surmised Hank. "He's got himself a little secret door."

Hank replaced the boards in the back wall and began to look around. To his delight, he spied a neatly stacked pile of bricks in the corner below an array of farm tools hanging on the wall. He gathered up the bricks and stacked them against the loose boards.

"Let's see him try to get in here now," said Hank. Satisfied his makeshift barricade was sufficient, he climbed back into the loft and bedded down for the night. Blocking out the sounds of war around him, he concentrated on how he was going to persuade Maurice and

Lily to help devise a plan to smuggle him out of France without severely endangering him or them. Thoughts of rough travel, disguises, and clandestine meetings with unsavory members of the French Resistance fired the young airman's imagination. This definitely had to be the next step, and it had to come sooner than later.

"Tomorrow," thought Hank before drifting off to sleep.

It was now the fifth night of the airman's stay at the Tessier farm. The hours passed slowly as the steady sound of gently falling rain played against the old barn's roof. Hank lay comfortably, half asleep up in the loft. His mind was filled with indiscernible visions. At one point he got up, lit the old rusty kerosene lamp Maurice had provided, and climbed down from the loft to urinate in the corner of the pigpen. As he finished, he glanced at the back wall and noticed that the bricks he had piled against the loose boards were gone! In fact, the boards themselves were missing, as well. He wheeled around and saw the little chubby French boy step out of the shadows. The lad stood motionless, with a face of stone. Hank reached inside his jacket to pull his .45 from the shoulder holster. To his horror, it was empty! From behind his back, the boy produced Hank's weapon and with both hands pointed it directly at the pilot's head. Hank rushed the boy and was enveloped in a blinding white light.

Hank snapped awake and sat upright. The barn was totally dark. He reached for his Zippo and sparked it to life. The flickering flame revealed the location of the kerosene lamp, which he promptly lit. Once the darkness was lifted away, the shaken airman came to his senses. He reached inside his jacket and found his weapon snugly secured inside its holster. In the pigpen below he verified that the bricks he had placed in front of the loose boards were exactly as he had left them. He had been dreaming—a dream that seemed all too real. Rattled, Hank sat on the small step that led up from the pigpen to the main barn floor and the cow stalls. As the minutes ticked away he did not return to the loft, but remained where he was in the soft comforting glow of the lantern. He didn't know what time it was, but knew morning couldn't be far away.

The sound of the rain subsided and the far-off artillery fire ceased. The first hint of morning light breached the overcast skies and released the grip of darkness. The barn was drafty and very chilly. Hank rose to his feet and zipped his jacket tight. Inside the Tessier cottage Maurice and Lily were still sound asleep. Hank walked to the front of the barn, unlatched the front doors, and peered outside. The grounds were eerily silent; it seemed that no creature had stirred to life. The ground was soft and damp with early-morning dew, and the air was thick with fog.

Hank looked over at the cottage and took one step toward it before stopping dead in his tracks. He turned his head in the direction of the meadow that led to the stone bridge. It was obscured by layers of fog, but something caught his keen eyes. Movement! The young pilot slipped back behind the barn doors and kept them open just enough that he could peer out.

Ghostly shapes slowly began to emerge through the gloom. First there was one, then two, then two more. They moved stealthily without making a sound, and their inconspicuous silhouettes remained masked by the fog. As they drew closer there was no mistaking their identities. Hank recoiled in terror at the sight of several German soldiers piercing through the morning fog toward the Tessier cottage. They were crouched low to the ground with rifles at the ready, like vicious hunters stalking defenseless and unsuspecting prey.

Realizing the imminent danger, Hank abruptly closed the barn doors and latched them shut, unaware he had caught the attention of one of the approaching soldiers. He raced to the back of the barn and stepped down into the pigpen. Using the wall of the back cow stall as cover, he got down on his belly, drew his Colt .45 pistol, and peered toward the front doors.

Outside the silence had been broken as the sounds of German voices began to carry through the fog. Hank listened intently as the voices became audible, seeming to come from all directions. Several *Wehrmacht* soldiers hustled about, surrounding both the barn and the cottage. Hank heard loud banging on the cottage door, followed moments later by Lily's terrified screams as the soldiers forced their way inside her home.

Hank cringed in anger at the sounds of Lily's horrified cries. His mind raced feverishly, unable to determine what was going to happen next. Crouched down in the pigpen at the back of the barn with a cow stall wall for cover, he gripped his pistol with both hands and waited for the inevitable. Suddenly, the door latches came undone and the doors slowly began to swing open. Hank peeked around the cow stall in terror at the sight of an emerging rifle barrel. The German soldier carrying it stepped into view, as did another right behind him. Hank pulled his head out of sight and pressed it hard against the side of the stall. The two Germans did not speak, but gave each other hand signals as they peered around and started to creep forward, with guns pointing the way.

Hank's heart pumped madly as pure adrenaline coursed through his veins. The soldiers crept closer until they were halfway to his position. There was nothing left to do. There was no place to run. This was it! The American sprang up from behind the stall and fired at the nearest advancing German. Two quick shots burst out of the barrel of Hank's Colt pistol, striking the German in the right arm and chest. Blood exploded from the wounds as the man recoiled from the violent impact. He hit the floor hard and dead, knocking the second soldier off balance. Before he could fully recover, Hank swiftly trained his weapon on the second soldier and squeezed off two more rounds. The first missed entirely, while the second ripped into the soldier's right shoulder, splattering blood across the wall. The soldier screamed in pain and dropped to his knees before crawling behind a stall partition.

The wounded German soldier cried out, "*Achtung! Achtung! Der Amerikaner ist hier! Kommen! Kommen!*"

Hank rushed to finish off the wounded soldier but couldn't get to him before another troop burst inside, spraying MP-40 machine-pistol fire. Hank leapt backwards, seeking the cover of the back pen and cow stall. The German continued to fire, ripping dozens of holes in the wooden panels around Hank. Deadly splinters shot out as the bullets impacted the stalls and pricked into Hank's exposed neck. Foolishly the German emptied his gun too quickly, forcing him to reach for a fresh magazine. This gave Hank the respite he needed. He jumped up and fired again, hitting the German before he could dive for cover. The bullet ripped into the German's neck, killing him instantly. Blood gushed from his severed jugular vein and pooled on the floor.

The wounded soldier in the stall continued to cry out for help. Frantic voices outside the barn grew louder and more confused. Hank again went for the wounded soldier but was greeted by two German troops who kicked in the front doors, firing their rifles as they came. Again Hank dove for cover. The Germans alternated their fire, keeping Hank pinned down and unable to get off an aimed shot. They aimed, fired, and recycled their bolt-action rifles with deadly precision. Each shot ripped through Hank's cover, coming closer and closer to finding its target. As he advanced, one soldier dropped his rifle to help the still screaming wounded man. As he did, the enraged American leapt up again and madly fired several rounds in the direction of his attackers. Two bullets struck the German still wielding his rifle. The impact knocked him back, toppling him mortally wounded on top of the fellow German struck earlier in the neck. Hank wheeled and fired three more rounds at the soldier who had stopped to help his wounded comrade, but missed badly as the soldier dove for safety next to his friend. The anxious American squeezed the trigger one more time, but the gun failed to discharge. The hammer dropped on an empty chamber. Hank was out of bullets! He raced for cover just as the last German soldier stormed in, firing his MP-40 machine gun. The spraying fire ricocheted off metal farm tools hanging on the walls, causing sparks to fly, and ripped through the walls of the barn itself. The noise caused by the gunfire, human screams, and commotion was deafening.

Hank ejected the spent magazine from his .45 and reached for his belt magazine pouch. He grabbed a fresh magazine and slapped it into the butt of his pistol. He drew back the slide, cocking the weapon, and rose up to fire at the marauding German with the machine gun. The sight of the American caught the German by surprise, and he dropped to the floor just as Hank fired off three quick rounds. The German returned fire, forcing Hank to duck for cover. As Hank dropped, he kicked over the still dimly lit kerosene lantern he had been using earlier. The flame touched off a small pile of hay and started to burn ferociously. The fire quickly spread to the side wall of the barn and started licking upward, toward the ceiling. The German with the machine gun saw this and started to back away. His comrade rose up and pulled to safety the injured German who had been struck in the shoulder.

The flames spread quickly and soon surrounded Hank in a massive furnace of deadly heat and flame. The Germans backed out of the barn, but continued to spray bullets inside. Coughing uncontrollably from the enveloping smoke, Hank fired back wildly, while kicking away the bricks covering the opening in the back wall. The fire grew intense as smoke billowed skyward and flames punched through the roof. The old barn was transformed into a blast furnace of death.

With one last mighty kick, Hank dislodged the bricks and the loose boards on the back wall. As the flames burned only inches from his body, he lunged toward the hole and squeezed through just as the roof caved in and collapsed. Dazed, but alive, he staggered toward the woods, coughing uncontrollably, thereby alerting the Germans to his position.

"*Halt!*" cried a uniformed SS officer. "*Legen Sie es hin!*" he commanded after catching sight of Hank's gun. He raised his Walther PPK and fired at the retreating American, who stumbled to the ground. Before he could get up, Hank raised his .45 one last time and fired, praying he still had some ammunition left in the magazine. Two bullets exploded from the barrel, forcing the unsuspecting German officers to hit the deck, but not finding any targets. Hank staggered to his feet, summoning all his remaining energy to run. However, there was nothing left. His lungs were full of smoke, his eyes were bloodshot from exposure to the point where he could barely keep them open, and he was too exhausted and disoriented to fight any more. He turned in the direction of the Germans and raised his empty gun expecting several bullets to crash into his body and end his traumatic ordeal.

Time seemed to stand still as Hank caught a glimpse of Lily and Maurice, in their bedclothes, lying face down in the mud, with their hands behind their heads. Over them stood a German dressed in a black, double-breasted suit with a white shirt and red-and-black striped tie. A bright red handkerchief protruded from his jacket's breast pocket. Atop his head was a black fedora and over his suit was a long, black, unbuttoned leather overcoat. He wore round spectacles and had a small, Hitler-like mustache. He wore a gold Nazi Party badge on his suit lapel. He was in his forties, with graying, oily, slicked-back hair. He was not especially tall or physically imposing; however, there was an unmistakable aura of evil about him.

Two pistol shots rang out from the uniformed SS officer's gun, cutting across the surface of the dazed airman's right forearm. Hank recoiled in pain as his extended arm gushed dark red blood. The pistol fell from his injured limb while his bloodshot eyes locked onto a German soldier rushing toward him carrying a Kar 98 rifle. The butt of the soldier's rifle crashed into Hank's skull, sending him to the ground half-conscious and bloody. He lay there for a moment, looking up at the sky. His eyes grew dim, but his ears captured the sounds of indiscernible German phrases, horrific cries of mercy in French, and the thunderous sound of the collapse of the burning Tessier barn. The final image he saw before losing consciousness was the menacing face of the bespectacled, Hitler-mustached German staring wickedly into his eyes.

Chapter 10

THE HOLDING CELL

The evening hours had slipped by without notice. The fire in the wood stove had burned down to glowing red embers while the darkness inside nearly matched that on the outside. A very tired and worn out Hank slowly rose from his chair and jabbed an iron poker at the nearly extinguished fire. Sparks flew up the stovepipe and flames quickly rekindled once the old man tossed in a few scraps of wood.

Matt Switzer sat on the sofa and finished scribbling notes on his pad. The young student, caught up in Hank's story, hadn't realized he had filled eleven pages. He put his pen down and flexed his hand to alleviate the cramp caused by writing so vigorously.

The old man looked at his watch. It was 11:22. He was alarmed at how long he had been talking and how late it had gotten without either he or his guest noticing. He wearily looked over at his young friend sitting on the sofa. The old man was quite finished for the evening and wanted to go to bed. In contrast, the young student viewed 11:22 as early in the evening and was now totally engrossed in the story the old fighter pilot was telling. He showed no signs of fatigue, and Hank sensed he wanted to hear more.

"Well, Matt, I suppose we should call it quits for now. It's pretty late and I've just about had it. Whaddaya say?" expressed Hank wearily.

"So they got ya," replied Matt, ignoring Hank's question.

Confused, the old man answered, "Beg your pardon?"

"They flushed you out of the barn … you exchanged shots … you were wounded … and they captured you, right?"

The old man, realizing that getting to bed was not going to be an easy task, rolled his eyes and replied, "Yes, Matt. They got me."

Not sensing the old man's fatigue, Matt continued to ask questions as Hank politely tried to wrap up the evening and head for bed.

"Well, what happened next, Hank?" asked Matt, his voice brimming with enthusiasm.

The old man stood up from his chair. "I think that had better wait for another time. It's late, and you should start back to Orono before it gets much later."

Matt looked down at his watch again and began thinking of ways to plead for more time, but the old man was already halfway out of the study.

"Hank, do you think you could just give me a quick idea of what happened next before I go? You know … to give me something to think about on the way home?" he asked.

Turning to his eager young student, Hank answered, "Not tonight. I'm too tired and I'm going to bed. Come back tomorrow afternoon if you like and maybe we'll get into things a bit further. But for now, just go home and get some rest. Surely you have some other commitments to tend to."

"Yeah … maybe you're right, sir," meekly replied Matt. "Could I hang around for a bit longer and organize my notes before I leave? I'd just like to get some personal thoughts down on paper before they fly right out of my head."

The old man looked at the youngster with a sense of pride and understanding that his story had made a meaningful impact. It made him feel good inside and helped restore his faith in the idea that Matt's generation wasn't completely apathetic and oblivious to the trials and struggles of those who had fought so hard for freedom all those many years ago.

"Sure. Take as much time as you need. Feel free to let yourself out. Just turn off the lights and make sure to lock the door when you leave. I'm going up to bed before I collapse right here," he said with a smile. With that, Hank pulled himself up the stairs and closed the bedroom door behind him.

The next morning the old man woke from a sound night's sleep at around seven o'clock. After showering and shaving he went downstairs to the kitchen and heated up the antique stove in preparation for breakfast. The cabin was quite chilly and Hank wondered if the wood stove in the study still had any embers left that he could use to rekindle the fire.

Entering the study he was startled at what he saw. Lying on his sofa, curled up in a shivering ball, was Matt Switzer! His notepad and backpack lay on the floor next to the sofa and his jacket was draped over his upper body like a blanket. Quietly Hank built a new fire and let his guest sleep while he withdrew to the kitchen. Soon the kitchen was overflowing with the pleasant smell of bacon and eggs cooking. Hank tried to be as quiet as possible, but the aroma of fried eggs and crisp bacon soon woke his young friend.

Matt shook the sleep from his system and wondered if his actions had been appropriate. Would Hank be furious that he had spent the night without permission? Would he kick him out and tell him not to ever come back? He didn't have to wonder long.

"You're up. Good. Come on into the kitchen and have some breakfast. You must be hungry, young fella," said Hank as he looked in at Matt on the sofa. Without a word, Matt first used the bathroom, then walked into the kitchen and pulled up a chair at the table in front of a plate of bacon and eggs and a bowl of Cheerios Hank had prepared for him.

"Want some juice?" asked Hank in a raspy voice.

"Yeah, that'd be great. Thanks," said Matt.

Hank poured Matt a glass of orange juice and sat down to eat his breakfast. Matt nibbled at his bacon, knowing he owed his friend an explanation, but not knowing exactly what to say. Finally he mustered the nerve to speak between bites.

"Ah, Hank, thanks for breakfast. I didn't mean to crash here last night. It's just that . . ."

Matt's voice trailed off. Hank swallowed a quick swig of orange juice and decided to put the student's mind at ease.

"It's okay, Matt. I don't mind that you spent the night. I was pretty tired and the last thing I woulda wanted to do was jump in a car and drive back to Orono. You could have asked me, though. The least I could've done was get ya a decent blanket."

Replied Matt, "I didn't plan to crash here, Hank. I just got so wound up in your story that I kept writing down notes and thinking of questions to ask and I lost all track of time. Before I knew it, my watch said it was way past one in the morning. I packed up my stuff and started to leave … but I was so tired that I figured I'd just stay here, hoping you wouldn't mind."

Hank looked at the young man. "Have you learned something from what I've told you so far? Because it ain't always easy for me to talk about these things, Matt. It would make me quite upset knowing you were just going through the motions of listening and not really hearing what I have to say about that very difficult time in my life."

Matt spoke right up. "Yes I've learned a lot. I'm not sure how much I can use, but I definitely know that I wanna hear more. I've taken lots of notes and I wanna learn what happened after you were captured. Plus I'm sure that your granddaughter would be happy to see the progress we've made since the first time we met. Don't you think so?"

"Well, I'll tell ya what I think, Mr. Switzer. I think you've shown me enough respect and interest in what I've had to say to have earned enough of my trust to hear some more. But it's not gonna be pleasant, young man, just keep that in mind. Okay?"

"Yes, sir. I'll keep that in mind," said Matt, unsure of what to expect.

"Okay, then." Hank started to clear away some dishes from the table and straighten up the kitchen. "What other commitments do you have today? Classes? Other appointments and such?"

"Well, it's Friday the twenty-first. There won't be much happening on campus today. I'm essentially done with classes, until final exam week, that is. I'm pretty set to just focus on this project. That's really what I want to do. I've got plenty of time this morning. And you?"

Hank leaned up against the sink with his arms crossed and looked up at the ceiling.

"I had one or two little things I wanted to do today in town, but they're not that important. I guess I can spare you some time this morning. Okay. Give me a few minutes to clean up and we'll continue where we left off last night," said Hank.

"Great," answered Matt. He went back to the bathroom to wash up before resuming his place on the sofa. He was joined a few minutes later by the old man who stoked the fire, cursed the unusually cloudy and cool April weather, then settled into his chair once again. The story continued.

Darkness. Total and unholy darkness accompanied by throbbing and numbing pain were the first sensations to register in the captured American's mind. Hank's head was a bloody mess. He had slipped in and out of consciousness several times since absorbing the full impact of a German rifle butt to the head. But now, to his dismay, he was painfully alert.

At first the pilot thought his head was bandaged to contain the blood dripping from his temple. He discovered very quickly, however, that the cloth wrapped around his head was just a blindfold. The oozing blood from his battered head had soaked into the blindfold, saturating it and adding to his discomfort. He sat in a wooden chair, his legs bound together at the ankles and his hands tied tightly behind his back. The ropes were so tight he could barely feel any sensation in his hands and feet. His head hung limp and he desperately wanted to pass out, hoping unconsciousness would end the pain coursing throughout his body. It didn't come, however, and the wounded pilot was forced to suffer, not knowing what was in store for him.

As blood dripped down Hank's cheek he listened intently for any clue that might reveal where he was. There was no sound of voices or machinery to be heard. It was silent in his unknown surroundings save for hauntingly intermittent drops of water falling into a small puddle behind him. The eerie drip fell in a rhythmic pattern that echoed loudly throughout the unseen chamber. It was cool, dark, and extremely damp. A stale, musty smell hung in the air and reminded Hank of the scary root cellar at his grandparents' house he had visited as a small boy. The mysterious, dank enclosure brought back the unpleasant childhood memories.

Hank realized he was locked in total darkness. Even blindfolded he could tell the room was devoid of light, natural or otherwise. His leather jacket was gone, as was his shoulder holster. His officer's shirt felt as if it had been ripped open in the front and there were irritating abrasions on his neck where someone had forcefully wrenched off his dog tags.

At length Hank's ears caught the faint sound of voices. He labored to listen, but couldn't make out what was being said. Soon the voices became more audible. As he strained to make sense of the strange voices, he realized they were in an unfriendly tongue—the ominous and threatening sounds of German.

Moments later the voices ceased. An eerie silence ensued. Seconds, then minutes ticked by. Hank's heart pounded in fear, not knowing what would happen next. Then, suddenly, the unmistakable sound of a large wooden door being unbolted and slowly opened pierced Hank's senses. Light poured into the room and the sounds of footsteps followed. The American captive was no longer alone!

"*Dort ist er,*" called out a voice. Hank felt hands loosening the knots of his blindfold.

"*Beeilen Sie sich!*" cried the voice, urging the man working on the blindfold knots to hurry. A moment later the blindfold fell off. Hank's vision was a blur as the sudden exposure to the light pouring in from the doorway forced him to squint and lower his head, preventing him from seeing who was in the room.

"*Danke. Gehen Sie!*" ordered the voice directly in front of Hank. The man standing behind him clicked his heels and walked away. The sound of the heavy wooden door closing, then being bolted again, echoed throughout the small chamber. Again the sound of dripping water was all that could be heard.

Hank lifted his head and opened his eyes wide. He was not alone and was terrified of the unseen monster lurking in the darkness so near to him and just waiting to strike! He strained to see who or what was in the room with him but saw only darkness. He couldn't even hear the mysterious stranger's breathing.

Then … footsteps! The sound of boot heels impacting what Hank could only visualize as cobblestones filled his eardrums. The monster in the dark room walked in circles around the chair, repeatedly, like a predator zeroing in on wounded prey before striking. It reminded Hank of the FW-190A pilot who circled around him before attacking while he helplessly dangled in midair from his parachute. Hank defied the growing fear inside him and resisted the urge to cry out.

The footsteps ceased and the next sound heard was a match scratching against a rough surface. Hank's eyes caught the glow of the match and followed the flame as it was delivered to the wick of a nearby candle. The candle came to life, its soft light giving the pilot's eyes time to adjust and capture his surroundings for the first time.

Hank surmised he was in some sort of holding cell. The walls, floor, and ceiling were stone and the only door, directly in front of him, was made from a very heavy, dark oak. Water seeped in from the walls and collected in small puddles on the floor. Against the wall stood a small, dirty, half-rotted wooden table and chair. On the table sat the lit candle in a wide-based candleholder, and in the chair, only partially visible, sat a shadowy figure dressed all in black with legs crossed.

The figure picked up the candle and stood. His face obscured from Hank's sight, he said, "*Es tut mir Leid, dass ich Sie habe warten lassen. Können Sie mir eine Auskunft geben?*"

Confused and unresponsive, Hank simply watched as the man again began to walk in circles around him. Each time he completed a revolution Hank was able to piece together more and more of who he was dealing with, although he could not clearly see his face. Then the monster spoke again.

"*Wie heißen Sie?*" he asked, holding the candle away from his face and continuing his orbit of his bound captive. "*Woher sind Sie?*"

Hank did not understand the words but understood without a doubt that he was being questioned and tested on some unknown level. Perhaps it was a preinterrogation interview. His initial feelings of fear gradually turned to frustration and irritation resulting from his inability to understand the German language being forced upon him. The German's tone of voice was neither harsh nor threatening. It was surprisingly mild-mannered. Nevertheless, the airman stayed on guard.

"*Wo sind Sie geboren? New York? Los Angeles?*" The German's mention of two U.S. cities piqued Hank's attention. He gathered he was being asked about home or possibly where he was from. He did not utter a word of reply; he merely watched as the German circled in and out of his sight.

"*Wie alt sind Sie? Zwanzig? Zweiundzwanzig?*"

Again Hank didn't say a word. He kept silent and motionless, making sure not to eyeball his captor.

The German stopped and took his seat next to the rotting wooden table. He placed the candle far enough from him so as not to fully reveal his identity.

"*Sprechen Sie Deutsch?*" asked the German, his tone elevated. "*Nein? Das ist schade.*"

Hank listened to the words, but continued to say nothing. His irritation grew with each comment the German spouted. He remained vigilant, however, and remembered his training that taught him to stay silent in situations such as this. The German would not have much more of it though.

"*Sprechen Sie!*" he shouted out, causing Hank to flinch. "*Wie heißen Sie? Woher sind Sie?*" he bellowed repeatedly, all the time staying seated in his chair. The young pilot decided to go against his tactic of remaining silent and employ a different measure of resistance. After listening to the German's harangue to the point he couldn't bear to hear another word, Hank spoke up.

"Mitchell, First Lieutenant, United States Army Air Force, 36243600," he sounded off, as if he were addressing a senior officer.

The German ignored the American's reply and continued to lurk in the shadows. Seemingly endless statements, questions, and snide remarks poured from the German's mouth. His tone was neither harsh nor threatening, but considerably annoying. The droning speech went on for several minutes.

Hank knew what was going on but was unable to deal with it. The German was using mild, yet provoking speech tactics to begin to break down his will and get in his head. The airman knew it was best just to keep silent. However, his fighter pilot instincts got the better of him. He couldn't remain defensive. He had to attack!

"Mitchell, First Lieutenant, United States Army Air Force,

36243600," he angrily sounded off again. Unimpressed, the interrogator countered with another series of verbal volleys that forced Hank to interrupt again with his name, rank, and serial number. The two went back and forth against each other in this fashion until Hank finally lost his nerve and verbally lashed out at his adversary.

"You fucking son-of-a-bitch! Shut up with that diseased Pig Latin bullshit! You wanna ask me some questions? Get some other bastard in here that can speak English, you Nazi piece of shit," railed Hank. "You hear me? Speak English or get the fuck out! I'm done listening to you!"

The German took some sadistic pleasure at the brutal stream of profanity unleashed against him. He paused to listen and interjected a devilish snicker at opportune moments that incensed Hank further.

"You heard what I said! Get an interpreter in here or leave me the fuck alone! Do you speak English? Do you understand English? Come around where I can see you, you bastard! You better hope I don't get these ropes off, pal, cause if I do, I'm gonna whip your Kraut ass! Do you hear me? Do you understand English, asshole?" roared Hank, the sweat dripping down his face and his throat growing hoarse.

Just then the German leapt from his seat, grabbed Hank's chair, and spun it around so Hank was staring directly into his face. Hank's eyes opened wide as he was caught by surprise at the face now no more than an inch away from his own. The next words uttered sent a cold shiver down Hank's spine.

"Of course I speak English, you bloody idiotic Yank; it is my native tongue! Now if you're quite through with your little childish spat, you're going to close that vulgar trap of yours and listen to every bloody word I say—that is, in fact, if you desire to live! Do we understand each other?"

The airman was speechless as the German slowly pulled his face away, keeping his eyes locked on his startled prisoner's. The German returned to his seat where he calmly sat down and crossed his legs.

Hank couldn't believe what he had heard. The German interrogator who had grilled him in fluently accented Bavarian German had just screamed at him in English, with a voice no louder than a whisper, and in an unmistakably British accent! The German said nothing as he allowed Hank to take in what he had heard. He pulled the candle closer to him, allowing Hank to get his first good look at whom he was dealing with.

The dark uniform was unmistakable, even to Hank, who had seen only black-and-white pictures of its likeness. The uniform was that of the "Black Order" and "Praetorian Guard" of Hitler's Reich ... the dreaded SS! Now facing the German, but still bound to his chair, Hank scrutinized his captor.

The German wore a tailored, prewar and older-styled, black *Allgemeine-SS* patterned, open-necked service tunic with matching black *Allgemeine-SS* peaked officer's visor hat with white piping. The hat bore the horrible metallic SS national eagle insignia. The ominous bird clutched the swastika in its talons, as its distinctive horizontal feathers extended outward. Just below the hat's eagle was the sinister skull and crossbones "*totenkopf*," or death's-head insignia so symbolic of the SS and the evil it represented.

The uniform bore a distinctive collar insignia. The right collar patch was completely black, devoid of any symbol. The left collar patch however, contained four diamond-shaped metal pips over a doubled-braided strip indicating the officer's rank. On the left breast pocket was a golden Nazi Party badge pinned above a Knight's Cross medal.

Beneath the coat was a brown shirt and a solid black tie. On the left arm, above the elbow, was a bright red sleeve brassard with a large black swastika within a white disc. Just below that was a curious symbol that caught Hank's eye. It was a solid black, diamond-shaped patch with the letters "SD" sewn in silvery white thread. Hank did not recognize this acronym and wondered why it didn't read "SS," as he was sure he was in the presence of an SS officer.

Hank's eyes glanced down at the leather belt with a smaller shoulder strap cutting diagonally across the chest. The buckle was circular and contained the design of an eagle atop a wreathed swastika, with words written underneath that Hank could barely make out and certainly did not understand—"*Meine Ehre Heißt Treue.*" The helpless pilot's eye was drawn to the pistol holstered on the officer's right side and the SS dagger in its scabbard dangling from his left. Even in the dim candlelight he could discern the awesome, yet primeval-edged weapon suspended from nickel-silver chains and adorned with SS runes, skull and crossbones, swastikas, and an ornate silver troddle. His fascination with the weapon grew to detailed but very brief thoughts of using it to cut himself free, then plunge it into the heart of his captor.

The SS officer sat patiently, deliberately allowing Hank to size him up. The man was in his fifties with graying, dirty-blond hair. His face was clean-shaven, wrinkled by time, and without scar. He legs were long and Hank estimated he was over six feet tall. He was also very trim, with a strong chest and back that belied his age. Hank stared at him without saying a word, just waiting.

The SS officer picked up the burning candle and positioned it behind him. He drew very close to the American and began to speak again.

"If you know what's best for you, you'll keep your mouth shut and listen to every word I say. You are alive right now because some very important people have decreed it necessary to keep you alive, for the moment. You have shot at members of the SS and killed several *Wehrmacht* soldiers. Those are serious crimes that under ordinary circumstances would have you castrated and hanging from a meat hook with piano wire wrapped tightly around your neck. But, fortunately for you, my associates are intrigued by Americans who fall from the sky—especially officers—and wish to get to know you a little bit better. Trust me, they will get to know you and your intentions better, even if it requires you to painfully lose a few body parts in the process, my young friend. Keep that in mind for now."

The German paused, allowing his last sentence to sink in. He kept his voice at a whisper and kept close to the young airman. Hank listened intently to the soft British accent, which was not unfamiliar to him. He had heard it before from English flying-officers he had met while stationed in North Africa and during his brief stint in the Azores. It sounded very upscale and refined, as if spoken by British royalty. It was truly the "King's English," not the Cockney accent associated with the working-class people of East London.

The whispering German continued, "I know who you are, so you can save that bloody name, rank, and serial number nonsense. It won't do you any good, no matter who you talk with, so drop it right now. Your dog tags are gone and soon your clothes will be destroyed, as will those pilot wings and leftenant insignia bars on your shirt. The one thing I want you to keep mercilessly clear is that all rights and freedoms under the Geneva Convention that you think you have do not exist. You are in the custody of the SS, and you no longer have any rights or protection granted by international law. You can be eliminated at any time. That is, unless you do everything I say. Then maybe, just maybe, you'll get out of here alive. Do we understand each other? Just nod your head if you feel most agreeable."

Hank didn't comply. Though he knew it wasn't a wise idea, he chose to answer verbally.

"Mitchell, First Lieutenant, United States Army Air Force, 36243600!"

With a mighty swing the German slapped Hank hard across his already bloody face. The pain from his throbbing head, wounded arm, and aggravated earlier injuries forced him into unconsciousness again. But the German was not about to let that happen and grabbed Hank by the hair, forcing his head up.

"You don't listen very well, do you?" he said, keeping his voice at a whisper. "I'm offering you a chance to live. If you want that chance to get out of here and see your family again back home in America, you had better start paying exceptional attention to me."

The German paused again and let go of Hank's hair. Hank fought every urge to pass out and kept his head held high.

The German said, "For I am all you have in the world right now. Without me, you're as good as dead. Mark my words flying-officer—good as dead!" The German sat back down and placed the candle on the table.

The suffering pilot next to him did not know what to make of the situation. He decided it was best just to keep listening, no matter how painful it was.

"Now, do you want my assistance, or shall I save my associates the trouble, and just slit your throat right here and now?" As the German spoke he put his left hand on his dagger.

Hank worked up his courage and inner strength to laboriously answer his captor. "Why would you want to help me? You're nothing but a goddamned Nazi that happens to speak English with a British accent. That trick won't work with me. I'm a United States Army Air Force officer. We ain't got nothing more to discuss."

"Oh, I think we do," replied the German, maintaining the perfect British accent. "You see, a few of my acquaintances from the local *Wehrmacht* command would love to meet the American who gunned down several of their comrades. Also, I feel it necessary to mention that I have acquaintances in the Gestapo who feel inclined to talk with you about why you're here and what you were doing at that nice old couple's farm. I trust you would tell them what they want to hear. Those old folks' lives would depend on it! I might also add that whatever they decided to do to you would pale in comparison to what they would do to that French couple."

Hank's head shot upright, as terrible visions of the Tessiers being tortured by the Gestapo flooded his mind. Were they still alive and in captivity like him? Could he help them somehow by cooperating with this peculiar officer? He had to believe Maurice and Lily were prisoners and that it was his duty to try to protect them, no matter what. His purpose now became clear. He had to find them and get them out. But how?

"I see I have your attention now," said the SS officer. "I understand your apprehension toward my offer to help. You have to trust me, that's all I can say."

"Who are you? Why would I trust you? You're a Nazi and you've given me absolutely no reason to believe this whole charade," said Hank, his pain worsening.

"Who I am is of no consequence to you. Why I am offering to help is of no consequence to you. You seek proof of my sincerity. Fair enough … here it is."

The German rose from his chair and slowly drew the dagger from its scabbard. Hank's heart began to race as the German held the knife against his throat. The terrified airman closed his eyes and waited for the slash that would end his young life. It did not come. Instead of feeling the dagger's sharp edge slide across his throat, Hank felt the sensation of the blade slash through the ropes that bound his legs and hands. As the cords went limp and fell to the damp and musty floor, Hank felt the tingling sensation of blood rushing back into his freed extremities. He wanted to spring to his feet and lurch forward at his captor, but his strength was gone and his head spun dizzyingly from the loss of blood. All he could do was sit there helplessly.

The German put away his ornate dagger and reached for his gun. He pulled the weapon from its holster and pointed it at Hank, who was freed, but still anchored to his seat by nothing more than the weight of his own limp body. With the barrel in his face, Hank recognized the gun as a Luger that looked to be in pristine condition. Many Allied soldiers fantasized about obtaining the prized pistol as a war trophy.

Suddenly the German turned the gun around and handed it to the stunned pilot. Hank was so taken by surprise at this gesture that his hand trembled uncontrollably, almost causing him to drop the weapon.

Still keeping his British-accented voice at a whisper, the German said, "Now you can take that, kill me where I stand, open that door that is not bolted, and try to shoot your way out of here, all the while not having a bloody clue where you are or how many men stand between you and certain death once the magazine is empty. Or you can hand it back to me and sit back down, knowing you'll be alive a bit longer, with the chance to get out of here and help that nice old French couple."

Hank summoned every ounce of strength, then wearily stood up and pointed the Luger directly at the German's head. His hand trembled and his mind was unclear. He tried desperately to pull the trigger and end the German's trickery, but he couldn't. He couldn't do it knowing there was some distant hope the Tessiers were still alive and needing his help. He lowered the weapon and dropped it at the German's feet before crumpling to the floor, weakened and disoriented.

The German picked up the gun and put it back in the holster.

He knelt down next to Hank and said, "That's the wisest thing you've done in your entire life. You remember that for as long as you live … Yank."

Just then German voices became audible outside the door to the holding cell. Instantly the SS officer began screaming at Hank in German.

"*Stehen Sie auf!*" he angrily shouted. He stood up and violently kicked him in the side, drawing his dagger just as the door to the cell opened and light poured in. Two SS guards entered the room, then snapped to attention, clicking their heels and throwing their right arms forward with a Nazi salute. The officer began yelling at them and pointed to Hank, who was moaning in pain on the floor. The guards saluted the officer again, picked Hank off the floor, and sat him back down in the chair. His bleary eyes caught one last sight of his curious jailer, silhouetted in the light shining in the doorway from the room beyond. The guards tightly wrapped the blindfold around his head and tied his hands and feet as before. They snuffed out the burning candle and left the cell with the mysterious officer behind them. He glanced at the dying American before closing the door, again encasing Hank in total darkness.

The airman did not expect to live much longer; his bleeding continued and he slipped in and out of consciousness. To his surprise, the door to the holding cell opened and in walked two Germans. One carried a leather bag while the other held a rifle. The man with the bag peeled off Hank's blindfold and untied his ropes. He opened his bag and pulled out bandages, a stethoscope, a syringe, and various bottles of medication. He produced scissors and cut away Hank's shirtsleeve. Probing delicately, he scraped tiny bullet fragments from Hank's forearm, then cleaned and dressed the wound with alcohol swabs and cotton bandages, applying stitches as needed. He bandaged Hank's head, stuck the syringe into his exposed arm, and forced a pill down Hank's throat.

After pressing the stethoscope against the American's chest, the SS doctor seemed satisfied and left the room. His companion then blindfolded Hank and tied him up.

The door closed, and Hank was alone again in total darkness, still not knowing where he was nor what was about to happen next.

Chapter 11

TRUTH AND DECEPTION

Water continued to drip down into small puddles on the dank floor of the holding cell. Lieutenant Hank Mitchell lay on the ground still tightly bound to the knocked-over chair, madly licking at the muddy pools of moisture on the cell floor. Entombed in total darkness, Hank had no conception of time or where he was. He would pass out, only to awake from hunger pangs and a parched throat. Though his wounds had been treated and pain reliever administered, he had not been fed or given water for what seemed to him like days. He was filthy, drenched in dried perspiration, blood, and dirt that gave off a foul, pungent odor.

During one of his conscious moments, Hank heard voices and the sound of the cell door being unbolted and opened. Artificial light once again poured into the cell. He sensed multiple voices around him as he was grabbed by the shoulders, lifted off the floor, and set upright. He squinted as unseen hands wrenched off the blindfold and his eyes tried to adjust to the light from the doorway. A large kerosene lantern was brought in and placed on the table, where it brightly illuminated the whole room. Hank blinked wildly as his keen eyes adjusted to the light and visions of human forms started to appear more clearly. He could make out two uniformed men standing in front of him. He recognized one as the mysterious, English-speaking officer who had questioned him earlier. The other he had not seen before, although he appeared to be an SS officer, as well.

The officer who had talked with Hank earlier turned his head toward the door and addressed an unseen guard standing outside.

"*Geben Sie mir ein wenig Wasser!*" he ordered. A moment later the guard appeared with a glass of water. The officer took the glass and held it to Hank's lips. He guzzled the water as fast as the German could pour it down his swollen throat. Hank coughed hard, trying not to expel a single drop of the precious liquid. When the glass was empty the officer turned again to the guard and said, "*Nehmen Sie das fort!*" The guard took the glass and exited the cell, leaving Hank with the two officers. Silence ensued as the men sized each other up.

"*Was hat er, Obersturmbannführer Steinert? Er spricht wenig,*" coldly remarked the unidentified officer.

"*Das ist doch ganz einfach. Er hat Angst, Gruppenführer von Schreiner,*" replied the other.

With a sinister snicker the first officer replied, "*Ah, ich verstehe.*"

Hank listened to the pair helplessly, unable to understand their conversation. He did, however, pick up on their names—Steinert and von Schreiner. He noticed that the officer who had spoken to him earlier in English was not wearing the black uniform he had worn previously, but rather an updated, field-gray version, with most of the military insignia and accoutrements minus the ornate dagger.

The second officer, von Schreiner, wore a similar uniform, but was superior in rank to Steinert. He had an air of arrogance about him, common to those in command, which profoundly exhibited itself whenever he spoke. His uniform also seemed superior to his comrade's. The black collar patches of his tunic carried mirrored pairs of silvery embroidered rank insignia that looked much like three feathers crossed at the base and pointing upward. The shoulder straps were standard SS pattern and had toxic, green-colored piping. His hat had the same *totenkopf* skull and crossbones device, and his lower left sleeve the same diamond shaped patch, with the letters "SD" on it. He wore a Knight's Cross medal just like his comrade's; his had small oakleaves and was worn around the neck. The latter sported a gold Nazi Party badge as well as a brightly colored, horizontal ribbon board above it.

Gruppenführer von Schreiner looked younger than Steinert and had black hair, but bore a black eye patch over his left eye. Hank recalled *Treasure Island*, the book he had been reading before he arrived in

England. Visions of pirates and Long John Silver swirled in his head as he wondered if this *SS-Gruppenführer* might be some sort of bloodthirsty pirate himself.

The two Nazis stood over the imprisoned American flyer, pointing to and gesturing at him. The *Gruppenführer* casually walked around Hank in a circle, with his hands gripped behind his back. He eyed Hank's rank insignia and commented to *Obersturmbannführer* Steinert, who shook his head affirmatively.

Von Schreiner's fascination with Hank ended abruptly, and he motioned for Steinert to leave. The mysterious English-speaking officer extinguished the lantern. The *Gruppenführer* hastily exited the cell and brushed past another man standing outside. Steinert stood in the doorway for a moment and angrily eyed the man before stepping aside and out of sight.

The airman looked up and instantly recognized the man now standing in the doorway before him. It was the Nazi agent from the Tessier farm! He was still wearing his black suit and red tie. He viciously scowled at the American, then shouted *"Schweinhund!"* before stomping off.

Hank stared in the direction of the open cell door with a heavy heart, not knowing what was to become of him or if he would be able to help the Tessiers, whom he hoped were alive. However, before he could formulate another thought, two SS guards entered the room and began slashing off all of Hank's clothes with long knives.

Still tied to the chair, the American was now completely naked, save for the bloody bandages that covered his wounds. The guards took away the tattered uniform and replaced the blindfold over his eyes. The cell door slammed shut, immersing Hank in total darkness once again. His cold, trembling, naked body pulsated with pain. He took deep breaths and prayed he would pass out. For the moment his wish would not come true.

As Hank helplessly languished in his cell, the two SS officers, Steinert and von Schreiner, made their way up a long, dimly lit stone staircase. At the top they entered an ornate corridor decorated with fine oil paintings, plush carpeting, and crystal chandeliers—a stark contrast with the setting they had just left. Several SS guards snapped to attention as the two walked past. As they navigated through several spacious and lavishly decorated rooms and connecting hallways, the pair eventually arrived at a set of large wooden doors opened for them by two SS guards standing on either side.

Steinert and von Schreiner now entered a large room filled with comfortable furniture, a fireplace, large bookcases overflowing with leather-bound books, a bar stocked with various liquors, and a resplendent wooden desk covered with papers and files and a bronzed nameplate that read "*SS-Gruppenführer* Gerhard von Schreiner." Massive paintings of the *Führer* and *Reichsführer-SS* Heinrich Himmler covered the walls. Large red flags bearing the Nazi swastika draped limply over wooden flagpoles flanking a towering leather chair behind the desk. Throughout the office were various symbols of National Socialism. A bust of Adolf Hitler perched atop a narrow wooden pedestal alongside a large picturesque window that overlooked the outside grounds.

Steinert looked out the window at the bleak sky. A solid deck of clouds yielded drizzly raindrops that gently rolled down the window. It eerily appeared like Jolieville was blanketed in an unnatural and perpetual gloom. It was as if God himself were channeling the most miserably foul weather systems to assault the tiny French town, as if to try to wash away all the evil entrenched within. While nearby towns and villages were being treated with warm sunshine, Jolieville seemed cursed with an unending stretch of dismal, rainy weather.

Von Schreiner sat down behind his desk and began shuffling through scattered files and papers littering the desktop. Steinert sat down in a facing chair and waited patiently. He had practiced this particular exercise of lingering many times before until it had become routine. Von Schreiner gathered a pile of papers filled with various requests and orders needing signatures and approvals. Like a callous automaton, the eye-patch-wearing Nazi grabbed the nearest fountain pen, unscrewed the cap, dipped it in an inkwell, and scribbled his name across the bottom of the first page in front of him, rubber-stamping a red-circled SS insignia next to it. The double sig rune symbol adopted by the SS resembled a pair of lightning bolts hurtling down from the sky.

Von Schreiner signed and stamped the next page without reading the detailed contents above his signature. He repeated this action continuously until the last page had been signed, stamped, and shuffled away from his view. He then sat back in his chair and rubbed his forehead. After a moment of silence he sat up, folded his hands on the desk, and simply said, *"Die Amerikaner?"*

Steinert came to attention and began speaking to his superior officer in a calm, eloquent manner. The two conversed on the subject of the captured American pilot for several minutes. Occasionally von Schreiner would rise and pace back and forth behind the desk, but never raised his voice. Steinert simply sat in his chair and calmly addressed his superior. After several minutes, von Schreiner walked to the bar and picked up a bottle of Hennessy cognac, poured two glasses, and gave one to Steinert. They held them up in the direction of a painting of the Führer, then drank heartily.

Before von Schreiner could pour another, the office doors burst open amid shouting protests from the SS guards standing outside. In stormed the black-suited agent. He ignored Steinert and rushed up to von Schreiner. Steinert turned and snapped his fingers in the direction of the baffled guards, who gave a quick Nazi salute and exited the room, closing the doors behind them.

"Eichner!" roared von Schreiner as the angered civilian-clad Nazi charged at him. Steinert stepped aside, his arms folded, as von Schreiner and Eichner clashed in a fury of deafening words and wild gestures. The two hollered at each other, often nose tip to nose tip, with neither wanting to back down. Steinert stood by calmly.

Steinert snickered to himself as Eichner pulled the handkerchief from his breast pocket and wiped away the perspiration from his forehead. Still seething, the Gestapo agent pointed to Steinert and voiced his displeasure in a cooler, yet more sinister manner. Von Schreiner immediately responded, then motioned for Eichner to leave the office. The disgruntled Gestapo agent adjusted his round spectacles and straightened his tie before striding to Steinert and looking him in the eyes.

"*Der Amerikaner ist meiner!*" he said in a low and sinister voice. Steinert said nothing, but stared right back at him without twitching. Eichner slowly backed away and walked to the doors, intentionally throwing them open with a harsh bravado that caused the guards outside to leap to attention. With a parting threat, he glared at Steinert and said, "*Der Amerikaner ist meiner! Heil, Hitler!*" The guards closed the doors as the man in black stormed off.

The two SS officers conferred for a few minutes until the distant sounds of sirens, anti-aircraft fire, and droning bomber engines could be heard. Steinert and von Schreiner stepped to the window. The view revealed much, through a window that was part of a grand French château atop a large hill overlooking a small French town not far from the coast. It was isolated, luxurious, and very defensible—an ideal spot for German invaders to set up, command, and occupy.

Steinert scanned the leaden sky as von Schreiner witnessed German troops and French civilians scattering like ants in the streets of the town below. Suddenly faint booms could be heard off in the distance—the sounds of bombs dropping. They were undoubtedly the work of agile low-flying American B-26 Marauders slicing in through the clouds to deliver their payloads before vanishing without a trace. Steinert had to admire the Americans for risking these hit-and-run tactics in such inclement weather. Von Schreiner only scowled and thrust the drapes shut. The two sat back down and talked while von Schreiner drew up and signed some orders that he handed to Steinert. For the moment, both men seemed pleased.

One man who was far from being pleased was Lieutenant Henry Mitchell. Strapped to his holding cell chair, naked and blindfolded, the subdued pilot could feel the faint tremors of distant bomb hits. The damp basement cell shuddered ever so slightly from the shock waves. For a second Hank forgot how cold, hurt, and hungry he was, as he delighted in the thought that some Germans close by might be catching hell from the distant bomber attack. Soon the tremors stopped and the pilot was left drowning in a pool of darkness and silence. He was hungry, but there was no food to be had. He desperately wanted to drink, but found himself too weak even to struggle for the muddied pools of water on the floor. He prayed he would fall unconscious—even permanently—and alleviate the pain wracking his body, but the damp chill in the air kept his naked body shivering and his mind running endlessly.

Eventually he did pass out; for how long he didn't know. At some point the cell door creaked opened, then shut again. Hank awoke to the sensation of his ropes being cut away from his hands and feet. As the circulation gradually returned to his freed extremities, he raised his numb and shaking right hand and painfully pulled off the blindfold.

His bleary eyes slowly focused on a dark, shadowy figure sitting in the chair across from him. A single burning candle atop the nearby table provided the only illumination in the room. From the dark corner a hand emerged gripping a tall glass of water. It pushed the glass into Hank's reach, whereupon the suffering airman seized it and speedily drank it down. Next his visitor gave him several small scraps of stale bread, which he hungrily gnawed at, quietly thankful his body was receiving some small form of nourishment. He wanted to speak but thought better of it, instead making sure every last crumb found its way into his mouth.

The next thing Hank felt was the sensation of clothing being dropped into his naked lap—a shirt, a pair of pants, a hat, and even an old pair of leather shoes. His weak, trembling hands sifted through the clothing. Afraid of making a wrong move, he turned his head in the direction of the shadowy figure seated at the table, his face purposely positioned away from the dim light. A few seconds elapsed, then …

"Put the clothes on," whispered a familiar British-accented voice through the darkness. Hank gathered all the energy he could and painfully got to his feet. His numbed arms and legs tingled madly as blood flooded into the shivering limbs. He rammed an arm through each shirtsleeve. With throbbing fingers, he painfully buttoned up the front. He then pulled on the pants and tucked in the shirt. There were suspenders attached to the pants that Hank strapped over his shoulders. He slumped back onto the chair and slipped his bare feet into the shoes. They were well worn and ripped in places along the base near the soles. The laces were frayed, but intact, and the size too big for his feet. It didn't matter, though. Hank was relieved he had things to put on no matter how ragged or abused they might be.

The voice from the shadows whispered again.

"Today is your most promising day, flying-officer. You're being transferred from here to more … shall we say … suitable living conditions."

Hank looked in the direction of Steinert, who sat in the chair, his legs comfortably crossed and his face obscured by the flickering light.

"And where would that be? A nice hotel in the heart of Paris? Oh wait, I forgot. You're actually an English Nazi. We must be going to jolly old London to feast on fish and chips and some English pudding with Winston Churchill, right?" said Hank sarcastically, his voice weak and raspy.

Unimpressed by the American's wisecrack, Steinert leaned forward into the candle's light with a face of stone. He stared hard at the American who could barely keep his head up. The peculiar Nazi slid his hand down over the right side of his waist until it came to rest on his holstered Luger.

"This is the last time I'm going to say this, so you had better listen and understand, flying-officer," seethed Steinert with little patience evident in his voice. "You are alive right now because of me. You have been given medical attention because of me. You have been provided clothing, food, and water because of me! You would be drowning in a pool of your own blood right now at the hands of the Gestapo if not for me. You have been reluctantly placed in my charge, and the reason you haven't been interrogated to death by now is because there are no English-speaking interpreters in this area."

"Well, you seem to speak English quite well," insolently cracked Hank.

"I don't have time for your bloody nonsense, Yank! Don't forget about your dear friends the Tessiers. Your only chance to help them is to cooperate with me, whether you like it or not! Now get on your bloody feet!" ordered Steinert, still managing to express his rage at a whisper.

Hank fell silent and gathered his strength. He stood up as tall and straight as he could, as if he were being addressed by one of his superior officers back home. He wanted to prove that even without a uniform or proper nourishment he was still a U.S. Army Air Force officer and demanded to be treated as such. The drained American airman stood toe to toe in a defiant standoff with the English-speaking Nazi. His haggard face grim and hard, he looked the Nazi squarely in the eyes. Visions of going for the Nazi's gun entered his mind, but he thought better of it. Steinert, not wanting his authority tested, grabbed Hank by the arm and spun him around. He picked up the ropes on the floor and bound Hank's hands together. Next he wound the blindfold tightly around Hank's head, causing it to throb with discomfort. Steinert then reached into his pocket and produced a large piece of cloth that he used to gag the unsuspecting man.

"In case you can't keep that big Yankee yap of yours shut," jeered Steinert. Hank's teeth bit down hard on the cloth that burrowed deep into his lips and cheeks.

Steinert called out for the SS guards who entered and shoved Hank outside the cell.

The only voices the airman heard now were German ones. He was hustled up the stairs and led through long corridors that echoed his footsteps and those of the ones forcing him along. Soon a door opened and filled Hank's nostrils with the scent of fresh air for the first time in what seemed like an eternity. More German voices surrounded him and the airman felt himself being forced up and into the back of some sort of vehicle, where he slumped down on the floor. He heard the voices of several German troops who climbed into the back and sat down with weapons at the ready. The sound of a tailgate being lifted and secured filled Hank's ears. He concluded he was in the back of a covered truck or troop carrier.

A German seated near him shouted out an order and banged on the floor with his rifle butt. An engine started up, exhaust belched out the tailpipe, and Hank could hear the sound of shifting gears grinding as the truck began to roll forward gradually picking up speed. At the foot of a long, sloping hill it came to a halt. After a brief conversation in German, Hank heard the sound of a metal gate being opened, and the truck rolled through the gate and started down a dirt road.

The soldiers sitting in the back with Hank chatted away and occasionally laughed. Some lit up cigarettes as the truck swayed back and forth down the road. Hank sat grimly silent and listened for any clue that might help reveal where he was going. The truck lumbered on down the dirt road. As the driver reached a sharp curve in the road, he downshifted and slowed to a nearly complete stop.

A sudden explosion rocked the front of the truck, blowing off the right front tire and sending fragments of jagged metal knifing upward through the engine. The damaged motor seized up, emitting streams of smoke and flame through holes in the hood. Minus the tire blown from the axle, the vehicle crumpled forward and down to the right.

Dazed and bloodied by the blast, the driver peered through the windshield just as a hailstorm of bullets slashed through the shattered glass and ripped into his body, killing him instantly. The five German SD troops hollered to each other and leapt out the back, only to be met by ferocious machine-gun fire that seemed to be coming from all directions. Two were hit and killed instantly before firing a shot, while the other three hit the ground and began firing their MP-40 machine guns wildly into the thick hedgerows. Not knowing what was happening around him, Hank hit the floor of the truck and lay as flat as he could as the sounds of ricocheting bullets and feverish cries punctuated the leaden air.

The three remaining Germans were no match for their unknown assailants. Hank heard cries of agonizing pain as they dropped their guns and crumpled to the ground. The attackers then fell upon the dead or dying Germans and plunged knives into their chests, making repeated deep, mutilating cuts. The pained German voices were quickly snuffed out and were replaced by those of men speaking French.

Inside the truck, Hank listened intently to the French voices. A man jumped into the truck and shouted, "*Ici, mes amis! L'Américain est ici! Vite! Vite!*" Someone grabbed Hank by the arms and helped him from the smoldering vehicle. With his hands still tied and the blindfold and gag still in place, the three men hustled the wounded and exhausted American down the dirt road until they eventually reached uneven ground. Hank felt bushes and tree branches claw at him from all directions until his liberators abruptly stopped. One of them dropped to his knees and cleared away thick brush and dirt on the ground. Hank felt the sensation of hands pushing him down into a hole. At first he instinctively resisted, but soon gave in. The three men crammed the unsuspecting American into the ground, then climbed in themselves before covering the hole from the inside. On his knees and with his hands still bound behind him, Hank was prodded forward from behind. He painfully crawled inch by inch, unable to see anything in the pitch black. He struggled to keep his balance. The three men following kept silent.

After crawling forward for several minutes, Hank reached the edge of the tunnel, where he heard the sound of running water below him. At the prodding of those behind him, the airman painfully slid down from the hole until his feet hit water and he was able to stand erect. The three men behind him popped out of the hole and stood up as well. One pulled out a knife and cut off Hank's ropes. Another untied the gag and pulled off the blindfold. The third clicked on a bright flashlight and shined it forward.

Hank gazed at the three who had saved him. They wore dark clothing and dirty scarves or handkerchiefs that hid their faces. All wore hats pulled down low to conceal their eyes. They looked like bandits hidden behind masks. Hank realized they did not desire to be recognized and instead he made an effort to focus on his surroundings. As best he could determine, he was in some sort of underground sewer. The foul stench assaulting his nostrils was overpowering and he heard the squeaks of rats all around. Before he could take in much more, one of the men pushed Hank forward into a side tunnel. After walking a good distance through the smelly muck and putrid water, the four men, led by the one wielding the flashlight, stopped at an iron ladder anchored to the concrete wall. The man in the lead clicked off the flashlight, climbed up a few rungs in the darkness, and stopped. He quietly unlatched a rusty iron trapdoor and struggled to push it open before climbing up and through. Hank followed, as did the two remaining masked men.

All four were now standing in a small room lit by a single electric light bulb dangling by a wire from the ceiling. It appeared to Hank to be a storage space. The walls were fashioned of stone, giving Hank the feeling he was at the bottom of an old well. Crates of liquor, assorted foodstuffs, dry goods, and other supplies marked in German and decorated with black swastikas were stacked in the corners. The last man to enter through the trapdoor swung it closed and slid a heavy crate over it with a mighty heave. The secret exit was now concealed, and the three masked men turned their full attention to the American.

The one closest to Hank pointed to a small set of steps partially hidden behind sacks of flour and sugar. The airman hobbled over to the staircase and looked up to see a small door, with no knob or latch, at the top. Only a faint outline and two tiny hinges all but invisible without close observation revealed that a door was there. At the silent urging of his new companions, Hank stepped up and pulled it open. He squeezed through and up into another room. His three hosts followed. The last man to enter sealed the door behind him and it invisibly blended into the wall. A bookcase slid over to conceal the spot where the secret opening was located.

Hank looked around, observing his new surroundings. This room was slightly larger than the one he had just left. It was sparsely furnished with a single bed, a small table, two wooden chairs, a small writer's desk, and the bookcase—with only four books on it—covering the secret door. The room had one electric light mounted on the wall and a small rectangular window high up by the ceiling and heavily covered by thick drapes. Accessible only by standing on the bed, the window allowed in merely a hint of natural daylight, just enough to see without the aid of electricity. The walls were old and the paint on them and the ceiling had peeled away in many places. Scattered pictures of French landscapes hung askew while a small square mirror hung over the table.

The three masked men conversed briefly, but said nothing to Hank. Two of the men left abruptly through the room's only visible door. Hank could hear their footsteps ascending wooden stairs. The third pointed at Hank and then to the bed. The weary airman understood the Frenchman's gesture and crumpled onto the bed, overcome with fatigue. The Frenchman nodded affirmatively and then made his exit, locking the door behind him. Hank instantly knew his newfound companions didn't want him to go anywhere—at least not unattended. It mattered little for the moment. Overwhelming mental fatigue overpowered his enormous physical pain and provided him some temporary relief with much-needed rest. Within minutes the injured and completely drained

American fell fast asleep. Lieutenant Henry Mitchell seemed safe—for the moment.

Time slipped by while the American slept. He dreamed he was back home, climbing up and down the rocky shore of Maine's picturesque coast. He was a boy again, squinting up at the clear blue sky and feeling the cool ocean breeze flow over his smiling face. He felt young, happy, healthy, and free—without a care in the world. It was a wonderful feeling—a feeling that appeared so real.

Suddenly the skies grew dark and the ocean breeze faded away. The ocean swallowed itself up and Hank was no longer the cheerful boy. He was a man stricken with pain, wearing secondhand civilian clothing, and crushed by the frightful uncertainty of the future. The image of peace and tranquility was gone, and Hank felt only the discomfort of his aching body. He lay on the bed awake, but with his eyes still shut, not wanting to open them for fear of completely shattering the image of the wonderful time and place in his mind.

However, peculiar scents and sounds filled his senses. One in particular caught his attention. It was the soft and distinct scent of a woman hovering very near. Hank slowly lifted his heavy eyelids, gradually revealing the face of a stunning young woman looking down at him. Hank's bloodshot blue eyes locked onto her clear, soft sapphire eyes and saw his tiny reflection in the lovely deep pools of crystal blue. The haggard, disheveled image he saw made him cringe and want to look away. Yet, he couldn't pull his eyes away from the intoxicating beauty standing so near to him.

Without saying a word, the young woman gently rubbed a warm, cleansing cloth over Hank's cheeks, neck, and forehead. Her touch was soft and inviting and fueled Hank's senses and curiosity. Her face was without blemish and her skin appeared naturally smooth and creamy to the touch. Her lips were full and lush, yet not too plump. They were sweetly formed like a little heart every time she showed a petite pearly smile. Her shoulder-length hair was blonde and very straight, partially hidden under a white head kerchief that allowed her flaxen locks to flow down the back and sides of her head while covering the top.

The young woman momentarily stepped back away from Hank to

soak her cloth in a steaming pan of hot water. This allowed the young American a more thorough look at his caregiver. His eyes ran up and down her body as she wrung out the cloth. He watched the water drip into the pan and tried to keep from foolishly gawking as the beauty turned back in his direction. He was enchanted by her slender, hourglass physique. Her body was proportioned beautifully, enhanced by feminine curves. Her breasts were full and firm and mostly hidden by her white blouse that wasn't fully buttoned to the top. Her legs were partially revealed beneath a well-worn, floral-printed, light blue skirt that looked as if it had been longer and fuller when it was new. The hem had been ripped away, pleasantly revealing more of the lower legs than had been originally intended. A small white apron fit snugly around her waist. She was a marvelously attractive woman, whom Hank guessed stood about five-foot-seven and was possibly in her early twenties. The pilot couldn't be happier with the splendid sight of this lovely female and briefly forgot about his bodily pain and the mysteriously dangerous predicament he was in as she continued to wipe the dirt and sweat from his face and neck.

"My name is Pauline. You are safe … for now," she whispered softly. Hank was relieved to hear words in English riding atop the young woman's breath as she spoke. Her accent was deeply French, but her English was comprehensible.

"Where am I? How did you find me?" asked Hank, attempting to sit up.

Pauline responded, "You are safe. We knew where to find you. That is all." She fell silent as she carefully removed the bandage from Hank's head. She cleaned the rifle-butt wound and applied a disinfectant that stung sharply, causing Hank to wince in pain. When she finished she repeated the treatment on Hank's injured arm.

"I must get you clean. The smell … how you say … unbearable?" said Pauline. Hank smiled faintly and couldn't disagree. He was filthy and desperately needed to bathe. But where?

"Okay, I understand," said Hank realizing his questions would have to wait. "First things first." He hauled himself to a sitting position on the bed. "Where can I get cleaned up?"

"Wait here and do not make a sound," quietly replied Pauline. The young woman stood up and walked over to the door. She turned the knob and pulled it open slowly so it wouldn't creak as it swung on its rusty hinges. Hank watched her slip out of view and couldn't help but feel physically attracted to her, even in his weakened state. Hank heard the door latch and lock as it was secured shut. Obviously his lady caregiver didn't want him to go anywhere either.

Moments later Pauline reappeared carrying a round metal washtub. She placed it on the floor in the center of the room. Without a word she left again and returned minutes later with a large wooden bucket of water that she poured into the tub. She repeated the process twice, then brought a teakettle filled with steaming hot water, pouring it into the tub and swirling the water to mix it to an even temperature.

"There," she said quietly. "It is not much, but it will do." Hank stood up and walked gingerly to the tub. He glanced at the clean water, then at Pauline.

"Please give me your clothes," she said as she laid a small bar of soap on the floor next to the tub. He unstrapped his suspenders and unbuttoned his shirt, handed it to Pauline, then reached for the zipper on the front of his pants, but hesitated. He turned his head and looked over at Pauline, who was staring at him as if she were in a trance. After a second or two she snapped out of it and turned her back in embarrassment. Hank pulled his pants down and slid his feet out of the oversized leather shoes. He handed both over to Pauline, who kept turned away.

"*Merci*," she said as she left and locked the door behind her.

Hank looked down at the tub and stepped in. It was much too small to sit in, so he crouched like a baseball catcher and splashed the warm water over his grubby, stinky body. He snatched up the soap and lathered himself, making sure to rub the suds into his face and hair. The compacted layers of dirt and grime began to melt away and Hank almost felt human again. He rinsed away the soap as best he could and stood erect, looking down at the once-clear water that now appeared nearly black as oil.

Hank reached for a dry cloth, dried himself off, wrapped a thin blanket around his waist, and sat on the bed and waited. His stomach growled, reminding him how hungry he was, while the pain of his injuries kept him from getting too comfortable.

Soon Pauline returned with more hot water in her kettle and a clean set of men's clothes. She handed Hank a white shirt, a pair of brown pants and suspenders, and a pair of rolled-up white socks. He dressed while she turned and attended the teakettle on the table. Steam gently rose from the hot water as she poured it into a metal pan. She did not face the American until she knew he was fully clothed.

"How do they fit?" she asked pointing to the shirt and pants.

"Quite well," replied the gracious airman. "It's been a while since I've had the luxury of putting on anything clean. Thank you."

Pauline smiled, but her face contorted in disgust as she spied the filthy water in the tub.

"Please sit down next to me," said Pauline who was seated at the table. She picked up the soap and produced a shaving razor from her pocket. "Please use the soap and … " Not being able to come up with the words, she gestured for Hank to wet and lather his scruffy face.

Hank reached for the soap and water and covered his beard with both. Pauline scooted her chair up behind his and tilted his head back. She carefully shaved away several days of growth from the American's face and neck. When she finished Hank rinsed and dried his newly shaven face. Pauline pulled a comb from her pocket that Hank used to tame his damp and disheveled hair. He glanced at the mirror and saw a face resembling the one he had seen in his barracks mirror just before leaving Jefferson Airfield.

"Is better … no?" said Pauline, looking at his reflection in the mirror.

"Yes," said Hank with a smile. "It's much better."

The airman stood and stretched his arms toward the ceiling. His stiff back cracked while twinges of pain rippled through his extended left arm and shoulder, causing him to wince. His right foot and ankle throbbed as well, forcing him to shift his weight onto his other foot. The injuries sustained during his bailout and parachute landing were again causing him discomfort. Feeling lightheaded, he sat down on the bed.

"You must tell me where it pains you," said Pauline, sitting down next to Hank.

Hank answered, "My left foot and right shoulder were hurt when I landed. I'm an American Army Air Force pilot who got shot down. I was cared for by an elderly French couple who treated my wounds. Eventually the Germans found and captured me after grazing my right forearm with a bullet and bashing my skull with a rifle butt." Hank pointed to each injury as Pauline shook her head in acknowledgment. She motioned for him to turn around and then massaged his back and shoulders to alleviate the discomfort.

Hank continued to tell Pauline how he happened to come to be in her care. He disclosed his name, rank, and serial number, then generalized all subsequent information and made sure not to give any specific details about the logistics of his failed mission. He mentioned the air battle and getting shot down. He told her about the Tessier farm, his eventual capture, and lastly, about his SS captors.

The young woman listened intently. She refocused her treatment to Hank's surface wounds, applying fresh bandages to his forearm and head, which were already healing. She then lifted his injured foot onto her lap and began to massage, manipulate, and probe it, looking for areas of discomfort. Hank lay back on the bed and thought about kind old Lily Tessier, who had provided the same wonderful treatment days earlier.

Hank's mind filled with questions and concerns. The thought of the Tessiers and their present unknown situation made him uncomfortable. He had to find out where he was, what was going to happen, and how he was going to help them. Thoughts of their safe recovery from the clutches of the Gestapo superseded all concerns of his own escape from occupied France. Questions started to roll off his tongue.

"Pauline, where exactly am I, and what's today's date? I really must know."

Pauline continued to rub his foot. She didn't look at him and hesitated before quietly answering. "You are not far from where you were captured and held by the Germans. This is a small town … " Her voice trailed off, and Hank sensed her reluctance to reveal much. He pressed her anyway.

"What is today? I need to know the date … please."

She answered, "Today is Saturday, the twenty-seventh of May, 1944."

The date somewhat startled Hank as he was completely unaware of how long he had been in German captivity. Several days had passed during his confinement and lack of consciousness.

He replied, "And the location? Where are we? What is this place?"

Pauline said nothing and did not look at Hank. Reluctantly Hank pulled his foot from her soothing touch and sat up next to her. He looked her in the eyes and repeated, "Where are we?" When Pauline again did not answer, the airman began to doubt her.

"Pauline, you and your associates are French Resistance, right?"

"*Oui ... Resistance*," she answered unconvincingly.

"Is this town called Jolieville?" asked Hank, as Maurice Tessier's map flashed in his mind.

Pauline stood up with her back to Hank and clasped her hands to her chest. When he repeated the question she meekly nodded her head. For the first time in days Hank had a clear understanding of where he was. He was still in Jolieville and, hopefully, so were the Tessiers.

Hank then asked, "How many of you are there? Where are the men who brought me here? How many German ... "

"Stop!" interrupted Pauline, raising her voice. She turned to confront him. Her face filled with serious concern, bordering on fear.

"Please ... no more questions. I have told you too much already. I can help you, but you must stop with the questions. Please," she pleaded. The young woman turned to look at the door as she waited for Hank's next words.

"Pauline," Hank said, "I've given you much information about myself and how I got here. If I seem too inquisitive, it's only because lives are at stake. The lives of the couple that helped me depend on my actions here and now. Time is the enemy ... and I don't have much time. I need your help badly ... and that help depends on what you can tell me!"

Pauline put her hand on the doorknob and answered, "I cannot tell you any more."

Hank replied, "Why not?"

Pauline opened the door and the next voice Hank heard was a

man's, speaking in a horrifyingly familiar British accent.

"Because she is not in charge. ... I am!"

The door swung open and Pauline stepped aside. Hank's eyes grew wide and his body stiffened as the terrifying figure of an *SS-Obersturmbannführer* stood before him. This time it was not immersed in the shadowy darkness of a dimly lit holding cell. Every detail was now clearly visible. The pilot ran his eyes up and down the field-gray SS uniform standing before him, then stopped and locked on the man's face. In a fraction of a second, every feature of his facade was burned into Hank's memory. Lieutenant Henry Mitchell and *SS-Obersturmbannführer* Steinert were thrust together once again!

Hank's fear instantly transformed to rage at the sight of the SS officer. Adrenaline surged through his body, causing him to leap off the bed and rush Steinert.

"No! Stop!" shrieked Pauline, as she threw herself between Hank and Steinert. Hank cocked his right arm, ready to bury his right fist into the German's face, but was abruptly stopped by Pauline and the sight of the black muzzle of Steinert's Luger pointed at his head.

"Please! Do not fight! He is here to help you!" pleaded Pauline while pushing Hank back toward the bed. Stunned at her words, Hank tripped on his own feet and fell backward onto the bed. He quickly concluded that he was once again a prisoner of the SS and decided to offer no further resistance.

Steinert holstered his pistol and spoke to Pauline in French. She responded in her native tongue, looked at Hank, then left the room, closing the door behind her.

"I trust you're well, Leftenant?" asked Steinert as he sat down in one of the wooden chairs. "You look as if you've been treated very admirably by my lovely young associate. Pauline is ... quite extraordinary when it comes to matters of healing one's body. Wouldn't you agree?"

Hank sat on the bed and said nothing.

Steinert continued, "I see that you're going to play that stupid game again. Silence can be a virtue in some circumstances, but it may not necessarily help you here. I can assure you of one thing—the more you cooperate, the better it will be for all of us. That includes you, Pauli her associates, me, and that nice old French couple. You do remember them, don't you?"

Hank's head perked up at the mention of the Tessiers. "Where are they?"

The cool-headed Steinert answered, "Keep your voice down. In case you haven't already noticed it, English is not the preferential language spoken in this part of the world. The less attention you draw to yourself, or to me, for that matter, the better things shall be overall. Mark my words."

Hank scowled at the SS officer and resisted every urge to lunge at his throat with both hands, in hopes of squeezing the life out of him.

"Your friends, the Tessiers, are under my care, much like you're under my care right now. If you want to help them, then you must do everything I say. There is no negotiation on that point, Leftenant."

"You can go to hell, you Gestapo bastard," replied Hank indignantly.

Steinert sighed deeply and stood up. He fumed, but chose not to verbally or physically attack the American. Instead he climbed up on the bed and pulled the blinds from the small window, letting in what little sunlight there was outside.

With a sinister chuckle, Steinert addressed the American, saying, "I am not Gestapo." He pointed to the window, then said, "Right now, on the other side of this glass, the Gestapo is tearing apart this town, searching for you! Only the constant interruption of bombs and fighter attacks from Allied air forces have kept the Gestapo from wiping out this entire town looking for you. I can see that you still don't trust me, and perhaps you never will, but the fact remains that your life is entirely in my hands. Know this: I orchestrated your rescue. You are sitting in the last and final bastion of resistance in this immediate area. It is comprised entirely of Pauline and her three male associates who so graciously gunned down six of my men to retrieve you and bring you here. I'll have you know that the lives of those SS men cost this town twenty innocent souls! A few innocent French dairy farmers happened upon the incident moments after you departed. Before they even had a chance to figure out what had happened, they were preyed upon by an SS security detail that rushed to the scene after hearing the explosion and subsequent gunfire.

Those poor French citizens were slaughtered on the spot. After they were identified, armed SS men found their families and murdered them, as well. If you would like to visit them, their fresh corpses are hanging by piano wire in the center of town, with signs around their necks warning whoever is still alive to see them, that killing sons of the Reich will only bring misery and death on those foolish enough to think otherwise. SS justice is as swift as it is brutal. You might want to consider what your freedom has cost this town and quite possibly several other towns in the vicinity this very day."

At this point, Steinert's tongue-lashing was interrupted by the drone of aircraft, distant anti-aircraft fire, and the familiar thud of bombs slamming into the ground. The room shook and Steinert stood back from the small window lest some stray shrapnel unexpectedly blast its way inside.

"The time is near. When and where is the ultimate question, though." Steinert turned to Hank and asked, "When is the invasion and where do the Allies plan to land?"

Stunned at the question, the young American replied with silence.

"No. You wouldn't know, would you? Even if you did I sense you wouldn't tell me … no matter how much torture I subjected you to," said Steinert. "Okay. This is how it's going to be. You're going to stay here until I decide what to do with you. Pauline and her associates will look after you and keep you hidden. If you decide to leave under your own free will, rest assured you will be captured and killed, if not by the Germans then definitely by the townspeople who will turn you in immediately upon your discovery. You're an American who is a stranger to this town and who doesn't speak any French. You'd stick out like a sore thumb. Just remember this: Only I know where the Tessiers are and how to help them. If you truly want to save their lives and your own, then you'd better start showing me some respect!"

Steinert moved to the door and knocked twice. Hank heard footsteps and the sound of the door being unlocked from the other side. Before it opened, Steinert turned to Hank and said, "I have something for you. Take it as a sign of good faith. You'll know what I'm talking about soon enough."

With that he left the room and stomped upstairs and out of the building. Hank stood up tall on the bed, peered through the small window, and watched the curious Nazi climb into his staff car with the help of his driver and another SS man, then speed away. Hank crumpled down onto the bed, not knowing what to think or who to trust. He felt surrounded by an inescapable web of lies and deceptions spun by persons unknown. Who were his allies and who were his enemies? Who was this mysterious English-speaking Nazi named Steinert, and what was his interest in Hank? Where were the Tessiers and how could he help them? Who could he trust and how was he going to get himself out alive? All questions a weary Hank Mitchell could not answer. He was again forced to continue doing the very thing he had done and despised since he was wrenched free from his battered P-51 Mustang—he had to wait.

Hours passed and it became dark again. Hank spent most of his time since meeting with Steinert listening to every sound he could hear coming from the world outside; however, he ultimately grew tired and fell asleep. As the evening darkness enveloped his small room, Hank heard the sound of soft footsteps and that of the door being unlocked and quietly swung open. He rolled over on the bed, terrified that someone was in the room with him, but he couldn't see who it was. The visitor struck a match and lit a candle. Its soft glow revealed the lovely face of Pauline sitting at the small table with a tray of food in front of her. Hank's heart raced at the sight of the strikingly beautiful young woman, while his stomach growled at the sight of a bowl of steaming soup, bread, and a water glass on the tray. He sat up and faced Pauline.

"Do not reach for the light switch. It is not safe to turn on the lights at night. Even this candle is dangerous," said Pauline as she motioned for Hank to sit at the table and help himself to the food she had prepared.

"*Mon Dieu*," exclaimed Pauline at the sight of the uncovered window. She rushed up and quickly closed the drapes that Steinert had so carelessly opened earlier. She angrily mumbled a few words in French under her breath before sitting next to Hank, now quietly spooning hot tomato soup down his throat.

"How do you feel?" asked Pauline in the glow of the candlelight.

Hank kept his head down and continued to eat.

"You are angry with me?" said Pauline. Still Hank said nothing while repeatedly lifting the soupspoon to his mouth.

"Yes … you have anger with me. Do you not trust me?" she asked.

Hank put down the spoon and after a moment's hesitation, decided to answer. "I'm very confused right now. I'm not sure who to trust. You've given me aid, food, and shelter, but for all I know, you and your associates are nothing more than Nazi sympathizers just waiting for the right moment to profit by turning me over to your Gestapo friend Steinert!"

"We are not friends to the Nazis! We do not help them in any way! They are filthy, brutal, murderous conquerors that must be obliterated from France forever! We are French Resistance and we fight Germany … just like America!" expounded Pauline with passion in her breath that took the airman by surprise.

"I don't believe you and I don't believe that English-speaking Nazi son-of-a-bitch!" exclaimed Hank with a thud of his fist on the table that caused his soup bowl to jump. "I wish you people would stop playing with me and just cart me off to some POW camp before I lose my mind!"

"Your life has been saved and you are with friends. I assure you of this," implored Pauline.

"Do all French Resistance members collaborate so closely with Nazis?" Hank asked with heated breath.

"You know nothing. You are an arrogant American who knows nothing of our struggle against Germany!" replied the uneasy young woman.

"I'm not blind, though! And I'm smart enough to figure out what the sight of a uniformed SS officer standing right in front of me means. It means that I am in a huge pile of shit, lady!" said Hank angrily.

Pauline did not respond. She sat motionless, contemplating the consequences of her next words. Hank arrogantly resumed eating.

She said, "He is not a Nazi. He … he is a British spy. He helps us fight for our country and our freedom. You must understand this?"

"Bullshit!" shouted Hank. "He's a Nazi, plain and simple! And even if you are who you say you are, then I fear for you and all of France because you just let the fox into the hen house! He's obviously got you all fooled into believing he's your friend when in reality he and the Gestapo have fully infiltrated whatever pitiful organization of resistance you've put together here!"

"Keep your voice down," pleaded Pauline. "There are informers everywhere!" She glared at Hank, then watched as he settled down again, before deciding to continue the conversation.

"He is not Gestapo," she said calmly. "And he has not … how you say … infiltrated anything. He works with us. He has given us much information about the Germans. He protects us and keeps us from the Gestapo and the death camps. In time you will see this for yourself. You will have trust, I promise you!"

"You're crazy. Just what am I supposed to do here? Stay locked in this room until the Gestapo breaks down the door? You speak of trust, then let's start seeing some right now. There are two people out there who desperately need my help. If you are who you say you are, then help me bring them to safety."

"You speak of the people who helped you after you were shot down—the Tessiers, *oui*? Herr Steinert has told us about them and your eagerness to help them. We can do nothing at the moment … not until Herr Steinert tells us," she said. "For now you must stay here. I will bring you food and attend to your injuries. Please do not try to leave. You will be killed if you do. Be patient, I beg you."

Pauline rose and walked to the door, turning to look at Hank with a sad, but understanding expression. The American, full of mistrust and frustration, stared deeply into her eyes. There was something about her that compelled him to trust her. She seemed so young and innocent. How could she be evil? Hank felt a strong physical attraction to this beautiful young woman—an attraction that could very well cloud his better judgment, but certainly couldn't be ignored.

Pauline said, "Goodnight," and opened the door.

"Wait," said Hank. "Steinert said he had something for me. Something that would be a sign of good faith. What is it? Do you have it?"

"Soon," Pauline said. "When you have shown *me* some trust." With that the young woman slipped out the door. As it closed, Hank heard the familiar sound of the door locking and footsteps heading upstairs.

Resigned to the fact he was still helpless and at the mercy of his captors, Hank settled for finishing his meal and trying to get a good night's rest. He blew out the candle and climbed into bed. For a moment he could hear the sound of distant droning bomber engines and anti-aircraft fire. Irritated, he covered his ears and fell asleep.

Chapter 12

THOSE WE TRUST

Hank Mitchell awoke from his slumber feeling restless and full of questions. He needed answers and desperately desired a plan of action to get him out of his current predicament. He was completely helpless and he knew it. Tumbling amidst all the thoughts and uncertainties pertaining to his present situation, he paused for a moment and wondered deeply about the rest of his air assault force. Brady was dead—there was no question of that—but what of Hendricks and Dandridge? Were they alive and well, back in England, or had they been blown from the sky with their ashes scattered to the wind? And what of Captain Wheeler and his bomber crew? Had they managed to ward off their attackers and hit the target before returning safely to Jefferson Airfield, or were they languishing in Nazi prison camps alongside countless other Allied air crews shot from the sky? Maybe they were all rotting and suffering in dark holding cells, courtesy of Herr Steinert—or even Pauline, for that matter.

Fighting his better judgment and doing the best he could to tune out the thoughts of his fellow airmen and the Tessiers, the unsettled fighter pilot began quietly rummaging through his room to see what he could find and use to his advantage. His search turned up nothing of interest or utility in the writing desk or under the bed. Hank quietly walked over to the door and tried the knob out of curiosity. Not surprisingly the door was locked and bolted. Undeterred, he turned his attention to the bookcase. He silently slid it aside looking for the secret door that lay hidden in the wall behind it. Amazingly, Hank couldn't find the edges! He ran his fingers up and down the wall, feeling for even the slightest imperfection, but found nothing. His eyes scanned the smooth wall looking for any type of bump, notch, or crack that might reveal the door's exact location, but again came up empty. Hank stood back in total bewilderment at how perfectly the secret door was hidden. Hank slid the bookcase back in place and realized his captors were more clever than he gave them credit for.

Frustrated, the airman collapsed on his bed and lay quietly. He closed his eyes and listened aggressively for any perceptible sound that might constitute a threat. He heard very little. Occasionally there was the sound of footsteps from upstairs accompanied by muffled indecipherable rumblings in French, but no voices in German, which provided a sense of ease.

As time passed Hank got up and paced back and forth. Ignoring all logic of safety, he stood on the bed and repeatedly peeked out the window. The small window was right at street level and didn't offer much of a view. Just an empty cobblestone street and a few buildings across the way that looked like deserted apartments. He could make out a few anti-Semitic signs and some dreary looking Waffen-SS recruitment posters, but nothing else that gave him any hope or encouragement. Some Nazi flags hung limply outside a few buildings in the soaking drizzle and seemed symbolic of the morose state the town was in. There was very little sign of life anywhere. The wet skies prevailed, and the sad little town seemed to soak up all the gloom the raw disagreeable weather rained down upon it.

As Hank peered outside he noticed a detachment of German troops march by, which made him immediately hunker down on his bed, out of sight. It was just as well. The sight of the *Wehrmacht* was not as depressing as that of Jolieville as a whole. The town looked tired and run down. Four years of war and neglect had left all the structures still standing appearing like gray ghostly shells—barren and devoid of life or purpose. The town was essentially dead.

Hank sat impatiently on his bed and waited. He could do nothing else, it seemed. His mind wandered back to Pauline. As much as he wanted to figure out her role and real intentions, he couldn't help but unwisely dwell on her stunning beauty. As much as he wanted to convince himself otherwise, he was enthralled with his new caregiver. Hank yearned to see her again, not necessarily because of any news or hot food she might share, but simply because he loved the feel of the nervous tingles that rippled through his stomach every time he pictured her face. He just hoped she was on his side and not some enticing piece of bait tantalizingly dangled in front of him, in hopes of ensnaring all he knew about his top-secret mission.

The hours passed slowly without mercy. Faint sounds of activity came from upstairs, but nothing readily distinguishable. At length Hank heard soft footsteps coming down the stairs. He stood by the bed and faced the door. Hank took a deep breath as it was unlocked and slowly swung open. Pauline's striking form emerged with food and water on a wooden serving tray. Hank trembled with delight, secretly overjoyed to see her and not Steinert. Without saying a word she motioned for him to sit down at the table and eat.

"Don't go," said Hank when Pauline turned for the door. "Please stay and talk with me for a while. I've spent so much time alone. I ... I really need to talk with someone, and I'd like to talk with you."

Pauline hesitated for a moment, then cautiously made her way back to the table. A somewhat irritated and impatient look was detectable on her face as she sat down and stared at the American.

Hank continued, "I want to apologize if I offended you earlier by what I said. You've treated me well in the short time I've been here, and perhaps I don't have all the facts straight. Regardless of what happens to me, I want to thank you for your kind treatment. I owe you some trust, although I hope you can understand my position and stubbornness. Put yourself in my shoes for a moment and ask yourself how you would feel and what you would think if our roles were reversed."

Pauline responded, "Lieutenant Mitchell, you have been through much pain. This I know. But your pain does not compare to mine. Your suffering does not compare to mine. You have been imprisoned in France for several days, yes? I have been imprisoned in France—my own country—for four years! You are a soldier, yes? A pilot? You fight the Germans in the air for very brief encounters only to return to the safety and comfort of your home base where you rest and wait to fly again. I fight the Germans every day and every night with little or no rest and in constant terror of being discovered and killed. I have seen countless acts of destruction and senseless murder. I have lost many loved ones and seen my country torn apart. Your country—America—is safe and has two vast oceans protecting it from its enemies. Bombs do not fall on New York City as they do around here every night! You ask me to see things from your shoes? Ask yourself the same question while standing in mine!"

Pauline thrust her chair back and abruptly stood up, tears streaming down her cheeks. She started for the door, but Hank grabbed her arm and pulled her toward him. She wrapped her arms around him and wept softly, her face buried in his chest. Hank warmly embraced her and gently tried to comfort her pain with a tender caress. He whispered soft words in her ear and slowly rocked her back and forth. He stroked her hair and wiped away the tears. He stared deeply into her tear-soaked eyes and tried desperately to resist all urges to kiss her. Finally he could bear it no more and slowly moved his lips toward hers. Just then noises from upstairs startled the two and Pauline pulled away from Hank's embrace.

"Later I will come to you and show you the trust you desire from me. *Au revoir!*"

As Pauline closed the door behind her, Hank heard the familiar sound of the lock and knew he was still imprisoned. It was late in the afternoon and all he could do was finish his soup and water. It sure tasted good. When finished, he lay on the bed and felt his heart race with delight as he kept thinking about Pauline and what she had said; moreover, what it meant.

Night came quickly, bringing more foul weather. The rain pelted heavily against the glass of Hank's small window, then stopped unexpectedly. The sound of anti-aircraft batteries was sporadic as the skies weren't flooded with Allied bombers—compliments of the offensive weather. Thick dark clouds madly churning in the atmosphere blocked out the stars and moonlight, causing Jolieville to be encased in total darkness. Even the weary German troops who normally patrolled the streets and outlying areas with their ferocious German shepherds tugging hard at their leashes, sought refuge from the miserable rain and eerie darkness. All seemed quiet and peaceful for the moment.

Hank lay quietly in the darkness. He had dozed off only to awaken to the sound of torrential rain pounding the street outside. He listened for any noise coming from upstairs but heard nothing. All was quiet, or perhaps the rain masked all sounds within earshot. Hank pulled the bandage off his head and rubbed the area where the rifle butt had struck him earlier. It felt better and seemed to be healing quickly. He detected a tiny gash with his fingers, but felt no blood. He unraveled the bandages on his injured forearm, discovering it, too, had healed enough that it was no longer bleeding or risked infection. The gunshot wounds and uneven skin were not pleasant to the touch, but at least he could move his arm without pain or loss of blood.

He heard footsteps. The door opened and soft candlelight pierced the darkness. Pauline's face, illuminated by the candle she was holding, had a radiant glow, enhanced by a touch of makeup. Hank stood up and silently admired the beautiful woman standing before him. She looked and smelled as if she had freshly bathed. Her head kerchief was missing, revealing the full beauty of her flaxen hair. She had changed her blouse to a newer red one, similar to the white one Hank was accustomed to seeing. Her skirt was clean and white and not hidden behind a dirty apron. A delicate red silk scarf knotted around her neck added a subtle hint of fashion to her natural beauty.

Stimulated, Hank tried to keep his natural urges in check. It had been a long time since he had been with a woman, and the anticipation and sexual excitement were becoming almost overwhelming. Sensing his desire, Pauline approached him, but before he could embrace her, the young Frenchwoman stopped his advance and broke the silence.

"No … just come with me now," she said. Hank noticed that she had not secured the door behind her, as she had done in their previous encounters. It was still wide open. His world was about to get a little bigger. Pauline turned and headed for the door. She led him up the dark staircase with only the little candle lighting the way. They reached the top only to find another door. Pauline turned the knob and the two went into another room. This room, a small kitchen, contained a sink, a large icebox, and two stoves covered with various pots and pans underneath cabinets and shelves filled with glasses, dishes, mixing bowls, cutlery, and cooking ingredients, such as flour and sugar. Hank noticed light coming from yet another room through an open door. He could also see what appeared to be the end of a bar. Pauline motioned for him to follow and the two entered a large room that Hank immediately surmised was the main dining area of a tavern or restaurant.

Pauline slipped behind the long bar and put down the candle, allowing the young airman to take in his new surroundings for the moment. Hank put his hands on his hips and slowly meandered to the center of the room, fully utilizing his keen fighter-pilot eyesight. The room was very dark and pitifully illuminated by a few scattered candles placed on round dining tables, or in small nooks on the walls and in the corners. The tables were covered with red-and-white-checkered tablecloths and surrounded by wooden chairs or stools. Electric lights atop small hanging chandeliers were turned off. Up front was a large wooden door flanked on either side by large rectangular windows covered by heavy, floral-printed curtains. A small coal-burning stove sat on a brick hearth located halfway down a side wall.

The rain continued to fall outside and an occasional clap of thunder crashed loudly through the uneasy French countryside. Hank turned toward Pauline behind the bar. On shelves behind her stood bottles of wine, champagne, cognac, schnapps, and other tempting spirits. Neat rows of shot glasses and beer mugs sat on a tray at the end of the bar beside a small barrel and wooden tap reeking with the sweet smell of beer. The aroma teased Hank's nostrils and made his mouth water for a small taste of home.

Pauline glanced at Hank in the dim candlelight and the young airman's thoughts wandered back toward those of a sexual nature. He felt urges he hadn't experienced in a long while and was eager to find out if the Frenchwoman had the same feelings of desire. He offered a smile and looked around, wondering what was to come next. Curiously, he noticed that Pauline was looking away from him now, her eyes fixated on a dark corner of the room. Confused, Hank looked into the darkness and saw nothing—until a tiny flame erupted from a struck match! Hank watched as the fire was pulled upward to meet the end of a cigarette hanging from a man's mouth. Soon the tip glowed ominously and the smell of smoke drifted in the still air.

Alarmed, Hank took a step back and turned his eyes toward Pauline. She did not return his glance and continued to look away. Sensing danger and betrayal, Hank leapt toward the front door. As he did, the sound of chairs being knocked over filled the room as Hank was violently tackled to the ground by not one, but three men.

"*Ne blessez pas lui!*" shrieked Pauline as she rushed from behind the bar. One of the men leapt to his feet and intercepted the young woman, pulling her back from the melee.

Hank struggled violently to ward off his unknown attackers. He swung his right arm at the nearest assailant and buried his fist hard into the man's jaw, knocking him off balance. As Hank tried to get up, another man jumped on him from behind. Pulled backwards, Hank's arms were quickly pinned down against the wooden floorboards. The man who had been struck in the face calmly collected himself off the floor and pulled out a knife, pressing it firmly against Hank's throat. The scuffle ended quickly, as the pilot realized he had no choice but to submit or risk having his throat slashed from ear to ear.

Pauline broke away from the third man's grasp and rushed to Hank's side, hollering at the knife-wielding assailant in French. He pulled the blade away from Hank's throat. Pauline helped the American to his feet as the three attackers calmly sat down at the nearest table. One lit up a cigarette and arrogantly puffed away. Dazed and dizzied by what had just happened, Hank expected the lights to come on any second, revealing a room full of uniformed Nazis with weapons pointed in his direction. To his astonishment, the men sitting at the table in the dim candlelight were not wearing Nazi uniforms, nor were they carrying guns.

Pauline's calm feminine voice broke the silence, saying, "It is all right, Lieutenant Mitchell. These are the men who helped you escape. They are my brothers."

Hank sat down at the table as the three Frenchmen stared at him. They were dressed in ragged, filthy, black clothing. Their faces were dirty and unshaven; their hair, disheveled and oily. Their appearance reminded

Hank of that of a coal miner or laborer. Pauline pulled up a chair and sat down beside Hank. She stayed close to him in a protective posture, much like a mother bear protecting one of her cubs.

"*Je m'appelle René*," said the first brother, extending his hand across the table for Hank to shake, which he reluctantly did. "*Bonsoir*," he added with a nod.

"*Je m'appelle Grégoire*," said the second brother, also extending his hand. The third brother, the one smoking the cigarette and holding the knife, said nothing. As Hank released Grégoire's hand he looked toward the third brother, who did nothing but glare with sharp annoyance at him. He appeared to be the oldest and from what the pilot could gather, he was most likely the leader of this motley crew.

Immediately Hank decided he didn't like this man. There was something foul about him. He wanted to rise up and drive his fist into the man's dour face. He let his own grim expression apprise the man of his distaste for his unhealthy attitude.

"*Christophe!*" said Pauline sternly. The unruly Frenchman looked at Pauline and scowled. Unfazed by his belligerent mood, the young woman began conversing with him in French. At first his responses to her flowing questions were terse and evasive, but they soon grew into longer, more heated uncompromising remarks. René and Grégoire shook their heads in disgust and backed their chairs away from the table as Pauline and Christophe argued on. Hank sat defensively and tried to translate the conversation, to no avail. Finally, Pauline seemed to gain the upper hand as her voice became the dominant one and Christophe appeared to steadily succumb to her will. Soon he fell silent and he crossed his arms and legs in disgust as his sister had the last word.

Turning to Hank, the young woman said, "Forgive my older brother. He has doubts … and questions."

Hank said, "Doubts? Questions? I don't understand. Questions about what? If anyone has questions about what's going on here, it's me! Before I start answering questions from him or anybody else, I think it's best you begin answering some of mine!"

"*Oui … d'accord*. That is fair," said Pauline. "Begin."

"What is this place?" asked Hank.

"This is our café," replied Pauline. "It is run by day by my brothers and me."

"The Germans allow that?" asked Hank, somewhat skeptical.

"*Oui*, the German officers come here often to eat and drink. They allow us to buy supplies from neighboring villages. We prepare food and liquor for the Germans and they pay us next to nothing for it! We barely make enough money to survive." Pauline hesitated then added, "But as you saw earlier when you were brought here, sometimes we help ourselves to German supplies."

Hank remembered the crates and sacks of supplies marked with German lettering and swastikas stored in the secret room he'd seen briefly upon his forced arrival.

"Why did you bring me here? What do you plan on doing with me?"

Somewhat puzzled by his questions, Pauline thought for a moment and answered, "We are French Resistance. You are an Allied pilot. It is our duty to protect you from our common enemy—the Germans."

"You're collaborators from what I see," responded Hank. "I think you work *with* the Germans, not against them. How do I know you'll protect me when the time comes? How do I know you won't offer me up to your Nazi buddy Steinert for a pretty sum and some extra sacks of food with Nazi markings on them?"

Annoyed and upset, Pauline put her hands to her head and tried to control her emotions. She wanted to speak but held her tongue. Christophe pulled her towards him and began pumping her with questions. She answered him with several statements, each compounding his anger and impatience. Even René and Grégoire, who had managed to stay civil, began to get aggravated by Hank's challenging comments.

When Pauline finished speaking, Christophe ripped the burning cigarette from his mouth and threw it at Hank. He stood up and spit right on the American airman. Hank thrust his chair backwards and aggressively stood up with balled up fists ready to strike. Pauline leapt to her feet and threw herself between the two men. She screamed at Christophe in French, then turned to Hank and commanded with a stomp of her foot, "Sit down! There will be no fighting in here! Not now and not ever! No and no." Hank wiped the spit off his shirt and flicked away the cigarette ashes. He calmly recovered his chair and sat back down, as did Christophe. Silence ensued. Glancing toward René and Grégoire, Hank noticed pistol butts under their jackets, visible even in the dim candlelight. Now all three armed Frenchmen seemed equally agitated with their American guest.

Audaciously, Hank broke the silence first and said to Pauline, "Why don't your brothers just speak up and say what's on their mind directly to me?"

She replied, "Why do you insist on making this so difficult? My brothers do not speak English. I must translate every word you say for them! It is not easy for me, especially since what you tell is very … how you say … discomforting to them."

"My apologies," sarcastically chimed Hank.

"My brothers do not trust you," said Pauline truthfully.

"I don't trust them," said Hank. "Or you, necessarily," he added.

Pauline translated for her brothers, who reacted with disgust toward the American. Christophe spoke and gestured for her to translate for Hank.

"My brother says that you have no right judging us. He says that he has risked his life and the lives of his brothers for you and countless other American and English pilots who have been shot down. You have no right to question our motives or our hospitality. We are fighting for our freedom and our very lives … and if you wish to keep yours, then you had better stop insulting our cause."

Hank replied, "You tell him that it's Americans and Englishmen who are fighting and dying daily to help free his country from Nazi rule. Pilots like me who risk their lives to help liberate your people every day. If it weren't for American airpower, backed by American industrial might, this war you're waging against Nazi tyranny would already be over and Hitler would've replaced the Eiffel Tower with a statue of himself!"

Pauline translated Hank's words to Christophe, who went on his own tirade. When he finished, René and Grégoire pounded the table in agreement, while Pauline, thoroughly disgusted, translated in English for Hank.

"My brother says that if America is so great and their weapons so powerful, then why does the sky rain American bomber crews and fighter pilots like yourself? Why is the French countryside strewn with countless numbers of destroyed Flying Fortresses, Thunderbolts, and Mustangs? Why do the only planes in the sky bear black German crosses and swastikas? Why do brave French Resistance men and women sacrifice their lives to bring incompetent fools like you to safety, when they would be better off fighting the Germans directly? Why should we waste our time trying to help you or your friends, the Tessiers, when it is obvious you think you are better than us and better off without us?"

Once again the mention of the Tessiers piqued Hank's interest. He wanted to fire back at Christophe and defend the honor of his country and the service, but thought it would be better to cool it for the time being. He had to help the Tessiers, and these people were his only chance. Cooperation now became imperative, he realized. Perhaps a bit of diplomacy and trust were necessary, even if deep down he felt otherwise. He went against his gut and extended an olive branch.

"Pauline, tell your brothers that perhaps I have been too judgmental. I apologize if I insulted them or France in any way. I understand and appreciate their struggles against the German invaders and am most grateful for the help and care shown to me while I've been here. However, my duty as a U.S. pilot is to try and make it back to Allied-held territory and get back in this fight as soon as possible. I need your help to make it back to England and to help save the lives of two of your citizens who risked their lives to hide me from the Germans."

Pauline translated Hank's English into French for Christophe. He sat back in his chair coolly and pondered his next move like a clever chess player. He spoke to Pauline, who translated for him again.

"Christophe wants to know what your mission objective was and how many other pilots were flying with you when you were shot down."

Suspicious, Hank hesitated for a moment. He then answered, "I was part of a flight of fighters protecting a B-24 bomber—a Liberator. I was flying a P-51 Mustang. Target and mission objective are classified. Tell him that is all I have to say about that unless he knows of any other members of my mission that might have been shot down and captured or picked up like me."

Pauline translated and Christophe immediately shook his head no. Hank thought to ask Christophe about Steinert and his family's involvement with the Nazi. However, he refrained, remembering what Pauline had told him earlier. He didn't want to interject anything that might disrupt the fragile alliance, though his suspicions and distrust lingered.

"What now?" asked Hank. "Are you going to help the Tessiers? How do you plan on getting me out of here? We're close enough to the coast, right? Can you get me on a ship that will put me in Allied waters?"

Pauline hesitated, then translated Hank's question to Christophe. René and Grégoire looked away and then got up from the table. The two men stretched and wandered over to the window, peering from behind the curtains to see whatever could be seen in the pouring rain. Hank looked back at Christophe and Pauline. Christophe gestured at Pauline as if to say that she should choose the next response to Hank, not him. Pauline looked at Hank and spoke.

"Lieutenant Mitchell ... *Henri* ... we cannot act to help your friends right now. We do not know where they are ... because Herr Steinert has not told us yet."

Hank dug down deep to control his anger and suspicions concerning the *SS-Obersturmbannführer*. His confusion mounted along with his frustration. Were these people collaborators, or were they truly working with a British spy infiltrator? It just seemed too far-fetched.

"I want to be able to trust you. But how can I legitimately trust anyone who follows directions from a Nazi and member of the SS?" he asked Pauline.

"You remember what I told you earlier?" she inquired.

"Yes," he answered, "but I can't in good faith believe that. It's crazy! How is it possible for the British to have planted a spy among Hitler's elite guard? There are strict rules and requirements to become an SS officer. Even the most ignorant fool that's ever picked up a copy of *Life* magazine knows that!"

Before Pauline could answer, Christophe grabbed her arm and told her he wanted her to translate Hank's words right away, which she did. He then told her what to say in return.

Pauline said, "You desire proof that he helps us. Here is your proof!" The young woman got up and went behind the bar. She reached down and pulled something from a shelf, wrapped in a dirty red rag. With both hands she carried it over to the pilot and placed it on the table in front of him. Hank reached out and unwrapped the rag. To his amazement, the object on the table before him was his own Colt .45 semi-automatic pistol. He picked up the weapon and examined it closely. It was undoubtedly his—the same one he'd picked off the equipment table at Jefferson Airfield. The very same one he'd used to gun down several German soldiers at the Tessier farm. He pulled the magazine from the butt of the gun and discovered it was fully loaded. He slapped it back in and pointed the gun in a safe direction but did not put it back down on the table.

"That is trust, *Henri,*" said Pauline. "Herr Steinert instructed us to give that back to you when the time was right. Undoubtedly you will need it. You will need these, too." Pauline reached into a hidden pocket under her skirt and pulled out another surprise that she dropped on the table in front of him. Hank rejoiced at the sight of two metal disks attached to a metal chain—his dog tags! He looked up at Pauline in happy confusion and thanked her before slipping the dog tags around his neck.

"Now, to prove to you that we are fighters who despise the Germans, you are going to help my brothers this evening."

"What do you mean?" asked Hank.

"There is a train station and a freight yard on the edge of town, not far from here. It is the only railway in or out of Jolieville. The Germans use it extensively to move supplies, weapons, and ammunition up to their coastal defenses. We must disrupt their operations and capture whatever useful supplies are on board. You can help, *Henri.*"

Hank thought for a moment and then asked, "Won't the train be heavily guarded? How would we be able to even get near it?"

Pauline responded, "Herr Steinert has arranged everything so that you, Christophe, René, and Grégoire will be able to get in and out without trouble. Follow Christophe's instructions. He will gesture if he needs to communicate to you to do something. Only take what you can carry. It is time to go now."

Hank's heart sank. A feeling of dread overwhelmed him. A trap? Could very well be. Choices? Not many. The young American stood up and looked deep into Pauline's beautiful eyes, scanning for any sign of honesty and sincerity. There wasn't time to find any, as Christophe pulled him away and toward the front door. René and Grégoire handed Hank a black hat and coat that he reluctantly put on. Then they strapped knapsacks onto their backs before tossing one to Hank. It was empty. The rain continued to come down hard and the American knew he would be wet, miserable, cold, and possibly dead very soon.

"*Vite, vite!*" said Christophe as he opened the front door and slipped outside with René and Grégoire close behind.

"*Henri,*" called out Pauline, "*Bon chance.*" The fighter pilot looked back at the beautiful young woman and saw the sincerity in her eyes he so desperately needed to see. He nodded his head and closed the door behind him.

Once outside, the four men hustled across the street and entered a small, open plaza, where on clear, pleasant days before the war, patrons of the café had likely gathered to enjoy their coffee and pastries. Benches and chairs surrounded small tables beneath neatly landscaped trees. A large stone fountain was present in the center of the plaza, yet no water had cascaded from it since the Nazi takeover.

Hank could hardly see anything, as the town was entirely blacked out. Christophe and his brothers squatted down in front of the fountain and pulled up a neatly concealed manhole cover. Hank waited his turn to descend into the sewer system as the rain pelted his already soaked clothing. Just as he started to enter the manhole, a German Mercedes with slit-mask headlight covers, designed to deintensify and deflect its headlight beams downward, slid down the street and stopped in front of the café. Frozen with just his head and shoulders protruding from the manhole, Hank dared not move, for fear of exposing himself. The driver got out and ran around to the other side, where he opened the door and snapped to attention. An officer with a peaked cap and long gray leather overcoat stepped out and under the café's red-and-white-checkered awning, just out of reach of the falling rain. The driver gave the Nazi salute, set a small brown wooden case down on the ground next to the café door, and got back in the car. He then drove around the corner and out of sight. The officer turned around as the door to the café opened.

Enough light shone from the café for Hank's keen eyes to identify the man standing there. It was Steinert! He removed his cap and tucked it under his arm. Pauline appeared in the doorway and confronted the SS officer. She willingly leapt into his arms and kissed him passionately. His hat dropped to the ground as the two stood for several seconds locked in passionate embrace. Steinert broke their hug and picked up his hat and the small case before disappearing inside with Pauline.

From across the street Hank watched, stunned, as his heart beat wildly with amazement and rage. He wanted to leap out of the hole, charge into the café, and unload every round in his gun into Steinert's head. That wasn't going to happen now, though. The three Frenchmen below him tugged at his legs until they pulled him underneath the street. Replacing the manhole cover, they made their way through the dank, foul-smelling sewer with low-powered flashlights that dimly illuminated their way. Hank felt helpless and uncertain all over again as he followed.

"What happens when those we trust turn on us like a pack of ravenous wolves?" he thought, his grip tightening around his reacquired pistol, while carnal visions of Pauline and Steinert together flashed through his racing mind. "What happens when a man is forced to accept the fact that he can't trust anyone or anything, regardless of what he is led to believe is true? In air combat, a pilot trusts and depends on his wingman to alert and protect him from any danger he can't see; however, down here—down on the ground—surrounded by known enemies and questionable allies, one doesn't have the luxury of a loyal and trusted wingman." Hank's mind raced with each step forward through the repugnant ankle-deep sewage.

Confused by what he'd seen and uncertain where he was going and why, Hank grappled with the thought of pumping a few rounds into his three French captors and thereafter taking his chances in finding a way out of France, pitting himself solely against whatever was thrust in his way, with however many bullets he was fortunate enough to have remaining in his pistol after René, Grégoire—and most importantly

Christophe—were reduced to nothing but three corpses lying face down in a sewer. The thought passed quickly though, and uncertainty set in again. He came to his senses and determined that patience and discipline were his best options—at least for now.

The four men trudged on through the dark underground sewer accompanied by the sound of sloshing water and squeaking rats. Occasionally they would have to stop and crawl through tight, rancid spaces before emerging into another connecting tunnel where they could stand and walk upright again. To Hank the disgusting and uncomfortable journey seemed to go on without end. Occasionally René would shine his light back toward him seemingly just to see if he was still with them, but not necessarily caring if he was. Finally, they reached a rusted iron ladder bolted to the concrete wall leading up to a steel grate. Christophe shined his light upward as raindrops cascaded down upon his face. Satisfied they were in the right place, he motioned to René and Grégoire with a wave of his hand. The younger brothers knelt down and started clearing away a small pile of rubble stacked in a corner. They removed stones, pieces of rotted wood, filthy saturated cloth, and other debris. Puzzled, Hank wondered what twisted form of treasure the two Frenchmen were hunting. Christophe looked away and just waited, uninterested.

After several minutes, René and Grégoire reached the bottom of the pile. Christophe shone his light downward, revealing a rusted iron door. Grégoire tugged upward on a latch and pulled it open with difficulty. René reached down and pulled up a large burlap sack, undoing a rope wrapped around the neck. He reached in and brought out a British 9mm automatic Sten machine gun that he handed to Christophe. He handed a second gun to Grégoire. Both men checked over the weapons, making sure they were loaded and ready to use. Hank expected René to pull one out for him to use as well, but was quickly disappointed. The remaining items were a few German "potato masher" hand grenades that he quickly stuffed in his belt.

Christophe looked at Hank and pointed his machine gun at him. Shocked, Hank took a step back and froze with fear. When nothing happened, Hank looked down and noticed that Christophe's gun barrel was pointed at the .45 tucked in his belt. Hank understood and pulled the gun out, cocking it in the process. With the flashlights off and machine guns slung, Christophe secured a large dirty scarf over his face, then cautiously started climbing up the iron ladder with his two brothers in tow. René and Grégoire likewise covered their faces. With some effort, Christophe was able to forcefully lift the steel grate up enough that he could slide it out of the way. He climbed out, followed by René and Grégoire. Hank felt the rain lash against his face as he climbed upward. When his turn came, he poked his head out and was amazed and terrified at what he saw.

Chapter 13

THE FREIGHT YARD

A German BR 41 locomotive sat motionless a short distance away from Hank's position. The large steam engine, curiously illuminated under prominent light towers, was hitched to a coal tender and several boxcars. A caboose with coils of razor-sharp barbed wire strung out beneath it was hitched on at the end. Steam swirled all around the base of the locomotive, while smoke gently wafted upward from its stack. A red Nazi flag emblazoned with a large black swastika in a white disc was attached to the very front of the engine.

Hank wondered just what type of precious freight it was hauling. He would find out soon enough, as his three French companions jerked him out of the sewer drain and quickly secured the steel grate back in place. Staying low to the wet, muddy ground, the four men scurried off, finding a small supply shack in a darkened and isolated corner of the freight yard.

Protected by the darkness and cover of the shack, the four men huddled down next to the wooden structure as Christophe whispered instructions to his two brothers. Unable to comprehend, Hank turned his attention back to the train and the general layout of the freight yard. Unlike the surrounding area, the freight yard was brightly lit up by fixed lights and sweeping searchlights atop covered guard towers. At the center of the yard stood a small ticketing office and sheltered waiting area, with an adjoining platform alongside the tracks for loading and unloading passengers and rail freight.

The train had not pulled up to this passenger platform yet. It was farther across the yard on a different set of tracks. Around the perimeter of the yard, makeshift fences consisting of small earthworks, cut timber, and rolls of barbed wire had been hastily put into place. A road led to a main gate at the front of the yard.

As further security, German shepherd guard dogs policed the perimeter of the yard tugging hard at their master's leashes. The dogs seemed unfazed by the rain soaking their thick brown and black coats and making their handlers miserable. They kept their noses to the ground, searching for the slightest hint of a foreign, unwelcome scent. They looked lean and hungry and as brutal as their human counterparts. Fortunately for Hank and his companions, the dogs were on the other side of the yard and hadn't detected them—yet.

As if on cue, René and Grégoire dropped down on their bellies and crawled in the rain and mud toward the boxcars. Hank watched as the two brothers slithered their way around the sweeping searchlights and clear of the sentries who had momentarily retreated to the shelter of their guard shacks across the yard and away from the train. René reached the half-empty coal tender and climbed between it and the engine, then disappeared in the shadows as Grégoire unlatched the door on the first boxcar and slipped inside, seconds before a German searchlight swept over the very spot where he had been standing. Satisfied that all was going according to plan, Christophe hugged the ground and clutched his weapon. He pointed the business end of the barrel toward the train and motioned for Hank to do the same with his pistol. They were to provide cover for René and Grégoire.

Minutes passed and there was no sign of either brother in or around the train. Christophe began to fidget impatiently. The guards and dogs could not stay in their sheltered shacks indefinitely and would soon resume their patrols, despite the cold, miserable weather. Suddenly an armed guard emerged from the caboose. He looked around for a moment, then retreated back inside his private shelter, out of the stinging rain.

Christophe focused his attention on the lit-up ticketing office where Nazi rail officials, the train's engineer, and two officers from a nearby army detachment had gathered to escape the rain. The window of opportunity was shrinking with each passing second, and it was only a matter of time before the whole rail yard would be bustling with activity, as the idling train would soon be moved onto the set of tracks adjacent the platform and unloaded. The operation could be exposed and the French perpetrators along with their American baggage undoubtedly caught and executed. Christophe's impatience was apparent as he looked toward the train, then back toward the steel drainage grate leading to the sewer.

"*Merde!*" he muttered as he checked his wristwatch. Suddenly Grégoire appeared from the front boxcar with his knapsack heavily loaded. He slid the door shut and latched it quickly. Christophe caught his brother's attention and motioned for him to return to the cover of the shack; however, the middle brother disobeyed and scurried to the engine instead. Christophe turned to Hank and pointed violently at the ground, indicating he wanted the American to stay put and not move. Hank understood and kept low.

Keeping one eye on the sweeping searchlights, Christophe darted into the shadows toward the locomotive. Hank watched him skillfully slip in and out of sight until he reached the engine, climbed aboard, and disappeared. Hank's attention was drawn back to the steel drainage grate. He hoped the escape route would go undetected long enough for Christophe to collect his brothers and allow the four of them time enough to get out of there. Wild thoughts of escaping by himself flashed through the pilot's head, but soon evaporated at the sight of a guard slowly meandering in his direction.

Long minutes passed as Hank awaited the return of the brothers. His anxiety heightened as a lone German guard approached his position. Clenching his Colt .45 with his finger tightly wrapped around the trigger, Hank had to think fast and make a fight-or-flight decision before it was too late. Just then the wind picked up and blew rain into the guard's face, causing him to stop and turn away. As he did, Hank left the cover of the shack and dashed over to the boxcar hitched immediately in front of the caboose. He ducked low and hugged the ground, managing to hide in a shadow that provided temporary cover. Hank knew he couldn't stay there for long as the guards and their dogs drew increasingly close.

At that moment a German truck rolled up to the main entrance gate—an *LKW Opel Blitz*. It seized the guards' attention and gave Hank a golden opportunity. Seeing that all the patrolling guards were momentarily distracted, Hank burst from his shadow, unlatched the boxcar door, and climbed inside before anyone noticed. He closed the door and drew a long breath, hoping no one had seen or heard him. Beams from the German searchlights penetrated small holes in the side of the beat-up boxcar. Rain dripped down from holes in the roof. Hank wondered if this car had been strafed by Allied fighters. He peeped through a hole and watched the German truck enter the freight yard. The guards stirred and the dogs barked as it rolled up to the boxcars located in the middle of the train. German soldiers hopped out, met by curious guards who directed them to the train. One by one the middle boxcars were opened and ramps lowered. Several soldiers began loading the contents of the boxcars directly onto the truck. Apparently someone felt there wasn't time to move the train into its correct position adjacent the platform to be properly unloaded.

Hank could make out the wording on several of the wooden crates: *Eigentum Der Deutschen Wehrmacht*, applied above the emblem of an eagle clutching the swastika in its talons. The light filtering through the cracks was just enough for his eyes to view his small compartment in some detail. The boxcar was relatively empty; only a few wooden crates stood stacked in the corner. As his eyes strained to take in his surroundings, his nose detected a curious and increasingly foul odor. At first he couldn't place the smell, but soon it became obvious.

"Urine," Hank murmured. He knelt down and touched the floorboards. They felt damp, almost spongy. Deep grooves cut into the wood gave the impression someone had gouged the floor with a chisel. Hank brought his fingers up to his nose, then turned his head away in disgust, realizing his fingers were now saturated with a repulsive mixture of puddled rainwater, urine, and feces.

"They must being moving livestock in these cars," Hank thought. "Pigs, cows, chickens, or something of that nature. But what are these crates for?"

Remembering his knapsack, and the nature of the mission as he understood it, Hank thought it best to try to open the crates and steal whatever contents were inside. That would certainly improve his standings with his new French associates. He approached the crates, which had no markings on them. Meanwhile, another *Wehrmacht* truck rolled up beside the train as more German soldiers appeared and worked their way from car to car, unloading ordnance and other war supplies. Hank looked down at his .45 and knew it was only a matter of time before they reached his car and discovered him. That would be the end.

He realized there might be something in the crates that could aid him in an escape attempt, some explosives or other weapons that might save his life. Possibly something that would at least take out more Germans than just his small pistol. Feverishly, Hank began to look for something that would help him open them. He crouched on the floor and pushed them away from the wall, climbing behind them to provide cover should the door open and soldiers enter. To his astonishment, he found a small crowbar secured to the wall by long, protruding pegs. He snatched up the tool and swiftly began pulling up the nails on the lid of the nearest crate. The sounds of the Germans outside grew louder, fueling his desire to expeditiously discover what was inside before the lead started flying.

One nail came up, then another, then another. Finally Hank was able to pull off the first lid. As he looked inside, disappointment turned to puzzlement. The entire crate was filled with nothing but eyeglasses of various sizes, shapes, styles, and colors. Most curious. He moved to the next crate. It was smaller and opened with less effort. The lid flew off and Hank plunged his hand inside, hoping desperately to find a machine gun or some hand grenades. He found nothing of the sort; the crate was filled with human hair! Long, colorful strands of blonde, black, and brown women's hair. Bewildered, he tried to rationalize why a crate of human hair would be on a German army train. The best he could come up with was that the Germans were using cut hair to make rope or something for the war effort, and this crate must have come from a German or a French barbershop.

With no time to lose, Hank moved to the third crate and wrenched off the lid. As he looked inside his heart sank again. It was filled with wallets, watches, purses, shoes, and other personal items. At first Hank paid no attention to these and started prying open the fourth and final crate; however, his curiosity got the better of him and he reached into the third crate and pulled out a wallet. He was surprised to find it filled with money and family pictures—black-and-white photos of happy, smiling faces. Hank grabbed several other purses and opened them, finding similar items.

"Damned thieves," he muttered as he dug through the crate, finding identification cards and papers all marked with what Hank recognized as the Jewish Star of David. "The Nazis are robbing the French Jews and hauling away all their possessions." What he couldn't understand was that the names on the identification cards were not French names. They appeared to be Polish or some other Eastern European persuasion.

With no time to spare Hank pried off the lid from the fourth crate. As the lid fell to the floor, he recoiled in horror at what he saw.

"My God!" Hank gripped his pistol with his right hand as his trembling left retrieved a small object and held it close to his eyes. There was no question what it was and absolutely no rational explanation why it was there. It was a tooth! A human tooth! The whole crate was filled with human teeth! Thousands of them! Upon further examination it became apparent what was so special about them. Each had a gold filling in it.

Unable to stand the macabre sight, Hank covered each crate quickly before slumping down on the floor. During his tour of duty in North Africa he had heard stories of Nazi atrocities committed against Jews throughout the conquered nations of Europe, but, of course, he had never been witness to any such crimes. His heart filled with rage as his mind raced with horrific images of beaten Jews robbed of all their possessions, crammed into boxcars like cattle, and hauled away into the night, where death awaited them at some undisclosed location. The smell of urine on the floor started to make him sick. Something had to be done—and soon!

Wondering what the French brothers were doing, Hank peered through a crack, his pistol at the ready. Waiting for a chance to open the door and make a run for it, his adrenaline began to pump furiously as he spied a larger truck—a German *LKW Büssing-NAG 4500*—roll alongside his boxcar. This time it was not *Wehrmacht* troops aboard; it was SS troops that filed out. These hardened men looked extraordinarily violent and disturbed. They wore right-collar patches and SS garrison caps bearing the sinister *totenkopf* symbol.

Met by several regular 7th Army soldiers, the SS contingent demanded entry onto the train—specifically Hank's boxcar. They brandished papers and shoved them in the faces of the *Wehrmacht* troops and guards. An *SS-Untersturmführer* collided with a *Wehrmacht Hauptmann*, who, after a minute of tense conversation, allowed the SS men onto the train. Several SS men headed for Hank's boxcar. Hank scurried behind the crates for cover and aimed his .45 at the door.

As if things weren't bad enough for the small band of raiders, the rain, which had provided them natural cover, began to subside. German soldiers who had previously sought shelter from the foul weather now ventured out into the yard. Several lit cigarettes and watched curiously as others loaded the trucks. The guard dogs grew restless and tugged at their leashes as though they had already identified a foreign and threatening scent from the locomotive. A few close to the engine began to sniff, whine, and growl. It was only a matter of minutes before all hell would break loose.

The door to the last boxcar slid open with a thud amidst the sound of callous German voices. An SS troop climbed into the car and shined his flashlight onto the crates.

"*Halt!*" he yelled, recoiling in surprise as the beam from his flashlight cut through the blackness and revealed the American intruder. Hank leaped up out of his crouch and fired two shots from his .45. The slugs burst through the German's chest before exploding out through his back in a shower of blood that lifted him off his feet, hurling him backwards onto the ground below.

"*Achtung!*" cried out the nearest German.

Just then, machine gun fire ripped across the freight yard and several *Wehrmacht* troops suddenly fell dead to the ground. The SS troops nearest Hank's boxcar wheeled in horror toward the locomotive as the three French brothers ran clear of the engine immediately before it exploded into a massive fireball of twisted metal and charred wood. Heavy metal fragments from the stricken engine shot through the air and sliced through both wooden building and human flesh like deadly shrapnel from a cannon's muzzle. The mighty explosion touched off the coal tender behind it, turning it into a blazing pit of fire generating coal-fed flames that flared skyward like a mighty torch. The concussion from the blast knocked many unsuspecting troops off their feet, while the nearest *Wehrmacht* truck was blown on its side and caught fire, as well.

Dazed and knocked down by the colossal explosion, the uninjured troops scrambled to their feet and fired their weapons in an unrelenting fury. A distant siren started to shriek while the guards in the light towers frantically tried to locate the intruders with their sweeping searchlight beams.

Hank watched in astonishment as the three French brothers ran hard across the yard, dodging gunfire until they reached the platform and the ticket office. Using the side of the building as cover, Christophe and Grégoire sprayed the grounds with machine-gun fire. The Germans dug in, finding cover behind the burning trucks while concentrating their fire on the office. Bullets whizzed past Christophe's head as he fired his Sten gun mercilessly until the magazine was empty. Grégoire stepped up his fire and was able to kill two German troops who dashed out into the open. René reached into his bag and pulled out several grenades that he hurled through a blown-out window in the ticketing office. The grenades exploded violently, killing or maiming all the officers and German rail officials who had sought cover inside. The office caught fire and started to burn, while German gunfire peppered holes through the platform and wooden office walls.

The SS men scattered and seemed to forget about Hank in all the confusion, instead turning their attention to the brothers wreaking havoc across the freight yard. Hank saw his opportunity and leapt from the car. He ran headlong for the supply shack and hit the deck as soon as he reached it. Machine-gun fire ricocheted around him as an SS man wielding an MP-40 spotted the American's escape and tried to cut him down. Hank returned fire, forcing the German out of his hiding spot. Locking on the German's silhouette, he squeezed off two more rounds, dropping the man dead in his tracks. Crouching by the side of the supply shack, Hank tried to stay out of sight, again eyeing the sewer grate.

In the center of the yard, the Germans were gaining the advantage. Using the burning supply trucks and scattered debris as cover, they inched closer and closer to the beleaguered brothers, who were quickly running out of options and ammunition. Machine-gun and rifle fire ripped all around them. Christophe fired back until he was out of ammunition. Grégoire managed several more bursts from his Sten, but was soon also out of rounds. The brothers looked to René for support, but found none from the youngest sibling, who lay wounded on the ground. Grégoire dropped to his knees, frantically trying to find where his brother had been hit. An exit wound on René's lower abdomen spilled blood across the platform. Grégoire did his best to stop the bleeding with a handkerchief while Christophe lobbed the only two remaining grenades at the approaching troops. The grenades exploded, but failed to kill anyone. It was all over. Christophe shouted profanities at the Germans, who crept ever closer to their position. In a defiant last gesture, he openly reviled Hitler, while Hank held his breath, expecting German gunfire to rip through Christophe's body and quickly end his life. The Germans yelled back and moved in for the final kill.

The fires raged wildly and there were still lights beaming down from the guard towers. Hank looked on helplessly as the remaining *Wehrmacht* troops and SS stepped onto the burning platform and closed in on the three French saboteurs. As they did, the unmistakable sound of fighter aircraft engines filled the skies. Before Hank could blink, heavy machine-gun fire strafed the freight yard, cutting down several German troops. The others ducked for cover. Seizing the opportunity, Christophe sprang to his feet and helped Grégoire get René up and moving. With their stricken brother in tow, the trio scrambled from the platform and darted across the yard, dodging fiery debris and scattered German gunfire. They reached the supply shack where Hank was waiting just as the fighters came around and strafed the yard a second time, knocking down two guard towers and blasting one of the German trucks sky high.

Christophe pointed to the sewer grate. Hank nodded, and he and the three brothers hustled to it. A dazed SS man saw the escaping saboteurs and yelled for them to halt. Hank raised his pistol and took him out with three quick shots. Christophe and Grégoire strained to lift the sewer grate while Hank covered them. Finally after tremendous struggle, the grate slid away and the two able French brothers climbed down to safety. They reached for René who was helped down by Hank. Finally it was the American's turn. He tucked his gun away and started to climb down just as another huge explosion rocked the freight yard, knocking what was left of the boxcars clear off the tracks. Heavy-caliber machine-gun fire continued to rain down on the yard from the mystery fighters above, destroying everything in sight. Cries of stricken German soldiers could be heard until the deadly barrage from above silenced them. The heat from the fires singed Hank's face, forcing him down the sewer ladder fast, but not before he had replaced and secured the grate.

"Mosquitoes," said Christophe, gasping for breath as he looked up at Hank. The American understood what was happening now that Christophe had made reference to the famous British night fighters. Their timing couldn't have been more perfect.

"*Vite, vite,*" Christophe added, indicating he wanted everyone to move out quickly—his brother's life hung in the balance. After taking every precaution to hide what little useful gear they'd managed to escape with in the hole under the rubble pile, the four men started back through the sewer as the sounds of muffled explosions continued above and behind them. René, half-conscious, clung to his brother Grégoire for support while Christophe, flashlight in hand, led the way through the filthy tunnels. Hank again brought up the rear. The trek back was much harder as exhaustion began to take its toll. The men slowly trudged through the murky, repugnant filth. Several times Grégoire pleaded for rest only to be relentlessly prodded on by his older brother, who was not about to let his youngest sibling die in a sewer.

After a spell of plodding through tunnels and squeezing through tight crawl spaces, Hank felt certain Christophe was leading them back through a different route than the one they had used getting to the freight yard. The young airman had had enough surprises for one evening and wasn't enthusiastic about another. He said nothing, but kept his pistol within easy reach. Soon the group entered a tunnel that brought smiles of relief to both Christophe and Grégoire. A familiar iron ladder leading up to a wooden trapdoor was a welcome sight. Christophe climbed the ladder, unlatched the door, and helped Grégoire lift René up. Hank climbed out last. As the trapdoor closed behind him, Hank recognized where he was. It was the secret storage room he had been brought to when he first arrived! Apparently Christophe felt it was the only safe way back to the café. Hank slid a crate over the trapdoor while Christophe climbed the small steps leading to the hidden hinged door. Before he could reach it, the door opened for him. It was Pauline, her face filled with worry, as well as relief at the sight of her brother. Christophe spoke to her quickly and she rushed to help René upstairs to safety. Without acknowledging Hank, Pauline rushed through his room with her brothers and slammed the door leading to the bar. The door locked again, leaving Hank trapped and alone. Unable to say anything, Hank secured the secret door and slid the bookcase in front of it just as he had seen his French companions do when they first brought him there.

Hank took out his .45 and slid the magazine out. He had one bullet left and made sure it was chambered and ready. He placed the gun on the table and started to peel off his filthy and soaked clothing. He stripped down to his underwear and tossed his dirty clothes in a heap in the corner. The young American was hampered by exhaustion, he was filthy and smelled awful, and his body ached with recurring pain from his earlier injuries. However, despite his physical discomfort, he couldn't stop thinking about Pauline and the ache he felt in his heart. He was becoming infatuated with her, and the thought of Steinert having her enraged him intensely. Her failure to acknowledge him upon his return only worsened the matter. He didn't understand why the pain in his heart felt greater than the pain in his body. Love was a powerful thing, if, in fact, it was love. The early hours of the morning were waning. Dawn was fast approaching. He lay back on his bed and fell asleep.

A short time later Hank was awakened by the sound of soldiers running down the street. It was early morning and the rising sun had emerged from behind several small clusters of clouds. Hank rose slowly from his bed and prudently peered out the small street-level window. The soldiers hustling down the street were a handful of regular *Wehrmacht* troops and not SS. Hank sank back down on the bed wondering if they were rushing to the scene of last night's raid or simply engaged in some sort of military exercise. They soon were out of sight and the street went quiet again.

As Hank rubbed away the deep exhaustion from his leaden eyes, his ears heard muffled footsteps and commotion upstairs. It was evident the café was open for business. As he pulled his hands away from his face, his tired orbs locked on a pleasant surprise sitting in the corner of the room not far from the door. It was the round metal washtub. Someone had recently placed it there while he slept. Gentle vapors of steam rose into the air, luring the American toward the warm, inviting water. Beside the tub on the floor was a clean towel and a bar of soap. Beside them lay his clothing from the night before, now clean, folded neatly, and accompanied by fresh undergarments. Hank wasted no time stripping off his dirty undergarments, and eased into the tub one foot at a time. He quietly splashed water on his shoulders, then washed thoroughly using a liberal amount of soap to remove the mud and sewer stench from his body. The hot water rinse felt good on his aching shoulder and ankle. He stepped out of the tub and toweled himself off. The tub water had turned from crystal clear to dingy brown. Hank didn't hesitate and urinated strongly in the tub, relieving himself. He got dressed in his freshly cleaned clothes and was again happily surprised to find a bowl of hot soup sitting on the desk. He promptly sat down and spooned the simmering potato soup down his hungry throat.

As the last swallow hit his stomach, Hank sensed he wasn't alone anymore. Standing beside the closed door watching him was Pauline. She leaned back against the wall with her legs crossed at the ankles and her hands clasped neatly in front of her. She said nothing as the bewildered airman tried to comprehend how she had managed to slip into the room undetected.

Hank's curiosity quickly turned to anger—an anger fed by deep pulses of heartache—painfully assaulting Hank at the sight of the young woman. He could do little to conceal his anguish and simply turned away from her.

"*Henri*? Are you all right?" softly asked Pauline.

Hank said nothing.

"*Henri*? Are you in pain?" She slowly approached him, his back still turned to her. She reached out and put her hand on his shoulder, wondering what the silent airman was thinking and why he was not answering her. Was he unable to speak because of some undetected wound?

Not able to stand it any longer, Hank turned, faced Pauline, and said sullenly, "I'm fine. Let me be."

"I do not have much time, *Henri*," Pauline said, "I must return to the bar and wait on our German customers who will become suspicious if I am gone too long. If you are in pain, you need to tell me now."

Hank sighed deeply as he looked into Pauline's blue eyes. He had to say something. He couldn't keep it bottled up inside any longer. She had an extraordinary effect on him, and he couldn't deny his powerful feelings for her, despite his inability to trust her. He decided to speak from his heart, no matter how unwise it might be.

"Yes Pauline … I am in pain," he answered her. "My mind is filled with distrust toward you, while my heart feels completely betrayed." He added, "I don't know whether to thank you for all your kindness, or shoot you dead right where you stand."

Horrified by Hank's words, Pauline stepped backward in disbelief. Her face froze in a scared, puzzled expression.

She said in an angry but controlled whisper, "*Mon dieu!* Was not last night's raid enough to convince you, *Henri*? Did you not see enough Germans die last night to be convinced that we are who we say we are? Have I not cared for you enough with hot food, water, and clean clothing? Have I not looked after your wounds and allowed you to sleep without fear of being captured by the Gestapo? What will it take to gain your trust, *Henri*?"

The young woman began to weep softly as she turned away. Hank brought his rage under control and remembered to keep his voice low.

"Do you like me, Pauline?" he asked.

Pauline turned to him and wiped the tears from her eyes. She wanted to answer, but was afraid to. Hank spoke again.

"I look at you and sense that you have feelings for me that match the ones I have for you. I see you, and I want to hold you and kiss you. When you're not here, I think of you constantly and wonder when I'll get to see your beautiful face again. I want to hold you now. I want to be able to trust you because I see in you the only chance I have of getting out of here alive. Please tell me if you feel the same way," he said as his insides trembled.

The young Frenchwoman found it hard to speak. Her tear-soaked frightened face did not portray the warm, inviting glow to which Hank had become accustomed. He was afraid of her answer. It finally squeaked out of her lips.

"*Oui,*" is all she could say. Even though Hank didn't understand French, he knew what that particular word meant and felt overjoyed when he heard it. He wanted to embrace her and kiss her lovely face all over at that instant, but couldn't, as evil visions of her with Steinert entered his head. He stayed vigilant, knowing he could still be in enormous danger.

"Does your lover, Herr Steinert, know that you have feelings for me?" asked Hank as his eyes wandered from Pauline to his gun resting neatly on the table. "Does it matter?"

Pauline's expression turned from sadness to one of disturbed confusion. She wiped away a tear and paused a moment before replying to Hank's insensitive question.

"What do you mean, *Henri?* I do not understand."

Hank looked her in the eyes and said, "Don't be that way, Pauline. Don't treat me like some ignorant fool who can't put two and two together. I saw him last night with you as I was being kidnapped and dragged down into the sewers by your brothers! I saw it all. The both of you looked awfully cozy together standing outside the door. I can imagine what fun you must have had once you got back inside!"

Hank felt his blood start to boil. His feelings for Pauline were stronger than even he himself realized. He was descending into a jealous rage involving a woman he hardly knew, yet was tremendously attracted to in ways he couldn't grasp. He had never experienced these powerful emotions before, yet they were now influencing his every judgment. The young beauty had that effect on him and it was dangerous.

"I have told you before to keep your voice down," snapped Pauline in a controlled tone. "You do not understand what types of danger are all around us!"

"What do you care?" replied Hank. "You're one of them. They won't hurt you. They'll just take me away when the time's right. Won't they?"

Pauline became visibly angry at Hank's remarks. She controlled her outwardly growing rage, but was not going to let him have the last word. With calm feminine composure, the young Frenchwoman spoke her mind. "You should not pass judgment on things you do not fully understand, *Henri*. What you saw last night was not necessarily what you think you saw. Do not judge me. You do not know me well enough to pass judgment on me. I have told you before and will tell you again that we are not German collaborators! We are French Resistance!"

Pauline started pacing back and forth. Hank watched her intently. She was visibly agitated and seemed quite sincere and determined in what she was saying. However, he couldn't help but wonder if she were truly trustworthy, or if he had simply fallen under the spell of a beautiful young actress. She continued speaking.

"Did last night's raid on the train station not convince you? We have given you food. We have given you shelter. I have cared for your wounds and shown you compassion that thousands of poor French souls dying every day in Nazi labor and death camps will never see! How dare you, *Henri*? How dare you?" she said as if she couldn't find any other words to express her dissatisfaction.

Hank said calmly, "I saw you with him. You held him. You kissed him as a lover does. He's a Nazi agent! He's a member of the SS and will most assuredly kill me when the time is right! He wants information from me. Information that could help the German war effort! I've got to get out of here! I've got to find out what happened to the old French couple that saved me. I have to help them if they're in trouble. Most importantly, I have to get back to England or some other Allied-controlled territory so I can get back in this fight! If you're French Resistance, then you're obligated to help me!"

"That is exactly what we have been doing, *Henri*," said Pauline coldly. "Do not assume you understand everything that is going on here. Do not think that you understand me either."

Pauline rushed up to Hank and kissed him firmly on the lips. Then she turned away and hustled to the door leading back up to the bar. As she opened it she looked back at Hank and added coldly, "My brother René is dead. He died last night for what he believed in ... liberty for France. You remember that, *Henri!*"

Pauline closed the door and was gone. Hank sank down on his bed and lowered his head. He was no closer to understanding his predicament than he had been at the moment of his capture. As he stared at the floor in a daze, he heard the door slowly creak open. He kept his head down and wondered what Pauline was going to say to him now. He quickly composed a thought in his mind and raised his head as the door closed.

"*Guten Tag.*"

To Hank's horror, standing before him in the familiar SS, field-gray uniform and peaked cap with his arms folded was Steinert! Hank quickly turned in the direction of his gun resting on the table.

"Don't bother with that nonsense again, because I really don't have the time," said Steinert in the familiar British accent. The daring airman jumped to his feet and grabbed the pistol off the table and aimed it at Steinert, who didn't flinch or make any attempt to stop him.

"I'll take my chances!" growled Hank as he sat back down on the bed, keeping the gun barrel trained on Steinert.

"As you wish, then." Sighing heavily and paying little attention to the weapon pointed at him, Steinert sat down at the small table, eyeing Hank determinedly.

"I have duties, you understand. I can't just keep showing up here and engaging in these stimulating little chats. Sooner or later you will be discovered, and I won't be able to protect you any more," stated Steinert in a low, serious tone. Hank made no reply.

"You still don't believe I am who I say I am, do you?" asked Steinert. Again Hank remained silent.

"I saved your life. I got you out of German captivity and delivered you right into the hands of the French Resistance. I gave you back your gun and your dog tags. I even allowed you to participate in a raid on the local train yard, resulting in the death of many German *Wehrmacht* soldiers and SS men … not to mention the destruction of the train, its military contents, and the actual yard itself. Lastly, you've been fed, clothed, cleaned, and cared for by the loveliest young woman in all of occupied France. One would think you owed me a bit of gratitude after all I've done for you. Wouldn't you agree? Quite distressing to me, actually. I thought you'd be a bit more gracious. What's more, the only thing I've asked from you is one simple piece of information that you for some unknown reason won't provide me. Let's try again, shall we? Where and when is the invasion going to take place?"

"Do you like fucking her? Is she your little collaborating bitch?" bluntly asked Hank, ignoring all else.

"You just don't understand anything, do you?" said Steinert. "You Americans know absolutely nothing about espionage. You can't see the bigger picture. You think only of yourself and your own immediate problems without considering for one second the grand scheme of things and how they impact issues that are larger than you could ever possibly imagine!"

Hank listened and could see Steinert was losing his patience. He was angry, but never raised his voice. The muffled sounds of German officers upstairs in the café could still be heard and it was apparent now, as it had been before, that Steinert, like Pauline and her brothers, didn't want anyone to hear him.

"Even though you hold that gun on me at this particular moment, it is I who am clearly in charge here, Leftenant Mitchell!" added Steinert. "The reason you are not rotting in some Gestapo torture chamber in Paris at this very moment, along with dozens of other citizens of this ravaged town, is because I was able to convince my superior, SS-*Gruppenführer* Gerhard von Schreiner, that the raid on the train station last night was actually not sabotage by the French Resistance, but rather a British aerial night attack! Those British Mosquitoes and I are the reason you are alive right now, Leftenant. I knew those fighters would be in the area last night, so I arranged for that train yard to be all lit up and the train to be delayed just long enough for a proper attack to be made. And, believe me, I know what was on that train!"

Hank took a moment to process all Steinert was telling him. His mind flashed back to the boxcar and the crates he'd seen filled with SS horror.

"If that train yard hadn't been destroyed last night, those boxcars carrying military ordnance to the Atlantic Wall might very well have been filled with French Jews, conscripted workers, and others seen as enemies of the Reich to be hauled back to Germany, put into concentration camps, and killed! You might have been on that train and taken straight to Natzweiler-Struthof if it hadn't been for me! You have no right to question who I am after all I've done for you, Yank! What will it take to gain some trust from you?" angrily seethed Steinert as his right hand came to rest on his holstered Luger.

The irascible young American paused again and slowly lowered his gun until it rested on the bed beside him. His guard was down and he knew it, but he needed to take a chance.

"You want me to extend you some trust? Then do what I've asked you to do before. I need to know if the old French couple that helped me is alive and unharmed. If you're truly who you say you are, then bring them here and out of harm's way. Give them the same protection and assistance that's been given me. You've claimed you've done that. Prove it to me! Bring them here and show me! Then maybe you'll have earned some of my trust, but not before," said Hank defiantly.

Steinert shook his head with a sinister chuckle. He stood up from his chair, folded his arms behind his back, and walked to the door. Without saying a thing he opened it slowly and checked to see if anyone was standing outside. No one was there. He reached around the corner and grabbed what appeared to be a paper laundry parcel tied in a flat square with twine. He closed the door and dropped the parcel at Hank's feet. The young airman looked down at it, then up at Steinert.

The *SS-Obersturmbannführer* said, "Open the parcel, Leftenant." Hank reached down and picked it up. He undid the knotted twine revealing a uniform and cap—an *SS-Sturmmann* uniform and garrison cap! "You've got ten minutes to shave and get dressed. I'll have Pauline bring you some hot water and a razor. She'll bring you appropriate boots as well."

Confused, Hank hesitated and was reluctant to follow Steinert's direction. Sensing this, Steinert spoke.

"I anticipated you'd bring up the Tessiers again. You want to help them? You want to make them feel all safe, snug, and secure? I do know where they are right now, so why don't we go see them together? I'm sure you've got nothing better to do," snarled Steinert. "Move! The clock is ticking!"

Chapter 14

THE TESSIER CONTINGENCY

Questions. Always more questions and precious few answers. As usual Hank did not know who to trust or what was going to happen next. Was he going to be set loose like a captured bird winging its way to freedom, or fed to the wolves like a sacrificial lamb? An unsettling wave of doubt and dread swept through his mind and caused his body to tremble. Could this be it? Was this the end?

Pauline reentered the room with a pan of hot water, some soap, and a shaving razor. Placing them on the table, she motioned for Hank to come close to her. Neither person spoke as Hank sat down. Pauline wetted and lathered his face, shaving him much as she had done once before. However, this time there was little warmth or care about her touch. She moved the razor across his face and neck with swift precision and a sense of urgency. Soon the pilot's stubble was gone. She then produced a comb and ran it through Hank's brown hair until it was straight and neat. After finishing, she stood up and pointed to the SS uniform. Hank toweled off his face and stood up.

"Get undressed, *Henri*," Pauline said. "I will help you put this uniform on."

Hank sensed the urgency in her voice and quickly undressed to his underwear. Pauline handed him the shirt, then the trousers. She buttoned the shirt properly and made sure it was tucked in according to German standards. She adjusted the collar and smoothed out any wrinkles. Leaving momentarily, she returned with a pair of boots and socks. As Hank adjusted the too-small footwear, Pauline finished by placing an SS garrison cap on his head. Hank stepped to the mirror and couldn't believe what he saw. He no longer looked like an American fighter pilot. He now resembled something far worse; he looked like a Nazi—something he'd never dreamed would happen in his worst nightmares. His heart sank and the fear of uncertainty set in again as the familiar SS skull and crossbones insignia sewn on the cap stared him in the face and set him on edge. Even the presence of the lovely Pauline did not put him at ease.

Moments later Steinert entered the room. He motioned for Pauline to leave and return to her duties upstairs. She left quickly, without acknowledging Hank. Steinert circled the American and examined the fit of the uniform. Everything looked in place and he nodded in approval.

"Take this," said Steinert as he handed Hank his .45. "Tuck it in back of your trousers and keep it hidden at all times." Hank did as he was told, forgetting the magazine was empty and only one shot remained in the chamber. "Now listen very carefully, Leftenant," said Steinert. "There is a car out front. You are going to pose as my driver. Follow me upstairs and out of the café. Stand straight and tall and do not say anything! Keep your eyes forward and open all doors for me. The dining room is filled with German army officers who would be more than happy to shoot you on the spot, so don't do anything foolish. Don't look at Pauline or her brothers. Just escort me to the car and drive away. I will direct you where to go once we're moving. Understand?"

Hank nodded as his heart pumped madly with fear. Steinert moved toward the door, then stopped. He turned to Hank and stared into his eyes. He paused a moment, then spoke.

"If you run, you will be gunned down. I will kill you. Do you understand? I've no time for any of your preconceived heroic notions of escape. I will shoot and kill you and it will be very easy for me to dispose of you and make up any story I like. Make no mistake, Leftenant, I am in charge, and you will do as I say or you will die. It is as simple as that! Now, let's go!"

Steinert opened the door and walked up the stairway. Hank felt his pistol secured and hidden against his back and followed the Nazi up the stairs. He also felt for his dog tags hanging around his neck and under his shirt. The sounds of foreign voices encircled him, as if he were stepping into a whole other world. The two men crossed through the kitchen, passed Pauline who was serving drinks from behind the bar, and stepped out into the crowded dining room. The room was filled with cigarette smoke and the smell of food. Hank was surprised and horrified to see the room so crowded with German officers. Many had come to the café to partake in a hearty breakfast. As he watched them eat, his keen eyes spied both *Wehrmacht* and *Luftwaffe* uniforms. He even noticed a man standing in the corner wearing what appeared to be a *Kriegsmarine* uniform. The room was so crowded that several tables had been pushed together, making it difficult to walk directly to the front door. Steinert waded through the sea of men standing in his way and kept Hank in close tow. He pushed a table or two out of his way and finally made it to the door, ignoring the few who had bothered to stand at attention and salute him.

Steinert stopped at the door and waited a moment. Puzzled, Hank stopped and waited, too. Steinert turned to the American and glared at him without saying a word. Suddenly Hank realized what was wrong and stepped up to the door, opening it for the higher-ranking Steinert. Outside, the skies were filled with puffy white clouds and the sun was shining. Parked directly in front of the café was a German staff car, a big black Mercedes-Benz 770 adorned with swastika flags on the sides and SS runes on the license plates. It was a convertible, although the top was up. Hank stepped to the rear door and pulled it open for Steinert to climb in. He then ran around to the front and climbed into the driver's seat.

The car was quite luxurious, inside as well as out. Hank sank down into the driver's seat and couldn't remember the last time he'd felt such comfort in an automobile. He put his hands on the wheel and hesitated, as if he didn't know what to do next. Sensing this and not wanting to draw any attention, Steinert started speaking authoritatively and directly at Hank—in German. After spewing out a few loud sentences, Steinert leaned forward and spoke softly into Hank's ear.

"Engage the ignition and pull away slowly. I will direct you where to go. Do not do anything that will unnecessarily draw attention to us! Now, let's go. Time is precious, and we don't have much of it to spare!"

Hank nodded weakly and looked at the dashboard. The car was unfamiliar to him and he felt as if he had just climbed into the cockpit of an experimental aircraft that had never been flown before and had no instruction manual. Even worse, the car was foreign, and the controls were labeled in German. The American took a breath and gathered himself. His meticulous gift for figuring out machinery, complex or otherwise, and how it operated kicked in just as it had done previously when he first climbed into the cockpit of the P-51D Mustang. He started the car, depressed the clutch, shifted into gear, released the brake, and slowly pulled away from the curb and into the street.

"Very good, Leftenant," said Steinert, adding, "Your file is very accurate."

An uneasy chill ran down the pilot's spine. Hank concentrated on his driving as he carefully maneuvered the car through the silent streets of Jolieville.

"Look around, Leftenant," said Steinert as the car wound its way through the narrow town streets. "This town is dead. Completely drained of all things good and natural by the oppressive hand of Nazism. No people out and about conducting business, no children playing gleefully in the street, not even birds singing in the trees—only a barren shell of a small town overrun by German troops and the SS."

He added, "Don't worry about being stopped by the French Gendarmerie, Leftenant. They don't exist here … not any more, at least. In fact, all French authority in this little town has been swept away and replaced by Germans. Not even the lowliest clerk in the town office is French. The Gestapo has made sure of that. And the Resistance? Obliterated. Except for one small remaining group comprised of three … no, excuse me, now two French brothers and one sister. One young, lovely sister." Steinert snickered to himself and pointed Hank in the direction he wished for him to steer the car. As Hank turned the wheel his mind wondered if the next bend would lead the car into a German ambush where he would be captured, tortured, and killed. His hands trembled on the wheel. Steinert picked up on this and shot Hank a sinister glare, as if to tease him and make him feel even more uncomfortable.

"Oh, by the way, do be careful with this automobile, Leftenant. It belongs to my superior, and he would be quite distressed if anything bad happened to it. I heard he shot his last driver because he found a small scratch under the door handle," said Steinert, playfully reveling in Hank's uneasiness.

As Hank navigated the narrow streets, he was happily surprised at the almost total absence of motorized traffic. Pedestrian traffic was at a minimum, as well. The only souls out and about were uniformed German military personnel. Once in a while Hank would spot a man or woman dressed in civilian clothing, and he wondered if they were French townsfolk. The town did appear dead. No other word described it better in Hank's mind—dead.

"Don't worry about having to stop at any military checkpoints, Leftenant. We won't come across any along this route," Steinert said as he lit a cigarette. He added, "There could be a roadblock if the occupying *Wehrmacht* units in this area are performing a drill, so don't be surprised if you have to stop. In that event, sit up straight, look forward, and for God's sake, don't say anything. I will handle whatever comes our way." Hank nodded and drove on, paying close attention to his driving.

Soon the car left the small town and began traveling down a dirt road. Massive hedgerows flanked both sides of the way, making it impossible to see anything on either side. The car twisted and turned as the road seemed to be deliberately constructed with sharp hairpin curves. Finally Hank turned onto a dirt road that left the maze of hedgerows and entered patchy woods. Hank slowed as the road became more unfriendly. It was not meant for motorized traffic, but for horse-drawn carts and carriages. It was mined with potholes, roots sticking out of the ground, and occasional stones that made travel in a car uncomfortable.

The shiny Mercedes looked extremely out of place, bouncing through the woods, along an old French dirt road. Surely it was designed for luxury and the freshly paved roads of Europe's finest cities. Hank carefully drove on until Steinert finally ordered him to stop. Hank set the parking brake and shut down the engine. Steinert motioned for him to get out, and the two exited the vehicle. Hank took a moment to glance around. Though he wasn't sure where Steinert had led him, he couldn't help but feel he had been here before. The thought gave him chills.

"Come with me, Leftenant," said Steinert as he walked toward a path leading into the woods. At the far edge Hank rushed ahead when he sighted an arching stone bridge spanning a slow-running stream. Suddenly the landscape made sense. The dirt road, the path, the stream, the bridge; Steinert had brought him back to the Tessier farm! Excited, Hank was hopeful he was about to be reunited with his old friends.

As the two men crossed the bridge, Hank's hopes began to fade. The meadow leading to the Tessier cottage was not green and lush like he remembered; instead, it was now blackened and charred. The old fence enclosing the property was entirely gone and there were no signs of life anywhere. Even Maurice's livestock was missing! Hank looked toward where the old barn and cottage had been. He was shocked to discover that the cottage was nothing but a pile of bricks and rubble. Without a word, Steinert walked in the direction of the debris. Hank quickly followed. The air possessed a rotten stench that Hank had never smelled before and caused his eyes to water. Faint traces of smoke lingered in the air. Soon he and Steinert were standing on scorched, earth, at the spot where the old Tessier barn once stood. Hank looked down and saw pieces of charred metal tools protruding from the blackened soil; these were all that remained from the vicious blaze that had brought down the barn. Distressed, he looked in the direction of the cottage. Burned completely, all that remained was a toppled brick chimney surrounded by unrecognizable charred remnants of the Tessier home. Hank looked at Steinert who stood behind him with his arms folded and a grim expression on his face.

"This is what you wanted wasn't it? You wanted to see your old friends? Hmmm? You wanted me to extend you some trust? Wasn't that it? Well, Leftenant, here they are. Why don't you say hello?" Steinert pointed to the heap of bricks. Hank moved cautiously as he approached the pile, only to recoil in horror at the hideous sight before him. At his feet lay two charred human bodies bound to a wooden pole that had been staked into the ground, but had burned at the base to the extent that it had snapped and toppled over. Tacked to the pole was a white sign with black lettering that read in German, "*Verräter des Reichs! Fotografien verboten!*" Underneath was a French translation: "*Traîtres du Reich! Photographies interdites!*"

Hank couldn't translate the words, but knew they conveyed a

hideous warning. Stunned and repulsed, he trembled and his stomach churned. The bodies were burned beyond recognition, although not completely to bare bones. The indescribable and unholy stench of charred human flesh hung in the air and forced Hank to turn away, his brain compelled to identify, catalog, and remember the brutal odor. His eyes started to water heavily as a helpless, yet enraged feeling overcame him. Without thinking, the American wrenched his gun free from beneath his SS uniform and wheeled around toward Steinert. Unexpectedly, the barrel of his .45 pointed directly at that of Steinert's Luger. Steinert had anticipated Hank's reaction and was ready to gun him down in an instant. His Luger held steady while Hank's Colt shuddered.

"You better be sure of yourself, Leftenant," said Steinert with a cocky twist to his British accent. "You only have one shot, and I never miss!"

His blood boiling, Hank responded, "You unbelievable bastard! You brutal, murdering, Nazi son-of-a-bitch! You Germans are the absolute scum of the Earth! You'll all burn in hell, starting with you!"

Hank cocked the hammer on his .45 and prepared to gun down Steinert in cold blood. The Nazi stood without moving a muscle. Calm and collected, he kept his weapon trained on the American, simply staring at the young pilot as if to subliminally suggest he knew Hank didn't have the guts to pull the trigger. The standoff lasted a few seconds more until Steinert decided to break the uneasy silence.

"You think I did this, Leftenant?" he said. "You are responsible for this tragedy, you bloody fool! Not me! Killing me will get you nowhere, nor will it give you any satisfaction. If you kill me, you'll never get out of here alive. If you shoot, you'll not only condemn yourself to death, but you'll also guarantee the deaths of Pauline and her brothers. I am your only hope. You have to trust me!"

Hank yelled, "How am I supposed to trust you? You knew they were dead from the beginning! You've known it all along! You led me to believe they were alive and could be helped. You played me for a fool this whole time. Why don't you just kill me? Get it over with and just kill me before I kill you!"

"I'm not going to kill you, Leftenant," said Steinert. "I'm not a bloody murderer, nor am I a Nazi! I am a British agent trying to do some good for King and country! I've helped many downed pilots to freedom—even arrogant Americans like you! I can get you out of here, but first I need your help. So, again I ask you, when and where is the imminent Allied invasion of the continent going to take place? What knowledge and details of the operation are you familiar with? You must tell me."

Hank shook his head in disbelief. He couldn't believe what he was hearing. His finger wrapped tight around the trigger, he began to squeeze harder and harder. He waited for the point of no return when the gun would discharge, leaving Steinert dead, thus ending the web of confusion he had so cleverly spun. Steinert spoke again.

"I need to have that information, Leftenant Mitchell."

Hank responded, "Go to hell, you Nazi cocksucker!"

"Very well," Steinert chuckled. "You're a good soldier, Leftenant Henry Mitchell of the phantom 23rd Fighter Squadron, 96th Fighter Group, 9th Air Force." Steinert noticed Hank's eyebrows rise slightly. "You know when to keep your mouth shut, even when there is a gun pointed at your head. Well, you don't seem to want to tell me anything about yourself or what you know, so how about I tell you a few things that might pique your interest? And then you can tell me if I'm right or wrong. Would you like to play that game with me, Leftenant?"

Hank said nothing, but kept his gun trained on Steinert, who showed no signs of lowering his weapon either. This Nazi agent was clever and Hank realized he had to be wary of all he heard. Anger and a general hatred for the enemy compelled the young pilot to pull the trigger; however, curiosity kept him from doing so. Hank wondered if it would get him killed. Maybe what he needed now was some good, old-fashioned common sense.

"I know who you are, Leftenant. I know why you are here. Quite frankly, I am thoroughly familiar with your so-called 'top-secret' mission. You were flying escort to a B-24 bomber sent to destroy a V-1 rocket site located near Martinvast, France. You took off from southern England from a base with designated call sign 'Gray Goose,' indicating Jefferson Airfield, not far from Portsmouth. En route to the target you were surprised by a flight of German fighters. Those fighters destroyed the bomber and all supporting fighters, including yours. However, before you had your Mustang shot out from under you, you were able to down two ME-109s—impressive, since they were your first air-to-air kills. You see, I know that during your previous tour of duty in North Africa you didn't have any air-to-air kills, only ground targets destroyed. Correct? Pity you got sick and had to return to the States. Pneumonia is never fun to deal with. It can kill you if you're not careful. You must be made from good hearty Maine stock. You'll have to show me that beautiful rocky coastline someday when this madness is over with. I must admit that your insistence to return to duty was quite admirable. You really came into your own as a fighter pilot during your time spent in the Azores before reassignment to the U.S. 9th Air Force. Must have been that superior British influence that got you on track."

Hank listened intently and began to relax his trigger finger. He became intrigued. Visions of Colonel Dexter's manila folder containing all his military files flashed through his head. His mind told him to stay vigilant and on guard; however, his arm was tiring and Steinert gave no indication he was about to lower his weapon first. The standoff continued.

Steinert resumed, "Your mission, dubbed Operation Vengeance, failed. You never reached the target and you bailed out of your fighter, sustaining only minor injuries. You eluded immediate capture and were fortunate enough to be brought here, where you received food and care from two poor old dairy farmers with anti-German sentiments— Maurice and Lily Tessier. You were safe and in good hands until you were discovered by two Nazi sympathizers—a young woman and her little boy. Her name is Yvette, by the way, and she's the mistress of my superior. The boy's name is Pierre and he's quite cunning."

Memories of peering through the Tessier barn peephole at the young woman and her plump son as they visited played like a movie through Hank's mind. He remembered the woman's long dark hair and blue-and-white floral print dress and how pushy and arrogant she seemed when met by Lily. More importantly, Hank remembered the fat little boy who got into the barn and must have somehow discreetly discovered him. He wondered if, in fact, it was the boy who was ultimately responsible for the Tessiers' execution. The Colt .45 slowly slipped downward as Hank took his eyes off Steinert, his mind racing as it processed the information being thrown at him.

Steinert continued, "Once you were given up to the Gestapo, they raided the farm with the help of the *Wehrmacht* and flushed you out of hiding. Amazingly, you weren't killed and you were brought to the SD and me under protest from the Gestapo. I, in turn, saved your life by arranging your escape and delivering you into the hands of the only remaining cell of French Resistance in all of Jolieville. After some excitement and the company of a beautiful woman, well … here we are. Is that accurate enough for you, Henry?" Steinert had effortlessly rattled off the facts of Hank's mission and personal file from memory. He lowered his Luger and carefully replaced it in its holster, folding his arms behind his back to stand straight and tall, in a soldierly posture as though someone were about to pin a medal on his chest. Hank raised his weapon again and pointed it at Steinert's heart. It was his turn to speak now.

"Yeah, that's accurate enough for me. It proves yet again that you're nothing more than a clever and manipulative Nazi agent who got his hands on some foreign intelligence—or, more likely, captured one of my flight's fighter pilots, or a bomber crewman, and tortured him into giving you details of the mission. How do you know he wasn't lying to you after you tortured—"

"Let's dispense will all this speculative rubbish, Leftenant!" interrupted Steinert. "You can stand there and second-guess me all you want, but the fact remains that you know what I'm saying is pure truth! There were no survivors from your ill-fated mission except you! The B-24 never made it to within a hundred kilometers of the target. It was shot down and exploded on impact, leaving a gigantic crater and no signs of any survivors. The largest piece of metal recovered from the crash site was the size of a pocketknife! Your Captain Charles Wheeler was a fool and an unstable lunatic to think he had a chance to hit the target and return to England safely with such a heavily loaded bomber. As for your P-38 Lightnings, both were shot down and both Leftenant Donald Hendricks and 2nd Leftenant Anthony Dandridge were killed. Also, as I'm sure you're already aware, 2nd Leftenant Stanley Brady was also shot down and confirmed dead by the attacking *Luftwaffe* pilots. You, Leftenant Henry Mitchell, are the only pilot reported to have bailed out of his aircraft."

Hank listened to Steinert and couldn't comprehend how he knew so much. How could a German agent have such complete information? Hank had to concede that even he didn't know the first names of his fellow pilots. Was Steinert truly privy to accurate secret information, or was he making things up as he went along? Hank had to hear more. He lowered his gun.

"I see I have your attention now, Leftenant," said Steinert. "Let me enlighten you further. Your mission may have seemed like a one-of-a-kind adventure, but I assure you it was not unique at all. Allied air forces have been attacking Nazi V-weapon sites for quite some time now. It's part of another top-secret operation called Crossbow. Martinvast itself has been hit several times. So many bombs have been dropped in or around that area that the French locals are cursing the Allies more than the occupying German forces. Your particular mission was more complex and much more sinister than you could ever possibly believe."

Hank sighed audibly and looked away. He felt lost and confused more so now than at any earlier point. He looked around at the charred and smoldering rubble. He breathed the foul air and yearned to see any sign of life around him. He found none. Not one bird, small animal, or even an insect anywhere. It was as if life all around him had stopped courtesy of Adolf Hitler's Third Reich. Just then the ground started to tremble as muffled booms could be heard in the distance. Hank looked up at the sky, wondering if he would see bombers dot the horizon. He saw nothing and couldn't determine the source of the disturbance.

"We should get back to the car," said Steinert. "Allied bombing raids in this area have stepped up considerably over the past few days and it isn't safe to be out in the open. Plus, German patrols come through here all the time. I'll also add that two men in SS uniforms pointing guns at one another and screaming at each other in English is also a very foolish thing, if we both expect to get out of here alive. Agreed?"

Hank nodded and gestured for Steinert to lead the way back to the Mercedes. He got in the driver's seat while Steinert climbed in the back.

Hank didn't turn around to face the *SS-Obersturmbannführer*; rather he tilted the rearview mirror at an angle so he could see Steinert's face in the reflection. Steinert continued the one-way conversation.

"Your mission was an experiment, Leftenant. A simple experiment. Not very long ago it was discovered that there were tiny, yet concentrated German spy rings operating in southern England. British Intelligence and your own O.S.S. eventually uncovered the cells of German spies. They constituted a serious threat to the secrecy around the planned invasion of Europe. All the German operatives were rounded up except for a few who seemed to just disappear. Our countries could not ascertain the extent of the damage and feared that the pending invasion plans may have been compromised. A plan was devised at the highest ranks to test the potential extent of the damage. A secret and unofficial bombing mission was planned through all the normal and proper channels, many of which included fictitious invasion chatter. The idea was to see how quickly and efficiently the information would be passed on to the Germans and how they would react. The plan called for the assembly of a strike force to bomb a V-1 site around Martinvast, France. A group of unlikely candidates was hastily thrown together around one of the suspected areas where the unidentified German spies were thought to be operating— Jefferson Airfield. Essentially a group of ordinary unsuspecting pilots were unknowingly plucked by U.S. and British Intelligence to volunteer for a mission that would deliver them straight into enemy hands and had virtually no chance for success."

Hank locked eyes with Steinert in the mirror. "Are you saying that my mission was a suicide mission deliberately planned to catch a few spies? Do you honestly think my government would simply throw away the lives of trained combat pilots and waste precious war materiel to discover a leak? That's crazy! Even if the plan had been put into place, and the enemy discovered and reported it, why would the U.S. Army Air Force actually go through with it and sacrifice pilots? Why not just fake the mission?"

Steinert chuckled. "Do you think you're someone special, Leftenant? How about your comrades? Are they special, too? Are their lives worth preserving at all costs? Let me tell you something. You all happened to be the right men in the wrong place at the wrong time. Start with your Captain Wheeler—an unlucky and unpopular flight-lieutenant with a reputation for being a bit unstable and getting a lot of his men killed. Seems to me like the perfect candidate to lead a suicide mission, as you put it. Then there are your wingmen, Brady, Hendricks, and Dandridge—all young and foolish, with little knowledge of the European theater. Kind of like you, Henry. You flew in North Africa and spent a long time at home away from the war. What do you know about occupied France or preparing for covert missions hastily put together with inadequate military hardware and untried crews who barely know each other? Huh? Does that make sense? What do you know about your wingmen? Next to nothing, I would wager. They were like you, Henry. They were fighter pilots with differing degrees of combat experience and had been scattered around the globe in different theaters of operation. They were not special, Henry—just like you. I'll tell you what you are, Henry. You are expendable."

Steinert's cold words struck deep into Hank's soul. He sat in disbelief and amazement at what Steinert was telling him. He didn't want to believe any of it and still had doubts, but the more he heard, the more frighteningly real it all seemed to become. He thought back to all the unanswered questions and concerns he'd had before the mission. All the things that didn't seem right or clear now were eerily and dreadfully starting to make sense—the lack of basic equipment and the general confusion on the base. Thinking back, nothing that occurred at Jefferson Airfield now seemed normal or routine. He began to understand. Still, questions abounded in his head.

"If what you're saying is true," he said, "how are you involved in all this? How is it that you know so much?"

Steinert paused a moment, then drew a long breath.

"Very well," he started off. "I am a British agent who has managed to infiltrate one of the most sinister and deadly organizations ever formed in the history of mankind—the SD."

"What's the SD?" asked Hank.

"The SD, or *Sicherheitsdienst*, is the security branch of the SS. My department deals with gathering and utilizing foreign intelligence for the

Nazi party. I am what you would call a lieutenant-colonel in a special, secret detachment of SD operatives stationed in the area and tasked with the mission of gathering information about the impending Allied invasion of the continent. My superior, *SS-Gruppenführer* Gerhard von Schreiner, who resides in the château overlooking Jolieville, is a rather vile and brutal officer whom you had the pleasure of meeting briefly while you were locked up in one of the château's filthy root cellars. He is extremely efficient and has systemically wiped out all resistance in this area, excluding, of course, Pauline and her brothers. All foreign intelligence concerning the impending Allied invasion is secretly channeled to him. The specifics and personal backgrounds of you and your mission were transmitted to him from his spies in England. I, of course, was made privy to all that information, which is why I know so much about you and why you're here. I also know that you have no chance of getting out of here alive without my help. You don't realize it now, but you have nothing to go back to in England."

"What do you mean?"

"You're dead, Leftenant," said Steinert. "The men, whoever they may be, who devised this mission assume you are dead. You see, the reason they couldn't just scrub your mission before takeoff and haul away the spies who revealed it to the Germans, was because they weren't entirely sure who the remaining spies were until you were well over France. My people in England secretly informed me of their names. They may sound a bit familiar to you. One chap was named Jamison, while the other went by Stevenson. Ring a bell, Leftenant?"

Hank was shocked at the thought of both Major Jamison and Lieutenant Stevenson as Nazi spies. It was unbelievable! How could it be true? Hank thought of all the interaction he'd had with the two officers and wondered about Lieutenant Dandridge's pre-mission accident in his P-38 Lightning. Was it truly an accident or an act of sabotage?

"What about Colonel Dexter?" asked Hank. "Was he a part of this elaborate plot, too? Was he the mastermind?"

"Hardly," replied Steinert. "Your Colonel Dexter was nothing more than a drunk who, according to my sources, cracked under pressure and put a bullet into his head soon after you took off. Jamison and Stevenson were taken into custody. They're either imprisoned, dead, or are being forced to feed disinformation to the Germans. All vital information regarding the 96th Fighter Group and core base personnel tied to Jefferson Airfield prior to your mission are right now being disposed of or scattered to the wind. I wouldn't be surprised if the base itself was being bulldozed at this very moment. Nothing is more vital to the Allies than maintaining the secrecy of the invasion plans."

While Steinert talked, Hank noticed that his right arm was draped over a small brown wooden case. With each sentence, Steinert seemed to pull the curious little case ever closer to his body, like a protective mother would her child after sensing danger nearby. Hank quickly recognized the case as the same one Steinert had with him the night of the train yard raid and had carried into the café after meeting Pauline at the door. The unpleasant memory of secretly witnessing their passionate embrace fired Hank's foul temperament toward the Nazi now sitting just centimeters from him.

"We need to help each other, and without delay, Leftenant!" urged Steinert. "I can only protect you for so long. Eventually the Gestapo will find and murder you without remorse. I know that Eichner was here the day you were captured."

"Eichner?"

"Eichner is the Gestapo agent who is thirsting for your blood. Many who've seen him don't live long enough to remember what he looks like. He's often dressed in a black suit and tie and wears spectacles and a hat. He and his agents have torn this town apart searching for you. They've terrorized the locals, dragging several of them out of their beds in the middle of the night ... many never to be seen again. They have no regard for the French or their possessions and enter homes freely, often violently and without restraint. They have unlimited powers of arrest and are fanatically loyal to the Reich. They're often dressed in plain clothes, but they're easily identified when seen."

Hank remembered back to the time when he tried to flee from the burning Tessier barn. He remembered the menacing face of the bespectacled, Hitler-mustached German dressed in black, staring wickedly into his eyes, before he blacked out. This must be the man

Steinert was talking about—the Gestapo agent. Hank also remembered the brief glance he got of him while still a prisoner in the dank root cellar.

Steinert continued, "Did you talk to him at all? Did he interrogate you before you were taken into custody? Did you reveal anything to him?"

Perplexed, Hank replied, "I never talked to him at all! I was too busy fighting for my life! I only saw him once before my head was nearly caved in by a German rifle butt. That's all I remember."

Unsatisfied with the pilot's response, Steinert furthered his questioning. "What about the Tessiers?"

"What about them?" snapped Hank. "They're dead, or hadn't you already noticed?"

"I mean, did you tell them anything?" Steinert exploded. "Did you tell them anything about who you are, what your mission was, or most importantly, where the invasion will hit?"

Hank was taken aback by the unsettled urgency in Steinert's voice. This was the first time he had witnessed the Nazi without his usual calm, arrogant swagger. He was used to Steinert acting as if he had all the answers and was the domineering puppeteer pulling the strings. However, the pilot now picked up the peculiar scent of fear in the curious Nazi's voice and body language. The only question lingering now was whether the fear was genuine, or an elaborate ruse performed by a clever Nazi agent to gain the advantage. Not wanting to get into a battle of wits that he felt sure he would lose, Hank decided his best defense against Steinert's line of questioning was simply to speak the truth.

"The Tessiers didn't speak English, and I don't know any French. Even if I wanted to tell them every detail of my mission, it would have been meaningless because they wouldn't have been able to understand me. I didn't tell them anything, anyway."

"Eichner doesn't speak English and neither do any of the soldiers who assaulted the farm that day," said Steinert. "However, he does have men who speak French, so any information you conveyed to the Tessiers could have been wrenched out of them before they were killed."

"You mean murdered!" Hank burst out.

"Yes, I do mean murdered!" snarled Steinert in reply. "Now, again,

Leftenant, are you absolutely sure you didn't tell them anything about the impending invasion? You must tell me the truth!"

Hank turned and faced Steinert. Again the unsettling urgency in the Nazi's voice caught him off guard. Though his facial expression looked hard and determined, it couldn't totally mask the glimmer of fear and uncertainty hidden deep beneath his menacing SS uniform. He clutched the small wooden box ever tighter. Whatever chess game Steinert was playing, Hank thought sticking with the truth was his best move.

"You've asked me the same question over and over again. Let me be absolutely clear on this point. I don't have any information regarding the planned invasion. I don't know where or when it will happen. How could I know? You said it yourself earlier—I'm cannon fodder! I'm expendable! I'm just an ignorant, sacrificial lamb served up on a platter so my guys could grab a few Kraut spies back in England. According to you, I've been lied to and betrayed by my own country. Why in the hell do you think they would tell me anything about the invasion? You're the son-of-a-bitch who seems to have all the answers! Figure it out for yourself!"

"Very well, Leftenant," Steinert said coldly. "We need to get back into town and away from this place before we're discovered. This area is considered off-limits. Pauline is expecting me back at a certain time. If we miss that time, then she'll assume something is wrong and quite possibly risk her own safety to find out what happened. We can't endanger her. Start the car and head back into town."

Hank's fiery temper began to seethe at Steinert's mention of Pauline. The thought of them together was enough to stir a violent, lustful rage within his soul. Jealousy overpowered his notions of common sense and he couldn't help but foolishly let his sentiments escape his lips aboard ill-chosen words.

"Yes, sir. We'll get you right back into town so you don't miss any opportunity to fuck your girlfriend! Tell me, Steinert, what's it like to fuck a girl half your age? Does it make you feel that much more important, knowing you're having sex with a woman young enough to be your own daughter? Do you Germans go after little schoolgirls and boys, too, or do you move straight on to livestock when—"

Steinert lurched forward from the back seat and grabbed Hank by the face, covering his eyes with his left hand. Before the startled pilot could react, he felt the cold blade of Steinert's ceremonial SS dagger pressed against his throat. Hank stiffened and was too terrified to even breathe. His hands rested on the seat and did not move. He fell silent and waited for the angry German to drag the blade across his throat and end his life.

"I've had just about all I can stand from you, Leftenant!" fumed Steinert. "If you continue to press me, I just may forget that I'm actually a civilized Englishman doing his duty for King and country and simply plunge this dagger deep into your gullet without thought or remorse, like a Nazi would!"

Frozen with fear, Hank said nothing. Steinert continued, "I'm only going to explain this once to you. If I have to explain it again a second time, the last thing you'll remember is the sensation of my blade severing your jugular vein!" Steinert paused. "As an officer of the SS, my responsibilities are complicated, my duty schedule intense, and my activities always monitored. However, there are certain privileges with rank. One of those privileges allowed me by my commanding officer, von Schreiner, a man who would have you shot on the spot for not properly giving the Nazi salute, is an occasional on-duty visit to the loveliest girl remaining in this cursed part of France. He has his mistress and I have mine. My relationship with Pauline protects her, her brothers, and their business. My reassurances to my superior have convinced him that they are not part of any French Resistance group and can be trusted as loyal collaborators for the Reich. Pauline's striking physical beauty and Aryan features offer even greater reassurance to von Schreiner, who is a fanatical believer in the Nazi laws surrounding Aryan racial purity. Her brothers have not been carted away to slave labor camps in the East because I have written orders protecting them! My signature below countless false documents stating their service to the Greater Reich of Germany has saved their lives and killed many Germans! In return, I get a base of operations to secretly plan sabotage and execute espionage against our enemy. Without Pauline's café, I would be virtually unable to carry out any covert activity against the Nazis. Without me, they would have been wiped out by the Gestapo months ago and all French Resistance activity in this area would have collapsed. That would have meant more ordnance and supplies readily brought up to reinforce the Atlantic Wall, and more human freight shipped east toward certain death!"

Sensing his victim was not about to grapple with him, Steinert eased his grip on Hank and slowly backed the dagger away from his throat. He calmly sat back in his seat and waited for Hank's next words. Hank rubbed his throat, making sure it was not bleeding, and again turned to face Steinert. He didn't reach for his .45.

The brazen fighter pilot said, "So you get to play your little spy games and you get the girl at the same time. Best of both worlds, as I see it. She lied to me about your relationship with her. I wonder what else she's lied about!"

Steinert fired back, "Get this through your bloody thick head, Leftenant. I have never had relations with that young woman. I have never so much as laid a finger on her! Our relationship is fictitious and for show only. If von Schreiner didn't believe she was my mistress and that I was fucking her regularly, then our whole cover would be blown and my operations compromised. Our fictitious sexual relations are the only thing that allows me regular access to the café without suspicion. I will also add that if I were not claiming Pauline as my own conquest, she would most certainly be enslaved at the château and defiled repeatedly by von Schreiner. He would have not one, but two mistresses. Personally the thought repulses me beyond belief. Think what you want of me, Leftenant, but I will not have you question the virtue or honest sincerity of that young lady! You challenge that again and I will not bother you with empty threats. I will merely put a bullet into your brain! Now start the engine and head back into town. If the Allied air forces are on schedule today, this area will most likely be struck directly in a short space of time, and I'd rather not be here when they arrive in force."

Silenced, frustrated, and confused as to what to believe, Hank started the Mercedes and turned in the direction of Jolieville. Along the way, the wind swirled through the treetops, dislodging some dead leaves from their broken branches. The leaves chased each other through the powerful gusts like fighter planes engaged in an intense dogfight. Hank's eyes followed them until they crashed into the ground and out of sight of the rolling car.

Breaking several moments of silence, Hank asked coldly, "What do you know about the men who attacked my flight?"

Steinert stared out the car window as he gathered his thoughts. He answered in an aloof manner and didn't turn his head to address Hank.

"You were hit by elite pilots of *Jagdgeschwader 2 Richthofen*, specifically hand-picked and tasked to intercept your flight and destroy you. They took off from a hidden, makeshift airstrip not far from here and simply waited for you and your chaps to waltz right into their trap before they torched you out of the sky. They knew exactly when and where to hit you, Leftenant."

Hank scowled and gripped the steering wheel as the car motored forward. The thought of being set up and used as a guinea pig turned his stomach.

"I'm actually quite impressed with the reports I saw after the fact, Leftenant. You alone were able to destroy two ME-109s piloted by two very experienced *Luftwaffe* officers. I expected there to be no German causalities at all; however, you proved me wrong. The P-51 Mustang fighter has sent ripples of concern up through the higher ranks of the *Luftwaffe*, all the way to Reichsmarschall Göring. You should feel honored, Henry," said Steinert smugly.

Irritated, yet still curious, Hank replied, "I got into a dogfight with the pilot of a *Focke-Wulf* 190. He came out of nowhere and attacked with a lethal precision I had never experienced before. I got close enough to him to see some kind of personal or group insignia on the engine cowling. It was the image of a wolf's head—a kind of silhouette in black on a white background. It was ferocious looking. Anyway, that FW-190 pilot was good—very good. He got the advantage on me and shot me down. I had one chance to get him, but I ran out of ammunition. I was too beat up, too tired, and out of ammo. That son-of-a-bitch tore my fighter apart and nearly killed me in midair after I bailed out!"

Steinert replied, "I know, Leftenant. I saw his report. A very seasoned and lethal officer of the *Luftwaffe* shot you down. The wolf's head on his fighter's engine cowling is his own personal insignia. He's shot down more enemy fighters than you could possibly dream of. He's quite proficient with the *Focke-Wulf* and uses it to its utmost lethality. You're lucky he didn't rip open your intestines with his propeller blades!"

Hank shook his head in disbelief while guiding the Mercedes past the maze of giant hedgerows leading back to Jolieville. It wouldn't be long before they were back in town and eventually at the café. The road smoothed out, allowing Hank to pick up speed. Out of the corner of his eye, Hank spied German troops milling about along the side of the road. Some watched the car go by, others just ignored it, while still others snapped to attention and gave it a Nazi salute.

"Don't mind the troops," said Steinert. "Just keep driving unless you're forced to stop."

Hank drove on, encountering more troops and vehicles, forcing him to slow to a crawl. The activity was unnerving, but he kept cool and did nothing to draw unnecessary attention to the Mercedes. Back in town, more soldiers appeared on the streets, forcing Hank to slow down again. Steinert leaned forward with a curious eye, trying to deduce exactly what was going on.

"What is it?" whispered Hank.

"I don't know," replied Steinert. "Something is out of sorts here. It's unusual to see such a large number of troops scattered on the streets in broad daylight. I'm not sure what's going on. It could be some sort of drill, or perhaps a nearby barracks got bombed. Just keep driving. Get back to the café as quickly as you can," said Steinert in an urgent whisper. "Hopefully, they don't have the road blocked off and checkpoints set up."

The Mercedes turned a corner and headed down a narrow street. Hank's eyes grew wide with horror. Both sides of the street were lined with hastily constructed wooden gallows where several human bodies, both old men and women, dangled from nooses tightly twisted around their necks! He counted ten, then twenty, then thirty. All hanged, all dead! Their swollen faces emphasized their anguish. Steinert kept a rigid expression as his eyes surveyed the faces of the unfortunate victims. Was Pauline among the dead?

Soft-spoken, yet direct, Steinert said, "Don't look at the bodies and don't make eye contact with any of the troops. They appear to be in just as much shock as we are. Most likely, they don't understand what has happened either. Just look straight ahead and drive. Get us back to the café."

Hank nodded and drove forward with caution. Soon they were past the rows of brutally executed French locals and on the street where the café was located. Several buildings in the area showed some recent, albeit minor bomb damage. Small groups of *Wehrmacht* troops with fire hoses battled rooftop blazes billowing plumes of gray smoke. Hank dodged some large chunks of rubble before managing to park directly in front of the café, which appeared to be free of damage. He noticed a weathered wooden sign hanging above the red-and-white-checkered awning and the small outside dining tables and chairs he hadn't noticed previously. It read, "Café LeBlanc."

"Oh, Lord, have mercy!" said Steinert in a controlled British-accented voice. Hank turned toward where many curious German troops had congregated in the small plaza across the street. As a few moved away from the plaza's center, Hank saw the large, stone water fountain and, more importantly, what was in front of it. Someone had erected a coat stand and draped over it a tattered, charred U.S. Army Air Force, type B-3 jacket and leather helmet with shattered goggles. He immediately recognized the seal-brown shearling gear and concluded it had come from a bomber crewman—possibly one of Captain Wheeler's crewmen!

Steinert sighed and said, "We need to find out what's going on here. Listen to me carefully, Leftenant. I want you to get out of the car and open the door for me. Once I'm out, step back and give me the Nazi salute. You've seen it done before, I'm sure. Stand up straight, click your heels, and extend your right arm outward. After that, get back in the car and avoid drawing any attention to yourself. If a soldier confronts you, do not say anything. Point at your throat and shake your head, indicating you have some form of injury and cannot speak. I will be back shortly and will keep an eye on you. Do you understand?"

Hank replied meekly, "Yes."

"Good. Then off we go," said Steinert.

Hank opened his door, climbed out, and opened Steinert's door. The *SS-Obersturmbannführer* stepped out, steel-faced and in control. The American played his part well and snapped off a decent Nazi salute.

Steinert ignored it and walked over to the plaza as Hank got back into the driver's seat. Momentarily, he thought of grabbing the mysterious wooden case Steinert had protected so carefully and now had left unguarded on the back seat. He thought better of it and simply watched as Steinert addressed the nearest *Wehrmacht* officer. After another Nazi salute, the young officer walked to the coat stand and began explaining something to Steinert. Hank watched intently as Steinert questioned him at length. A moment later another officer appeared; however, this time it was Steinert snapping to attention and giving the Nazi salute first.

The senior officer was a younger man wearing a black leather coat over his uniform. He had on top of his head a peaked officer's cap. Both his hat and jacket bore *Luftwaffe* insignia that Hank recognized. The two men talked for a few minutes, while examining the macabre display in front of the fountain. As they finished, the *Luftwaffe* officer casually saluted Steinert, then walked into the café. The *Wehrmacht* troops gradually dispersed. Steinert approached the Mercedes, triggering Hank to jump out and salute him again.

"Get in," growled Steinert, his teeth firmly clenched. Both men got back into the car and slammed the doors shut.

"What's going on?" asked Hank calmly.

"It appears the SS has been busy today," said Steinert. "I've seen public executions before, but this seems more extreme than usual. Normally, bodies are displayed in the town center, not randomly lined up and down the streets—and never this close to the café. The killings appear to be random reprisals for the death of an SS man killed in an air raid earlier this morning. SS troops rounded up these innocents and hanged them out of pure rage. I wouldn't be surprised if the Gestapo pitched in and used the search for you as an excuse to kill another thirty-plus people—again! God only knows how many others were taken away and killed out of sight this morning!"

Hank lowered his head in grief.

Steinert added, "Eichner is ruthless. He'll stop at nothing to find you. A downed American pilot is a valuable treasure in the eyes of the Gestapo. My superior is no better. Even though he and Eichner despise one another, he has powerful friends in high places who protect him, and no mercy for those he considers weak. He was an *Einsatzgruppen* commander at the start of the Russian campaign in 1941 and oversaw the brutal killings of many Russian political commissars as well as thousands of innocent Polish and Russian peasants. Death is his ally, as well as his alibi. He'll do whatever it takes to carry out his orders and accomplish his mission. He placed me in sole charge of you, and I let you escape. Not only is he furious with me, he also has to contend with *Kriminalrat* Eichner and the Gestapo, which enrages him further. So you can see we're not in a very good spot here, Leftenant."

"What about that U.S. gear hanging on the coat stand?" asked Hank.

"That's another interesting story. The man I was talking to is an *Oberst*—excuse me, colonel in the *Luftwaffe*. The jacket came off a waist gunner from your bombing mission. It seems that after you were shot down, your friend in the *Focke-Wulf* 190 fighter joined in on the final minutes of the attack on the B-24 Liberator. Before the plane was 'sorted out,' the 190 pilot used his 20mm cannon to blow open a hole in the side of the bomber. It took an extra shot to blast through the additional armor plating, but he managed well, it seems. One of the waist gunners jumped free from the open hole and plummeted to his death. Apparently he didn't realize the bomber was too low for his parachute to properly open and function in time. His body was found, stripped, and that's what is left of his existence. Propaganda used to frighten those who don't believe in and obey the Nazi ideology!"

Numbed, Hank sat still and said nothing. He watched as the streets cleared and wondered just how much danger he was really in, and if he fully understood the consequences affecting himself and those who had helped him if he were caught. The brutality of the people he was dealing with now had become crystal clear. Not only were Eichner and von Schreiner's enemies swiftly executed, but their corpses were grotesquely put on public display to instill terror into the hearts of those who dared defy them. Never before had Hank witnessed such a savage act of inhumane cruelty. He thought of Pauline and the extreme risks she and her brothers faced every day, and that gave him a greater appreciation for all they had done for him—an appreciation still buried deep in a cavity of uncertain mistrust.

"What does the SS hope to gain by showcasing a U.S. bomber jacket? Isn't it terrifying enough that they line the streets with strung-up bodies of murdered, innocent people?" asked Hank.

"Isn't it obvious, Leftenant?" replied Steinert. "They're using the remains of that pilot gear to scare you out of hiding. They're hoping that whoever sees that will give you up to them before more blood is shed! They are determined to recapture you. The Gestapo wants you because you are an American, and Americans are rare prizes. My superior wants you because he realizes you may possess information vital to the impending Allied invasion."

"Yeah? And what is it *you* want?" defiantly asked Hank.

"I think it's best we get you back inside and out of sight, Leftenant," replied Steinert coldly. "I have plans for you. Don't question me any further if you know what's good for you!"

Hank turned around to look the *SS-Obersturmbannführer* in the eye. The two men stared at one another frigidly. Hank noticed Steinert's arm grip the small wooden case tightly. The standoff ended and the two men got out of the Mercedes and entered Café LeBlanc. Hank felt a nervous twinge in his stomach as his eyes rested on Pauline, who was behind the bar serving hot coffee to a small gathering of *Luftwaffe* personnel. She glanced at Hank and Steinert as they entered, but paid no attention to them. At the center of attention was the *Luftwaffe Oberst*, with whom Steinert had conferred just a few minutes earlier. Three other lower-ranking *Luftwaffe* officers, listening intently to the story he was telling, surrounded him. Steinert stopped, as did Hank right behind him. The *SS-Obersturmbannführer* wanted to hear what the *Luftwaffe Oberst* had to say.

The cocky pilot spoke in a confident, condescending tone as he told his story. He gestured with his hands to represent two fighter planes embroiled in a dogfight. His audience clapped and cheered when the story reached its climax. Even Pauline applauded enthusiastically as the pilot concluded his tale of heroism in the heat of battle.

Hank scrutinized the cocky pilot and instantly developed a hatred for the man who undoubtedly was singing his own praises about the damage he had inflicted on the Allied air forces. He was a tall man, in his thirties, with black hair and a neatly cropped mustache. He brimmed with arrogance and supreme confidence in himself. He acted as though he were some sort of celebrity and expected to be treated as such. He swallowed his last sip of coffee, then looked at his watch before hustling out the door with his entourage in tow. The room was now empty and Pauline let out a sigh of relief.

Steinert walked to the front door and looked out the window. With the mysterious wooden case in hand he said something to Pauline in German and prepared to make his exit.

"Goddamned Kraut pilot," said Hank, agitated at the *Oberst*'s bragging. "One day he'll get his. Mark my words—that son-of-a-bitch will get his!" Pauline looked away.

"You should have a little more respect, Leftenant," sneered Steinert, still looking out the window. "That was the man who shot you down and nearly snuffed out your life! I'd be careful what I say around men like him!" Steinert gave one more order to Pauline in German and left the café. He opened his trunk, put the small wooden case inside, got back into the Mercedes, and drove off.

Stunned at what he just heard, Hank turned to Pauline, not knowing what to say or what he was supposed to do next.

She said, "Go back downstairs to your room. Take off your SS uniform and leave it outside the door. I have left your clothes for you on the bed. Put them back on and wait. I will bring you some food later. Christophe and Grégoire are secretly away and will return soon. Be patient. You will know what to do soon. This is a critical time for you and for us, as well. Now go."

Hank nodded and headed down the stairs. Halfway down he stopped and turned around. Pauline was standing at the top, watching him with a look of compassion and confusion. He wanted to go to her and sensed she wanted the same, but he didn't. He continued down the stairs and into his room. Pauline turned away and went back to the bar, hoping for the best in an uncertain future.

Chapter 15

AN UNCERTAIN FUTURE

S teinert sat patiently alone in von Schreiner's opulent office. Upon his return to the château, the *SS-Obersturmbannführer* had received a message that he was to report to his superior at once. Steinert had gotten messages of this sort in the past; however, he sensed this meeting would be anything but routine or pleasant. His stomach began to churn in reluctant anticipation of von Schreiner's eventual appearance.

Von Schreiner burst into the office, causing Steinert to leap to attention and thrust out a Nazi salute followed by the usual, "*Heil Hitler!*" The *SS-Gruppenführer*, adorned in his customary field-gray SS uniform, rushed to his desk and sat down, motioning for Steinert to do the same.

The two men started to talk. At first they calmly went over routine issues and duties, but then the conversation turned in a direction Steinert had feared. Von Schreiner began to express his displeasure in the way Steinert had handled the situation involving the American pilot. His anger only intensified when he mentioned the Gestapo's involvement. He demanded that Steinert resolve the current situation, thus getting the Gestapo and the dangerous Eichner off his back before something truly disastrous happened.

Silence ensued once von Schreiner finished his harangue. Steinert felt uneasy, but refused to show any weakness that he knew would only fuel his superior's displeasure. Both men stood up in unison, staring at one another. The sheer evil that could be unleashed from the eye-patch-wearing *SS-Gruppenführer* was undeniable and terrifying to the point where Steinert didn't even feel comfortable raising the question of why so many townspeople of Jolieville had been slaughtered and left hanging in the streets. Instead, he simply saluted his superior and marched out of the office without any sort of acknowledgment from the disgruntled von Schreiner.

As the doors leading out of the *Gruppenführer's* office opened, Steinert stopped and caught a glimpse of a familiar figure standing in the corner smoking a cigarette. The man, dressed in a black suit and red tie beneath his black leather overcoat, dropped his cigarette and stepped on it as he cast a sinister smile in Steinert's direction. He tipped his black fedora and entered the office. The doors shut behind him. Eichner was meeting with von Schreiner alone, which made Steinert extremely uneasy, especially after his unpleasant encounter. He looked away and turned toward the nearest wall as a gray pallor washed over him.

The *SS-Obersturmbannführer* quickly collected himself and strode away. He had duties to perform and he wasn't about to waste any time. He made his way through the common areas of the château until he reached a room under guard. The guard snapped to attention and allowed Steinert to enter. Inside, Steinert walked over to an expansive bookcase and reached into the stack to release a lever. It triggered a mechanism that slid a wall of books aside, revealing a hidden dark stairwell. He stepped into the stairwell as the door slid shut behind him and walked down a winding stone staircase dimly lit by fluttering electric lights barely kept on by an old failing generator. At the bottom an SD man sitting behind a wooden desk supporting stacks of files, a typewriter, a telephone and a small dim lamp saluted him. The SD man reached under the desk and pressed a buzzer, unlocking a large metal door hidden in the shadows down the corridor. Steinert pushed open the metal door, which abruptly closed and locked behind him once he had entered.

Steinert stood overlooking a large, secret-operations war room abuzz with SD staff of various ranks, performing their duties with typical German diligence. Lining the walls were tables laden with heavy radio equipment, telephone switchboards, chattering teletypewriters, and secret code-breaking machines. Lit up on the walls were massive maps of Germany, France, England, and Norway—even a smaller one of the United States. Each map showed current information on *Wehrmacht* troop deployments, *Luftwaffe* airfields, *Kriegsmarine* surface ship and

U-boat locations, local areas of known French Resistance, possible enemy embarkation strongpoints in England, and other targets of interest, including many areas simply marked with a star of David.

In the center of the room lay a gigantic map of England supported on an equally imposing oak table. Several points on the map were marked red, including many in southern England. One particularly interesting area was curiously marked "FUSAG—Patton." Several men looked over this table and used wooden pointers to move around small markers indicating potential targets of covert espionage or brute military force. The intellectuals in the SD loved to strategize and play out their chess-like war games using such large models. They delighted in scheming and strategizing where the enemy was and how to surprise and liquidate him—an exercise especially admired by Department VI of the SD, the branch tasked with foreign intelligence gathering and espionage.

On the far wall were large photographs of prominent Nazis like Hitler, Göring, and Himmler, but also high-ranking SS leaders including Ernst Kaltenbrunner, Walter Schellenberg, and the universally feared and despised SS martyr Reinhard Heydrich, the brutal former head of the Reich Security Main Office (or RSHA). These Nazi figures were surrounded and glorified by brightly colored swastikas and other symbols of the SS and National Socialism. There were no windows here as the room was located deep in the carved-block, stone substructure of the château. Incandescent desk lamps and some internally illuminated machinery brightened the shadowy room. The eerie substructure of the château resembled a cavernous medieval dungeon.

Steinert walked to his cramped desk at the head of the room. After acknowledging some salutes and a few *Heil Hitlers*, he removed his officer's cap, sat down at his desk, and began shuffling through mounting piles of intelligence paperwork. He only read what was pending with regard to the inescapable, cross-channel invasion he felt was menacingly near. To his surprise there was nothing marked "urgent" and nothing that seemed alarming. All the intelligence gathered and summarized in neat paragraphs on official SS stationery in front of him seemed rudimentary—almost as if it weren't real, but a fabrication. Steinert thumbed through many more pages, searching for some hidden pattern or irregularity, but couldn't find one. He looked at his telephone for a moment—then two, then three—and was curious as to why it wasn't ringing. He looked around the room, closely observing his intelligence officers as they carried out their duties. The radio operators huddled close to their equipment, listening intently to wireless traffic through their headsets. The telephone switchboard operators directed calls with speed and precision as the switchboards lit up. Some SD personnel read teletypewriter information and relayed it to others who adjusted markers on the wall maps, especially the large map of England on the center table. Everyone seemed busy and all seemed routine.

Steinert slowly rose from his chair and became fixated on a row of codebreakers sitting at individual workstations with their backs to everyone else. Code books and piles of paperwork lined shelves above them. Teletypewriter machines, radio transmitters and receivers, and, most curiously, strange-looking portable typewriter devices with round metal rotors protruding from the tops of them kept the codebreakers busily engaged in their work.

Each codebreaker wore a headset and listened sharply to the radio airwaves for coded Allied messages. They monitored strange portable devices that resembled a cross between an ordinary typewriter and a small cash register. The device was the cornerstone of Germany's armed forces secret communications.

It was called Cipher Machine E, but was more commonly referred to as "Enigma." It had a typewriter keyboard located below a multi-lettered porthole over a lamp board. When a key was pressed, electric current flowed, illuminating a lamp at a specific lettered porthole behind the keys. Above the lettered porthole were three rotors, or drums, on a shaft with the alphabet around the outside. The rotors were set in specific positions on an axle and directed current via hidden wiring in a manner that resulted in a lit-up portholed letter different from the one pressed on the keyboard. The result was a coded message the Germans touted as impossible to crack. To make matters more difficult for would-be codebreakers, daily "cipher keys," issued several times over the course of a day, were necessary to break the code. These keys consisted of specific knowledge needed involving the order of the rotors on the machine's shaft, the position of the movable rings on each rotor, and the specific connections involving the plugboard. These settings applied to only one particular signal's network at a particular time, making the job of correctly intercepting and deciphering messages nearly impossible.

The Enigma machine could both send and receive ciphered messages. Once Enigma had enciphered a message, it was transmitted via radio using Morse code. If enemy forces intercepted the Morse-coded message, it was seen only as a nonsensical jumble of letters and thus deemed worthless.

Steinert began inspecting the codebreakers' daily intercepted and freshly deciphered enemy radio traffic printed out on teletypewriters and not yet delivered to his desk. The deciphered intercepts he saw lacked substance. When he asked for certain intelligence messages received from England, he was met with blank stares and questionable excuses. Most importantly, there was nothing available concerning the cross-channel invasion. Frustrated, he ordered the codebreakers to provide him with copies of the daily Enigma cipher keys for all branches of the German armed forces. Each handed him the day's cipher keys marked down in secret codebooks. Steinert carried them to his desk to go over them more thoroughly before turning to the piles of paperwork that needed his attention.

Hours had passed when Steinert looked at his watch and realized how late it was. He rose from his desk and exited the secret operations room. Pausing for a moment, he walked down the damp and poorly lit corridor instead of ascending the stone staircase out of the dungeon. His jackboots echoed through the darkness. The château's vast basement was filled with small cell-like rooms. The foundation was part of an old French medieval castle that had been destroyed centuries earlier. Once unearthed, architects and engineers had restored the foundation and incorporated it into the modern-day château atop it. Prior to the war, the previous owner had hoped to turn the space into a vast wine cellar, but the SS had since destroyed all likelihood of that.

Steinert passed the holding cell that had kept Hank a prisoner during their first encounters. He looked inside and found nothing but cold, damp, empty space. He continued on until he reached another large doorway hidden in the shadows. He was in an area that was off-limits to all except a privileged few. There was no guard at this door and no checkpoint to contend with. He reached into his pocket and pulled out a long metal key. Inserting it into the keyhole, he turned it until the lock opened. He then took a breath, opened the door, then closed it immediately once he was inside. Encased in total darkness, he reached into his pocket again and pulled out his lighter. Sparking to life, the tiny flame provided enough light for him to find a nearby ornate candelabrum. One by one, he lit its multiple candles.

As the candles glowed, the darkness subsided just enough to reveal the room's boundaries and contents. Brushing aside some cobwebs, Steinert gazed at his surroundings. The room was large—much larger than most of the grandest rooms in the château above—and filled with Nazi plunder. Precious French artwork consisting of fine oil paintings, priceless marble statues, richly colored and woven tapestries, rolls of fine silk, and ornate jeweled sculptures rested precariously on exquisite antique furniture dating as far back as the Renaissance. Large sacks overflowing with precious gems, coins, and countless varieties of jewelry lined the walls. Boxes and crates were stamped with eagles clutching swastikas and marked "*Reichsmarschall H. Göring.*" Stacks of stolen paper currency and bags of French francs and British pounds lay scattered throughout the room. A large golden chalice detailed with shiny jewels sat precariously out of place on the edge of a little wooden table. It was filled with ancient gold coins of unknown origin—another of many victims of Nazi thievery in France.

Other items of culinary privilege and luxury included priceless bottles of French Bordeaux wine and Hennessy cognac, as well as canned caviar and pâté, L'Espadon sardines, Colombian coffee, Indian boxed teas, and exquisite Swiss chocolates. Several dozen boxes of Cuban cigars were piled up in the corner. Steinert carefully maneuvered his way through the stacks and piles of plundered riches, using the candelabrum to light his way. He noticed the collection had grown since he had last seen it and wondered just how much his superior had secretly kept for himself. He cracked open an unmarked crate and held the candlelight close, revealing the remarkable contents. Solid gold ingots neatly stacked one on top of another magically glistened in the dull light. Steinert felt like a pirate who had just opened a buried treasure chest. Resisting avarice, he replaced the lid on the crate and instead acquired the one real treasure he sought. He opened a box of Cuban cigars and placed two in his pocket, silently cursing the fact that there wasn't a proper humidor to store them in. Lastly he grabbed a bottle of wine, snuffed out the candles, and swiftly made his exit from the hidden treasure room.

As he locked the door behind him, a dull thud caught his attention. Dust and dirt gently filtered from overhead while the dim electric lights in the corridor flickered. Steinert looked up, realizing the Allies were bombing close by again. He walked along the corridor to the stone stairway leading to the secret library entrance. In no time he was up the stairs and back in the opulent surroundings of the château. The booms and thuds were louder upstairs and several SS personnel were scurrying about as the château shook from nearby bomb impacts. The lights flickered off and on and Steinert could hear glass breaking in the kitchen. Then all was quiet again. The bombing was over as quickly as it had started, not even giving the Germans enough time to reach their bomb shelters.

Steinert shrugged off the event and made his way to the front entrance. He ordered the guard on duty to call the nearby motor pool and have his car brought up immediately. As he waited, he adjusted his uniform and pulled on his cap. Minutes passed and he began to grow impatient. He turned around to pull up a nearby chair, but was surprised to see his commanding officer standing right behind him.

"*Gruppenführer,*" said Steinert with a casual smile and a quick click of the heels as he acknowledged his superior officer.

"*Wohin fahren wir, Peter?*" asked von Schreiner.

"*Café LeBlanc, mein Herr,*" replied Steinert as he fortuitously held up the bottle of wine and Cuban cigars.

Von Schreiner let out a sinister chuckle and put his right arm around Steinert's shoulders. He crassly asked him a few off-color questions concerning Pauline, then reminded the *Obersturmbannführer* of his duties to the Reich. He snickered again and looked up the tall, winding staircase that led upstairs to the lavish bedrooms and guest quarters.

Steinert glanced up and saw an attractive feminine figure standing at the top of the stairs, holding a full wine glass and gazing seductively down on von Schreiner. She wore a blue-and-white floral-print dress, nylons, and high-heeled black dress shoes. She had shoulder-length black hair and her face was well made up. Steinert had seen her before and knew exactly why she was there. She was von Schreiner's French mistress, and it appeared that he required her services for the evening.

"*Gerhard, je vais au lit,*" said the young mistress as she sauntered out of sight, in the direction of the *Gruppenführer's* luxurious quarters.

"*Bis morgen,*" said von Schreiner playfully patting Steinert on the back, snatching one of the Cuban cigars from his pocket as he did so. The *Gruppenführer* then vanished up the ornate wooden stairway. Steinert thought for a moment and wondered if his superior was slightly drunk. The front entrance guard motioned that his car had arrived.

Steinert left the château and looked up at the dark sky. The day was far from over. For the moment all was quiet. There were no sounds of bombs or German anti-aircraft fire. All he heard was his Mercedes engine idling. As his driver ran to open the door for him, Steinert was caught by surprise as a chubby little boy with chocolate covering his face leapt out of the car and ran laughing into the château. A female SS secretary chased him down, calling out, "Pierre!"

Steinert shook his head in aggravation, looked up at the dark château's master bedroom window, and wondered if the boy's mother was having a good time. The driver slammed his door shut and ran around to get into the driver's seat. Steinert ordered him where to go and the car motored in the direction of the Café LeBlanc. Neither man noticed the car that slipped in behind them in quiet pursuit.

Steinert pondered his situation as he rode along, his head down and his left hand gently rubbing his temple. An uneasy feeling washed over him. His usual methodical and diabolical thought processes could not immediately pinpoint the source of his nagging concern. The Mercedes maneuvered the twisting roads on the way to Jolieville, then wound through the streets of town, carefully avoiding heaps of rubble and damaged military vehicles. Steinert looked out the window. Even though streets were dark and no lights could be seen due to the mandatory curfew, the stench of death was all too apparent. In the pale moonlight, Steinert could make out the ghastly silhouettes of the hanging dead. Orders had been given to keep them in plain sight to incite terror. But who had given the order? Was it von Schreiner and the SD, or Eichner and the Gestapo?

Steinert snapped out of his trance as the car came to a halt outside the darkened Café LeBlanc. He stepped from the car and looked toward the fountain across the plaza. The American gear was still hanging untouched on the coat stand. Retrieving the small wooden case from the trunk, he tucked it under his arm and ordered the driver to return to the château. As Steinert approached the entrance to the café, the door opened before he had a chance to knock. The Nazi agent slipped inside, unaware his movements were being observed by two shadowy figures sitting in a parked car just down the street.

It was Christophe LeBlanc who had let him in, not Pauline, whom he had expected. Christophe, unkempt and in his normal surly frame of mind, began challenging the *SS-Obersturmbannführer* with an onslaught concerning the recent murders of the innocent townsfolk. The remarks devolved into a heated argument in French, rousing Pauline from downstairs to attempt to diffuse the situation. She forcefully interjected and suggested they sit and calmly discuss matters before more trouble ensued.

Steinert placed his wine bottle on the table and motioned for Pauline to get some glasses. The young woman retrieved wine glasses from behind the bar and fixed a small serving tray of cheese. Steinert uncorked the bottle and poured a glass for each. Pauline sipped her wine and looked at her brother.

Christophe spoke first, expressing his concern about the recent killings and the danger of harboring the downed American pilot, whom he still did not trust or like. He voiced his anger and dismay about the death of his brother, René, and the secretive, dishonorable fashion in which he and Grégoire had to dispose of the body. Christophe and Pauline had become uneasy after inquisitive German officers who frequented the café brought up the whereabouts of René. Christophe railed about Steinert's secretive nature and unwillingness to share information. He felt the Gestapo's dragnet was slowly descending over the café and Steinert was becoming powerless to protect them. He spelled out several different scenarios he felt were crucial for their survival, including giving up the American pilot. Pauline jumped to her feet and angrily protested.

Steinert had heard enough. He swallowed the last splash of wine in his glass, slammed it down, then stood up with his wooden case and walked into the kitchen behind the bar. Christophe stood up and cursed Steinert openly, calling him a coward and announcing the conversation was not over. He said that Grégoire had grievances as well, and would share them once he returned from his supply-gathering mission. Christophe spit in Steinert's direction and cursed everything German.

The Nazi stopped, placed the small wooden case on the bar, then calmly walked over to Christophe and drew his Luger, pointing it directly at the Frenchman's head. The unarmed Christophe froze. Pauline recoiled in horror and covered her mouth with her hands, unable to take a breath. Steinert, with a face of stone, held the gun hard and steady. He calmly reminded Christophe that he was in charge and nothing would change unless *he* decided it would. He told him the overall situation was under control and not to worry. Lastly he added that he didn't appreciate the Frenchman's attitude, and if it didn't change, he would gladly blow his head off. After a few silent tension-filled seconds passed, Steinert lowered his pistol and ordered Christophe out of his sight. Stunned, the Frenchman slowly backed away and disappeared up a narrow staircase hidden behind a curtain in the back of the room. It led to the family quarters above the café where the LeBlanc brothers slept.

Pauline scowled at Steinert. Her heart raced and perspiration glistened on her forehead. Regaining her composure, she walked behind the bar and quietly began cleaning up. Steinert sighed, picked up his case, and walked into the back kitchen, where he opened the doorway leading downstairs. Halfway down he stopped and looked at the locked door at the base of the stairs leading into Hank's room. It was dark and quiet. Steinert surmised Hank was asleep. The Nazi ran his hand along the wall and felt for a little groove. When his fingers slid over the correct spot, he pushed on the wall. A secret door, completely invisible a second earlier, popped open, revealing a small room. Steinert stepped into the room and flipped on a light switch, revealing cramped quarters containing one wooden desk and chair. On the desk was a large radio complete with headset and Morse code keying device. The equipment was capable of both receiving and transmitting messages—secret or otherwise.

Steinert turned on the radio and waited patiently for it to warm up. As it hummed to life, a whisper of static flowed through the headset. Steinert put on the headset and listened attentively while slowly tuning in the radio dials and scribbling notes. As the late evening hours ebbed away, Steinert meticulously listened for specific radio traffic. His patience turned to frustration as the uncoded messages proved of little significance. The seemingly endless rows of randomly coded letters he had written down had worn both his mind and his pencil down to a dull point. He cast his notes aside in anger and glanced at the mysterious wooden case on the edge of the desk.

Steinert stood up to stretch. His back ached and he felt all his fifty-two years heavily piled upon him. Each day he looked in the mirror he felt he was becoming more wrinkled and his blond hair increasingly gray. These things were disquieting and made him yearn for earlier times and his younger, more vibrant years. He bent over and opened the wooden case. Inside was an unmarked and unaccounted for German Enigma machine.

Steinert powered up the device and began recalling the cipher keys he had seen and memorized earlier in the day. Fearing they would be changed very shortly, he set each rotor to its precise position and began deciphering the various rows of meaningless coded letters into an intelligible message. He soon had a grouping of short messages similar to those he had seen in the secret operations room. There was nothing of importance. Steinert read the decoded messages over and over, trying to discover any deep, hidden meaning he might have missed. He found nothing.

Discouraged and tired, the *SS-Obersturmbannführer* buried his head in his hands and took a moment to rest and reflect. The uneasy feeling he had experienced earlier at the château came back to him. His mind began conjuring unpleasant visions of Eichner and von Schreiner and the dangers both men could unleash when provoked. The man who had repeatedly professed being a British agent to Lieutenant Henry Mitchell and had earned the trust of the only remaining cell of French Resistance fighters in Jolieville looked upon the swastika emblazoned on his arm and began to wonder just who, in fact, he really was and which side he was truly on. A moment passed and he snapped out of his reverie. He got back down to business and switched from deciphering to enciphering.

Steinert began typing encoded messages on the Enigma machine, carefully noting each key that was depressed and the corresponding letter that lit up on the lampboard. Next he keyed his coded message over the radio airwaves in Morse code, ending with the code name "Windsor." He sat back, closed his eyes, and waited patiently for a response to reassure him, liven his spirits, and give him some much-needed direction. It did not come. An hour passed and the airwaves were silent. No faint Morse signals, no coded message of reply. Instant responses were unrealistic to expect and it took time for initially transmitted messages to be decoded and analyzed, but he had cleverly worded his message in an alarming tone intended to trigger a quick response.

Steinert's intended audience was across the English Channel, nestled secretly in a series of obscure huts northwest of London. The place was called Bletchley Park. There, dozens of English codebreakers, linguists, mathematicians, and spies conducted covert wartime operations against Germany's Enigma radio traffic and spy network. The codename for deciphered Enigma was "Ultra." Ultra was Steinert's intelligence lifeline and something he depended on for his very survival. He frequently scanned the airwaves for faint messages directed to him from his personal contacts at Bletchley Park. He, in turn, provided pertinent German intelligence to Bletchley through specially coded Enigma traffic that he had personally designed and that the Germans intercepted and simply dismissed as garbled transmissions from one of their own sources. The system had worked perfectly up to now.

Steinert looked at his watch and saw that it was 2:10 a.m. on what was now Tuesday, May 30, 1944. He was mentally drained and physically exhausted. He needed sleep badly in order to resume his normal duties, which were to commence in a few short hours. Realizing that the answers he sought were not forthcoming, the weary agent shut down his radio equipment, boxed up the Enigma machine, turned off the light, and slipped away from the hidden room, making sure there were no indications he had been there. Once in the stairway, he again looked toward Hank's room. It was still dark and quiet. He made his way up the stairs and into the kitchen where Pauline had left a few dim candles burning to brighten the way for him. He used one to light his Cuban cigar, which he puffed on vigorously. In the quiet still of the dark early morning, Steinert sensed he was not alone. He looked into the main dining room and saw Pauline in the shadows. She quietly walked toward him.

"*Es ist Zeit zu gehen*," she said

"*Wie sagen Sie das auf Englisch?*" Steinert chuckled smugly.

Not amused by his retort, Pauline dipped her head in silent disgust, unable to cloak her apparent disdain for him and her own overwhelming fatigue.

"My dear, don't you ever sleep?" Steinert confidently asked, his burning cigar clenched firmly in his teeth.

"Why do you speak English to me?" asked the weary young woman, who appeared as if she might collapse from exhaustion at any moment. "It is dangerous."

"Why not, my lovely? It is my native tongue, as you know," Steinert replied, unwilling to suppress his English accent. He chuckled and added, "Lots of things are dangerous, my divine French rose. You of all people should know that by now."

Pauline, her mind wracked with weariness and still shaken over the evening's earlier argument, said nothing. Steinert placed his hand on her cheek and brushed away a strand of blonde hair from her eye. He puffed a huge cloud of smoke from his cigar, went behind the bar, and reached for a hidden telephone. He cranked it to life and talked briefly with a subordinate in German. After hanging up he looked at Pauline.

"My car will be here in a few minutes. After I'm gone, inform your brothers I have a little task for them. I'll let them know what it is when the time is right. Our guest will be included, as well. See to it that he's well rested and up for the challenge. In the meantime, I want you to repose, my darling. Don't worry about Eichner and his Gestapo thugs. I have everything well under control. Go about your daily business and do nothing that attracts attention to this establishment. I'll see about getting those hanging corpses out of the streets. If I know the local *Wehrmacht* commander as well as I think I do, he'll be filing a complaint in person sometime today. Von Schreiner will most assuredly delegate the authority and responsibility to me. Not to worry, my dear. Do you understand me?"

"*Oui,*" replied Pauline, her head still down.

"*Très bien,*" answered Steinert sarcastically, loudly adding, "*Ich muss jetzt gehen,*" in German.

Soon Steinert's Mercedes arrived. As the SS driver jumped out of the car, Steinert opened the front door of the café. The driver snapped to attention. Steinert glared back at Pauline, who dropped her tired, melancholy appearance and hurriedly ran to embrace him. She threw her arms around him and kissed him hard on the lips. She stepped back and looked at him with passion in her eyes and a lustful smile on her face. The *SS-Obersturmbannführer* returned the smile and walked to the trunk of the car that the driver had opened for him. He placed the Enigma machine in the trunk and hopped into the back seat. They exchanged waves as the car pulled away and drove out of sight. Back inside the café, Pauline closed and locked the front door. As she did so, she looked out the window and noticed another car seemingly come out of nowhere and follow Steinert's Mercedes. She wondered where it had come from and what it was doing so near to the café at such an early hour of the morning. Not wanting to think anymore about it, she went to the back and pulled away the curtain revealing the stairway leading up to her quarters above the dining room.

Pauline started up the stairs, then stopped. Pausing for a moment, she found herself walking back around the bar and through the back kitchen. She quietly lit a candle and carried it downstairs toward Hank's room. At the door she paused again and listened for any signs of life inside. All was quiet. Her hand trembled as she slowly pulled back the bolt, turned the doorknob, and pushed the door open. She tiptoed to the table, set down her candle, and sat facing the bed, her hands folded in her lap. Hank lay peacefully but was awake. The sounds of the sliding bolt and turning doorknob had woken him up. Hank knew it was Pauline. Somehow he sensed some kind of passionate unbridled emotion radiating from deep within her soul, compelling her to stay.

Hank lay on his left side with his face toward Pauline. He kept his eyes closed but could sense her soft eyes running over his darkened facial features gently resting on the pillow. He wondered if she found him to be very handsome and if she wanted to say something. She reached out and discreetly stroked the young man's hair, afterward lovingly gliding her fingers across his exposed cheek.

Hank stirred and took a long, soothing breath. His eyes opened as the light from the candle revealed the beautiful silhouette of the young Frenchwoman. His heart leapt at first, but then he felt an enormously warm and calming sensation sweep over him. He gingerly sat up and rubbed his eyes. He wanted to speak, but the words didn't come to him. He wanted to reach out his hand to the young woman, but he remained frozen. He felt as helpless as he was confused. Instead, he waited for Pauline to reveal her intentions.

Pauline reached out and touched Hank's cheek with a tender, inviting caress. Hank reached up and placed his hand over hers. He sensed she was in anguish and that bad news was about to come his way. Her head dipped as she prepared to say something. Hank's heart started to pound as his mind raced to remember exactly where his .45 was and if it was within quick reach. He feared he might have to use it. Just then Pauline broke her silence.

"I am so very tired, *Henri*," she said. "I want to lie down and forget about this nightmare war, but I cannot. It haunts me when I sleep and it haunts me when I am awake. It is always there. I cannot escape it!"

Hank wanted to reply, but again the words didn't come to him.

Pauline continued, "I am tired of war. I am tired of death. I am tired of lies and I am tired of this place! Herr Steinert was here. He has a task for my brothers and you. He did not say what. As he left, I noticed a strange car behind his. I have never seen it before … it worries me! He fought with Christophe earlier about the bodies hanging in the streets. It is too much for me to handle right now. I am so very frightened!"

A small tear formed in the corner of her left eye and gently rolled down her cheek. Hank was unsure where this was going, but the wall of cautiousness and skepticism he had built to withstand the lovely Pauline started to crumble like particles of dust in the wind. It was gradually replaced by genuine sympathy and remorse for her plight. He knew his guard was down, but he couldn't stop the overwhelming feelings that were boiling over in his body and soul.

All the harsh words and accusations Hank had hurled at her in days past without pity or thought reverberated in his mind. He had heard her explanations and witnessed her acts of kindness. She had cared for his wounds, provided him with clean clothes, and fed him and kept him safe. Throughout all this, Hank's conscience had kept him wary and on guard, as if this was all a clever plot to gain his confidence, then violently strike out against him when the opportune moment arrived. While he still wasn't fully convinced of her sincerity, the blazing fire that ignited inside him every time he was in her presence could not be extinguished and seemed to overrun all other rational thoughts or emotions foolish enough to step in its path. Whether he trusted her or not, his fiery passion for her could no longer be contained!

Hank's wide eyes locked onto Pauline's. He slowly leaned over and closed his eyes, only to feel the gentle caress of her soft lips press against his. He reached out and wrapped his arms around her, pulling her body close to his. The two began to kiss torridly without restraint. Hank's lips feverishly maneuvered from Pauline's lips to her cheek, then her ear, and then down to her neck. Pauline's smooth feminine skin was heavenly to his touch, only inviting him to want her more. Pauline softly groaned in delight with each caress from Hank's exploring hands. He could feel her passion for him grow with each passing second until she unexpectedly pulled away from him.

Hank sat up and swung his legs over the side of the bed. He looked at Pauline, who pushed the chair aside and stood before him. She had a twinkle of seduction in her eyes that caused Hank to become extremely aroused. She returned Hank's gaze, then started to slowly disrobe. With all the sexual feminine grace and poise any man could ever desire, Pauline removed her blouse, skirt, and all her undergarments until her exquisitely gorgeous, undraped form glowed in the soft candlelight. She was more beautiful than Hank had ever imagined any woman could be. Her nude form paralyzed him to the point where he could not breathe. His body was motionless except for the passion growing in his shorts! His physical arousal was so pronounced it became inescapable to notice. Pauline smiled and looked away in giddy, girlish embarrassment. Her laughter was good, as it helped ease the tension between the two. Hank stripped off his shirt and shorts, revealing himself fully to the woman before him. He stood up and embraced her again. Their lips locked as their arms wrapped around each other like anacondas. The two were ready to give themselves to one another and nothing was going to stop them now.

Hank's hands began to adoringly explore every inch of Pauline's body. They came to rest on her warm and inviting, supple breasts. Pauline responded in kind, as her hands tenderly ran up and down Hank's smooth chest and lower abdomen. Without breaking their loving embrace, the two slowly sank down onto the bed and wriggled their way in between the sheets. Hank carefully maneuvered his body on top of Pauline's and smothered her upper torso with deep passionate kisses. Hank sensed her overwhelming desire for him through her intimate body language and soft spontaneous vocalizations. His heart throbbed with pleasure and heightened sexual tension unlike anything he had ever experienced before with a woman.

Hank couldn't hold back any longer and repeatedly entered the young French beauty with as much strength and masculinity as his body could muster. With each powerful thrust, a potent sexual energy was unleashed that fueled his mind and body with an emotional rush comparable only to the overpowering spectrum of feelings he had experienced while flying in the heat of combat. The onslaught of pleasurable physical emotions intensified rapidly as the two moaned with mutual delight. With each moment of passion, Hank felt the urge in his rigid lower extremity build like rising water behind a dam until Hank couldn't hold back any further. The dam burst, unleashing a torrent of liquid ecstasy driven home with each passionate thrust. The two lovers climaxed together and eventually fell apart from one another out of sheer exhaustion.

Hank and Pauline lay next to each other on the small bed. Each smiled happily and breathed heavily. Few words were exchanged, but what was said was both tender and reassuring. Both were tired and covered with a moist film of perspiration; however, neither wanted the joyous sexual experience to end. One casual little soft kiss invited another, until the two lovers were locked in each other's passionate embrace once more. Both recouped what little energy they had left and continued to make love through the early morning until both dropped off into a deep sleep, buried in each other's arms. As the two lovers slept, the candle, still a flicker on the table, gradually grew dimmer until the wick was totally enveloped in wax and snuffed out. Although it was still dark outside, morning with all its unpleasantness was near.

Chapter 16

THE NEXT TARGET

On Tuesday, May 30, 1944, dark clouds and unsettled rainy weather obscured the morning sunshine. Hank Mitchell awoke to the muffled sounds of people moving about upstairs. He wearily opened his eyes and sat up in his bed. To his dismay, he was alone. The young pilot began to wonder if what had happened earlier had been real or just a dream. The tangled sheets on the bed and his naked body offered him some reassurance. He saw the washtub near the locked door, filled with warm water and soap. Piled next to it were his clothes, neatly folded. On the table he saw the familiar serving tray with soup and potatoes awaiting him.

Hank washed and dressed as quickly and quietly as possible, then promptly finished off all the food left for him. His spirits and his physical strength were at their best since his unceremonious arrival in France. He raised his arm and stretched his lower back and shoulders until his muscles sang with relief. There were still twinges of discomfort in his back and shoulder, although both had improved greatly. The pain and swelling in his foot had subsided to the point where it was hardly noticeable. His injuries had been well cared for and the fighter pilot was grateful for the timely care he had received, first from the tragically slain Lily Tessier and more recently by Pauline LeBlanc. He plopped back down on his bed and did his best to relax. He fiddled with his Colt pistol, removing the single remaining bullet from the chamber, then putting it back again until he surmised he was making too much noise and put the weapon back down on the table. Bored and impatient, he realized he had to do what he hated the most—wait. His thoughts turned happily back to Pauline. He couldn't wait for her to reappear. He prayed it wouldn't be much longer.

Upstairs the mood was quite different than normal. It was a little after seven o'clock. A few German *Wehrmacht* officers milled about in the main dining area. Some drank coffee while others looked out the rain-speckled window at the grisly sight occurring outside. The officers looked on as several elderly men and women of Jolieville painfully lifted and loaded corpses onto wooden carts just outside the café. Pauline casually caught a glimpse through the window as she served the Germans their coffee and breakfast.

Pauline heard some of the officers say that the order had gone out to clear the streets of the dead. She watched as the unlucky civilians chosen for the gruesome task appeared neither physically nor mentally fit for the arduous job. Many wept openly under the physical and emotional strain, while others hid their faces behind scarves and kerchiefs, hoping to hide their grief and filter out the foul stench of death deeply permeating the air. The German troops overseeing the job kept their distance and did not lend any assistance. One by the one the bodies were cut down from the makeshift wooden gallows and stacked onto the carts. The bloated and bloodied bodies drew hundreds of buzzing flies that only added to the misery. Once the bodies had been taken down, the wooden structures they had hung from were also removed and carted off. The weeping townspeople strained to push the heavily laden carts along the bomb-cratered and rubble-strewn streets as no horses were available to help pull the loads. The work looked unforgiving and was only going to get worse.

As Pauline poured coffee for two officers seated by the window, she overheard one say that orders had been issued to take the bodies to the rural outskirts of town and bury them in a secret, unmarked mass grave to be dug by the townsfolk themselves. The other responded by saying that two SS troops had thwarted an earlier attempt by *Luftwaffe* personnel to take down the U.S. bomber crew gear from the coat stand by the stone fountain. He said they were told to leave it in plain sight or risk being arrested by the Gestapo. Pauline cringed, then casually walked away.

On the top of Jolieville's highest point of elevation stood the grand old French château now commandeered and infested by the SS. *SS-Obersturmbannführer* Peter Steinert sat at his desk upstairs in his palatial quarters gazing at his surroundings. His eyes swept back and forth, methodically scanning the large room and all its contents. He had grown tired of looking at the gloomy afternoon weather through his unsightly blast-taped window. Neither the untidy clutter on his desk nor the immobile fountain pen in his hand drew his attention. His mind was elsewhere. He looked at his watch, then at the clock hanging on the wall. No matter how hard he tried to focus on completing the endless paperwork in front of him, his mind wandered and he felt out of sorts.

Steinert stood up from his chair and looked down at his desk. He examined the exact position of every pen, pencil, piece of paper, rubber stamp, paperclip, letter opener, file folder, index card holder, magnifying glass, rolled up map, SS paperweight, and his other Nazi desk trinkets. He carefully opened his desk drawers and systematically went through all his files and other belongings with the patience and care of an expert detective at a fresh crime scene. He crossed from behind the desk to the middle of the room, where he examined every wrinkle in the window curtains and every fold of his bed sheets and blankets. His eyes wandered down to the red carpet underneath his jackboots and scanned every imperfection and imprint that could have been made by feet other than his own. He gazed up at the crystal chandelier hanging above him, then at the finely upholstered sofa and matching chairs and coffee table. He examined the walls and the hanging artwork, looking to see if a single picture was a fraction of a centimeter out of place.

His careful visual examination completed, Steinert sat down in one of his chairs, an unsettling urge silently gnawing away inside. He deeply felt something was wrong, yet could find no physical evidence of it. All seemed normal on the surface, but what lay beneath felt like a rotten structure ready to collapse at any moment. The thought was unnerving, and he couldn't shake the feeling that something drastic was about to jar his world in an unimaginable fashion. He envisioned enemies closing in all around him and precious few options to pursue or escape routes to follow. What was worse, he really didn't know who his true enemies were! He wondered if the distinction between friend and foe had become so obscured that the two really had no meaning anymore.

A moment passed. He closed his eyes and put his ears to work. He sat and listened for any little thing that didn't sound right. He particularly listened for noises that sounded manmade. All was quiet until he heard thundering little footsteps outside his door. He opened the door to discover a familiar chubby face looking up at him.

"*Ah, Pierre, bonjour!*" he said in French to the young boy huffing and puffing hard to catch his breath. "*Comment allez-vous?*"

"*Bien!*" replied the young Pierre with an impish grin.

The boy turned to dash away in a mischievous and playful manner, but was abruptly stopped when Steinert firmly placed his hand on the boy's shoulder. Steinert, not one to waste an opportunity, seized a golden one both in his mind and with his hand.

"*Pierre, avez-vous faim?*" Steinert asked.

"*Oui, j'ai faim!*" enthusiastically replied the boy.

"*Bien. Entrez-vous, mon petit ami,*" Steinert said while escorting the boy into his room and closing the door behind them. Pierre's curiosity was piqued, as he had never seen the inside of the *Obersturmbannführer's* personal quarters. He slowed his youthful gyrations just enough to take in this new and uncharted territory. Removing his peaked officer's hat, Steinert placed it on the young boy's head and watched as it fell down over his eyes. The boy chuckled with delight as he pulled it above his eyes.

"*Heil, Hitler!*" cried the little boy as he stuck his right arm out stiffly with a Nazi salute.

"*Heil, Hitler!*" Steinert responded in kind. The SS-*Obersturmbannführer* looked ominously at the boy's playful face underneath the evil death's-head skull and crossbones insignia, then motioned for him to sit in the "big boy" seat behind his desk. The boy happily plopped down in the chair and tried to look official and grown up underneath his newly acquired SS hat. Steinert pulled up a chair next to him.

"*Pierre, où est votre mère?*" Steinert curiously asked the boy.

"*Je ne sais pas*," Pierre answered.

Picking up on the boy's clever ploy, Steinert grinned, then reached toward the bottom desk drawer. He pulled it open and shifted the contents until he found what he was searching for. Pierre looked on with curious delight as Steinert placed a small wooden box on the desk, just out of his reach. Steinert opened the box as the young boy strained to see what was inside. He wiggled and squirmed in his chair, but his stubby legs couldn't touch the floor and push his fat little frame up high enough. He was unwittingly trapped in his chair, which Steinert had deliberately pushed in to prevent the boy from escaping.

Steinert tantalizingly wiggled his fingers, then snatched a rectangular object wrapped in white cloth from the box. Pierre reached out to grab the item, but was quickly thwarted by Steinert. Steinert carefully unfolded the cloth, revealing a dark bar of Swiss chocolate. Pierre's face lit up with enthusiasm. The fat little boy looked at Steinert with sad yearning, hoping his little act would convince the man to give up his confectionery treat.

Steinert simply asked again, "*Où est votre mère, Pierre?*"

The boy smiled and shook his head, as if to say the game wasn't over quite yet. Steinert reached back into the box and pulled out another bar of chocolate still in its wrapper. He placed it next to the exposed bar and again asked, "*Pierre, où est votre mère?*"

"*Je ne sais pa*s," playfully replied Pierre with a laugh that indicated he didn't want the game to end.

"*Pierre, est-ce que vous aimez le chocolat?*" asked Steinert.

"*Oui, j'adore le chocolat!*" said Pierre, drool appearing at the side of his mouth.

Steinert reached into the box again and pulled out yet another bar, accompanied by a tin of L'Espadon sardines and a shiny silver can opener. Pierre stared at the stash of goodies as if he were in a hypnotic trance.

"*Donnez-moi le chocolat, s'il vous plait, maintenant!*" pleaded Pierre.

"*Répondez à ma question*," said Steinert. "*Où est votre mère?*"

"*Avec le Gruppenführer dans la chambre à coucher*," said the boy.

With that, Steinert motioned to Pierre that he could have the chocolate. The greedy boy tore into the first bar. Steinert took advantage of the distracted lad and cleverly pulled the rest of the goodies from his reach. He needed this game of bribery to go on a bit longer. With fragile poise and lighthearted delicacy, Steinert posed additional questions that gradually became more serious; however, they came across as nonthreatening and playful, as if the entire conversation was just a fun game being played by two friends. After each useful answer the child gave, came an additional sweet reward from Steinert. He kept him engaged and interested with the food he offered and with the various interesting sights and objects in his quarters. Steinert eventually let Pierre out of his chair and allowed him to race around the room. The boy climbed over and under the king-sized bed. He hopped onto the ornately upholstered chairs and rolled around on the lush rugs. He examined the books in the bookcase and put his hands on everything. The obsessively neat and organized Steinert took this in stride and allowed the boy his fun, for he wanted to keep him happy and occupied.

Pierre eventually calmed down. His poor physique coupled with his sugar overload caused his energy levels to sharply spike, then abruptly crash, leaving him sluggish and dazed. He sat down on the bed and leaned against one of the bedposts while he wheezed heavily. Steinert made his move. He sat down next to Pierre and resumed his subtle questioning. He asked Pierre if he liked his room and the nice things in it. Pierre said he did. Steinert then asked if other people liked his room. People such as his mother, or the *Gruppenführer*, or the man who often wore a black suit and red tie. The chubby little boy who had playfully and eagerly answered Steinert's questions earlier now became quiet and evasive at the mention of the man in the black suit and red tie. Steinert picked up on this and changed his line of questioning, so as not to inadvertently frighten or discourage the boy. At the same time, he was intrigued at the boy's reaction to the casual mention of Eichner.

Steinert gathered as much information from Pierre as he could before reaching the point of tipping the young lad off and revealing his true intentions. He abruptly ended his questioning and gave Pierre a pat on the back. He retrieved a small gift box from his top desk drawer and handed it to the boy. Pierre's face lit up as he opened the box and removed a shiny gold circular Nazi Party badge. Steinert pinned it to the boy's shirt before giving him a stiff Nazi salute. Pierre beamed with glee. He sprang up and marched around the room, trying to emulate the Nazi goosestep. Steinert smiled and handed the boy his chocolate before allowing him to leave the room. Without saying "*merci*," Pierre flung open the door and raced into the hallway, eager to show off his new pin to anyone interested in seeing it.

Steinert stepped outside his door and put on his cap after wiping a small chocolate stain from the visor. As he looked toward the top of the grand open staircase, his eyes rested on the sight of a beautiful woman patiently indulging her child, who was thrusting his new prize in her face. The woman looked at the gold badge with disingenuous interest masked by a false smile. She uttered a few encouraging words bathed in phony excitement before sending the boy on his way to discover something else of curiosity that would occupy his time and free her of any parental obligation. As Pierre quickly scurried out of sight, the woman looked up and spotted Steinert eyeing her.

The attractive young woman cast a seductive glance as her eyes met Steinert's. She was dressed in a stylish, revealing, and somewhat disheveled red dress, white gloves, and red high-heeled shoes. Her dark hair appeared tousled and her makeup faded. Steinert folded his arms across his chest as she sauntered over to him.

"*Bonjour, Monsieur Steinert*," said the Frenchwoman in a casual, tempting tone that caught the *Obersturmbannführer* by surprise.

"*Bonjour, Yvette*," Steinert replied. The smell of the woman's Parisian perfume was overpowering and caused the unsuspecting Steinert to casually turn away, in hopes of inhaling a quick breath of untainted air. The two exchanged inconsequential pleasantries laced with sexual innuendo until Yvette grew bored and drifted away down the stairs. Steinert wondered just how much control Yvette enjoyed over von Schreiner and how she used it to her advantage. He wondered how much his commander's mistress knew about the activities in Jolieville and what sort of threat it posed. He wondered how dangerous she was and exactly what sort of destruction she could bring down on someone if provoked.

He knew who and what she was, but he had sparse few details about her past and knew nothing about her recent activities. He wondered if she worked and associated with other French Nazi collaborators, independent of von Schreiner and SS control. Finally, he wondered who Pierre's father was and if he was still a loyal French citizen, a soldier, a member of the French Resistance, a Nazi collaborator, or dead.

Steinert's concentration was abruptly broken as von Schreiner emerged from his bedroom. The Nazi SD chief stepped into the hallway and straightened his tunic, adjusted his trousers, and brushed off his SS officer's cap before placing it on his head. The younger officer shot Steinert a devilish smirk that quickly turned to a hardened glare. Steinert snapped to attention and gave the Nazi salute as his superior approached him. He couldn't help but stare at von Schreiner's piratical eye patch and wonder about the evil hidden behind it. Von Schreiner casually returned the salute and began to address his subordinate intelligence officer.

The two men offhandedly discussed the day's order of business. As von Schreiner spoke, Steinert could smell the cognac on his breath, as well as Yvette's pungent perfume on his uniform. The *Gruppenführer* ended the conversation suddenly and began to walk away without saluting or giving the customary "*Heil Hitler.*" Steinert stayed at attention. Von Schreiner stopped in his tracks and turned back towards the *Obersturmbannführer*, ordering Steinert to report to his office in two hours. The thought did not sit well in Steinert's mind, and he retreated back into his quarters once his superior was out of sight.

Steinert sat on his bed, uneasy and lightheaded. He reached to his nightstand to retrieve a bottle of aspirin in the drawer. As he did he stopped suddenly and reached for his pillow. He pulled it up to his face and inhaled deeply. His nostrils identified a faint scent trapped within the fibers of the pillowcase. It was unmistakably that same smell that had assailed his nostrils a moment earlier—the scent of Yvette's perfume! Steinert's heart sank. She had never been in his quarters. He knew this was a fact. There was absolutely no legitimate reason for her to enter his room.

Steinert's mind began to run feverishly. He once again began to look for any signs that his room had been searched, but aside from

Pierre's uneasy reaction to the earlier mention of Eichner and the faint scent of Yvette's perfume on one pillowcase, he could find no smoking gun. A feeling of isolation swept over him as he felt he could trust no one. However, his duties called as he looked at his watch and realized he had to get moving.

Steinert pulled himself together and collected the large pile of paperwork on his desk. He clipped the papers together in a file folder and exited his room, making sure to lock the door behind him. He hustled down the grand staircase to the library that contained the secret entrance to the underground intelligence center.

The clandestine war room, as usual, was abuzz with activity. Staff were poring over maps, listening to radio traffic, and tending Enigma machines. Steinert began sorting through an unusually large stack of classified Luftwaffe documents on his desk. Finally he summoned his staff officer and quizzed him as to why there should be such an extensive pile of documents.

The officer explained that a huge volume of British radio traffic had been recently intercepted stating the exact positions of several secret *Luftwaffe* airstrips meant to engage and repel any attacking forces during the impending Allied invasion of the continent. The decoded messages also stated that the British intended to eliminate these airstrips prior to the invasion. The time and the method were not given.

The staff officer thumbed through the pile and pulled out a communications sheet from the German High Command in Berlin. It was a copy issued to all local *Luftwaffe* commanders to move their aircraft and pilots away from the targeted areas and disperse them to safer locations. There was also a list of the targeted sites and the *Luftwaffe* units assigned to them. Attached was a list of coordinates and locations showing where each unit was supposed to immediately relocate. The orders were dated two days prior. Steinert dismissed the junior officer with a wave of his hand and began examining the comprehensive list.

Time passed quickly. Steinert, buried in his paperwork, glanced at his watch and realized it was nearly time for his meeting with von Schreiner. He knew he mustn't be late. Minutes later he was sitting at attention outside von Schreiner's office. The telephone rang on the desk of a nearby SS secretary. When she hung up the phone she told Steinert the *Gruppenführer* was ready to see him. Steinert rose, removed his officer's cap, and entered the office. Von Schreiner was seated behind his desk. Steinert snapped to attention with a click of his heels, a stiff Nazi salute, and a lively, "*Heil, Hitler!*" Von Schreiner did not respond in kind, but kept shuffling through the paperwork in front of him, only managing to casually raise his finger and point Steinert down to a chair.

The *Gruppenführer* didn't indulge Steinert today. The cognac did not pour freely, nor was there any exotic food or cigars as there had been during previous meetings. Von Schreiner's palatial office, filled as it was with so many luxuries and elegant symbols of National Socialism, now felt like a prison to Steinert; a prison from which he was not sure he could escape. At length von Schreiner finally cast aside his papers.

He rose from his chair and began to verbally assault Steinert. He railed about his incompetence involving the still-at-large American pilot and the mounting pressure from the Gestapo—specifically, from *Kriminalrat* Otto Eichner. Von Schreiner reminded Steinert of the friction between his SD and Eichner's Gestapo. The two Nazi agencies, although both a part of the all-powerful RSHA headed by Ernst Kaltenbrunner, embodied the struggle between State and Party authority. Each organization had similar and overlapping duties, and each tried to assert power over the other, utilizing different spheres and angles of influence. Von Schreiner, with all his influence with top Nazi officials, including the *Reichsführer-SS* Heinrich Himmler, could not deflect indefinitely the powerful arm of the Gestapo and its almost limitless faculties of arrest. It was a point he drove home with deadly accuracy with references to his own neck being on the chopping block. Eichner's belief in total separation between the SD and Gestapo made working conditions between the two elements nearly intolerable.

Von Schreiner issued an ultimatum: The missing American be in SD custody within a week, or he would no longer be responsible for interfering with Gestapo activity concerning that particular matter. The way von Schreiner worded his sentiments was enough to send a chill down Steinert's spine; however, he held fast and did not show the least sign of weakness.

Von Schreiner didn't let up. He began to review the details of the secret mission concerning the American airborne strike force. The failure to acquire useful information regarding the time and location of the imminent Allied invasion infuriated him. Reminding Steinert of his command and their top-secret purpose in France, von Schreiner vehemently stressed that the capture of the American for interrogation was vital to gain insight as to where and when the Allies would strike. Von Schreiner was very displeased with Steinert's handling of the situation and the lack of useful follow-up. Von Schreiner snatched a pile of SS rubber-stamped papers from his desk and threw them at Steinert. The *Obersturmbannführer* flinched as the large stack of papers collided with his chest and then scattered to the floor.

Von Schreiner went on to stress the importance of vital intelligence. He emphasized the importance of the military presence in the area, particularly the hidden *Luftwaffe* airstrips needed to launch fighters against any Allied attack from the sea. He specifically mentioned the special *Luftwaffe* unit that spearheaded the attack on the failed American bombing mission and how it would play a primary and critical role in repulsing an Allied invasion from crossing the English Channel and hitting the coast of occupied France. As he continued his harangue, Steinert took notice of how the *Gruppenführer*'s tirade drifted into many different subjects, only to refocus on the importance of the *Wehrmacht* presence in and around Jolieville, particularly the *Luftwaffe* and its hidden fighter airstrips. He surmised that his commander's growing fear of the imminent Allied invasion was putting an added strain on him, perhaps negatively influencing his decisions and putting too much reliance on the *Wehrmacht* to save his skin, once Allied troops started to hit the beaches. He silently wondered how he could use that to his advantage.

Von Schreiner paused for a moment and sat down behind his desk. He scowled at Steinert, who couldn't help but scrutinize the black eye patch covering von Schreiner's left eye. Steinert had heard all the stories behind the origins of the eye patch. He knew that von Schreiner had worn it since 1941, when he was an *Einsatzgruppen* commander on the Eastern Front. His clandestine killing units would fall in behind the regular German Army and "cleanse" the newly conquered areas of any elements suspected of being enemies of National Socialism. Blood-soaked soil and horrible, murderous atrocities were evident wherever the *Einsatzgruppen* marched. Their undisciplined and monstrous behavior sickened even the hardest and most ruthless *Wehrmacht* commanders who cringed whenever these unholy, fanatical soldiers of Nazism were attached to their army groups.

Steinert had never seen any official paperwork stating that von Schreiner had been wounded in battle. Neither had he heard stories from SS men who had served with or under him, claiming why he wore the patch. He only knew that official SS files prior to 1941 had pictures of von Schreiner with two perfectly good eyes. SS file photos of von Schreiner on the Eastern Front following the launch of Operation Barbarossa and the invasion of Russia showed him wearing it. Though Steinert's facts were sketchy and incomplete, at best, he clung to a theory that seemed ambiguous, yet entirely plausible. When he was first assigned to von Schreiner's foreign intelligence post in the west, Steinert had been briefed on the newly appointed *Gruppenführer*'s reputation for ruthlessness and intimidation. After meeting him and learning about his past, Steinert got a taste for how von Schreiner enjoyed exposing and preying upon a person's weakness—a skill he no doubt perfected during his ruthless days in Poland and Russia. Von Schreiner possessed a unique quality for instilling unrelenting fear in people. This fear sparked an internal fire in those who served him. Fear and intimidation were useful emotions when ordering men to do the unthinkable. Von Schreiner needed his men to be brutal and follow his orders without question; thus, he had to possess intimidating qualities. Perhaps those evil, internal characteristics were intensified outwardly via a simple yet cleverly diabolical accessory. Simply put, Steinert theorized that his commanding officer wore an eye patch over a perfectly good eye to get his men to fear him and fight harder for him. A very simple ploy, yet brilliantly effective.

The brief silence between the two was abruptly broken as von Schreiner reinvigorated his verbal assault on Steinert with new business. The *Gruppenführer* pulled out paperwork revealing signed, written orders issued to select *Wehrmacht* units to remove and properly dispose of the slaughtered townspeople left to hang on the makeshift gallows in

Jolieville. Von Schreiner flung the papers down on his desk in front of Steinert, who recognized his own freshly inked signature at the bottom of the pages. The *Gruppenführer* worked himself up into a frenzy as he hurled obscenities at his subordinate officer, shouting at Steinert that he hadn't the right or the authority to issue such an order. He told him he had no business interfering in such matters and that involving the German Army in SS affairs without higher orders was a dangerous and borderline punishable offense. He highlighted this point by removing his Walther PPK pistol and placing it on the desk with the barrel pointed directly at Steinert. The *Obersturmbannführer* made it a point not to make any sudden movements or show any outward emotion that could be construed as weak or fearful. He merely sat stone-faced and motionless. It was his best defense.

Von Schreiner finished his speech by threatening Steinert not to disobey orders or overstep his authoritative bounds again. To do so would encourage strong reprimands and potential action by other authorities outside the realm of the SD. Steinert took the comment to mean he would be arrested and turned over to the Gestapo if he created any more waves for his superior. Almost out of breath, von Schreiner stood up, red in the face and breathing heavily, and ordered Steinert out of his office. Steinert stood up, saluted his superior, did an about-face, and calmly walked to the door. As he reached for the knob his superior fired off one last threat. Von Schreiner told Steinert that he felt he was spending far too much leisurely time at Café LeBlanc. He then hypocritically inferred that the company Steinert sought while there was not becoming of a German SS officer. He ordered Steinert to drastically reduce the number of visits and restrict his business to matters benefiting the preservation of the Reich— specifically, finding the escaped American pilot.

"*Jawohl, mein Herr! Heil, Hitler!*" Steinert responded with an accompanying Nazi salute. Steinert left the office fully composed, making sure not to show any fear, as he knew it would be used against him. As he walked away from von Schreiner's office, his mind started to formulate ideas. The *Gruppenführer's* orders repeated themselves in his head, yet he chose to suppress them. Realizing his neck was truly on the line and the deadly consequences surrounding disobeying his superior,

Steinert began to ponder the thought of unleashing a new emotion he hadn't been able to express openly for a long time—defiance.

The next day, Steinert performed his duties and obeyed his orders in exemplary fashion. He did nothing either to create waves or draw unnecessary attention to himself.

Early on the morning of June 1, Steinert sat at his desk in the secret intelligence-gathering room, attacking piles of backed-up intelligence paperwork. Most of it contained useless, outdated information, unworthy of even being reported; however, it had to be examined and filed, per standard procedure. He quickly grew weary of the countless irrelevant files that littered his desk. He ordered the most recent Enigma cipher keys, for all military branches, placed on his desk for review. He went over the codebooks, then returned them to their proper place.

Frustrated, Steinert decided it was necessary to pay Café LeBlanc another visit. He would make the trip there much later in the day, without von Schreiner's knowledge, and preferably when he was occupied with his mistress. Steinert only hoped Yvette and Pierre hadn't left the château. It was immaterial anyway. He had made up his mind. He was going to the Café LeBlanc despite the danger.

That afternoon, Steinert's junior intelligence officer reported that he had been monitoring a peculiar coded broadcast from the BBC. It was a repeating message in the form of poetry. Steinert picked up a headset and listened to the message. He closed his eyes, took in every word, and committed them to memory, ordering the *Untersturmführer* to decode the message and transcribe it for him at once. Minutes later Steinert had the complete message. It was something he recognized immediately— the first line of the poem "*Chanson d'automne*" by Paul Verlaine. Steinert was very familiar with it, but had no idea what it meant or for whom it was intended. He could only speculate. After a minute of thought and a round of orders to his staff, he folded the transcript, put it in his pocket, and left the intelligence-gathering room, headed to von Schreiner's office.

Back at von Schreiner's office, Steinert alerted von Schreiner's secretary to the urgency of his visit. The secretary nodded and picked up her telephone. After a brief conversation, she hung up and motioned to Steinert that he could enter the *Gruppenführer's* office. Steinert took a breath, entered, and gave the Nazi salute followed by *"Heil Hitler."* Von Schreiner was wearing his formal black *Allgemeine-SS* uniform, rather than the more customary field-gray version. As he rose from his desk chair Steinert noticed he was also wearing his ceremonial SS dagger— very curious, indeed.

Steinert showed his superior the intelligence transcript of the poem. Von Schreiner told Steinert he was already aware of the British broadcast—it had been relayed to him earlier by his secret contacts within the local *Wehrmacht* headquarters. Steinert suspected he was lying. Von Schreiner told Steinert that the German High Command had been notified and several military units in northern France had been put on alert, particularly units of the 15th Army in and around the Pas-de-Calais. He claimed to have in his possession written orders to that effect from high-ranking *Wehrmacht* Field Marshals, including Rommel and von Rundstedt. Again, Steinert felt that von Schreiner was simply lying to appear in control of the situation.

Suddenly, thundering booms echoed in the far distance. Both men went to the window and could faintly hear distant air-raid sirens. The Allies were again bombing in inclement weather during the day. It wouldn't have surprised Steinert if an entire battalion of Allied troops suddenly marched up to the front door of the château and knocked! Von Schreiner closed the drapes and launched into talking about other matters. He informed Steinert that he had received word earlier that Hitler had removed the German Army's military intelligence unit, the *Abwehr*, from the control of the *Wehrmacht*. A bit stunned and intrigued, Steinert listened carefully to what he said next. Von Schreiner then imparted that the *Abwehr*'s chief, Admiral Wilhelm Canaris, had been dismissed and that all secret service and intelligence gathering activities had been placed under the control of the *Reichsführer-SS* Heinrich Himmler and the SS, in general. Von Schreiner told Steinert to expect added duties in the coming weeks and to be prepared for high-ranking Nazi official visits, possibly in the next few days. He did not specify who or when, but dropped important SS names including Ernst Kaltenbrunner, Walter Schellenberg, and even Himmler.

Von Schreiner poured two glasses of schnapps and offered one to

Steinert. The smell of alcohol was already detectable on von Schreiner's breath. After guzzling down the last swig of schnapps from his glass, the *SS-Gruppenführer* ordered Steinert to leave and resume his duties. Steinert put down his glass, gave the Nazi salute, and went on his way.

Down the hallway he noticed a familiar feminine figure standing alone, holding a slow-burning cigarette. Beneath a large, stylish ladies hat, complete with colorful ribbons and flowers, stood the *Gruppenführer's* mistress. She was wearing a revealing dress accessorized with smooth silk stockings, sparkling jewelry, and voluptuous makeup. She looked up and smiled seductively. Steinert nodded, then turned and walked away, knowing Yvette would be occupying von Schreiner's time during the evening, making it easier for him to slip away undetected. He wondered how much information his superior had revealed was truth and how much pure fantasy.

As daylight hours gave way to evening, Steinert looked out his chamber's window. The skies were still dark and gloomy, but free of Allied bombers and fighters. Steinert, off duty but still wearing his field-gray uniform, looked out toward the blacked-out Jolieville. He gathered a few things and made his way down toward the motor pool. On his way, he silently walked past von Schreiner's personal quarters. He heard muffled music from behind the door accompanied by sounds of drunken laughter easily identified as both male and female. It was apparent that von Schreiner was pruriently occupied for the evening. Steinert couldn't have asked for a better scenario. He slipped outside without arousing the concern of the SS guards on duty.

At the motor pool, he spotted his personal Mercedes parked in a corner. The officer on duty confronted him. With a salute and a nervous crack in his voice, the young officer admitted he wasn't expecting any evening departures. Steinert reassured him that nothing was wrong and simply said he was going out for the evening with classified orders and didn't require a driver. The officer clicked his heels and escorted the *Obersturmbannführer* to his car. Steinert climbed in and drove off. When he reached the outer gate he presented his identification papers to the guard, who immediately raised the gate's rail and let him pass without question. Steinert was now on his way to Café LeBlanc. What he didn't realize was that he was not alone. A mysterious car began a silent pursuit.

The sun had set but there was still enough light to navigate the roads leading into Jolieville without the use of headlights. The town was dark as ever and showed no signs of life. No street lamps were illuminated nor any electrical lights visible inside any local residence. Von Schreiner had made sure, with cooperation from the local *Wehrmacht* commanders, that strict blackouts would be in effect each night until further notice. It was an inconvenient and irritating order, but one that was adhered to without question, especially since Allied air raids had noticeably increased in recent weeks.

Steinert pulled his car up in front of Café LeBlanc, surprised at the lack of military checkpoints he assumed he'd have to cross going into town. He grabbed the wooden case from the trunk and instinctively looked around to see if anybody was watching him. He saw no one. He quietly knocked on the café's front door, but nobody answered. He knocked again, waiting another minute before a stone-faced Christophe opened it.

Steinert and Christophe glared at each other before retreating inside. Christophe closed and locked the door. The café was drowned in darkness except for a few dimly lit candles providing just enough light for a person to safely get around. At first Christophe said nothing. He only stared at the small wooden case, knowing exactly why Steinert was there. Eventually he spoke up and told the *Obersturmbannführer* they needed to talk. Christophe and Grégoire had heard the BBC broadcast earlier and knew the Paul Verlaine poem had some significance pertaining to the impending invasion, but since they were entirely cut off from the closest French Resistance cells, they couldn't decipher what the message meant.

Steinert simply told Christophe to wait, and that he'd have instructions for him later. Christophe seethed with anger as he didn't appreciate being ordered around by Steinert. Not wanting Steinert's Luger waved in his face, Christophe again reluctantly retreated to his quarters above the café. Steinert watched him go, then descended the main staircase behind the bar and kitchen. He ran his hand along the wall until he felt the groove that revealed the hidden door. Once discovered, he entered the secret room to set up his Enigma machine.

Steinert put on his headset and listened to the BBC radio traffic flooding the airwaves. Per his routine, he recalled the cipher keys he had memorized earlier at the château, then began configuring the Enigma device, setting each rotor to its proper position. He sent several coded messages prefaced with the code name "Windsor" to his contacts in England. The outgoing messages, coded brilliantly, were very direct and straight to the point. He wanted to know when and where the Allied landings would occur. He also requested instructions on how to prepare for the event. Lastly he sent messages in hopes of simply reestablishing the routine communications with England that had strangely ceased several days earlier. As before, the airwaves were silent. There was the occasional coded message, but there were no messages from his personal sources in England.

Steinert began to grow impatient. He felt time was being wasted and that he needed to act audaciously. He began sending encoded messages revealing the locations of the hidden *Luftwaffe* airstrips and the threat they posed to any Allied landing in the area. He then relayed the new coordinates identifying where these fighter units were to be relocated. A separate message went out asking for verification. Time passed with no response. Frustrated, he put together a tersely coded message giving his intention to sabotage one particularly vital airstrip. He gave the coordinates and the approximate time of the action, then requested a separate attack by low-flying British Mosquito night fighters in and around the area to mask the action, thereby taking responsibility away from the French Resistance that could spark horrific SS reprisals on the civilian population. He falsely relayed that there would be several other concealed targets of opportunity in the area that could be taken down easily by fighters rather than by sabotage. The destruction of the targeted airstrip by the Resistance would act as a lighted beacon that would guide the fighters to the important nearby targets of opportunity, thereby serving a mutually beneficial dual purpose.

Steinert ended with emphasis on the code name "Windsor," then sat back in his chair. It was a bold plan, one that may have overstepped his authority. Nonetheless, he felt it needed to be done. A bold action was necessary to jolt some response and clear up any miscommunication. At least that was what he hoped. He stayed at his secret monitoring station for two more hours before giving up and powering down his equipment. No response and no other information was forthcoming from Bletchley Park. It did not bode well for the SS-*Obersturmbannführer*, who decided it was time to share his plan with the LeBlancs and their American guest.

Steinert secured the secret room, climbed the stairs, and entered the dark dining room. Fumbling for a candle, he heard distant booms and accompanying air raid sirens. Some German troops scurried down the street, but he paid them no mind. He lit a candle and made sure all the curtains were drawn—then a second candle. Soon there was enough dim light to suit him. Steinert placed the Enigma machine on a dark corner table and walked behind the bar, found a bottle of red wine, uncorked it, then bent down to retrieve some wine glasses under the bar. As he stood up, the two LeBlanc brothers emerged from the curtain concealing their stairway, rigid and silent, their arms crossed and crooked scowls across their faces. Steinert felt their anger and wondered if they were inclined to jump him the second he let his guard down. Without a word, he motioned for the two to sit down at the corner table.

Downstairs, behind his closed door, Hank Mitchell was enjoying Pauline's warm embrace. The two lovers had spent as much time as possible together in the privacy of Hank's room. Pauline brought him fresh food, clean water to drink, and unsoiled clothing. She also continued to care for him with soothing massages and warm baths. Her visits often led to some form of sexual exertion. Although Pauline tried to be as discreet as possible, her amorous actions did not go undetected. Both her brothers knew what was happening and were displeased. The American airman was becoming even more disliked than before.

"I hear something upstairs," Hank whispered in Pauline's ear as he looked at the closed door. The two were in bed together wrapped in each other's arms. "Do you think it could be trouble?"

"I do not know," whispered Pauline. "I must go and find out," she said while crawling out from under the bed sheets, her naked silhouette framed in the soft glow of the candlelight. She reached for her dress and slid it on over her body, then silently opened the door and tiptoed up the stairs, hiding just out of sight in the kitchen. She peeked over and saw the three men seated at the corner table. Pauline could tell her brothers were not happy. She listened intently to what was being disputed.

"What's going on? What are they saying?"

Pauline turned around sharply and saw Hank crouched down close behind her, stealthily watching the secret meeting.

"Be quiet and do not move!" firmly whispered Pauline. "I do not want them to see us!" The two eavesdroppers continued to observe.

Christophe grew agitated several times at Steinert's instructions. The disgruntled Frenchman turned his head away and spit in disgust. Steinert poured the Frenchmen a glass of wine to ease the tension. Grégoire accepted his drink and finished it at once. Christophe was reluctant and held his glass suspiciously, as though he suspected the uniformed SD officer had poisoned the libation. He placed the glass on the table. The conversation continued with Steinert expressing his plans and issuing orders in fluent French.

"What are they discussing? I can't understand what they're saying," expressed Hank.

"Shhh," said Pauline, whispering in Hank's ear, "Herr Steinert is giving my brothers a new task to … how you say … carry out? He is also reminding them that he has taken care of the removal of the bodies in the streets that had Christophe enraged earlier."

Just then Christophe slammed his fist onto the table, sloshing some of the red wine from the glass and staining the red-and-white-checkered tablecloth. Grégoire fidgeted in his chair while Steinert fired off some harsh words, tapping his index finger on the table as if he were pointing to something specific.

"What's happening? Tell me!" Hank demanded in a whisper.

Pauline turned to him and said, "Herr Steinert wants my brothers to destroy a German airstrip tomorrow night. It is a very dangerous mission. Christophe does not like the plan."

She paused to hear more of the conversation. She then continued, "Christophe is angry and does not feel this mission is necessary. He and Herr Steinert are arguing about the location of the German airstrip.

Herr Steinert is telling Christophe that the airstrip is at a new location. Christophe is insisting that it has not moved. He says he knows this to be true, but does not say how. Also they argue about a message heard over the radio. Christophe feels it is about the invasion, but Herr Steinert will not discuss it, which makes Christophe very upset."

Christophe folded his arms angrily and turned away from the table, shaking his head. He turned back and spoke to Steinert, who, in turn, shook his head in disagreement. Grégoire meanwhile remained silent and began to take an interest in the small wooden case on the table just within his grasp. The younger brother reached out in an attempt to open it. Instantly Steinert drew his Luger and pointed it directly at Grégoire. The brothers threw back their chairs and raised their arms. Pauline trembled in terror while Hank stayed frozen. Steinert snatched the case and tucked it under his arm. He kept his gun trained on the two brothers and barked out one final order before retreating out the door.

Christophe and Grégoire started arguing. Both were upset and uncertain about the task at hand. Suddenly Christophe looked in the direction of the kitchen and spotted the two spies. He rushed over and grabbed Pauline by the arm and pulled her into the open. Hank jumped up to help her, but Grégoire stopped him and pushed him into the wall. Pauline angrily wrestled free from her older brother's grip and started to argue with him in French. Their voices elevated and she showed no sign of backing down. Christophe ranted and raved until his face turned red. He fired off one final statement to his sister then turned and pointed a forbidding finger at Hank before withdrawing to his room. Grégoire turned to his sister and expressed some choice remarks of his own, only to be thoroughly rebuffed, then dismissed by her. He went upstairs to join his brother.

Not knowing what to say or do, Hank looked blankly at Pauline. She explained, "They are going to destroy the airstrip tomorrow. They do not think they will come back alive. You are to go with them, though they still do not trust you or want you here any longer. They are furious with me and they know of our relationship. They want you to go, but I will not let them send you away!"

Pauline embraced Hank and started to weep softly. He could offer little comfort. Again he was being placed in harm's way, with no mention of a plan to get him out of occupied France and back to Allied England. As he held Pauline in his arms, he continued to wonder what his fate would be and if he truly was with friends, or surrounded by wolves in sheep's clothing. It was late, the candles began to flicker, and the two lovers crept back down the stairs and behind the closed door of Hank's room. Pauline locked it from the inside. For the first time she was more afraid of her brothers breaking in than the Gestapo.

Chapter 17

THE AIRSTRIP RAID

June 2, 1944. The day had been oddly quiet, with scarcely any German soldiers or Nazi Party officials patronizing Café LeBlanc. Normally the café would have had a modest number of gray-green-clad officers and enlisted men milling about with food and drink in between duties. Today, however, was very different. Odd as it was, it was a welcome blessing as it gave the LeBlanc family more time to prepare for their upcoming nocturnal activities. Fortunately for Pauline and her brothers, the clear and sunny weather seen earlier in the day had taken another turn for the worse. The evening skies filled with menacingly tenebrous clouds that obscured the sun and let loose torrential downpours that drenched the Earth below. These intense pockets of moisture, fueled by unpleasant gusts of wind, tore through the French countryside, abating only occasionally to a steady drizzle.

Soon the café was empty. Not wanting to entertain any late-night drunken stragglers, Christophe bolted the front door and drew the curtains. He switched off the electrical lights and lit small candles, giving the place the appearance of being closed for the night. The foul weather, chaperoned by the eerie darkness of the blacked-out town, furnished an uncomfortable feeling to many residents who remedied the problem by staying home and out of sight behind locked doors.

Christophe retreated to his bedchamber above the main dining room, unaware he was being watched. His young sister silently followed him up and hid outside his room. The door was closed but Pauline cleverly got down on her knees and peeked through the keyhole. She could see and hear everything. Grégoire, already in the room, was gathering supplies and packing knapsacks with weapons, ammunition, explosives, and other stolen German military stores that might be useful during the upcoming raid. The two brothers looked at one another grimly. Christophe stopped Grégoire from what he was doing and began going over a plan for the raid—a new plan!

Christophe began by spelling out his distaste and distrust for Steinert. He felt their arrangement with Steinert was becoming increasingly invalid and that the arrogant, purported British agent was thinking way too much like a Nazi to suit his taste any longer. He had grown very wary of the sudden lack of information-sharing and strongly felt something monumental was about to happen that would undoubtedly destroy the fragile alliance.

Grégoire took a long drag on a cigarette and added that he felt Steinert was leading them into a trap by setting up a bogus target. Furthermore, if captured, the presence of the American fugitive would certainly seal their doom in some horrible Gestapo torture chamber. Christophe agreed that Steinert could no longer be trusted. Both agreed that a raid would occur that night, but not according to Steinert's design.

Christophe's plan was both elaborate and devious. They would take the American with them to where Christophe felt the genuine target was located and not where Steinert had indicated. They would destroy the target and kill the American in the process, after which they would return to Café LeBlanc and sadly explain to Pauline the young American's demise at the hands of the Germans. Fearing immediate Nazi reprisals, Christophe would convince her that they had been exposed and betrayed by Steinert and had to flee at once, or risk being captured by the Gestapo. They would then gather whatever belongings they needed, set fire to Café LeBlanc, and stealthily work their way out of Jolieville and into the rural countryside, in search of other existing cells of French Resistance. Once safely among their fellow patriotic countrymen, they would wait for their ultimate liberation at the hands of the impending Allied invasion that Christophe was convinced would occur any day.

Grégoire nodded in approval of his older brother's plan, beamed a malicious smile, and continued to pack ammunition and German potato masher–shaped stick grenades into three knapsacks spread out on a small table. Christophe looked at his wrist watch and exclaimed, "*Bientôt!*" He pulled back a closet curtain revealing several British 9mm Sten machine guns that he checked over meticulously and then lined up on a table. The two Frenchmen continued their preparations, unaware that their plans were now known!

Pauline was aghast. She trembled and could barely breathe. She stood up and quietly made her way downstairs. She didn't know what to do next. Her mind filled with conflicting feelings of familial loyalty and burning passion for her newfound love. She couldn't let her brothers murder Hank, but then again, how could she prevent it without ultimately causing their demise? She knew she had to do something as time was quickly slipping away. For the moment she composed herself. She would prepare for the raid as planned, and work on a solution that would be for the betterment of all.

Pauline found Hank some dark clothing that she hoped would better conceal him in the late-night raid. Knowing her brothers would be dressed mostly in black, she wanted him to have the same advantage. In the dim light of his small room, Hank changed into the clothes and carefully fed stubby .45 caliber bullets into the magazine of his Colt pistol. He slapped the magazine into the butt of the weapon, then loaded the two spare magazines with extra bullets Pauline had left for him. He was grateful he still had his gun and didn't question how Pauline had been able to supply him with the right ammunition. He slipped the pistol into the back of his pants and the extra magazines in the front pockets, then sat back and nervously waited for what was to happen next.

Moments later, the door unbolted and swung open slowly. Hank looked up, expecting to see Christophe's miserable visage staring at him with disdain, but was curiously surprised to see Pauline. Momentarily confused, then horrified beyond belief, Hank stood up to confront his lover, who was dressed in a baggy pair of black men's pants held up by a tightly wrapped belt and black suspenders. She also wore a white man's shirt buttoned all the way to the top and a dark-brown leather coat. A white scarf around her neck and her hair pinned underneath a black beret gave her a masculine appearance. Heavy boots on her feet and black grease smeared on her face completed her ensemble. She looked the part of a French Resistance fighter ready for action.

"What are you doing? You can't go!" objected Hank.

"I am going," replied Pauline, "and do not try to tell me no."

"This is crazy! I can't let you risk your life! You can't possibly understand the dangers involved in a mission like this! It's too much for a woman to handle! You have to stay here where it's safe," insisted Hank.

"You do not tell me what to do, *Henri*," snapped Pauline. "I have experienced more danger than you could ever imagine. I have served and I have killed those who would do me and my family harm. This I have done for France and this I will continue to do until we are free again. This is my duty and you will not stand in my way. There are dangers all around us, *Henri*. Some are obvious, others are hidden. The worst threats are those that are not easily seen or understood. *You* are blind to these dangers … and *I* must keep you safe … for I fear no one else will!" She stormed out and up the stairs.

Hank became agitated and paced back and forth. He didn't want Pauline put in harm's way, but slowly began to realize there was very little he could do to stop her. He just hoped that her brothers, who commanded more authority in the matter, felt the same way he did. Perhaps they could force her to stay behind? Hank tried the door, only to discover it was bolted shut. Apparently his newfound love didn't let her burning desires impair her better judgment. It was still best to keep the American locked up behind closed doors and out of sight. Her protective nature had intensified since he was first brought to her.

Hank heard voices in French upstairs. He put his ear to the door and made out angry conversation between Pauline and her brothers. Though he couldn't understand the words, he definitely understood the tones. For once, he hoped Christophe would win the battle. Hank pulled his ear away from the door when he heard footsteps coming down the stairs. The door was unbolted and Grégoire appeared. "*Vous!*" the Frenchman said, pointing at Hank. "*Venez avec moi maintenant!*" he demanded while motioning for Hank to follow. "*Vite, vite!*" he added impatiently.

Up the stairs they went, through the kitchen, and into the main dining room. There stood Pauline behind the bar, arguing with

Christophe. Each pointed a finger at the other as they exchanged unsavory words laced with dark undertones. Grégoire ignored the family spat and busied himself checking over the contents of the knapsacks. Christophe pointed an accusing finger at Hank, while continuing his verbal assault on his younger sister. Not backing down, Pauline matched every phrase and unflinchingly stood her ground. Even though Hank couldn't understand French, he knew what was being discussed and could see that Christophe was steadily losing this oral sparring match with his sister.

His arms flailing, Christophe gave it one last effort, his bulging eyes looking as if they would pop out of his skull. It was no use. Pauline sidestepped, outwitted, and outmaneuvered her brother's demands using courage, honor, and common sense. She was going on this raid and that was final! Christophe raised his hand to slap his sister, but abruptly stopped, poured himself a glass of whiskey, and swallowed it with malice while glaring at Hank. He then hurled the glass onto the floor and watched it shatter. Grégoire looked at him and said, "*Nous ne pouvons plus attendre.*"

"*D'accord. Regardez ici,*" icily replied Christophe. He snatched up a burning candle and placed it on a nearby table, then produced a scrap of paper from his pocket and laid it out. The others huddled around and looked down at the hastily drawn map—Christophe's assault plan. He detailed precisely how he wanted the raid carried out and what everyone's assignment was. Having reconnoitered the area and the secret airstrip earlier, he knew the best way to get in, inflict the most damage and causalities, and get out. Once the eldest brother finished, his younger siblings nodded in agreement.

"*Nous partons!*" Christophe barked. Grégoire strapped on his knapsack. Christophe did the same. Pauline went to the bar and reached under, producing a Spanish .38 Llama automatic pistol, which she tucked into her belt. Hank noticed that the weapon looked very much like a smaller version of his Colt .45. Christophe reluctantly handed his sister the third knapsack, which she strapped on her back. He gave nothing to Hank. Pauline snuffed out all the low-burning candles, encasing the café in near total darkness. As the tiny raiding party slipped out into the rainy night, Hank wondered if the secret sewer route was to be their destination again.

Pauline hustled over to Hank. "Stay close to me at all times. Christophe and Grégoire will lead and we shall follow. They will carry out the sabotage and we will … how you say … cover them. Now come, my love!" Hank nodded and the two hurried along in pursuit of the older LeBlancs. "*Quel temps horrible!*" Pauline cried, looking upward.

In front of the center plaza fountain across the street from the café, Christophe and Grégoire pulled up the neatly concealed manhole cover leading down into the sewers. The American flying gear was still drooping on the nearby coat stand, untouched and weighted down heavily by the rain. The sight of it angered Hank. He made a move for it but was stopped by Pauline.

"No, *Henri*! Do not be foolish! Leave it or we could all suffer later!"

Christophe and Grégoire slid the manhole cover aside and motioned for Pauline and Hank to drop down first. Grégoire climbed down next. Christophe was last to enter. He took a moment to scan the streets for any sign they had been spotted, then pulled the manhole cover back into place. Flashlights in hand, the brothers took the lead and headed into the depths of the sewer. The dimly lit flashlight beams barely cut through the darkness, but Pauline had faith in her brothers' knowledge of the tight maze of tunnels and crawlways that lay before them. The water level was high due to all the recent rains, and the stench was overpowering. Hank could hear the squeaking of dozens of rats lurking in hidden corners.

The group trudged along without saying a word and making as little noise as possible. After traveling for a while they reached a tunnel where Christophe stopped and raised his light until it illuminated an exit point.

"*Voila,*" said Christophe. "*C'est tout droit,*" he added. Ahead lay a low drainage pipe where wastewater was rushing out. The exit pipe was at the base of a stone wall that looked as if it had been built fairly recently. It was large enough in circumference for an average-sized man to crawl through, but the water flooding through was dangerously high in volume.

"*Quatre mètres,*" said Christophe to Pauline and Hank indicating how far they'd have to crawl through to reach the other side safely: four meters.

"*Après vous, Christophe et Grégoire,*" Pauline said, motioning for her older siblings to go first. Christophe scoffed at her and boldly got on his belly, crawling headfirst into the pipe. His head and knapsack were nearly submerged below the rushing putrid water. The flood of the draining water carried him swiftly through to the other side. Hank heard a faint splash above the loud "whoosh" of running water that drowned out virtually all other sound.

Grégoire crawled in next. He accidentally swallowed some water and choked it up loudly. After coughing for a minute, he put his head down and let the water whisk him away. Pauline hesitated, making sure her knapsack was tightly secured before climbing into the pipe. She looked at Hank, then at the running water. She was scared, but crawled in headfirst and was gone.

Hank listened for the faint splash that meant she was safely through, but heard nothing. All at once he heard thrashing sounds and incoherent, water-choked calls for help.

"Damnit! She must be stuck!" thought Hank frantically as he crawled into the pipe and reached out blindly for Pauline. The water current had slowed due to the human blockage, so Hank had to pull himself along until he reached her position about halfway through. Her legs were thrashing as she tried to spin herself free from some immovable debris that had snagged her knapsack. Hank managed to grab her legs and, with one mighty twist and shove, was able to free her like a cork from a champagne bottle. In the process her knapsack ripped open, aiding in her escape. She splashed down on the other side with Hank right behind her.

Sensing something was wrong, Christophe hurried to his sister's aid and pulled her out of the stream where the sewer drainage pipe was emptying. Hank splashed down seconds later, stood up in the chest-high water, and pulled himself out to meet the others. Christophe held Pauline in his arms while she coughed violently, trying to expel the dirty water she had inadvertently ingested. Hank reached out to touch her face but

Grégoire stopped him and motioned for him to stand back, out of the way. After a few minutes, Pauline's coughing ceased and she was able to stand on her own. She retrieved her beret and embraced Hank in gratitude for saving her life. The American did not receive any thankful recognition from the male LeBlancs, who huddled together on a patch of wet grass and mud, draining the water from their knapsacks, hoping it would not render all their explosives and small arms useless.

"*Où sommes-nous?*" Pauline asked Christophe between coughs. The two whispered for a moment as Christophe tried to ascertain if Pauline was well enough to proceed with the mission. Grégoire kept his eyes and ears alert, while Hank simply tried to gauge where they were. He reckoned they had emerged from the Jolieville sewer system at some remote drainage outlet on the far outskirts of town. They were by a stream that presumably led to the coast and eventually emptied into the ocean. They were definitely clear of Jolieville, amidst a patchy wooded area. Hank had a feeling that they would be striking out into the woods. His instinct would soon prove correct.

Christophe and Grégoire took the lead again and proceeded southeast into the woods with dim flashlights cutting a narrow path through the rainy darkness. There was no distinct path to follow, yet Christophe seemed confident in the direction he was heading. They ducked under tree limbs, climbed over thick, exposed tree roots, and scampered through small open fields.

The rain subsided and occasional breaks in the night sky revealed a hint of moonlight. At the edge of the forest they reached a muddy, sunken dirt road. Heavy tire marks carved into the earth caused Christophe to quietly rejoice. He had found what he was looking for! He reached into his knapsack and pulled out his Sten machine gun. Grégoire and Pauline did the same. All switched off their flashlights and it was apparent to Hank, clutching his .45 pistol, that danger was not far away.

The group followed the road into another patch of forest, beyond which Christophe saw dim lights on the horizon. Quickly he signaled the others to get off the road and into the adjacent woods, then led them on a course straight for the lights. The group cautiously slithered along, watching for any sign of trouble. Christophe stopped and hunkered down behind a large rock that provided adequate cover for all four raiders. He pointed to a dim glow in the distance. It was a large, covered German truck with a rumbling generator in tow. The truck's bed had been transformed into a mobile barracks with two windows on the side and electric light shining through them. Long, heavy cables snaked out from the generator and connected to other trucks hidden under camouflage netting just off the road.

Just beyond the vehicles was a rectangular clearing in the woods. It was the hidden airstrip, just long and wide enough for German fighters to scramble in and out. Hank scanned the area feverishly. Nestled in the dark, shielded by tall trees and heavy camouflage netting, sat German fighter aircraft. Even though they were hidden brilliantly, Hank's extraordinary eyesight and intimate knowledge of fighter plane design easily picked up the familiar shapes of the chocked wheels, landing gear, propeller blades, wings, and cockpit.

Four hidden ME-109 fighters sat opposite the small airstrip, ready for action. Hank looked down to what he considered the base of the airstrip and noticed another fighter cleverly hidden and apparently lined up to be the first in flight, should the need arise. He surmised it was probably the aircraft of the senior pilot on scene—possibly the group leader. He determined it was not an ME-109, but rather a *Focke-Wulf* 190! His veins coursed with excitement. He wanted to inspect the "Butcher Bird" up close. Maybe even jump into the cockpit and make a daring escape flight back to England! As enticing as that seemed, he squelched the notion when he looked over at Pauline. Besides, he knew that Christophe had other ideas in store for these particular German aircraft.

It was just after midnight. There was no sign of human activity along the airstrip, though Hank knew there had to be a sentry on duty somewhere. Perhaps the miserable weather had forced the Germans to retreat inside the trucks for shelter and rest. There was no telling how many Germans were on-site at this secret airstrip, but it didn't matter. Regardless of the number, the team was prepared to kill anything that moved.

The elder brother readied his machine gun and wrapped a dirty red scarf around his head to cover his lower face. Grégoire did the same. The two brothers whispered to each other, then Grégoire cautiously crouched down and moved off toward the airstrip. Christophe told Pauline to stay behind and provide machine-gun cover when the shooting started. Christophe pointed at Hank and beckoned for the American to follow him. Hank looked at Pauline, who reluctantly said, "Go with Christophe. He will place you where he wants you. You are to provide cover for him."

Hank nodded and grasped his pistol. The two men started toward the nearest truck. Light from the window in the back of the covered bed of the truck enabled them to see in more easily than the Germans could see out. To their astonishment, no one appeared to be guarding the area. Satisfied for the moment, Christophe pointed to Hank, indicating for him to stay where he was while Christophe got closer. Hank nodded and crouched at the ready. He looked back for Pauline but couldn't find her position through the darkness. Christophe dropped to the ground and crawled under the truck. He pulled a grenade from his knapsack and kept it at the ready as he pointed his machine gun across the airstrip in the direction of the parked, hidden ME-109s. He waited.

Across the strip Hank could just make out the figure of Grégoire, who had begun slicing through the camouflage netting of the first fighter in line. Satisfied that enough of the fighter was exposed, he began to place grenades under it. With the planes fully fueled and tightly grouped together, Grégoire was about to unleash a fiery surprise upon the Germans.

Just then the back door to one of the parked trucks swung open. Two Germans stepped out, lit cigarettes, and began to converse. Belly down in the grass and mud, Christophe aimed his Sten at the unsuspecting Germans and waited. Not far back in his hidden position along the tree line, Hank also watched the Germans. Unsure what to do, he kept his Colt at the ready and knew it was better to wait and let the Frenchmen's plan unfold rather than start any aggressive action of his own.

The two Germans finished their cigarettes and tossed them onto the wet, muddy ground. Curiously, they weren't armed. As Hank observed them, he deduced they were most likely mechanics or standard *Luftwaffe* ground crew personnel. He watched them closely with pistol at the ready. He took comfort knowing Pauline sat poised to strike from behind if the need arose.

The Germans reentered the truck and came back out carrying two high-powered light stands and two *Wehrmachtskanisters*, or jerry cans, of gasoline, dropping the fuel next to two empty steel fuel drums and lugging the portable light stands to the base of the airstrip. One set up the lights while the other strung a heavy-duty cable from the lights back to the rumbling generator. Once connected, the lights came to life, illuminating the *Focke-Wulf* 190 fighter and a good portion of the airstrip. Christophe crawled up behind the truck's tire trying to stay hidden as the new electrical light partially illuminated the vehicle under which he was hiding. Grégoire stayed concealed behind the ME-109s farther down the airstrip while Hank and Pauline were still safe and veiled in the woods not far from the edge of the tree line.

The two Germans gathered their toolboxes and started some early-morning maintenance on the FW-190. Hank strained his eyes to study the lit-up fighter plane. His heart sank into the pit of his stomach. He recognized the dapple-gray paint scheme, yellow color on the engine cowling's underside, and yellow rudder. Carelessly he moved out of his assigned position and drew closer, where he could see better through the trees. He looked long and hard at the upper engine cowling. Incredibly, the American pilot spied the insignia forever impressed deeply into his subconscious—the hideous black wolf's head outlined in white! A voluminous range of emotions tore through his body as his heart pumped wildly and his mind raced feverishly. Suddenly Hank was falling again, trying to escape a mad German pilot murderously trying to strafe him out of the sky! The actual enemy fighter that had nearly ended his life weeks earlier was sitting only a few short meters away from him. Hank wondered if the fiendish hotshot pilot Steinert had so arrogantly pointed out to him days earlier at the café was also nearby.

More uniformed *Luftwaffe* personnel soon emerged from the trucks. These men were clearly pilots and officers, not just mechanics. Standing together, some smoked while others talked quietly. One man picked up a full jerry can and poured a little fuel into an empty steel drum. He then dropped a lit match into the drum, igniting the fuel and producing a large flame that flared out of the barrel. Other pilots scrounged for broken limbs, leaves, tree bark, and anything else that would burn and tossed them into the drum. The men now had their own makeshift campfire that gave off light and heat during the cool, damp morning. The four of them swapped combat flying stories by holding up their hands to simulate fighter planes sweeping through the skies.

The mechanics finished working on the FW-190 and retreated into their truck for a respite from the chilly morning air. The pilots continued to stand around the fire while other *Luftwaffe* men armed with slung MP-40 machine guns began to appear. Hank silently cursed at the sight of armed troops. The opportunity to strike first and hard with total surprise had gone by the wayside.

Hank glanced across the airstrip in the direction of the ME-109s to see Grégoire hastily positioning grenades in key locations under each of the four 109 fighters. Keeping the last German Model 24 stick grenade for himself, he moved away to a safer distance. With his machine gun slung, he clasped the grenade, unscrewed the base cap, grabbed the dangling porcelain ball attached to a pull cord, and gave it good hard tug. This dragged the roughened steel rod inside through the grenade's igniter, causing it to flare up. Its five-second fuse was now burning. Grégoire hurled the grenade at the base of the first plane and dropped to the deck for cover. Seconds later the grenade exploded, tearing away a large chunk of the ME- 109s tail section, causing it to collapse and the nose to point upward toward the sky.

The blast shocked the Germans, who cried out in alarm and scrambled toward the stricken fighter. Christophe's Sten machine gun roared to life as he fired several bursts at the unsuspecting *Luftwaffe* personnel. Two Germans dropped to the ground dead, while the others scattered, running for cover as they tried to comprehend what exactly was happening. The explosion brought several *Luftwaffe* troops scurrying from the trucks, armed with rifles and machine guns. Christophe took aim again and fired, killing or wounding three others. Unfortunately for him, his position was now revealed and several troops hit the deck and began firing in his direction. Bullets ricocheted off the underside of the truck all around him. Seeing his brother was in danger, Grégoire emerged from the woods, firing his Sten and effectively cutting down several Germans in a murderous crossfire. However, more German troops began to arrive from hidden positions and unseen vehicles farther down the airstrip. They found cover in the early-morning darkness and slowly advanced on Christophe's and Grégoire's positions, as both Frenchmen continued to return fire.

Meanwhile, still hunkered down in the woods, Hank watched the graphic firefight with a feeling of helplessness. He held his pistol, ready to shoot, but found no targets. Suddenly a voice came from behind!

"*Henri!*" said Pauline as she crouched down beside him, "We must destroy those planes!" Hank looked over at the ME-109s and saw that Grégoire's grenade had only damaged the first one. The anticipated chain reaction had not happened! The initial blast did not touch off the other grenades or ignite the fighters' fuel tanks. One 109 sat damaged, but not on fire, while the other three looked unharmed and still serviceable. "I will go and destroy them with my machine gun and grenades," said Pauline.

Hank grabbed her arm and hissed, "No!" He spun her around and opened her knapsack, discovering there were no explosives in it. The grenades had fallen out through the rip caused by her ordeal in the sewer drainage pipe. All she had left were some extra magazines of ammo for her machine gun.

"I'll go, Pauline," shouted Hank over the sounds of shouting Germans and machine gun fire. "I have an idea, but you gotta stay here and cover me!"

"No, you cannot go," shrieked Pauline. "You will be killed!"

"I know what I'm doing! I'm faster and stronger than you, and I'll make it. You just need to cover me with that machine gun! You have to trust me because I'm trusting you," Hank said, patting Pauline's gun, indicating that he hoped she was a good shot. Pauline weakly nodded in compliance and raised her weapon in the direction of the advancing German gunfire. Hank took a deep breath and dashed onto the airstrip, grabbing a jerry can of gasoline with his free hand and firing his Colt toward the Germans with the other. Pauline rose up out of her crouch and fired her Sten, spraying bullets across the airstrip. She fired wildly, hoping to knock down as many Germans as possible in hopes of keeping Hank's path clear.

From their positions Christophe and Grégoire watched as Hank sprinted across the airstrip in the direction of the 109s. German bullets whizzed by his head and slammed into the damp earth by his fast-moving feet. He reached the cover of the damaged 109 and unscrewed the cap of the jerry can as gunfire continued to pelt his location. He poured the gasoline all over the ground, soaking the grenades. He then sloshed what little remained on the damaged tail of the 109. When the can was empty he tossed it aside and dashed for cover as German gunfire increased all around him. Turning, he raised his pistol and fired it at the stricken fighter. The bullet ripped through the fighter's fuselage. Nothing! He aimed again, but this time at an angle. His finger squeezed the trigger, causing another bullet to explode out of the barrel. The shot ricocheted, producing a spark that ignited the gasoline! A trail of flame flared up and spread rapidly, catching the attention of both the Germans and the LeBlancs. The intense exchange of gunfire waned for a few seconds as the grenades under the German fighters were enveloped in flame, then touched off one by one, causing a massive chain reaction of explosions that obliterated the parked aircraft. The concussion and heat of the blast knocked Hank backwards off his feet. He hit the ground hard and dazed.

Christophe and Grégoire scrambled from their positions across from the burning plane wreckage and sought cover with Pauline along the edge of the tree line. The Germans, disoriented and disorganized, continued to hurl gunfire in their general direction, but were unable to kill or injure their attackers. The four ME-109s were now completely enshrouded in flames. Suddenly the ammunition they carried began to explode, sending fragments of lethal shrapnel and fire in all directions! Then, the fuel inside the fighters ignited, delivering the most lethal blow. What was left of the 109s blew sky high in a massive fireball of death and destruction. The blast shot large pieces of red-hot metal across the airstrip, striking two of the parked trucks and knocking them on their sides. One caught fire and began to burn intensely.

The small remaining force of German *Luftwaffe* troops desperately tried to reorganize and fight their way up the airstrip to their attackers' position and eliminate them. Some were wounded, others struggled with their weapons, while all were overwhelmed and confused by the rapidly unfolding violence and destruction.

Christophe and Grégoire conferred briefly, sizing up the situation. Pauline interrupted them, concerned for Hank's safety. She was ignored. The brothers looked down the airstrip and quickly determined the German threat to be five or six troops still alive and capable of continuing the fight. They disregarded the wounded Germans as their screams of pain slowly diminished with the inevitable forthcoming of death. The *Luftwaffe* troops still standing crouched low and slowly worked their way to the burning wreckage at the top of the airstrip, firing sporadic bursts in the direction of the LeBlancs' position to cover their advance.

Christophe wanted to eliminate the troop threat, then completely destroy the remaining vehicles and equipment still intact farther down the strip. He saw the silhouette of an aviation fuel truck that he wanted to blow sky high. He also wanted to salvage any useful gear or weapons before departing. Then there was the prize jewel that needed to be destroyed—the *Focke-Wulf* 190, illuminated by the still-running light stands, remarkably untouched by gunfire or shrapnel.

Pauline stood up and started to make for Hank's last position somewhere near the burning *Messerschmitts*. Christophe abruptly grabbed her arm and pulled her back. Grégoire reloaded his Sten and returned fire at the advancing Germans. Christophe told Pauline he would go and help Hank. He needed her and Grégoire to make their way down the airstrip, take out the remaining *Luftwaffe* troops, then shoot up the German vehicles and equipment that were still operable before they could all flee to safety. Pauline hesitated. She was suspicious of Christophe's plan, but was in no position to dispute it as the enemy gunfire increased all around them. Grégoire pulled her toward him and the two scurried into the dark cover of the tree line. Pauline watched in horror as Christophe readied himself, then dashed across the airstrip toward the burning ME-109s. The Germans shouted for him to halt, to no avail. German rifle fire cut through the air but could not find its mark. The Frenchman made it safely to the other side. He started to look for the American.

Farther down the line Grégoire made a daring move. He emerged from the tree line and sprinted across the airstrip just a few steps in front of the German position! The Germans were caught by surprise and could barely react in time to aim their rifles. Some even recoiled backward in stunned surprise and dropped their weapons. Grégoire disappeared into the darkness just before a terrific blast of machine gun fire cut down every remaining troop from behind. Suddenly all was quiet. Pauline emerged out of the darkness. Smoke wafted upward from the barrel of her empty Sten machine gun as she looked over her kills. The plan had worked. Grégoire had gotten in close enough to distract the Germans so Pauline could flank their position and get in behind them. Her Sten had done the rest. The German troop threat was now eliminated—at least for the moment. Grégoire came out into sight. He nodded in approval of his sister's work, then pointed out the next targets that needed to be destroyed. Grégoire began to search undamaged vehicles for supplies and possible German intelligence. As he did, Pauline slipped away down the airstrip toward the FW-190 fighter, looking for Hank and Christophe.

Not far away she saw Christophe searching the woods near the flaming wreckage of the 109 fighters. The flames gave off good light, and it was only a matter of minutes before the elder Frenchman discovered Hank's motionless body. Pauline froze, and watched her brother kneel down beside Hank. She could tell he was alive, but very dazed, as if he had temporarily slipped out of consciousness. Hank tried to sit up and clear his head, but Christophe pushed him back down hard. With Hank now helpless, the Frenchman pulled out a large knife! Pauline, frozen with fear and indecision, watched helplessly as Christophe raised his knife high above his shoulder! She tried to cry out but her voice was paralyzed. She could barely breathe as her hands began to tremble uncontrollably as she attempted to point the barrel of her Sten at her eldest brother!

"*Au revoir, monsieur*," he said. "*Et c'est la vie!*"

Suddenly a single shot rang out! A bullet from behind ripped through Christophe's right shoulder. The stricken Frenchman slumped forward, falling on top of Hank. The executioner's knife slipped harmlessly from his hand. From the shadows emerged an unidentified figure. Pistol in hand, he crept past the two bodies, keeping his eyes focused on one thing—the *Focke-Wulf* fighter! Out of the corner of his eye he spotted Pauline. Still in shock and unable to act, the frightened woman watched as he made his way to the aircraft. Sensing her helplessness, the man fired two shots in her direction, causing her to hit the deck and drop her weapon. He then began to check the fighter for damage while keeping his gun raised in Pauline's direction. Sensing she would be killed any second, Pauline managed to roll to the side of the runway, after which her overwhelmed mind shut down and she blacked out!

Hank felt pressure from Christophe's weight on his own upper body. He managed to push the body to the side, not knowing whose it was or what had happened. He took a breath, slowly sat up, and rubbed his head, waiting for the dizziness to clear. His vision slowly came into focus. The first sight he saw was the lit-up FW-190 and the unidentified man tearing down the camouflage netting from around the plane, then moving the light stands and wheel chocks out of the way. Hank looked closely. He was definitely a pilot, dressed in *Luftwaffe* flight gear under a leather jacket. He appeared to be an officer, as well. Beneath his garrison cap was a face Hank had seen before and instantly recognized. It was the hotshot pilot whom he had encountered at the café days earlier—the flier who had so effectively shot his Mustang out of the sky! The American pilot couldn't believe the coincidence.

Without thinking clearly Hank got to his feet and with pistol in hand lurched blindly toward the German pilot. His emotions ran wild as he staggered onto the airstrip, raised his gun, and prepared to shoot at point-blank range. The German wheeled around and knocked the .45 from Hank's hand. Hank threw a hard punch, but missed badly. The German tackled the American and wrestled him to the ground. The two rolled around in the mud, kicking and punching at one another, each hoping to seize the advantage.

"Know who I am?" yelled Hank as he rolled on top of the German with his hands clenched around his neck. "American ... I'm the American!" he seethed. "You tried to kill me before. Now I'm going to kill you!"

"*Schweinhund!*" gasped the German pilot. With great effort he broke free from Hank's grasp, struggled to his feet, and hit Hank with a vicious punch to the face that sent the American reeling backward, onto the ground. He followed with a brutal kick to Hank's gut that caused the American to curl up in agonizing pain. The German reached for his pistol but felt only an empty holster! His gun had been lost in the struggle. Not wanting to waste any more time, he staggered back to the FW-190, climbed onto the wing, opened the cockpit canopy, and scrambled inside. With his hands racing over the controls, the radial engine came to life with a bang. The propeller began to spin, gradually picking up speed. Hank could hear the roar of the plane's engine and painfully pulled himself off the ground. He had only seconds to do something and he knew it! Glancing around, he glimpsed his Colt .45 pistol. He released the magazine, retrieved a full one from his pocket, slapped it in place, and drew back the slide. Gun in hand, Hank staggered in front of the FW-190 and defiantly raised his weapon.

From the cockpit the German stood up and saw the American standing before him. Shaking his head in disbelief, he sat down, securing the cockpit canopy and preparing to take off. The BMW 801D-2 radial engine roared to full power just as Hank fired a volley of shots. Several rounds struck the propeller and ricocheted into the engine. Sparks flew and smoke began to rise from the damaged motor. Undeterred, the German pilot pushed the throttle forward and the plane began to roll toward Hank. Hank kept firing at the engine and cockpit until his gun was empty. As the 190 thrust forward, Hank dove out of the way. The fighter slowly gained speed as it rolled down the airstrip. Hank looked on as fire spit from the damaged engine and licked back toward the cockpit. Still, the fighter gained speed and momentum, determined to get into the air. Then, without warning, the damaged propeller blew sideways off the engine and sliced deep into the left wing. The impact caused the plane to skid. The left-side landing gear crumpled and the wing dug deep into the ground. The fighter cartwheeled, turning into a fiery inferno just before violently exploding halfway down the airstrip. The hotshot *Luftwaffe Oberst* was no more!

Hank watched the brilliant display of destruction and took some satisfaction in the thought that justice had been served. He had avenged the deaths of his fellow pilots and gotten personal payback by destroying the man and machine that had nearly taken his own life weeks earlier! Farther down the strip Grégoire emerged from a German truck, stunned at the awesome destruction of the German fighter. He approached the burning wreckage to make sure the pilot was dead. Hank looked to the side of the runway and saw Pauline on the ground. He staggered over to her and held her in his arms, hoping she was all right. Slowly her eyes opened as she regained consciousness! The two embraced lovingly. Hank could sense Pauline was shaken up but couldn't detect any visible injuries. He told her he was a little banged up, but okay. Grégoire, stunned Hank was still alive, checked on his sister, then started down the airstrip in search of Christophe. He was drawn to the plane wreckage first.

"We should leave here at once," urgently said Hank. "Where's Christophe?"

"I do not know," answered Pauline, still not thinking clearly. She picked up her Sten, then the two moved into the cover of the tree line, on the opposite side of the strip from where Christophe lay. Pauline, unsure what to do next, looked down the airstrip toward Grégoire. He started to move away from the plane wreckage just as rifle shots rang out! Grégoire, struck from behind, dropped to the ground with a bullet wound in his right leg. German army troops suddenly appeared from the woods at the base of the airstrip. Pauline recoiled in terror as soldiers surrounded her injured brother. One kicked Grégoire's Sten machine gun away, while another ripped his knapsack from his back. Grégoire, helpless and in severe pain, put his hands up and offered no resistance. The German army troops saw the multiple *Luftwaffe* dead and cautiously made their way up the airstrip to investigate.

"My machine gun is empty! I have no more ammunition," exclaimed Pauline as she ditched her Sten and dropped her knapsack. All she kept was her fully loaded .38 Llama automatic pistol. Hank reached into his pocket and pulled out his last magazine.

"I've got one more full magazine and that's all," he said, reloading his weapon. The two looked at each other helplessly, then at the advancing troops. Fifteen soldiers were coming their way and it was impossible to determine how many might be behind them, just out of sight!

"*Achtung! Kommen Sie hier!*"

Pauline and Hank cringed at the sound of German voices so close to them. They watched as two German troops hauled a body from the woods and dropped it on the airstrip. It was Christophe! For a moment Hank assumed he was dead. To his amazement, he slowly sat up. He wasn't dead! He was badly hurt from the bullet wound in his shoulder, but the injury wasn't fatal. Instead of being dead, he was a prisoner.

As the Germans clustered around, Grégoire was brought next to Christophe. Both had their hands tied behind their backs. Their scarves had been wrenched from their faces and turned into blindfolds, and they were forced to kneel on the ground. Bright red blood oozed from their fresh wounds. Two German troops stood guard over them, while the others fanned out with handheld lights to search the area further.

"We can't help them," Hank said, looking at Pauline. "There are too many soldiers. We can't fight them with the limited firepower we have. We'd be killed or captured the second we exposed ourselves. We need to get out of here quickly!"

Pauline thought a moment, then agreed. The only recourse would be to appeal to Steinert and have him intervene before Christophe and Grégoire were hauled away and executed as terrorists and enemies of the Reich.

"*Oui.* We must go now! Hurry," insisted Pauline. The two slowly made their way back toward the sunken road. Without a light the going was difficult. Behind them were loud German voices moving all over the place. Like angry bees buzzing around an agitated hive, the Germans intensified the search for those who had wrought havoc on the secret airstrip. As Hank and Pauline blindly made their way along, Hank looked behind them and saw several flashlight beams cutting through the darkness.

"I hope you know where you're going," he said worriedly.

"Stay silent!" anxiously scolded Pauline. She grabbed Hank's arm and pulled him in the direction she wanted him to follow, moving swiftly even though she was unsure of her steps. It was Christophe had who chosen the route that led them to the target, and it was Christophe who knew the best route back. Pauline would have to trust her good instincts and sense of urgency to get them out of danger. The task would not be an easy one!

The two fumbled their way through the dark woods and somehow found the sunken road they had followed getting to the airstrip; however the pursuing Germans were not far behind. The growing sound of their voices and the long, piercing beams from their flashlights revealed their advancing positions. They were getting closer and the danger to Hank and Pauline was escalating. Pauline hesitated. A decision had to be made quickly! Pauline pulled Hank down into a crouched position before whispering in his ear.

"*Henri*, we cannot go back the way we came. Christophe always plans the easiest way to the target. He almost never returns the same way. I do not know how to get back down into the sewers! We could not get back through the drainage pipe, even if I could find it, and I cannot," she dejectedly admitted.

"What about this road?" asked Hank. "Where does this sunken road lead? Do you think it leads to somewhere near Jolieville?"

"I do not know, *Henri*," Pauline answered. "The Germans must use it. It must lead to somewhere close to a town or village. We cannot be too far from Jolieville."

"We don't have much choice. We can't risk getting lost in the darkness … and without flashlights we don't stand a chance. All roads lead somewhere. I say we find out where this road takes us," suggested Hank. Pauline weakly concurred.

"*Halt!*" cried a German trooper. Suddenly Pauline and Hank were blanketed with a beam of light. They had been discovered! Pauline sprang up and fired her .38 Llama pistol. Two shots ripped into the chest of the German soldier, who fell, mortally wounded. His flashlight dropped as well, taking the light off Hank and Pauline.

"C'mon!" exclaimed Hank. He took Pauline by the hand and dashed into the darkness down the sunken road. They could still hear angry German voices behind them, as other *Wehrmacht* troops scrambled to the spot of their fallen comrade. German Kar 98 bolt-action rifle shots ripped through the air in random directions in hopes of knocking down the fleeing duo. Several whizzed by Hank's head, but none hit the mark.

Pauline was equally fortunate. Three German soldiers gave chase, but the darkness soon swallowed up Hank and Pauline. The two had managed to successfully evade their pursuers.

As the unsettling sounds of German gunfire faded away in the distance, Hank and Pauline groped their way together through the darkness down the sunken road, unsure of what potential dangers lay ahead. Darkness severely impaired their vision, but the depressed earth of the sunken road kept them on a straight course. The two clung to each other for warmth and support. They were cold, wet, hungry, exhausted, and still in unfamiliar surroundings. They discussed the wisdom of spending the night hiding in the hedgerows and finding their way back to Jolieville at daybreak, but decided to press on in the dark and take their chances.

After an agonizingly slow hour's walk, they reached an intersection. A wooden T-shaped signpost, with arrow-shaped boards sticking out horizontally in opposite directions, could barely be seen. Unable to read the sign in the gloom, Pauline reached into her pants pocket and pulled out an old cigarette lighter. Her thumb tried to spark it to life with no success. She blew on it and tried igniting it again—nothing. She kept at it until finally a spark flew up, producing a small glowing flame. She held her weak little torch up to the sign, which read, "Ste. Mère Eglise et Jolieville."

"*Bon!*" said Pauline with a sigh of relief on her cold, quivering, lips. "Ste. Mère Eglise is down the road in that direction and Jolieville is that way."

"Do you know where we are now and how to get back to the restaurant?" asked a shivering Hank.

"*Oui.* If we follow this road to the northwest it will lead us into Jolieville, only a few kilometers away. We need to be careful. Soon this road could be filled with German patrols! Come … we must keep going, or all will be lost. It will not be light for a few more hours."

The pair headed down the road in the direction of Jolieville. The faint smell of the morning dew hung in the air and Pauline knew their journey was not far from over. After a seemingly endless hike, filled with several dashes into the patchy woods at the first hint of an unfamiliar or unfriendly sound, they reached the immediate outskirts of Jolieville and a paved road. Now familiar with her surroundings, Pauline took the lead and the two cautiously made their way into town, knowing full well what would happen to them if they were caught outside after curfew. Strangely enough, some of the town's streetlights were on, making it easier to find the way. Pauline wondered why the strict blackout conditions were not being enforced. She got the unfortunate answer when German vehicles and troops began slicing their way down a lit up street!

Hank and Pauline hit the deck and crawled into a nearby dark alley. The column passed and seemed to be headed out of town. Hank wondered if they were going to the secret airstrip. He also wondered about Pauline's brothers, just how much trouble they had stirred up, and the unavoidable negative repercussions that would result. The situation had changed drastically. The two ducked and dashed in and out of the shadows as they made their way across town. Pauline moved with catlike reflexes that Hank tried to mimic. They managed to stay out of sight of the occasional German sentry patrolling the streets. Eventually they reached Café LeBlanc. Hurriedly, Pauline unlocked the front door and shoved Hank in. She dashed inside, slamming the door shut before locking it. She raced to the bar and lit a candle to provide some light. She and Hank collapsed on the floor behind the bar under the glow of the candle. They embraced and held on to each other tightly. It was just after 3:00 a.m.

"*Henri*, we must get cleaned up now. We must prepare for what is to come!"

Hank sensed the anger and urgency in Pauline's voice. He hauled himself up, his body weary and his head throbbing with pain. He sat down in a chair and waited for Pauline's instructions.

Pauline hung a sign outside Café LeBlanc that read in French and German, "Closed Until Further Notice." She hurried back to the kitchen and began heating water. She stripped out of her filthy clothes and motioned for Hank to do the same. He undressed, giving his clothes to Pauline, who promptly hid them. They then went into Pauline's quarters behind the kitchen, bathed, and put on fresh clothing. Pauline put on her simple everyday dress and apron. Next they cleaned away every hint of the outside world from the bathroom and what had been tracked onto the dining room floor. Once everything looked in order and to Pauline's satisfaction, the two sat down to rest.

"We have no choice now. We must wait for whatever comes to us," Pauline said solemnly.

"What does that mean … exactly?" asked Hank.

"We must wait for Herr Steinert. He is the only one who can help us now. He is the only one who can protect us. When he returns, he will see the sign I put out front. It is a call for help and he will know what it means. Only he can keep us out of harm's way. Only he can save my brothers … if it isn't too late," she said, her head dropping and her voice trailing off with uncertainty.

"I don't trust him," said Hank.

"I know. But we are in no condition to do anything now but wait. We will lock down the café. Come now, we must rest," said Pauline, taking her lover by the hand and leading him down to his bedroom.

Chapter 18

AN ATYPICAL INVESTIGATION

The clock on Steinert's bedroom wall read 3:20 am. The *SS-Obersturmbannführer* was still awake and seated at his desk in his personal quarters. He couldn't doze and wasn't inclined to try, even though he was quite tired. His uniform was unbuttoned and his tie hung loosely around his neck. His disheveled appearance matched his unclear mind that was compromised by lack of sleep and a half consumed bottle of cognac. A scattered pile of unfinished paperwork was rumpled beneath his elbows. He held his head in his hands, rubbed his temples, and looked at the unfinished bottle within arm's reach. His eyes wandered around the room, laboring to discover anything out of sorts. Soon, everything appeared to be out of place. Visions of Gestapo agents in his room rummaging through all his files and possessions occupied his every cloudy thought.

Suddenly the door burst open! Startled, Steinert instinctively reached for his holstered Luger, as he wheeled around to face whoever was about to confront him. Standing before him was von Schreiner! The *SS-Gruppenführer* looked almost as disheveled as Steinert. He was wearing his black SS trousers and jackboots. His coat and cap were missing, and his brown shirt was partially unbuttoned. Suspenders dangled loosely around his legs, causing Steinert to wonder how he would react if his superior's pants suddenly fell down around his ankles. The thought almost caused him to chuckle out loud.

Von Schreiner informed Steinert that an airstrip of vital importance to the Atlantic Wall coastal defenses had been attacked just a few hours earlier. Word had reached his office that saboteurs were responsible and that prisoners had been taken and were being held on the spot by regular German army troops. He ordered Steinert to take a car out to the location immediately, interrogate the prisoners personally, disassociate and eliminate the army's involvement in the matter, identify the culprits and their purpose, reveal any immediate threats against the Reich, then deal with them accordingly, without involving Eichner and his Gestapo. He added that one of the prisoners could be, or could have knowledge of, the missing American pilot he so desperately wanted back in SD hands. He reminded Steinert of one of his earlier threats—that the week he had given him to find the American was waning fast, and the consequences of failure would not be pleasant.

Steinert asked which airstrip had been hit and where he specifically needed to go. He asked what details were known about what had happened and how he should carry out the investigation, only to be interrupted by his drunken superior officer.

"*Was haben Sie? Stellen Sie nicht so viele Fragen!*" shouted von Schreiner. *Stehen Sie auf! Es ist Zeit zu gehen!*"

Steinert began to gather files into his leather briefcase. His commander informed him that the area hit was the most vital airstrip. He emphasized the word "vital," then added the word "*Richthofen.*" After hearing that, Steinert knew exactly what von Schreiner had been railing on about. Steinert nodded understandingly, then innocently went about gathering his things, making sure he didn't let on that he knew anything further about what had happened earlier.

"*Ich muss jetzt gehen,*" said Steinert. Von Schreiner stared at him almost toe-to-toe, as if he were a prizefighter sizing up his opponent, before abruptly departing without issuing any further orders. What the drunken *Gruppenführer* failed to notice throughout the entire awkward visit was Steinert's right hand, casually resting on his holstered Luger. It had never moved from it until the *Gruppenführer* was out of sight.

Steinert exhaled, then composed himself, straightened his uniform, and washed his face. Briefcase in hand, he made his way down the stairs and out the front door where he was surprised to find no car or driver waiting for him. He stood impatiently in the darkness for several minutes until he could stand it no longer. Steinert briskly made his way to the motor pool. Upon entry, the SS officer on duty confronted him, unaware of his orders. Hesitating, the officer saluted Steinert, then fetched the keys to his vehicle. Steinert swiped the keys away and climbed into the driver's seat. Pressed for time, he didn't wish to be delayed any longer.

The Mercedes roared to life and Steinert sped away, through the main gate security, then toward Jolieville. The morning darkness coupled with the Mercedes's dimmed slit-mask headlights forced Steinert to drive slower than he desired. The car motored along into the darkened town. Steinert tried to shake off the effects of the alcohol that impaired his keen thought processes. Almost unintentionally, the Mercedes came to a sharp stop in front of Café LeBlanc. Steinert hesitated, contemplating why he had chosen to stop there first. It was risky, dangerous, and might not yield any fruitful information. He didn't need to be there at all; moreover, under the circumstances it was extremely dangerous to be seen there. Nevertheless, Steinert recklessly embraced the risk and went up to the front door. Before he had the chance to knock, he noticed the sign hanging on the door. He pulled out his lighter and read the words Pauline had written through the tiny orange flame. He instantly knew what they meant and thought for a moment. He looked through the café window and saw nothing. He wanted to force his way inside, but hesitated. Suddenly an odd feeling overcame him. He backed away and got back into his car.

Just then the darkness and silence of the morning was pierced by a *Wehrmacht* troop transport noisily making its way through the narrow town streets. Steinert warily looked on as the truck stopped just across the street, near the plaza. He observed the driver get out and open a map, which he held under a flashlight. An officer appeared and looked over the driver's shoulder. Steinert deduced the young German officer was an army *Hauptmann*.

Curiosity swept over the *SS-Obersturmbannführer*, who brazenly got out of his car with his briefcase and approached the *Wehrmacht* truck. As the *Hauptmann* caught sight of Steinert, he shined his light on him, then leapt to attention with a Nazi salute and a click of his heels. Steinert casually acknowledged the show of respect and started to question the young German officer.

"*Wie geht es Ihnen?*" Steinert inquired pleasantly.

"*Gut, Obersturmbannführer,*" replied the *Hauptmann* after taking a moment to identify Steinert's rank.

"*Entschuldigen Sie, Hauptmann! Wie heißen Sie? Woher sind Sie?*" Steinert asked.

"*Hauptmann Hans Kranz. Munich, Obersturmbannführer,*" tersely and cautiously answered the young officer.

"*Ah, ich verstehe,*" Steinert replied, with a smile and reassuring nod of his head

Realizing that his peculiar presence, timing, and SS rank had put *Hauptmann* Kranz on the defensive, Steinert starting doing everything in his power to charm and put the officer at ease without embarrassing him in front of his men, who were casually observing the conversation from the back of the open truck.

"*Können Sie mir eine Auskunft geben?*" Steinert asked as he gently pulled the young *Hauptmann* aside and away from the idling vehicle. The officer signaled his driver to get back into the truck and toss him the map.

"*Ich habe keine Zeit,*" *Hauptmann* Kranz respectfully stated.

"*Das ist überhaupt nicht wahr,*" Steinert continued. His tone was nonthreatening, but it reflected his superiority in rank and sent a subtle message to Kranz that he wasn't going anywhere until all of Steinert's questions had been answered to his satisfaction.

Steinert questioned the *Hauptmann* about his current orders and where he was going with a truckload of troops. Kranz explained there had been a violent occurrence at a nearby *Luftwaffe* airstrip and his orders were to take a detachment of men to the scene and help secure the area. He added that the location of the airstrip was not well documented by his commander and they were having a hard time locating the exact position on the map and the best travel route to get there. Steinert motioned for Kranz to show him the map. Kranz opened it and the two squatted down near the ground like a pair of baseball catchers looking it over with flashlights.

Steinert began to debate the positions on Kranz's map marked in red. Kranz pointed to the final destination marked with a red X, where his army intelligence officer had indicated the *Luftwaffe* airstrip to be. Steinert shook his head and informed the young officer that he had been placed in charge of the investigation and that his SS intelligence was far more accurate and reliable.

Kranz defended the validity and accuracy of his intelligence and its pertinency to his mission. He added that the locations of select *Luftwaffe* airstrips including the one in question were well-guarded secrets and known only to certain local military commanders, including his own. Steinert scoffed at the claim and challenged Kranz by foolishly exposing his own top-secret SS intelligence documents showing the original locations of all *Luftwaffe* airstrips in the area and where they had been moved to. Kranz stood his ground by listing the army intelligence contacts he had worked with and their impeccable service records. He refused to believe he had been given incorrect information and had no knowledge of any *Luftwaffe* airstrips having been moved. He further asserted somewhat defiantly that Steinert's intelligence was misleading, if not altogether false.

Steinert began to lose his temper with the confident young *Hauptmann*, but did not expose his growing rage. Kranz skillfully played his final card by summoning his driver, who hopped out of the truck and snapped to attention. Kranz told Steinert that the enlisted man standing before him had driven to the very location they were looking for just twelve hours earlier. He had delivered aviation fuel and other supplies and had chatted with some of the pilots, who gave no indication they were going anywhere soon. He mentioned one particular pilot who was quite cocky and bragged about several enemy fighters he had recently shot down in his *Focke-Wulf* 190.

Steinert paused a moment, then asked why the driver was now having difficulty locating the direction of the airstrip. "*Sie müssen die Wahrheit sagen,*" he told the driver sternly. The driver explained that he had traveled there in the daylight and that the route looked different and confusing in the dark. He assured both Kranz and Steinert that after studying the map he had gotten his bearings and was confident he could now get there. Steinert again was silent.

Kranz, losing both patience and time, respectfully insisted he had orders to carry out and must leave immediately. "*Ich freue mich, Ihre Bekanntschaft gemacht zu haben ... danke,*" said Kranz hurriedly, without any trace of sincerity on his breath. He and his driver climbed back into the truck and rumbled down the road. Steinert, thoughts racing, dashed back to his Mercedes and drove after the truck. He kept a fair distance behind, but made no attempt to hide his pursuit. As he intently concentrated on following the vehicle in front of him, Steinert again failed to notice the mysterious car stealthily pursuing him from Café LeBlanc.

With heavy thoughts weighing on his muddled brain, Steinert kept well behind the lumbering LKW Opel Blitz. So many questions needed answers ... he didn't know where to begin. The first was soon to be revealed as the troop truck turned off onto the sunken road. As Steinert followed down the dark and rough thoroughfare, he saw manmade lights and huge fires cutting through the predawn darkness. Simultaneously, heavily armed German troops emerged from hidden positions within the surrounding woods. Commands filled the air while soldiers flocked around the truck, directing it where to park. The truck eventually lumbered to a complete stop and all its troops hurriedly jumped off. *Hauptmann* Kranz got out, as well, and immediately began issuing orders after conferring with another soldier already on the scene. Kranz glared smugly back at Steinert's car, then raced off. Steinert looked through the woods at the raging fires and could plainly make out burning aircraft and vehicle wreckage. He glanced at his intelligence report once again and verified that he was definitely not at the location where he thought he needed to be. It was obvious that Kranz's intelligence was genuine!

A soldier angrily knocked on Steinert's car window with his rifle muzzle. Steinert opened the door and stepped out. Realizing who Steinert was, the low-ranking soldier snapped to attention. Seeing the chaos, Steinert ordered the soldier to take him to the ranking officer in charge. The soldier quivered nervously and said nothing.

"*Was haben Sie?*" said Steinert. "*Sprechen Sie!*"

The soldier gathered his wits and mustered up a simple response. "*Folgen Sie mir, Obersturmbannführer!*"

He led Steinert through the woods and onto the airstrip where troops were fighting to douse the flames from the burning vehicles and aircraft, fuel stores, and parts of the woods that had caught fire, despite the soggy weather. Others combed the surrounding area, looking for traces of evidence that might reveal those responsible for the destruction.

"*Warten Sie hier!*" said the soldier as he hurried off to find his superior. Steinert stood calm amidst the surrounding chaos. He glanced at the burning debris and sniffed the smoke-filled air, then turned his head in the direction of a *Wehrmacht* officer hastily headed toward him.

"*Es tut mir Leid, dass ich Sie habe warten lassen,*" said the *Leutnant* with a Nazi salute. Steinert returned the salute and asked the junior officer if he were in charge. The man introduced himself as *Leutnant* Oskar Becker and indicated that, for the moment, he was in charge. Steinert told him that as an officer of the SD he was now in charge of the investigation and they should find someplace to talk privately. Becker agreed and led Steinert to an undamaged covered truck, where they were treated to a dry, warm, comfortable place to sit and talk. Steinert wanted to get as much information from *Leutnant* Becker as he could before *Hauptmann* Kranz made his presence known and decided to pull rank on the unsuspecting Becker.

Steinert pulled a pad and pencil from his briefcase and began taking notes. At first he asked general questions, which increasingly grew more specific in nature. The more he asked, the more evasive Becker's answers became. Each enquiry Steinert posed seemed to make Becker more and more uncomfortable. This piqued Steinert's interest, and he knew he had to play his hand just right in order to get the truth.

Steinert asked how many *Luftwaffe* survivors there were from the attack and Becker stated none. Confused, Steinert demanded to know how Becker and his men came to be in this particular area. Becker's head sank and he let out a troubled sign. He explained to Steinert that he and his men had just been transferred to the area a few days earlier from a reserve army unit in Berlin. They had orders the day before to engage in a training exercise not far from the town of Ste. Mère Eglise. During the exercise, Becker confessed that he had gotten his men lost. Rather than seek help and bear the shame, he marched them blindly through the darkness, not knowing where they were heading. By chance they happened on the commotion of the airstrip raid and bravely engaged the forces threatening the soldiers of the Reich.

Becker's voice swelled with courage when he began discussing the details of the battle with the unknown saboteurs. Steinert continued to take notes and asked how many saboteurs there were. Becker stated he didn't know for sure, but estimated a group of twenty or so. Steinert saw through the lie and Becker amended his statement, claiming he only saw four for certain. He then proudly blurted out that he had two prisoners in custody. Steinert ordered that they be isolated and not questioned by anyone but him. Becker confidently stated that he had already passed along orders to that effect and that the prisoners were being held under heavy guard in the back of a damaged truck. No one had interrogated them yet, including himself.

Steinert ordered Becker to take him to the prisoners. The two exited the truck and walked down the airstrip toward another that was damaged on the outside, but still intact. The troops had the fires under control and were gradually beginning to restore order. *Hauptmann* Kranz was off in the distance giving orders and helping set up a portable radio transmitter to reestablish communications with other local *Wehrmacht* command centers.

Becker put the guards at ease and opened the back door. Steinert anxiously looked in. Seated in the darkness, bloodied, bound, gagged, and blindfolded were Christophe and Grégoire LeBlanc. Both looked haggard and beaten. Their heads hung in silence as if they knew the end was near. Steinert shined a flashlight on them to verify their identities for himself, then closed the door tightly. He pulled Becker off to the side and privately grilled him further. He expressly asked the *Leutnant* if he or any of his men had ever been to a town called Jolieville. Becker's response was no. Steinert then asked if either man had any identification papers on him. Becker replied they did not. Steinert asked if he had had any conversation with the men in custody, or if they had volunteered any information. Becker answered that neither man had said anything before being bound and gagged. He added that the prisoners' wounds hadn't even been attended to, simply because there hadn't been time.

Steinert nodded in approval and told the impressionable *Leutnant* that he would now take the prisoners with him for additional interrogation and that SD personnel would solely conduct any further investigation of the area, with orders going out to all local military commanders not to interfere. Steinert ordered the area cleared of all *Wehrmacht* personnel once the threat of fire spreading had been eliminated. The area was to be treated like a crime scene, not a battlefield, thereby releasing the *Wehrmacht* of all investigative duties. There would be no mention of prisoners being taken. All enemy forces had been killed or executed by firing squad—no survivors, thus no prisoners. This order would be relayed to everyone on scene and earnestly obeyed. This took Becker slightly aback, but he stood silent and made meticulous notes of Steinert's orders. Those orders also caught the ears of the nearby *Hauptmann* Kranz, who did not want to recognize Steinert's authority. He labored to raise direct radio communication with his commanding officer.

Steinert then began to wheel and deal with Becker. He assured him that his cooperation would reap rewards and that his heroic exploits would not go unnoticed. Steinert said he would arrange for Becker and his men to be praised for their actions and there would be no mention of their getting lost. A glowing propaganda piece would immediately be written on their behalf and sent to their commanding officer. Steinert ingeniously and effortlessly conjured up tales of Becker and his men bravely fighting off hordes of armed French traitors, thirty or so, who were all gunned down by him and his men for the glory and protection of the Third Reich. The SS propaganda would be priceless. The more Becker heard Steinert lie, the better and prouder he felt.

Becker beamed with delight at the thought of becoming a hero and absorbed Steinert's every order like a wet sponge. He was now putty in Steinert's hands. The crafty *SS-Obersturmbannführer* then ordered Becker to place a hood over each prisoner's head before escorting them out of the holding truck and into his Mercedes. Under guard, both wounded Frenchmen moved slowly and in agonizing pain until they collapsed next to the Mercedes. They were shoved onto the back seat, their hands bound behind them and their legs tied together. Their mouths were still gagged and faces hidden under hoods secured at the necks by rope.

Hauptmann Kranz hurried over to the car and immediately began to protest the release of the prisoners into Steinert's custody. He claimed that as the highest-ranking *Wehrmacht* officer present, he had authority to issue orders. He further stated that the whole situation fell under the jurisdiction of the *Wehrmacht*, and he insisted Steinert wait for further orders from his superior officer. Steinert laughed at the futile attempt of Kranz to seize control. He immediately barked orders reasserting his rank and the power of the SS. He then decreed that *Leutnant* Becker was now in charge of the area and his orders would be carried out without question. Failure to comply would result in serious reprimands by the Gestapo. The mention of the Gestapo silenced Kranz, who decided it was wiser to bite his tongue rather than risk infuriating Steinert any further. The young *Hauptmann* still harbored silent frustration at how very oddly the situation, especially with the prisoners, was being handled. He ended his exchange with Steinert by giving him a Nazi salute before disgustedly walking away.

Steinert restated his orders to Becker and went over the cover story one last time. He told Becker the SS would provide photographs of fresh French corpses to show evidence of the imaginary battle. He even went as far to say that real corpses could be provided if the situation called for them. In return, the clever Steinert insisted on Becker's unconditional help and support if called for under any circumstances. The *Leutnant* agreed without hesitation. The mold had been set and Steinert was convinced he had handled the situation well and covered his bases in a detailed and thorough manner. It was now time to take the next step.

Steinert refused Becker's attempt to dispatch a guard detail with him and asserted that he had everything under control. Before leaving, Steinert posed one last question of *Leutnant* Becker. He asked him if he or any of his men had seen or heard any enemy fighters in the skies overhead during or after the firefight. Becker simply said, "*Nein.*" He added that he and his men were fortunate as the bright fires could have attracted marauding enemy night fighters that could have hit the area hard and killed a lot of Germans. Steinert saluted Becker, got in his car, and started the drive back to Jolieville.

Daylight started to break through the overcast skies as Steinert's Mercedes rumbled down the sunken road. Reaching the turn for the main road leading into Jolieville, Steinert stopped the car, checked for any German motorized or foot traffic, then pulled into a small clearing, somewhat hidden by adjacent bushes and low-hanging tree limbs ideal for concealing a vehicle. He reached into his boot and pulled out a small folding pocketknife, with which he cut off the gags and blindfolds from Christophe and Grégoire. For the moment, he left them bound at the wrists and ankles.

The two brothers seemed relieved to see Steinert; however, both were angered, fearful, and confused at what had happened earlier.

"*Où est Pauline?*" painfully asked Christophe. His wound was getting worse and the blood loss was starting to make him dizzy.

"*Je ne sais pas,*" answered Steinert somewhat sarcastically as if he deliberately wanted to play with Christophe's mind.

"*Où est ma soeur? Mort?*" Christophe demanded irately.

Grégoire remained silent as Christophe glared at Steinert, who matched his defiant eyes with a heated stare of his own.

Steinert answered again with, "*Je ne sais pas, monsieur!*" However, this time he deviously added with a snicker, "*Avec votre ami, Henri … probablement?*"

The mention of Hank incensed Christophe even further. He turned his head and gritted his teeth at the thought of the American possibly still alive. Grégoire tried his hand with the *Obersturmbannführer* and began conversing in a more polite, respectful manner, in hopes Steinert would do the same. He didn't get far, as it was evident Steinert wanted to control the conversation, particularly the questioning.

Steinert grilled the brothers on what had happened during the raid. He got little response. Their answers were simple and obvious. Christophe repeatedly kept trying to find out the whereabouts of Pauline. Steinert cleverly avoided answering Christophe's question. Though he had seen the secret distress call sign on the door of Café LeBlanc, he still didn't know if Pauline, or Hank, for that matter, was okay. For all Steinert knew they both could be lying dead on the main dining room floor.

After bickering for several minutes, Steinert determined the conversation was yielding little useful information. As the dark skies brightened with the rise of the morning sun, Steinert felt it was best to move on and continue the conversation elsewhere behind closed doors.

He ignored Christophe's request to untie his and Grégoire's limbs and simply headed back toward Jolieville.

Christophe grew increasingly indignant and began derogatorily questioning Steinert. Christophe asked why his location of the hidden airstrip was correct and why Steinert's intelligence report was wrong. He then made subtle accusations implying that Steinert had deliberately led them astray. Christophe picked away at Steinert, citing even the smallest of irregularities in their past dealings as purposely and deliberately damaging to the French Resistance. He brought up the recently coded broadcast message from the BBC and accused Steinert of withholding vital information. He questioned Steinert's relationship with his sister, making scandalous remarks while also claiming that his dealings with the American pilot were less than reputable. He even questioned Steinert's loyalty to England and his identity as a spy. He went as far to say he felt Steinert was just a pawn at the Gestapo's disposal and his SD rank meant nothing.

The angry Frenchman continued his tirade. Grégoire quietly struggled to free himself from his ropes. Christophe recklessly inferred that Steinert needed the LeBlancs more than they needed him. He railed at Steinert, stating his own importance and power, especially once the Allies landed in France. After exhausting what was left of his strength, Christophe fell silent. He scowled and winced in pain while Steinert drove on, showing no response or emotion. Christophe hurled one last disparaging remark at Steinert, praising his own countrymen and their valiant struggle against the Nazis, while condemning the English as weak, bumbling cowards who ranked just below the Americans in total lack of competence. Just then Steinert casually turned his head to the left and fiercely jerked the steering wheel, causing Christophe and Grégoire to fall over on the seat. He skidded the car off the main thoroughfare and sped down a smaller, less-defined dirt road. A minute later he came to a screeching halt, leapt out of the vehicle, threw open the back door, grabbed Christophe by his wrists, and hauled him out of the car. Bound, wounded, and off balance, Christophe was at Steinert's mercy. The enraged Steinert threw Christophe to the ground and kicked him in the stomach so brutally it knocked the wind out of him. Steinert hauled the helpless Frenchman into a ditch and drew his Luger.

"You will never again question my authority or insult me or my homeland, you bloody, fucking frog! I've had quite enough of your intolerable nonsense and am not going to stand for it, or you, any longer! You think I need you? You think you're the one with all the power? You best think again, you ignorant ass!"

Christophe gasped for air as he tried to make sense of the English words. He didn't understand them and simply squeaked out, "*Vive la France!*"

"*Auf Wiedersehen, Schweinhund!*" shouted Steinert.

A bullet ripped from the barrel of Steinert's Luger and blew a hole clean through Christophe's forehead, killing him instantly. Grégoire cried out in fear, causing Steinert to wheel around and go after him, as well. He hauled the wounded, helpless middle LeBlanc brother from the car and violently silenced him with a Nazi executioner-style shot to the back of the head.

Steinert stared at the corpses for a moment, then realized he had to work fast. The morning light had arrived and soon the area could be crawling with German patrols. Steinert, unprepared for what he had just done, hastily dragged both bodies into a patch of nearby woods, using loose soil, mud, leaves, tree bark, and broken limbs to conceal them. Once he was satisfied they were sufficiently hidden, he covered the blood trails with mud, picked up the two spent shell casings, cleaned himself off as best he could, then got back into the car and drove away, simultaneously looking in every direction to make sure he wasn't being secretly watched.

Steinert coldly motored back into Jolieville. As he navigated the narrow streets his senses took in nothing. They had become dull and unresponsive to any form of external stimulus. Steinert's eyes saw only the route in front of him. His ears heard only the sound of the Mercedes's engine, and his nose detected only the faint odor of dirt and mud caked on his jackboots. Death was in the air, and for once Steinert was incapable of handling it. His clever mind that ordinarily functioned with extreme precision and attention to detail was now barely able to keep the car on the road. Like a master chess player, Steinert was always able to stay three steps ahead of his opponent and maneuver his way through any tight situation that posed a threat to him. However, now he had gotten sloppy, and his razor-sharp faculties had become so dull and clouded it was uncertain if he would live to see another dawn. His fatigued brain, crying mercifully for sleep, was barely capable of remaining alert enough to get him back to the château. Nevertheless, the car motored on.

Back at the château, Steinert returned to the motor pool. Still in a deep fog, he parked, collected his briefcase, and staggered to the main entrance, ignoring all those with whom he came into contact. Inside, he stopped to ask the whereabouts of von Schreiner. The duty officer, one of von Schreiner's aides, informed Steinert that the *Gruppenführer* was not awake yet and that he was to wait for further orders to come at a later time. Thrilled he didn't have to make his report to von Schreiner immediately, Steinert acknowledged the junior officer's salute, then staggered up the staircase to his room where he collapsed on his bed. The combination of consumed alcohol, the unexpected and deadly twist of events, and the almost total lack of rest forced Steinert to immediately pass out into a deep sleep. Sleep was the only escape … for the moment.

Inside Café LeBlanc, Hank and Pauline had gotten little sleep. The constant worrying forced Pauline out of bed and Hank to sit up. Pauline kept her Llama pistol close, praying she wouldn't need to use it. Hank could sense the fear of the unknown painfully gnawing away at her stomach. Where was Steinert? What had happened to her two brothers? Were they still alive or dead? Was the secrecy surrounding the LeBlancs' resistance operations completely compromised? Would the Gestapo burst through the front door at any minute? Many questions raced through his mind. The answers all relied on one common denominator—Herr Steinert—— the man he distrusted the most.

Hank knew Pauline was determined nothing could be done until the outside world came to them. Either Steinert would appear and provide them with news, or some unknown would reveal itself, forcing a confrontation. He feared for the time being they would remain barricaded inside the shut-down café and out of sight. Fortunately, no German military or police personnel had challenged the closed sign hanging on the front door. They were safe for the moment, or at least it appeared that way.

Around noontime Pauline went into the kitchen and prepared a simple meal of potato soup for Hank and herself. She brought the food into Hank's room. The American was stretched out on his bed, quietly contemplating the grim situation and trying to ease some of the dull pain still lingering in his head and body. The sight of Pauline instantly lifted his spirits and he sat up enthusiastically as she handed him a bowl of soup.

"Thank you," he said as she sat down next to him on the bed. She looked at him affectionately with a weak smile and nodded. The two then hungrily ate their soup. Pauline took away the bowls, then snuggled up to Hank on the bed. She kissed him on the mouth and then began rubbing his temples, hoping to massage away any pain from his battered skull.

Hank closed his eyes and felt the dull aches in his head begin to subside. Pauline had an uncanny healing touch that Hank's sore body craved. She gently worked her hands down the sides of his face and onto the back of his neck. She rubbed hard, loosening his stiff neck until it cracked and all the tension was released. Next she removed his shirt and went to work on his upper back and shoulders, making sure to give extra attention to the tender left one.

She took off his shoes and massaged his feet, working her fingers skillfully between his toes. Hank's blood circulation increased as his heart beat rapidly with anticipation. He couldn't hide it any further. He pulled Pauline to him, wrapped his arms around her tightly, and pressed his lips firmly against hers. He kissed her lips and her cheeks, then her neck. He slowly pulled up her blue skirt and positioned her on top of him until he felt he would burst out of his pants! Pauline reached down and slipped off her undergarments, then skillfully helped relieve Hank of his trousers. She embraced him again and slid her exposed soft femininity to his awaiting hard masculinity. The two groaned with delight upon penetration and the ensuing sexual rhythm established with each pelvic thrust. Hank undid Pauline's blouse and caressed her exposed breasts before pulling her lips back to his. He rolled her over on the bed and stripped off every stitch of her clothes until her gorgeous naked form filled his field of vision, as well as every crevice in his lustful imagination.

The two made love over and over again until both were forced to lie back on the narrow bed and rest from sheer exhaustion. They took long, cleansing breaths and held each other close. For a short, blissful time, both were oblivious to the burgeoning dangers surrounding them. For once they didn't feel like combatants, soldiers, spies, or even hunted prey in a hostile world gone mad with war. For one special moment in time they were simply two young people in love, and what a wonderful feeling it was! It was a feeling both wished would last for eternity.

As time passed and day turned to night, the euphoria of love began to wane and harsh reality slowly crept back to the forefront of Pauline and Hank's thoughts. Both got dressed and stayed behind the closed door of Hank's room. They discussed endless scenarios of what could be happening at that moment. Pauline talked about her brothers. Hank, although he expressed outward sympathy, did not share any of Pauline's concern. As she talked, Hank sensed something was wrong. She sighed and told Hank she distrusted many of the things her brothers had done recently with regard to him. That distrust brewed anger that channeled feelings of betrayal and resentment. She told him the bond between flesh and blood was strong, but the fiery passion of a newfound love was just as powerful. She admitted she wanted to save her brothers, but not at the risk of losing him. In her rational mind they were already dead, but in her emotional heart they were still alive. What she said next left Hank dumbfounded.

"*Henri*, I am quite certain my brothers meant to do you harm," she said, trying to hold back her tears. "I overheard them plotting to kill you before the raid. I heard them talking upstairs behind closed doors. I did not want to believe it. I did not think it could be true. I did not know what to do except stay close to you and try to keep you safe. I failed you, Hank … I truly failed you, my love."

Hank, not knowing how to respond, simply asked, "How did you fail me, Pauline?"

"I saw you lying helpless on the ground. I saw Christophe by your side ready to plunge a knife into your heart. I froze … I couldn't react. I did not know what to do! I saw that German pilot shoot Christophe, and then he shot at me. The next thing I knew, you were by my side helping me. I must have been unconscious."

"You were," said Hank, adding, "You've never failed me, Pauline. Your brothers … they've failed you. They're more dangerous to us alive than dead. You must realize that."

"I know, but what can I do?" cried out Pauline. "They are my brothers! I cannot just kill them! Perhaps Herr Steinert . . ."

"Will do nothing," said Hank, finishing Pauline's last sentence. I doubt either of your brothers are still alive. And even if they are, I doubt that son-of-a-bitch Kraut Steinert will lift a finger to help them. We need to think of ourselves, Pauline."

Pauline softly wept. Hank understood her conundrum concerning her brothers. Family bonds ran deep, he knew that. But he sensed she knew they were dead and all it would take was some time for her to accept it. There was further talk of Steinert. The mention of his name made Hank's blood boil, and the distrust he felt for him still ran deep, despite any assurance Pauline could provide. Hank had grown to trust Pauline, yet he still saw nothing but a deceitful, conniving Nazi in Steinert. Nevertheless, Steinert was the wild card and the only figure who could shed any light on the current situation.

Hank insisted the best route was simply to pack up, slip away undetected, and take their chances together, in hopes of finding shelter with loyal French Resistance cells outside Jolieville. He was more than content with leaving Steinert and whatever remained of the LeBlanc brothers far behind. Pauline was apprehensive. She argued that it was too risky and flawed. Without knowing exactly where to go, how to get there, or whom to trust, the idea was simply not feasible and would inevitably result in capture and certain death for both. She insisted on a more formal and well-thought-out plan with a specific goal and an even more specific way of achieving it. Hank couldn't argue her logic or her desire for planning. She was far more versed on how to survive under extreme circumstances than he. Living and surviving among such a brutal enemy for so long had made her more of an authority on the matter, which Hank had to respect.

After lengthy discussions, both agreed that preparing to leave abruptly on their own was necessary. However, they also agreed that they had to wait for Steinert's eventual appearance. Pauline reasoned that under the circumstances it was the safest thing to do and their best chance for survival. Hank reluctantly agreed, but not without expressing his sincere distrust of the man yet again. He sensed that Pauline, although wise in her reasoning concerning Steinert, was still clinging to the hope that her brothers were alive and that she would eventually be reunited with them. Both knew that only Steinert could reveal their fate. The thought did not sit well with Hank for many reasons, although he didn't openly protest simply because he felt the LeBlanc brothers were already dead. He remembered the deceptive game Steinert had played with him involving the grisly fate of the Tessiers and thought the same scenario might play out for Pauline. Hank kept silent and honored Pauline's request. They would wait for Steinert. The mere thought of the *SS-Obersturmbannführer* caused Hank to instinctively reach for his .45. He checked it over and made sure it was fully loaded.

The two spent the rest of the day quietly gathering vital supplies— clothes, foodstuffs, weapons, ammunition, fake identity papers, money, hidden valuables, and other useful items. They brought everything down into Hank's room and stored it in the secret chamber leading into the sewers. As night fell, Pauline and Hank finished their preparations and hunkered down for the night. There had been little German activity that day. No unexpected company tried to enter the café, permitting Pauline and Hank to remain safely hidden. Pauline kept the café enshrouded in darkness and didn't allow Hank to leave his room. Steinert could show up at any time and Pauline wanted to be the first to meet him.

As time passed, however, it became less and less likely the *SS-Obersturmbannführer* would appear. Pauline took the opportunity to clean herself up and prepare some food for Hank and herself. The young woman descended into Hank's room with a tray of bread, cheese, some cooked potatoes, and a bottle of red wine. The two ate the hearty meal under candlelight. To conclude the pleasant evening, Pauline produced a large pan of hot water and shaved Hank's face and neck. When she finished the two fell upon each other in passionate embrace and made love once again. Later they fell happily asleep, unconcerned for the moment about what fate had in store for them.

Chapter 19

SPRINGING THE TRAP

Steinert lay face down on his bed. He had slept continuously throughout the day, the night, and into the next day. On Sunday morning, June 4, a knock came on his door. The groggy *Obersturmbannführer* awoke and squinted at the clock on the wall. It was 9:45. He jumped up, trying to tidy his wrinkled and disheveled uniform. He gave up and answered his door. Von Schreiner's aide clicked his heels and tried not to notice Steinert's unsoldierly appearance. Steinert dreaded the sight of the aide and hoped he hadn't come to escort him to von Schreiner's office for an immediate report on the airstrip investigation. Instead, the young aide informed the *Obersturmbannführer* that he had been taken off the duty schedule for the day and was ordered to stay at the château until von Schreiner called for him.

Steinert snatched the piece of paper from the aide and read von Schreiner's order. He was shocked to see that it was dated Sunday, June 4! He had been asleep for more than twenty-four hours. He read it again, looking for any mention of disciplinary action or reprimand, but found none. Von Schreiner's aide added that the *Gruppenführer* had been called away the previous morning and he was scheduled to return much later in the day. Steinert inquired as to what business the *Gruppenführer* was currently engaged in, only to get a vague and terse reply that it was official business for the greater glory and protection of the Reich. Steinert retreated behind his chamber door and pulled himself together, taking time to get cleaned up and put on a fresh field-gray uniform. He had some food sent to his room, as well. Steinert then retrieved a typewriter from the deep bottom desk drawer. After several long moments of thought, he fed a sheet of paper into it and began to peck away at the keys, commencing his official report to von Schreiner regarding the airstrip investigation. As he typed, he began to realize that it was more fiction than fact, but under the circumstances, that's exactly what it had to be.

The deeper he got into the report, the more he wondered where von Schreiner was and what was going on. He dared not leave the château for fear of severe reprimand for disobeying orders, should von Schreiner suddenly arrive and discover him missing. The fact that he was taken off duty on a Sunday was not altogether odd; he had been off duty on Sundays before, but this time it didn't sit well with him. Deep down inside something felt very wrong. His suspicions grew, as did his speculations. He needed solid information and direction, but not from von Schreiner, nor his own intelligence staff; he needed it from Bletchley Park.

Steinert desperately wanted to get over to Café LeBlanc to access his hidden radio equipment and the Enigma machine. He wanted to scan the airwaves for vital Ultra information from England. He gravely desired to reestablish communications with his covert contacts in Bletchley Park and gather information on the situation in his area. Hopefully, they would have pre-invasion instructions for him to carry out. Something … anything … that gave him a clue as to what was going to happen and when. As strange as it seemed, Steinert above all else yearned for a feeling of normalcy and routine to settle back into his life. He hadn't had that feeling since contact with Bletchley Park had been lost and von Schreiner's behavior had become more peculiar. The fact that Eichner and the Gestapo had been silent and relatively absent around Jolieville had Steinert concerned the most. Where was the Gestapo and what was it up to?

Steinert's thoughts turned to Pauline and the American. He had to get to her to find out what she knew. He wondered if she was still alive. He wondered if Lieutenant Mitchell was still with her. Was he dead? Was he injured? Was he on the verge of capture? What was Steinert going to tell Pauline about her brothers? As the questions swirled in Steinert's head he continued to type his fabricated report. As he typed the impressive lies, he conjured up a batch of equally influential ones he planned to tell Pauline, and even Hank, if necessary, when next they met.

Steinert spent the rest of the day finalizing his report. He also spent a great deal of time scheming plans to get to Jolieville and into Café LeBlanc. As night returned, there was still no word from von Schreiner.

Suddenly a knock came at the door. It was von Schreiner's aide. The young officer greeted Steinert in the customary respectful manner, then gave him another written order, together with the next day's duty schedule. The order stated that von Schreiner wanted Steinert's report on the airstrip raid tomorrow at 6:00 p.m. Von Schreiner also requested that various other intelligence reports be gathered and summarized. The process would take some time and test Steinert's bureaucratic skills. Last, it read that von Schreiner was having a dinner meeting with several important and distinguished members of the SS security and intelligence community at 9:00 p.m. the following evening. Select SS and Nazi Party officials from Berlin were going to be in attendance, as well. Steinert's presence was mandatory and appropriate dress was required. Specifically, von Schreiner indicated that he wanted Steinert to wear his pre-war, black *Allgemeine-SS* uniform. Steinert shook his head at the thought and couldn't understand von Schreiner's fascination with the obsolete outfit that was now worn mainly by foreign *Waffen-SS* units on the Eastern Front.

Before he dismissed the junior officer, Steinert asked him if von Schreiner had returned to the château. To his surprise, the officer said he had. He had come back an hour earlier and was resting in his quarters. He had given orders not to be disturbed. Steinert peered down the open hallway. He saw light coming out from under von Schreiner's closed bedroom door and wondered if the order applied to his mistress, as well. The junior officer suggested to Steinert that he make himself available at a moment's notice in case the *Gruppenführer* needed him. Steinert indicated he would be available for the rest of the evening and closed the door. His room felt like a prison. Angered at a lost opportunity to sneak out while von Schreiner was away, he began to prepare for the next day's events.

At Café LeBlanc, Pauline made one final check of the dining room before retreating to Hank's room. She crawled into bed with him and whispered happy sentiments. Hank thought about pressing the issue to leave again without waiting for Steinert, but decided to wait until morning. Even then he wasn't sure it was the right subject to bring up. Nevertheless, he knew something had to be done soon or else both would assuredly be discovered and captured by the German Army or Gestapo. Hank wasn't thinking clearly either. He was in love, too, and more enamored with the moment than concerned with the dangers of the unknown future. The two lovers held each other tight and made love before drifting off to sleep.

Steinert awoke with first light on the morning of June 5. He dug out his black SD uniform and carefully put it on, making sure every detail was represented properly. When he finished he looked in the mirror for any imperfections. Everything seemed in place. The brown shirt and black tie; the black trousers and jacket; the silvery white buttons and shoulder cord; the bright red, white, and black swastika brassard on the left arm; the highly polished black jackboots; the holstered Luger on his right hip; and the SS dagger in its scabbard dangling from his left hip all made up the finished uniform. The last touch was the black SS officer's cap Steinert placed on top of his head. He now looked like a complete Nazi.

Steinert gathered his files and headed for the secret-operations war room. On the way, he noticed several house staff scampering about, cleaning, moving furniture, and hanging decorative Nazi art and Party symbols. He entered the main dining hall and discovered several SS staff in white waistcoats and gloves preparing and setting the large oak table for the evening's feast. As he descended the dark stone stairway down to the secret intelligence center, he was met by several other SS in white waistcoats and black trousers carrying boxes of luxury items from the hidden treasure room. Von Schreiner was most definitely looking to make a grand impression on whoever was going to be in attendance later that evening.

Buzzed in through the secure door, Steinert went straight to his desk and began sorting through paperwork, looking for any useful recent intelligence. He checked in with his staff and had them gather the information von Schreiner had requested. Then, following his normal routine, he requested to see the daily Enigma cipher keys for all branches of the German armed forces. These he secretly memorized. Once complete, he settled into his normal duties, issuing written orders and analyzing intercepted foreign intelligence.

The hours slipped by and Steinert kept a close eye on the time, to make sure he would not be late for his superior's six o'clock meeting. He spent his time wisely, cleverly crafting the words he would use when making his oral presentation. He wasn't sure what to expect from the *Gruppenführer*. There were many unknowns in play. The only way to determine where things stood between the two SS officers was through a meeting with candid discussion, a proposition that struck a chord of fear within him. Steinert hoped von Schreiner's lustful preoccupation with wine and women, combined with his premature ambitions for higher rank and power, would cloud his perceptions just enough to keep Steinert from being totally exposed for what he was. The airstrip raid and subsequent investigation report would be the true test—a test Steinert knew he had to pass in order to survive.

Looking forward, Steinert knew he had to get to Café LeBlanc as quickly as he could. He had to know what the situation there was, and time was most assuredly running out on him. He feared what would happen if Pauline started to make decisions on her own. He greatly feared what would happen if his American pilot were still alive and what horrendous ideas would blossom from his foolish mind. He wanted to maintain control and authority over what remained of his little espionage empire. The entire situation was like a fragile house of cards. One wrong move, and the entire covert framework he had gruelingly built over the past few years would come crashing down around him in horrific catastrophe.

Steinert racked his brain to find the nearest window of opportunity to sneak out and get to the café. He thought perhaps after dinner, when all of von Schreiner's guests had departed, the opportunity would arise to slip away undetected. He was hoping the alcohol would flow freely before, during, and after dinner. That would certainly help his chances of getting out without much notice. Lastly, he hoped Yvette would be in attendance, as her presence would be a welcome distraction for von Schreiner. Steinert got up and stretched, walked to the center of the room, and examined the large map of England laid out on the big oak table. He stared at it almost as if he were in a hypnotic trance. He reached down and placed his right hand on London, where it rested for several long seconds. He pulled his hand away, returned to his desk, gathered all his reports, and made his way back upstairs. It was nearing time for his dreaded meeting.

The château was filled with activity as the final preparations for dinner were being made. The scent of slow-cooked ham, turkey, and roast duck pleasantly filled the air. Swastika-emblazoned flags, black banners with white SS sig runes, Hitler and Himmler portraits, and other emblems of the Third Reich decorated the château's interior. Steinert was surprised at the enormous preparation taking place. Von Schreiner was clearly trying to make a lasting and favorable impression.

Steinert briefly glanced outside at the fading light of day. The weather was less than perfect. Strong winds pushed dark clouds across the gray skies, whipping the rain into a driving frenzy that buffeted the windows of the château. Night was approaching. He straightened his tie, brushed his jacket, and made sure his hat was on securely before approaching von Schreiner's closed office doors. Von Schreiner's female SS secretary greeted him, alerting von Schreiner to the waiting *Obersturmbannführer* Steinert's presence. Steinert drew a deep breath, lifted his head, squared his shoulders, threw out his chest, and entered his master's office.

SS-Gruppenführer Gerhard von Schreiner, seated behind his desk, did not immediately rise to greet his deputy commander. Steinert walked over to greet him with a strong military posture. He stopped abruptly before the desk and snapped to attention by clicking his heels and throwing his right arm outward with a customary Nazi salute. Von Schreiner acknowledged the salute and held his hand up in reply, slowly rising from his chair to look over his subordinate. Steinert realized that he hadn't seen his superior since the early morning of the third, when he'd barged his way into his bedroom, drunk and disheveled. Now he appeared much different, resplendent in his black SS uniform adorned with medals and ribbons. He was clean-shaven and completely sober. The bar in the corner looked untouched and there was no sign that the *Gruppenführer* had been drinking.

Von Schreiner put Steinert at ease and both men sat down. Von Schreiner sat behind his desk while Steinert sat in a chair across from the desk. The *Gruppenführer* asked for Steinert's written reports, which he started to read over. After a few minutes of silence, he began to haphazardly flip through the pages before tossing the paperwork onto his desk. He glared at Steinert and asked him to report in his own words on what happened.

Steinert began to detail his findings during the investigation of the attacked airstrip. He told von Schreiner that after arriving at the scene he found the area to be in chaos and poorly controlled by the German *Wehrmacht* forces present. Upon his arrival, he took immediate charge of the situation and questioned the *Wehrmacht* officer in command. He identified the officer as *Leutnant* Oskar Becker. Steinert explained that the airstrip had been attacked by a small group of French terrorists who managed to inflict heavy damage and casualties to the *Luftwaffe* personnel present. He reached for his written report and pulled out a page listing casualties and equipment lost.

Leutnant Becker and his men were engaged in a training exercise nearby and were alerted to the attack after hearing explosions and gunfire. He and his men immediately responded and were able to reach the scene in time to repel the terrorists and take the two leaders into custody. Steinert extolled Becker's efforts and bravery by suggesting he and his men be commended and decorated for their actions and service to the Reich. Steinert, of course, failed to mention the fact that Becker and his men were originally lost and stumbled upon the action by pure luck.

Von Schreiner shook his head and cut Steinert off before he could continue. The *Gruppenführer's* interest turned to the identity of the terrorists and, more importantly, the prisoners. Steinert stated that the number of terrorists was unknown, but believed to be very small. Once the fires were under control, Becker's men went on a relentless search of the surrounding area but came up with nothing. No bodies were found.

Steinert persuasively theorized that several French terrorists could have been killed or wounded and simply not found or helped away by uninjured comrades. He stressed this was his belief.

Von Schreiner grew impatient. He asked Steinert directly about the prisoners and why they were not in his custody. He also demanded to know if one of them was the American. Steinert had anticipated this; however, he hesitated and merely fumbled a simple "*Nein.*" It was not a sufficient answer.

Von Schreiner crossed his arms and glared at Steinert, as he waited for a more detailed explanation. Steinert put his exceptionally organized mind into motion and swiftly composed himself. He started again. He made it clear the American was not one of the captured pair and his whereabouts were still temporarily unknown. Steinert was quick to add that it was unlikely the American was causing any grief to the German forces in the area. He most likely was curled up in a ditch, half dead, and rotting away, having been betrayed and abandoned by whomever was foolish enough to have initially seized and sheltered him. He praised von Schreiner's accomplishments regarding the elimination of French Resistance in Jolieville and how this had spawned an environment that thrived on Nazism and was thoroughly toxic to enemies of the Reich. Those terrorists who had freed the American were most likely dead. No French inhabitant of Jolieville had the spine to harbor an enemy combatant, and Steinert assured von Schreiner it would be only a matter of days, if not hours, before he would present him with the American— dead or alive.

The *Obersturmbannführer* shifted the subject away from the American and onto the prisoners. He reported that he had interrogated both men privately. They were both Frenchmen and self-proclaimed members of a French Resistance cell with origins in the distant French city of Caen. Their organization had become so fractured and decimated that their members had scattered to the wind and were being forced to carry out suicidal terrorist activities that mainly resulted in certain death or capture by superior German forces. The men in question were drifters who had managed to elude German authorities during their travels. The attack on the airstrip was unorganized and happened by chance.

Its effectiveness was the result of surprise and pure luck. Steinert added that the number of terrorists could not have totaled more than ten. The majority of these men were undoubtedly dead and their bodies would be recovered within the next day or so. Any survivors who had temporarily eluded capture were certainly injured as a result of Becker's swift counterattack and would be rounded up immediately by SS personnel currently waiting for orders to be dispatched in and around Jolieville.

Steinert mentioned his ideas concerning the raid's propaganda value. He suggested that the SS inflate the number of enemy dead to around thirty and strategically plant the bodies of freshly deceased French citizens at the scene. The bodies could be taken from local morgues and put to good use. Photographs and news stories could be manufactured and distributed extolling Becker's heroism and downplaying the number of German dead. The propaganda value would be invaluable; moreover they could make up any feasible story they saw fit to create. Steinert argued the point enthusiastically before moving on.

As Steinert spoke he made constant references to his written report. He showed von Schreiner the names he'd fabricated for the two prisoners plus a brief history of the two. He quoted their intelligence as being below normal and similar to that of a Pole or a Russian. True "*Untermenschen*," as he put it. They were easily interrogated and incapable of trickery or hiding vital intelligence. He concluded by stating that he had easily extracted all necessary information from them, deemed them to be a non-threat, then dealt with them in the proper manner. He went on to specifically report that he had both terrorists shot in the back of the head and their bodies disposed of by way of conflagration. He considered the matter officially closed.

Von Schreiner rose from his seat and began slowly pacing back and forth. He started to talk about his past, specifically his days during the early stages of the war when he was an *Einsatzgruppen* commander whose unit was attached to Army Group South during the invasion of Poland, and later Russia. He spoke of the brutality and unwavering loyalty he instilled in the men he commanded. He bragged that under his brilliant detective work and his uncanny ability to motivate his men under harsh circumstances, his command claimed remarkable death totals.

He described how his unit would secure rear areas of conquered Polish territory after the *Wehrmacht* had initially fought through it. He would then cleverly utilize local inhabitants to help reveal and isolate any undesirables in the territory, namely Jews. Those undesirables were swiftly dealt with in a beastly manner until all of them were wiped clean from the region. They would then move on and repeat the same process with impunity. He described the mass killings with an unnatural delight. He reveled in the monstrously creative ways of taking human life, many of which he claimed were his own ideas. He spoke of numerous ways of torture, mass executions by firing squads, public hangings, personal suffocations, mass drownings, mass roundups followed by confinement in public buildings that were subsequently torched and allowed to burn until nothing remained but ashes, and even mass poison gassings.

Steinert's stomach began to turn as his superior flaunted his emotionless abilities to snuff out innocent human life. Von Schreiner continued by quoting numeric death tolls, rattling off the names of obscure Polish towns and villages and how many "enemies of the state" had been liquidated by men under his command. His eyes lit up when stories of his forces shifting into Russia poured from his lips. He bragged that that was when the most purposeful service was done for the Third Reich. Not only were Jews exterminated, but also disloyal Russian peasants, captured Soviet NKVD agents, Soviet political commissars, partisans, filthy gypsies, homosexuals, the mentally ill, and any other class of people deemed undesirable by the Reich. His unit was an unstoppable killing machine that had free rein to carry out its duties, no matter how ghastly.

Von Schreiner chuckled about the time a few top *Wehrmacht* commanders had complained to Hitler about the actions of the *Einsatzgruppen* on the Eastern Front. He mentioned how men like *Generalfeldmarschall* Gerd von Rundstedt, then commander of Army Group South, now ironically Commander-in-Chief West, was appalled by *Einsatzgruppen* activities in Upper Silesia and demanded disciplinary actions be carried out immediately. Von Schreiner laughed out loud when he told Steinert that Hitler simply removed control of occupied regions from the military and placed Nazi *Gauleiters* in control, thereby giving the Party total jurisdiction. Von Rundstedt was sacked and replaced by *Generaloberst* Johannes Blaskowitz. Von Schreiner laughed again when he mentioned that Blaskowitz fell prey to Hitler, as well, when he dared complain about the *Einsatzgruppen*! His removal was cleverly orchestrated by Hans Frank, the brutal head of the General Government in Poland.

Steinert remained silent, wary about where von Schreiner's line of lecturing was going. He had endured long-winded speeches from his superior before, but this one seemed different, and frightening. Steinert stayed stone-faced and made no indication he was anything but totally at ease. Von Schreiner ended the reminiscing of his gruesome *Einsatzgruppen* experiences by citing what a great detective he was and how brutally efficient he was in discharging his duties for the greater glory of Germany. It was these qualities, he stressed, that got him recognized and promoted to bigger and better things. He deviously added that his unmatched ability to read people, coupled with his total lack of trust of anyone, had made him the successful leader he was today. He pressed the final point home by twice pounding his fist onto his desk.

The *Gruppenführer* went silent for a moment and sat back down behind his desk. As his uncovered eye locked with Steinert's, he started to thump his chest with talk of his self-perceived greatness that was going to propel him on to higher, more distinguished roles and responsibilities within the SS. Party loyalty, coupled with tenacious, if not ruthless ambition was key in advancement. His work in the past, in addition to the remarkable work he was doing now, was going to land him a higher-echelon role within the SS. He even suggested the powerful title of *Höherer SS-und Polizeiführer* was one he might inherit. Steinert stayed motionless and didn't allow himself any emotional reaction. He found the *Gruppenführer*'s mention of possibly becoming a Higher SS and Police Leader to be absurd and was growing weary of listening to his superior's unsubstantiated boasting. Moreover, he still was unsure about where all this lecturing was going.

Von Schreiner's focus on his own self worth and adulation gradually shifted to Steinert. The *Gruppenführer* started to contrast his own successes with Steinert's failures. He pointed out his displeasure with his deputy commander's handling of the situation regarding the still-at-large American. "Unacceptable" and "disgraceful" were the words he repeatedly used to describe Steinert's handling of the assignment. He maliciously picked up Steinert's written report and slammed it down hard into his wastecan. Steinert went back on guard, knowing he was about to be attacked more heavily. The *Gruppenführer* summarily listed what he considered to be a string of failures by his *Obersturmbannführer*. The American was always at the core of the issue, but somehow Steinert began to suspect that things were going to get a lot worse as the long disciplinary lecture intensified.

Steinert listened as von Schreiner's voice changed from one of loud disciplinary displeasure to one of growing suspicion. Von Schreiner began to question some of Steinert's activities outside his normal duties. He questioned all the time he had spent at Café LeBlanc, in addition to his undocumented movements in and around Jolieville. He specifically asked about Pauline LeBlanc and where her true loyalties lay. He had suspicions concerning her and her establishment. Steinert said nothing. Von Schreiner stated his growing displeasure with Steinert's relationship with Pauline and told him that it had negatively affected his ability to carry out his duties.

Von Schreiner accused Steinert of being too lax and careless with his responsibilities. Lately his intelligence gathering had become substandard and useless. Von Schreiner asked why that was. Steinert gave no reply. Von Schreiner again brought up the recent airstrip raid. He pointed out details in the *Obersturmbannführer's* findings that, to him, just didn't make sense. He mentioned *Leutnant* Oskar Becker's name, but then curiously asked why there was no mention of a *Hauptmann* Hans Kranz anywhere in the report. Steinert kept silent. Von Schreiner told Steinert that he recently had the pleasure of meeting *Hauptmann* Kranz and enjoyed listening to him recall the events of the other night that in some cases were in direct conflict with what Steinert had reported. Von Schreiner did not go into detail and instead let Steinert stew for a moment. Von Schreiner leapt at the opportunity to challenge his subordinate's keen mind. Still Steinert remained calmly silent.

Von Schreiner continued to pick away at Steinert's report, pointing out how implausible it was for a small disorganized group of French terrorists to take down the most secret and vital *Luftwaffe* airstrip in the immediate area. He stressed the role these particular pilots had in the destruction of the recent American strike force. He continued to harp on Steinert's carelessness and made an obscure comment that a careless SS officer could easily let his guard down when traveling and not realize he was being observed and followed. A chill ran down Steinert's spine. Von Schreiner's hands gestured wildly and his condescending remarks toward Steinert grew more fierce. His body language resembled that of the Führer during one of his frenzied speeches. Steinert listened as his superior admonished him about some specific trivial infraction, then spouted off about something totally unrelated. The ranting seemed to go on endlessly. Two full hours had gone by and soon von Schreiner's dinner guests would start to arrive.

Seemingly out of nowhere, von Schreiner asked Steinert how he got to the secret *Richthofen* airstrip. Genuinely confused by the question, Steinert began to reach for his written report but von Schreiner abruptly stopped him. Before he could begin to compose an answer, the *Gruppenführer* cut him off and began to ask rhetorical questions. He didn't understand how Steinert could have arrived at the right location when he specifically gave him intelligence marking the wrong location. Steinert was stunned at the comment, but said nothing. Von Schreiner asked why Steinert stopped at Café LeBlanc first. What purpose did that serve? He then brought up *Hauptmann* Kranz again. He began listing incriminating testimony from Kranz against Steinert. All of it was convincing lies fabricated by the angry *Wehrmacht Hauptmann*, who had taken advantage of an opportunity to get back at an SS officer who had angered and insulted him. Von Schreiner had personally interrogated Becker also, but from a Gestapo jail cell where he was presently incarcerated!

Steinert knew now that anything he could say, whether true or a lie, wouldn't exonerate him in von Schreiner's eyes. The participants involved had twisted or destroyed the truth to such an extent that no one could believe anything the other said. More importantly, von Schreiner had created his own perverted version of the truth, and everything and everybody else was simply cannon fodder. For Steinert to try to defend his position was irrelevant and would be extremely dangerous. Steinert sat firmly in his chair, contained his fear, and was most interested in just how much von Schreiner knew about him now! He needed to know the full extent of the damage. He decided to remain mute and force the *Gruppenführer* to act first.

Von Schreiner stated his superiority as an intelligence officer and how he trusted no one. He bragged how that gave him a greater insight into the minds of both his enemies and his friends, which allowed him to be in control of every situation. He listed his opinions of Steinert's shortcomings as an intelligence officer—and spy! He ended the list by asking how a man who had achieved such high rank within the SD could be so inept and foolish that he allowed himself to be followed without realizing it. Steinert's heart sank as von Schreiner reached into a desk drawer and presented his deputy commander with two enlarged photographs showing the bodies of Christophe and Grégoire LeBlanc lying right where Steinert had crudely hidden them! The *Obersturmbannführer* glanced at them casually and waited for von Schreiner's next move.

The confident *Gruppenführer* had one more card to play. He coolly reached down into his lower desk drawer and placed the contents onto his desktop, directly in front of Steinert. The *Obersturmbannführer's* eyes opened widely; he couldn't believe what had been placed in front of him! His heart pumped madly at the sight of his secret Enigma machine. Checkmate!

Steinert made no sudden moves, yet found himself staring down the barrel of von Schreiner's pristine Walther PPK pistol. Steinert's holstered Luger was in easy reach, but he made no move for it. Von Schreiner had the clear advantage.

Suddenly both men heard some commotion near the main entrance to the château. Von Schreiner's guests were starting to arrive. Cars sloshed through large puddles as they passed through the main gate toward the motor pool. Muffled yet soothing sounds of Mozart started to play from a phonograph set up outside the dining room.

Realizing that time was growing short, von Schreiner stood up and ordered Steinert to do the same. He commanded his captive to turn around and put his hands together behind his head. The *Gruppenführer* snatched Steinert's Luger, tossed it onto his desk, and began to circle his prisoner while throwing out random questions. He asked Steinert who he really was and who he worked for. Great Britain? America? The French? He asked how many languages he spoke and whether he was born in Germany. He told him he was a fool to think he could outwit National Socialism and the SS and he would not live long enough to see any benefits from his crimes committed against the Third Reich. Von Schreiner assured him he would see to it the Gestapo would interrogate and torture him until he spilled every secret within his very soul and his death would be slow and painful! The same fate was awaiting Pauline LeBlanc and the American pilot she was hiding at Café LeBlanc. They were his treat, intended for *Kriminalrat* Otto Eichner and the Gestapo. The two men who despised each other had made an unusual alliance and collaborated to help one another. Von Schreiner would reap the rewards of Steinert's capture, while Eichner would get credit for the American. Thus for once the Gestapo and SD worked together.

Von Schreiner continued by praising Steinert's cover. He admitted he could find no paper trail or records of any kind showing that he wasn't who he said he was. However, he added he would enjoy finding out, no matter how long the torture lasted! He would see to it personally. He would use every means at his disposal to obtain every shred of information Steinert possessed, no matter how horrific! Von Schreiner, irritated by the soothing sounds of Mozart, cranked up his own personal phonograph with his free hand. As he placed the needle on the spinning record, the sounds of his favorite composer, Richard Wagner, filled his office. Steinert expected the piece to be Wagner's "Ride of the Valkyries," which he often played; however, this time it was "The Flying Dutchman." Von Schreiner turned up the volume and seemed to revel in the piece's dramatic passages.

With pistol still pointed squarely at Steinert, von Schreiner barked at his prisoner, glorifying Hitler and National Socialism and how the artistic works of Wagner were a supreme tribute to the success of Nazism.

He praised himself yet again and explained how that very evening he would become a hero, once he revealed his prisoner as a spy to his esteemed guests. He would parade his captive in front of his superiors like a caged animal. After he told his brilliant story of how he personally took down a spy within his own midst, he would lock Steinert away in the very root cellar that had previously held the downed American pilot!

Von Schreiner pushed his pistol's muzzle deep into Steinert's gut and stood nose-to-nose with him. Steinert glared back at his eye-patch-wearing foe. Von Schreiner sneered and sinisterly whispered how much he would enjoy getting to know Pauline LeBlanc personally and how he hoped Eichner would bring her to him still all in one piece—at least below the waist! With that the *Gruppenführer* chuckled. Adrenaline pumping through his body, Steinert saw his one risky opportunity. Acting on blind instinct and fear, he thrust his head forward and crashed his skull directly into von Schreiner's! The violent blow caught the *Gruppenführer* by surprise and sent him hurtling backwards onto his ass. His pistol flew from his hand and clattered onto the hardwood floor. Steinert lurched forward and leapt on top of him, wrapping his hands firmly around the *Gruppenführer*'s throat. Von Schreiner tried to cry out, but couldn't muster enough breath to be heard over the blaring phonograph.

Steinert squeezed the *Gruppenführer*'s throat with all his might, but von Schreiner attacked his own throat in the same fashion and he could feel his own windpipe gradually being closed off. The winner of this death match would be determined by who had the strongest grip and the most endurance. The two rolled over several times, but neither could gain the advantage. Steinert slammed his right knee deep into von Schreiner's crotch, causing him agonizing pain and forcing him to loosen his grip. He again tried to call out for help, but couldn't. Steinert, feeling his own strength waning, made a desperate move and clawed for his ceremonial SS dagger dangling from its scabbard. He grasped it with his right hand while his left still kept von Schreiner's throat pinned to the floor. Realizing what was about to happen, the *Gruppenführer* made one last-ditch effort to protect himself. He took one hand from Steinert's throat and madly reached for the dagger about to strike at him. His reaction was too slow, and Steinert was able to cover the *Gruppenführer*'s mouth with his left hand, then drag the blade across his now-exposed throat with the right! Blood gushed as von Schreiner's life was snuffed out. His grip on Steinert's throat went limp until his hand fell away harmlessly. His body twitched and went motionless. His eyes went dark, and like a fountain, his severed jugular vein gushed blood onto the floor.

Steinert gasped for air as he climbed off the fallen *Gruppenführer*. He looked down at his dagger and read the insidious inscription now covered in bright red blood—*Meine Ehre Heißt Treue*. He wiped away some of the gore, returned the blade to its scabbard, and looked down on the lifeless SS-*Gruppenführer*, Gerhard von Schreiner. He had murdered one of the greatest monsters he had ever known, and it gave him an indescribably sinister feeling of evil warmth and joy. For a moment he almost felt paralyzed. Momentarily the eerie feeling passed and his sharp, rational mind kicked back into gear. He had to work fast if he was going to stay alive!

Steinert was aware there were most likely several SS guards just outside the office doors waiting for some sort of signal from the *Gruppenführer*. He listened to the commotion of arriving guests and decided his violent actions had not been yet discovered. As Wagner loudly played on, Steinert crept over to the doors and locked them, then silently retrieved his Luger and his SS cap that had been knocked off his head during the struggle. He had to get out quickly and the only exit was through the large window. He set the volume of the phonograph to its highest level and went to the window. He used his dagger to cut away large pieces of the drapes, which he wrapped around his right hand. He then punched away the bottom right corner of the window. He was able to skillfully make a hole big enough for him to squeeze through without noisily destroying the entire pane and alerting the nearby SS guards. His feet hit the ground and he dropped to a crouch as he tried to determine a viable escape route. The rain continued to fall steadily.

Steinert's black SS uniform helped him blend into the night's darkness. Knowing the château's perimeter was completely enclosed by a large iron fence that was too high to climb over, he started across the grounds toward the front gate. He was aware of the guards who patrolled the grounds with German shepherds. Even though it was apparent the alarm hadn't gone out yet, his uniform, hands, and part of his face were covered with fresh bloodstains. There was no way he'd avoid being detained if confronted by a guard. He had to get away undetected. The only way out was directly through the heavily guarded front gate.

Hugging the ground, Steinert watched as a stream of cars was slowly let through the front gate. Their slit-mask headlight covers greatly diminished the headlight beams, but the light could still fully expose a man if he crossed in front of them. Awaiting the right moment, he scampered across the long driveway, then crawled down the sloping lawn through the rain-soaked grass and mud parallel to the driveway toward the gate. He crept on his belly as he watched vehicle after vehicle roll by. A few meters from the gate's rail, he hid behind a small sculpted hedge and drew his Luger. Only two sentries and no dogs attended the gate. Steinert knew that he had to move fast, as it would only be a matter of minutes, if not seconds, before von Schreiner's body was discovered and the alarm would sound. The grounds would be locked down in the ensuing chaos, virtually guaranteeing his immediate capture. Timing was critical!

Shooting wasn't an option. Shots fired would only hasten the alarm. He had to get out undetected. As the last Mercedes rolled away toward the motor pool, Steinert was presented with an unbelievable stroke of luck. A large, covered truck rolled up to the lowered railing. Both sentries climbed onto the cab's running boards and shined lights onto the driver. Steinert could hear them talking. The driver explained the truck was full of crates of cognac and champagne that had to be delivered immediately on the orders of von Schreiner. The driver pleaded that he was late and had to get to the château right away or risk being arrested. The guards chuckled and brazenly entered the back of the vehicle, partially to escape the rain, but mostly to inspect the crates. The driver reluctantly joined them.

Now was Steinert's chance! With all three men preoccupied, he made a dash for it, slipping under the lowered railing and racing down the road, into the darkness. The sound of the idling truck's engine helped mask his hurried footsteps. He looked back toward the gate and watched the truck pass through. As he suspected, each guard happily held a bottle of cognac.

Steinert now had to make the trek into Jolieville on foot without being discovered. He had no idea how long it would take. Unspeakable thoughts of Eichner and Pauline LeBlanc filled every crevice of his mind and motivated him to move quickly. It was now well past nine o'clock and soon every SD and Gestapo official would be looking for him!

Back at the café, Pauline and Hank had spent most of the day arguing about what to do. The more Pauline felt they should wait, the more Hank became convinced they should go. Hank had originally agreed to wait for Steinert, but his patience had run out. The time wasted arguing took precious time away from preparing an escape plan. Now it was dark and ideal for a breakout, but the two remained at odds about what to do and were still unprepared to leave their shrinking island of safety. Angry, Hank stressed the need for action in spite of the risks. Leaning more toward caution, Pauline insisted they both give Steinert one more night. Hank didn't agree, but again felt Pauline had greater wisdom and experience in such matters. He deferred to her.

With a lit candle, Pauline made her way through the dark main dining room, checking all the windows and the front door to make sure they were locked and secure. She warily peered outside to see if she could spot any unusual or threatening activity. All was quiet. Hank, sick of his jail cell of a room, felt more emboldened and had started to move about the café more freely, even carelessly. Pauline, having let down her guard and better judgment, had not reprimanded him for doing so.

"We can't do this forever, Pauline."

The startled woman wheeled around to find her American lover standing directly behind her.

"Sooner or later we're going to have to leave this place—for good. You know that," Hank said solemnly.

"*Oui*," replied Pauline with a touch of despair on her lips. "But you should go back to your room now, *Henri*."

Hank put his hand gently on her shoulder and said, "It'll be okay. No one will hurt you as long as I'm alive. I promise."

A small tear ran down the young woman's face as she motioned for Hank to return to the safety of his room. She told him she would join him there soon and just to be patient and silent until that time. Hank nodded in agreement and quietly retreated. He went halfway down the stairs then stopped. After a few seconds passed he got down on his belly and stealthily crawled back up into the kitchen and then into the dining room. He hid behind the bar in the dark and kept his eye on Pauline. She put her candle down on a table and sat alone in silence for several minutes. Hank watched her as she collected her thoughts. He knew she was wondering what was ultimately going to happen to them. Her whole family was dead. He knew it was true, but did she? There was no reason to hold out any hope for her brothers' safe return. All was lost in that regard. Where was Steinert? What was the right move? Sit and wait, or strike out into the darkness to the coast in search of the Resistance? All these questions bounced through his mind until his head began to ache.

The anxious girl sighed heavily and started to get up. As she moved, Hank noticed her attention become focused on something outside the window. She sat back down and slowly pulled back the drawn curtain and peered into the darkness. Hank stood up without being noticed and stared out the window. His eyes zeroed in on a tiny orange glow that seemed suspended in midair. Pauline quickly blew out her candle, immersing the café in complete darkness. Hank deduced the glow was from a lit cigarette inside a parked car across the street! Pauline strained her eyes as did Hank. It was definitely a German Mercedes, although he couldn't tell if it was Steinert's. Hank wondered if it was him sitting in the front seat, smoking and just biding his time, waiting for the right moment to make a dramatic appearance as he had done so many times in the past. Pauline sat there like a statue and surreptitiously stared at whoever was watching her. Hank silently slid back down behind the bar out of sight.

Steinert hustled along the roads leading into the center of Jolieville. He was soaked by the rain that continued to fall and covered in mud and bloodstains. He used the massive hedgerows as cover and was thankful the few German patrols he encountered were motorized and drove by him fast enough that he wasn't seen. The rain helped provide a natural cover, while the black uniform helped camouflage him further. He was a fugitive, knowing von Schreiner's body had to have been discovered and the alarm sounded by now. He was far enough away from the château that it was out of sight, but not necessarily out of earshot. The sound of alarms, whistles, and angry men with barking dogs would commence at any moment! He listened intently but heard nothing. He trotted on, knowing his strength wouldn't hold out at such a hurried pace. He realized his only chance to avoid detection and get to the café in time was to commandeer a vehicle—and quickly. He had to take some risks.

Steinert's mud-caked boots finally hit pavement as he neared the main road that led to the café. As he turned a corner and rounded a small building he came to an abrupt stop. Bright headlight beams from a Volkswagen VW Type 82 *Kübelwagen* illuminated him fully. Steinert raised his right hand to shield his eyes from the blinding light. As he did, the sounds of German voices filled the air!

"*Achtung! Halt!*" cried out a soldier. Steinert lowered his hand as the headlights were dimmed. A second later he was hit by two flashlight beams. He assumed he had stumbled onto a roadblock of some sort. It was not uncommon for *Wehrmacht* troops to set up random checkpoints leading into town. They did it often as part of war games, or other forms of military drill. However, this was the first time Steinert had encountered one as a fugitive. He believed he was doomed as it was certain this roadblock was initiated to capture him. Steinert casually positioned his right hand over his holstered Luger and waited for what was to come next.

Two *Wehrmacht* troops cautiously walked up to Steinert. They were wearing greatcoats and steel-green, M1940 helmets as protection from enemy threats and, more importantly, the foul weather. As soon as both saw Steinert's uniform they snapped to attention and curiously saluted. Steinert deduced they must be unaware of his identity and were probably just confused as to why an *SS-Obersturmbannführer* was out for a walk in such dismal weather. Ironically, at that moment, the rain stopped. Steinert looked up at the sky and noticed a hint of the bright full moon behind a large cloudbank. A favorable omen?

"*Sind Sie schmerzen, Sir?*" asked one soldier as he dubiously looked at the smeared mud and bloodstains on the soaked *Obersturmbannführer's* uniform.

"*Nein. Gut. Danke*," Steinert replied tersely. Unable to quickly conjure up a story about what exactly he was doing, he hesitated and waited for the troops to make the next move.

"*Wohin fahren Sie?*" asked the curious one.

"*Café LeBlanc*," blurted out Steinert without thinking clearly.

"*Sind Sie schmerzen, Sir?*" repeated the curious soldier, unable to understand why there were red bloodstains and mud covering Steinert's uniform. Even the rain hadn't fully washed away either from his face and hands. "*Brauchen Sie etwas?*" he added with concern.

"*Nein*," answered Steinert. Then he reversed his answer and pointed to the car blocking the road. "*Ich braucht es.*"

Puzzled, the soldier looked at Steinert and asked, "*Was sagen Sie? Was brauchen Sie?*"

Steinert quickly got his head straight and whipped up a story. He explained to both men that he had been in a bad car accident and had been walking for several kilometers. His driver was killed and the blood on his uniform was from his driver's smashed skull. He further explained that he was a bit dazed, but had to get to Café LeBlanc as quickly as possible to meet a fellow officer who had ordered him there for a critical meeting.

As Steinert was recounting his story, a telephone rang inside the soldier's makeshift guard shack next to the road. Steinert noticed it was sitting next to radio equipment on a small table. The other soldier walked over to answer it, while the first went on asking questions and nodded his head as Steinert figured he was finally beginning to buy his story. The soldier quickly offered to give the *Obersturmbannführer* a ride to the café, which Steinert immediately refused. He stressed needing to go by himself and promised he would return the vehicle as soon as he could. The soldier hesitated. Steinert insisted he didn't want to order the soldier to give up the vehicle, but he would if it came to that. Having heard that, the soldier snapped to attention and was about to grant Steinert's request until he heard his comrade hang up the phone and yell out, "*Halt!*"

The soldier in the guard shack raised his Mauser Kar 98 rifle and pointed it directly at Steinert! In response, Steinert grabbed the soldier closest to him and used him as a human shield just a split second before the second soldier fired. The bullet ripped through the unsuspecting soldier's neck, killing him instantly. His body went limp and slid down to the ground, leaving Steinert exposed. The German frantically worked the bolt action on his rifle. The spent shell casing ejected from the chamber and a new bullet was recycled in its place. Just as he locked down the bolt and squeezed the trigger, Steinert's Luger pumped two rounds into his chest, The second rifle round fired harmlessly into the air, and the German slumped forward and fell dead.

Knowing there wasn't a minute to lose, Steinert raced to the *Kübelwagen*. He leapt into the driver's seat and frantically tried to start the motor, giving it too much gas and flooding the engine. The car wouldn't start! It sputtered and wheezed as the engine failed to turn over. From inside the car he could hear the telephone in the guard shack ringing again. There was also lots of very audible yet indiscernible chatter coming over the radio. Steinert had stirred up a bee's nest of unbelievable proportions and it wouldn't be long before every German in Jolieville would be after him! He struggled to start the engine of the *Kübelwagen*. It was one little piece of German engineering that might ironically save his life!

Back at the café, Hank watched Pauline look on in terror as three shadowy men emerged from the Mercedes and cautiously approached the front entrance. As they drew closer, enough moonlight shone through the clouds to reveal that none of them was a uniformed Steinert. Pauline slipped away from the window and retreated to the front of the bar, not seeing Hank crouch down out of sight. He remained hidden in the shadows, tucked in a corner behind the bar with his eyes glued to Pauline and what was happening

Suddenly there was a loud pounding on the door!

"*Öffnen Sie die Tür!*" a loud and frightening voice demanded. The command was followed by another assault on the door's wooden frame. Pauline knew she had been seen, so she courageously summoned the will to unlock and open the door. The three men stepped inside. Pauline, weak in the knees, staggered three steps backward before regaining her balance. The leader of the shadowy trio slowly stepped into view. Pauline's nerves fluttered with fear as the devilish Gestapo sociopath spoke.

"*Guten Abend, Fräulein LeBlanc*," greeted the venomous Otto Eichner, his words soaked in wickedness as they oozed out of his smug mouth and across his thin lips. He was dressed in his usual black suit with red-and-black striped tie beneath his black leather overcoat. His golden Nazi Party badge was pinned on his suit lapel just above the red handkerchief poking out of his jacket's breast pocket. He glared at Pauline through his round spectacles as he scratched his tiny mustache. He didn't remove his black fedora, nor did he do anything to make himself or Pauline more comfortable. Eichner simply stood before her in an imposing stance, ignoring the fact that he was slightly shorter than she.

"*Das Café ist geschlossen*," meekly stated Pauline.

The three intruders burst out laughing. Pauline watched as the other two Gestapo agents, dressed similarly to Eichner, fanned out behind their boss. They slowly took in their surroundings, eyeing every detail as if they were waiting to find something—or someone! One agent located the overhead electric light switch and turned it on. Instantly, light bulbs atop the small hanging chandeliers illuminated the room. Hank froze but saw he hadn't been spotted yet. He could see that the agent by the light switch wore an open, brown leather overcoat with a slung MP-40 "*Schmeisser*" machine gun protruding from inside. The other, dressed in a dark brown suit with no overcoat, didn't have a visible weapon, although Hank was sure he had a pistol concealed somewhere on his person. The agent positioned himself by the front door, stood cockily aloof, and lit a cigarette.

Eichner began to intimidate Pauline with a series of hard, direct questions. To her consternation, every one revolved around Hank! Eichner repeatedly asked where the American was hiding. As he assailed the young Frenchwoman with his unending questions, he forced her to back up until she was pinned between him and the front of the bar. Pauline, speaking in her best German, denied having any knowledge of a fugitive American pilot and was quick to mention Steinert's name in her defense and the defense of her family establishment. Eichner laughed out loud again, then lashed out in a fiery rage, stating that Steinert was no longer in charge of the goings on at Café LeBlanc and his corpse was already lined up next to both of Pauline's recently killed brothers! Pauline gasped for air and became speechless. Fear overpowered her every emotion, and she couldn't muster any words of defense to counter Eichner's ruthless verbal barrage.

The machine gun-toting agent stepped up to the bar and grabbed a bottle of cognac resting on the counter top. He picked up a shot glass and poured himself a drink. Eichner pointed to the bottle and said, "*Geben Sie es mir!*" The agent handed it over and stepped away. Eichner slowly turned the bottle over and poured the remaining contents onto the floor. Then without warning he hurled the bottle at the shelves behind the bar, breaking several other bottles of liquor. Pauline flinched, but didn't try to break away from Eichner's hold on her. To her added horror the Gestapo beast began picking up stacked shot glasses and started randomly tossing them onto the floor. The sound of glass shattering was unnerving. Eichner continued his psychological attack on Pauline with more questions laced with physical-sounding threats. He pinned her harder and harder against the bar.

Pauline continued to stall by trying to remain brave and saying nothing. Eichner became intense. As he spoke he pressed his crotch deep into Pauline's. Simultaneously, his threats sounded sexually violent in nature. He started to fondle her aggressively. Pauline was mortified and paralyzed with fear. The two accompanying agents, each snickering with delight, showed no compassion for the helpless Frenchwoman. In fact, they eagerly looked on as if poised to indulge their darker sexual appetites when their boss was finished with Pauline.

Eichner reached into his overcoat pocket, pulled out a knife, and slowly raised it to Pauline's pounding chest, using the blade to pluck away her blouse buttons, one by one, until her breasts were almost completely exposed. He whispered disgusting-sounding threats in her ear as he made tiny slashes into her blouse and skirt. A moment of silence passed before Eichner's slim patience ran out. He raised the blade to Pauline's throat! Her eyes grew as wide as hen's eggs and she dared not even breathe. Eichner's men stayed motionless as they watched with sinister anticipation, unsure of exactly what was going to happen next.

"*Wo ist der Amerikaner?*" Eichner violently shouted at Pauline. A tear ran down her cheek, but she bit her lip and said nothing. Eichner snarled at her defiance and simply said, "*Auf Wiedersehen, Fräulein!*" As he prepared to plunge the knife blade deep into her throat, Hank suddenly leapt up from behind the bar and pressed the barrel of his Colt .45 into the center of Eichner's forehead! Taken by surprise, the shocked Eichner recoiled, dropped his knife, and froze in place after slowly raising his hands. A rageful and defiant look was chiseled on his face. The Gestapo agent with the machine gun quickly raised his weapon and pointed it at Hank. Simultaneously, the second agent by the front door reached into his suit and produced a Walther P-38 pistol that he aimed at Hank. Eichner barked out an order. "*Nicht schießen,*" he shouted.

"Don't fucking move," ordered Hank with gritted teeth, as he looked Eichner square in the eyes and kept his gun pointed at his forehead. Pauline slipped away from Eichner's clutches and retreated behind the bar, positioning herself behind Hank and within reach of her .38 Llama concealed on a shelf underneath the counter top. She made no sudden move to go for it, but kept herself ready.

"Remember me?" furiously asked Hank. "I sure as hell remember you! The shoe's on the other foot now, you bastard! Your ass is mine!"

Eichner simply sneered at Hank, further fueling the American's rage. He didn't want to talk any more; he just wanted to fight! Without warning Hank wheeled to his left and fired a shot at the machine gunner. The bullet tore through the gunner's right shoulder, knocking him backward into the wall. The MP-40's barrel kicked upward and discharged, spraying a hail of machine gun fire into the ceiling and knocking out most of the overhead lights. The agent nearest the front door couldn't get off a clear shot and ducked out of the way of the falling glass. The dining room went dark. Eichner retreated toward the front door, knocking over tables and chairs for cover. Hank fired two more shots, barely missing Eichner and the Walther-carrying agent, both of whom found protection behind knocked-over dining tables. Eichner reached under his coat and pulled out his PPK pistol, angrily returning fire. The agent with the P-38 did the same.

Hank and Pauline took cover behind the bar. Bullets pinged off the bar and wall, ricocheting in every direction. Pauline picked up her pistol while crouching for cover. Eichner shouted orders to the machine gunner still on the ground and in pain and shock. His shoulder was shattered and he couldn't move his right arm. He was losing lots of blood fast. He reached for the gun with his left arm, raised it toward the bar, and pulled the trigger, causing the gun to spit out sporadic bursts of inaccurate fire. German 9mm pistol fire ripped into the wooden bar, punching holes through the frame and shattering glasses and bottles. Pauline and Hank had to hit the deck for cover amidst the intense ricocheting gunfire. Eichner directed the second agent to move closer, to get a better shooting angle. He scurried toward the bar and ducked behind a table while firing his Walther P-38, pausing only to seek cover and reload.

The machine gunner fired off one last burst before his gun went dry. Dazed by the loss of blood, he tried unsuccessfully to reach for a fresh magazine. Pauline sprang out from behind the bar and pumped a bullet into his gut, putting an end to his threat. She took aim at the second agent and fired several rounds in his direction, while Hank continued to exchange shots with Eichner. Pauline's battle with the second Gestapo agent climaxed when she heard the hammer on his Walther fall on an empty chamber. With all her courage she emptied her weapon into the upended table he was using for cover. The shots ripped through the wood and tore into the agent's head and chest, killing him instantly. He toppled over in a pool of blood. Pauline ducked back behind the bar and looked for more bullets for her now empty pistol. Hank continued to trade shots with Eichner. In one mad flurry, Eichner fired the remaining bullets from his PPK directly at the section of the bar Hank was using for cover, but none of the shots found its mark. Hank and Pauline could hear the gun's hammer click repeatedly on an empty chamber.

"Pauline, he's out!" shouted Hank. "But so am I," he added as he hurriedly fumbled to find another magazine.

"My gun is empty, as well," she angrily replied, "and I will not let him get away!" Suddenly she got to her feet and leapt over the bar.

"No, Pauline! Wait!" shouted Hank, thinking she was going directly after Eichner before he had a chance to escape through the front door. "He doesn't know we're out of ammo and he may still have that knife!"

The brazen Frenchwoman fearlessly jumped on the dead machine gunner and yanked the gun from his lifeless grasp. With incredible precision and speed she removed the spent magazine, found the spare under his coat, and slapped it into place. Hank bravely jumped up and kept his unloaded Colt trained on Eichner's position, to pretend he was covering Pauline. Pauline pulled back the machine gun's bolt and prepared to unleash an unholy barrage of fire on the man who had just threatened her with words describing unthinkable acts of sexual torture, violence, and murder. However, as she raised the gun to fire, Hank glimpsed an orange flame shooting up from behind Eichner's little fortress of cover. During the gunfight he had managed to grab an intact cognac bottle that had fallen off a nearby upended table and stuff his red handkerchief down the neck, creating an instant firebomb! Eichner lobbed the Molotov cocktail directly at the bar. The bottle shattered, splashing fiery flames across the floor and igniting the alcohol spilled earlier from other damaged bottles! The flames and the accompanying heat forced Pauline and Hank to recoil and seek cover. Eichner saw his opening and made a dash for the front door. Pauline fired a burst from the MP-40 through the flames. The bullets missed their mark, as Eichner made it outside safely.

"C'mon, Pauline! Down the stairs!" shouted Hank as the fire continued to spread rapidly. Pauline leapt over the bar and took Hank's hand. The two dashed through the kitchen and down the stairs, back to Hank's room.

"Grab whatever you can carry, and we'll use the secret exit and escape through the sewers," hollered Hank as he slapped a fresh magazine into his gun and made sure his dog tags were still hidden securely in his shoe.

Pauline slung her machine gun and added, "Everything we need is in the secret storage room! We must get to it quickly! Hurry!" The smell of smoke hung heavy in the air, and the glow of the spreading fire intensified above them. They had no time to waste!

Hank pushed aside the bookcase, revealing the secret door. Pauline popped it open and the two descended the small ladder leading to the secret storage room. Hank reached for more .45 caliber ammunition while Pauline filled her skirt pockets with money, fake identity papers, and some scraps of bread. She hurriedly put on her leather coat to cover up her torn blouse. Hank threw on an old brown suit coat over his white shirt and suspenders and stuffed some bread into the pockets. He then heaved with all his might and pushed the large storage crate off the hidden iron trap door. He pulled up on the handle. To his shock and dismay, the rusted iron door wouldn't open! Hank pulled again, but couldn't free the stubborn hatch.

"It's rusted shut!" said Hank. "I can't budge it!"

"Try again, *Henri*!" pleaded Pauline as smoke from the fire upstairs began to pour down into Hank's room.

Hank gave it everything he had and ripped the rusty handle clean off the door! Both looked on in terror as there was now no way to pry open the door. It was sealed for good, leaving the terrified couple precious few options for escape.

"There's no time now, *Henri*! Leave it and come quickly before we are trapped!" exclaimed Pauline, as she pulled the American back up the ladder and into his room. She dashed to the door leading upstairs, only to be stopped by an impassable wall of fire and smoke. She slammed the door shut, temporarily stopping the steady stream of smoke. Both could hear the sound of the café's heavy support beams beginning to buckle and knew that the entire roof could collapse at any moment.

Coughing heavily from the smoke-filled air, Hank saw only one remaining option. He jumped up on the bed and tore down the drapes covering the small, rectangular window. It would be tight and painful, but it was just large enough for someone to squeeze through—he hoped! He shattered the glass, using the butt of his pistol. Pauline gathered the bed sheets and wrapped her arms and hands with them to protect herself. With a boost from Hank, she swept away as much jagged glass as possible.

"Okay, you first!" commanded Hank, as he held Pauline by the waist and lifted her up to the window. Pauline unwrapped her hands from the sheets and pulled herself up and partly through the window. Hank was shocked at how difficult it was for Pauline's tiny frame to fit through the opening. Nevertheless, she persevered and painfully wriggled through and onto the street, safe for the moment. She immediately dropped to her stomach and reached through the window, grasping for Hank's hand. Hank looked at the closed door leading upstairs and saw it had caught fire. Within minutes he would be dead!

"Hurry, *Henri*! *Vite, vite!*" cried Pauline as she watched the flames enveloping the entire café.

Hank peeled off his coat and handed it through the window. He emptied his pockets and handed out his gun to Pauline's outstretched hands. Carrying nothing, he leapt to the window and tried to pull himself through. Pauline grabbed his arms and tugged with all her strength. Hank twisted and wriggled, but couldn't clear his shoulders through the small opening! He dropped down to the bed, and tried again from a different angle. Pauline pulled hard, but couldn't drag him through. The pain got to be too much and Hank had to abort the attempt again. He turned and saw the entire doorframe and part of the wall were now on fire! His mind raced, and he didn't know what to do next.

Outside, by the front of the café, Eichner had scrambled across the street, back to his Mercedes. He fumbled around inside the car until he found the spare bullets he needed to reload his PPK. Cocking the weapon, he got out of the car and stood by the driver's door. He laughed malevolently as the flames burst through the front windows and part of the roof caved in.

The intense wall of heat from the raging fire pinned Eichner against the door of the Mercedes. He put up his left hand to shield his face from the inferno. The heat forced him to turn his head and look away. As he did, he spotted a pair of dimmed headlights pointed right at him. Suddenly a pair of tires squealed and the unidentified vehicle lurched forward directly toward him! In a split second the stunned Gestapo agent jumped out of the way and dove into the center of the street. His PPK pistol flew out of his hand and clattered across the pavement, into the shadows. Sparks flew as the unidentified vehicle clipped the Mercedes and then skidded out of control, hitting a curb then smashing to a stop against a darkened street lamp. Eichner looked up and saw that the vehicle was a German *Kübelwagen*! The driver, a bit dazed, stared at him and struggled to get out of the car. Eichner leapt to his feet, raced to the car, ripped open the door, and grabbed the driver, hauling him out and manhandling him down to the ground. The light from the blazing café fire illuminated the street, clearly revealing Eichner's would-be assassin!

The black-clad Gestapo thug laughed heartily at the sight of Steinert doubled over in pain. His head was cut and bleeding and he was dazed. Steinert reached for his Luger and managed to get it out of its holster, but before he could take aim, Eichner fell upon him and kicked the weapon out of his hand. He followed the first kick with a second that landed square into Steinert's gut and sent him reeling in agony.

"*Stehen Sie auf!*" Eichner barked with delight. "*Was haben Sie?*"

Steinert desperately tried to get to his feet to defend himself, but each attempt was met with more punishment from Eichner. The Gestapo agent continued to brutally pump kick after kick into the helpless Steinert. The final blow put him flat on his back, motionless and groaning in pain. Eichner stood over him, asserting his superiority and continuing to verbally harass and berate him.

"*Machen Sie es sich bequem, Peter!*" said Eichner sadistically. "*Wie sagen Sie das auf Englisch?*" he asked. "*Sind Sie Engländer? Amerikaner? Sprechen Sie!*" Steinert said nothing. Eichner then pointed to the burning café and said, "*Die Amerikaner? Ich hatte bereits das Vergnügen!*" Eichner told Steinert he was going to enjoy watching him suffer as he languished in a Gestapo torture chamber while every ounce of information was painfully and forcefully extracted from his brain. Eichner then turned to hunt for his PPK he was sure was on the ground nearby.

Steinert, garnering every last unit of strength in his battered body, fueled on nothing but pure emotion, struggled to his feet and tackled the unsuspecting Eichner from behind. Both men hit the pavement hard as the flames from the burning café raged behind them! "*Schweinhund!*" hollered Steinert as he grabbed Eichner by the throat with his left hand, and then buried his right fist into his face, knocking his head back hard against the street. Eichner's nose gushed blood. The Gestapo thug was stunned, but not out of the fight! He kneed Steinert in the groin, freeing his right arm that he swung violently at Steinert's head. His fist caught Steinert on the side of the forehead, knocking him off. Eichner got to his feet and staggered over to the injured Steinert. He kicked him hard again in the side of his gut. Steinert, the wind knocked out of him, gasped for breath, as blood started to drip from the corner of his mouth.

Then, like a European football player lining up a penalty shot, Eichner drew his foot back and prepared to cave in the right side of Steinert's face with one mighty blow. As his leg swung into motion, Steinert, like a skilled goalkeeper, brought his hands up and caught Eichner's foot! Jerking with all his remaining strength, he pulled Eichner back down on the ground. The Gestapo agent fell on his back and hit his head hard on the pavement. Now it was Steinert's turn! He leapt to his feet before Eichner could react and began to ram his jackboots deep into Eichner's side. Eichner rolled over several times to get out of the way, but Steinert managed to stay within reach. The evil little man cried out in pain, but luckily his rolling on the street had put him within arm's reach of his PPK!

Eichner lurched for his gun and managed to get hold of it. Steinert leapt on top of him and grasped his right hand before the Gestapo thug could aim the weapon. The two rolled over on top of each other several times before ending exactly where they started. Eichner fired two rounds, but Steinert was able to keep the weapon pointed away from him. Steinert then made a desperate move. He remembered his SS dagger dangling from its scabbard and went for it with his free hand. Steinert wrenched it free and raised it high! Eichner reacted quickly and used his free left hand to catch Steinert's right before he could plunge the blade deep into Eichner's face. Now it became a test of will and strength. Both men had weapons in their right hand and both men used their left to fend off the other. It was unclear who would win this deadly contest.

Meanwhile, on the other side of the café, Lieutenant Henry Mitchell continued to struggle for his life as he desperately tried to escape the burning inferno. He had tried to wedge his way through the narrow window, but couldn't get his broad shoulders to fit through. Pauline tugged and pulled with all her might, but was unable to bring her lover to safety. Hank dropped down to the bed below in futility. His body was doused in perspiration as he felt he was being roasted alive! The fire spread closer and Hank knew it would be only a matter of minutes before he would be overcome and killed by the smoke and flames.

As Pauline screamed for Hank to try again, the American had a radical idea. He bluntly slammed his left shoulder into the smoldering wall. He yelled out in pain, but continued to bang his shoulder against the wall as Pauline begged him to stop. Finally, with one mighty slam, Hank accomplished his goal. His left arm sagged downward awkwardly—he had dislocated his shoulder! Pauline finally understood what he had done.

With his able right arm, Hank reached up to the window and grasped Pauline's hand, telling her to pull as hard as she could as his legs pushed upward. With all his strength, Hank squeezed his shoulders through the window opening. His dislocated shoulder sagged just enough to allow him to fit his upper body through the devilishly small space. Pauline pulled hard. Soon Hank was halfway out. Parts of the ceiling crashed down just as Hank yanked his legs through and out to safety. Pauline quickly patted down his legs as his pants were smoldering. The two got to their feet and scampered across the street, away from the raging inferno. Hank collected his coat and gun from Pauline. She kissed him hard, happy and relieved that they made it out safely.

"Come, *Henri*, we must hurry before the streets are filled with Germans!" said Pauline. "This way!" The two hustled around to the front of the building, where they stopped dead in their tracks.

Still locked in a life-and-death struggle, Eichner yelled out in pain as another shot rang out from his pistol. Steinert, still on top of him, bellowed mightily and broke free from Eichner's weakened grip. He plunged his SS dagger deep into Eichner's right eye socket. The Gestapo thug screamed in agony and fell silent. Completely exhausted, Steinert rolled off of him. He lay in the street, dazed and gasping for breath.

"My God!" said Pauline as she put her hand to her mouth.

"C'mon, let's get out of here," Hank said, tugging Pauline's hand with his good arm.

"No. We have to help him," she insisted.

"Are you crazy? We can't trust him! Just leave him and let's get out of here! We can make it on our own! We don't need his help any more," Hank implored.

"No, *Henri*! You are wrong! We need his help now more than ever," said Pauline. "He can guide us to safety and get us through the German lines. He knows where the Germans are located. He knows what places to avoid. He knows where we can find transports. We must help him! We must all get away together! Look at what he has just done!"

Hank looked at the grisly body of the man who had just tried to kill him. The dagger impaled in his skull gave small testament to Steinert's true loyalty. Hank resisted saying so, but he felt there was little choice. They had to move and move quickly if any of them had a chance for survival.

"Okay, just be careful and be ready for anything. I still can't bring myself to trust that Nazi son-of-a-bitch!" Hank's right arm and shoulder throbbed with agonizing pain, but he gritted his teeth and ignored it long enough to raise his .45 at Steinert. Pauline rushed to the *Obersturmbannführer* and helped him to his feet.

"Jolly good to see you, my lovely," said Steinert in his charming British accent. "We had better take our leave of this place and without hesitation. Get in."

Steinert picked up his officer's cap and put it on. Pauline and Hank hurried to the Mercedes and climbed into the back seat. Steinert got into the driver's seat from the passenger's door as the driver's door was jammed shut from the earlier impact of the *Kübelwagen*. He sat there a moment with his head back trying to block out the pain. Pauline attended to Hank, popping his shoulder into place with a mighty crunch. Hank cried out in pain. His arm tingled and he did his best to keep it motionless.

"Do you need my help, Herr Steinert?" asked Pauline, seeing the blood drip down from his cut forehead. Hank squeezed her hand, indicating he didn't want her tending to the stricken *Obersturmbannführer*.

"No, no, my dear. I'll be as right as rain and fine as paint in just a moment. I just need to get my wits about me before we dash off into the darkness. Give me just a minute," said Steinert as he fumbled with the car's ignition.

Hank impatiently and angrily spoke up, saying, "Well, in that case, I've got something I need to do while you get your wits about you!" Hank threw open the door and dashed into the open plaza. Pauline screamed for him to come back, but it was too late. Hank rushed up to the fountain and kicked over the coat stand supporting the charred U.S. Army Air Force jacket, leather helmet, and shattered goggles. He kicked away the stand, neatly folded the jacket, laid it on the edge of the fountain, and placed the helmet and goggles neatly on top of it. Now it looked more like an honorable memorial rather than a morbid display of foreboding cruelty. Satisfied, he hurried back to the car.

"That was very stupid, *Henri!*" scolded Pauline. "Do not do something like that again!"

Steinert started the car and drove away. At that moment, what remained of the café's roof collapsed. The walls came crashing down, spilling charred timbers, shattered glass, metal, and other remnants of the burning building into the street. The collapse sent an avalanche of debris onto the spot where the Mercedes had been parked a moment before! Hank and Pauline looked back in amazement at the utter destruction.

Steinert concentrated on the road and secretly tried to figure out where they were going and what they were going to do. Hank questioned Pauline about Eichner. Still a bit shaken, she told him all the terrible threats he had made. The streets of Jolieville were coming alive with curious French locals and German troops wanting to investigate the blaze. Steinert looked at his watch and saw it was now well after midnight. He was still a hunted man. As he slowly drove through the streets toward the outskirts of town, he heard the faint sounds of German anti-aircraft batteries. It was not an uncommon sound, but for some reason, it didn't feel right this time. The sound of droning aircraft engines could also be heard, but the sound of aircraft passing overhead usually subsided after a minute or two. This particular sound seemed to go on forever, as if the skies were filled with endless numbers of planes. Steinert eventually maneuvered the Mercedes to the dirt roads outside of town, abruptly stopped the car, and got out the passenger's door. Hank and Pauline, not understanding the situation, did the same. Steinert looked up and saw white-hot tracer fire arching skyward from hidden *Flakvierling-38* anti-aircraft batteries below. Higher still, hundreds of roaring Allied planes filled the skies—an incredible sight! The air armada, though not fully visible, sounded endless. Steinert knew this was not a typical bombing raid. It was something else altogether. This was the invasion!

Chapter 20

A MEANINGFUL LESSON

Matthew Switzer was thunderstruck. He couldn't move nor find any words to describe what was going on in his mind. He sat amid a scattered pile of handwritten notes and other papers, but hadn't even realized he had stopped writing long ago. Hours had passed and he had done nothing but simply listen in sheer awe and amazement. Never in his life had he heard such a story. Hank Mitchell had calmly and patiently described in extraordinary detail the frightening and disturbing events surrounding his secret mission, yet even he was unaware of the awesome impact it had had on his curious listener.

Neither teacher nor pupil had realized how quickly the hours of the day had slipped by. It was early in the evening now and neither had even stopped for lunch. Hank knew he was at a good stopping point in his story, and he figured it was time for a break and a change of subject. The old man slowly rose from his chair and stretched his weary bones. He excused himself, made a quick bathroom visit, then returned to breathe life into the wood stove by adding some hearty, old, dry oak. Soon the fire sparked anew.

"You know, sometimes I just hate April," said Hank as he looked out the window at the gray, overcast sky. Matt looked at him and said nothing. "April hits ya with all sorts of promise and hope … then often disappoints ya with all kinds of gloomy, rainy, chilly weather. May as well still be winter, as far as I'm concerned, by gorry. It's supposed to be spring, right? Some nights it sure don't feel like spring. Maybe I'm just getting old. Ayuh, sometimes I just hate April." The old man chuckled, waiting for some sort of response from his young guest.

Matt tried to think of something to say. Normal conversation and pleasantries eluded him. His mind was on sensory overload trying to visualize, understand, and digest all the compelling information Hank had conveyed to him. He sat like a zombie. Hank, realizing the effect his tale had had on Matt, made a decision. He shuffled over to the sofa, collected Matt's papers, and neatly put them into his backpack. He patted Matt on the back and spoke to him directly, hoping to snap him out of his trance.

"Say there, fella. Why don't we knock off for the night. You should get home and rest up. You know—take a break from this. Whaddaya think?" Hank waited for a response but got only a sluggish, confused look from Matt. Worried, Hank became more direct. "Now c'mon there, fella. It's Friday night, and I'm sure you've got more enjoyable things to do than hang around with an old, broken-down fool like me! C'mon, let's get your stuff together and get you on your way. There must be dozens of pretty girls waiting for you back in Orono. Don't want to keep them waiting, do ya? You'll wanna go out and get some pizza or something and catch a movie … right? That'd be fun?" said Hank as he helped Matt to his feet and handed him his backpack.

"Yeah … I guess I need to get going," said Matt as he seemed to snap out of his trance. "I, uh … I should, uh … head out, I suppose. I need to get back to campus and uh … you know." Matt's voice trailed off as he scratched his head. He knew he had to leave, but something compelled him to stay. He had to hear more. He yearned to learn more and was excited about it. It was a feeling he couldn't explain.

"Boy, I'm sure beat. Do yourself a favor, Matt, and never grow old. It's just one thing after another," Hank said with a powerful yawn. The old man was hunched over and rumpled looking. He was clearly very tired. The long hours of recalling the past had taken a toll on him.

"Thank you for your time today, Hank," Matt said, as he shook the old man's hand. "When do you think we could meet again and talk some more?" he asked, knowing he needed to hear the rest of the story.

Hank sighed. "I don't know if that's a good idea, son. Maybe I've said too much already. It's not a good idea to get too carried away. Some things are better left untold."

"But you just can't stop now!" Matt exclaimed. "I have so many more questions and notes to take. I need to understand things better before I start to write my paper. We can't just stop now! This is important to me."

Hank sighed again and shook his head. He wondered if the course he had set out on was the right one. He'd seen the immaturity and lack of interest when they first met, which made him skeptical; however, he had noticed a marked turnaround in the young man's attitude during the time they had spent together. He had started this, and he knew that it was only fair to finish it. He only hoped his inner demons wouldn't become Matt Switzer's, as well. The nightmares were hard enough for the old man to cope with; he didn't want to be responsible for unleashing something worse on a younger, more impressionable mind. He decided to allow matters to progress a bit further and see how his pupil reacted. He felt what he had to impart was important and needed to be said to the younger generations before it was too late. He hoped Matt understood that and would put his newfound knowledge to good use in a mature and responsible way. That was the best he could hope for.

"Okay, come back tomorrow and we'll try and finish up. We'll see how things go and how much time we have. I want you to pay good attention and leave here knowing a thing or two. Got it?"

"Yeah, I got it," said Matt with a smile. "I already am leaving here a little wiser, I think."

"Not too early tomorrow!" yelled Hank as Matt started to drive away. Matt waved his hand and was soon out of sight. Hank went back inside and headed to his bedroom to settle in for an early night. He was exhausted and didn't care how early it was. He just had to sleep. He prayed his dreams wouldn't be filled with the horrors he had experienced so many years ago!

Matt made it back to Orono and his room in Chamberlain Hall. The Friday night parties were already underway. Music blared from stereos and thirsty undergrads emptied beer bottles left and right. Matt was oblivious to it all. He slammed his door shut and immediately picked up the phone. He dialed Michelle Kessler's number and couldn't wait to talk with her. As the phone rang he felt it was a good time to keep up with his part of their arrangement. He just hoped she wasn't busy and had some interest in meeting him in a nice, quiet place where the two of them could talk uninterrupted. He tried to picture what she was doing and what she was wearing. His heart leapt when she picked up the phone with a simple, yet lovely "Hello?"

Matt drove back to Bar Harbor early the next day. The skies were overcast and it felt unseasonably cool again. The Rabbit chugged along and came to a stop in Hank Mitchell's driveway. With renewed enthusiasm and curiosity, Matt eagerly knocked on Hank's door. The good night's rest he had gotten following the warm and pleasant conversation with Michelle had calmed his nerves and allowed his mind to reset and refocus. The old man opened the door and let his friend in. After exchanging pleasantries, Hank showed Matt to his normal place on the sofa in the study and sat in his chair opposite the wood stove. A crackling fire produced a comfortable warmth that evenly circulated throughout the room.

Matt started his tape recorder and readied his pen and notepad. His elder companion did not noticeably match his enthusiasm. Matt sat unaware his teacher had not passed a good night. The tales dredged up of unpleasant times from long ago had taken their toll on him. The nightmares, once almost forgotten, had returned to terrorize the old warrior without mercy, robbing him of precious sleep. Nevertheless, Hank maintained a strong demeanor and was determined to finish what he had started. He was about to pick up his story right where he left off, but surprisingly his young friend spoke first.

"You know, Hank, I'm so grateful that our country was completely protected by both the Atlantic and Pacific Oceans during the war. I've been doing some studying, and it's a relief to know we weren't threatened at all. I can't imagine what it would have been like if we had to fight on our own soil. Boy, were we fortunate!" said Matt.

Hank shook his head in disbelief. "Exactly what history book were you reading, son? There might be a tiny shred of truth to what you just said, but the rest is just a load of bull!"

Surprised, Matt replied, "What do you mean? The U.S. wasn't ever attacked—except for maybe Pearl Harbor, and that wasn't even a state at the time—right?"

"Just stop right there, Matt, because what you're saying simply isn't true," said Hank. "Yes, the mainland United States never suffered a major enemy attack during the war. However, you might be interested to know that a Japanese sub surfaced and shelled the Pacific Northwest and caused some damage early in the war. The Japs also inflated and released several thousand high-altitude balloons with explosives attached to them. Some of these balloons crossed the Pacific and made it to the United States. Some detonated and caused wildfires out West. There were even some American casualties. So, ya see, the largest ocean in the world couldn't protect us. I won't even get into what those poor souls in Hawaii at Pearl Harbor had to endure on December 7, 1941. You research that on your own, fella. And while you're at it, look up Wake Island and read about the battle our Marines and several American civilians had to fight there. You'll be surprised at what you find out! Mark my words!"

"Wow, I never knew any of that. Is that true?" asked Matt.

"Yes, it's true. Sometime you go over to that library on campus and you look up Alaska. Read about two little islands called Kiska and Attu. You'll learn something that will really knock your socks off and open your eyes. I won't spoil it for ya."

Matt scribbled down the information and wanted to ask more questions. He hesitated for fear of saying something stupid. He didn't know Hank wasn't finished. The old man switched gears, as well as oceans. His focus shifted from the warm Pacific to the cold Atlantic.

"Let me tell you something else, son," Hank continued. "The entire U.S. Eastern Seaboard was at risk from the very start of the war until the last shot was fired. We were so overconfident and ill-prepared that we suffered many losses at sea that could have been easily prevented. The Germans had submarines prowling up and down the East coast in groups called wolfpacks. These wolfpacks used the bright lights of our coastal cities to spot the silhouettes of U.S. merchant vessels making runs up and down the coast. Those U-boat skippers had a field day torpedoing and sinking countless unarmed ships in waters ranging from New England to the Gulf of Mexico. Our government and the Navy should have instituted blackouts all along the coast from the first day of hostilities. Damn stupid they were at the time!"

"Did they eventually fix the problem?" Matt asked sheepishly.

"Ayuh, the Navy finally got its head out of its ass and started up the convoy system. They used warships to escort and protect the freighters along the coast and over to England and back. It became very effective up until the end of the war. We also smartened up quick and turned the damn lights out, too!" replied Hank.

"I guess I never knew about any of that. I didn't grow up learning about it. I was never around anything like that," said Matt.

"Never around it! Where'd you say you were from again?" asked Hank with astonishment.

"South Portland is where I grew up," answered Matt reluctantly, as if he knew he was going to get hit with a bomb.

"Oh my Jesus!" said Hank with a hearty laugh. "You must be fooling me, kid! I grew up in Cape Elizabeth—you do know where Cape Elizabeth is, right?"

"Yeah, 'course I do," replied Matt.

"Have I got a story to tell you … but first let me key you in on a few important facts," said Hank. "Ever been out to any of the islands in Casco Bay?"

"Yeah, my parents and I would take the ferry out of Portland and go over to Peaks Island every now and then in the summer when I was little," answered Matt.

"Okay, that's good," said Hank. "Then you must have seen Fort Gorges, right?"

"Yeah, it's out in the middle of the bay," said Matt, unsure of his answer.

"Yup, kinda," said Hank. "Did you know that it was built between 1858 and 1864? It was armed and manned during both the Civil and Spanish American Wars. I betcha didn't know that submarine mines and various other types of munitions were stored there to combat those pesky German U-boats I mentioned earlier."

"No, I never knew that. I never really knew what it was used for or why it was built at all," Matt said, embarrassed.

"Wait right there," Hank instructed. The old man got up and

retrieved a Maine atlas from another room. He placed it on the coffee table in front of Matt and sat down next to him on the sofa. Thumbing through the pages, Hank found the one showing maps of the Casco Bay islands. He then proceeded with his geography lesson.

"Okay, this is Jewell Island right here," he said. "It essentially was a coastal artillery battery during the war. A couple of concrete observation towers still remain today, if I'm not mistaken. Ever see one of those? I'm surprised you never been to Jewell. It's an unimproved state park today and the kids love to camp out on it. You got a girlfriend?"

"No, not at the moment," reluctantly said Matt with thoughts of Michelle running through his head.

"Over here is Bailey Island," said Hank, moving his finger along to the right spot. "It had observation towers on it, too. They were always looking for enemy vessels. One tower even had some sort of radar antenna on it, disguised as just a plain old wooden structure. There was also a gun battery placed at the tip of the island for defense. Ever hear of the Cribwork Bridge?"

"No, what's that?" asked Matt.

"You go out to Bailey Island sometime and check it out for yourself. It's pretty neat. She was built in 1928 and is the only one of her kind in the world, my friend."

"I'll do that," said Matt.

"Here's Long Island," Hank continued. "Couple of schooners were deliberately sunk off Long Island by the Navy. They were used as protection to block enemy subs and torpedoes. All harbor entrances were lined by anti-sub nets."

Matt sat and listened intently. He'd had no idea the war was so close to his very place of birth!

Hank continued his lesson. "Long Island was also used as a naval refueling station. It had three fifteen-hundred-foot piers and these huge underground fuel tanks that serviced and accommodated vessels of the Atlantic Fleet. Ships would anchor north of the island and steam right through Hussey Sound," said Hank as he showed Matt the route with his wrinkly pointer finger.

"That's really impressive, Hank," Matt said as his eyes perused the pages.

"Here's Diamond Cove, which was the site of the former Fort McKinley. It was manned during both World War I and World War II. The officers' barracks were renovated for private housing, I believe," said Hank as he rubbed his chin. "There were observation towers on Cushing Island, too, I believe. And you must have seen the old fortifications at Fort Williams by the lighthouse and at Two Lights State Park? Both those places are practically in your backyard."

"Yeah, I seen 'em, but nobody ever told me what they were for," Matt said.

"Well you need to go do some exploring on your own when you get home. Learn about the gun battery 201 at Two Lights. Go explore Fort Williams. Don't rely on me to tell you about it all. Learn about Fort Scammell on House Island, too. There is so much history relating to the war right near your own home. Go out and discover it! We weren't safe and secure like you commented earlier. The Germans were operating in the Gulf of Maine on countless occasions and posed a real threat. You want to know why they had such an interest in this area?"

"Yeah," said Matt eagerly.

"Because in 1941 the Navy designated Casco Bay as a vital fleet anchorage. They authorized the establishment of a U.S. Naval Frontier Base in Portland. That base grew to an enormous naval station that serviced thousands of U.S. sailors and hundreds of vessels. You may not believe this, but both the Army and the Navy designated it as the most important naval base in the entire United States!"

"That's incredible!" exclaimed Matt. "I had no idea."

"Research it some more when you have the time," said Hank. "You'll be amazed at what you find. The Navy didn't want the American public to panic so they never publicly recognized the threat. The truth is we were tangling with U-boats out in the Gulf of Maine pretty regularly. Do yourself a favor and research a small U.S. warship named the USS *Eagle* PE-56 and a German submarine called U-853. You'll find that story quite intriguing, I'll bet. Piece together what you find out and make up your own mind about what really happened. There's many conflicting accounts in the record books on that one."

Matt wrote notes on his pad as Hank closed the atlas and went back to his more comfortable brown recliner across from Matt.

"Ever hear of a place not too far from here called Frenchman's Bay? How about Hancock Point?" quizzed Hank.

"No," replied Matt with a sigh, feeling stupid.

"Well, you might be very surprised to learn that those Nazi U-boats I was telling you about did more than hunt U.S. merchant vessels along our coast," expressed Hank. "Some of them brought spies and saboteurs to our very shore!"

Matt's eyes widened. He had read all the textbook assignments in class about the historic events of World War II, but none of them ever involved his home state of Maine. Reading about the major battles and political intrigue in Europe and Asia was not all that interesting to him, as they were events that happened long ago in places far away. Now the scenario was much different. He wasn't in a classroom reading from a textbook about places and events he had never heard of. He was hearing stories about the greatest conflict in history that occurred in the last place he ever expected—his home state of Maine!

"Are you saying that German spies were dropped off here?" asked Matt, pointing his index finger downward. "How could that happen? What was their mission? How could they—"

"Just listen, be patient, and I'll tell ya what I know," Hank interrupted.

Matt sat back on the couch looking like an excited child waiting for dessert to be served. Hank got up and opened the Maine atlas again. He flipped to a page showing maps of Bar Harbor and Mount Desert Island, with inserts showing surrounding areas. He pointed out Frenchman's Bay and Hancock Point. He then showed Matt just how close both were to the very spot he was sitting. Once Matt got an understanding and appreciation of the geography involved, Hank resumed his seat and started to tell his story.

"In September of 1944, a German IXC/40-class submarine designated U-1230 departed Kiel, Germany, with two spies aboard," told Hank. "Their destination was Maine. The agent's names were Gimpel and Colepaugh. You might be interested to know that Colepaugh was an

American!"

"What a minute, one of the German spies was an American? No way," protested Matt.

"Ayuh, William Colepaugh was an American, by gorry," stated Hank. "He was born in Connecticut and even went to MIT. He was pro-German, though, and his big mouth probably got him into trouble around these parts. He hopped on board a Swedish ship, taking a job as a kitchen helper. As you can imagine, that was a perfect way for him to cross the Atlantic and get to Europe to help the Nazis. He made it to Portugal, where he met up with the German consul in Lisbon and stated he wanted to help Germany. They eventually shipped him to Paris, then on to Berlin, where SS Major Otto Skorzeny interviewed him. This guy was Hitler's favorite commando and was famous for rescuing Mussolini after his own people imprisoned him. Anyway, Colepaugh eventually was educated at an SS training school and that's where he met his future spy mate, Erich Gimpel."

"What's this guy Gimpel's story?" curiously asked Matt.

"Erich Gimpel was considered by many as the most accomplished spy to make it into the U.S. He spent a lot of time in Peru sending along secret information about shipping traffic to a contact in Chile. As I understand it, when America entered the war, he and a bunch of other Germans got deported from Peru to Texas where they were interned for several weeks before being shipped back to Germany. Once back there he resumed his spy role for the Nazis."

"So the Nazis gave him a mission to spy on the United States?" asked Matt.

"Ayuh," said Hank. "They teamed him up with Colepaugh and ordered them to find out about our country's atomic bomb program. You know what I mean, right? The Manhattan Project?"

"Yeah, I learned about that in high school. That was Los Alamos, right? With that guy—Oppenheimer, that was his name, wasn't it?" asked Matt.

"Yeah, that's right," Hank replied. "Well, they crossed the Atlantic in that sub and got into the Gulf of Maine after being at sea for nearly two months. On November, 29, 1944, that sub sneaked a dozen miles up

Frenchman's Bay and came to a stop near Sunset Ledge, on the western side of Hancock Point. Around 11:00 p.m. the sub's conning tower broke the surface of the water a couple hundred yards offshore and out popped Gimpel and Colepaugh. A rubber raft was inflated and the two were supposed to row themselves ashore. However, the tether broke and a couple of uniformed *Kriegsmarine* sailors had to row them in and then take the raft back to the sub! It's interesting to think about. Those two sailors most likely were carrying weapons and probably went back to that sub bragging to their buddies about how they were the first uniformed and armed combatants of the Third Reich to set foot on American soil!"

"So Gimpel and Colepaugh got ashore! What happened next?" Matt asked eagerly.

"The U-1230 slipped away undetected, and Gimpel and Colepaugh made their way up through the woods to Route 1," relayed Hank. "Now it was late November, ya gotta understand. It was dark, cold, and snowing at the time. These two guys were walking along the road in a remote area late at night in bad weather dressed in light topcoats and carrying suitcases. They didn't exactly blend in, ya understand. What's even crazier is the fact that their cover worked, believe it or not!"

Matt asked, "What was in the suitcases? Explosives, guns, weapons?"

"Money mostly," answered Hank. "They had around sixty thousand dollars on 'em. They were expected to stay a while, I guess. Anyway, as they walked down Route 1 they actually were spotted by a couple of cars that didn't stop. Guess the locals were more concerned with minding their own business. The first was driven by a woman named Mary Forni. She saw 'em and kept going. She was coming home from a late-night card game. The second car that passed 'em got a good look, too. A kid named Harvard Hodgkins, who was a neighbor of Mary Forni, was coming home from a dance at a place called Townsend Hall. He kept going, too. Curiously enough, Harvard's dad Dana was a Hancock County deputy sheriff. Mary called the Hodgkins' house to alert Dana of what she thought was kinda odd behavior. Turns out that Dana was away at a hunting camp, doing some guide work. Mary talked to Mrs. Hodgkins and confirmed through her that Harvard had seen the curious-looking men that evening as well. He did admit he thought it was all very strange, but gave little thought to it. What's even stranger was that a third car did stop when it came across them. It happened to be a taxicab from Ellsworth! You know where Ellsworth is, right?"

"Yeah, I've driven through Ellsworth before," said Matt.

"Well, our two spies took that cab thirty-five miles to Bangor and hopped on a train down to Portland around 2:00 a.m. After getting a bite to eat they then took another train down to Boston around 7:00 a.m. In Boston they got some rest, bought some American clothes, and jumped on another train to New York City the next day. It was quite remarkable that in a span of thirty to forty hours they had traveled from an inflatable raft on a muddy beach in middle-of-nowhere, Maine, to the largest and possibly most important city in the world at the time!"

"That's amazing, Hank. Nobody detected them. Nobody suspected they were spies? Was their cover eventually blown? Did they ever get caught? What happened after they got to New York?" asked Matt.

"Well, once in New York they found a place to live and set up camp suitable for their spy operations. They went undetected for quite a while, actually," Hank stated. "Believe it or not, their cover was quite good. Deputy Hodgkins came home from the hunting camp a few days after his son and Mary Forni had spotted them. His wife told him about the phone call, and he did find some tracks in the snow leading up from the shore at Hancock Point. It convinced him to contact the FBI in Bangor. The spies ran into more bad luck after the sub that initially dropped them off drew attention to itself. Ya see, the U-1230 was still lingering off the coast when our two German spies were just arriving in Manhattan. That sub torpedoed and sank a Canadian freighter called the *Cornwallis*. Well, that was enough to alarm the Boston FBI. They sent agents up to Maine to investigate, because they feared the sub could've dropped off spies along the Maine coast. Those agents eventually connected with Mary Forni and Harvard Hodgkins, who described to them what they had seen."

"So Forni and Hodgkins were able to help the FBI find and capture the German spies?" Matt asked.

"Naw, it wasn't that simple," said Hank. "It didn't happen like you'd see in some movie today. The reality was a lot less exciting. No high-speed car chases or bloody gun battles. What happened was that Colepaugh got scared. He took off on his own from the apartment with the suitcases and all the money! Colepaugh made a beeline for Grand Central Station. Gimpel returned to the apartment and discovered Colepaugh had flown the coop. He went to Grand Central Station and miraculously found the suitcases in the baggage area. He nabbed the bags and took off. Colepaugh traveled to an old friend's place and foolishly admitted he was a German spy. Well, his friend called the FBI." Hank was unable to hold back bursts of laughter.

"So the FBI came and nabbed Colepaugh," said Matt confidently.

"Ayuh, they grabbed him and went on a manhunt looking for Gimpel," responded Hank. "Gimpel was captured on December 30, 1944. Both men were tried and sentenced to death by hanging. But by the time their date of execution came around, President Roosevelt had died and all federal executions were suspended for several weeks. Later, President Truman commuted both sentences to life in prison rather than death. Both men served a number of years and were released. You might be surprised to know that both men are still alive and well today!"

"You're kidding!" exclaimed Matt. "How does that happen? They were enemy spies looking to steal our atomic bomb secrets. How could they have not been executed eventually?"

"Life is funny and strange, my young friend. Life is as forgiving as it often is cruel. Ayuh, no rhyme or reason to things," pondered Hank.

"That is an incredible story, Hank," said Matt. "I never realized something like this ever happened around here during the war. I wonder why a story like that isn't included in the history books? It's important and relevant, as far as I'm concerned. It's remarkable! Nazi spies in Maine during World War II! You just never hear about things like that. Truly incredible."

Hank sank back down deeply in his chair and rubbed his face. Matt could sense the wheels spinning in his mind. The old man paused long enough for Matt to take down more notes and get more comfortable. Matt wondered if the old man was beginning to recall more painful memories from his own ordeal in France. As pleased as he was to hear about the little Maine spy drama, Matt secretly couldn't wait to find out what happened next in Hank's own horrific adventure.

"You think that story was incredible, do ya?" inquired Hank. "Well, how'd ya like to hear about something even more incredible?"

"Yeah, absolutely," replied Matt, trying to contain his growing enthusiasm.

"Okay, listen closely and you'll learn some pretty astounding things, Mr. Switzer," said the old man.

Fully expecting to be brought back to 1944 France, Matt settled in to hear the inevitable conclusion of Hank's tale. What he started to hear instead was something different. Hank didn't return to France of 1944, but rather stayed in Maine of 1944. Soon both teacher and pupil were again engaged in the art of oral history, and this time it was the summer of 1944 in Cape Elizabeth, Maine.

Ted Browne found himself overheating and cursing as he waddled down Shore Road. The short, obese man, dressed in a navy blue suit and matching bow tie, lifted the fedora from his mostly bald head and wiped his sweaty brow with a dingy handkerchief. He silently cursed the hot early September weather, as well as the continued gas rationing that had forced him to leave his Buick at home in his garage. The middle-aged man hated walking and despised exercise in any form. He was not up to the task this morning and didn't wish to carry out his current assignment.

Ted Browne was the Truancy Officer for the Pond Cove Elementary School in Cape Elizabeth. The hot Tuesday morning of September 5, 1944 saw him puffing his way toward a remote house off Shore Road on a rocky outcrop overlooking Pond Cove. It was the first day of school and Mr. Browne was on his way to the residence of Skip and Jessica Wilson. As the portly truant officer neared the quaint little home, a cooling ocean breeze picked up and swept over his sweaty face. Two high-soaring seagulls arced in the air above, then flew out of sight. Browne arrived at his destination and walked up the driveway to the side door of the Wilson home. Skip Wilson's brown 1936 Hudson was parked in the driveway. Browne caught his breath, wiped his head again, and prayed his heart wouldn't explode out of his chest. He knocked twice on the door. There was no answer.

Browne turned away and looked out over the ocean. The view was breathtaking, and he was pleased that such a nice family like the Wilsons were treated to such an extraordinary view. He had met Skip and Jessica on more than one occasion. The young couple were in their late thirties and had ten-year-old twins in the fourth grade—a boy named Francis and a girl named Lena. They were both well-behaved children who minded their parents and teachers in a well-brought-up and respectful manner. Both were very good students and studied hard in school. They had blond hair, blue eyes, and wonderful smiles that always made others want to smile back, no matter what their mood.

Browne always thought that children were simply younger versions of their parents, both physically and emotionally. He considered that a child's attitude, personality, and appearance were direct results of his or her parents' upbringing. The Wilsons were a model of his theory. The father, Skip, was a good-looking man, with broad shoulders and a lean frame. He was over six feet tall, with blond hair and a handsome, clean-shaven face. He was amiable and well respected in the community. He worked as a clerk at the South Portland Post Office. It was the place where everyone saw him the most and knew him best. Many local residents commented on how pleasant a man he was, but were surprised at how much he seemed to keep to himself. Some speculated that he was embarrassed and ashamed of some unknown illness that had kept him out of the Army. To avoid questions about it, he simply avoided people when he felt it necessary.

Skip's wife Jessica was equally liked throughout the community. She was an attractive woman, with dark shoulder-length hair and a naturally pleasing face. She had a trim figure and appeared much younger than her actual age. She was a lover of fashion and popular music and was known by several other women of the community to be enthralled with Hollywood starlets, such as Greta Garbo, Rita Hayworth, and Betty Grable. She loved to wear makeup and put on fashionable dresses and real silk stockings. Sometimes people heard Cole Porter playing on her phonograph and wondered if she were happily dancing in her kitchen. She was often gossiped about by several of the local ladies, but rarely in a bad way. She was, in fact, a very sweet, caring woman.

Jessica Wilson was seen as a good mother who kept an orderly household and looked after her children with love and admiration. Her kids played well with others and never got into trouble. She never let them run wild about the neighborhood and they were scarcely seen, except when visiting a friend's house. Like her husband, however, Jessica was viewed as someone who liked to keep to herself. The family was active in the community and often helped with charitable organizations, church functions, and local war bond drives, but were seldom seen otherwise. They had few visitors, and those who had been inside their place seldom got past the living room. Regardless, they were a well-liked household and seen as no different than any other typical New England family. Those who knew them best knew they had moved to Cape Elizabeth from Portland in early 1940.

Browne knocked again. He was there to find out why the Wilson children were not in school. All the other fourth-graders had made it to class on time, and it was odd the Wilsons were absent, especially on the first day. To Browne's knowledge, Francis and Lena had never missed a day of school, and their teacher Mrs. Sherman was concerned they might be sick. She felt it necessary to advise Principal Parlin, who, in turn, dispatched Mr. Browne to investigate.

Browne called out, "Hello? Mrs. Wilson? Are you home?" He knocked on the door once again and was surprised as it swung open freely. Browne poked his head inside and called out again for Mrs. Wilson. There was no reply. He was about to turn and leave when he smelled something peculiar—and dangerous. He stepped inside, through an entryway, into the living room. The kitchen beyond was half-filled with a hazy, smelly smoke! He rushed down the hall and saw that the gas stove was lit and charred food was burning in fry pans and pots on top of the burners. A window above the sink was cracked open, allowing some smoke to escape, but most of it remained in the kitchen. Browne immediately threw open the window and turned off the burners, covering his mouth with his sweaty handkerchief while the smoke vented and the room gradually started to clear. He looked around the kitchen and saw that the table was set and half-eaten food was spoiling on the plates. An open bottle of milk left on the table gave off a terribly sour odor. Browne kept his nose and mouth covered as he looked on in bewilderment.

"Hello! Is anybody home?"

Not understanding what was going on, Browne made his way through the other rooms of the house. He went back to the living room and looked at the fireplace. There was a hint of wood smoke in the air. He picked up a poker and dug through the ashes. Small red glowing coals indicated the fireplace had been smoldering for some time. Browne walked down another hallway to the children's bedroom. The beds were not made up. There were some toys and a few articles of clothing on the floor. A book lay open on top of a desk and a half-empty glass of milk sat next to it emanating a foul odor. Browne opened a door leading into the master bedroom. An open *Life* magazine and two expensive-looking dresses lay on top of the bed, which was made up. The closet was open, and everything seemed in place. In the bathroom the tub was filled with room-temperature water and two folded towels lay on the sink. Back in the living room, Browne looked at the furniture for signs of other things out of place. A newspaper lay folded over the arm of Skip's favorite chair. Browne picked it up and saw that it was last Saturday's. He put it down, then noticed the family radio in the corner. It was on, but the volume had been turned down to the point where one couldn't hear anything. Just then, he realized that several lights were on despite the ample daylight coming in through the windows.

Enough was enough. Browne knew something very strange was going on and he decided to get help. He went back into the kitchen, where a candlestick telephone stood. He picked up the receiver only to discover the phone wire had been cut. It was useless! Browne rushed out the side door and hurried toward the nearest neighbor's house, wondering if the Wilsons had been kidnapped! Or maybe they had fallen victim to some other horrible crime. It all seemed very odd.

The distressed truant officer chugged a short distance down Shore Road to the nearest house. He found the owner at home, an old widow, and told her what he had discovered. The woman knew the family from church and showed Browne where her phone was. She also commented that she hadn't seen the family at church the previous Sunday. Moments later the operator connected Browne to a dispatcher with the Cape

Elizabeth Fire Department who told him they would contact the local constable's residence and send him out to meet him at the Wilson house. Browne thanked the woman and headed straight back to the Wilson house. Feelings of dread and anxiety floated through his mind as he walked back to the Wilsons' door. He not only felt concern for what may have happened to the family earlier, but he also began to fear for his own immediate safety. He decided to wait outside by the road.

Some time passed before a car drove into sight. Browne waved him over. The constable parked and got out. He identified himself as the officer-in-charge and said his name was Rob Marley. He wore a blue policeman's uniform and hat. He carried a polished whistle, a billy club, and a notepad and pencil—nothing more. Browne identified himself and explained what he was doing at the Wilson home and what he had seen inside the house.

"I think something terrible may have happened to the whole family!" he exclaimed. "I don't understand where they could be. You know, maybe we should call over to the post office and see if Skip reported to work this morning … ahhh … he could have walked, you know, and … "

"Just a moment, Mr. Browne," said Marley. "Let's take things one at a time here and not jump to any conclusions. Perhaps I should go inside and see what's what first?"

"Yeah … I'll come with you," Browne replied with mild apprehension.

At the door Marley shouted out, "Police! We're coming inside if anyone is in there!"

"Nobody's in there, I checked already," said Browne.

Browne led the way inside and pointed out every peculiar sight he had previously encountered. Marley scratched notes on his pad. After going through every room, both regrouped in the living room. Marley finished writing and put his pad back in his pocket.

"What do we do now?" asked Browne.

"Well, there's not a lot we can do at the moment," replied Marley.

"What does that mean, exactly?" said Browne.

"There's no evidence of foul play, and the house doesn't appear to be burglarized. I'll admit some things do look out of sorts, and the cut phone line is peculiar … but, all in all, I don't consider this a crime scene. We should leave and wait to see if the Wilsons come home. Meantime I'll check the post office, see if Mr. Wilson arrived for work today, and make out a report."

"That's it?" Browne asked loudly. "They could be in real trouble! Think of the kids, for Christ's sake!"

"Sir, for all we know the whole family could be out on an all-day picnic. Maybe they decided to extend Labor Day a bit and celebrate longer. Ever think of that? Maybe they just left the house in a rush and weren't thinking. I guarantee we'll see them later today, all safe and sound," assured Marley.

Browne sighed deeply and threw up his hands in disbelief. The officer motioned he wanted to leave, but Browne hesitated. Something caught his attention—a sound he didn't recognize. He put up his index finger, signaling a need for silence. Marley humored him and stood still. Browne walked down the hall and stopped at a doorway he had overlooked, thinking it was just a pantry closet. On closer inspection he could tell it was a door that led into the basement. Listening carefully, Browne heard a peculiar yet faint clicking sound from behind the door. His heart sank as fear of the unknown gripped him. He slowly reached for the knob as a voice behind him called out.

"Mr. Browne, I've other duties I need to perform today, and I'd like to get going now, if it isn't too much trouble," said Marley impatiently. "I wouldn't worry about this matter, but like I said I'll make out a report and check back here later. Will that satisfy you?"

"Yeah, I suppose it will," said Browne as he opened the basement door, looked down the dark stairway, and listened again for the clicking sound.

Marley slowly made his way out the door and yelled, "You coming, sir?"

"Yes, just give me a minute. I want to check one last thing," said Browne. Marley sighed and walked out. He leaned up against his car and waited for Browne to appear.

Browne, sweating profusely, nervously edged his way down the dark staircase. There was just enough light from the hallway to reveal an overhead bulb with a dangling pull cord. That was Browne's goal. Like a child afraid of the boogeyman, Browne summoned up enough courage to race to the light and pull the cord. The light bulb came to life and illuminated the dark and windowless basement. Ted Browne took a step back and gasped at what he saw! Instantly his body was gripped with fear while sheer horror paralyzed his panic-stricken face.

"My God!" he yelled and turned to run back up the stairs. As he did, the chubby little man tripped over a cord that triggered an explosion! The house rocked; windows were blown out and doors blasted off their hinges! Outside, Marley was knocked to the ground by the concussion. He quickly got to his feet and raced back inside, shouting out for Mr. Browne. He got no reply. Fire erupted from the basement and smoke filled the house. Marley raced back out and jumped into his car, speeding away to alert the fire department and report what had happened.

Shortly thereafter two fire trucks, one from Cape Elizabeth and one from South Portland, arrived on the scene. Within a short time crews of regular and volunteer firefighters had the blaze under control and were able to save the house from total destruction. Rob Marley returned with three other constables and began questioning the small crowd of onlookers who had congregated nearby to witness the excitement. The bystanders were abuzz, asking questions about what had happened and the whereabouts of the entire Wilson family. The constables weren't getting many answers, as nobody seemed to know what was going on or why. One fact did surface: a few mentioned being at the post office earlier and not seeing Mr. Wilson there. The constables grew frustrated as the mystery deepened. Suddenly a man shouted out from the gathering.

"I know where they are! I know what happened! They gone! I saw 'em! They run off into the sea!"

Everyone present went silent and turned to see who had hollered out so assertively. He was well known, but not well respected—a slovenly drunk and drifter whom everybody knew. His name was Otis Thorpe, but everyone called him "Odie." He was a loner who mostly meandered about the towns of South Portland and Cape Elizabeth looking for odd jobs and people gracious enough to give him a handout or a place to stay for the night. He was dirty and unshaven; his clothes were filthy and smelly. His black hair was unkempt and needed to be cut, and his face looked aged even though he was only forty. He rarely had any money or desire to earn it until it became absolutely necessary. It was rumored that apart from his alcoholism, Odie suffered from some mental illness, though no doctor had ever clinically diagnosed him. He was a complete mess, but he had more to say!

"They run off into the sea at night! I saw 'em. I was right over there when it come for 'em! I saw the whole damn thing right from just over there," Odie said while vigorously pointing to a spot by the edge of the water.

"Odie, you been drinking?" asked Marley.

"Naw, I ain't had nothing to drink today, Mr. Marley," replied Odie without any apparent slurring of his words. "I seen what happened! I swear I seen it! It come for 'em! It come up between Smuggler's and Pond Cove and it stopped right out there! It was Saturday night around nine-thirty. It come and took 'em away!"

"What came for them? What are you saying, Odie?" asked Officer Marley.

"It was a submarine, damnit!" Odie exclaimed. "A Goddamn Nazi sub come up out of the water and took 'em away! I seen it! They run outta their house together and made a straight line right to the beach! I watched 'em! They didn't take nothing but the clothes on their backs! They left the lights on and everything! They run down to that spot over there and get into this rubber raft that two guys rowed over from the sub. Then they all rowed back, got in the sub, and vanished. I seen everything!"

A few people chuckled at Odie's story, but not Marley. He listened intently and took down more notes on his pad. He turned to another constable and said, "Stan, take the car back and get some more help out here. Call the coroner's office in Portland and see if you can get him out here right away. We've got at least one body in the house and things are getting crazier by the minute. Contact the South Portland police and then try Portland, if necessary." Stan nodded, got in his car and drove off.

Odie wasn't finished. He said, "It was a Nazi sub, I tell ya. I seen it! It was lit up by the light of the full moon the other night! I seen it come up! White caps rippled against the base of the hull! It was huge! I thought we was being invaded!"

"Okay, okay, Odie," said Marley. "Thank you for your observation. We'll look into it. Why don't you stick around for a while with me? Everybody else needs to go home. We need to keep everybody out of danger here, people! Let's disperse, please."

The crowd started to move away when all of a sudden one of the volunteer firefighters who had entered the house came bursting out. He vomited and then informed his superior that he had found body parts all over the basement! Marley moved closer to hear the conversation while motioning for the crowd to back away even further. The firefighter was gasping for breath and was obviously shaken up. He looked up at his superior and said, "That's not all, sir. I seen other things down there, too!"

The crowd strained to hear what the distressed firefighter was saying. Most couldn't catch the words, but all could see the aghast look on Rob Marley's face. He became insistent that everyone leave at once and go home. He watched every person exit the scene save only himself, two constables, and a dozen firefighters. The mystery at the Wilson house was becoming more intriguing by the minute!

"So what was down in the basement?" eagerly asked Matt Switzer, who had become captivated with Hank's latest tale.

"No one knows, Matt," replied Hank. No one knows much of anything about the truth behind that story. That story was told to me by a man who claimed he was in the crowd at the Wilson house at the time it burned. He told me the story in 1965, just before he died. He was someone who knew my parents a long time ago. His name was Edgar Reeves, and he was a widower who lived alone and would visit with my mother from time to time. My father died in 1936, when I was eighteen."

"What else did he tell you?" asked Matt.

"Well, he told me everything I just told you, of course, but he did mention other things, too."

"What other things?"

"He said that after a day or two passed, a man knocked on his door. He was dressed in a suit and identified himself as FBI. He asked old

Edgar to please come with him, which old Edgar did. Edgar told me he was taken to a building in Portland and was led into a large room with no windows. Inside that room was every other person who had been at the scene of the Wilson house fire the day it burned. Cape Elizabeth constables, South Portland police officers, firefighters, and any curious onlooker who happened to walk by during the course of the day were there—all, that is, except Otis Thorpe. Edgar said the room was filled with FBI agents and men dressed in U.S. Army and Navy uniforms. He said that every person in the room was ordered never to discuss what they had seen or heard that day. If anyone did, they would be accused of threatening national security during war time and arrested."

"That's incredible. What else did Reeves tell you?" asked Matt.

Hank continued, "He told me that everyone signed a document swearing secrecy and that the official story would be printed in the papers the next day. That story would state that Ted Browne was killed in the basement of the Wilson house after their furnace unexpectedly exploded in a freak accident causing the fire. He was investigating the children's absence from school that day and found reason to enter the home, where he met his ill-fated demise. As for the Wilsons, the group was told they were alive and well and had made the decision to move away after the fire. They salvaged what they could and left town to pursue a better life someplace else. Everybody wished them well."

"Huh?" said Matt. "What does that mean? I don't understand. They wished them well?"

"Matt, according to Edgar, those people were told that the Wilsons simply left town and that everybody in that room knew they left town. Nobody knows what really happened to them. The government simply forced a story of the fire on the witnesses and ordered them to accept it and not say anything to the contrary, or risk being arrested. Claimed it was in the best interest of national security and such."

"So they forced them to lie and keep quiet," stated Matt.

"Essentially, yes," replied Hank. "Edgar Reeves was seventy-six years old and ill in 1965, and I guess he figured he wouldn't live long enough to be arrested if the story got out. He claimed I was the only one he ever told it to."

"Did he tell you anything else?" Matt inquired.

"Ayuh, he said Rob Marley was never the same man after that whole incident. Claimed he couldn't look himself in the mirror without feeling ashamed to a degree. He said that Otis Thorpe simply disappeared. Local rumor was that the FBI carted him away for serious questioning. It caused him to break down completely and be incarcerated in some federal asylum. Reeves said Odie was dead serious about what he saw and that he was sober that day."

"What was Edgar's take on the whole situation? What did he believe happened?" asked Matt.

"Edgar told me that he believed that Skip and Jessica Wilson were German-born Nazi spies who had infiltrated the U.S. and operated under deep cover for many years. He said that he'd bet money on the fact they were ordered back to Germany just as things really started to go bad for the Nazis. The timing made sense when you think about it. It was September of 1944. Our forces were in Europe and pushing on the borders of Germany. Paris had been liberated and Hitler's empire was crumbling fast. Edgar told me that he and many others firmly believed that that family rushed out of their house during the night and boarded a German IXC/40 submarine sent to pick them up. They then disappeared forever as soon as that sub's conning tower slipped under the waves."

"Was there any mention of anything else of interest?" Matt asked with unbridled curiosity. "Like what was seen in the basement?"

"Ayuh, Edgar told me he secretly met with other witnesses at the house that day, excluding Rob Marley, the fireman that was seen vomiting, and his superior. They all discussed things they thought they heard when the fireman emerged from the basement and conveyed what he saw."

"Like what? What did they hear?" Matt eagerly inquired.

Hank sighed and tried to recall.

"Oh, there were all kinds of stories, Matt. Most I'm sure were simple fantasy," the old man said. "Ted Browne's body was down there for sure. Edgar said he thought Browne set off some booby trap that triggered the explosion. He said others thought they heard the fireman say he saw charred radio equipment and all sorts of Nazi paraphernalia, like flags and pictures of Hitler and such. One woman claimed she heard the fireman say there were charred bags of stolen mail down there and lists of local residents and their families."

"Is that all?" asked Matt.

"No. There were other stories too," Hank said with an uncomfortable sigh. "Some claimed the fireman said he saw dead, naked, and dismembered bodies stacked up in a corner. There were rumors that there were torture devices down there, as well. Some claimed they heard the fireman say he saw the Wilson children down there. They were dead, of course, and burned. Other gruesome things as well."

"Well, like what, Hank?" asked Matt impatiently.

"Look, Matt, a story becomes interesting when it's told over and over again and embellished to the point where it almost becomes completely unrealistic! I don't know what was down in that basement! I wasn't there! Only Rob Marley, an unknown fireman, and his unlucky supervisor on duty that day know what was discussed with certainty. Only that fireman who went down in that basement knows for sure what he saw, and I don't think he's ever going to tell anyone, even if he's still alive today. Rob Marley's dead. I do know that. He died in a car accident in 1972. As for the supervisor, I don't know who he was, or if he's alive today either! My point is, don't read into every gory tale you hear. People like to make things up. It makes them feel more important sometimes. Don't let your imagination run wild. I'm sure there was a lot of unpleasant stuff down in that basement, but don't immediately equate it to some ridiculous slasher movie! Life is hard enough as it is without adding that gruesome nonsense into things!"

"Okay, I'm sorry, Hank. I let my curiosity get the best of me. I apologize if I seemed too insensitive," admitted Matt, as he lowered his head shamefully. "How did it all end?"

Hank regained some composure. "Edgar claimed that the FBI sealed off the area for a short time and that nobody was allowed anywhere near the half-burned Wilson house. It was essentially quarantined. The FBI spent many days there before leaving for good. The house was gutted and then demolished several weeks later. A new house was built on the site years later. As far as I know, Edgar was the only person who talked."

"Wow. That's a really unusual and amazing story, Hank. Everything you've told me is just off the hook! I can't process it all. Spies, subs, intrigue, fighter planes, sabotage, battles in faraway places, the Gestapo and SS … "

"Maybe we should take a break now, Matt. I feel I've overloaded you with too much," said the old man.

"Okay," replied Matt. "But just for a little while. We are going back to France, right? You have to tell me what happened in France. I insist."

Hank knew what he had to do. He wanted to end everything, but he owed it to his young pupil to finish what he started. It would take a lot out of him, but he would finish the story of his own harrowing experiences in France. He just hoped it wouldn't painfully affect Matt's impressionable young mind! The two grabbed a snack from the kitchen, rested a while by the wood stove, then settled in. Matt waited patiently for Hank to begin.

Chapter 21

THE ROAD TO RIGEAULT

Steinert, Pauline, and Hank gawked skyward in awe at the monumental aerial spectacle unfolding above them. Large V-shaped formations of black-and-white-striped C-47 transport planes, several towing gliders, rumbled endlessly overhead. The sky was lit up all around them by white-hot tracer fire pouring out of German anti-aircraft batteries scattered across the countryside. Hank observed as several planes broke formation, increased their speed, and took evasive maneuvers to avoid the deadly barrage hurled up at them from the ground. Many planes could not escape the streams of white-hot lead and burst into flames before crashing. Hank watched in horror as one C-47 caught fire and burned like a blowtorch. Pieces of the stricken plane seemed to burn uniformly and fall away from the main fuselage one by one. After watching the grisly sight for a moment, Hank realized with alarm that what he was witnessing was not burning pieces of the plane falling to the ground below, but rather burning men!

"Paratroopers! They're dropping paratroops," called out Hank.

Just then a violent explosion threw all three to the ground. Hank struggled to his feet and looked to the rear of the Mercedes. A C-47 had violently crashed on the road several meters behind them and exploded into a ball of red and orange flames! The sound of advancing and disorganized German troops echoed in the distance.

"Let's get the bloody hell out of here, you two!" Steinert hollered at Hank and Pauline. Awestruck and without thinking, all three jumped back into the car. Steinert peeled away down the road and drove farther inland, leaving the coast and Jolieville far behind. The car bounced up and down over the uneven road.

"Where exactly are we going?" Hank demanded.

"We're going where this road takes us, Leftenant," answered Steinert. "Out of immediate danger."

"That's not very specific or reassuring, Steinert!" Hank roared back. "I mean, what's the plan? Where are you taking us? As far as I can tell we're heading farther inland! That's not exactly the direction I want to be going right now!" Hank clutched his pistol. Pauline saw this and reached down, putting her hand over his in calming fashion.

Thinking quickly, Steinert responded, "The farther away we travel from the immediate chaos, the better chance we have for finding a way out alive! We can't just abandon the car and go happily gallivanting through the dark countryside in hopes of running into an English or American paratrooper and just expect them to lead us to safety!"

"Why not?" fired back Hank. "That sounds like a perfect idea! I can't think of anything better than to run into an American soldier right about now!"

"Then you're a fool, Leftenant!" Steinert exclaimed. "Use your head for once! I'm in a bloody SS uniform! How happy would an American soldier be to see me coming his way in the dark? He'd love nothing better than to gun me down without hesitation! After a moment of pause he added, "If this is truly the start of the invasion, every German soldier in the area will be mustered up immediately and sent to their post. We have a far better chance of running across armed Germans than Americans! If that happens, I have a chance of talking or ordering our way through any trouble. I can make up any story about how the car was damaged, why I have blood on my uniform, and why you two are with me. Now just sit tight. Hopefully we can avoid any major disruptions or German troop movements along this road. I know of a secret German airfield not terribly far from here where there's Ju-52 aircraft. It's not heavily guarded and the small German *Luftwaffe* force there will be preoccupied with other matters … "

Hank looked on as Steinert struggled with what to say next.

"I'll gain us access to one of the planes and we'll use it to make our escape! We'll take it by force, and you can fly us to safety over England.

We'll crash-land in a field, if necessary, before any Allied fighters discover our presence. Or we could parachute to safety once we know we're over friendly territory and … "

Steinert's voice trailed off again and he fell silent. Hank and Pauline both frightfully realized he was groping for ideas, and had no concrete plan for their escape. The two looked at each other, then back at Steinert, who was concentrating on the road. Hank wanted out of the car immediately and secretly gestured his intentions to Pauline. The young Frenchwoman shook her head no and gestured that it was still better to wait and stay together—at least for the moment. Hank kept his hand firmly on his pistol, sensing he would need it very shortly.

Steinert drove on amid scattered bursts of anti-aircraft fire and the continuing sound of droning aircraft above. He sped up the car every time he happened upon a pocket of disorganized German troops working their way along the road in the opposite direction. They made no attempt to stop the car, nor did Steinert make an effort to attract their attention. Hank and Pauline grew more and more uneasy at the sight of all the activity increasing around them. The farther the car traveled the more anxious both passengers became.

The Mercedes continued to plow down the road at a frightening speed, crossing a tall bridge spanning a severely flooded canal that had overflowed into the surrounding fields. The Germans had purposely opened the locks at La Barquette to flood the lowlands, discouraging airborne paratroop drops, and to deceive overhead reconnaissance flights. The nearby swollen Douve and Merderet Rivers had turned solid acres of cow-grazing meadows into swampy areas of deep-water marshes. Hank watched as the car passed road signs indicating they were not far from the city of Carentan. He noticed Steinert steer away from it and continue along more rural roads that weren't flooded leading to the southwest.

As Steinert turned down an open stretch of rural road, Hank's patience ran out. The American pulled out his weapon and raised it to the back of Steinert's head. Pauline cried out, "No, *Henri!*" Just then the car veered off the road and was rocked by a small explosion! The car had hit a landmine strategically placed on the side of the road. Steinert lost all control and the Mercedes rolled over on its side into a ditch. Dazed, Steinert was able to crawl out through the passenger door and collapse onto the road. Seconds later Hank emerged through the passenger-side rear door, drawing up and out the limp body of Pauline!

The girl was unconscious and injured. The two men placed her lifeless body on the side of the road. Hank frantically started checking for gross injury. Her forehead was bleeding and so was her lower left abdomen. Hank tore away her ripped and bloody blouse to discover that a piece of shrapnel from the explosion had torn through her side. The blow to her head had rendered her unconscious and her heartbeat and respiratory rate were slowly diminishing.

"My God, no!" cried out Hank in shocked disbelief. Tears ran down his cheeks at the thought of losing his love. Steinert drew his dagger and cut away at Pauline's blouse, using pieces of the garment as a bandage to help stop the bleeding.

"Here, push down hard and keep pressure on the wound," he said to Hank, who immediately did as he was told. The distraught American airman looked down at Pauline's face through his tears and prayed to God she would open her eyes and speak to him again. He begged God for her to be okay. He couldn't bear the thought of losing her. Not now and not ever!

Steinert stood up and looked around. As he did, gunfire ripped through the air! Steinert dropped quickly and lay flat on the road. Hank rolled over and tried to shield Pauline with his own body. Bullets pinged off the side of the upended Mercedes. Out of the darkness two German troops ran up onto the road and fired their rifles at movement on the other side. Gunfire was exchanged for several seconds until distant screams were heard, followed by silence. Both German troops lowered their weapons. One ran off into the direction he had fired. The other approached Steinert as he slowly got to his feet. The German soldier slung his rifle and snapped to attention once he identified Steinert's SS uniform in the moonlight.

As the soldier conversed with Steinert in German, a second soldier appeared, dragging a corpse. It was an American paratrooper! Hank couldn't bring himself to look at his deceased countryman. His thoughts were on only one thing. He concentrated on doing everything he could to help his beloved Pauline, who was slowly slipping away like a picked flower beginning to wilt.

The soldiers signaled some of their comrades hiding in the adjacent field. A moment later a horse-driven wagon pulled up next to the Mercedes. Two Germans jumped off the wagon and pushed Hank aside. To the young airman's relief, they appeared to be medics. One reached into his pack and pulled out fresh bandages, which he quickly applied to Pauline's wound. Steinert directed the medics to place Pauline in the wagon and take her to the nearest *Wehrmacht* medical facility or aid station. He was just about to issue another order when the worst possible thing happened.

As the medics began to lift the lifeless Pauline into the wagon, one lost his grip. Her upper torso hit the ground hard. Hank sprang to his feet and yelled, "No! Be careful with her! Goddamn you!" He pushed the clumsy medic away and cradled Pauline's head in his arms. Unaware of what he had said and to whom he had said it, Hank was oblivious to the danger he had just created and focused on Pauline as if nothing else in the world mattered.

The soldier nearest Steinert turned to the *Obersturmbannführer* and exclaimed in amazement, "*Was ist das? Er ist ein Amerikaner?*"

"*Ja,*" simply replied Steinert. The soldier took a step back, but before he could raise his rifle, Steinert drew his Luger and pumped a bullet into his chest at point-blank range, killing him instantly! The second soldier brought up his rifle but couldn't squeeze off a shot before Steinert had fired, putting a bullet through his skull. The startled horse whinnied and reared at the sound of the close gunfire but didn't bolt. The two unarmed medics tried to run for it, but were stopped by Hank and his Colt .45 pistol. They raised their hands in surrender.

"Stop! Help her!" pleaded Hank. Steinert stepped up with his gun raised and ordered the medics to load Pauline into the wagon and give her medical treatment.

"*Achtung! Sie ist Deutsche! Helfen Sie ihr!*" he commanded.

The medics lifted her into the wagon. As they prepared to drive off, Hank shouted out, "We can't just abandon her! We can't just leave her with them!"

Steinert shouted to the medics and, with the barrel of his Luger, persuasively motioned for them to leave. The horse took off in the direction leading to the coast, while Steinert angrily turned to the frantic Hank Mitchell.

"No! No," the distraught Hank yelled, as the wagon pulled out of sight.

"They're her only hope, Leftenant! If she stayed here much longer she'd be dead! They'll attend to her. I told them she was German. With luck, she'll revive and will communicate to them in German. She's clever enough to take care of herself! If you hadn't been so bloody stupid and opened that dumb American yap of yours, things might have worked out differently! As it is, this is our only option!"

"You're a son-of-a-bitch! How could you!" sobbed Hank, unable to comprehend anything but the loss of his beloved Pauline.

"I suggest you control yourself and deal with the situation swiftly, Leftenant, before we both wind up dead! If that happens, neither one of us will be any good to Pauline! I suggest we start moving—now." Steinert picked up a German rifle and motioned for Hank to follow him down the road further inland. He hesitated for a minute, then walked over to where Pauline had lain. He picked up a piece of her bloodied blouse and handed it to Hank.

"Here, Leftenant," Steinert said as he handed the young airman the shred. "Wrap this around your neck and tie it tight. It will make it appear as though you were wounded and will give you a plausible reason why you can't speak. That will come in very handy if we happen upon any more Germans! Now let's be off! We need to find a serviceable aircraft and get the hell out of here!"

"What makes you think I can fly us out of here in a German plane? Who's to say we'll actually find one in all this madness?" asked Hank, trying to suppress his emotional pain after tying the blood-soaked cloth around his neck.

"Because you're a quick study, Leftenant! It was in your file! You have an uncanny knack for figuring out things of a mechanical nature—particularly airplanes. I have faith in your abilities, which is why I'm risking my neck to keep you alive," Steinert growled.

Hank reluctantly tried to pull himself together. He looked down at the dead American paratrooper lying in the road and reached for his weapon. The slain American soldier was a young private who barely looked twenty years old. He had a Thompson M1A1 submachine gun slung around his chest. Hank picked it up and held it at the ready as he and Steinert began cautiously walking down the road with only the moonlight and distant German anti-aircraft fire to guide them. Hank mournfully looked back with thoughts of Pauline and prayed she was all right. Bursts of small-arms fire filled the air as the sky continued to light up with hot tracer fire from German gun batteries. Strange as it seemed, Hank was no longer a fighter pilot. He had now become an infantryman in a very hostile world, surrounded by the enemy!

The two crept along the road using the moonlight to guide them. Several times Hank had fleeting thoughts about gunning down Steinert and taking his chances finding American paratroopers who would help him. But he realized that chances were they would run across many Germans before any Americans. He thought again of Pauline and realized he needed Steinert as much as Steinert needed him! The two formed an unusual symbiotic circle that both privately had to acknowledge if they were to have any chance of survival.

The two walked for an hour, managing to avoid contact with anyone. The droning planes overhead had temporarily ceased and they heard nothing but sporadic small-arms fire. Unexpectedly, things got more interesting. Steinert's jackboots suddenly splashed into water. The road ahead was flooded, and a large expanse of deep, marshy terrain lay in front of them, effectively stopping their advance.

"That way," said Steinert, pointing in a direction leading to higher ground. Hank nodded and motioned for Steinert to lead the way. The pair slogged across a marshy area that had once been a solid, thriving meadow, leaving the road far behind. They paused for a moment. Both were very tired and in pain.

Without warning the two men heard movement in the grass not far from their position. Both readied their weapons and froze like statues, peering into the darkness to see what dangers might be lurking nearby.

All was eerily silent. Suddenly Hank thought he saw a shape move. He brought the Thompson to his shoulder and looked down the barrel into the darkness.

"Flash!" an American voice called out with authority. Steinert pointed his rifle in the direction of the voice and motioned for Hank to keep silent.

"Flash!" repeated the voice with greater volume. Hank started to say something, but hit the deck instead as heavy machine-gun fire sprayed through the air toward him! Steinert fell to the ground in pain as gunfire shredded the air above him.

"Hold your fire," boomed a voice from the distance. As quickly as it had started, the firing ceased and the next sound heard was U.S. paratrooper jump boots rapidly hitting the ground.

"Don't shoot! Don't shoot! Hold your fire! I'm an American, for God's sake!" hollered Hank, face down on the ground. A second later he was surrounded by several U.S. paratroopers, their faces smeared with black camouflage paste. Hank was rolled over quickly and saw the business end of an M1 Garand rifle pointed at his cheek!

"We got an injured Kraut here!" called out a paratrooper standing over Steinert. "Holy shit, he's SS!" exclaimed the soldier at the sight of Steinert's uniform.

"Don't shoot! I'm an American! I'm with you guys! I'm a pilot—"

"Shut the hell up!" interrupted the paratrooper with the Garand. "Sir, they're down. You need to come see this!"

Out of the darkness emerged an American officer. He was weighed down heavily by paratrooper gear, and Hank could clearly see the American flag armband on his right upper arm. Hank looked at his blackened camouflaged face under his M2 helmet. He too carried an M1A1 Thompson submachine gun. Hank couldn't see any rank insignia, but automatically assumed he was a lieutenant or a captain.

"Get 'em up and on their feet," the officer ordered. "Get those weapons away from them and check 'em for intelligence!" he ordered.

The four other paratroopers pulled Hank and Steinert onto their feet. Steinert groaned. It was apparent he had been hit by the initial gunfire. He grabbed onto his lower right side and Hank saw blood oozing from the fresh wound, but Steinert didn't say a word and didn't let on how hurt he was.

"Kraut's got a Luger!" joyously exclaimed the paratrooper searching Steinert. "Hot damn, I've been dying to see one of these babies," he said after close inspection. The trooper happily tucked the weapon in his belt and continued roughly going through Steinert's pockets. He removed the SS dagger and handed it to his buddy, who seemed impressed and glad to have it as a souvenir. Steinert's hands were pulled behind his back and hastily tied with some extra parachute cord. His SS officer's cap was knocked off his head and stepped on by one angry trooper.

"This one speaks English, sir," said the trooper searching Hank. He went through Hank's coat pockets and removed all the contents, including some money and scraps of bread. "He's carrying a .45 too," he added. He handed it to the officer, who examined it closely and stared curiously at the fighter pilot. Then he pointed Hank's own .45 right at him!

"You speak English?" the officer asked calmly.

"Yes, I'm American," Hank responded quickly. "I'm a fighter pilot. I flew a P-51 Mustang and was shot down a few weeks ago."

"What's your outfit?" the officer asked with the pistol still trained on Hank's face.

"I was originally with the 232nd Fighter Group, 44th Fighter Squadron of the 9th Air Force in North Africa. I was transferred to the 23rd Fighter Squadron, 96th Fighter Group when I volunteered to be rotated to the ETO. I was shot down weeks ago—"

"I never heard of either of those fighter groups," interrupted the officer as his thumb drew back the hammer on Hank's weapon.

"I've got proof of my identity!" Hank blurted out. "My dog tags are in my shoe! Check my shoe!"

The officer paused a moment, then said, "Taylor, get him down on the ground and check both shoes. Collins, you and Mills watch the perimeter for Krauts. I don't like how exposed we are. Parker, keep that SS piece of shit subdued. He's an officer and I want him alive for the time being."

"Yes, sir," replied Private Taylor. Hank was pushed down hard onto the ground. Taylor wrenched off his shoes. As the second came free, the moonlight illuminated the small metallic dog tags as they fell to the ground. Private Taylor picked them up and handed them to the officer, who squinted to read what was imprinted on them.

"What's your name, rank, and number?" asked the officer.

"Mitchell, Henry, First Lieutenant, United States Army Air Force, 36243600," said Hank.

"What a relief. I don't have to salute you, Lieutenant, 'cause I'm a captain," said the officer, still pointing the .45 at Hank's head. "I got just one more question for you, Mac. How many career home runs did Babe Ruth hit?"

Hank paused a moment in fear, then silently thanked God he was a baseball fan. "Seven hundred and fourteen home runs from 1914 to 1935," he blurted out.

The captain paused again, then seemed satisfied with Hank's answer and slowly lowered the gun.

"You a Yankees fan, sir?" Hank bravely asked the captain.

"Naw, I'm from St. Louis," he answered.

"Good to hear, because I'm from New England, and I think Ted Williams is gonna be the greatest player of all time. He'll shatter every batting record Ruth ever put up!" Hank said confidently.

The captain turned from Hank and looked at Steinert, who appeared weakened from his wound and stayed defiantly silent.

"English?" asked the captain. Steinert said nothing.

"Yeah, he speaks English—"

"I didn't ask you, Ted Williams!" said the captain. "English?" he repeated. Again Steinert stayed silent. Puzzled, Hank wasn't sure what Steinert was up to. He grappled with the thought of turning against him and making up lies to further incriminate him in the eyes of the American paratroopers; however, he couldn't do it. Steinert was clever and could easily reveal information or lie about him, putting him in a bad spot. Also, Steinert could be essential in locating Pauline. This forced Hank to realize he couldn't jeopardize Steinert's life because that could cost him hers. Lastly, Hank considered the thought that Steinert might actually be who he'd said he was all along—a British spy!

"One last time, Kraut! English?" ordered the captain.

"*Nein*," responded Steinert.

"Private Taylor, give Teddy Williams back his shoes and pick up that Thompson he was carrying. Tie his hands behind his back. Both these guys are coming with us," said the captain.

"Yes, sir, Captain Wade," replied Taylor.

"Sergeant Parker!"

"Yes, sir!"

"Did you find any useful intelligence on this uniformed Kraut?"

"No, sir. Just this identity booklet."

Captain Wade looked at Steinert's SS *soldbuch*, read his title of *SS-Obersturmbannführer*, and realized he had a rather high-ranking officer in his presence.

"Collins, Mills, you got guard duty. Keep an eye on these two. Either one tries to run … gun 'em down!" said Wade. "Taylor, take point. Push up into the high ground. We got to get out of this marsh."

"Yes, sir," responded Taylor, as he started to move out. Sergeant Parker came up to Captain Wade.

"Is taking prisoners a good idea, sir?" Hank overheard Parker ask.

"No, it isn't," whispered Wade, "but they may be useful later. Right now we gotta find out where the hell we are. We gotta get our bearings and haul ass to our objective before our guys hit the beaches! We're running outta time. It'll be daylight soon and this place could be swarming with Krauts then. Our whole damn stick got scattered to the wind, and I don't recognize a single landmark in this area. So far we only have five guys from our company. We need to find the rest, get to our objective, and successfully carry out our mission. However, the first thing we need to do is get the hell out of this marsh and on solid ground."

Parker nodded in agreement and Captain Wade's small band of airborne assault troops stealthily made their way through the early-morning darkness to higher ground. Hank and Steinert were kept bound and closely guarded. Small bursts of gunfire echoed in the distance, but no enemy troops collided with the small airborne force and their prisoners. After slogging along for about an hour, Private Taylor in the lead position called back to Captain Wade and informed him he could see a village ahead. Wade moved up to the front. Both men peered into the distance and spotted a church spire seemingly rising up toward the heavens with each step forward. In the first dim light of dawn, Wade's small force cautiously entered the unknown village.

"Stay alert and watch for Germans!" Wade ordered.

His men fanned out for closer inspections of several small houses randomly clustered near the church, which itself was not very imposing and looked to be several centuries old. One by one, curious inhabitants, mostly elderly, came out of their homes with lit lamps or candles and greeted the American airborne troops.

One skinny little man wearing a suit and tie walked up to Captain Wade and enthusiastically said, "*Bonjour, mes amis! Bienvenue! Vive les États-Unis! Il n'y a pas ici Allemands!*" The man began to shake Wade's hand as others in the village crowded around the paratroopers.

Knowing none of his men spoke French, Wade smiled at the French citizens and called out, "Does anyone speak English? English? Does anyone understand what I'm asking?"

The confused villagers looked at one another, unable to comprehend. Just then a villager, angered by the sight of Steinert's black and bloodied SS uniform, struck Steinert from behind, knocking him down, then swore and spit on him in disgust. He then turned to Hank and started to push him around. Hank, though not wearing any uniform, was immediately guilty by association. The villagers branded him a collaborator and wanted his head as much as Steinert's. Captain Wade motioned for Sergeant Parker to intervene. The wily sergeant quickly broke up the angry crowd and gestured that the two bound men were prisoners. The crowd reluctantly backed away.

"Parker, see if you can find some kind of jail or other secure building to lock these two away for the time being. Get one of these people to help you. Have either Collins or Mills stand guard when you find a location."

"How am I gonna do that, sir? Nobody here can speak English."

"Just jump up and down if you have to! Use body language to describe what you need. Someone will figure it out! Better yet, go find me a local who can understand English! Now move out!"

"Yes, sir," said Parker as he started to move Hank and Steinert with the muzzle of his Garand. Two French villagers followed, trying to understand what Parker was asking for. Steinert said nothing and continued to conceal the pain from his injury. Hank wanted to speak out but thought it wiser to remain silent for the time being. His heart sank, as once again he knew he was a prisoner with an uncertain future.

Captain Wade watched as Hank and Steinert were marched out of sight. The skinny man in the suit and tie kept babbling on gleefully, seemingly unaware or simply not caring that Wade couldn't understand and was ignoring him. Wade stayed alert, concerned about possible enemy positions nearby. Long, dull, muffled booms could be heard from miles away, and the wary captain knew the Normandy beach landings would be starting soon. He couldn't discern whether the noise he was hearing was ordnance being dropped from bomber aircraft or shells from heavy naval gunfire. Either way, he knew he had to do his job and secure his objective soon! He called out to his small group of men.

"Fox Company! Front and center!" Wade ordered. Private Collins, Mills, and Taylor hustled up to their commanding officer. "Okay, here are my orders. Collins, go find Parker and see where he's detained the prisoners. You got guard duty. Have Parker find me, once the prisoners are secure. Mills, Taylor, I want you two to reconnoiter the area and report back any immediate threats to our position. Stay within the village limits. I don't want you two to wander off too far. For God's sake, find a local who can speak English and have that person find me immediately. Stay close and stay safe! Don't do anything stupid like get killed! Move out!"

The three men replied with a hearty, "Yes, sir!" then hustled to carry out their assignments. Wade gestured to the skinny man in the suit, indicating he wanted to find a place indoors to talk. The man understood and broke up the crowd of villagers. Wade had determined this man was a figure of authority in the village, possibly a minor official or mayor. The man led him into a nearby cottage where Sergeant Parker soon joined them.

"*Je m'appelle Anton Durant*," said the skinny man. "*Je suis le maire*," he added, again happily shaking Wade's hand.

"Anton?" quizzically asked Wade.

"*Oui.*"

"I'm Captain Joseph Wade, Fox Company commander, 2nd Battalion, 501st Parachute Infantry Regiment, 101st Airborne Division, of the United States Army. Pleased to meet you, sir."

"*Tres bien! Tres bien, Joseph,*" replied Anton, acknowledging Wade's first name.

"This is Sergeant Jeffrey Parker," said Wade as he pointed at his noncommissioned officer.

"*Bon,*" said Anton with a pleasant nod. The curious Frenchman examined Wade's shoulder sleeve insignia, intrigued with the "Screaming Eagle" patch that represented the 101st Airborne.

Wade pulled out a map from one of his jacket pockets and unfolded it onto a nearby table. Anton lit up an old oil lamp and drew it near. The three men huddled over the chart, Wade pointing to numerous spots marked in red ink. The marks indicated Captain Wade's unit objectives on D-Day. The base of the map showed the town of St. Côme du Mont along Highway N13. Wade pointed out the town and then moved his pointer finger to the locks at La Barquette to the southeast. He likewise put his fingers on nearby marked bridges spanning the Douve River, repeatedly tapping on these marks, indicating this was where he and his men were supposed to be. Wade then put up his hands and shrugged his shoulders while looking around in confusion. The pantomime worked. Durant slipped on a pair of glasses and looked closely at Wade's map.

Durant pulled Wade near and became less jovial and far more serious. He studied the marked spots, then put his finger on the table below and off the edge of the map! He tapped his finger on the table and said slowly and lucidly, "*Voici Rigeault.*" He then called off names, while pointing to their map locations with his finger. Each time, his finger dropped lower and lower toward the base of the map. Finally he put his finger back on the table below the map where he had placed it before and said, "*Voici notre village, Rigeault.*" He repeated the name "*Rigeault*" several times, while pointing to the ground. Wade nodded his head in acknowledgment. Parker looked at the map again and began calculating mathematical formulas in his mind.

"How far, Sergeant?" asked Wade with a deep sigh, leaning against the table with his head down.

"It's tough to say, sir," replied Parker. "We're obviously nowhere near our drop zone and well south of our objective. We're on the wrong side of the Douve River and from what our friend here is indicating, this village called Rigeault is anywhere from sixteen to twenty kilometers southwest of our objectives, sir." "Give it to me in miles, Sergeant," said Wade impatiently.

"That would be roughly ten to twelve miles off target, sir. Clearly we weren't released anywhere near our DZ."

Wade shook his head in frustration and disbelief. He pulled Parker off to the side. The two stood and conferenced for a moment, recalling what had gone wrong upon entry into France.

Wade said, "I was at the door looking out. We hit a huge cloudbank, and I could feel the plane bank slightly to the right. When we came out into the clear again, all I could see was a wall of tracer fire filling the sky! It looked like one helluva Fourth of July fireworks display. Never seen anything like it."

"I was further back and couldn't see anything, but I remember the plane throttling up and climbing to gain altitude," Parker recalled. "A few of the guys behind me fell on their asses!"

"It wasn't much longer after that when we got hit. Ground fire took out the left wing engine. It burned like a torch," recalled Wade. "We started to weave back and forth. Pilots musta lost control, as well as their nerve. God only knows how far off course we got before they signaled the release. I saw that light go green and I just leapt out into all that fire! The wind just ripped me right out of that C-47."

"Yeah, it took forever to hit the ground. The prop blast blew my damn leg bag off, and I lost most of my gear. Then I landed in neck-high water!"

"So did I," Wade replied.

"You know, sir, I wonder if the Pathfinders even properly marked the DZs? They had direction-finder radios, Eureka sets, and Holophane lights."

"Everything happened so fast. I don't remember seeing any lit-up Ts on the ground before we jumped. Just darkness and tracer fire," said

Wade.

"Well, if the Pathfinders didn't do their jobs, then everybody could be lost. Right, sir?"

"We can figure out what went wrong another time, Sergeant. Right now, we have bigger problems to solve," said Wade.

Just then Wade heard several muffled challenge calls and responses coming from outside. "Flash!" followed by "Thunder!" seemingly in all directions. Wade, Parker, and Durant hurried outside to investigate. It was just before dawn.

The three men watched as American paratroopers entered the village from all directions, looking for friendly faces and other men from their units. First a dozen or so, then more and more made their way into the village. Most were armed, some were not. All were tired, wet, and apparently just as lost as Captain Wade and his men.

Private Mills and Private Taylor worked their way through the crowd and up to Captain Wade and Sergeant Parker.

"Sir," said Private Taylor, "we've got friendlies coming in from all directions. A mixture of units from different companies. They're not even all from the 101st, sir! Several are 82nd Airborne, sir!"

"Jesus, these misdrops are worse than I thought. They scattered us all to hell and back!" said Wade. "Have you come across anyone with significant rank?"

"A lieutenant here and there, sir. A couple sergeants and one corporal. The rest are mostly enlisted men—privates."

"Nobody outranking me?"

"No, sir. Not yet, at least."

"Any sign of enemy activity?"

"No, sir," spoke up Private Mills. We did a quick patrol of the perimeter and found no sign of the enemy. It's a small village, fortunately. We also spoke to a few paratroopers coming in. They didn't see any signs either. This whole area is mostly flooded, sir. A lot of the men struggled to get here without drowning."

"Very well. Listen up!" yelled Wade. All the paratroopers milling about stopped and turned toward the captain. "It'll be daylight very shortly! We're all a bit confused and disorganized at the moment.

However, I have a good fix on where we are and where some of us need to be. Try to locate others from your specific companies, especially officers. Pass the word and have them report to me! Stay within the village. I want the area secured! I want squads assembled and walking the perimeter! Locate every road, path, or other entryway into this village and secure it. Any contact with the enemy needs to be reported immediately. This village seems to be mostly surrounded by flooded areas. You all look like you struggled hard to get here. Don't do anything foolish, like strike out on your own to try to reach your objectives. Let's develop a plan first! We're all in the same boat! Further orders to follow. I'm just as anxious as you are to join the war, but let's be smart about it and get a plan together before running off into the fray. Understood?"

Several nodded in agreement and shouted, "Yes, sir!"

"Good," replied Wade. As the men started to organize, Wade shouted, "Does anyone here speak French? I need a French interpreter. Anybody? Who speaks French?"

One paratrooper emerged from the group and hustled up to the captain. He snapped to attention and saluted.

"Corporal Timothy Rioux, sir ... 82nd Airborne. I can speak French," he said.

"Are you completely fluent in French, soldier? How's your accent?"

"Yes, sir. I speak French perfectly. I was brought up in Shreveport, Louisiana, speaking both French and English."

"Very well. I need you to stay with me and act as my liaison and interpreter," said Wade. "Taylor, Mills!"

"Yes, sir," they said nearly in unison.

"I want you two to climb to the top of that church. Looks like there's a bell tower up there. Use it as a lookout and observation point. See if you can get a good lay of the land. Report any threat or friendly activity. I'll see if I can find a good sniper to join you up there. Move out!"

"Yes, sir," they said again before hustling off.

"Parker, Rioux, you both come with me now. Anton?" said Wade, pointing back at the cottage they were in previously. Anton nodded and followed the others back inside. Moments later they were joined by four lieutenants, all from different companies within the 101st and 82nd divisions. The men all sat down around the table as daylight started to pour in through the windows. Captain Wade sat between Durant and Rioux and started asking questions. Rioux translated the questions for Durant, who answered them.

"This man is Mayor Anton Durant, sir," said Rioux. "He's the mayor of this village called Rigeault."

Durant continued to speak while Rioux translated.

"This is mostly an agrarian community," translated Rioux. "Mostly self-sufficient dairy and vegetable farmers. About eighty inhabitants. The village is small and not very modernized. There is a small general store, a dairy, and the church located near the center of town. Some of the narrow roads are paved, but most are just dirt. There was telephone service, but the Germans cut all the lines long ago. Only a few homes and small businesses near the village center have electricity, and running water is unreliable, at best. The houses on the outskirts are not wired or plumbed. There are no cars here, except for the mayor's, and the Germans took it when they arrived in 1940. There are plenty of horses and carts available, though. The Germans control the locks at La Barquette to flood the lowlands. Approximately three quarters of the farmland in Rigeault has been underwater, causing the farmers severe problems. Most major routes into the village have been flooded, but there are smaller, more rural roads that provide access in and out. Mayor Durant can show us exactly where these are."

"Good. What about the Germans? What kind of resistance can we expect? How large of a force is in this area?" asked Wade. Rioux posed the question to Durant, who paused before answering. Rioux speedily translated sentence by sentence for Captain Wade.

"He says the Germans never set up any type of garrison. There are no soldiers posted here, and there never have been. On occasion, German troops do pass through as part of military exercises and to take food. However, he says they don't ever stay long. Too much of a hassle for large numbers of troops and vehicles because of the flooded, swampy terrain."

Rioux paused a moment, processed more of what Durant was saying, then continued.

"But the mayor here does believe the Germans will come through the village very soon because of the one major highway they use to travel through Carentan and up to the Normandy coast, Highway N13, which is not completely underwater and very serviceable for motorized infantry and tanks. Mayor Durant says Rigeault sits astride a road that connects to Highway N13 from the southwest. He believes German units will use this road because it's not clearly marked on maps and is little known, except by the locals."

"I'm familiar with Highway N13," said Wade as he examined his map. "My company was ordered to seize and hold two small bridges spanning the Douve River, set up demolitions, and hold back any German reinforcements heading for the beaches to hit our invasion force. We were dropped on the wrong side of the river and too far to the southwest. Several of our airborne forces should be fighting in and around Carentan by now."

Wade paused a moment, then asked more questions. Durant answered Rioux, who turned back to Wade.

"Mayor Durant says he believes he can convince the villagers to help us out. They can provide us with food and shelter for as long as necessary. He says he wants to hold a town meeting in the church to discuss the matter and hold a vote," said Rioux.

Captain Wade thought a moment then nodded in approval. He then asked, "Where's the mayor's office?" Rioux translated the question, then chuckled after hearing Mayor Durant's reply.

"This is it, sir," said Rioux. "His house doubles as his office, I guess. Small village, that's for sure! He wants to go and start assembling the villagers right away, sir."

"Very well. Corporal, go with the mayor and assist in every way possible. After all the people are gathered and waiting, come find me and I'll join the mayor before he starts the meeting."

"Yes, sir." With that both Rioux and Durant left the cottage. Captain Wade removed his helmet, uncovering the white captain's bars painted on the front that had been mostly hidden by camouflaged netting. For a second he wished he weren't the ranking officer in charge. A second later he was damn glad he was! The confident captain sat back down at the table and called a war meeting with the four lieutenants present and Sergeant Parker.

"I've decided our best course of action at this time, based on the information available," said Wade, studying his map. "We're going to stay here in Rigeault, set up defensive positions, and defend the village from enemy aggression."

Silence ensued for an uncomfortable amount of time. The men seemed a bit stunned at Wade's decision. Nobody spoke until a lieutenant from the 82nd decided to ask a question.

"Sir, I'm 2nd Lieutenant Riley from the 82nd. May I ask why you feel staying here is the best course of action? We all have specific missions to carry out, and I for one would rather try to reach our objective than stay here, sir."

"This is how I see it, men," said Wade. "Listen up, because I'm only going to explain this once. We're a good ten to twelve miles from our drop zone. I'm speaking for the 101st, of course, but I'll wager that you boys from the 82nd are well off target, too, right?"

The two lieutenants from the 82nd nodded after studying Wade's map.

"Since we were so badly misdropped, we're going to do what I feel is the most sensible thing right now to stay alive and contribute to the invasion as a whole. This village is almost completely surrounded by flooded and marshy terrain. In order for the majority of us to reach our initial mission objectives, we'd have to trek directly northeast and travel a distance of several miles over uneven ground that's flooded. Most areas can't be crossed without a raft or boat. How many of your men parachuted into water above their heads? How many brave souls drowned early this morning?"

The room went silent. The four lieutenants dropped their heads, painfully pondering Wade's questions. Sergeant Parker, who had not taken a seat at the table earlier, stood in a corner with his arms folded, listening to his captain speak.

"What about the heavier equipment?" continued Wade. "If we did strike out immediately as a group to face that flooded terrain, we'd have to leave all the heavy mortars and .30 caliber machine guns behind. I'm sure the Krauts would just love that when they passed through here later on!"

Wade got up from the table and started to pace back and forth in the small room.

"A second option would be to move out toward the road that connects to Highway N13 leading to Carentan. Well, gentlemen, assaulting Carentan isn't my unit's objective, and that route will take us longer to travel and possibly put lightly armed U.S. airborne infantry up against mechanized and more heavily armed German infantry. I don't want to risk putting these men's lives up against a column of Tiger Tanks!"

The junior officers began to understand where Wade was coming from.

"If we stay here and defend the village, we'll get support from the locals. They can feed us, shelter us, and provide necessary intelligence that will allow us to put some serious hurt on the enemy. If we organize immediately and dig in, we can disrupt any German units passing by and force them to engage us. This will allow our forces an easier time breaking out from the invasion beaches. The more time we give them, and the more Germans we kill before they can get to the beaches, the greater chance we have of surviving and linking up with our forces as they press inland. Our overall mission as airborne infantry is to disrupt and prevent Kraut reinforcements from attacking the seaborne forces landing on the beaches. Following my plan, this is essentially what we'll be doing. We may not be able to accomplish our original assignments, but at least we'll be contributing to the greater goal by killing Krauts and protecting our men on those LCIs!"

The others in the room started to nod in agreement. The plan made sense and it seemed it could work. Lieutenant Riley stood up and saluted Captain Wade.

"We're with you, sir. What are your orders?"

Wade answered, "We're gonna need to recover as much equipment as possible." He thought for a moment, then continued, "We've got several bundles of equipment just sitting out there somewhere in these marshes. We're gonna need to retrieve as much as we can. Perhaps the villagers can help us out. I'll ask the mayor to spread the word and ask all those physically able to search the area and bring us as much of our gear as they can find. They certainly know the area better than we. They can also show us the best spots to place our guns and set up ambushes. Their help could be invaluable, and we'll show them our gratitude by defending this place and driving off all threats. That is, if they agree to cooperate, which we'll find out soon. Clear?"

"Yes, sir!" was the unanimous reply.

"Very well," said Wade.

A moment later Corporal Rioux returned. He saluted Wade and gave an updated report.

"Sir, Mayor Durant has spread the word throughout the village. The townspeople are all assembling in the church. The mayor requests your presence."

Wade went to the window and saw several groups of villagers walking toward the centuries-old Roman Catholic church.

"Okay, you officers come with me. We're gonna find out just how cooperative and useful this newly liberated little French village is!"

Wade adjusted his helmet so it sat securely on his head, slung his Thompson over his shoulder, and led the way to the church with his men confidently following behind. There was plenty of daylight now and Wade thought anxiously about his men still scattered, lost, and aimlessly wandering about the French countryside. His thoughts drifted to the brave troops assaulting the Normandy beaches and the bloody hardships they were undoubtedly enduring. He hoped he was making the right decision!

The paratroopers entered the church and approached an old wooden podium up front. Mayor Durant was already there, looking firm, resolved, and poised to orate a great speech. Standing behind him was a young village priest. Captain Wade stood off to the side as the townsfolk squeezed into the little church. Once the pews were filled the rest ringed the back and sides.

Wade was impressed by the old house of worship. It was well kept—clean, orderly, sturdy, and possessing an old-world charm that was captivating. He was fascinated by the numerous religious icons and stained-glass windows that caught the early-morning sunlight. Mayor

Durant cleared his throat loudly to silence the buzz in the crowd.

"Ten-hut!" ordered Wade. The four lieutenants snapped to attention in a line behind him. "Sergeant Parker, go watch the door. I don't want any uninvited guests crashing this party. Corporal Rioux, stay by me."

"Yes, sir!" said Parker as he worked his way to the front entrance with his rifle at the ready. Rioux stood next to the captain ready to translate Durant's speech.

As the crowd fell silent, Mayor Durant began, speaking clearly and calmly like a father addressing his family. He came across as a good leader concerned about the safety and well-being of his people. Captain Wade grew confident he would get the help and support he needed. The captain turned to Corporal Rioux, who began to translate in a low whisper.

"Sir, he's explaining who we are and why we're here. He's declared that the liberation of France is finally underway and that we've come to drive away the scourge and tyranny of Nazism from occupied Europe."

"I hope they don't expect us to have it all done by the end of the day," Wade whispered to Rioux, who couldn't help but crack a smile.

Durant continued to speak and Rioux proceeded to translate.

"He's now telling them of the importance of assisting us, the Americans. He's expressing that our journey here, although fortunate for them, was not part of our original battle plan. He expects lots of hard fighting to occur all across France within the next several days, and he feels it's every Frenchman's duty to help the liberators fulfill their objectives and fight the Germans wherever they may be. He considers our presence here a blessing and a sign from God."

Rioux stopped a moment and then added, "He's now referring to us as angels dropped from the heavens."

Wade could tell that Mayor Durant was a gifted speaker and a good salesman, both critical to being a successful politician. He hoped what the mayor was pitching would strike a convincing chord with the people. It seemed to, as many began murmuring and nodding.

As Durant continued speaking, his speech and body language became more sullen and he appeared concerned.

"Captain, he's now getting to a difficult point," said Rioux. "He's explaining that while our presence here is a blessed gift, he knows what will happen if the Germans arrive in force and discover that the villagers have been helping us. There will be horrific reprisals, resulting in torture, interrogations, and executions."

The church fell silent as Durant paused to emphasize the point.

"The mayor doesn't want to put anybody directly in harm's way. He's not going to force anyone to assist us. He wants to hold a vote right now to decide whether or not we have the village's support."

Wade tensed up as the room grew loud and filled with multiple conversations. It became apparent there was some uncertainty and fear amongst the assembly. Several shouted out questions. Mayor Durant called for order. He then motioned for Captain Wade to come and stand next to him. Wade and Rioux made their way to the podium next to Durant and took questions from the audience.

"Sir, this man would like to know what assurance he and his family have that they won't be slaughtered when the Germans arrive and we immediately pull out because we're outnumbered," translated Rioux.

"Corporal, be sure to translate my reply word for word. No mistakes. We have to be clear here. Understand?" said Wade.

"Yes, sir. Go ahead, sir," said Rioux.

"Everyone, my men are doing their duty and deploying right now. They are setting up defensive positions along the town's perimeter. They are digging in, with orders to defend this village. We are not going anywhere. We are going to fight whatever threat comes our way. We have a duty to protect French civilians, as well as our own soldiers who are valiantly risking their lives to liberate you all. Americans, Englishmen, Canadians, free Frenchmen, and other allied forces are all fighting hard for your liberty right now. We will not abandon you in the face of a German threat. We are pledged to help you, but we, in turn, need your help."

Wade paused a few seconds as Rioux finished translating his words to the townspeople. Mayor Durant nodded agreeably and most seemed satisfied with Wade's pledge. A woman spoke up next, directing her question directly to Captain Wade.

"Sir, this woman wants to know specifically what is required of the townspeople. What sort of help do we require?" said Rioux.

"My men will need to rely on you heavily," answered Wade. "They'll need food and shelter. Whatever food you can share with my men will be invaluable. Whatever shelter can be provided will only boost their morale and make them want to fight harder for you. Don't be afraid of the soldiers. Talk to them. Tell them what you know about the Germans. Show them where you've seen the Germans. Point out places for them to hide. Show them good spots to set up ambushes. Help them keep you safe."

"My friends, the most important thing you can do for us at this moment is to go out into the marshes and other surrounding areas and look for equipment bundles that were lost when we parachuted in. We need you to find and recover for us as much equipment as possible. These bundles contain weapons, ammunition, navigational aids, maps, clothing, and food. The more you find and bring back to us, the more easily we can defend this village. Please help us. You know the area better and won't raise as much suspicion if you're observed by the enemy in the process."

Rioux emphasized the captain's request and the people seemed to want to cooperate. Mayor Durant pledged his personal help, then asked for a vote, first from those in favor of helping the Americans. The room resonated with loud approval. Only a small handful expressed their dissension. Mayor Durant told Captain Wade that he would organize the equipment-bundle search parties and also arrange for the village women to begin disseminating food to the soldiers as quickly as possible. The captain shook his hand, and the crowd of townspeople clapped and cheered as the paratroopers exited the church.

"Well, that went better than I had hoped," Wade said. Addressing his lieutenants, he continued, "We got a lot to do in a very short time. I want the four of you to split up this village into four sectors corresponding with the four directions on the map. Each one of you will be responsible for a sector. Decide amongst yourselves which one to take and deploy what manpower you have evenly and accordingly. Organize the men into tight units. Put as many together from the same companies as possible. I want tight and cohesive defensive positions. Get it done, gentlemen.

Report back to me in an hour. I want to know head counts, weapons and ammo dispositions, and morale. Hopefully by then we'll have some food and more of our equipment. Understood?"

"Yes, sir," was the response.

"Good. Move out. Parker, you and Rioux stay with me. It's time I paid a visit to our two mystery guests."

Chapter 22

FIRST CONTACT

Lieutenant Henry Mitchell and *SS-Obersturmbannführer* Peter Steinert sat together on short, stubby, rickety wooden stools that creaked with every little movement of their tired bodies. Their hands were bound behind their backs and their feet rested in thick mud strewn with dirty straw. They were being held in a small stone building with a high, arching, leaky wooden roof. Caged behind rusted iron bars, it was obvious to both that they were in Rigeault's sole jailhouse. The tiny prison consisted of three decaying holding cells and an office for the village Gendarme who was curiously missing. A lone window let in natural light.

The jail was damp and moldy. Two of the three cells were so heavily saturated with moisture they were unusable. Large patches of black mold covering the walls gave them a putrid smell. The third was not much better. Hank sat quietly. He didn't feel the acute pain in his shoulder, lower back, or in his wrists. His thoughts were solely on Pauline. He prayed she was safe and getting the medical treatment she desperately needed. Nothing else mattered to him.

Hank watched as Steinert breathed heavily and winced in pain as his untreated injury continued to take its toll on him. He was sweating profusely, while drops of blood dripped onto the muddy hay at his feet. Hank could tell the bullet lodged in Steinert's side was causing him excruciating pain and impairing his thoughts.

Steinert carefully tried to position his body so the wound oozed as little blood as possible. He ignored Hank completely. Eventually, the pain became so unbearable that Steinert silently renounced all manner of strength, tolerance, and dignity, and slid off the rickety stool, collapsing into the muck and filth. He painfully turned on his good side, keeping the wound out of the mud and retarding further blood loss.

Suddenly the jail's front door was unlocked and swung open. Captain Wade and three others walked in. Hank looked up earnestly while Steinert turned his head away, not wanting to look at the Americans. Wade hesitated a moment, then said, "Sergeant Parker, why don't you take a walk around the village perimeter. Find out what's happening with the defensive preparations. Report back to me after you've covered the entire area. Take Corporal Rioux with you and keep a good eye on him. I don't want to lose our interpreter under any circumstances. Got it?"

"Yes, sir. I'll see what I can find out."

"Collins, why don't you step outside for a few minutes, too? But before you do, open up this cell."

The private nodded, unlocked the rusty cell door, and swung it open.

"Hope you boys are nice and comfortable," said Wade as his jump boots squished down into the mud.

"Captain, I'd like to talk to you," said Hank.

"That's why I'm here, Ted Williams ... or whatever your real name is," said Wade as he leaned up against the wall and crossed his arms, ready to listen.

"I mean I'd like to talk to you in private, sir."

"What about your Kraut buddy there? Does he have something he'd like to say to me first?"

Wade waited for a response from Steinert, who said nothing. Hank looked over at him and continued to wonder why he didn't speak up in English. The more Steinert resisted, the more Hank wanted him to cooperate. He believed that Steinert was his only chance to save Pauline.

"All right, Teddy. Stand up slowly," said the captain as he drew his .45. "Come with me."

Wade led Hank out of the cell and slammed the iron bar door shut behind him. He pushed Hank outside where Collins put his rifle on him.

"It's okay, Collins. I got him. Stay here and keep an eye on our friend from the SS. I want to talk to him, too. If you know of anyone around here who speaks German, let me know. I'm taking this one to the mayor's cottage."

"Understood, sir," Collins replied with a salute.

"That way," pointed Wade, indicating the direction he wanted Hank to walk. Hank, hands still bound at the wrists behind his back, marched off with a .45 pointed at his back.

Minutes later they arrived at Mayor Durant's cottage. It was open and unoccupied. Wade instructed Hank to sit down at the table.

"Okay, Teddy Williams, I don't have much time. Start talking, and it better be something I want to hear," said the captain.

Hank recounted for Wade his career in the Army Air Force, from his first tour of duty in North Africa through his arrival at Jefferson Airfield. The captain listened patiently and closely, looking for any disjointed gaps in Hank's story. Hank described what little he knew of Jefferson Airfield and gave a brief description of his last mission. He didn't discuss the top-secret nature of the mission or mention any of the unanswered questions and intrigue Steinert had divulged to him earlier. Hank told about his battle over France and how he'd been shot down. He spoke of his injuries and how Maurice and Lily Tessier had helped him. He told of being captured by the Gestapo and his escape with the aid of the French Resistance. He mentioned Café LeBlanc and particularly Pauline. He went into great detail about how Pauline had looked after and hid him from danger. He talked so passionately and caringly about her that Captain Wade began to grow impatient. He said nothing about her brothers and didn't mention the raid on the Jolieville train station or the secret *Luftwaffe* airstrip.

"All right, just hold on one minute," said Wade. "All I really want to know is what you know about that Kraut we got locked up. Why did we find you two together ... armed?" he asked. "You said he speaks English, and it was obvious to me that you were helping each other when we opened fire on you! You're not in uniform, and in my book that makes you look pretty damn suspicious, regardless of how well you can tell a story! You need to be very clear about what you say next, Ted Williams! Do we understand each other?"

Hank hesitated, and then looked Wade square in the eyes. He

thought of Pauline and her safety. He thought of home. Most importantly he thought of his honor and duty to his country. He made a decision. He would divulge the truth. Nothing more and nothing less. He would accept his fate thereafter.

"His name is Steinert. He interrogated me shortly after my initial capture by the Gestapo," said Hank. "He said he was a British agent posing as an officer of the SS. He claimed he arranged my escape and delivered me into the hands of the LeBlancs who ran the café. Pauline LeBlanc told me on many occasions that he was a British spy and used the café as a base to run clandestine operations involving the French Resistance in and around the town of Jolieville."

Captain Wade took out his map and unfolded it on the table. He scanned it for a minute until he found the little town.

"Do you honestly believe this man draped in an SS uniform is who he says he is? A British spy?" Wade asked Hank candidly.

"I've had my doubts ever since I met him, sir," replied Hank. "I've wanted to kill him on several occasions, but I never did, because he's always been able to produce information to make me believe he might very well be who he claims he is. I have no doubt that Pauline LeBlanc believed in him. There is no question in my mind that she's as fierce a fighter as the French Resistance has ever produced. I pray she's still alive."

"Why do you fear she's dead?" asked Wade.

"The three of us fled together when the Gestapo raided the café. I witnessed Steinert kill a Gestapo agent. Pauline and I got in his car and we drove off. The car hit a landmine and Pauline was injured and unconscious. We were discovered by German soldiers who Steinert ordered to help Pauline. I foolishly gave us away by speaking English. Steinert protected us by shooting the armed soldiers. He then ordered the unarmed German medics to take Pauline away in a horse-drawn cart and treat her wounds. He told them she was German. It was then that I realized he could be the genuine article."

"Then you ran into us. Right?" said Wade.

"Yeah, you could say that," answered Hank.

"What were you expecting to see happen? Where were you going?"

"Steinert said he knew where there was a German airfield nearby.

The plan was to somehow get onto a German Ju-52 and have me try and fly us out of here. It was definitely a long shot, and I don't think even he believed it could work."

"I'd say that was one helluva long shot," said Wade. "Damn crazy idea, if you ask me."

"Sir, with respect, the last several weeks of my life have been nothing but damn crazy! I can't say with any certainty whether that man locked up in that cell is an SS agent, a British spy, or fucking Adolf Hitler in disguise! What I've come to accept is that there is enough evidence to warrant keeping him alive to bring him before the proper authorities and find out once and for all! He's my only hope for finding Pauline LeBlanc. I owe my life to her and I have to find her! Steinert undoubtedly has the information and resources to find out where she was taken and how we can … "

"Now just hold it right there!" interrupted Wade. "I'm not convinced *you* are who *you* say you are, Teddy Williams! I don't trust you as far as I can throw you." He added, "And I sure as hell am not going to give any son-of-a-bitch Kraut decked out in an SS uniform the benefit of the doubt about his identity! He's the enemy and so are you until I decide differently!"

Wade grew increasingly agitated. He got up from the table and started to pace, pistol in hand.

"You sound more concerned with this mystery woman you keep yapping about than anything else, and that makes me really wonder why, under the circumstances," Wade said.

"She saved my life! She kept me hidden and out of danger! I love her and I'm going to help her! I *am* who I say I am! You have my dog tags! That's me! I'm an officer in the United States Army Air Force!" shouted Hank.

"I got news for you, you son-of-a-bitch! You aren't going to do shit! I don't care who you say you are or what those dog tags read! You're nothing but my prisoner! Maybe you hadn't noticed, but I got much bigger problems to deal with! I don't have time to try and figure out who you really are and what your story is. You're in civilian clothes and were found armed and walking, apparently of your own free will, with an equally armed uniformed Nazi. In my book that doesn't add up and doesn't match the behavior I'd expect to see from a downed American pilot!"

Wade sighed heavily and stopped pacing. He took a minute to calm down.

"What did you fly?" he quietly asked.

"My last bird was a P-51 Mustang. Brand new she was. I've flow P-40s and P-47s, but nothing has come close to that Mustang. She just galloped across the sky! Man she was smooth!" said Hank.

Wade walked to the door and stopped. His back turned to Hank, he said, "I want to believe you. I really do. It's like I said, though; I got bigger problems to worry about right now. You're not going anywhere at this time, and neither am I, for that matter. If by some miracle we get out of this place alive and in one piece, I'll turn you over to the proper military authorities and have your identity verified. That's all I can offer you. In the meantime you're going back to your cell and will be kept locked up and under guard."

"Well, I guess I have no choice," mumbled Hank.

"No, you don't," said Wade. "I got just one last question to ask you. Who won the heavyweight boxing championship title from Max Baer in June of 1935?"

Hank thought for a minute, then answered, "That was Jimmy Braddock at the Madison Square Garden Bowl in Queens, New York."

Wade reached into his pocket and pulled out Hank's dog tags. He tossed them on the table in front of him and reached for the knife tucked away in his boot. He cut the ropes from Hank's wrists and said, "Take those dog tags. Put 'em around your neck and wear 'em like an American pilot should. I'll try to get you some food. For now, you're going back to your cell."

Wade opened the door and motioned for Hank to step outside, where Wade spotted Private Mills and yelled for him to come over.

"Private Mills, where ya off to?" asked Wade.

"I was going to spell Private Collins on guard duty, sir," answered Mills. "Taylor's got the bell tower pretty well situated, and there really isn't much room up there for two, sir."

"I understand. Taylor will be my eyes in the tower. Return this prisoner to his cell. Have Private Collins bring the Kraut in uniform to me. Right here. Got it?"

"Yes, sir. Right away, sir," said Mills. The young paratrooper led Hank back to the jail.

Minutes later the door burst open. Both Collins and Mills were supporting Steinert, who could hardly walk under his own power. Steinert crumpled down into the seat across from Wade, unable to hide his agony. His muddy, sweaty, blood-soaked uniform gave off a most foul odor.

"Sir, he's hurt bad. Got a bullet wound in his side. He's bleeding quite a bit," said Mills.

"That's all, Private. You're both dismissed. Mills, go back and keep an eye on our guest in the jail. Collins, stand guard outside. I'll call for you when I need you. Nobody gets in until I'm done with the prisoner unless it's a dire emergency. Understood?"

"Understood completely, sir," answered Collins. The door slammed shut and Wade sat alone with a haggard, weakened Steinert. The captain stood up and reached into one of his many pockets. He pulled out a small first aid kit and dropped it on the table. With his knife he cut Steinert's ropes from his wrists and opened up the medical kit. Steinert watched with anticipation as he desperately yearned for some pain relief.

"You know, there must be a hundred of us G.I.s running around this village right now," said Wade as he unraveled a bandage, took out a sulfa powder packet, and laid his canteen on the table. "But I'll be damned if I've seen a single medic yet."

Steinert looked down at the medical gear on the table but said nothing. His side throbbed with unbearable pain, but he remained stoic.

"Your friend says you speak English. I'm hoping he's right because I don't speak German and that could make for a very hard conversation between the two of us."

Steinert again said nothing.

"I'm no doctor and I really couldn't give a shit whether you live or die right now 'cause I've been trained to kill Nazi bastards like you on sight. However, I'm thinking that maybe we can help each other out. You just help yourself to my meager medical kit here, and maybe in exchange for my overwhelming mercy, you could see your way to provide me with some much-needed tactical information. Would that be fair? Hmmm? After all, you are a British agent, right? And you do speak English, right?" asked Wade with a hint of sarcasm.

Steinert said nothing, but did reach for the medical supplies. He took off his SS coat and ripped away at the hole in his shirt where the bullet had torn through. After using water from the canteen to rinse the wound, he applied the sulfa drug powder. It stung and caused him to wince. Lastly he wrapped the bandage several times around his waist and tied it off to prevent further blood loss. He made no attempt to remove the bullet lodged in his side.

"Good," said Wade. "Now I hope you don't welch on your end of the agreement. But then again, you're a Nazi—you're used to breaking agreements! You do understand me, don't you? Don't you?" shouted Wade as he trained his .45 right at Steinert's face. "If you don't acknowledge me in some way in the next sixty seconds I will splatter your brains all over the walls of this room!"

Steinert paused, then finally broke his silence.

"Yes, Captain, I do speak 'The King's' quite well. It is my native tongue," said Steinert in his flawless British accent. He said it so well that Captain Wade was temporarily taken aback.

"Well, I'll be damned. How interesting," said Wade. "What other parlor tricks can you do?"

"I wish to speak to an officer of His Majesty's armed forces," Steinert asked, his breathing labored.

Wade listened closely to Steinert's accent. He had spent many months in England, stationed in Wiltshire, training for D-Day with the rest of the 101st Airborne. He had become accustomed to hearing many subtleties in the various English accents that surrounded him daily, and he recognized Steinert's accent as a variation he had heard before. It wasn't compelling evidence of his true identity, but Wade deemed it a curious coincidence.

"I'm afraid I can't help you there," said Wade in response to Steinert's request. "There ain't nobody in these parts but us Yanks."

"Surely, British commandoes parachuted in with you Americans? There must be a British command set up somewhere."

"Different zone of operation. Different objectives. It's unlikely we'll come across any Brits anytime soon. Let's play another game. How 'bout *I* ask the questions and *you* answer them?"

Steinert winced with pain and tried to get comfortable in his chair.

"Who are you? Do you really claim to be a British spy? If so, what organization are you a part of? Why are you here and what was your assignment?" asked Wade.

"Captain, I really don't wish to waste our time together. You have pressing matters to attend to, and I fear the nature of my wounds are severe enough to terminate my life in a very short time frame. Having said that, I must humbly again ask to speak to an officer of the British armed forces either face to face or via radio communication."

"I just explained to you that you don't have that luxury! You'll talk to me and tell me what I want to know or suffer the consequences. There is no second choice!" barked Wade.

Steinert sighed with pain and shook his head, acting as if he were a man talking to a brick wall.

"Let's try something else, then," said Wade with growing impatience. He took out his map and laid it out in front of Steinert. "This is the village of Rigeault, not far from Carentan. What kind of German forces are in this immediate area? Infantry? Armored? What kind of troop strength can I expect to encounter in the next few hours? If you can point out legitimate German strongpoints on this map and help me determine what I'm up against, I'll see to it you're treated with leniency as a POW and not summarily executed because you're a member of the SS. Trust me, I got plenty of guys who would love to pump a bullet into an officer of the SS!"

"Captain, I must speak with one of my own. You must allow me access to an officer of His Majesty's forces."

"Goddamn it! Haven't you heard a word I've said?" snapped Wade with pistol in hand. "Your request is denied! You either talk to me and answer my questions or you can go right back into that jail cell and rot! If that's the case, you better pray one of my men doesn't get an itchy trigger finger and accidentally shoot your ass on the spot! Now, once again, who are you? Who do you work for? What kind of German forces are deployed in this area?"

"Then we have nothing more to discuss, Captain. I really have no information to convey to you, sir. My position within my country's organization does not permit me to discuss past operations, intelligence, or even identify myself to anyone, much less a lowly captain leading a disorganized band of American paratroopers. You may shoot me if it will make you feel better, Captain, but I seriously doubt murdering me in cold blood will afford you any pleasure. You don't strike me as that sort of chap, and you would be killing an ally whether you believe me or not!"

Wade fumed, but kept his emotions in check. He knew he still had the upper hand and figured it was time to move on to more pressing concerns.

"Private Collins, get in here!" shouted Wade. The door swung open and through it came Private Collins brandishing his Garand rifle.

"Collins, take this piece of shit back to his cell with the other prisoner. Do not provide either with food, water, or medical aid unless ordered to do so by me. I want a continuous watch on these prisoners. Rotate with Mills in four-hour shifts. Nobody is to see these prisoners unless authorized by me. If either tries to escape, kill both of them. Is that understood?"

"Yes, sir," replied Collins. With that, he forced Steinert onto his feet and marched him back to his cell where Hank was waiting. The two prisoners were reunited again and locked away in filthy solitude.

Time passed and D-Day was slowly slipping by for the paratroopers in and around Rigeault. As evening came, Captain Wade, his four lieutenants, Sergeant Parker, Corporal Rioux, and Mayor Durant huddled inside the mayor's cottage. They stood over the mayor's dining table staring at Wade's map, together with a hand-sketched map of the immediate area.

"Sir, we've established a solid defensive perimeter around the village covering all directions," said Lieutenant Riley. He pointed to the hand-sketched map and showed Captain Wade the locations of the American strongpoints. "At present we have approximately eighty-six men patrolling the area. A jumbled mix of 101st and 82nd personnel. The men are digging in and bringing all available weapons to bear—mostly assorted personal small arms and grenades. As of 0400 hours no heavy 81mm mortars, bazookas, or .30 caliber machine guns have been recovered. Small arms ammo is sufficient for the moment. The men are carrying tiny K rations and chocolate, but they're hungry and need to be fed, sir."

"Corporal Rioux, ask the mayor what's being done to distribute food and to aid in our equipment retrieval," ordered Wade.

Rioux posed the questions to Mayor Durant, who promptly perked up and launched into an extended narration.

"Sir, the mayor says he appealed to all the women in the village to share whatever they have in their pantries and to cook up as much available food as possible. The plan for distribution is to have the children of the village deliver the food to our troops using covered baskets. The children will draw less attention if they're observed in the open by the enemy and each will be armed with a story of where they're going and what they're doing if they get stopped."

"Good. Go on, Corporal," said Wade.

"Mayor Durant says that he organized search parties amongst the adults and assigned certain locations for them to scour the marshes for our equipment bundles. He says this has to be handled by the adults, so as not to endanger the children, who might inadvertently discharge a firearm or set off a charge of TNT or Composition B. Also, he says that this part of the operation needs to be done more discreetly, as adults are more likely to be stopped and questioned if observed in the open by the Germans. He assures me that both food dispersal and equipment retrieval are happening right now."

"Very well," said Wade as he looked down at the map. "Parker, what do you got for me?"

"Sir, I've just come from the bell tower. Private Taylor is well situated. He has a good vantage point and excellent visibility in all directions. We found him a good pair of binoculars, and he'll be able to get the alert out quickly if he spies any enemy movement in our direction. So far, he reports no contact with the enemy."

"Captain, I've reconnoitered the area to the southwest, which falls in my command sector, and I found the road that connects to highway N13," said Lieutenant Riley. He added, "I've placed a squad of men in a well-covered position along the road, armed with M1A1 Thompson submachine guns, M1 Garand rifles, and one BAR with bipod. They're in an area I feel most likely will be encroached upon first by the enemy. Runners will speed word back to us as soon as contact is made with the enemy. I have no doubt that will be soon. Sporadic small-arms fire has been heard all day outside the village perimeter."

"Very well, Lieutenant. Keep me informed. Sergeant Parker?"

"Yes, Captain."

"What's our communications status?"

"All communications are down. The village phone lines have all been cut externally. We haven't found any working radios either. All we've found were smashed in the drop. The few radiomen in the village all reported they lost their equipment as soon as they jumped out of their C-47s."

"Great. For all we know our entire invasion force could've been pushed back into the sea! Goddamn!" exclaimed a very frustrated Captain Wade. "Gentlemen, thank you for your hard work and timely organization. I feel we're gonna have a helluva fight here soon. Report back to your men and do everything possible to get them adequately fed, rested, and armed! Show leadership and courage. That's all I ask. This cottage is headquarters from now on. All intelligence and pertinent information needs to come here. If I'm not here, find me! That's all for now. Do your duty, gentlemen. Dismissed!"

The four lieutenants saluted and filed out of the mayor's cottage. Mayor Durant spoke to Corporal Rioux and then went out the door. Wade looked at Rioux.

"He said he wanted to go check on the progress of the food preparation and dispersal," Rioux told Wade.

"Good. He's been very helpful," replied Wade. "Parker?"

"Yes, sir."

"Take me around the village perimeter. I want to assess our strengths and weaknesses personally. Rioux, you come too. I may need you."

"Yes, sir," said both. Captain Wade slung his Thompson and followed Parker out the door with Rioux in close pursuit.

Soon the sun started to sink downward in the sky. The villagers of Rigeault worked meticulously to aid the American paratroopers under the leadership of the unimposing Mayor Durant. Children of all ages bravely scurried about into the evening carrying covered baskets of bread, cheese, milk, and vegetables to the grateful paratroopers. Smart and cautious, they knew what routes to take and when to take them.

The adults of Rigeault did their part, as well. Old men and young women fanned out into the marshes looking for the precious equipment bundles. It wasn't long before the first one was found. An old man bravely jumped into deep water and pulled it up from the bottom. With help from a friend, he hoisted it onto solid ground and carried it back to the village, turning it over to the first Americans they saw. They eagerly tore into it and found a Browning .30 caliber machine gun and ammunition.

The yields of the search were many: machine guns, ammunition, mortars, mortar shells, explosives, medical supplies, and tools. Everything that was salvageable was put to good use by the paratroopers busy fortifying their defensive positions. Some of the women of the village picked up silk parachutes with thoughts of turning them into lovely dresses and other articles of clothing.

Captain Wade returned to Mayor Durant's cottage at dark. He had inspected the line with Sergeant Parker and found everything to be in order. Several paratroopers were given shelter in cottages and barns while others stayed on the line and watched the perimeter. Thunderous booms were heard off in the distance and the sky lit up with remote anti-aircraft fire or German 88mm artillery fire. The enemy was not far away, leading Wade to believe his fight might be upon him sooner than he hoped.

The captain ate a bowl of soup by dim candlelight, then rested by leaning back in his chair. He was extremely tired, but could not readily fall asleep even after the mayor offered up his own bed. Wade had issued orders to alert him the second contact was made with the enemy, and anticipation kept him anxiously awake. For now, though, there was nothing he could do but wait.

Inside the tiny Rigeault jail the two prisoners lay in near total darkness save for two candles Private Collins had lit and placed on the office desk. Hank stretched out on one side of the floor while Steinert lay parallel on the opposite. Hank's thoughts continually focused on Pauline, interrupted only on occasion by thoughts of food that was never delivered by Captain Wade. Steinert's condition slowly and steadily deteriorated. Blood seeped through his dirty bandages while throbbing pain rippled through his infected wound. The bullet lodged in his side was slowly poisoning his blood with a steady stream of harmful, multiplying bacteria.

Hank watched the sweat pour from Steinert's head and listened to his occasional coughing. It was obvious he was running a fever and needed immediate medical assistance. Hank himself was in poor condition, as well. He was greatly fatigued and extremely sore from his old wounds. His head throbbed and his empty stomach cried out in protest. His pain intensified with every thought of his beloved Pauline. The mental anguish he suffered matched every ounce of physical pain coursing through his battered body. He tried to relieve it all by getting some much-needed rest. Soon his eyes closed and the young fighter pilot fell asleep.

Hours passed and Hank awoke to the sound of a voice. His eyes fluttered open and focused on Steinert, who looked like he was suffering from a bad nightmare. The dim candles still burned in the background, giving Hank just enough light to witness Steinert's ordeal. His eyes were shut, but his head and body convulsed. He mumbled disjointed words, but didn't appear conscious. Hank listened closely and tried to make sense of what he was hearing. Steinert's mutterings included "England," "murder," "betrayal," "von Schreiner," "Ultra," and "Bletchley." Other words seemed to be English names completely unknown and unfamiliar to him, including "Colchester" and "Winterbotham." Several other indiscernible phrases emanated from Steinert's mouth accompanied by one word repeated over and over ... "MI6." Hank listened and tried to deduce the significance of "MI6." Was it a code of some sort? Hank had no idea.

Suddenly Steinert's eyes opened widely and life seemed to shoot into his body like a bolt of lightning. His hands shook as he turned his head to Hank. Their eyes locked and Steinert, without warning, coughed and said, "My country has betrayed me just as your country has betrayed you! We're both going to die here! Victims … just victims … of an unseen force controlled by an unseen power in a world gone mad!"

"My God, who are you?" asked Hank with stunned curiosity. "Who are you?" he repeated. "What's your real name?" He had finally accepted the fact he could be talking to a genuine British agent and not an operative of the Nazi *Sicherheitsdienst*!

"God has nothing to do with it," coughed Steinert. "The Devil does! My name is *SS-Obersturmbannführer* Peter Steinert!"

"*SS-Obersturmbannführer* Peter Steinert doesn't sound like a very English name to me," Hank said sarcastically. "I've had enough of your endless layers of bullshit! Why don't you try again? Tell me what your name is, you lying Nazi son-of-a bitch!"

Steinert glared at the smug American pilot. He propped himself up and struggled to clear his head. Hank had purposely played the role of agitator to get Steinert to reveal as much information as possible in his weakened state. Steinert coughed loudly and spit up some phlegm. He forced out heated words.

"You want to know my name? You want to know my *real* name? Does it matter that much to you?" Steinert managed a chuckle between his coughs and labored breathing. "My real name? It's been so long that I don't even think I remember it any more. I suppose the end is near enough so it really matters little. My name … my real name … my English name is Nigel … Nigel Shepley. So there you have it, Leftenant. Do with it as you wish. It has no meaning for me any more."

"Pleasure to meet you, Nigel," Hank said with little sincerity. "I'd introduce myself and tell you all about me, but you already know everything there is to know about me, so it would be a waste of time I'm afraid."

Steinert, unamused by Hank's sarcasm and continued distrust, simply tried to make himself more comfortable.

"We seem to have lots of time to spend together in this cell," said

Hank. "Why don't you indulge me? Tell me about your past, where you're from, for whom you really work, and how you ended up in this jail cell with me. We both can benefit from a little conversation at this point, I think."

"I have nothing more to say to you, Leftenant," wheezed Steinert. "I've told you far too much as it is. You only hear what you want to hear. You only believe what you want to believe. There's nothing further I can say that will change your opinion of me or convince you of my true identity. Neither my past words nor my past actions have swayed you, from what I can see. I've done my part for King and country and look where it's gotten me. I'll never see home again. England has betrayed and abandoned me just as America has betrayed and abandoned you! I'm just a ghost now … a ghost just like you!"

"I'm not a ghost and I think I've done my part for *my* country, blowing up German train yards and airstrips—and killing Krauts like you," said Hank.

"Oh yes, I suppose I owe you a great deal of thanks for both those operations," said Steinert sarcastically. "If it weren't for me you'd have been dead long before now. Those British Mosquitoes saved you after I arranged for the train yard to be lit up, and the LeBlancs would have most assuredly done you in had I not intervened after that clumsy airstrip raid."

"What do mean by that? What happened to the LeBlancs?" Hank asked.

"They got in my way. They questioned my judgment. They challenged my authority. That … well, let's say *that* was something I couldn't allow."

"So you killed them. You had them brought to you as prisoners and you had them killed," said Hank.

"No, you bloody idiot. *I* killed them! They became a threat and a liability to my whole operation, so I dealt with them accordingly. What you don't understand is that I was there after your little airstrip raid. Von Schreiner tried to lure me into a trap by sending me to the wrong location. I saw him meet with Eichner privately and I'm sure they hatched out a scheme to trap me. Von Schreiner questioned my loyalty and had me followed by the Gestapo. By sheer luck, I ended up at the right airstrip."

Steinert then proceeded to tell Hank in detail about his dealings with *Hauptmann* Kranz. He told him about *Leutnant* Becker and how his men had stumbled onto the location at just the right time. He divulged the whole cover-up scheme he had devised with Becker and how he had taken Kranz out of the picture––or so he thought. Finally he told Hank how he had cleverly taken Christophe and Grégoire into custody and how he dealt with them later.

"My God, you did murder them," said Hank.

"I eliminated them for the greater good, Leftenant, just as I did both von Schreiner and Eichner!"

Hank started to feel uneasy, but was intrigued enough to want to hear more. He indulged Steinert, taking advantage of his sudden willingness to talk and his weakened state.

"Tell me more," said Hank, while wondering if what he was about to hear was the truth or just a pack of lies orchestrated into a plausible story by a clever Nazi––a Nazi hoping to impress his American captors and perhaps save his own skin.

"I returned to the château and commenced preparing my written report. Von Schreiner wasn't available right away, but I met with him later. I sensed something was wrong but kept my composure. In his office he heard me out and reviewed my report, but then he decided to play mind games with me. He talked about his past when he was an *Einsatzgruppen* commander on the Eastern Front and his reputation as a brutal officer. He was trying to intimidate me while also basking in his own perverted form of self-adulation."

Steinert went on to describe the details of his meeting with the *Gruppenführer*. He told Hank about von Schreiner's formal dinner party preparations and his aspirations for promotion. Then the story took an interesting twist as Steinert began to reveal precise details about von Schreiner's suspicions toward him.

"The *Gruppenführer* continued his mind games by tearing apart my airstrip raid report. He had found out about my manipulation of Becker by meeting with Kranz. Kranz gave him a much different account of what had happened then I did. Then he produced pictures of the deceased LeBlanc brothers, proving I had been put under surveillance and followed. He accused me of being a spy while wondering how I showed up at the right airstrip when he purposely ordered me to the wrong one."

Steinert continued his story by describing von Schreiner's speech and threatening mannerisms in rich detail. He talked about being placed under arrest with the sounds of Wagner blaring in the background. He told Hank about his fight and eventual murder of the *Gruppenführer*, sparing none of the graphic and gory details of his demise.

"What happened next?" asked Hank. "How did you get away?"

"I smashed through a window and escaped the grounds undetected. I made it to a checkpoint on foot and killed the two soldiers present. I stole their car and drove directly to Café LeBlanc where I encountered the building in flames and Eichner fleeing into the street. After observing him, I proceeded to try to run him down. Failing to kill him, I crashed the car and was dragged out onto the street. Eichner and I fought. He said he'd enjoy watching me tortured. In so many words he told me I was either an American or English spy and that he was now in charge. We wrestled, punched, and kicked one another and … well … you saw how it ended."

Sitting perfectly still listening, Hank was amazed at the amount of detail Steinert shared in telling his story. Still not convinced it was the truth, Hank nevertheless wanted to hear more.

"What about Pauline? What happens to her?" implored Hank.

"She's dead, Leftenant. There's nothing that can be done for her, me, or even you! Soon every paratrooper in this village will be wiped out and there's nothing you or I can do about it! It matters little. I'll most likely be dead before that even happens. You'll be right behind me!"

"I don't give a damn about you!" said Hank. "How do we get to Pauline? How do we help her?"

"We don't! We just wait to die! There's nothing else, you bloody fool! You couldn't protect your ill fated flyers from certain destruction, you couldn't save the Tessiers from their demise back in Jolieville, and you can't save the life of your beloved Pauline LeBlanc! *C'est la vie*, Leftenant. Such is life!"

Hank fell silent. A feeling of helplessness overcame him. His body went limp as his emotions turned to utter despair. Steinert's words struck deep. All he had left was a narrow glimmer of hope that Pauline was still alive and being cared for and that someday soon they would be reunited. Steinert coughed loudly and said no more. Hank lay back and eventually fell asleep.

He was awakened later by Steinert's delirious blathering. It was morning; daylight shone in through the jail's only window. Steinert rambled on in a semiconscious state, spitting out fragmented sentences and phrases. The names "Rodney Colchester" and "Winterbotham" were said repeatedly. "Pauline LeBlanc" and "Gerhard von Schreiner" were mumbled often, too, as well as "Enigma," "Ultra," "MI6," "SOE," and "Hitler." The declining man who earlier had identified himself as an Englishman named Nigel Shepley went off ranting uncontrollably in German only to switch back to English, calling off names of towns and cities like Plymouth, Portsmouth, Dover, Manchester, and London. Hank took it all in, not knowing what to make of it. He wanted to simply dismiss it as mindless ramblings from a man gone delirious, but he couldn't. There was innate structure embedded in the nonsensical digressions that Hank didn't understand, but couldn't ignore.

Captain Wade visited the jail and went inside. He looked down upon his two filthy, worn-down prisoners. Private Mills joined him.

"Sir, the Kraut ain't doing so good. He's coughing up a storm and barely moving. I think he's dying, sir," said Mills.

"Yeah, that wound is a nasty one. I'm surprised he's lasted this long. Have the prisoners been any trouble?" asked Wade.

"No, sir. No trouble at all."

"Good. Private, go scrape up some food and water for them. I know I saw a well around here somewhere. Get to it quickly, and get yourself some food if you haven't eaten already this morning."

"Yes, sir," replied Mills with a salute before he left Wade alone with the prisoners.

"Captain!"

"What is it, Teddy?"

"Sir, this man needs a medic," said Hank looking at the unconscious Steinert. "He's dying. He keeps jabbering on about all sorts of things. I can't piece together what's important and what isn't, but maybe if you kept him alive, he might give you some important tactical information or some definitive clue as to who he is. If he is, in fact, a British spy, then we can't just let him die like this! He could have information vital to the war effort!"

"Yeah, and I'm sure he's gonna help you rescue your sweetheart, too, right?" said Wade sarcastically. The captain sighed heavily and said, "I have no medic. This village doesn't even have a doctor! Hell, I can't even locate a working radio or telephone! We are cut off, Teddy Williams. I already talked to your friend earlier when he was more lucid. He had absolutely no interest in talking to me, even after I gave him access to my medical kit. He gave me nothing in return. He can lie there and rot for all I'm concerned! He's lucky, and so are you, for that matter, that I'm giving him food and water. Right now, as I see it, he's your problem and not mine. If you want to keep him alive, then be my guest and try! If he has vital information to share, I'd love to hear it! Right now I have bigger problems to deal with."

Just then Private Mills returned with scraps of bread and a full canteen of water.

"Here, take this," said Wade, handing the provisions through the bars to Hank. "Eat up. I may want to talk to you some more later in private, Teddy Williams."

"Yes, sir," said Hank respectfully as he gave Wade the proper salute. Wade gave a curt nod in acknowledgment and stormed off. Mills resumed his guard duty while Hank tried to bring Steinert back to consciousness by forcing him to sit up and gently slapping his face. Steinert's eyes eventually opened. Hank fed him pieces of bread and gave him several swallows of water before taking the rest for himself. He wasn't sure if the nourishment would help, but he knew it couldn't hurt. Hank looked at Steinert's wound underneath the blood-soaked bandages. The skin around the wound was black and purple. A foul odor of decaying flesh hung in the air and blood continued to leak from the bullet hole. He couldn't do anything to treat the wound as he had nothing to work with.

He placed Steinert back on his side, to try to make him as comfortable as possible. There was nothing left to do now but wait.

Captain Wade inspected his lines along the perimeter of the village and was happy at what he saw. His men had maximized their efforts and put up the best possible defensive positions. There was little else to do now but wait until the inevitable arrival of either friendly forces or the enemy. Soon night was upon the defenders of Rigeault. Those who could sleep did so, while the rest stayed nervously awake, listening to the monstrous sounds of war edging closer with each passing moment. Captain Wade retreated to the mayor's cottage, not knowing what tomorrow would bring.

As the morning sun rose on Thursday, June 8, D+2, 2nd Lieutenant Riley lit a cigarette and crouched beside the vital road connecting to Highway N13 leading to Carentan. All was quiet—for the moment. Riley's squad of eight took shelter behind thick bushes and trees that lined both sides of the road. The Americans were sufficiently hidden and had a prime section of the roadway covered with deadly fire. Riley used his lone BAR man as his primary base of fire. He set him up prone with the M1918 Browning Automatic Rifle on a bipod. The gun's muzzle, pointed down the road, would easily shred any enemy threat on foot. Riley covered the prone man with brush and grass to conceal his position.

Time passed slowly and Riley's men tried to stay alert. They had been fed earlier and had sufficient amounts of ammunition; however, they were on edge and yearned for some action. Lieutenant Riley was about to leave his position to check on another group of men under his command closer to the village when a faint noise caught his ear. Instantly he put up his hand, signaling his men to go silent. He listened intently as the sound grew. As the seconds ticked away, he realized what the ominous sound was. Riley quickly signaled his men to get ready. Guns were locked and loaded instantly with muzzles aimed in every direction. Riley took cover as he watched a cloud of dust kick up down the road.

Suddenly the danger revealed itself in the form of two German BMW R75 heavy motorcycles with sidecars barreling down the road. There were armed troops in each sidecar—a total of four men. The motorcycles downshifted and braked entering a slight curve in the road that brought them in range and directly into Riley's kill zone.

"Fire!" shouted Riley with mad fury. His BAR man, the first to act, squeezed the trigger, sending a deadly barrage of .30-06 Springfield rifle cartridge fire slamming into the approaching vehicles. Both drivers were knocked off and killed instantly. The motorcycles careened out of control and smashed into one another before tipping over and spilling the sidecar soldiers. Before the upended Germans realized what had happened, the rest of Riley's squad opened fire, dropping them dead in their tracks.

"Cease fire! Hold your fire, goddamn it!" commanded Riley, not wanting his overzealous troops to waste ammo. "Move in slowly! Make sure they're down!"

The paratroopers cautiously crept out from under cover to inspect the carnage they had inflicted. Riley examined one dead body. He saw SS sig runes on the right collar patch and immediately began to search the corpse for identification papers. He pulled out the German's *soldbuch* and looked it over. He couldn't read German, but was able to make out enough to cause a shot of painful fear to rip through his adrenaline-laced heart!

"Get those cycles off the road! I want 'em out of sight immediately!" Riley ordered. "Same with the Kraut bodies! Get me their ID papers and any other intelligence they have on 'em!"

The lieutenant collected the material and ordered his squad back to their combat-ready positions. Riley took off running back to Rigeault. He arrived at Mayor Durant's cottage, where he burst through the door and into the dining room. Captain Wade, Mayor Durant, and Corporal Rioux were all present and alarmed at Riley's abrupt entrance.

"Sir, we've made first contact with the enemy!" said Riley, trying to catch his breath.

"Where and how many?" returned Wade, "I need as much detail as you can give me, Lieutenant." Wade opened his Airborne-issued map as well as several other hand-drawn maps of the village and its defenses. The two men hunched over the table while Rioux explained to Durant what had happened.

"I was witness to the whole thing myself, sir," explained Riley as he recounted what had happened in precise detail. "My squad covering that damn road connecting with Highway N13 on the village outskirts took down four Germans on motorcycles with sidecars. We took their identification papers."

Riley handed Wade the captured *soldbuchs* along with some maps and other papers.

"Corporal, go find someone who can read German and translate these written notes. Preferably one of our guys and not a local."

"Yes, sir," responded Rioux, who exited the cottage quickly.

Riley continued, "I'm not sure, sir, but I think we encountered a small element of a reconnaissance battalion. Part of a probe, possibly? According to these papers and from the uniforms I saw, they're definitely *Waffen-SS*. There could be a whole division out there … possibly an armored division."

"Yeah, I would agree with that, Lieutenant," added Wade. "Looks like an *SS Panzergrenadier* division," he said, holding one bloody *soldbuch* up to his face for a closer inspection. "They're definitely mechanized and they're bound to have some armor."

Lieutenant Riley shot Captain Wade a concerned look. "Just what do you think we're up against here, sir?" he asked.

"Combined arms formations," said Wade. "*Panzergrenadier* divisions are almost as lethal as full-blown armored *Panzer* divisions. One *Panzergrenadier* division could have up to six battalions of truck-mounted infantry, possibly a battalion of tanks, a complement of artillery, heavy assault guns … and God only knows what else," replied Wade somberly. "Their lethality depends on their strength. They could be severely lacking in able-bodied troops and equipment. Like I said … God only knows. What I do know is that we sure as hell don't have the troops or the equipment to hold back an entire goddamn division!"

"What are your orders, sir?" Riley asked.

"Lieutenant, split up your squad and lead half of it farther down the road. The other half will remain in their current position. Reconnoiter and try to determine how close the enemy is and what its strength may be. Move immediately. Understood?"

"Yes, sir," replied Riley. "Sir, what's the name of that damn road we're defending?"

Wade looked at his map and saw no designation for the road connecting to Highway N13.

"I don't see a name. From now on it's gonna be called Hitler's Highway," Wade decreed. "Move out, Lieutenant. Report back to me as soon as possible."

Riley saluted and rushed back to his men stationed on Hitler's Highway. Wade glanced at Mayor Durant standing meekly in the corner. He said something to Wade in French. Wade didn't understand, but definitely knew the fight was about to begin!

Captain Wade and Mayor Durant left the cottage together. Durant scurried about informing the villagers to get inside and protect themselves from the impending conflict. Captain Wade summoned runners to alert every paratrooper position of possible action. In doing so he came across a paratrooper with a sniper's rifle. He ordered the trooper to follow him to the church bell tower where Private Taylor was still scanning the area.

"Taylor, this is Private Falk from the 82nd. He's gonna give you some cover up here. Claims he's a great sniper," Wade said. He added, "We've made contact with the enemy from the southwest. I need you to spot and report any enemy movements immediately. Since we've got no radio communications at our disposal, I'll post runners in the church. Use them to speed word to the mortar crews. You're gonna be our eyes. We'll need you to tell the men manning the mortars where to direct their fire. Understood? You're the key, Taylor. You're vital to our survival."

"I understand, sir, and I won't let you down," said Taylor. "But, sir, I need to inform you that even from this high vantage point, my view of the road to the southwest is mostly obstructed by trees and tall hedgerows. It'll be difficult to spot approaching men and vehicles."

"I can see that, Private. Do the best you can and use your ears, too. Listen for anything that sounds like heavy vehicular traffic like tanks and trucks. They're slow and pretty damn loud. That should help you be able to get a fix on their position without actually seeing them. Falk here is going to cover your ass if any Krauts get too close. I'll be back to check up on you two later. Stay alert."

"Yes, sir," replied both men in unison.

Wade climbed down and returned to the mayor's cottage. Corporal Rioux was waiting to report that he was unable to find someone who could read German. Frustrated, Wade sent him back out again to look. The captain began to pace back and forth like a caged animal at the zoo. He could only sit tight and wait for Lieutenant Riley's report.

Some time passed before Riley made it back to his squad of eight stationed on Hitler's Highway. They reported no further enemy sightings. Immediately Riley took four men armed with Thompsons and Garands and cautiously led them down the road, away from Rigeault. Lieutenant Riley, carrying a Garand rifle and a .45 pistol, took point. They moved quietly down the road until they were out of sight of their fellow paratroopers. After about two kilometers they reached a sharp curve in the road. Riley and his men hugged the side of the road using trees and hedgerows as cover. They turned the corner and froze dead in their tracks!

"*Achtung! Amerikaner!*" a voice shouted in German. Riley and his men had just stumbled across a spot littered with German infantry and a few vehicles towing artillery.

"Fire!" yelled Riley. Thompson submachine guns blazed to life, cutting down several unsuspecting Germans. Riley hurriedly squeezed off a few rounds from his Garand before yelling out, "Fall back!"

The five Americans turned and ran back up the road. Fifty heavily armed German soldiers were too much to take on. The Germans, initially caught by surprise, quickly regrouped and returned fire. Two of the five paratroopers were hit and mortally wounded. Riley and the three others returned fire, but were hopelessly outnumbered. Some of the Germans rushed to pursue them, but were abruptly ordered back by their commanders. Soon Riley and his men were safely out of range and out of harm's way—at least for the moment.

The surviving Americans made it back to their lines without further incident. Riley put his men covering Hitler's Highway on high alert and told them that enemy contact was imminent. He issued orders for them to remain at their posts and harass any enemies trying to get through their lines. He then rushed back to Rigeault to report to Captain

Wade. It was now getting late in the day.

Wade again met with the winded and shaken Lieutenant Riley, who felt as if his exhausted legs were about to fall off. Wade told him to sit at the mayor's table and catch his breath.

"Sir," said Riley, his hands shaking, "we got a little over a mile down the road and ran into about fifty German troops and a few vehicles. We surprised them as much as they surprised us! We opened fire and took a few out. I ordered an instant retreat, as we were sitting ducks out in the open. The Krauts killed two of my men, sir," he said forlornly.

"Did the Germans give chase? Did they go after you?"

"Not really, sir. They stopped firing after we got far enough back up the road."

"Great. It's what I feared. They know we're here and they're massing troops to hit us hard. They're not coming until they're good and ready," said Wade. "That could be a day or an hour from now. Good work, Lieutenant. Get back to your men. Report back if the situation changes."

Riley stood up and gave Wade a weak salute. He said nothing and returned to his position along Hitler's Highway. Wade revisited the various strongpoints along the village perimeter, putting each location on high alert. The sun was beginning to set, and Wade prayed there wouldn't be a night attack. When he returned to Durant's cottage, Corporal Rioux and Sergeant Parker were there to update him and remain by his side. Rioux was still unable to find anyone who could read German. As the evening turned into night, Wade could feel the uneasiness within the village. Loud thuds and booms off in the distance made it clear the Germans were lobbing mortar fire in their direction. The fight would be upon them tomorrow. That was certain. Wade looked at the intelligence papers seized earlier, then turned his head in the direction of the Rigeault jail.

Chapter 23

THE BATTLE FOR RIGEAULT

A ll through the night and into the early-morning hours of June 9, the Germans tried to soften up the area around Rigeault with mortar fire and artillery. Constant reports from runners came into Captain Wade's headquarters. The German fire was not being accurately directed onto American paratrooper positions and the lines were holding. There were no casualties reported, only minor structural damage to some of the village homes on the outskirts and some dead livestock. A frustrated Captain Wade left the jail after an unsuccessful attempt to extract information from Steinert regarding the intelligence papers. Wade still had no idea of the size and strength of the German force lurking just outside of Rigeault.

The American mortar crews dug in and readied themselves. They eagerly waited for word from Private Taylor in the church bell tower that the enemy was within range. The fire from the limited number of long-range German 88mm artillery pieces was not well placed, giving the Americans hope for a chance at close-quarter combat. They needed to draw the enemy near, in order to destroy it.

As the clock struck noon, the German mortar and artillery fire stopped completely. Lieutenant Riley, still stationed with his ambush squad on Hitler's Highway, felt uneasy when the guns went silent. He figured his position would be the first to be hit. He desperately wanted to send a runner out to request reinforcements for his six-man squad, but there was no time. Minutes later the sound of SS *Panzergrenadiers* was heard advancing along the road toward Riley's position. The lieutenant counted about thirty soldiers poised for a direct assault. He yelled out strongly, "Wait until they're in range! Short, controlled bursts! Don't waste ammo! Use your grenades!"

Suddenly the Germans were upon them! Riley's BAR man opened up with a deadly barrage of lead that hit the advancing troops hard. The surprised attackers, dressed in camouflaged SS uniforms, hit the deck while returning fire. Riley and his men lobbed a few grenades in the enemy's direction, lifting several caught in the explosions right off the ground. Riley's men, armed with Thompson submachine guns, sprayed a relentless stream of hot lead toward the attackers, sending multiple Germans to their deaths.

Several minutes into the intense firefight, the Americans held the advantage! The strong base of fire provided by Riley's BAR man, coupled with his two men armed with Thompsons, forced the unsuspecting and uncoordinated German attack to temporarily falter. However, the determination and fanaticism of the *Waffen-SS* troops would not be denied!

Slowly the Germans gained the advantage. One of Riley's machine gunners took a bullet through his head and dropped dead. Another rifleman screamed in horror as a bullet ripped through his leg, slicing his femoral artery. He died in seconds from massive blood loss. The Germans slowly continued the advance on the entrenched American position, using the flanks and their superior numbers to outmatch the paratroopers. Riley, madly firing his Garand rifle, watched the ammo clip pop out with a clinking sound, indicating his eight shots were gone! He was reaching for a new clip when a German bullet tore into his left shoulder. He recoiled in pain as another American riflemen dropped dead not far from him. He looked at the charging Germans. There was nothing else he could do.

"Fall back! Fall back!" he shouted at the few surviving troops in his decimated squad. "Covering fire!" he ordered as his men got up from their positions and started falling back toward the interior defenses of Rigeault, making sure to cover their retreat with as much flying lead as possible. Riley's lone surviving Thompson machine gunner sprayed as much fire as feasible to protect the rear. The BAR man wielded his long, heavy weapon with deadly efficiency, killing and wounding several

German soldiers trying to outflank the retreating Americans.

Soon the Germans overran the American position on Hitler's Highway. They had managed to dislodge the paratroopers, but at a heavy and bloody cost. Twenty *Panzergrenadiers* lay dead to just four American paratroopers. Lieutenant Riley and his men pushed hard back toward Rigeault, eventually reaching a fortified position defended by two machine-gun nests bristling with recently recovered Browning .30 caliber machine guns. The soldiers positioned there were under Riley's command, as well, and thirsted for some action. The wounded Lieutenant positioned his surviving defenders alongside the machine-gun nests and ordered them to dig in.

"Don't give those bastards an inch!" he shouted. "Cut 'em down the second they get in range! Stand fast! All hell will be coming this way shortly, and I'm going to arrange a rude awakening from above!" said Riley as he sprinted off in the direction of the Rigeault church. His defenders reloaded their weapons and readied their grenades, peering down the open fields watching the advancing *Panzergrenadiers* regroup and try to bring up additional troops with heavier weaponry.

Lieutenant Riley, bright red blood running down his arm, got to the church amidst the confusion and panic and climbed up to accost Private Taylor and Private Falk.

"Private! The enemy is approaching from the southwest!"

Taylor grabbed his binoculars and could see German troops cautiously probing toward Riley's machine-gun nests.

"They have superior numbers, but haven't brought up any armor yet. Observe and direct mortar fire on their positions the second they get in range. Break up their formations as they advance. Don't give them an opportunity to get organized and attack our lines in force! I'm going to inform the captain and have runners from each mortar crew standing by to relay fire coordinates based on your observations. Clear?"

"Yes, sir," responded Taylor.

"You," said Riley, pointing at Private Falk, "Give him cover with that sniper rifle and assist the runners! And make sure at least one of you is watching the field at all times!"

"Understood, sir!" Private Falk said as he pointed his weapon and peered down the scope in the direction of the German threat.

Lieutenant Riley descended the bell tower. At the front entrance of the church he ran into Captain Wade, who was giving orders to Sergeant Parker. Riley saluted the captain and reported on the recent engagement with the enemy. Just then Private Taylor stuck out his head from high up in the bell tower and shouted out that the enemy was advancing and within mortar fire range, yelling out the proper direction of fire.

"Parker, alert the nearest mortar crew and put some fire in the sky now! I want a constant rain of lead dropping down on those sons-a-bitches! Get word out to all the mortar crews! I want to see runners in constant motion directing coordinates to the mortar crews from Taylor's observations! Get on it now, Sergeant!"

"Yes, sir," Parker said as he took off running.

"Are you hurt bad, Lieutenant?" Wade asked, noticing Riley's blood-soaked arm.

"It's just a scratch, sir. I'll be okay. Permission to rejoin my men?" the brave young lieutenant requested.

"Yeah, get moving. Report back to me if the situation changes for the worse. I have to check in with the other officers. So far, to my knowledge your sector is the only one to be hit," Wade responded.

Just then the sound of distant 81mm mortar fire was heard. The paratrooper mortar crews unleashed their fire with devastating results, inflicting heavy casualties. Several poorly coordinated German assault formations fell victim to the accurately directed shells. American machine-gun fire ripped through their ranks as quickly as they advanced into the crosshairs, stunning the enemy troops not hit by the deadly mortar barrage raining down on them from above.

With Private Taylor successfully directing the mortar attack, and the entrenched paratroopers stubbornly defending their positions with steadfast bravery and determination, the disorganized German infantry assault began to crumble. The *Panzergrenadiers* fought savagely, but couldn't gain a foothold past the overrun ambush position. Several failed maneuvers to flank the American defensive positions cost the Germans dearly in human lives. Dozens of German soldiers lay dead or wounded on the fields of the southwest approaches into Rigeault. The American defensive perimeter around the village had been successfully defended and remained intact. The line had held, with only a few American injuries and even fewer casualties. The scattered remnants of the failed *Panzergrenadier* attack retreated to solid German-held positions.

The afternoon sun began to drop lower, bringing a lull in the fighting. D+3 was winding down. Captain Wade sat in his headquarters listening to his lieutenants report on the situation. Only the southwestern sector of the village had been hit. The north and east positions had not been engaged. Lieutenant Riley sat across from Wade. A private from his company attended to his wounded arm.

"I think I got it, sir!" exclaimed the private. "Looks like just a fragment," he added as he extracted a small, distorted piece of lead from Riley's stricken arm. The lieutenant grimaced in pain while the private washed the wound with water, applied a packet of sulfa powder, stitched up the hole, then wrapped a bandage around the arm.

"How many casualties did we suffer today?" asked Wade to the group.

Only Lieutenant Riley spoke; the other three had nothing further to report. "Sir, I lost nine men killed in action and I have over eighteen wounded."

"Where are they being treated?" asked Wade with a heavy sigh.

"In the field, sir," answered Riley, adding, "We have no medics and no designated aid station, so the wounded are being looked after by their fellow paratroopers at their posts."

"That's unacceptable!" Wade bellowed. "Corporal Rioux?"

"Yes, sir," answered Rioux.

"Ask Mayor Durant if there is a hospital in the village."

Rioux turned to Durant and asked, "*Avez-vous un hôpital?*"

The mayor shook his head sadly and replied, "*Non, il n'ya pas d'hôpital dans Rigeault.*"

"He says no, sir. They ain't got a hospital."

"Then ask him what the largest building in the village is. We're going to set up an aid station to collect our wounded."

"*Quel est le plus grand bâtiment en Rigeault?*" Rioux asked the mayor.

"*L'école,*" answered Durant after a few seconds of thought.

"He says it's the school, sir."

"Good. Take the mayor and have him show you where the school is, Corporal. After that, find Sergeant Parker. Inform him that I want him to organize the school into an aid station and to start bringing our wounded up there immediately. Tell the mayor that we need some women to act as nurses and help care for the men. Gather all the medical supplies you can. Take this private with you, too. You've just been promoted to head surgeon, soldier," said Wade, pointing to the man who had just attended to Lieutenant Riley's wound.

Wade finished, and the three men left.

"Lieutenants, get back to your forward positions," ordered Wade. "Riley, take some men covering the north sector and reinforce your positions in the south. Send some men over to the east sector, but only if absolutely necessary. I don't want to be spread too thin. Get the wounded out of harm's way. See to it, gentlemen!"

The four lieutenants saluted and hustled out, leaving Wade alone. Moments later the sound of artillery shells crashing into the ground in and around Rigeault shook Wade right out of his seat! He raced outside and noticed some houses in the distance were burning as a result of German artillery shell impacts. The citizens of the village responded quickly, forming bucket brigades to attack the flames. Wade raced uphill to the church where Private Taylor was busy yelling out instructions to runners below on where to direct mortar fire.

"What the hell's happening?" demanded Wade after climbing to the bell tower to confront Taylor.

"Look, sir!" Taylor said, as he handed the captain his binoculars and pointed to the southwest in the direction of Hitler's Highway. Wade's binoculars focused on two German trucks that had rolled up towing 88mm artillery pieces. The Germans were now firing heavy artillery into Rigeault.

"Get some mortar fire onto those guns!" ordered Wade.

"Yes, sir, we're working on it now, sir. We may have to move closer, as those guns may be out of our range, even if we crank the tubes all the way up!"

Wade looked on as more massed German infantry began to assault American positions on the outer perimeter to the south. The fanatical camouflaged *Waffen-SS Panzergrenadiers* didn't wait for the artillery to cease before hurtling forward into the fight. Wade observed Hitler's paramilitary soldiers fan out and attack American positions with relentless tenacity and reckless courage. They countered the constant fire from the American .30 caliber machine-gun nests with their own MG-42 machine-gun fire. The massive barrage from the German MG-42 caught some of the American paratroopers by surprise, forcing them to hug the ground for cover and allowing the Germans to advance.

Despite their superiority in numbers and firepower, the Germans made little headway and couldn't break through the American lines. They attacked in uncoordinated waves that withered away before the Americans' well-placed defenses. Dozens of *Panzergrenadiers* fell, charging the line. Some paratroopers were killed in the attack; however, the ones that fell were quickly replaced with a man held back in reserve. Lieutenant Riley, whose men were taking the worst punishment, managed to plug every hole the Germans were able to create. The massed German assaults couldn't punch through the American lines. They soon had no choice but to fall back and lick their wounds or risk being destroyed.

Captain Wade observed and directed the battle from his elevated vantage point in the bell tower. American shells rained down, killing groups of *Panzergrenadiers* that presented juicy targets. Wade, Taylor, and Falk cheered in delight as mortar shells plastered the German artillery pieces and the trucks that had towed them into position. The trucks exploded, setting off nearby artillery shells that blew the 88s skyward in a dazzling ball of flame.

"Jesus Christ, we nailed those son-of-bitching guns!" cried Wade, with binoculars pressed to his eyes. "Damn, that's just what I wanted to see! Good work, Taylor!"

"Thank you, sir," sighed Taylor with relief. "It looks like the Krauts are falling back, sir! Looks like we held 'em off!"

"Yes we did, Private ... but they won't be gone for long. We just gave 'em a bloody nose. They'll be back very soon ... and God help us!" said Wade as he started to climb down the tower. "Keep a close lookout tonight, Taylor. I got a feeling we're not done here."

Wade exited the church amid a mad fury of activity. He looked on as several French villagers scurried about, alive with activity. Several houses were on fire from the German shelling. Many were busy fighting the flames, while others bravely hauled ammunition to the American front-line positions. Still others helped move and carry wounded paratroopers to the newly established aid station in the local schoolhouse. Wade followed a group helping the wounded to the school. As he entered he ran into Sergeant Parker, who was supervising the situation.

"Captain, sir, we've cleared out all the desks to make room on the floor for the wounded. Still, as you can see, this schoolhouse isn't very big, but it's the best we can do. The village women are donating bed sheets and pillows. Corporal Rioux has also requested them to bring in all medical supplies they may have and to help comfort the wounded," Parker reported. He added, "Currently we have twenty-six wounded. I don't know how many have been killed."

"Last count I had was nine killed," Wade said while looking around the classroom-turned-emergency room. "That's bound to have changed by now." Several wounded men were bloodied and groaning in pain. "Do what you can. Keep this place orderly and utilize everyone you can find with any kind of medical background. Scrounge up every aid kit out there."

"Yes, sir. I'll take care of everything, sir."

Wade patted Parker on the shoulder, then abruptly left. He headed back to Durant's cottage. He knew it wouldn't be long before his four lieutenants in the field would be looking for him with their reports. Time passed as Wade and his men endured another long lull in the fighting. After sunset, only the fires from the burning buildings illuminated the village surroundings.

A single oil lamp burned in the mayor's cottage to provide light at Wade's war table. The exhausted captain listened to his lieutenant's reports as sporadic gunfire echoed in the distance. Occasionally the gunfire would intensify as the Germans launched white-hot, slow-burning flares that would light up the sky and reveal American positions. Wade looked out the window at the chaos while his men reported the situation.

The casualty lists were tallied, showing twenty-eight wounded and eighteen killed out of the original eighty-six paratroopers defending Rigeault. The lines had held, and the Germans had been successfully repulsed. Morale among the men was good, but ammunition was starting to run low, according to Lieutenant Riley, who had absorbed the brunt of the German attack. The other three lieutenants agreed. All told, it was estimated the American defenders had killed or wounded upwards of two hundred German soldiers, all confirmed as being part of the 17th SS *Panzergrenadier* Division.

Mayor Durant, accompanied by Corporal Rioux, expressed through the corporal that his people were scared and there was talk among some of leaving the village to find safety elsewhere. He added that many others were committed to staying and helping, and would continue to feed and shelter the Americans until the last man was killed. Mayor Durant also stressed that there were still brave souls searching the marshes for equipment bundles, even though the Germans were extremely close and the danger to their safety had increased substantially.

Captain Wade took in all the reports and feedback. He ordered his men to return to the lines and be prepared for several smaller, probing actions from the Germans. He anticipated the entire perimeter would encounter some type of small-arms exploratory attacks from the Germans during the night. Everyone agreed and hastily returned to the lines. Wade sat alone for an hour or so. He tried to sleep, but couldn't. He picked up his Thompson and decided to inspect the American defensive line.

On the other side of the village, two men lay in their cramped prison cell wondering what was happening on the outside. Fire from a nearby burning building cast some light through the barred jail window. Frantic voices shouting in French could be clearly heard though not understood by the curious Hank Mitchell who lay awake listening and trying to comprehend the situation. His cellmate, the feverish Steinert, coughed heavily, grasped his aching wound, and rambled on in a low, delirious tone. Hank had ignored much of what the dying Steinert had mumbled and groaned earlier, but he now began to take more of an interest.

Steinert mumbled the name Nigel Shepley several times, along with other names that also ended with Shepley. He called out the names of streets, street numbers, and places, all with English-sounding names. He referenced the names Colchester and Winterbotham over and over and often said the word Bletchley as well. It all meant next to nothing to Hank. In Steinert's delirious state he referenced both the past and the present, often speaking in both English and German. In one instance he went on in English about vacationing in the Bavarian mountains as a child with his family, then in another he switched to German and rambled on nonsensically about things Hank couldn't understand. It all sounded like some strange code.

This went on through the night. Hank tried vainly to make sense of something that might help uncover just who Steinert was. The dying man slipped out of consciousness and fell silent. Gathering what he had learned from Steinert's ramblings in English, Hank got an idea. He got up and grabbed Steinert under both arms and propped him up into a sitting position, with his back against the wall. He lifted his sagging head up and gently slapped each cheek.

"Wake up, Nigel!" he said with authoritative enthusiasm, "it's me, Nigel. It's me, Rodney Colchester, your superior. And I want your report … now!"

"Operation Vengeance underway. Downed American pilot located by female operative. Captured and incarcerated at château," said Steinert mechanically and monotonously as if drugged or in a trance. Hank listened as Steinert gave account of the various rooms of the opulent château in detail. He started with the dungeon-like chamber filled with treasure and valuables of stolen Nazi plunder. He described the root cellar and the long stone stairway leading up through the various and lavishly decorated corridors leading to von Schreiner's office. In describing the layout and contents of the *Gruppenführer*'s surroundings, Steinert told about Eichner barging in and the heated exchange between the Gestapo agent and von Schreiner.

Steinert went on to tell about subsequent meetings with the *Gruppenführer*, oftentimes just rambling on about how displeased and suspicious von Schreiner was of him. He described the secret war room in the depths of the château and his procedures concerning monitoring and obtaining secret Enigma codes and other intelligence. As if preaching to a group of Allied codebreakers and engineers, Steinert went on to describe the inner workings of Enigma, specifically how the mechanism itself functioned.

Hank listened with a look of astonishment when he heard Steinert report about his clandestine activities in the secret radio room at Café LeBlanc. He couldn't understand how Steinert had slipped in and out so secretly. He was amazed Pauline had never mentioned this to him. The thought of Steinert sending out secret Enigma radio traffic further fueled his speculation as to whether he was in fact a brilliant British spy or just a clever Nazi agent. Steinert was so thorough with his story that he mentioned even the most insignificant of details such as retrieving Cuban cigars, seeing Yvette with von Schreiner, and finding Pierre playing in his car.

Hank continued to listen, confident that his ruse was working. Steinert droned on, revealing as much detail as he could. He was noticeably weak and his thinking severely impaired, but Hank was confident Steinert actually thought he was being debriefed by the man he'd mentioned earlier--Rodney Colchester. Before Hank could ask another question, Steinert spoke up and began revealing more information and experiences.

"I spent a good deal of time in my room, sir. I felt the Gestapo was on to me and I looked for clues that would indicate my room had been searched. The boy, Pierre, came in and we played a little game. I asked him questions. When he gave good answers I rewarded him with goods—chocolate and such. I saw Yvette in the hallway afterwards. I smelled her perfume and later discovered the same scent on my bedroom pillow. I knew something was askew and needed to stay on guard. I continued my duties in the war room and met with von Schreiner later on. He continued to berate me and express his displeasure in the way I handled my responsibilities--especially with the American who was still at large. He took pleasure in reminding me of his brutal past."

Steinert rambled on about the speculative details behind von Schreiner's eye patch and how he used it to instill fear in others. He then reported on going back to the war room and receiving information about the Paul Verlaine poem broadcast on the BBC. He discussed in detail reporting it to von Schreiner, then sneaking away to Café LeBlanc.

"I confronted Christophe LeBlanc, who repeatedly challenged my authority," said Steinert. After sorting him out I returned to the radio room and tried to make contact with Bletchley Park--to no avail. Frustrated, it was then that I decided to authorize the raid on the German airstrip."

Steinert's eyes slowly and painfully opened. His labored breathing intensified, and he coughed up some blood that splattered on Hank's chest. The young pilot was unfazed and stared Steinert in the eyes. He repeated his command, again using the name Rodney Colchester. Steinert, dazed and unable to think clearly, spoke.

"Yes, sir!" he said in a sick, gravelly voice.

"Listen carefully, Nigel," Hank said, trying to imitate a British accent, "I need you to continue your report. Tell us what happened."

Steinert's eyes rolled into the back of his head and he continued to cough. His speech became nonsensical and disjointed. Hank had a hard time following what came next.

"Americans ... on time ... mission information intercepted ... Jamison . . ." Steinert's weak voiced trailed off, prompting Hank to hold his limp head up and force him to continue.

"Go on, Nigel. This is important. Uh, intelligence needs to confirm your report. Please continue!" Hank said with a terrible British accent.

"Fighters ... bomber downed ... Jamison ... Stevenson ... confirm," he said as his head slumped forward, "Go with retaliation sweep ... Bletchley ... need a ... " Steinert trailed off again, but Hank kept up the pressure and urged him to continue.

"Confirm! Von Schreiner suspicious ... need orders ... talk to me! Where is Bletchley? Damned American! Why? Why! Not safe. Not safe any more! Nothing is safe! Acknowledge my bloody signal!"

"It's okay, Nigel," Hank said reassuringly, "Tell us about Pauline LeBlanc. We need to help her. Tell us how to help her now."

"Invasion ... when is invasion ... not safe here! Enemies everywhere! Gestapo knows all ... von Schreiner ... not safe ... Eichner

… Pauline!"

"Yes, Pauline … how do we help her? We need to bring her safely back to England, Nigel. How do we do that?" asked Hank, doing his best to maintain the charade.

"Bloody American fool! Pauline … lovely … dead … they're all dead!"

"She's not dead, Nigel," Hank calmly responded. "She's being looked after by the German Army. You sent her away with them. Where are they helping her? How do we get to her?"

Steinert laughed with delirium. A sudden clarity seemed to emerge on his face.

"I want to go home, sir. I can't do this any more. I want to be with my family while I still have some memory of who they once were! God knows I'm not sure of who I am any more! Take me out of this bloody nightmare! Let me go home sir … back to England. I want life to be like it used to be. I want my father to be proud of his son and the service he did for King and country. I want to see the white cliffs of Dover one last time! Give me my life back! Give me back my identity! MI6 can keep all the rest!"

Hank listened in silence. Steinert's head slipped back down.

"Nigel? Nigel?" said Hank, loudly trying to rouse him again and make him continue to talk. It was no use. Hank thought of one more little ploy and shook the dying man aggressively, saying, "Steinert! Steinert!"

Suddenly, German began to flow from Steinert's lips. Hank sat back and listened to him ramble on in German. At one point he broke out into an SS fight song. Hank felt he was sharing a jail cell with a schizophrenic! One moment he was with an Englishman named Nigel Shepley, while the next he was with a German named Peter Steinert.

Whoever this man was, he grabbed Hank by the shirt, pulling his face close so they were both nose to nose. "God save the King," he shouted emphatically, followed by a chilling, "*Heil, Hitler.*" He slumped over and fell silent. Hank, stunned, sat back in the mud and filth and refocused his attention on the happenings outside in the village. Light from burning buildings still dimly illuminated the jail through the window. Random gunfire could be heard in virtually all directions, together with muffled voices speaking both French and English. Hank desperately wanted to know what was going on. His thoughts shifted from Pauline to Captain Wade.

Along the village perimeter, the captain was dealing with his own problems. His earlier predictions had turned out to be true. The Germans were probing all along the American lines with small-unit, hit-and-run tactics. White-hot, slow-burning incendiary flares were shot up to reveal the hidden locations of the dug-in paratroopers. Sporadic small-arms gunfire continued through the night. Captain Wade patrolled the American lines all night, making sure to inspect both the American interior and exterior defensive positions. The worst was to come at first light.

On the morning of D+4, Private Taylor sent a runner to find Captain Wade and bring him to the bell tower. Wade rushed to the church and climbed the tower, where Private Taylor frantically passed him the binoculars. Wade's heart skipped a beat at the sight he saw to the southwest.

Taylor said, "Captain, the Germans have broken through Lieutenant Riley's outer defenses. They've advanced far enough toward the village where we can observe their every move now. Reinforcements have been sent from the northern sector to help stop the German advance and prevent the inner lines from buckling altogether! We just received word from a runner that the heavy machine-gun fire has temporarily halted the German advance, but they're seriously low on ammo and don't know how much longer they can hold out!"

Wade focused his binoculars on the battlefield below him. He watched German infantry clash with his paratroopers at close range. Guns blazed furiously and men dropped left and right. Soldiers on both sides fired until they were out of ammo, forcing them to resort to hand-to-hand combat, using knives and whatever else they could find as a weapon. Some ripped off their helmets and threw them at the enemy! The one-on-one combat carnage was appalling, but it was not the worst of Wade's problems.

"Captain, focus your glasses further to the southwest," instructed Taylor, adding, "We have big problems moving up our way!"

Wade was terrified at what he saw. At the same time, a combative fire burned inside of him fueled by a rush of surging adrenaline. Through his binoculars he observed the Germans move up another 88mm artillery piece that appeared to be just out of range of American mortar fire. It was towed into position by a *Sonderkraftfahrzeug 7* half-track! Just behind it arrived another German armored *Sonderkraftfahrzeug 251* half-track, deploying more troops into position.

"Goddamn Hanomag!" Wade exclaimed as he watched German troops pour out of the vehicle. The *Sd.kfz. 251* was perhaps the best-armored half-track of the war, and the Germans had it!

"Captain, look over there!" shouted Taylor as he pointed to the southeast.

Moving up through the fields into prime firing positions were two *Sturmgeschütz IV* assault guns! The four-man-crewed tank killers were deadly, self-propelled weapons. The Germans now had armor on the battlefield that thoroughly outgunned anything the Americans could hurl back at them! The awesome sight of the German *StuG IVs* made Captain Wade wonder just how much armor was being held in reserve and just out of his sight. How many ferocious Tiger and Panther tank commanders, standing in open tank turrets, lay in wait behind some hill, itching for orders to be unleashed upon the unsuspecting Americans? He didn't have time to ponder it. Seconds later an unrelenting barrage of shells rained down on Rigeault from the 88mm gun! It was joined by fire from the two *StuG IV* assault guns that blasted away at American defensive positions. German infantry then let loose a storm of mortar fire that forced every living thing in its path to dive for cover. The ground shook violently with every impact, causing the villagers to run and seek shelter from the deadly salvos.

Wade ordered, "Get every mortar tube available and direct as much fire as possible on that enemy armor! Find the range and plaster those positions with everything we've got! I don't want to see a single mortar tube silent! When they bring up infantry, hit 'em just as hard! Get word out to the runners to have every soldier with a bazooka, heavy machine gun, mine, or any type of demolition to get their ass up to Lieutenant Riley's south sector! I want as much firepower as we can muster in line to meet the German threat!"

Just then Private Falk fired his sniper rifle. Wade looked down and off in the distance at a dead German who had somehow managed to make his way through the paratrooper defenses and within Falk's crosshairs!

"Good shot, Falk!" praised Wade, slinging his Thompson and preparing to climb down from the tower. "Hopefully, they won't get as close as that, but if they do, drop a few more of those bastards for me … right between the eyes! Taylor, we're all depending on you! Keep those fire directions clear and keep the runners moving! I don't know how long we'll be able to hold!"

"I understand, Captain. I'll keep 'em shooting straight," promised Taylor.

As Wade climbed down he heard Taylor yell out mortar fire directions to a runner on the ground who quickly slung his .30 caliber M1 Carbine and sprinted off to his mortar crew. Another runner came to the captain with a message from Lieutenant Riley, begging for reinforcements. Wade sent the runner away with assurances that help was forthcoming. Shells burst all around him, forcing the captain to seek shelter or risk being killed himself. He hustled back to Durant's cottage, weaving his way through frenzied groups of French citizens bravely trying to combat the village fires and help the wounded to the aid station in the schoolhouse. Back at headquarters, he started to formulate contingency plans for a total pullout. Amidst the deafening chaos around him, his ears could pick out explosions well off in the distance, meaning his own mortar crews were returning fire—hopefully with deadly results! Machine-gun fire chattered away, and grenades exploded, kicking up earth all around. Just then the lieutenant commanding the northern sector of the village defense burst into the cottage.

"Sir, request permission … "

"Have your lines been hit yet?" Wade asked interrupting the lieutenant in midsentence.

"No, not yet, sir, but we've observed … "

"Take every available man off the line and transfer them immediately to Lieutenant Riley's command in the south. Strip your line down to the thinnest possible defense. Take all the heavy weaponry and explosives you have and rotate it over to Riley. They're catching hell right now in the south!"

Just then an artillery shell exploded outside the cottage, shattering the windows and throwing both the captain and the lieutenant to the ground. Both men slowly got to their feet.

"Are you okay?" Wade asked the lieutenant, who appeared very shaken up.

"Yeah, I'm not hit," said the lieutenant as he checked himself for wounds.

"C'mon, get to your position and transfer your men. Send them south. That's where the trouble is. Use the church as a landmark, if they need direction. The church is on the highest ground, and they'll be able to spot the German threat from there!"

"Yes, sir. I'll see to it immediately, sir!" the lieutenant replied before rushing off.

Another shell burst in the air close to the headquarters, forcing Wade to leave the cottage and stay mobile for his own safety. He made his way to the western sector, finding his men engaged in a firefight with small, scattered units of SS *Panzergrenadiers* doggedly fighting through the marshes. The paratroopers held their positions in the west, inflicting heavy casualties. Wade moved on to the northern sector, where he personally witnessed his men pull out and rush to the south, leaving only a skeleton defense behind. He then zigzagged through raining German artillery and assault gunfire to inspect his lines in the eastern sector. The fight in the east was nearly as intense as it was in the south as the Germans recklessly tried to flank the American positions. All along the American lines Wade could see advancing German infantry. Through a pair of borrowed binoculars, he observed more mechanized German infantry in trucks and on motorcycles slowly moving forward across the fields. To his dismay, the flooded marshy areas were mostly north and west of Rigeault, which was the American paratroopers' only legitimate direction of retreat. He ordered his men to stand fast while simultaneously assisting a mortar crew to fire several rounds in succession. The American fire had the proper coordinates, but not the range. The Germans had figured out the effective range of the American mortars and kept their vehicles and armor just far enough back to keep them from being hit.

"Damn!" Wade shouted, realizing his only long-distance offensive threat was becoming ineffective. "Keep firing!" he ordered, "Wait until their infantry gets in range, then blow 'em to hell! Use your grenades, too … every last one of 'em. Show me what kind of arms you got!"

"Sir!" cried a sergeant manning a .30 caliber machine gun, "We're almost out of ammunition! We've got one .30 cal already gone dry!"

"Short, controlled bursts, Sergeant!" Wade responded. "Make sure they're in range! Take weapons and ammo off the wounded before they're evacuated to the aid station! I'll get word out to conserve and share ammo!"

Wade left his own grenades for his men, then headed back to the church. He needed a better view of the battlefield as a whole. His men were holding the line, but he didn't know how much longer they could hold out before their positions were overrun. The situation was growing desperate! He had to make a command decision very soon.

Wade arrived at the church severely out of breath as 88mm artillery shells exploded all around him. In the bell tower he found a harried Private Taylor frantically identifying German movements and yelling out commands to any runner who was present below. Private Falk aimed his sniper rifle in several directions, trying to get a bead on any German soldier within range.

"Captain!" shouted Taylor, "I sent a runner looking for you fifteen minutes ago! I'm glad you're here! I've got several things to report. You need to see this, sir!"

Wade looked through his binoculars in the direction Taylor was pointing. One of the self-propelled *StuG IV* assault guns had completely broken through Lieutenant Riley's inner defensive perimeter! The gun continued to blast away toward Rigeault, while the remaining paratroopers fought savagely against the *Panzergrenadiers* who had fallen in behind the tanklike vehicle and were using it as cover.

Suddenly American mortar fire rained down all around the gray-green German assault gun. Wade saw the vehicle so clearly through his binoculars that he could easily make out the black German cross on the side, as well as the black shield and fist divisional insignia that represented the *17th SS Panzergrenadier Division Götz von Berlichingen*. The lethal American mortar fire killed both friend and foe fighting close to the gun, but by a great stroke of luck, one shell struck the assault gun in the left-side tracks, blowing the steel tread apart and sending deadly shrapnel slicing through the air! The tanklike weapon was now immobile and vulnerable.

Wade observed several of his men gun down lingering *Panzergrenadiers*, and then pounce on the *StuG IV*! One paratrooper bravely pulled the pin on a grenade, then rammed it down the gun's barrel. He leapt out of the way as the barrel exploded, rendering it twisted and useless. The other paratroopers jumped up on top and readied their guns as the top hatch opened, venting smoke and flame. The four-man crew, dazed and choking from the smoke and fire inside, tried to scramble out, but were stopped as an American soldier pulled a pin from his grenade and dropped it through the open hatch.

"Fire in the hole!" he yelled, while jumping clear. An explosion rocked the vehicle, killing everyone inside and making it totally inoperable. The *StuG IV* burned like a torch! Wade pumped his fist at the awesome sight. His joy was short-lived, though, as he observed his men fight bravely, but start to fall back toward the village under the weight of superior German numbers, which kept hitting them with wave after wave. Captain Wade watched as his flanks started to cave in and a steady stream of German troops began to work their way up to the village from the hole in the defenses the disabled *StuG IV* had created. He cursed loudly and barked orders to both Taylor and Falk. The American sniper was busy firing shot after carefully aimed shot at the advancing Germans!

"Both of you get out of here as soon as the situation dictates that it's absolutely necessary! Understand? Fall back to the north sector if you can't find any friendlies! This is the last time I'm climbing up here! Good luck to both of you!" Wade said, as he slipped through the trapdoor and slid down the ladder to the stairs leading down and out of the church. As he hustled outside, he was knocked off his feet by German mortar fire. Everywhere buildings were burning and people were running and screaming, trying to escape the deadly onslaught! Wade leapt to his feet and readied his Thompson. He knew it was time to get into the fight alongside his men.

The captain hustled down the hill from the church to the southeast toward the heaviest fighting. He took cover behind a damaged stone wall, alongside several other paratroopers who had fallen back under heavy enemy fire. Wade raised his Thompson submachine gun and sprayed several bursts of fire at the advancing Germans. His men, armed with Garands and carbines, kept up a steady volume of fire, forcing the Germans to take cover from the deadly barrage. The paratroopers covered each other when it was time to reload. Captain Wade emptied his first magazine and quickly reached into his ammo pouch for a fresh one. Locking it into place, he swung his weapon over the stone wall and blanketed the area with hot lead. Several Germans fell dead or wounded under the intense fire, but they were still slowly gaining ground and dislodging the Americans from their positions.

A paratrooper firing next to Wade was hit and killed by German fire. A second took a bullet to the shoulder and collapsed in agony. Before Wade could turn to help him, a German rushed him with bayonet in hand! The *Panzergrenadier* gave a deafening war cry and plunged the bayonet toward Wade's heart! The captain deflected the blade away by swinging his gun. He then whipped the muzzle around and pumped several shots into the attacker, killing him instantly! The captain turned around and saw several other Germans moving toward his position from different directions. He fired again, realizing there were far more Germans around him than Americans!

"Fall back! Displace and fall back now!" he shouted at any paratrooper within the range of his voice. He started to move back away from the stone wall and toward the village. He kept firing in all directions at every camouflaged German he saw. As he and his men retreated, Wade saw the second and still-operable *StuG IV* grinding its way toward the village, blasting away at everything in sight. In the distance he saw the Germans move up smaller artillery pieces and unload more troops from the armored *Sonderkraftfahrzeug 251* half-track.

Suddenly a violent explosion rocked the area. In horror, Captain Wade looked up the hill behind him to see the bell tower obliterated by 88mm artillery fire! A second shell ripped through the base of the old church, causing most of it to collapse in a massive heap of burning rubble. Finally, a third shot from the large German gun blasted through what little remained standing of the centuries-old structure, catapulting chunks of twisted burning shrapnel through the air. Taylor and Falk were dead, and the paratroopers' primary observation platform and mortar-directing fire center was now totally destroyed! There was no way for the remaining American mortar crews to accurately direct their fire down on German positions. Wade's defenses were falling apart, and it was time to consider more drastic measures.

Amidst a torrid volley of enemy fire, Captain Wade and several of his men retreated up the hill and took up defensive positions in and around the strewn rubble of the church. For the moment, his beleaguered and exhausted troops had the advantage of the high ground. They could concentrate their fire down on the Germans who had to make their way uphill to enter Rigeault. Wade sent out orders to pull every last man from the northern sector and place them in locations to the south. Wade would fortify his positions facing the advancing *Panzergrenadiers* with every soldier and weapon at his disposal.

The paratroopers moved with lightning speed. With the outer defenses completely gone and all his men forming a new inner perimeter to stop the German breakthrough, Wade frantically barked out orders to his men busy setting up new .30 caliber machine gun, bazooka, and mortar positions directly facing and in full view of the enemy. Surprisingly, after the destruction of the church and the rapid American pullout of all their smashed outer and select inner defenses, the German assault came to an abrupt halt. From his position behind a heap of rubble on the high ground, Captain Wade observed the German movements through his binoculars. He was relieved the shelling had stopped, but knew something far more sinister was about to happen.

"Sons-a-bitches are preparing for one final push," said Wade to a sergeant from the 101st crouched next to him. "That German prick of a commander who's somewhere down there," said Wade pointing his finger in the direction of the enemy, "is holding back just long enough to lick his wounds and then concentrate all his firepower and troops for one final strike. He intends to wipe us all out, even if it means obliterating this village from the map. I can just feel it, Sergeant. I can just feel it!"

"Sir, shouldn't we consider evacuating while we have the chance?" asked the sergeant. "We're dangerously low on ammo and I don't know just how much longer we can hold out, sir."

"Not yet, Sergeant. I'm not running from this bastard yet! I'm going to make him pay for every square inch of real estate he tries to take from me!" Wade said defiantly. "Somebody find me Lieutenant Riley!" he shouted loudly.

"Lieutenant Riley's dead, sir," answered the sergeant. "He got hit by a mortar round. Goddamn near blew him to pieces. I saw the whole fucking thing, sir! One minute he was firing his weapon, giving out orders, and the next minute he was gone. I took over command of his defensive position after he died, sir."

Wade groaned angrily and then said, "Very well, Sergeant, carry on." The sergeant hustled away and helped set up a machine-gun position. Wade looked on warily, noticing the men had practically no ammunition available for it.

"Lieutenant!" called out Wade upon seeing the beat-up officer he had put in command of the eastern sector.

"Sir!" he replied.

"Take charge here until I return."

"Yes, sir!"

Wade made his way through the village and past the schoolhouse. He could see the activity around it and knew several of his men and French civilians were inside. He had no time to stop, though. He kept on until he was spotted by Corporal Rioux, who rushed up to him.

"Captain, sir!" said Rioux trotting next to Wade.

"What is it, Corporal?"

"Sir, several of the townspeople are beginning to evacuate to the north. They know the Germans are advancing on three sides of the village and they're afraid. Still others are staying and helping with the wounded. What are your orders now, sir?"

"Corporal, find yourself a weapon and get your ass up to the front line! We need every man that can fight right now. I don't need a translator at this time! Where's the mayor?"

"He's at the aid station, sir, helping with the wounded."

"Good. What about Sergeant Parker?"

"He left the aid station earlier and joined the fighting."

"Very well. Now get going, Corporal! Go join the battle, too. That's what you jumped into France for, right?"

"Yes, sir!"

Corporal Rioux did an about-face and raced off in the direction of the American lines. Captain Wade sprinted through the burning buildings and rubble-strewn village streets until he reached his destination—the Rigeault jail. Standing outside was Private Mills, still on guard duty.

"Mills! Get up to the south sector of the village! We got heavy action that way, and I need every man available to fight! Get going!" ordered the captain.

Mills checked his rifle, saluted the captain, and ran toward the trouble.

"Mills!" Wade shouted after him. "Where's Collins?"

"I don't know, sir," replied Mills, turning back. "He didn't relieve me at his scheduled time. He may have joined the fight!"

"If you see him, tell him to get his ass up to the front! Get back here and give me the key to this shithouse!"

Mills raced over and handed Wade the key that unlocked the outer wooden door and the cell. Wade went inside and quickly opened the cell door. He looked down at Hank and Steinert. Both were lying in the mud and filth and not moving.

"Teddy Williams! Get up! I need your help!" ordered the captain. Hank slowly rolled over and sat up. He looked awful and smelled worse. He was tired, hungry, dehydrated, and full of despair.

"C'mon, stand up," said Wade, as the frightening sound of artillery fire started up again. Hank slowly rose to his feet.

"We're under heavy German attack. We're about to be beaten to a pulp, and the village is on the verge of being overrun. Our flanks are paper-thin and we're running low on ammunition. We have many wounded and killed. I don't have time for a long speech, so I'm simply gonna ask you to join this fight with me. I need every man."

Hank looked sullen and confused and didn't know quite how to respond. He tried to speak, but the words wouldn't come.

"Lieutenant!" shouted Wade, "I need your help! Lieutenant Henry Mitchell of the U.S. 9th Army Air Force, I need your help now! Prove to me you're who you say you are and let's go do our duty as United States officers! That's an order, lieutenant!"

Hank stood at attention and slowly saluted Captain Wade. He nodded and acknowledged that he would fight!

"Okay, then," said Wade reaching behind his back and producing a familiar Colt .45. "I believe this belongs to you," said Wade, as he handed Hank his gun. "It's fully loaded, but I don't have any extra mags. We're gonna have to scrounge for ammo very shortly. Come with me, and we'll find you a rifle!"

"Yes, sir," returned Hank in a raspy voice that prompted Wade to hand him his canteen of water. Hank guzzled it down.

"Let's go," said Wade, as more and more artillery shells rained down on the stricken village. "I just hope the Nazi prick leading this attack is running low on artillery shells!"

"Yeah, that would be a good thing, sir," responded Hank weakly.

"Wait," said Wade as he stopped just before going out the outer door. "What about him?" He pointed to Steinert, who lay motionless on the ground with his back turned to the cell door.

Hank turned to look at Steinert, then back at Wade.

"He won't fight, sir. It doesn't matter which side he's on anymore," Hank said.

"You don't think he'll join us even now with all hell breaking loose?" Wade asked.

"No, sir," Hank said. "He won't be joining anyone … because he's dead. He died during the night, sir."

Both men paused a moment in silence and looked at the filthy rotting corpse of the man in a black SS uniform whose true identity remained a puzzling mystery. He wasn't the *SS-Obersturmbannführer* working in a clandestine foreign intelligence operation, nor was he the clever British spy under heavy cover, assisting the tiny cell of French Resistance in the French town of Jolieville. He was now just a corpse wrapped in an enigma in a small, filthy French jail that would undoubtedly become his tomb. Everything he was and everything he had become was now lost forever. Hank prayed Steinert's demise was not a death knell for his lost beloved, Pauline.

"Let's go, Lieutenant Mitchell!" ordered Captain Wade. With that the two men exited the jail and made their way toward the fighting. Panic and chaos surrounded them at every turn. The streets were filled with fleeing civilians and heaps of burning rubble. Wade was having a hard time getting his bearings, since so many buildings had been hit by artillery fire, making them unrecognizable. The two pressed forward, however, and managed to stay alive under the fierce artillery barrage showering down on the village.

Captain Wade and Lieutenant Mitchell got through to the American line dug in around the ruins of the church on the high ground. Wade knew this would be the last stand. This was his Alamo! The paratroopers kept up a strong curtain of fire that was pinning down several German units trying to break through. A mortar crew, set up close by, fired off its last three remaining shells, inflicting little damage on the advancing enemy. Ammunition was running critically short.

"Someone get this man a weapon!" ordered Wade. One paratrooper rolled over the man lying next to him. He had been shot and killed and was lying on his gun. The paratrooper picked it up and tossed it to Hank. It was another Thompson submachine gun.

"You do know how to use that, don't you, Lieutenant?" asked Wade, still testing Hank's identity and knowledge of all things American.

"Absolutely, sir," responded Hank as he pulled back the bolt, cocking the weapon. The young airman now turned infantryman looked down the barrel through the simple sight and squeezed the trigger, filling the air with deadly .45 caliber bullets!

Captain Wade took cover and joined the attack with his own M1A1 Thompson. The military version of the infamous gangster-glorified Tommy gun belched out an unmistakable rat-a-tat-tat, causing the enemy to duck for cover. With Garand and carbine rifles, coupled with machine-gun and submachine-gun fire, the Americans held fast on the high ground, not allowing their lines to break. Unfortunately, their unmatched bravery and determination could not last without bullets.

One by one the paratroopers' guns went dry. Cries of, "I'm out!"

surpassed the cries of, "Incoming!" Wade's own Thompson went dry. He reached into his ammo pouch, pulled out his last stick magazine, and slapped it in place, but did not resume firing. He looked up and down the line and watched his mostly unarmed men getting killed or wounded. Barely a single rifle was firing.

Hank scrounged through the pockets and ammo pouches of the dead paratroopers around him and found only two loaded Thompson magazines. He reloaded his weapon and put the spare in his pocket. He then looked to the captain. There was nothing left to do.

"Pull out! Everybody fall back to the village! We're pulling out! We're pulling out now!" shouted Wade, waving his arms madly. One by one the paratroopers retreated into Rigeault, firing until their ammunition was gone. Every German heavy gun and mortar suddenly fell silent, as the order was given for an infantry attack. The SS-*Panzergrenadiers* began to regroup in force and make their way up into the village.

Captain Wade led a fighting retreat into the village streets. From the west, south, and east his fragile lines began to cave in, and the Germans slowly pushed the paratroopers northward, back into the village. Panicked village residents sought refuge anywhere they could to avoid the fierce battle between the retreating paratroopers and the advancing *Panzergrenadiers.* Bloody and savage fighting occurred everywhere as the Germans entered Rigeault. Many American paratroopers fixed bayonets on their rifles and violently charged the attacking Germans as a last resort to save their lives and fend off the enemy. The tactic was brave, but futile. None of Wade's men would surrender, as they knew they would be given no quarter by *Waffen-SS* troops!

Fires raged from burning buildings, while explosions and gunfire rocked what remained of the tiny village. Wade and Hank led their ragtag group of paratroopers through the streets amidst the chaos and past the blown-out buildings, using whatever they could for cover, while desperately trying to keep the advancing Germans back. Those still with ammunition fell to the rear, providing covering fire that allowed those carrying empty weapons a chance to get farther away unharmed. The armed paratroopers took up positions amidst the rubble and set ambushes for the Germans trying to navigate the cratered and rubble-strewn streets. The Americans would strike, then strategically fall back, following in the general direction of the retreat. The tactic worked and bought time for everyone to escape.

"This way!" shouted Wade, who could now see the flooded marshes lying on the outskirts of Rigeault's northern border.

"Look out!" shouted Hank, pushing Wade aside and firing a burst from his machine gun. His fire cut down two *Panzergrenadiers* about to toss their Model 24 stick grenades into Wade's group. The captain turned to Hank with a stunned look of gratitude.

"Keep moving! Displace!" the captain yelled. The leaders of the group finally escaped the congested chaos of the narrow village streets and crossed an open field that led them directly to the edge of the marshes. The water seemed to stretch for miles in all directions, shallow in some spots and very deep in others. There was no other way to go but through the marsh. Wade turned and looked back at his men fighting hand-to-hand with the Germans, using knives, bayonets, and even their helmets. They were being pushed to the brink.

"I wonder if this is what Custer felt like," said Wade as he looked at Hank and raised his Thompson.

Hank did the same and gave the captain a nod before saying, "Welcome to the Little Big Horn, sir."

With that, both men cried out and charged toward the action with reckless abandon.

Suddenly a massive roar was heard overhead, followed by a thunderous boom. Wade and Hank froze in their tracks and looked skyward, catching a glimpse of a glorious sight slicing through the air. Two big beautiful silver P-51D Mustangs bearing black-and-white invasion stripes on their undersides dropped down out of the heavens, releasing bombs on the German positions! Massive explosions caught the Germans off guard and forced them to stop dead in their tracks and look for cover.

"C'mon! Get out of here! Move it! Move it!" commanded Wade while madly waving his men across the field to the edge of the marsh. The Americans made a dash for it, just before the Mustangs winged over and came back around. The paratroopers out in the open wisely hit the deck, as they knew what was about to happen! The pilots flying the Mustangs cut loose their six Browning .50 caliber machine guns and strafed everything that moved on the ground. The Germans made easy targets as they scampered back toward Rigeault looking for cover. The Mustangs roared overhead, ripping the *Panzergrenadiers* to pieces with multiple strafing runs. Having pinned down and eliminated most of the *Waffen-SS* troops on the ground, the Mustangs quickly moved on to bigger, juicier targets. Suddenly free from the German troop threat, the remaining American paratroopers scrambled to their feet and formed a group at the edge of the marsh.

Hank continued to scan the skies watching for the beautiful fighters that had saved them all from certain death. He listened hard and heard more thunderous explosions to the south. Overhead another pair of fighters emerged, this time Republic P-47 Thunderbolts also bearing black-and-white invasion stripes. They, too, headed southward.

"They're going after the German armor!" shouted Hank excitedly. Though none of them could see it, the mighty American warplanes pounded the German armor south of Rigeault. All the 88mm artillery guns, the armored *Sonderkraftfahrzeug* half-tracks, the operational *StuG IV* assault gun, and all the trucks and motorcycles of the mechanized *17th SS Panzergrenadier Division Götz von Berlichingen* were blown sky high by the marauding fighters. After the planes were through, all that remained were scattered pockets of shocked, disorganized German *Waffen-SS* troops climbing out of the ruins of the decimated village!

The day was slipping by quickly and night would soon be upon France once again. Realizing this, and not knowing where the Germans would strike next or when, Captain Wade led his surviving band of paratroopers into the marsh, followed by a small group of villagers who feared returning to Rigeault. Wade made a quick head count. He had twenty-eight of the eighty-six paratroopers left with him and about fifteen villagers. He didn't know how many of his men left behind in the village were dead and how many were wounded. He led the way, slogging through the marsh in mostly chest-deep water.

Chapter 24

NEARING THE END

"We slogged our way through those damn marshes all night," said Hank, looking over at Matt Switzer on the sofa. It was now evening in Bar Harbor, and the old man slowly rose from his chair to click on a lamp. The fire had died down again, prompting Hank to open the wood stove and poke around at the coals until they glowed a dark red. He dumped a fresh log on the fire that soon flared up and brought life back to the hearth.

"Chest deep in water and couldn't see a damn thing in front of ya," continued Hank as he eased back into his chair. He looked outside at the still gloomy, wet Maine weather that reminded him of his ordeal that night back in France. "I couldn't stand it," he said, adding, "There were threatening sounds all around us. We were cold, wet, filthy, and unsure of where we were going. Captain Wade led the way, and eventually, by the grace of God, I believe, we got across the marshes and stepped foot on solid ground. By daybreak we stumbled upon a patrol of men from the 506th PIR of the 101st Airborne. Captain Wade knew most of them, even though he was from a different regiment, and heartily shook each and every one of their hands. God, he was so relieved to see them!"

"So what happened next?" asked Matt. "Was that the end of things pretty much?"

"Well, it sorta was for me and the French civilians for the most part," Hank answered, tapping his finger on the armrest of his chair. "You see, we were all taken to a spot where the paratroopers had set up a sort of collection point and command station inside another village they had liberated. We were fed and looked after. Things were still so chaotic that I wasn't even treated like a prisoner anymore. I was considered just another French refugee and wasn't paid much attention to. I wasn't a fool, though. I stayed as close as possible to Captain Wade at all times. I figured he was the only one who could help me. Late in the day a major from the 506th took Wade aside. He brought him into this bombed-out house, sat him down, and debriefed him thoroughly. I casually sat outside under a blown-out window and listened to their whole conversation undetected. I wanted to know exactly what Wade was telling this major about me."

"What did you overhear?" asked Matt anxiously.

"I heard a lot," said Hank. "Captain Wade musta talked for two straight hours. He told that major everything that happened in that little French town called Rigeault from the second we first arrived to the moment we got out of those damn marshes. I was amazed at the detail he gave that officer. He talked about the meeting at the church and how the villagers were so cooperative and brave in helping recover equipment. He talked meticulously about his men—Parker, Mills, Collins, Taylor, and others like Rioux and the mayor ... ahhh ... Durant—and how they followed his orders and how brave and helpful they were during combat facing incredible odds. He described the battle in detail as he saw it unfold from the bell tower and from the constant reports he got from his officers and men. He went on to personally extoll the efforts and bravery of a Lieutenant Riley whom he felt deserved the highest praise for his conduct and discipline during the battle. He felt if it weren't for Riley's actions, both as a fighter and as a courier of vital information about the enemy's strength and movements, all would have been lost. He went over casualty figures and constantly urged the major to send forces back to the village to recover wounded he was forced to leave behind in a schoolhouse. I could tell this upset him, but according to what I heard the major say, there was nothing that could have been done at that time."

"Wow, what happened next? Did Wade go back to Rigeault for his wounded?" asked Matt.

"No, Captain Wade and his men got their orders and joined the assault on the nearby town of Carentan. There was heavy fighting on June 10 and 11. The 101st Airborne Division entered the town on June 12, and basically mopped up what was left of the German defenders.

They were part of the 6th *Fallschirmjäger* Regiment, I think," pondered Hank for a moment. "A German paratrooper force," he added.

"Me and the rest of the refugees were taken into Carentan and put under the guidance and care of the 101st Airborne and the U.S. 2nd Armored Division, which was also in the area and helped take apart the advancing Germans at a place dubbed Bloody Gulch near Carentan. Look that one up, too," instructed Hank.

Matt wrote down all the information in his notebook, then paused to ask a question.

"Hank, what happened to Rigeault after the attack? Was the village destroyed? Did the *Panzergrenadiers* reoccupy it? Do you know what happened after you left?"

Hank thought a moment, then answered, "I really don't, Matt. I never heard anything about it again after I got back home."

Hank sat back and reflected for a moment. Matt didn't say anything as he could see Hank was feeling uncomfortable. The old man looked away and then spoke again.

"I can say this, if the Nazis did reoccupy the village and they found that aid station, it's almost certain they killed every last wounded paratrooper they found there. Quite possibly they lined up a good many French locals and killed them, too, for helping those wounded men. God only knows how many innocent souls suffered through that unimaginable situation. Wade lost fifty-eight paratroopers, either killed or wounded, in Rigeault. It was estimated the 17th SS *Panzergrenadier* Division lost upwards of four hundred men during the assault. I did some research on the battle many years later."

Hank dipped his head and bit his lip. Matt could see the strain on his face as he fought back the tears. He remained quiet and waited for the old man to compose himself.

"Sometimes I imagine that those Mustangs and Thunderbolts that swooped down out of the sky and saved us that day drove the Germans off for good. Or maybe they killed them all? I pray that American ground forces got there in time to help as well … before any mass Nazi reprisals against the French. I just don't know … I just don't know whatever became of that small French village. I hope it's still there today. I really do," he said, choking back the tears in his eyes and the lump in his throat.

Matt felt for the old man and found himself a little choked up, too. He didn't know what to say next. He felt as if he should try to comfort Hank. But what could he say? He wasn't there, and he couldn't fully understand his pain. Words seemed meaningless.

After moments of awkward silence, Hank broke the tension. "I guess you probably want to know what happened next?"

"Well, I was kinda wondering ... yeah," Matt said weakly.

"I was kept in Carentan for days with the American occupation force there. Captain Wade told the major everything he knew about Steinert and me and our curious situation. I assume Wade turned over Steinert's identity papers. I heard Wade tell the major everything that was discussed during Steinert's interrogation. It gave me no more insight as to his true identity, however. Fortunately I had proof of mine. I still had my dog tags. Wade made sure of that. Basically I was treated like a downed Allied pilot—which of course I was—but I didn't have the freedom of movement I expected. I wasn't under guard, but there was always an armed soldier near me who never let me out of his sight. Days went by, and as the Allied forces solidified their Normandy beachhead, I got transferred from place to place, not ever really knowing where I was or why I was there. Most of the time I had hot food, an occasional shower, and a bed to sleep in. I was happy as a clam. Of course, the war continued and eventually I was taken to an Allied command center right on the coast of the landing zone, codenamed Omaha Beach. That was where our soldiers took the most casualties after hitting the beach on D-Day. The Germans had a well-trained and equipped infantry division there called the 352nd. They were a tough nut to crack, but our boys got 'em!"

Hank reflected again, then continued, describing the sights around Omaha Beach.

"I had never in my life seen so many ships! They were constantly offloading supplies, men, Sherman tanks, trucks from Ford, Chrysler, and General Motors, fuel, ammunition, guns, and everything else a man could imagine! The trucks rolled on endlessly, delivering supplies up to the front lines. Overhead, there were always fighters providing air cover.

That's where I wanted to be, I tell ya!"

"So what happened while you were at Omaha Beach?" asked Matt as he continued to take down notes.

"They kept me there for a long time," Hank said in an agitated tone. "I was questioned by numerous officers. One by one, they paraded in front of me. Some were pleasant, while others were real sons-a-bitches! No matter what their demeanor was, though, they all asked the same goddamn questions over and over again! I told them everything I could recall. I told them the truth! I gave them every detail I could, yet nothing was ever good enough. I wasn't free, so to speak. I became a prisoner of my own army."

"So what did you do?" asked Matt.

"What could I do?" responded Hank. "I was detained for a long time. The troops got bogged down in the hedgerow country of Normandy and put together a plan called Operation Cobra. It commenced July 25, which happened to be the same day I was put on a ship back to England. Once there I was taken to an unknown airbase and questioned further. They threw everybody at me. I was questioned by uniformed officers of the USAAF and the RAF. I told them all about what had happened to me in France. I gave them every honest detail I could. The only thing I held back was the purpose of my mission, which was top secret. That little detail really set them off, but I never divulged what the mission was. Besides, I had a feeling they already knew everything, anyway. I was sure of it. They kept me there for weeks while they played their little games. They were particularly interested in my dealings with Steinert. A lot of demanding questions revolved around him."

"Did they really interrogate you hard? Was it painful?" asked Matt sheepishly.

"No, it was nothing like that," Hank said with a little chuckle. "They didn't rough me up or anything. In fact, what happened next was kinda strange and enjoyable, believe it or not. One day I was met by a full-bird colonel, who told me he was sorry I had been so badly inconvenienced and that I would be integrated into a new 9th Air Force fighter group as soon as he could arrange it. In the meantime, he told me I was granted extended liberty for my invaluable service. I knew he was full of shit, but what could I say? He was a colonel and I was just a lieutenant, right?"

"So what happened next?"

"I was given a sharp new uniform and some money. They gave me both British pounds and American dollars. I was put on a bus to London, where I checked into a nice hotel and did some sightseeing. It was really strange sightseeing in London where the *Luftwaffe* had done so much damage, but I managed to get around okay. The people were generally pleasant and upbeat, even after all they had endured. After a while I noticed men in plain clothes were following me. Their suits were easy to spot and they stayed with me everywhere I went, trying to go unnoticed. I never could lose them, and I really never tried to. They followed me into every shop, theater, and tavern. Even though I knew what was happening and the presence of those agents, or whoever the hell they were, bothered me, my mind was still only on one thing and one thing only."

Matt sat back and knew instantly what Hank was referring to. He purposely stayed away from the subject, out of respect, but secretly desired to know more about it. He would let Hank bring it up and discuss it—when he was ready.

"When my liberty was up," Hank said, "I was conveniently picked up at my hotel by MPs in a jeep and brought back to that airbase. Next I was put in front of a General What's-his-face and told my 'testimony,' as he put it, had been thoroughly reviewed and I was hereby ordered never to speak of it again. I was ordered never to talk about what happened in France or anything at all pertaining to the time frame just before and after I was shot down. And you know what, Matt? I never did ... until now."

Silenced ensued. Matt didn't know what to say. He had sensed he was hearing something important from the first time Hank started to speak days earlier, but he'd been either too ignorant or immature to understand just how important Hank's story really was! A sense of privilege swept over Matt like a wave over the bow of a ship in a storm. He couldn't believe that in fifty-six years, Hank had never told anybody what he had just heard. He felt honored and a bit wiser.

Hank adjusted his glasses after rubbing his tired eyes with his wrinkly hands. He coughed, then looked as if he still had more to tell. He could see he had really reached Matt Switzer and hoped the recollection of his war years had added to his knowledge and maturity.

"That general promoted me to captain right there on the spot," relayed Hank. "He then told me that I was going to be reassigned to an Air Force pilot training program back in the States. I was to become a flight instructor at a base in California. I respectfully protested and requested another combat assignment with the 9th Air Force. The last thing I wanted to do was go home and be an instructor, confined behind some damn desk!"

"What did they say?" asked Matt.

"They said that since I'd been shot down, I couldn't be sent back into combat over Europe. The risk was too great. They didn't want me to be shot down again and recaptured. They claimed I had suffered enough and my services were needed elsewhere. In all fairness, it was common practice in the Army Air Force not to send recovered, downed airmen back into combat. I reluctantly saluted the general, accepted my promotion, and took my new assignment. A week later I was flown back to Washington, D.C., where I was yet again questioned about my little adventure in France. This time, however, it wasn't a bunch of uniformed brass hats doing the questioning; rather, it was a bunch of suited agents from the FBI. They eventually got what they wanted from me, and I was then free to report to my next post, which was an airbase in the southern California desert called Muroc Army Airfield. It later was renamed Edwards Air Force Base."

"I've heard of that place before," said Matt confidently. "Didn't the space shuttle land there years ago, or something?"

"Yes. And I'm not surprised you've heard of it. A lot of experimental aircraft were tested out there. Look it up when you get back to Orono. And look up a man named Chuck Yeager. You'll be impressed by what you read about him."

"Yeah, I will," said Matt as he wrote down Yeager's name.

"Anyway, I became a flight instructor at Muroc Army Airfield. The Boeing Stearman Model 75 biplane was our primary trainer for those just starting out. Later on I trained men how to fly fighters like the P-47 Thunderbolt, the P-39 Airacobra, the P-40 Warhawk, and, of course, the P-51 Mustang, which was my favorite. I myself became a test pilot for some of America's first jet-powered fighters like the Lockheed P-80 Shooting Star. So that's where I spent the rest of the war. I was honorably discharged in early 1946."

"Where did you originally learn how to fly, Hank?" Matt asked curiously.

"Oh, I got interested in planes as a little kid. When I was ten, I used to bug this guy who had an old World War I surplus Curtiss JN-4 Jenny biplane he had converted into a crop duster. He owned a lot of open farmland and he used to take me up flying with him. Well, after a while he began to teach me how to fly the thing. Turns out I picked it up rather quickly. I had the knack for that sort of thing. As I got older, I used to fly it solo. He let me fly it as a reward for helping him do chores and such. He was a kind man and a World War I veteran, too. He flew in the Great War."

"When did you know you wanted to join the military? Did you always want to be a fighter pilot?" Matt asked curiously.

"Well, that's another sad story, Matt, but I'll tell ya about it because I feel it's important," Hank said with a sigh. The old man sat back comfortably and slowly closed his eyes. Matt watched and listened, fearing that Hank was about to take him back to a place that was very painful once again. This time the year was 1936, when Hank Mitchell was a mere teenager.

The eighteen-year-old boy slowly walked through the Maine woods, cutting across apple orchards and grassy fields on his way home from a disappointing day at school. It was late October and the air was crisp. The fallen leaves rustled and crunched loudly underfoot, as the sun slowly dipped toward the horizon, lighting up the sky with beautiful red-and-orange clouds that matched the brilliant colors of the fall leaves on the ground. The trees were mostly bare, giving the woods a creepy feel. The daylight was dwindling fast, and Hank Mitchell knew he needed to get home without further delay.

He walked slowly, with his head down, watching his feet trample the well-worn path that cut through the woods leading to his house. He felt depressed and he wanted to drop the schoolbooks he was carrying and simply crumple to the ground in despair. He didn't, though. Perhaps he felt it was more important to get home safely, lest his mother worry. Or perhaps it was a bit of uneasiness caused by the eerie woods with night quickly approaching. The young Hank's active imagination would often be fueled by his surroundings, especially when he was alone in a peculiar place. As Hank continued to stagger along through the woods, he imagined himself as the fictional character Ichabod Crane, nervously traveling home with dreadful thoughts of the terrifying Headless Horseman appearing to challenge him! It was a scary thought for a very young man with an overactive imagination, but it kept his mind off his real problems.

Hank emerged from the woods and crossed a vast apple orchard leading to a road. After following the road a bit, he arrived at his residence in Cape Elizabeth, Maine. He glumly walked up the long driveway and saw his father working on the family car—a black, 1930 Model A Ford. His father looked up from under the hood and watched his son walk up the driveway. He could tell something was wrong and put down the wrench in his greasy hands. He picked up a rag and tried to wipe away most of the filth, but it did little good. His white shirt and black suspenders were covered in grease. His forearms, exposed by his rolled-up sleeves, were also blackened from engine grime. He wiped the sweat from his face and stuffed the rag in the back pocket of his tan trousers.

"Kinda late this evening, ain't ya, son? Mother was getting worried. I saw her looking out the window for ya. Were ya off flying again?"

"No, sir," Hank said gloomily, with his head down and his shoulders slumped forward.

"Well, where ya been, Hank? Is something wrong? You look kinda sour. Something bad happen at school today?"

"Dad, what's wrong with me?"

"Whaddaya mean, son?"

"I mean, what's wrong with me? I'm pleasant to everybody I meet at school. I study hard and never fool around in class. I pay attention and always try to do my best. I always help other kids, and I treat every girl I meet with class and respect."

"I know that, son. You're a good boy, and I'm proud of you. What's this about?"

Hank sighed and leaned up against the Model A.

"Well, the Harvest Moon dance is this Friday night. I asked Ashley Libby if she might like to go with me. We're decent friends. I talk to her a lot in class, and we laugh a lot together. We have common interests and …"

Hank's voice trailed off. His father patted him on the shoulder. He knew where the conversation was going.

"I waited until after school and wanted to walk her home. She said that was okay and we started walking. I was kinda excited and just came right out and asked her if she would go to the dance with me. She stopped and gave me this weird look. I didn't know what to make of it at first. She paused for a second and declined the invitation. She told me she thought I was real nice, but that she wasn't interested in dating me. Before I could even ask her why she didn't like me, she told me she had to hurry home, then took off, just leaving me where I stood!"

"I'm sorry, son, that was kinda mean of her. Not very becoming of a young lady, if ya ask me," said Hank's father.

"I don't know what to do anymore, Dad," said Hank, his voice choking up. "I'm as nice as I can be, but that just doesn't matter. The girls must see me as plain, ugly, and boring. I ain't got nothing the girls like. I don't have any money, or fancy clothes, or a car. I just feel like a fool. All I wanted to do was take a girl I like to a crummy dance! It's not like I'm asking for too much, is it?" Tears started to well up in Hank's eyes.

"I understand you're unhappy, Hank," his father said, "and I know what it feels like to be hurt by a young lady who ya got feelings for. But you can't dwell on it, son. You have to accept it and move forward."

"I know, Dad, but this seems to happen to me all the time. Am I that undesirable? Do I deserve to have my feelings crushed every time I want to court a girl? I don't understand what's wrong with me."

"Nothing is wrong with you, Hank. You're a good son, and ya treat people with dignity and respect. You conduct yourself like a bright young man should, and I'm always impressed with your attitude and work ethic. You're ambitious and your love of flying is a positive thing. I'll bet Ashley Libby would change her mind about you if you took her up flying."

"I can't even get her to go to a dance with me. What makes you think she'd want to ride in an old biplane?"

"Don't let it bother you, son," sighed Hank's father. "You take things awful hard sometimes. You got a big heart and you make good decisions. Use that brain of yours. There are lots of other girls out there. Someday soon you'll find the right one and realize she was worth the wait. Trust me on that."

"It just hurts Dad."

"I know it does, Hank. No man likes to feel rejected. But we all do at certain times in our lives. Your mother turned me down several times before we eventually started going together. Bet you didn't know that!"

"No, I didn't," replied Hank.

"Sure she did. But I kept my head up. Over time she saw me for the person I really was on the inside, where it counts." Hank's father turned and faced his son, who was still visibly upset. "Henry, never let anybody change who you are and never let nobody tell you you're not good enough—man or woman. You follow your heart and your conscience and you'll never go wrong. And never give up. That doesn't just mean girls, either. Never give up on anything in life. Do that and I'll always be proud of ya. Someday I know you're gonna be a great pilot and have a career in aviation. You're gonna meet a great girl, get married, and have lots of kids. And I'm gonna be a grandpa," he said with a smile.

"Howard, send Henry inside, please! I need some help in the kitchen," shouted a woman's voice from an open window.

"Okay, Marilyn. He'll be right in," Hank's father replied.

"Better get on up to the house. I gotta wrench on this old Ford a bit more before it gets too dark."

"Thanks, Dad," said Hank as he gave his father a hug. "I'm glad we talked."

"Ayuh, that's okay, son. Now go help your mother. Oh, and speaking of help, I need your help on Saturday, clearing out some debris and fallen trees in the orchards. You available?"

"Well, I don't have a date with a girl, so I guess I'll have to settle for helping you," Hank said sarcastically.

"Don't start that again! Now go on and let me finish up with the car," said Howard, putting his head under the hood and wrenching hard on the engine. "She's been runnin' funny and I don't want her to quit on me out on the road tomorrow."

Hank started to walk toward the house. Behind him his father tried to loosen a stubborn, rusted bolt on the engine block. He wrenched on it with a powerful turn that strained his body beyond its limits. Howard let out sharp cry of pain, then slowly crumpled to the ground cradling his right arm with his left.

Hank turned around and raced back to his father. One side of his father's body was completely limp while the other trembled uncontrollably. He cradled his head in his arms, frantically asking, "What's wrong?"

"Son!" his father called out in a strained and broken voice that sounded strange to Hank's ears, "Remember what I said! I'm proud of you! I always will be!"

Seconds later the trembling stopped, and Howard Mitchell slipped away, dying in his son's arms. Hank tried to bring his father back, but could neither say nor do anything that helped.

"Dad, don't leave me!" Hank cried out, "Please come back!" But it was too late. He started to sob as he pulled his father's face close to his chest. A moment later he heard his mother scream and race outside. The two wept together, not being able to fathom what had happened, or why. Howard Mitchell was gone forever.

"*The doctors that examined* him later said a blood vessel burst in his brain. My father died of a stroke in my arms when I was eighteen years old on that day in October 1936," Hank said to Matt as he sullenly finished his story.

"My God," said Matt, "I had no idea. You mentioned your dad's death once before, but I never realized how he died and that you were right there! I'm so sorry you had to go through that."

Hank continued, "It was tough on both my mother and me at first. We owned a large piece of farmland and an apple orchard that my father worked on a good part of his life. He was mostly a farmer, and we sold a lot of the produce we grew on our farm, but apples were the biggest part of his income. We grew corn and strawberries and all sorts of other fruits and vegetables. My father had to hire extra help at harvest time, as you could understand. I, of course, helped out considerably as a boy."

"Did your business survive?"

"Yes, but it was a terrible struggle after my father died. I had ambitions to go to college, and my heart wasn't in becoming a full-time farmer," confessed Hank. "My mother realized this and sold a lot of our land, keeping only the acres needed to sustain a much smaller operation. It was hard on both of us, but we managed, and I did go to college."

"Was that when you realized you wanted to be a professional pilot?"

Hank wrinkled his brow and clasped his hands together near his face as he pondered the question. After a moment of reflection he gave his answer.

"When my father died, I had a deep feeling of urgency within me. That feeling made me want to go after and accomplish everything I wanted in life," Hank professed. "I knew he wanted me to go to college, and I knew he was always pleased and excited about my flying. That brought him some sort of joy I could never explain, because as far as I knew, he had never been up in a plane his whole life. I guess it was around that time when I figured I wanted to be a pilot. Ya gotta remember, Matt, airplanes in those days were still considered a new, emerging technology, with massive potential for growth in the field of aviation. It was a smart move, I thought, and a good way to help support my mother."

"Where did you go to college?"

"I got a scholarship to UMO, the very same school you're attending now," said Hank proudly. I studied Aeronautical Engineering and graduated with a degree in that field."

"So you got a job as a pilot, or something, after you graduated?"

"No … I'm getting to that. Be patient and let me explain things, Matt," said Hank. "When I graduated, it was the spring of 1940. World War II had already started, and Hitler's tanks were rolling all over Europe, while the Japanese were violently expanding their empire in Southeast Asia. The United States declared neutrality and wasn't officially involved in the war, although we were secretly and openly helping the British and the Chinese. At the time, people thought differently about the military. It was more of an honor to be in the service back in those days. People realized that war was coming and their lives would be affected in one way or another. Men eagerly looked to join up, even before Pearl Harbor. I made a decision to do my part, as well, and join the Army Air Corps. In order to do that, I had to have some college under my belt, be at least twenty, and be single. Well, by 1940, I had all those bases covered. One last major hurdle I had to overcome was to join the Civilian Pilot Training Program."

"What was that?" asked Matt.

"It was a government-sponsored flight training program put together to increase the number of qualified pilots in the country," Hank answered. "You see, countries all over the world were trying to build up their air forces in anticipation of war. Nations who control the skies control the battlefield, you understand. Roosevelt knew that America had to increase the number of trained pilots, too. The Civilian Pilot Training Program was set up around college campuses to encourage students to learn how to fly. By that time, I had decided I wanted to be a military aviator. Specifically, I wanted to be a fighter pilot."

"So it was then that you knew what you wanted to be and where you wanted to go?" asked Matt, furiously taking notes.

"Yes. You could say that," replied Hank. "I successfully completed the CPTP and enrolled in the United States Army Air Corps in late 1941, not long before the Japs hit us at Pearl Harbor."

Hank rose out of his chair and stretched his tired back. He looked outside at the chilly, overcast sky and silently cursed the long stretch of inclement weather that was putting a damper on spring.

"Ya want something to eat? A snack or a beverage? I need a little something from the kitchen," he proclaimed.

"Yeah, sure, Hank," Matt said, "Whatever you have will be fine," he added while organizing a pile of written notes and changing the microcassette in his recorder.

"Okay, then," Hank replied as he shuffled down to the kitchen.

Matt took a moment and stood up to stretch. He warmed himself by the stove and looked at Hank's fascinating painting of the epic dogfight between the Mustang and the *Focke-Wulf*. As he studied the painting, his eyes were drawn to the framed photographs on the mantel below it. Matt picked one up—a color photograph of a young man in uniform, posing in front of an American flag. Matt looked closer and deduced it was a U.S. Marine, dress-blue uniform.

Matt put the picture down and looked at another. This one was of a young woman dressed in a colorful and outlandish outfit that reminded Matt of a 1960s hippie. The last picture was a family photo. He held it up and looked at it closely. It seemed relatively old, but was in very good shape.

"That's a picture of me and my family."

Matt turned to see Hank place a tray of tuna fish sandwiches and potato chips on the coffee table in front of the sofa.

"Help yourself," said Hank, nibbling on a sandwich and picking at some chips. "Here, let me see that picture."

"Here you go," said Matt. "Who are the other folks standing in front of you?"

Hank swallowed a bite of sandwich, then answered, "The woman by me was my wife, Karen. The young woman is my daughter, Brittany, and the young man was my son, Thomas."

Matt picked up on Hank's usage of the past tense. His mind wandered back to France at the mention of Hank's wife. He wanted to ask his elder friend a question or two pertaining to a certain individual, but decided not to pry. Both sat down in their places and paused to eat. After some time had passed and bellies were filled, Matt decided to be brave and ask a little more about Hank's family.

"Do you mind telling me a little bit more about your family, Hank? I feel as if I don't know anything about them. You told me a little about your mother and father. What about your own family?"

"Okay," said Hank. "I met my wife, Karen, at a train station in Portland. I was given some liberty and decided to fly home to visit my mother back in Cape Elizabeth. I flew from California to Boston, where I took a train up to Portland. It was a very special date. When I got to Boston it was May 8, 1945. People were celebrating in the streets everywhere, it seemed. The war was coming to a close, because Germany had formally surrendered. I got on the train and rode up to Portland. When I got off, people were celebrating on the platform. They were just jumping up and down hugging and kissing one another. I was in my captain's uniform and noticed this attractive young woman standing by herself on the platform. We looked at each other and she smiled at me. I walked over to her, took her in my arms and kissed her hard on the mouth. I don't know why I did it, I just did. I guess I got caught up in the moment. It was a momentous time. That God-awful war in Europe was finally over!"

"Wow, what did she do? Did she slap you or something after you kissed her?" Matt asked.

"Nope, she smiled again and I said, 'We did it, we really did it. We stopped those Nazis from spreading their poisonous ideology all over the world. Thank God!'"

"Then what happened?" asked Matt with a little smirk.

"Well, after proper introductions were made, she told me she was waiting for a girlfriend to meet her at the station. Apparently she worked nearby. The friend never showed, so I took her to dinner that evening. We talked and became acquainted with one another. She lived in Portland, and I saw her several times while on liberty. I spent most of my time with my mother and the remainder with her. When I reported back to my post in California, we wrote letters to one another almost every day. We fell in love. After I was honorably discharged from the Army Air Force in early 1946, I went back to Maine and married her."

"Hmm, that's a nice story," Matt said. "What about your kids?"

"Thomas was born in 1947. Brittany was born in 1950. They were both wonderful, well-adjusted kids who had a very peaceful and happy childhood during the 1950s. My family and I were living in Portland at the time. With my military days behind me, I became a flight instructor at the Portland-Westbrook Municipal Airport. You know it now as the Portland Jetport."

"That's interesting, Hank. You no longer had any interest in military aviation?" Matt asked.

"I was done with war. I had endured so much, seen too much, and killed too many. I wanted no part of war ever again. Ironically, though, I was approached by the United States Air Force in 1951, by then a completely separate and independent branch of the military, no longer just a part of the army. They wanted me to join up again and train to fly F-86 Saber jets. We were embroiled in the Korean War at that time. I refused. I had a wife and kids and was through with war. Besides, there were other things going on … "

Matt noticed how Hank's last sentence trailed off, indicating it was something he didn't necessarily want to talk about. The young student, ready to listen, decided he would tactfully press the issue.

"What other things, Hank?" he asked.

Hank sighed softly. At times he regretted telling Matt as much as he had. He realized that there was little he could hold back now. The truth was powerful and sometimes painful. He had known that for a long time now. He began to explain.

"Remember when I told you earlier about being observed and followed while in London?" asked Hank.

"Yes," replied Matt. "You thought they were agents of some sort, right?"

"Yeah, they were," said Hank, "and I received a lot of the same treatment when I got home."

"What do you mean, Hank?"

"After leaving Washington, D.C., on my way to California, I began to notice that I was still being followed. It seemed that no matter where I went, one or two guys wearing suits and hats were always nearby. It didn't matter if I was in civilian clothes or uniform, I was always being casually observed by somebody."

"Who were they, Hank? What did they want? Why were they following you?" asked Matt like a boy wrapped up in a good detective novel.

"Government men—CIA, FBI. I was never really sure, but I knew it had to be one of those intelligence organizations. They watched me all throughout the 1950s."

"What did you do about it?"

"There was really nothing I could do, Matt," Hank said. "You have to understand that things were different in those days. Ya couldn't just come out and challenge everything and say whatever you want like people do today. America was not the boiling cauldron of political correctness that we live in today," Hank said, rolling his eyes. "You had to watch what you said and, more importantly, watch what you did in those days. Some things you just couldn't do without serious repercussions. I wasn't going to risk the good reputation or the safety of my family by openly challenging forces I didn't comprehend. I was a military man, and I knew how to follow orders and fight, but I wasn't prepared to take on the American government and its law enforcement."

Hank popped a few more potato chips into his mouth followed by a quick swig of water.

"Besides, I was never harassed or threatened. I decided that as long as I followed orders and never discussed what had happened to me in France during the war, that my family and I would be okay. I never fully knew why I was being watched, but I always figured it was because of that one top-secret mission and my ordeal in the short weeks leading up to D-Day."

"What was the issue?" Matt inquired. "What did they think you'd reveal? What was the threat?"

"I don't know, Matt," Hank responded. "The military is funny at times. They have a tendency to make up problems that don't really exist, while creating imaginary enemies at the same time. Keeps them in business, I suppose."

"So, how did you handle it?"

"I was a good citizen. I followed my orders and ignored the surveillance as best I could. I just basically lived my life like I would've, even if they hadn't been there. Fortunately nothing ever came of it, and by the early 1960s I noticed they had moved on to more important matters, because the surveillance had ended. I wasn't being followed anymore."

"So things were good after that? Tell me about your son and daughter," requested Matt.

"We had a good, normal life in the 1950s. I enjoyed my work at the airport and was given the opportunity to learn to fly multi-engine planes. Into the 1960s, though, things started to change. I took a job with

TWA as an airline pilot. I had to learn to fly multi-engine jet planes, which kept me away from home for long stretches. It put a strain on my relationship with my wife and kids. For a long time I wasn't home a lot. When I became an airline pilot, I was flying all over the country all the time. For a while I hardly ever got to see my family. I put my passion for flying above the needs of my family. Before I knew it, they were all like strangers to me. By the late sixties, my son Thomas had become quite opinionated, politically. He had very conservative views and was pro-military, which I didn't mind at first, but soon realized was becoming a problem. He became embroiled in the situation over in Vietnam and decided he wanted to join the Marines, so he could fight and 'help preserve democracy from the clutches of communism,' as he liked to put it. He graduated from high school in 1965 and instantly enlisted in the United States Marine Corps, against my wishes."

"You didn't want him to serve in the armed forces?" Matt asked, puzzled. "I thought you'd be proud of a decision like that. Didn't he want to fly, too?"

"No, it was nothing like that!" Hank snapped back. "When I was home and had chances to talk to him about it, all we did was argue! He had some grand notion of marching off to war and serving his country like his father and uncle had in World War II. He had this overflowing and false sense of patriotism. He saw war as splendid and glorious and not what it really was—a horrific waste of life and precious resources. He wanted to march off behind a cause that I didn't agree with, and he always used the argument that my brother-in-law and I had done the same thing when we went to war. I tried to tell him that things were different in those days, and the threat was a lot different. In my day, the country was united and a real danger was evident. I had to remind him we had been attacked! We were attacked at Pearl Harbor by the Japanese while Hitler and his Nazis were conquering Europe. A legitimate threat to the free world existed from Imperial Japan and Nazi Germany. I told him we were fighting a different war, as a united nation for the right reasons!"

"How did your son respond to that?"

"He saw no difference between what happened in Europe in the

1940s and what was happening in Southeast Asia in the 1960s. He simply substituted the spread of communism for fascism and Ho Chi Minh for Hitler. There was nothing I could say or do to convince him of the mistake he was making. He had it in his mind that our involvement in Vietnam was just and righteous. He didn't want to hear that it was *just* a civil war between the north and south, and he didn't want to hear that we had no right interfering in a conflict that would cost American lives. His mind was made up. He wanted to enlist and he wanted to be a Marine. He had no interest in flying. He wanted infantry … God, did he want infantry. Nothing else could compare. Nothing else was good enough. I told him that killing a man face to face was a lot different than a fighter plane shooting down another fighter plane. He knew of the nightmares I had, but that didn't sway him one way or another. Against my wishes, he enlisted in the Marines just after he graduated high school. He went through basic training and was sent to Vietnam. He was killed when his platoon got ambushed by the Viet Cong during a routine patrol in the jungle. That was in 1967. He was only twenty years old!"

"I'm sorry Hank. I don't know what to say. I didn't want to … "

Hank interrupted, "It was a long time ago, Matt. I do have a lot of good memories of my boy. I only wish he were still with us today. You would have liked talking to him. He was actually quite a bright and funny young man—when he wasn't talking politics. I miss him very much."

"What about your daughter, Hank? Was she like your son, too?"

"Good Lord, no!" exclaimed Hank with a sarcastic laugh. "Brittany and Thomas couldn't have been more different. Britt took a totally different view of life in the 1960s. She had more radical and liberal views. She was against anything to do with the military or mainstream America. As she grew into her teen years, she became very rebellious and outspoken. She was a peace activist who opposed all involvement in Vietnam, even while her brother was still alive and fighting over there. His death only strengthened her anti-war convictions. She wore crazy clothing and went on protest marches wherever she could find them. She eventually became a full-blown hippie. She dropped out of high school and left home one day to ride across the country in some damn 'freedom bus.' Her mother and I didn't know of her whereabouts for several weeks until one day she sent us a postcard from San Francisco. We couldn't fathom what she was doing out there, and we really didn't want to know," said Hank sadly.

"What happened to her?" Matt wondered aloud.

"Well, fortunately nothing too serious. We heard from her from time to time, and as the years went by she grew out of the hippie phase and straightened out her life. In the late 1970s she married a nice, successful man named Michael Kessler, who did a lot for her and showed her how wonderful life can be. They had a daughter named Michelle. I believe you know who she is? Right?"

Matt smiled at the mention of Michelle. "Yeah, I know Michelle. I think she's great. I like her a lot," said Matt, trying to conceal his growing feelings for Hank's granddaughter.

"You ought to like 'er," said Hank confidently. "She's a marvelous young lady with a good head on her shoulders. She's kind and caring and goes after what she wants in life. I love spending time with her, and I know she's going to be a success out in the real world. You should spend more time with her, boy. Some of her good characteristics might rub off on you!"

"Gee, Hank, I was thinking the same thing," Matt said, as lovely visions of Michelle danced through his mind. "If you don't mind my asking, what happened to your wife, Hank?"

"We divorced in 1970. The death of Thomas, Brittany leaving home, and my absence put her over the edge. I was never home. She was alone all the time. She couldn't handle it. We fought a lot and eventually decided to get divorced. When it became official, she kept the house in Portland and I moved around the country wherever TWA wanted me to go. I became a 'company man' and flying was my life. I didn't care about anything else. It was a bad time, now that I think back on it. I eventually retired for good in 1983. I bounced around a while and wasn't in touch with my family at all.

I then learned through a friend that Karen had died of cancer. I returned to Maine to attend the funeral, which is where I reunited with Brittany and her new family. Michelle was just a little girl then, and it was the first time we had met. I moved back to Maine and stayed close to my daughter. We got to know each other again and reconciled our differences. For the first time in a long while, I had a family. In 1990, Brittany and her family moved to Bangor, and I moved to Bar Harbor. I've been here ever since. I'm close to my family, and that's all I care about now."

"That's a good thing, Hank. Sometimes I think we take our family for granted and we forget about the truly important things in life. Before you know it," Matt said quietly, "the things we really cherish the most are gone, and we regret not doing or saying things differently. I can relate to that, though I hate to admit it."

"You make a good point, Matt," said the old man. "Remember this, though: It's never too late to change things. People can change for the better. All it takes is a little courage and self-determination. Life can be hard, but it also can be wonderful. Ya just gotta go after what you desire most with a good, honest effort!"

"I think you're right, Hank. Talking with you has made me realize a few things about myself—particularly my academic career," Matt said as he gathered up and neatly organized his notes.

"Well, my young friend, where are we at now?" asked Hank as he realized it was getting late and Matt was picking up his stuff.

"I think I have enough material to utilize and research. I should be able to begin writing my paper. I have so many great ideas in my head that I can hardly wait to start. It's weird … I never wanted to sit and write a paper so badly in my whole life. Generally, I can't stand the idea of writing a research paper, but now I really feel enthusiastic, and I owe it to you, Hank," Matt confessed.

"Well, I'm glad you feel that way, Matt," replied Hank with a grin. "At first I thought you were another one of those kids who didn't take anything seriously and couldn't care less about life. But after talking with you these past couple days, I've come to realize you do have a good head on your shoulders and do genuinely respect others, which is very important to me. You're a lot more mature than I originally thought. It just took a while to get it outta ya."

"Thanks, Hank. I do respect you and all the hardships you've had to endure in life. It's truly remarkable. Thank you for sharing your difficult memories with me. I know it was hard, and I respect your courage. I mean that sincerely!"

Matt paused a moment, then couldn't hold back. He had to ask the question that he knew would pain Hank the most. He just couldn't leave without knowing what happened.

"Hank … I'm sorry. I just have to know. Did you ever find out what happened to Pauline LeBlanc?"

Hank's face instantly darkened and his shoulders sagged. He slumped back in his chair and silently stared at the fire for several minutes. Matt cringed, sensing he had finally crossed the line and damaged his new friendship. He didn't dare to speak or move.

Hank sighed heavily and his eyes welled up. Still staring at the fire, he mustered up all his remaining strength. "I never saw her again," he stated bluntly, biting his bottom lip to hold back the tears.

Matt searched for something supportive to say, or just an excuse to leave quickly and ease the situation. He looked helplessly at Hank and was sorry he ever asked the question.

"I tried to get anyone who would listen to help find a way to locate her. I pleaded this request over and over to every officer who questioned me. None of them wanted to hear it, though. All they cared about was that bastard Steinert and what I knew about him, and my contacts with any fool in an SS uniform! They never once showed a bit of compassion or concern regarding her plight! She was simply a name with a number on a piece of paper."

"You never found out what happened to her?" Matt asked meekly. "Not even a clue in the years after the war?"

"No, nothing. I prayed the German medics who took her away cared for her. I don't know how severe her wound was, but it was bad enough, I guess. If only I had kept my damn mouth shut that night!"

The tears started to flow down Hank's cheeks and for the first time, Matt got a real sense of how deeply the old fighter pilot loved her. Hank pulled out a handkerchief, wiped his eyes, and blew his nose before stuffing it back into his pocket.

"I prayed our troops overran the German positions where she was being treated and that she was brought into protective custody. I musta gone through a hundred different scenarios in my mind about how she could have been spared. Every vision I had ended happily, of course," Hank said, while shaking his head negatively. "I thought about her every day! I thought about all kinds of ways to try to find her, but there was always something or someone standing in my way. Once I left France I could never get back there to search for her! I had my good days and my bad days. At times I tried to forget her and I was fine, but then there were days when all I did was think about her and I could barely function. Though I never actually returned to France to search for her, I did make several inquiries as to her potential whereabouts in the form of letters to SHAEF. God, I even appealed to Eisenhower himself in a letter!"

"Did you ever get any responses or clues?"

"No. I don't think a single letter went through to its intended recipient. I think both American and English intelligence agencies like MI5, MI6, and the OSS intercepted and disposed of them. Remember, I was being heavily surveilled at that time. I had nowhere to turn for help. I prayed she would emerge one day and find me. She never did, though. Life goes on, Matthew Switzer. The war ended, I was reassigned, went home, got married … that's how it went. I never knew what happened to the woman I loved and who saved my life in so many ways, so many years ago! The more I dwelled on it, the more I painfully and bitterly accepted that that beautiful young woman who had endured and suffered so much, most likely slipped away on the back of that horse-drawn cart. She was probably dumped on the side of the road and left to rot well before she could get any medical help," Hank said with obvious pain. "I would've given my life in an instant if it would have saved hers!"

Matt paused to reflect for a moment, then slowly and quietly began to get ready to say his goodbyes. He thought the time was right and that his old friend had endured enough suffering for one day.

"Later in life she would often come into my thoughts, and I desperately wanted to know what had happened to her. But out of respect for my wife and family, I never vigorously pursued it. I tried to let that memory fade away forever. I never knew what her final fate was, just as I never discovered the true identity of Steinert. For every detail he gave me that alluded to the fact he was indeed a British agent, two more details would pop up convincing me he was just a clever Nazi. I have no more clue to that man's real identity than that of Jack the Ripper! The only thing I do know is that my knowing of his existence was important enough to have my life watched by covert agencies, foreign and domestic, for over a decade! That is truly something to think about, Matt!"

Hank paused as he recalled other details. "I once researched the town of Jolieville during the German occupation. I studied everything I could find about the SS and Gestapo presence there. I researched the château, Gerhard von Schreiner, and Otto Eichner. I researched *Jagdgeschwader 2 Richthofen.* I found some limited information on Rigeault and the battle fought there. I read some heroic exploits about Captain Wade and Lieutenant Riley and how they directed the battle. I tried to learn all I could about the occurrences that happened during the time I was over there. However, I found nothing about Café LeBlanc or any French Resistance movement in that area."

Hank paused for a moment then continued, "I did learn the fate of one woman in France you might be interested to know. After the Allies liberated Paris in August of 1944, I saw a newsreel in a theater in London. It showed images of French female Nazi collaborators being marched through the streets. They had swastikas painted on their foreheads and their heads were shaved! One woman caught my eye. I looked closely and discovered that it was the same woman who I saw at the Tessier farm when I was in hiding—Yvette! I guess she got hers. I never did find out what happened to her chubby little brat, Pierre!"

"That's really amazing, Hank. I can't tell you how sorry I am to hear about Pauline. I wish things had been different. I also can't tell you how much I appreciate all you've done for me. It's been a real eye-opening experience," said Matt as he stood up and slung his L.L. Bean backpack over his shoulder.

Hank pushed himself up and out of his chair and shook Matt's hand.

"Good luck with your paper, son," he said, walking Matt to the door. "You'll have to let me read it one day after you're graduated."

"That's a deal, Hank. I hope to talk to you soon," Matt said.

"Okay, then. Get back to Orono and get some rest. Lord knows I need some myself."

"Have a good night, Hank."

Matt walked through the darkness, not realizing how late it was. He climbed into his old car and sped away into the night, back toward Orono with a heavy heart and a lot on his mind.

Chapter 25

THE MACALLISTER REPORT

Matt woke up in his dorm room early Sunday morning, April 23, and bounced out of bed. He showered and dressed long before there was any kind of commotion on his floor. He smiled, realizing this was probably the earliest he had ever been up on a Sunday in the entire four years he'd been in college! There was a spark about him this day. He was excited and enthusiastic about his assignment—for once!

The enthusiasm was energizing; however, his mood dampened when he unloaded his backpack. Dozens of loose wrinkled papers, paperclips, reference books, microcassettes, notepads, pens, pencils, his recorder, and every other piece of stationery he had taken to Hank's place fell out onto the floor in a disorganized heap. Matt shook his head and quietly wished he had a laptop computer. He gathered up the mess and placed it all on his bed. The finished research paper was there lying in that mess. It just had to be organized and polished into a refined work worthy of Dr. MacAllister's high standards.

Matt was excited about the next step. It was time to call in Michelle and put her teaching and organizational skills to good use. Matt thrilled at the opportunity to see Michelle and to get her help. He hoped it would be beneficial for her, as well, considering her desire to write and submit an extra-credit report before final exams. He picked up the phone and called the Chi Omega sorority house. Michelle answered the phone pleasantly, causing Matt's heart to beat a little faster. The two talked for a few minutes, then set up a time to meet.

In an attempt to get a head start, Matt decided to go through his notes and put them in chronological order. He wanted to make Michelle's job a bit easier. He began reading what he had written down. The more he read, the more concerned he became. There was a lot of material to pore through, and the job wouldn't be easy; however, that soon became a secondary concern. He began to remember all the horrible and sometimes disturbing things Hank had reluctantly shared. He also remembered that Hank had never told anyone about his wartime experiences. Michelle had told him days earlier that her grandfather would never speak of the war in her presence. He now faced a difficult problem. How could he share his research material with Michelle without exposing all the terrible things he had written down? How could he respect Hank's wishes, knowing his old friend would not want Michelle to be privy to all the horrors he had gone through?

Matt started to formulate a plan. With his handwritten notes and reference material in order, like a clever censor he rewrote a cleaned-up version of Hank's experiences, purposely omitting the grisly details. He focused on the broader arc of the story, while maintaining focus on the interesting, yet less personal events, molding his original notes into something presentable, workable, and shareable with Michelle. It took hours, but he knew it was well worth the effort. He wasn't going to expose Michelle to anything that would go against her grandfather's wishes. At the same time, he would give her plenty of material that she could teach him to put together into a solid research paper.

About an hour before Matt was to meet Michelle at Longfellow Library, he finished his crafty revisions. All the audiotapes he'd recorded of Hank's conversations would stay behind. He gathered his material and decided to walk to the library to think about what to say. He arrived just after 7:00 p.m. and went up to the quiet third floor. He soon found his friend sitting at a secluded table. She waved and stood up. She was wearing jeans and a black T-shirt. Her hair was pinned up and to Matt she looked absolutely beautiful!

The two sat together and exchanged pleasantries, talking about their weekend and their plans prior to finals week. Then it was time to get down to business. Michelle pored through the tangled mess of notes. Matt explained how he hoped to craft the paper and Michelle showed the best way for him to structure and attack it. Matt guarded Hank's secrets like they were Fort Knox, cleverly diverting Michelle's attention from the specific subject matter and seeking her guidance on proper writing form and techniques.

The two spent hours going over the notes. At times, Michelle would stop being the teacher and question Matt about how he and her grandfather interacted. She herself took lots of notes as Matt provided her with the answers she sought. It was a productive session that left both happy and satisfied. They walked to the library exit just as the building was closing for the evening.

"Thank you, Michelle, for all your help," Matt said. "I don't know where I'd be right now without you. You've done more than I ever could have hoped."

"You're welcome, Matt," Michelle warmly replied with a smile. "You've given me a lot of good stuff, too. I know I can apply this into a nice little extra-credit report. That always looks good in the dean's eyes!"

"Awesome," said Matt. "Hey let's plan on meeting again to compare notes. Tomorrow I'm gonna really buckle down and start cranking on my paper. After I get through most of the first draft, I can tell you how it's going and which writing and listening methods I used. How's that sound?"

"Yeah, sounds good. It can be like a little interview, where I ask you how my teaching methods have applied to your work and such. It'll be great. Good idea, Matt."

"Cool. Well … I'll call you sometime this week."

"Yeah, that works. I have some sorority functions to help out with before school ends, but we'll figure out a time."

"Good … hey, are you hungry, Michelle?"

"Starving! I've barely eaten all day. I've been trying to lose some weight so I can fit into a new dress I bought."

Matt smiled and said, "Let's go over to Pat's. I could use a slice of pizza. Whaddaya say?"

"Love to! Let's go."

On Monday morning, Matt arose early, fired up his computer, and started writing his research paper. He managed to avoid all distractions, primarily the television. Michelle had helped him form a good starting outline that he utilized efficiently and thoroughly. Matt took the information Hank had given him and combined it with material he gathered from sources from the library and on the Internet. Matt retold much of Hank's story in a more concise, analytical, and informative manner, quoting the old man several times. Knowing Michelle would most likely read the paper, he left out the details concerning the truly horrible things Hank had endured. Instead, he talked about similar experiences written in the history books that were more widely known, particularly those involving the SS. He found himself truly interested and intrigued with the piece of work he was crafting, and his enthusiasm grew with each completed page.

Matt took an occasional break, but never strayed too far from his computer. His friend Bobby called a few times to bug him and try to drag him to lunch and dinner. Neither attempt was successful; Matt was content with microwaving food in his room. Eventually Bobby gave up and left Matt alone to work.

Other than occasional breaks to attend classes, for five solid days Matt worked steadily. By Friday night, April 28, he had completed the first draft. As he saved the file on his hard drive, he couldn't help but be amazed at the length of the paper—fifty pages! He had never in his life written something so lengthy and comprehensive. Moreover, he had never written with so much personal interest and pride. It was tough, but at least the first hurdle was over. He knew he had to edit and polish the piece into a final draft worthy of Dr. MacAllister's scrutiny.

Matt picked up the phone and called Michelle. She didn't answer, so he left a message, asking if she were free Saturday night for another meeting. He hoped she would get back to him right away. He understood why she wasn't home. It was Friday night and time to kick back and have some fun.

Matt was pleased to get a call from Michelle right after breakfast Saturday morning.

"Matt, why don't you stop by the Chi Omega house around nine o'clock this evening. We have a formal tonight at one of the fraternities. Kinda last-minute thing. I told the girls I'd help out and attend, even though I wanted to work on my extra-credit paper tonight. Anyway, we're all going out to get our hair and makeup done and shop for dresses. Just show up around nine. I'll be back by then. Sound okay?"

"Yeah, no problem, Michelle," Matt said. "You do what you need to do and I'll be sure to be on time."

After hanging up the phone, Matt thought about Michelle and the formal at the frat house. He wondered if she had a date or, even worse, a boyfriend! He became a bit depressed at the thought of her going out and having a good time with another guy. He had never thought to ask if she had a boyfriend. He thought way back to when he first saw her the night he was drunk at the party. He jealously wondered if she had been with someone that night. He liked her a lot and couldn't wait to see her; however, he knew his feelings would be crushed if she were to reveal she had a boyfriend. He tried to put it out of his mind.

That evening, Matt printed his paper and placed it with his notes in a folder in his backpack. He showered and shaved and started to put on a T-shirt and jeans, but then stopped. He reached farther back into his closet and pulled out a white dress shirt and black pants. He found a rich blue tie and put it on as well. He wiped the dust from his black dress shoes and put them on last. He chuckled, as he never thought he'd wear a tie even one day while in college!

The night was clear and the stars twinkled as Matt walked from his dorm to the sorority house. It was going to be a long stroll, but he didn't care. It helped clear his mind and build up the excitement of his anticipated rendezvous with Michelle. He thought of clever quips and interesting little facts that would be sure to put a smile on her face. The closer he got to the sorority house, the more he felt as if he were picking up a date rather than meeting someone for a study session.

He arrived at the house a little out of breath just before nine. He rang the doorbell and waited. A girl in baggy sweatpants and a hooded sweatshirt opened the door.

"Hi, I'm here to see Michelle Kessler. I'm Matt Switzer."

"Oh, yeah, she told me you were coming. She's not back yet. She should be coming shortly, though. Why don't you come in and wait for her up in her room?"

"Yeah, that's fine," said Matt.

"Follow me," said the girl, leading Matt up the stairs. "This is Michelle's room. She doesn't share it with anyone. Me and a few other girls are the only ones home, and we won't bother you."

"No problem at all," said Matt.

"That's a nice tie, by the way," commented the girl. "Michelle loves that color." She smirked as she walked out and closed the door.

Matt rolled his eyes and put his pack on the floor by the bed. The small room wasn't much larger than his cramped dorm room. It was impeccably neat and showed a woman's touch. The walls were pink with flowery hand-painted designs. The rugs, window curtains, and bedspread were frilly, puffy, and accented with feminine colors and taste. Matt moved several stuffed animals aside and sat on Michelle's neat bed. He tried to remember the last time he had consciously made his own bed. He couldn't remember!

Matt made himself comfortable and got out his paper. He had begun reviewing it when he heard some muffled commotion downstairs. Soft words and giggles preceded a single set of footsteps climbing the stairs. Matt stood up and faced the door as it slowly opened. His eyes opened wide at the gorgeous sight that stood before him. Michelle entered with a bright, welcoming smile. She was wearing a very revealing little black dress and matching spike-heeled shoes. Her brown hair was curly and her face was accented perfectly with just the right touch of makeup highlighting her big brown eyes and red lips. Matt was stunned and tried his best to keep his eyes on her face and not her cleavage or her legs!

"Hi," she said with a flirty little wave. "Have you been here long?"

"No, not at all. I just got here a few minutes ago."

"Wow, you look nice with your tie on. I love that color blue," she said. "You didn't have to dress up, you know."

"I know. I kinda wanted to just for fun. I figured since you'd be all dressed up that I should be too, so we'd match," Matt said with a smile.

"Aw, that's nice," Michelle replied with a cute smile. "Well, I was going to change into something a little more comfortable ... "

"Oh, don't do that!" Matt blurted out uncontrollably, quickly adding, "You look absolutely stunning, if you don't mind my saying so! Please don't go out of your way on my account. Besides, if you get changed, that'll make me feel fashionably lonely!"

Michelle laughed, "You're too cute. Have it your way. Let's get started, shall we?"

Michelle put down her purse and pulled up a chair next to the bed. The very sight of her sitting down and crossing her legs was enough to drive Matt wild! He kept cool, though, and stuck to business. Michelle reached for some notes on her desk, as well as a pen. Matt had never seen a woman look so studious and glamorous at the same time! He tried to purge his mind of all the dirty thoughts racing through it. It got easier once the two started talking about their work.

Michelle hit Matt with several questions about his prep work before writing the paper. Matt went through all his procedures and told her about every detail he found useful. Michelle jotted down his answers on her notepad. She started reading his paper, making corrections on every page. She was swift, yet meticulous in her work. Matt was amazed at how professional and thorough she appeared. She had the tools and mannerisms of a real teacher. She read through his paper in less than an hour, making written notations throughout.

"This is good work, Matt," Michelle said. "Your paper is well organized. It flows quite well, gives a lot of detailed information, and generally tells a pretty good story. There are a lot of historical terms and things I don't understand, but in my opinion it's a decent piece of work. It just needs some polishing before you write the final draft."

"Thanks, Michelle, that's nice of you to say. I worked hard on it all week," Matt replied. "Your grandfather and I had a good conversation over the course of a few days. He told me a lot."

"Yeah, I can see that," she said. "He must have given you a lot of good topics to research."

"Yeah, he did. He was real helpful, and we talked about a lot of his experiences as a pilot and an officer in the war."

Matt quickly ended his last sentence, for fear Michelle would press him for more details about her grandfather. Unfortunately, that's exactly what she did!

"What did he tell you specifically about his own experiences?"

she asked curiously. "Tell me about what you discussed and how you bonded. I'd like to understand how the two male generations interacted." She sounded like a real teacher, or even a psychologist.

Matt knew the true test was upon him. He crafted his answer carefully. He told Michelle about her grandfather's early love for flying and how he went to college already knowing how to fly. He told her about his time in the Civilian Pilot Training Program and his eventual acceptance into the U.S. Army Air Corps. He went on to talk about his tour of duty in North Africa and the Mediterranean. He mentioned Hank's bout with pneumonia and his insistence on returning to action once his strength returned. He described his assignment to England and his mission over France, making sure never to mention his being shot down or captured. Matt's paper made reference to an American pilot being shot down over France and captured, but he never revealed that this was her grandfather. He merely said her grandfather spoke about what happened in general when pilots were shot down over France.

He ended by telling Michelle about Hank's time as a flight instructor and his years as a commercial airline pilot. Again he purposely left out the personal stories and the family problems later in his life. He added that he and Hank had got along very well after working through the somewhat rocky start. He was pleased with meeting Hank and learned a lot about him and his generation. They bonded well and became good friends, which made Michelle very happy.

It was getting late, and the two put away their notes and papers. They started to talk casually about other fun and more appealing things. They talked on into the night, sharing laughs and flirtatious moments. After a while they realized it was after midnight.

"Well, I guess I should think about heading back to the dorm. It's getting late and you probably are dying to get into something more comfortable than that dress."

"Yes, I am," Michelle replied with a smile. "Where did you park, by the way?"

"Oh, I walked."

"You walked?"

"Yeah, I thought it would be a fairly short hike, but quickly learned otherwise."

"Well, I guess I could drive you back to campus," said Michelle.

"Yeah, that would be good. I'd appreciate that. Thank you so much for all your help, Michelle."

"Aw, you're welcome. Thank you for all you've given me. I appreciate it very much, too," she said.

Michelle opened her arms and gave Matt a hug. He wrapped his arms around her and hugged her back. As the two embraced, Matt's heart began to race and his level of arousal rose so quickly that he acted without hesitation. He pulled Michelle close and kissed her very tenderly on the lips. The scent of her sweet perfume hung in the air. He expected her to pull away, but she didn't. She kissed him back with a depth of passion he hadn't felt in a very long time. Matt slowly moved his lips onto her cheek and then her neck. Michelle responded positively, sending out all the right signals. Matt's hands started to wander up and down the back of her black silk dress. Matt's lips slowly worked down Michelle's neck. His hands reached down until they discovered the bottom of her dress. Both hands latched on and slowly began to pull it upwards.

"We can't!" Michelle said abruptly, pushing away and pulling her dress down. "It's too soon. I like you a lot … and I really do want to … but it's too soon and it's so late. We just can't … not here and now."

Matt composed himself, trying to coolly hide all signs of male arousal in his pants.

"I understand," he said maturely. "I like you a lot, too, and I want it to be right for the both of us. Don't feel weird. We have all the time in the world."

Michelle smiled and gave Matt another quick hug.

"Let's get you and the One-Eyed Sailor home," she said, unable to resist picking on Hank's state of arousal.

"You just won't let that one go, will ya," he replied with a chuckle as the two exited Michelle's room and found their way outside to her white 1997 Ford Escort. Soon Matt was back at the dorm with another confirmed date to meet Michelle later in the week. As his head hit the pillow, she was all he was thinking about and all he could possibly ask for!

Monday was May 1, and the official start to finals week. Matt had two exams to take in classes he knew he was going to pass, regardless. He put little effort into preparing for these tests. He instead devoted the majority of his time to cleaning up his research paper. With Commencement on Saturday, the 6th, he knew he was running out of time and his graduation fate rested in the hands of one man and one man alone—Dr. MacAllister.

Matt spent Monday revising and finalizing his paper. He couldn't resist inserting a few gruesome details of Hank's personal experiences— now that Michelle was out of the picture. By Tuesday morning he was finished and printed the final draft. He put the finished work into a leather binder and delivered it directly to Dr. MacAllister's office, leaving it with his administrative assistant. She smiled and placed it with the papers others had dropped off earlier. Matt breathed a sigh of relief and hustled to his final exam in Political Science.

By Thursday afternoon Matt was officially done with all his finals. He plopped down on the bed in his dorm room and smiled happily, knowing his scholastic career was finally coming to an end. He savored the good feeling. He napped a bit, and then the phone rang. He anxiously answered with an energetic "Hello," thinking it was Michelle. To his disappointment, it was his mother informing him of the family's plans for graduation. Once Matt was clear about everything, his mother said she looked forward to seeing him on Saturday. Matt hung up the phone and plopped back on the bed. His thoughts happily returned to Michelle Kessler.

An hour passed and the phone rang again. Matt hopped up and answered.

"Hello?"

"Yes, is this Matthew Switzer?" the voice on the other end inquired.

"Yes, it is."

"This is Gretchen Beals calling from Dr. MacAllister's office. I'm his administrative assistant."

"Yes, hello. What can I do for you?" Matt asked.

"I'm calling on behalf of Dr. MacAllister. He would like to see you in his office at four o'clock this afternoon if possible. He says it's quite urgent."

Matt looked at his watch and saw that it was just after three.

"Ah, yeah, I can, I suppose," he said, nervously adding, "What is this in regards to if I might ask?"

"I'm not at liberty to say, Mr. Switzer. He did say it was urgent, and that's all I really know."

Matt sighed and felt his stomach start to churn. "Please tell Dr. MacAllister I'll be there at four."

Less than an hour later Matt found himself sitting in a chair outside Dr. MacAllister's closed office door. He could hear MacAllister working inside, but dared not make his presence known prematurely. He looked over at Gretchen Beals, who shot him a reassuring glance.

"He does know you're here, Mr. Switzer," she said with a slight smile that did not make Matt feel any better.

Matt heard the sound of a chair being pushed back and he knew the moment of truth had arrived. The door swung open and there stood Dr. Edwin MacAllister. Matt stood up to greet him.

"Come into my office and take a seat, Mr. Switzer," said MacAllister, sternly and without pause. Matt followed him in and sat down across from his desk.

Dr. MacAllister was a short man in his fifties with a trimmed, gray beard and gray hair parted down the middle. He wore large metal-framed glasses that weighed heavily on his rather stubby nose. He always dressed in a tan or gray suit and tie. Today happened to be a tan suit day. He was not a stylish man, by any means, nor did he care to be. His clothes looked like they had been in style around 1980 and some would even debate that. He was also a man not concerned with idle chitchat or socializing. He was a hard-core educator who honored a simple "sink or swim" policy. Those who passed his courses truly earned their marks. The man got down to the business at hand.

"Mr. Switzer, I recently finished reading your research paper for my Contemporary American History independent study course." He reached into his desk drawer, pulled out Matt's leather binder, and tossed it onto his desktop.

"The paper is the reason I called you here," he said. "You're the only senior in my class of twelve students, so I read your paper first."

Matt sat up straight in his chair and alertly listened to every word MacAllister was saying. He was worried, but held out hope that the news about to hit him wasn't entirely catastrophic.

"Frankly, I'm perplexed and disappointed at this very poor piece of fabricated nonsense you handed in earlier, under the guise of a historical research paper!"

"I'm afraid I don't understand, sir," said Matt, genuinely troubled.

"That doesn't surprise me," returned MacAllister demeaningly. "It's obvious that you never read any of the books I assigned and recommended for the semester and it's also obvious you didn't comprehend the assignment either, which I thought was quite plainly spelled out."

"Sir, I thought I understood the assignment just fine," said Matt. "I did find the topic you assigned me to be a bit vague and large in scope," he added. "But … "

"Just stop right there, Mr. Switzer," ordered MacAllister, holding up his hand. "The topics I assign for historical research are purposely broad in scope, because I wish to test and examine the student's interpretation and execution of the assignment, based on what they've learned from my class and the outside readings I expect everyone to study. Again, from what I read of your feeble paper, it's obvious to me that you have done nothing in preparing this paper but research and expound upon boring, well-known facts that any middle-school student could copy from an encyclopedia or plagiarize off the Internet!"

"That's not true at all, sir," Matt said defensively. "The bulk of my paper was taken from oral history. I interviewed and questioned a living World War II veteran. He gave me a wealth of information regarding a first-hand account of the G.I. experience in Europe during the war."

"Oh, yes, I got quite a thrill reading about the trials and tribulations of Lieutenant Henry 'Hank' Mitchell, Mr. Switzer! If I didn't know any better, I'd think you majored in storytelling or creative writing, because you certainly have a vivid imagination for action and adventure tales!" said MacAllister quite gruffly. "Unfortunately, these little hopped-up fantasies are so far-fetched and unrealistic that I have no recourse but to believe they were just concoctions of an overactive imagination from a student who has watched far too many Hollywood war movies!"

"That's not the case at all, sir," cried Matt. "I worked very hard on that paper, and everything written in it is based on facts and truth. None of it is made up at all!"

"I find that very difficult to believe, Mr. Switzer. You obviously have no conception of contemporary American history and no idea of what your assignment was intended to have you produce! I see no reference to my lectures or my class whatsoever in this paper, which leads me to believe you didn't take my teachings very seriously. This fighter pilot 'character' you created and built up around a series of historical events has no real basis or credibility in history. This paper might make the beginnings of a low-budget adventure film or novel, but it has no merit in my course. You have shown me a complete lack of respect and no legitimate research at all into the true facts around the American G.I. experience in Europe during World War II. I have no choice but to give you an F on this paper and fail you in this course! You will not graduate, as you won't have sufficient credits. You'll have to take the course over again during the fall semester, then prove to me that you can learn and apply what I have taught you. That is all! This meeting has put me behind schedule, and I have other legitimate papers to read and grade."

MacAllister pointed Matt to the door. The young student got to his feet, stunned at what he had heard and knowing he had to do something about it, although at the moment he could think of nothing but firing back at the miserable little man before him for the lack of respect and trust he showed.

"I'll go now, sir, but you are dead wrong in your shallow assumptions, and I'll prove it to you and this university before I leave here for good! You've just insulted not only me, but a veteran of World War II who fought and sacrificed for his country in ways you'll never understand, no matter how much 'research' you do! You can fail me and not allow me to graduate, but I won't allow you to trivialize or insult Henry Mitchell, Bar Harbor resident, alumnus of this university, father, husband, aviator, and World War II veteran!"

"Get out, Mr. Switzer! I've had enough of you this afternoon," said MacAllister callously and without remorse.

With that, Matt abruptly left the office and stormed out of the building. His mind raced as he tried to think of where to go and what to do next. After wandering the campus, he eventually cooled down and returned to his dorm room. First things first, he decided. He called home and discussed what had happened with his parents. After a lengthy two-hour discussion during which Matt explained his meetings with Hank and the basis of his paper, his parents urged him to meet with Hank again and explain what had happened. His father reasoned that that course of action might clarify things and help remove some of MacAllister's doubt, especially if Hank were to meet him personally. Matt's mother, furious, threatened to drive to Orono and confront MacAllister in person. Only after some pleading from Matt and calm reasoning from his father did his mother finally relent. She was understandably upset after realizing her son would not be participating in the upcoming graduation ceremonies on Saturday.

"Mom, it's okay," reassured Matt. "I'm going to get this straightened out very quickly. I know what I need to do, and I will graduate. Maybe not Saturday with everybody else, but I will graduate! Don't worry. I'm sorry it has to be like this … I really am!"

"Son, I have faith in you and your mother does, too," said Matt's father. "Keep us informed and we'll come up and get you as soon as you need us to."

"I was supposed to be out of the dorm on Sunday, Dad," Matt said. "But that could change, depending on the outcome of this last History course. I'll call you as soon as I deal with the problem."

"Okay, son. We'll be waiting to hear from you. Good luck."

Matt hung up and immediately dialed Michelle's number. She picked up right away and was happy to hear from him until he explained what had just happened. Michelle agreed that the best thing to do was go and see her grandfather again and get his help.

"He can go see Dr. MacAllister with you and explain his role as the primary source in your research," Michelle explained. "Dr. MacAllister can't just dismiss my grandfather as a product of your imagination! That's absurd and completely disrespectful! He has no right to blindly make that claim and not acknowledge the hard work you did writing that paper."

"Yeah, I agree," said Matt. "Do you think your grandfather would help me out in a pinch like this?"

"Of course he would," said Michelle. "He's the sweetest, nicest, most generous person I know. He's also a fighter and hates to see any kind of injustice! I know he'll do everything he can to help you out."

"You know something, Michelle?" Matt said, "Somehow I already knew that myself. I really didn't even need to ask you that question."

"Call him up right now, Matt," she said. "Go see him as soon as possible. I'll go up with you if you want me to."

"No, that's all right, Michelle. You need to finish your paper and get ready for graduation. Besides, this is something I need to do alone."

"Okay … if that's the way you want it," she said.

After a brief pause, Matt said, "Michelle, about the other night … I'm sorry if I started to get a little out of hand or overstep my bounds. I just like you so much and think you're such an amazing person. I really want to see you again before you graduate and leave campus. I just need to deal with this ugly business first. I wish I didn't have to, and I wish I could march right next to you on Saturday."

"It's okay about the other night, Matt," said Michelle with a happy little tear in her eye. I really like you, too, and I definitely want to see you again! Call me as soon as you can after you see my grandfather. We'll figure this out together. We make a pretty good team! I can't wait to hear from you!"

"I can't wait to *see* you," Matt answered. "I'll call you as soon as I can, Michelle. Bye!"

"Bye, Matt!"

Matt hung up and found Hank's number in his wallet. He dialed it and listened to the phone ring several times before a familiar, raspy voice answered with a pleasant, "Hello?"

"Hi, Hank, this is Matt Switzer calling."

"Well, hello, Matt," said Hank. "What can I do for ya?"

"Hank, I'm sorry to be calling you like this, but I have a problem, and I need your help."

"What kind of problem?"

"It's in regards to the history paper I wrote. My teacher is under the impression that the work I did is made up. He doesn't believe you're a real person. He thinks you and the conversations we had were something I just created out of my imagination!"

"Oh, my Lord!" said Hank with concern, "What's gotten into people these days?"

"He's a very tough teacher, Hank, and he's known for being a bit of a pompous asshole, to say the least! Sorry, I didn't mean to … "

"That's okay, Matt," Hank said with a chuckle. "What do you need from me?"

"Hank, could I ask you to come to Orono and meet with the man with me? Maybe together we can straighten this thing out. As of now he's failed me, and I'm not going to graduate on Saturday!"

"Oh, I think I can do that," said Hank, adding, "I can still drive, and I'll talk to him tomorrow, if you like. I was planning on visiting with Michelle and the rest of my family at the graduation on Saturday."

"That would be great, Hank. Should I set up a time for us to meet Dr. MacAllister?"

"No, I think it's best if I see him alone," Hank said. "It might make matters worse if you're there with me. Might seem as if we're ganging up on him, and that could make him extra defensive. Let me handle it myself, and I'll contact you as soon as I can. I think that's the best strategy for now. I'd like to see just how much of a pompous asshole this fella really is!"

Matt laughed and said, "Thank you, Hank. I really appreciate it. I appreciate everything you've done for me. I'm sorry I have to drag you into this mess."

"That's okay, son. We'll get this cleared up so you can graduate. I promise. I'll call you tomorrow and let you know how the meeting went. Okay?"

"Okay, Hank. And thanks again," said Matt, after giving Hank the phone number to Dr. MacAllister's office. After he hung up, he sat back and waited. There was nothing else he could do.

On Friday afternoon Matt found himself on the phone with his mother.

"No, Mother, there's no reason for you guys to come up here.

Nothing's changed yet," he told her. "Mr. Mitchell told me he'd meet with Dr. MacAllister." Matt paused to listen to his mother's questions, then added, "Yes, I assume it's today. Look, there's nothing else I can do just now, so please stop worrying. I'm not going to march tomorrow. I won't march until I know I've passed every course and met all academic requirements. I'm sorry, but please let me handle this. I'll call you guys as soon as the situation changes … I promise. Bye, Mother!"

Matt hung up, wondering if Hank had made it to campus yet. He wondered if his old friend had even been able to set up an appointment with MacAllister. As it grew later in the day, Matt found himself pacing about his room. He felt like a caged animal and had to free himself or go crazy. He went outside and decided to go for a walk around the campus. He walked along the routes that had taken him to his classes in years past. He noticed subtle things that had changed over the last four years and how others had stayed remarkably the same. The walk helped clear his mind. He steered clear of Dr. MacAllister's office, as he didn't want to be reminded of his unpleasant situation.

Matt returned to his room after eating supper in the commons by himself. He avoided his friend Bobby because he didn't want to talk about MacAllister or failing his class. Bobby wasn't graduating on time either, and Matt suddenly felt very embarrassed to be lumped into the same category as his friend! He flipped on the television as a distraction, then picked up the phone and called Michelle. There was no answer at the sorority house. Matt assumed the girls were participating in some function in preparation for the end of the school year. He really needed to talk to Michelle.

An hour later his phone rang. It was Michelle!

"Matt, what happened?" she asked. "Did you talk to my grandfather?"

"Yes, he told me he would meet with MacAllister and try to straighten things out. I assume it was today, but I don't know. I hoped he had talked to you."

"No, he didn't call me … but I talked to my mother in Bangor earlier, and she told me he would definitely be at the ceremony tomorrow. I want you to come and see me tomorrow just before graduation. I'll make sure you touch base with my grandfather, in case you don't hear from him tonight."

"All right. I don't want to keep you. I'm sure you have a lot of things to prepare for tomorrow," said Matt. "Hey, did you finish and turn in your extra credit paper?"

"Yes, I turned it in yesterday. Unlike your teacher, my professor seemed very pleased with the extra work and effort," Michelle said happily.

"Good. I'm glad. That makes me feel better, believe it or not," said Matt. "I definitely will see you tomorrow just before Commencement, Michelle. Sleep well tonight … tomorrow you'll be a college graduate! Congratulations."

"Don't count yourself out so soon, Matt," said Michelle before adding, "My grandfather always gets results, and he won't let you down. I know he won't."

"I'll see you tomorrow, Michelle … and thanks again!"

Chapter 26

GRADUATION AND OTHER FINALITIES

Saturday, May 6, dawned bright and sunny. Hundreds of family and friends of graduating seniors flocked to the University of Maine to witness Commencement. In his dorm room in Chamberlain Hall, Matt Switzer dressed and prepared for meeting Michelle. He hadn't heard from Hank the day before and was concerned. The anguish of failing and not marching had finally passed and he now was more concerned with his scholastic reputation than anything else.

Matt hustled down to the football field where the ceremonies would be taking place. It was nearly eleven o'clock. He wove his way through the massive crowds, searching for Michelle. He bumped into several teachers and friends he knew well, but didn't stop to talk for long. His priority was to find Michelle.

"Matt!" cried a sweet feminine voice from the crowd. Matt turned and saw Michelle waving at him. He waved back, then hurried to her. "Hey, you," she said. "I'm so glad I saw you."

"Yeah, me, too," said Matt. "You look very lovely in your cap and gown!"

"Thanks," she replied with a smile. "I see you wore your shirt and tie again."

"Where's your grandfather?" Matt asked.

"He's over there, talking to my mother and father," said Michelle, pointing. "C'mon, let's go meet them quickly. We have to line up to march in a few minutes, and I don't have much time."

"Okay, let's go."

"Mom, Daddy, Grandpa!" shouted Michelle. Matt followed as

Michelle led him over to her family.

Matt walked right to Hank impatiently, but before he could say anything Michelle spoke up.

"Mom, Daddy, this is my friend, Matt Switzer."

"How do you do," said Matt shaking the hands of both Michelle's parents. Just then the final call was given for the graduating students to line up.

"You'd better go, dear," said Michelle's mother. "We're going to go find seats on the bleachers," she added, indicating they were in a hurry to get situated before the ceremonies started. Michelle looked at Hank and Matt and went to get in line.

"Hank, what happened? Did you get a chance to talk to Dr. MacAllister?" asked Matt desperately. "You never called."

"Yes, I did, Matt," Hank replied affirmatively. "I saw him late yesterday afternoon. By the time we were finished, it was very late and I was tired. When I got home I went straight to bed, and that's why I didn't call you back. I'm sorry, but I knew I'd see you today."

"Well, what happened? What did he say? Did you explain everything to him? Where do I ... "

"Settle down, Matt. I understand your need for an explanation right now, but this isn't the time or place to get into it," said Hank. "The graduation is starting now and we need to go find our seats," he said, shuffling off in the direction of his daughter. Matt followed.

"Well, when can we talk about this, Hank?" Matt asked with genuine concern.

"Let's meet tomorrow, Matt. I'm going to be spending the day with Michelle and the family. We're having a party tonight in Bangor to give her some presents and have a nice dinner. My daughter wants some exclusive family time this afternoon and evening. She told Michelle not to invite any of her girlfriends. Come to my house tomorrow around noontime. I want to show you a few things and take you somewhere I think you'll enjoy. It's supposed to be a nice warm day. Okay?"

"Yeah, I guess that works," Matt returned. "C'mon, I'll help you to your seat."

The graduation ceremonies started. The speeches were long and it seemed like forever before everything came to a close. The crowds of people dispersed following the final congratulations to the spring class of 2000. Michelle and her family left for their own private celebrations, leaving Matt behind. Matt knew Michelle would ask her grandfather what happened with MacAllister. He also knew that Hank wouldn't say a word about it to her. He knew he would respect his privacy. Matt resigned himself to the fact he would just have to wait another day before he learned his fate. He wanted to confront MacAllister again and get it over with, but realized that would be a poor decision. It was the weekend, anyway. All campus offices were closed.

Matt spent the rest of the day packing up his room. He spoke to his dorm's resident director, who told him it was okay if he stayed a few extra days past Sunday. Matt was relieved, as it allowed him to keep his parents at bay without their worrying too much about him or his living situation. He called his mother and again reassured her and said he'd have an answer for her soon. It was a struggle, but he convinced her again to sit tight and not travel up to Orono just yet.

Matt got up early Sunday morning and made the drive back to Bar Harbor, arriving just before noontime. The sun was shining and it was, in fact, a decent and warm day unlike the previous ones Matt had spent in Hank's cabin. No fire would be needed in the wood stove today. Matt walked up to the cabin and bumped into Hank, who came out to greet him before he had a chance to climb the steps and knock on the door.

"Hey there, young fella," he said warmly. "Let's hop in your car and go for a little ride. Whaddaya say? It's a great day."

"All right," replied Matt, a bit confused. He noticed Hank was carrying a picnic basket and an old suitcase. "Where we going?" asked Matt as they climbed into the Rabbit.

"Oh, I thought we'd go to Acadia. It's a great day for visiting the park. We can talk there in relative peace. Lord knows, the damn tourists haven't started invading the state yet. Won't see that until Memorial Day, thank goodness."

Hank directed Matt where to go, and the old car chugged along Route 3 into Acadia National Park. Neither said much, except for some small talk about the graduation and Michelle. Hank made it clear how proud he was of his granddaughter and what a great time the family had celebrating together. It was a very happy day for the eighty-two-year-old man. Matt was pleased, but still his thoughts revolved exclusively around his own predicament.

Their first destination was the top of Cadillac Mountain, the highest elevation along the eastern coast of the United States. As they drove to the summit, Hank mentioned that during certain times of the year, Cadillac Mountain was the first place in the U.S. to see the sunrise. Matt parked the car and the two got out to walk around. Hank took a deep breath and pointed out Bar Harbor in the distance below. Matt was awestruck by the natural beauty around him. Looking at the ocean and the surrounding islands, he couldn't help but be impressed by the indescribable sights. Tiny boats zipped along the ocean surface, while wispy banks of low-hanging fog hugged the coastline and shrouded some of the offshore islands.

Hank offered Matt more interesting facts about Cadillac as the two walked along the rocky trails. Matt assumed Hank had chosen this place to talk and waited for him to sit down somewhere and start. However, just as Matt was about to ask, the old man started back for the car, telling Matt it was time to travel to their next destination. Puzzled, but interested, Matt agreed.

The next stop was Jordan Pond. Hank showed Matt the Jordan Pond House Restaurant, not yet open for the season. Hank and Matt walked around slowly with Hank showing his young friend spectacular views of Penobscot Mountain and the unique "Bubbles," twin peaks overlooking the north end of the pond. Matt was fascinated and wanted to take a closer look at the pond. He and Hank walked down along the water's edge. Hank explained all the fun things a person could do on the pond and on the hiking trails nearby. Matt wanted to hike around the pond, but Hank talked him out of it, claiming his old bones couldn't take the pounding. As they drove away Hank again assumed the role of tour director. They drove around the twenty-seven-mile Park Loop Road, the primary route when touring Acadia by car. Hank pointed out Thunder Hole, Sand Beach, and other scenic little nooks by the road.

Matt couldn't believe he had spent so much time in nearby Orono and never once visited this amazing place. He thought how great it would have been to have known about Acadia's true beauty years earlier. He could have explored it in greater detail. He thought how nice it could be to bring Michelle here for a date.

The car motored on until Hank directed it to its final location. Matt pulled off the road and the two got out. Hank picked up his picnic basket and suitcase. The men walked up to a sign that read, "Ship Harbor Nature Trail." Hank shuffled forward and led the way through the woods to a magnificent rocky point overlooking the ocean and nearby islands. They found a comfortable place to sit and look out onto the ocean. Hank opened the picnic basket and gave Matt some bottled water, a tuna fish sandwich, and a small bag of potato chips. Matt chuckled to himself and wondered if that was all Hank ever ate!

"This place is really spectacular," Matt said. "I can't get over just how beautiful it is. The ocean, the trees, the blue sky, everything … just everything is a tremendous sight to see. It's very peaceful, too," he added.

"Yes, indeed," Hank responded. "I really love this place. I told you once that every now and again I like to paint. Well, I've painted many things from this very spot. I used to come here a lot. This place always seemed to help me forgot about the horrible things I saw and experienced during the war. It brought me some peace, ya know. I can't ever get enough of Acadia. It has to be one of the brightest and most beautiful places in all of Maine. I just wish there weren't so many damn rude tourists that come here in the summer!"

Matt thought for a moment and wondered if Hank had brought him to Acadia to help soften the terrible news he was about to receive. Time was up, and Matt wanted to know what had happened. Before he could ask, though, Hank spoke again.

"I saw your Dr. MacAllister late yesterday afternoon. I never called him directly. I just showed up on campus and asked where his office was at the visitor's center. Fortunately, when I got to his office, he hadn't left for the day. I caught him coming out and introduced myself. I asked him for a moment of his time and we went into his office to talk."

"Did he ask you a lot of questions? Did he mention me or talk about my paper in … "

"Settle down, Matt! Every now and again you show that loud impatience I despise. Listen and let me talk. I'm gettin' to the point. I'm old, remember. Old people slow down in many ways. You'll discover that one day, son."

"Sorry," said Matt.

"I identified myself and confirmed to Dr. MacAllister that it was I who gave you all that information. I brought him this suitcase and showed him everything inside."

Hank opened the case while Matt peered inside. Hank pulled out many old documents showing information about him while he was in the service. He showed Matt his enlistment papers, as well as his official discharge papers. He showed him old yellowed documents summarizing his training and his deployment with the 232nd Fighter Group of the 9th Air Force. He showed him old black-and-white photos of himself in North Africa, where he saw his first combat. He pulled out an old 232nd patch he had removed from an A-2 leather jacket he wore, as well as other little trinkets, including his flight wings and original rank insignia bars—all from North Africa. Lastly, he produced his dog tags he had managed to keep with him all through the war. Matt held them up and looked at them closely with awe.

"That's great, Hank," said Matt handing Hank's dog tags back to him. "Did he finally believe you were who you said you were?"

"Yes, I think so."

"What did he say about the paper, then? Did he say he would pass me, now that he knew I didn't make all this stuff up?"

"Well, no," said Hank.

"Why not? What happened?" Matt asked.

"I asked Dr. MacAllister if I could read parts of your paper that he disliked and questioned the most. After I read through a lot of it he started to make his own case, in a very gruff manner, I might add. In your defense, Matt, I agree with you on the point that that guy is a pompous ass!"

"What did he say?"

"Well, it seems that you incorporated a lot of my story from France into your paper."

"Yes, I did," said Matt quizzically.

"Well, Dr. MacAllister found a lot of what you wrote about to be unbelievable, even though you summarized a lot of it without going into too much horrific detail—which I'm glad you didn't—except in some parts, I noticed. He believes that you made it up, or more specifically, that I told you to make it up because it couldn't have really happened. He accused you of being a bit of a plagiarist and a storyteller, rather than a history student. He then made accusations that I put this nonsense into your head, thereby making me a coconspirator in this whole affair. After he finally came down off his high horse, he had us both failed and not graduating!"

"Well, I hope you set him straight again, Hank," Matt pleaded. "You did tell him that all you told me was real, right?"

Hank paused a minute, then said, "It was an interesting story, wasn't it, Matt? I mean you really got into it, didn't you? You showed a great deal of interest the more I talked, didn't you? Your whole attitude seemed to change, the more I told you. I guess that's what a good story will do to people."

Matt's heart sank. The life and soul just seemed to drain from his body, as he tried to comprehend what Hank was trying to tell him. Maybe, just maybe, his old friend had done nothing but make up a fantastic story that was no more based in reality than a child's fairy tale!

"Hank, I want to understand something here," Matt said slowly and clearly. "That story about you being shot down and your ordeal in France was all true, right? The story about the spies landing in Maine was true. I looked that up. Tell me the rest really happened and you weren't just making up a story to waste my time! You told MacAllister it was all true, right? France, Steinert and the SS, Pauline, Rigeault, all was real, right?"

"No, I didn't tell him that. It was a great story, though, wasn't it?" Hank asked. "Maybe I should become a novelist and write a book. How's that sound?" Hank asked in a low voice, like a child would use to try to cover up a mistake in front of an angry parent.

"I don't believe you!" shouted Matt. "I trusted you! How could you lie to me and make up such a ridiculous bullshit story! Do you get off on yourself, spewing out shit like that to guys like me? Does it give you pleasure to see me crash and burn, you bastard?"

"Now just stop right there, fella," fired back Hank. "First of all, you better calm down before one of us gets hurt here, and I do mean physically, Matt! I may be old, but I do come down hard when I'm not given the proper respect I deserve! And secondly, I want you to ask yourself a question before you jump to any conclusions! You listen to me good, Matt! Do you honestly think that I could have made up such a gruesome and horrific story? What decent human could ever conceive of such a terrible tale? I still suffer from nightmares, even after all these years! I have more emotional pain and scars than you'll ever feel in your entire life! Yes! Yes! That whole goddamned experience did happen! It was real! I wish it wasn't, but everything I told you was the truth! I didn't make up or embellish one single piece of it!"

"Then why didn't you tell that to Dr. MacAllister?" asked Matt, "So he doesn't totally destroy my chances at passing his course and graduating!"

Hank looked Matt square in the eyes and said, "Remember what I told you before you last left my cabin? I told you that I had never told those stories, particularly my experiences in France, to anybody—ever! You are the first person ever to hear it! That was a top-secret mission, Matt. I was under orders never to discuss it with anyone, ever. Remember the FBI agents who shadowed me all those years? How could I tell a college professor all that stuff I told you? I shouldn't even have told you about it! Even at eighty-two years old, a soldier doesn't disobey orders, much like an exposed Nazi guilty of war crimes doesn't escape prison or execution just because he's ninety years old today! Do you understand me, son?"

"Everything you told me was real, then?" Matt asked Hank, knowing deep down in his heart that nobody could have made up such a tale without being deeply disturbed.

"From the depths of my soul, I swear it was all real, Matt. You have my word as an officer, a gentleman, and a friend," Hank said, trying to fight back the tears in his eyes. "I guess I told you what I did because I felt it was important to pass it on to somebody, so the sacrifices of my generation during that unspeakable war wouldn't be forgotten and just scattered to the wind like so many secret, shredded government documents."

"I believe you, Hank," Matt said with a sigh. "I've spent too much time listening to what you've said to doubt such terrible happenings. I've seen the pain on your face and I know it's real. Somehow, I just know it. But the question remains, where does that leave me now? MacAllister still doesn't believe the work I put into that paper is genuine, right? I'm still not graduating, am I?"

"At the moment, no, Matt ... I'm sorry. The grade still stands. But before I left his office, I told your Dr. MacAllister that he was making a huge mistake and that old servicemen like me don't abandon their friends. I told him I was going to seek out the proper university administrators and appeal the grade and the paper to them and their judgment, no matter how long it takes. With that said, I will help you in any way I can to make things right and clear you of any defamation. I suggest we go to the president of the university himself first thing Monday morning and explain what happened. Maybe, just maybe, I'll disobey my orders twice in a lifetime, if that will get you off the hook. Hell, if the MPs, the CIA, or the FBI come after me now, they won't be too impressed at this eighty-two-year-old fart! And I'll take my lumps just like any good soldier should!"

"Let's hope it doesn't come to that," said Matt, managing a small but encouraging grin. "Thanks, Hank. I'm sorry I doubted you. By the way, I think I'm in love with your granddaughter."

Hank looked at Matt, chuckled, then said, "Does she know that? Well, I hope she knows what she's getting herself into if she does! She's a good girl and you're a decent boy. Treat her right. Treat her in a respectful manner that would make me proud." Matt smiled and shook his head. "My goodness that's a glorious sight out there," Hank said. "Makes me wish I'd brought my paints and some canvas."

The two friends, generations apart, fell silent again and together looked out across the peaceful waves gently lapping against the rocky shoreline. Matt looked out over the water with an uncertain future. He wondered what was going to happen and where he would end up, once his problem was resolved. Then for a brief moment, the young man soaked in all the beauty around him and had a brilliant moment of clarity. He may have failed a college course, causing a speed bump in his progression into adulthood, but he realized that, in doing so, he had learned a much more important lesson about life, the people who lived it, and the sacrifices they had made so that *he* could have a brighter future. Suddenly, he felt more mature, more responsible, and much wiser than he had ever felt before in his life. And, in the end, for Matthew Switzer, nothing else seemed more important.

ACKNOWLEDGMENTS

My sincere thanks to all my friends and family, long past and present, who have provided me with inspiration and support throughout my life, and have contributed to this story. Special thanks to my parents, Jane and Gene who raised me to be the person I am today. To my brother Mark, my sister-in-law Kathy, and my two nephews Will and Jack who have enriched my life and contributed (albeit unknowingly) to this story and more to come.

A special thanks to my Aunt Katherine and my Uncle Peter who have shown me so much of the beautiful state of Maine and imparted so many interesting, meaningful, and inspiring stories about the state's rich history.

I would also like to send a special thanks to my Uncle Peter for all the countless hours he spent providing feedback and editorial support in reviewing this book's rather lengthy and untamed first draft. If not for all his initial efforts, this work would have taken much longer to come to fruition.

Lastly I'd like to thank all the staff and other support personnel associated with Maine Author's Publishing. Their talented and professional organization is a shining example to the self-publishing industry

ABOUT THE AUTHOR

CHRISTOPHER MORIN was born, raised, and currently resides in Portland, Maine. He received a B.A. in Journalism from the University of Maine at Orono. He is a history enthusiast and has enjoyed creative writing since penning his first short story back in second grade.